The Adventures of Doctor Eszterhazy

THE ADVENTURES OF DOCTOR ESZTERHAZY

by Avram Davidson

dustjacket painting by George Barr
interior drawings by Todd Cameron Hamilton

Owlswick Press Philadelphia

Trade edition: ISBN 0–913896–28–4
Limited, signed, & slip-cased edition: ISBN 0–913896–30–6

CONTENTS:

To George Scithers, who encouraged these stories . . .
Blame him!

THE FISH UNTURNED: AVRAM DAVIDSON

A Foreword by Gene Wolfe

That I have never paid him homage face-to-face is my own fault; I saw him and failed to recognize him. Strolling down a hotel corridor at Norwescon, I happened to glance into a crowded room party. A single face stood out as though lit by a spotlight, leonine and framed in glowing white hair and snowy beard; I knew at once that it was the face of a great man. For half an hour I puzzled over it, and at last realized that it was Davidson's — I had not known he was at the convention, and had rarely seen his picture. When I returned and talked my way into that party in the hope of shaking his hand, he had gone. I have not seen him since, though I have admired him for decades and he lives just a few blocks from my friend Elliott Swanson.

Talents are bestowed by a generous hand; it would be vastly more difficult to find someone with none than to find a talented writer. Davidson has genius, a quality that is rare indeed. He is unique, by which I mean simply that his very best work (of which there's a great deal, much of it in this book) could never be mistaken for that of any other writer. And he has integrity, which is as water and air to genius. Allow me to explain.

When I was much younger, I longed to learn to paint. I did not, because my art teacher impressed on me, with the unshakable authority of a woman of twenty-six addressing a boy of thirteen, that the only subjects a true artist would condescend to paint were utterly commonplace things, principally bowls of fruit. (I remember this teacher's showing us a still life that included a dead rabbit. She criticized the inclusion of the rabbit as a surrender to popular taste.)

Much as I wanted to paint, I did not in the least want to paint bowls of fruit.

Though I don't enjoy admitting it, there's something to be said for my old art teacher. Many of the most acclaimed artists do indeed confine themselves to painting bowls of fruit, wealthy ladies in pearls, and meadows nibbled by sheep — things no one would pay a penny to see. (They do it, I think, because of the art critics, but that's another story.) And many of the most acclaimed writers are like those artists, writing about crises so small that the average reader would forget them in his hurry to get to work. They're praised for it, they're petted by their illustrious publishers, they're given professorships at Harvard and Princeton, and they are forgotten ten years before they are dead.

Now let me tell you a secret you may have guessed already: It's easier to paint a peach than a dragon. It's easier to write about a timid adulterer than to tour Hell or Averno with Vergil. And it's much, much safer.

Davidson never plays it safe, never angles for the approval of publishers and professors. He refuses to write in a way that would bore him if he were the reader. When you and I were young, Reader, every new story was a fresh exploration of the universe, in which we were alternately warmed by the familiar and thrilled by the exotic. Davidson writes in such a way that it shall be so for us again — he is himself the canal linking the Ister with the Danube. Permit me.

Through the high and far-off times, O best beloved, there flows a mighty river men call the Ister, having its source in the country of the Celts who live near the city of Pyrene beyond the Pillars of Heracles, and at long last giving up its waters to the Euxine at Istria (that beautiful city praised by Pliny). This river, the Ister, is now identified with the Danube.

I say, "is now identified," because the Danube is clearly not the Ister, as it neither rises in the country of the Celts, nor flows at last to lovely Istria, nor empties into the Euxine; rather the Danube rises, as every schoolboy knows, in the Black Forest of Germany and empties into the Black Sea at Sulina. Plainly then the two are not the same river, and must be linked (as they now are) by a canal or channel through "the endless and legend-haunted fens of the Vloxlands" — the canal we call Avram.

A difficult writer? Oh, yes, indeed. But only because he so seldom does what we expect. An imperious writer, certainly, and not merely when he writes of Scythia-Pannonia-Transbalkania, the empire adorned by Dr. Engelbert Eszterhazy. And yet we all come to him at last, when we have grown bored with the rest; and with him we remain.

The few writers whom we read with continued pleasure become our friends, although we may never encounter them outside their own pages. Silly people, as you have no doubt observed, insist that their friends be much like themselves, and at once drop a "friend" who cheers for the wrong team or buys at any one of the many incorrect supermarkets. It is not so with the wise. You may know them by many things, but most of all by this: that if ever they introduce you to some very dear friend, that person will prove to be the very last person you would have guessed.

In Davidson's "The Lord of Central Park" there soon comes a marvelous moment when Arthur Marmaduke Roderick Lodowicke William Rufus de Powisse-Plunkert, Eleventh Marquess of Grue and Groole in the Peerage of England and Twenty-second Baron Bogle in the Peerage of Scotland, Sixth Earl of Ballypatcoogen in the Peerage of Ireland, as well as Viscount Penhokey in the Peerage of the United Kingdom, Laird of Muckle Greet, Master of Snee, and Hereditary Lord High Keeper of the Queen's Bears, sweetens the air of his cave a bit by burning "a packet of frankincense that my friend, Osman Ali the Somali, sent me not long ago." There is something — indeed, there is quite a lot — to be said for the fact that the Laird of Muckle Greet eventually weds a Dutch pirate-grandmother. But there is much more to be said for his having such a friend as Osman Ali the Somali. Osman Ali is the friend we should all have, just as Avram Davidson is the author we should all read.

In "The Dragon-Skin Drum" (a story about a story that is really no story at all), Mr. Wong the translator explains that at the emperor's feasts "they only served the fish on top. As it was beneath their dignity to turn the fish over, the rest was left to the servants.

"See," he concludes, "how proud and haughty the Manchus were. Now everything is democratic."

And the gunnery sergeant, an old China hand, asks, "Does Jong Gay Shoo give his servants half his fish?"

So is it with you and me. Everything is democratic. We have writers very like ourselves, and thus books and stories that we ourselves might as easily have written. We need not kowtow to *them.*

But they do not give us much to eat; so let us feast with the emperor awhile instead. Then when some wide-eyed boy asks whether we actually *know Avram Davidson,* we shall be able to reply, as old Mr. Chen might have replied, "Oh, yes. I have bowed to him many times."

— July 1989

CORNET ESZTERHAZY

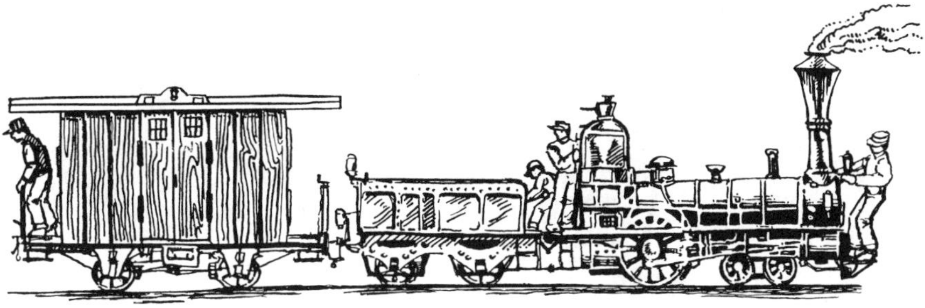

Thou, eye-bitten, hag-ridden, elf-shotten, anse-rotten:
Under the wolf 's paw, under the eagle's feather,
Under the eagle's claw, ever mayest thou wither.
— Anglish Spell

I, eye-clear, hag-dear, elf-sustained, anse-unblamed:
Over the wolf 's paw, over the eagle's feather,
Over the eagle's claw, may I ever have good weather.
— Northish counter-spell
from *The Book of the Troll-Hag (Trulldhaggibouger)*

It was the year that the bears were so bad in Bosnia.

The year that the bears were so bad in Bosnia and Queen Victoria actually said, "We are not amused," was a year very crucial in the affairs of Far-Northwestern Europe, as well as those of Scythia-Pannonia-Transbalkania.

The always-tremulous Union of Scandia and Froreland was once again in a state of perturbation, the Frore Nationalists now insisting upon a separate Bureau of Weights and Measures, and the Scands (entirely as a matter of principle, having nothing to do with the imposts on stockfish and goat-cheese) resisting this under the well-known motto, **Where will it end?** That Froreland and Scandia constituted "Two Gloriously Free Monarchies Conjoined by One Single and Magnanimous Monarch" was a truth as well-known as it was troublesome. The monarch at this time was Magnus IV and III, "Staunchly Lutheran and Ever-Victorious King of the Scands, Sorbs, Goths, Lapps, Lipps, and Frores; Protector of the Skraelings, Terror of Iceland and Ireland, and Benefactor of the Butter Business"

— known more generally as *Magni* — the reaction of the King to this most recent and non-negotiable demand, was to put down his glåg glass and offer to "settle the matter once and for all" by shooting dice for Froreland with the Khan-Tsar of Tsartary — Finnmark and Carelia to be the counter-stakes. This sporting suggestion was met with a most ringing silence all round about the Arctic Circle.

Hence, the train of cars departing from the Finnmark Station in St. Brigidsgarth at a most unusual hour: the Conjoint Cabinet of the Two Kingdoms had met in secret session and decided to send the Terror of Iceland and Ireland, Benefactor of the Butter Business, on an immediate and unofficial tour for the benefit of his health . . . Magnus being notoriously a martyr to bronchitis, liver-complaint, and elf-shot. . . . The incognito title selected was that of Count Calmar; the Royal preference for Great-Duke Gåtterdamurung being stiffly and decisively discouraged by Aide-de-Camp Baron Børg uk Børg.

As the journey was unofficial and had been almost unannounced (the *Court Circular*: The King has retired to the rural areas for a period of time), there was neither a military nor a civil sendoff: only two tiny groups; both on the wrong platform, with two banners: a new one, reading **Swearing Eternal Fealty to the House of Olaus-Olaus-Astridson-Katzenelenbågen-Ulf-and-Olaus, Froreland Demands a Separate Bureau of Weights and Measures**; and an old one, barely legible, representing the forlorn hope of **A Fourteenth Full-Bishop For Faithful Froreland** — this last was really getting very scuzzy and should have been replaced long ago — and would have, only it was "stained with the Blood of the Martyrs" — that is, of Adjutant-Bishop Gnump, always excessively prone to nosebleed. (He did indeed die, at the age of 87, during the royal absence, an advent marked by public mass recitations of the Shorter Catechism by all the as-yet-unconfirmed schoolchildren of the two kingdoms — even including the Unreconciled Zwinglians, by special dispensation of their Vicar-at-Large, who stipulated only that at the beginning of the famous and controversial Consubstantiation Clause they were to "pause perceptibly before continuing.")

For the first two days of the journey, "Count Calmar" had done nothing but drink champagne and play boston with his Aide-de-Camp; the third day he spent in bed (not in berth: in *bed*: even kings incognito do not travel without maximum basic comfort). Fairly early on the fourth day, the train drew to a slow, steamy halt at a station in what appeared to be a largely industrial suburb of a moderately large city; Magnus peered and blinked. "Is *this* Antibes?" he inquired, dubiously.

"No, Sire," said Baron Børg uk Børg. And cleared his throat.

"*Not* Antibes. . . . Cannes?"

"No, Sire. Not Cannes."

"*Not* Cannes. Oh! *Nice*! No . . . not Nice. . . ."

"*Not* Nice, Sire."

Magnus considered this, slowly. Very, very slowly. Next he asked, "Then where?"

"Sire," said Baron Bðrg uk Bðrg, who had been awaiting this moment, entirely without enthusiasm, for a long, long time; "Sire: Bella."

"Oh," said Magnus. "Bella." He scraped his tongue against his front teeth. He examined the result. Then, with a sort of convulsion, he leapt to his carpet-slippered feet. "*Where?*" he cried.

"Sire. Bella."

The silence was broken only by the **tchoof-tchoog, tchoof-tchoog** of a very small shunting locomotive, about the size of a very large samovar, in the adjacent marshalling yard. On the platform the assistant station-master was yawning, buttoning his tunic, and eating his breakfast bread-and-goosegrease. A much younger man in a much smarter uniform came walking up quite rapidly. Someone in a frock-coat and a red, blue, and black sash stood by, blinking tiredly.

"*No* palm trees," muttered Magnus. Then, "For God's sake, Bðrg, get me a glass of glðg," he said. "And tell me where the devil we *are* . . . for a moment I thought you said 'Bella'!"

". . . Sire. . . ."

The Conjoint Cabinet had decided that Scythia-Pannonia-Transbalkania was quite a good idea. "Perhaps," suggested Royal-forensiccouncillor Gnomi Gnomisson; "Perhaps Magni can learn from a sovereign who rules three countries, how to manage, anyway, Jesus Christ, *two*." All the other ministers muttered, "Hear, hear!" and pounded firmly on the green table. (The Special Minister for Frorish Affairs had actually muttered, "Froreland demands a separate Bureau of Weights and Measures," but he pounded just as firmly as the rest.)

"May you be buggered on an ice-floe by an impetuous polar bear!" cried Magnus; "At eight o'clock in the morning with a tongue like a stoker's glove! I cannot meet an Emperor!"

". . . Sire. . . ."

"But why is he coming here incognito?" asked Ignats Louis (King-Emperor of Scythia-Pannonia-Transbalkania). "He has never come here cognito; why is he coming here incognito?"

The Minister of Ceremonial Affairs had not become Minister of Ceremonial Affairs for nothing. "Because he is a Lutheran, Sire, and it is Lent," he said, as smoothly as though these facts had not just occurred to him. "Your Imperial Majesty could not officially receive a Lutheran during Lent."

"No, he couldn't, could he," observed Ignats Louis, who sometimes had trouble with pronouns. "Poor old chap's a Lutheran, isn't . . ." he paused a moment, swept on. "Well, well, so be it and be it so. *Lent.* Pontifical High Divine Liturgy this morning again, eh. Tell the Right Reverend Mitred Protopresbyter to keep the sermon short."

Then he put on his morning uniform saying slowly, "King of *where?*"

"But he is after all the King of Scandia and Froreland," said the Scandian and Frorish Ambassador. Again.

"Not according to my Official Intimations," said the Minister, slightly rustling the documents in his hand. "According to my Official Intimations, he is, after all, a Count Calmar."

"Quite so, Highness; quite so. But, actually, he is, after all, the King of Scandia and Froreland. . . . You know. . . ."

"When the King of Scandia and Froreland actually and really visits my country as such, he will actually and really be received as such. *After all.* Willingly. Gladly. *When,* however, he comes as Count Calmar, he can be received only as Count Calmar. That is what an incognito is all *about,* my dear Thorbringsson, you know," said His Highness the Foreign Minister, in a lower and sympathetic and presumably less official tone of voice. "They should have thought of that in St. Brigidsgarth."

"Of course they should have," admitted the Ambassador; "however: they *didn't.* Meanwhile, Count Calmar is arriving in Bella, and — in, of course, the strictest confidence — I may tell you that Count Calmar *is* the King of Scandia and Froreland. *Is* he to be met at the station *only* by the Customs, the Immigration, and the Pest Control? I put the matter to you."

The matter so put to him, the Minister of Foreign Affairs agreed that it would not do. The matter so put to the Minister of Ceremonial Affairs, he also agreed that it would not do.

"But, Holy Saint Ulfilas! *Two* merry-andrew monarchs, *both* arriving this same morning, and *both* incognito! For my sin, for my sin, for my own most grievous sin!"

Foreign Affairs paused in his departure, looked at Ceremonial Affairs with slightly raised eyebrows. "Really! Oh you poor chaps! Well, but who is the other?" For total reply Ceremonial Affairs performed an expansive gesture, intended presumably to outline a very large (and very female) figure. Foreign Affairs threw up his hands, rolled his eyes. "For your sin," he said, dolefully, as he departed, "for your sin, for your own most grievous sin!"

It was rather a quiet moment in the Stand-by Equerries' Waiting Room. Some were slowly having breakfast off the buffet. Some sat reading the newspapers, either morning, or of the previous evening. Some sat sipping coffee. Some merely sat. The traditional loaf of large peasants' bread (stale, traditionally) had not been thrown at a single noisy junior.

Enter: a page. "Summons for two," said he.

This was greeted with the equally traditional groan. Then someone asked, "What's the task?"

The page [without referring to his paper]: "Dowager Margravine of the Ister, one. Count Magnus —"

The Equerries [with a real groan]: "Her Fatness! *Ooohh!*"

"Margrave of the Ister" was one of the lesser titles of the King-Emperor, but not only was his mother long deceased, she had never even been Margra*vine* of the Ister. But all knew who had been . . . long before the late and sincerely lamented Queen-Empress (Ignats Louis was a widower). . . .

An inattentive Equerry: "Why are the scrambled eggs so tough? Cook! To the galleys!"

An attentive Equerry: "Oh Christ, it's my turn. Will no one save me from this frightful fate?"

The Page: "Why 'frightful'? You go meet the Public Train at the West Station, you bob and do the 'Highborn and Noble Lady' lay and all the rest of that cow-puckey, she bobs back, one of her witches comes forward with the charity-pyx, you drop something in, you fall back, some nobly-born nun takes over and takes them away; you come back and sign in and recover your donation from the Clerk of the Privy Purse, you sign out and collect your one-half gold-piece and you've got the rest of the day off and can go get bonked at Miss Betty's —"

Cries of: "Boy! Presumptuous boy! To the galleys! Flog the boy!"

Another Equerry [holding out his hand]: "Gimme Fat Emmy!" [Receives the paper summons and departs, accompanied by ribald hoots and howls.]

Yet Another Equerry: "I shall take the other task, Page. Give here."

This was a young man with a fresh and open face on which sat a light beard and moustache, plus, to be frank, a few freckles. Unlike the majority of equerries, who had on the dun undress jackets which would be changed for dress whites before leaving for duty, he was already wearing his dress white jacket: and on it were pinned the ribbons of a few campaigns. A palace saying had it, "To face a cannonade requires a brave heart and a steady hand; and so does drinking morning coffee in a dress white jacket." Another Equerry yet leaned over and looked at the official SUMMONS TO DUTY. "Who in the Hell, now, is Count Magnus Olaus of Calmar? — besides being a noble of the Kingdoms of Scandia and Froreland? Hey, Engli?"

Engli said that they would see, wouldn't they? His senior read on, " 'Arriving at the North Station,' at the North! Like a consignment of rendered lard! '— with two companions of rank and three servitors.' Hm, isn't that the country the polar bears come from? Mind you don't go back with them and freeze your boboes off. . . . Bye. . . . Who's got the morning *Journal* with the new *román* in it?"

"I have, trade you for an Egyptian cig, I'm all out. Ta. Here you are. Funny chap, Engli, eh?"

"Funny, but nice. Oh, good: *From the French. Translated.* Mm. . . ."

The usual torpor regained rule over the Stand-by-Equerries' Waiting Room.

Emma Katterina hoisted up her skirts . . . not very far . . . and bobbed a curtsey . . . not a very deep curtsey . . . a station-master, even with a high silk hat, was, after all . . . a station-master. But he had bowed. So she had curtseyed. She repeated the motion, somewhat like all the tents of Kedar being pitched at once, when the Equerry bowed. And she repeated it a third time when the abbess of the Convent of the Purposefully Impoverished Ladies of Noble Rank Being Now the Wee Sisters of the Sacred Crown and Humble Servants of the Very, Very Poor — repeated it considerably more deeply — curtseyed to her. A certain amount of attention was paid her arrival on the Public Train (the public paid rock-bottom rates for a racking, creeping journey, but the public trains ran once a day in each direction over every inch of track belonging to the Royal-and-Imperial Ironroads, and reservations were never necessary); but, though more than one person in the station either bowed or curtseyed, her presence in the capital was so well known as not to attract very much attention; and she did not attend further to such further attentions as she did get. She next embraced the Lady-Abbess and to her, and to her small suite, said, "Let us briskly walk. The Mamma is, truth to tell, rather chilled."

By "The Mamma," she meant herself.

To the station-master and the Equerry she gave a very thin smile and a very sly glance out of the corners of her tiny eyes, as if to reassure them how she valued their formalities; then she swept out. The station, with its smells of crowds and steam and smoke, like a somewhat smaller and somewhat cheaper version of the Baths of Caracalla done in wrought-iron and smoky glass, was now permitted to resume its usual, and commercial, functions. The 18th century had made a brief appearance. Now the 19th had taken over, once again.

Having seen their baggage into the hydraulic elevator at the Grand Hotel Windsor-Lido (the Scandian Count was merely incognito, not slumming), the Equerry next saw them into the hotel's dining room. Magnus was feeling rather better. Bôrg uk Bôrg was stiff. Bôrg uk Bôrg was always stiff. And Kopperkupp, the private secretary, had

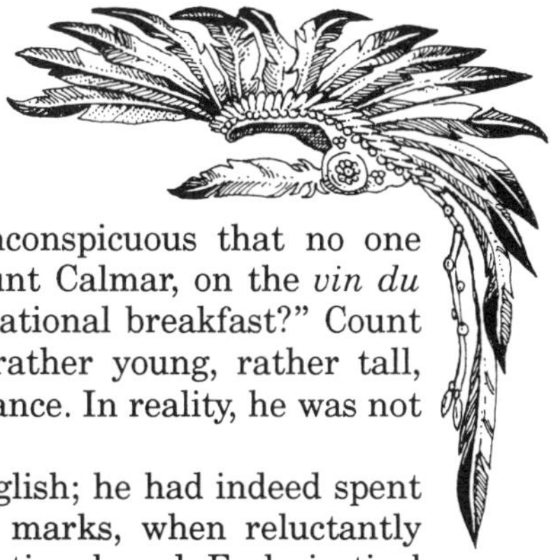

spent so many years making himself inconspicuous that no one noticed he was there. "I assume that Count Calmar, on the *vin du pays* principle, is desirous of trying the national breakfast?" Count Calmar merely looked at him. He was rather young, rather tall, rather blond, and rather rough, in appearance. In reality, he was not really rough at all.

"What is it?" he asked. He spoke in English; he had indeed spent many years in the study of French; his marks, when reluctantly wrested from the Department of Educational and Ecclesiastical Affairs, proved to be a straight, undeviating, uninflected **D**. The Scandian Parliament, in an absolute fury, had deprived him of his traditional right to dispense the marriages of those under thirty who lacked parental consent; but the Frorish Parliament, on the principle that "French is a language spoken in brothels," refused to do any such thing.

"What is it? Well, there are really two national breakfasts. The first one is dark bread spread with goose-grease. The other is boiled blood-sausage with boiled potatoes. Eh?"

"Nay."

"Oh, but Count Calmar. The blood-sausage is so delightfully strong-smelling. The boiled potatoes are served cold and have such a delicately blueish tinge. As for the goose-grease —"

"Surely, Cornet Eszterhazy, you jest."

"Well, Count Calmar, yes I do."

Count Calmar guffawed. Then he groaned and put the palms of his hands over his eyes. Eszterhazy went on to say, "Seriously, I would recommend a new-laid egg, a cup of strong, clean coffee of the Mocha-Java blend . . . toasted light bread spread with pure sweet butter and Scottish marmalade . . . and . . . perhaps . . . with coffee . . . a spoonful of white rum. Eh?

Count Calmar said, "Aye."

Baron Bo̊rg uk Bo̊rg after a moment said, "The Count Calmar is desirous of informing himself of the social and political principles whereby your own country, Cornet Eszterhazy, is enabled to encompass so successfully, how shall I term it, populations non-homogeneous in nature. This question naturally concerns us in our own Two Kingdoms." This statement so perfectly summed up, perhaps exactly, the desires of Count Calmar, that he said nothing whatsoever.

Cornet Eszterhazy said, "Hmm." After a while he added, "When we have finished breakfast, we might go for a ride. Or a walk."

Count Calmar said, "Aye!"

Cornet Eszterhazy next observed that one of his new-found friends' servants seemed rather odd . . . "For a servant, I mean. Nothing against his character, of course. He wears an odd sort of cap, and —"

"Ah, that is Ole," said Calmar, with an indulgent chuckle.

"His name is not really 'Ole,' only we call him so. I don't recall his real name," Bårg said. "The cap is part of his national costume. He is a Skraeling, a man of some importance among his own people —"

"Sings songs," Calmar said, looking around rather wistfully . . . perhaps trying to find the social and political principles of his host-nation; perhaps for more white rum.

Eszterhazy, having but slightly breakfasted with the Equerries, had joined in eating the same items suggested for his guests. And drinking. He felt benign. Felt . . . also . . . interested. "A . . . a Skraeling?"

Bårg and Calmar nodded. Something faintly flickered nearby. Eszterhazy believed that Kopperkupp had also nodded. "Yes," Bårg said. "A people of unknown provenance, anciently if not aboriginally established in the northern parts of both our kingdoms; from having intermarried with the Scands and Frores they have lost much of a distinctive physiognomy while yet retaining some elements of their old traditions. Traditionally they are entitled to be represented at court; hence Ole being with us, ahem."

"He supplies the Sovereign with, at each meal, an egg of an Arctic tern," said Calmar.

Eszterhazy politely raised his brows; Bårg said, "Of course this is not possible except when the Sovereign bi-annually visits their territories. Elsewise it has been commuted to a duck's egg."

"I see. . . . What else *does* the man do, then?"

"He blacks the boots," said Bårg, somewhat curtly.

It was arranged that Bårg and Calmar (and, presumably, Kopperkupp) would make a very brief call at their Embassy — "To be sure," the Frorish Nationalists said, "we must have our own Embassies some day. But first we must have our own Bureau of Weights and Measures!" — that Bårg and Kopperkupp would remain for whatever business need be. And that Calmar would then/there meet the Equerry-Cornet. And that they two would go off. Somewhere. Somewhere (it was discreetly understood) respectable.

The political education . . . perhaps re-education . . . of "Count Calmar" need not begin that very day. Perhaps the very next.

As the Northern visitors wished first to make some slight adjustments to their dress — a change of dress-coats, perhaps, the ribbons of an order — Eszterhazy would wait below, and meet them in the grand lobby. He watched them as they departed; watched the waiter arriving with more coffee; watched as a tall, thin man in tweeds arose from a nearby table and trotted — there was no other word — trotted over to Eszterhazy's table and snatched up one of the egg-cups and held it close to his eye. "Extraordinary," he said. "Extraordinary." Then, suddenly aware that his conduct might just possibly be considered other than entirely ordinary, he turned to Eszterhazy and begged his pardon. This was granted.

"Sir," the man said. "I am Regius Professor of Natural History at the University of Oxbridge. *Who* would have expected to find this on a table of an hotel in the capital of Scythia-Pannonia-Transbalkania!"

"But why so, Professor?" asked Eszterhazy, slightly put-out, and slightly amused. "We do not live on locusts here. I myself, generally speaking, eat an egg a day. At least one egg."

The Regius Professor of Natural History at the University of Oxbridge turned to him a face displaying the utmost astonishment. "But surely not the egg of an Arctic tern?" he asked.

Bårg was not eager to relinquish Magnus, but was obliged to agree that the younger man did indeed require to stretch his legs and breathe fresh air after more than three days in a railroad carriage. Still, he did ask where . . . "generally speaking" . . . they planned on going. Eszterhazy acknowledged that this was a very fair question. He stroked his fair and as yet rather sparse moustache. "I had thought," he said, "that we might commence with the Imperial Institute of Political and Social Economy."

"Yes, yes!" — Bårg.

"After a perhaps not over-tiring visit, hmm, next perhaps the Royal Ethnical and Ethical Museum. . . ."

"Excellent!" — Bårg.

"After that . . . well, although, alas, the Diet is not in session, still, a visit to the gallery will display the exquisite nicety with which the national and linguistic and political affiliations are delineated by means of a system of color-codes unique in Europe; the seats being upholstered — for example — in off-white for the Scythian Conservatives all the way through beige for the Hyperborean Monarchial Democrats —"

"Very good, very good!" — Bårg.

"There was some rumpus once upon a time, with the Slovatchko Christian Socialists and the Pan-Imperial Unified Socialists each demanding red; however, this could not be granted, red being the traditional color of the Pannonian Ultra-Conservative Agrarians; and in the end, the Slovatchko Christian Socialists accepted puce and the P-I. U. Socialists, mauve. Perhaps this might interest Count Calmar?"

"Cornet, it cannot fail to do so." — Bårg. (Grimly)

Magnus, later, had fallen into a silence, but by and by he began to look about with some interest at the passing scene and its presumably polyglot peoples. Just then the young Cornet lifted his light malacca walking-stick and gestured towards a stolid granite building across the street. "Imperial Institute of Political and Social Economy." Magnus's face fell at once, but his guide went on, briskly, "Well, so much for the Imperial Institute of Political and Social Economy; we have commenced with it. Now at the end of this alley, which leads towards the river, there is a place of public pleasure officially licensed under the name of The Pint of Port, the quantity which is sold there for three-tenths of a skilling . . . officially . . . actually the drink consists of the washings of expressed grape-hulls mixed with a small amount of low-grade potato-spirit, in consequence of which the place is commonly called The Pint of Piss. Its accommodations are rude, its ambience is coarse, its customers are very often totally depraved, and —"

"Take me there at once, *do you hear?"* said Count Calmar.

It was perhaps an hour and a half later that, as they strolled on through the Sunken Square (Ignats Salvador had intended a palace but died just as the excavation was completed), a large old woman performed a full-formal curtsey of archaic manner as she came upon them; and Magnus, automatically, gave her a full-formal bow. He had taken a number of steps before he gave a start, started to turn around, caught his new friend's amused eye, and asked, "Who was *that?"*

Down deep in a dungeon . . . that is, down deep in what had long ago *been* a dungeon for the confinement of forgers of the petty currency (and served them right) but was now a cellar for the storage of merely moderately harsh wine — the sort which corner grocers fix up with sugar syrup and advertise as **From Our Own Vineyard in the Country** . . . a device which fools no one but indicates that the stuff is not too bad: the worst poison almost invariably being labeled as **Imported From Oporto in the Land of the Portagews, DELICIOUS!** . . . three men sat at a bench before a table spread with machinery. Presently, "The works is almost ready," said one of the men. He wiped his brow with the sleeve of the denim jacket he wore.

"And then, " said another . . . pausing, as if he relished the words . . . "and then: **Ka-BOOM!** "

"Death to the tyrant!" cried a third. They returned to their employment.

After a moment, one of them said, "One hears . . . One hears rumors . . . one hears rumors that the tyrant may already *be* dead —"

"Nonsense!"

"Lies, spread by the tyrant's toadies!"

"The works! Let us get on with the works, and not dawdle over granny-talk!"

For a while they toiled on, jewelers' loupes in their eyes, so cautiously weighing gunpowder, so carefully adjusting clock-work, so deftly fastening wires, turning tiny screws — "But why, if the tyrant is not dead, has he not been seen riding his Whitey horse as always? One hears that, for days now, he has not been —"

"Enough, babbler! The works!"

The room was large and dark; only where they worked was there light. Somewhere, neither near nor far, water dripped. Another man spoke. Diffidently. "It is of course essential that the tyrant be destroyed. But he is not trustworthy. Suppose that just at the time the works go off, just at the door of the Infants' Infirmary in the Hospital for Children of Palace Servants, the tyrant is up in the throne room, trying on crowns — and not bringing sweets to the invalid infants?"

There was a murmur. There was a voice saying firmly, " 'Suppose?' suppose. We shall suppose he will be there."

Gaslight hissed.

Now in lower voice the same one resumed the same theme. "It is a terrible thought that the children would have died in vain. . . ."

Once more the firm voice. "That would be the tyrant's fault. If he had no servants they would have no children. It is the enemy who determines the conditions of the war."

They all nodded, bowed their heads, worked on. There were no further interruptions.

In a room in a tower not more than a kilometer away, three other men glanced up from their map and looked out the window. One of them gestured with his pointer. "The vehicle in question will at the time appointed cross over the Italian Bridge disguised as a fruit-and-vegetable wagon. They expect to enter the Royal and Imperial Palace grounds without trouble via the back central passageway, and to stop just at the door of the Infants' Infirmary in the Hospital for Children of Palace Servants. There several crates of produce will be unloaded in order to add an air of verisimilitude to the scene. Then, one by one, the men are going to leave the scene. The brakes and wheels will have already been tampered with so the vehicle cannot easily be moved. At three o'clock, as usual, the King-Emperor enters the Hospital to visit for fifteen minutes, said visit includes the Infirmary, and the infernal machine is to be set to go off at a quarter after three." He gestured towards a clock.

The men were all in uniform; but it was a curious sort of uniform, entirely bare of any adornments whatsoever. One of the men asked, "How accurate is the report?"

"Our secret agent assures us that it is quite accurate."

There was such silence as was not dispelled by the sounds of the great capital city below, muted by distance into one continual murmur, like that of some far-off and unbroken surf. Then someone said, "This is a terrible vision."

Someone else slightly shrugged, said, "All the visions of the Jacobins are terrible. That is why they must all be destroyed, they and their visions together, whatever names they employ: democrats, socialists, republicans, reformers, anarchists, conservatives — as though the present system were worth conserving! It is re-action which alone may save us all. A reaction which will totally sweep away such diabolisms as representative government, religious toleration, and all the rest of it. Mud! *Mud!* Every change which has come about since 1789 has come up from the mud, and back down into the mud it must go."

Someone cleared his throat. "You are quite sure then, companion, that it is not our duty to inform the August House?"

"Certainly not! The Jacobins must be destroyed and it is by exactly such an action on their part that shall come about a reaction, a revulsion which shall destroy them. All of them! They shall all die! Let the mobs arise and do this; then we shall destroy the mobs!"

The view from the tower window encompassed all the nearby Gothic Lowlands; one of those present said: "I see the Gothic Lowlands in flames . . . then all Scythia . . . Pannonia, too: then Transbalkania —"

"Scholars say," another murmured, "that it was the Gaetae of Dacia who were the ancestors of modern Scythian Goths and thus neither the Visigoths nor Ostrogoths; but scholars also say the descent is from the Gauts of South Scandia . . . and do not scholars also connect the Getae of Ovid's lines, *Haec mihi Cimmerio bis tertio ducitur aestas Litore pellitos inter agenda Getas* with those Geats which the Beowulf informs were centuries before encountered on the North and Baltic Seas? Scholars *do.*"

"Damn all scholars! Let the scholars burn, too!"

A throat was cleared. "The Emperor is not a scholar . . . what of the Emperor?"

The reply was brief. "The Emperor is a saint and has a place prepared for him in Heaven. Let the war go on."

"But —"

"It is the enemy who determines the conditions of the war. Let the war go on."

"Who was *that?*" asked Magnus.

The young Cornet-Equerry smiled. "*That?* That is Emma Katterina."

"Who?"

Emma Katterina. Her mother may have been "the barmaid of Bratislava," for that matter the mother of Don John of Austria had been "the laundress of Regensburg": unlike Don John, whose father was Holy Roman Emperor, Emma Katterina's father was merely a backwood noble in a barely united severalty of backwood thrones — again, however, and unlike Don John: she was of legitimate birth.

The Sunken Square, as Magnus quickly glanced, had the appearance of a valley of sorts down the middle of which rushed a river in spate, only breaking its flood to divide and roll round a black crag.

Looked at more slowly, the river was revealed to be the usual throng and the rock to be moving against it as it parted: vast and unmistakable was the immense figure of Emma Katterina, Dowager Margravine of the Ister, Dowager Great Duchess of Dubrovnik, and Titular Queen of Carinthia . . . a.k.a. Tantushka, Mammushka, Fat Emmy, Her Fatness, and Great Katinka: from head to toe in fusty black slowly growing green for years, and accompanied by what was for her a train of state: "three witches and a priest," as they were popularly described. She was also the widow of the half-brother of Ignats Louis, King-Emperor of Scythia-Pannonia-Transbalkania, as the Triune Monarchy was now called. Her parsimony was notorious; even now she was walking all the way across Bella in order to avoid the two-*kopperka* fares on the tram. Earlier, later, other sovereigns might negate this or that with some such phrase as **It is not Our pleasure** or **La Reyne s'avisera**; Emma Katterina accomplished it with the words, "Mamma wouldn't let." Metternich himself had shrugged his defeat by her, Francis Joseph would greet mention of her name by slowly rolling his head from side to side and uttering pained little moans. Bismarck —

Emma Katterina was not only immensely tall, immensely fat, immensely charitable (which was where her pensions mostly went); she was also immensely ignorant. She had certainly never heard of Darwin or Pasteur. It is doubtful if she could have placed Scandia, let alone Froreland, on a map; but, face to face with their Conjoint King, she had recognized his face at once. She had curtseyed. The effect was somewhat as though the Alps had curtseyed. Magnus bowed. Emma Katterina passed on by. Her moles bristled and her chins flowed. Then she crossed herself. Then she spat. Three times. A king was a king.

And a heretic was a heretic.

She knew her duty.

"Who was *that?*" asked Magnus again.

"Who was *that?*" someone else, far across the Sunken Square, asked his companion. " 'Tantushka'? Tell us something new. No: who was that she bobbed to? *No.* Fool. Does she bob to everyone? *Find out who she bowed to.*"

"Why was The Mamma pleased to bob and spit just now back there a bit?" asked one of the "witches," surtitled the Baroness Bix and Bix.

"The Mamma saw that that there youngling was a far-off king; The Mamma knows the faces of all the kings in Christendom," nodding firmly as she strode along, said Emma Katterina; "and emperors, too, even Of Abyssinia, who is in Asia, and Of Brazil, which he is in Africa. *Oh* yes!"

"*Oh* yes!" echoed the second "witch," surtitled the Countess Critz.

"The Mamma she cuts them kings's faces out of the penny papers and pastes them up in the excuse me."

"And what far-off king the youngling was?" asked the third "witch," surtitled the Highlady Grulzakk.

Emma Katterina shrugged. "The King of Koppenholm, somethinglike," she said. "The Mamma spit, after-like, what because, because he's a Calvinist: to burn," and here she spat again . . . without malice. "Nicelooking boyling, yes."

"In Koppenholm," the Chaplain said, screwing up his scrannel jaws, and unscrewing them down again, "the people there, may the canker eat, are said to be, allegedly, Lutherans, some say." The Chaplain may have been a bigot, but he was a tactful one.

"Lutherans are the worst kind of Calvinists," said Emma Katterina, nothing fazed. "Doctor Calvin was a doctor, in Paris-France," she explained to her suite. "And he turned heretic, for what because? Because for what he wouldn't buy a bishop's dispensation to marry his first cousin's nephew's niece. The Queen of Navarre, of blessed memory, she argues with him till she could see green worms with little red heads; but no and no and no! 'For Heaven's sake, Dr. Calvin,' says she, 'buy the bishop's dispensation, what does it cost, a richman like you?' But no and no and *no!* 'I'll not have no dispensation,' says he, 'though the heavens may fall, and what's more,' says he, 'I'll not have no bishops, neither!' "

Gasps of horror and disgust greeted this revelation of total depravity. "So the Queen of Navarre, of blessed memory, who was minding the schloss while her brother was off a-fighting the King of Ireland, she condemns him of course to be burnt at the stake for Unitarianism without benefit of strangulation. So off *he* runs, with his codpiece a-flapping atween his knees, not stopping till he gets to Gascony, where he changes his name to Doctor Luther, but the Elector a-sends him a packing. Nextwise he settles down in Switzerland, where their brains be all addled from the snows; Zwingling, he calls himself then. 'Away with all bishops!' says he. And there hasn't been no bishops in Switzerland from that day to this, which is the reason them Switzers has to come down into France or Liechtenstein for to receive Confirmation. Come here incognito, it seems, this boy-chick, which it means, without no uniform, so that republicans and other anarchists won't fling dirt in his face; what it means to be a king these days.

"Or a queen," she added. And slowly shook her massive head.

Somewhere under its roof-slates the Grand Hotel Windsor-Lido maintained a dormitory and a row of cubicles for the housing of its employees and the servants of its guests; "Old Skraelandi" did not bother to see where he was to be quartered according to the

G.H.W.-L.; he knew his place and his place never varied: whether it was the turf beneath a reindeer-hide tent or the thick Belgian carpet of an elegant hotel, he slept across the threshold of his sovereign's chamber. Somewhere far away amidst the moors and marshes of Skraeland, so void of landmarks to the outside eye, was a small hollow amidst a grove of dwarf willows. Here the child was born to whom the shaman gave the name of Eeiiuullaalaa. No one could have expected the pastor of the State Church, charged *ex officio* with the registration of births in his vast parish — he lived 100 kilometers from that willow-girt hollow — no one could have expected him to have spelled *Eeiiuullaalaa* correctly and so perhaps he hadn't; the Skraelings, being largely illiterate, would not have known the difference. *Largely* is, however, not *entirely.* The shaman knew how to spell it and he had spelled it — once — in runes carved onto a piece of reindeer horn, which he had entrusted to the infant's parents, strictly cautioning them not to show it about lest someone use it to work a spell upon the babe. The shaman had been the infant's uncle or great-uncle, and in celebration of the event he had gotten drunk on Hoffman's Drops (if "drunk" was quite the word to describe the effects of that antique but still potable and still potent mixture of brandy and ether, of which it was said that, "Three drops will paralyze a reindeer, four will kill a bull-elch, five would stun a polar-bear, six would bring a musk-ochs to its knees, and seven make the troll-hag smile"); so perhaps he had not spelled it correctly, either.

The boy did not grow tall, for the Skraeling are not a tall-growing people; but he grew, and, growing, learned deer-craft from his parents, and from his old uncle or great-uncle learned leech-craft and elf-craft and troll-craft; other things he learned, too, even the general names for which the Skraeling do not tell to others. And when a time came, and it did not come often, to select a shaman to go and live with the King and protect the King from harm (the incumbent shaman knowing he was now of an age to die), the young man suddenly and successively had visions and dreams of such a potent and indicative nature that every shaman in Skraeland agreed it was this one who must go. At the Court he took care of the sacred egg, of preparing charms for going under the threshold or under the bed, of beating the *toom-toom* if necessary and of blowing the eagle-whistle if necessary (these last two had not been necessary), and of chanting protective chants. And as indication of the trust the Court of the Scands and Frores had in the Skraels, they allowed him full charge of the care of the Sovereign's boots, shoes, and slippers: a *most* important magic! Each night as he rubbed off the dust or scraped the dirt or mud from the royal footgear, and by observing where the King had been, was able to decide where the King should be: *Bear him well, well, bear him well, well, well,* he would murmur, as he rubbed into the footgear of the King of Scandia and Froreland the tinted, scented grease they had provided him. Once, in the time of the previous king, John XII and XI, he, "Ole Frori," as they called him casually at Court, had observed on the twice-royal buskins, traces of a marl which could have come only from the estate of a certain high-born (and beautiful) lady known (though not to John XII and XI) to be a double-agent in the pay of both the Russians and the Prussians. Such elf-craft he performed upon every single item which the King ever wore upon his feet that the King went not thither ever again. Nor knew why not.

It was all quite different from the prolonged twilights, the sky-capped plains of golden moss over which the antlered herds drifted like dark clouds, the night-welkin covered with the quivering mantle of the boreal witch-lights; but the ancestors had told him in dreams both dark and clear that he must serve the King: and serve he did, although scarcely the King knew that he was being served — and how he was being served, and how well, the King did not know at all.

And certainly the King did not know, as he idly sought his casual pleasure in this strange city, that the last of his servants sought the King, tirelessly shadowing him from street to street, concealment easy in this forest of buildings to one who had concealed himself in and on the unforested moors of Skraeland.

"But would republicans and other anarchists come here to Bella for to hurt the youngling king?" one of the "witches" asked.

"The Mamma wouldn't let," said Emma Katterina, firmly. Then — "That big dump there, is for us, not?"

"*Royal and Imperial Bureau of Parks, Forests, and Lands,* ah-hah," said the Chaplain. Marble and granite and an entire range of mansarded turrets; they turned towards it.

The Mamma's lips moved; she had no need of notebooks. "In Ritchli, eleven paddocks, grazing rights, commuted: cash. In Georgiou, firewood rights, gathering of, commuted: cash. In Apollograd, that's in Hyperborea, twelve fields for geese and goats, which they made a park of, ah how the Pappa, now in Paradise, enjoyed for breakfast the goose-grease therefrom: the fees therefor, commuted: cash. Three deer-parks in Pannonia and a Hunt-the-Hare there also, commuted: cash. All due this quarter fortnight past, uccage, soccage, copy-hold, frankpledge, assigned Turkish Tributes, mum-mum-, *what?* One hundred and thirty-five ducats, eleven skilling, thirteen pennies, one half-penny — *plus interest* — from the big dump, here." She ignored the vast front steps and headed for a side door at street level.

Inside, one clerk-bookkeeper looking up through the glass half of his office door groaned, "Oh God, here she comes!"

"Her fatness! What! Have you computed her interest? *Do it at once!*"

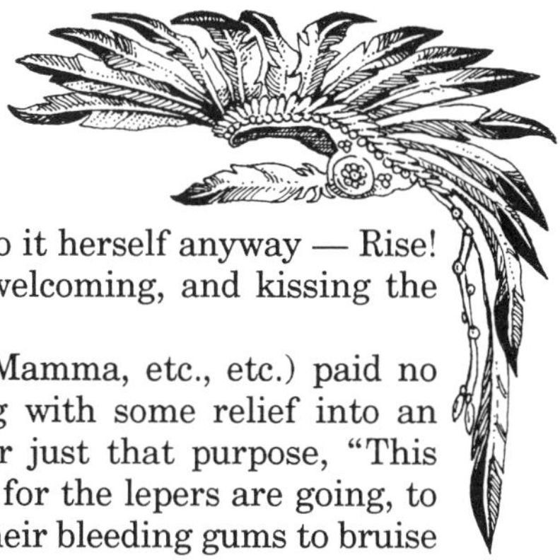

"Too late, too late — besides, she will do it herself anyway — Rise! All rise! Your Titular Majesty! Humbly welcoming, and kissing the hands and feet!"

The Titular Queen of Carinthia (Big Mamma, etc., etc.) paid no attention. To her suite she said, sinking with some relief into an immense and heavy chair kept there for just that purpose, "This quarter, the pensions from this big dump for the lepers are going, to pay for supplying loaves, they shouldn't their bleeding gums to bruise upon the hard and stale — *Writer!*" this to the clerk-bookkeeper, "The abacus!" There were at that time in the secluded Hospital of Saint Lazarus, less than one hundred patients; most people in the Triune Monarchy (". . . fourth-largest Empire in Europe . . .") scarcely knew there were any, anymore: but the Titular Queen of Carinthia knew every one of them by name, and with each click of the abacus-beads, she baked for them a loaf of bread.

Not feudal dues alone had been commuted; galley-slavery in punishment for crime had been commuted: into forced labor at the Royal and Imperial Shipyards (a courtesy plural, there was only one). Indeed, the term "ships' carpenter" had so much come to mean a convict, that genuine ships' carpenters termed themselves "maritime wood-workers." There was indeed talk — emanating, no doubt, from such sophisticated sources as Vienna, Berlin, Paris, and the American city of Philadelphiapennsylwania; talk that such forced labor was terribly old-fashioned, and that those convicted of offenses against society should be held in special institutions where they might learn to be *penitent,* and thus to *reform.* But for the present, such advanced ideas had yet to penetrate into the legal system of Scythia-Pannonia-Transbalkania; and burglars and forgers and manslayers not hanged continued to haul and hew and saw and scrape and caulk and paint: and if they declined to do, they were flogged until they ceased to decline. Bruto Alarits had declined . . . for a while . . . but not for a very long while.

It had been two years since he had finished his sentence. For a while he had found employ as a maritime woodworker in a private yard, but his employers had been finicky, objecting to the disappearance of tools and nails, and that had been that. Bruto was by then rather too mature to enter an apprenticeship in the pickpocket line and so had alternated casual labor with casual theft — smash and grab, grab and run — the lot. He was clever enough not to be caught again, but . . . perhaps he was not so clever as he thought . . . not enough to be prosperous. Finally he had drifted into a sort of padroneship over lesser, weaker, more stupid thugs, enforcing a sort of organization and system, maintaining a sort of terror over those who did not appreciate the advantages of the system but perforce went along with it. Sometimes he strolled through factory and warehouse districts, accompanied often by his second-in-command, one Pishto-the-Avar, eye cocked for stealables. He would not himself steal; he would assign others. He would find a fence. He would exact commissions. Sometimes he would lounge around the streets.

Sometimes he lounged around the Sunken Square.

To call Pie-Petro's place "a low dive" was to be not judgemental, but exact. The place was not only low in a social sense, it was low in a topographical sense as well, having originally been built at the bottom of a ravine and the ravine largely filled in and another storey built onto the original building . . . but the entrance remained where it had first been, and down the several pairs of stairs Bruto now walked in a thoughtful manner. Inside the dive it was dim — what else — and the sole gas-lamp emitted as much smell as light. Petro, sallow, squat, silent, had discovered a trick of business from which he had never seen any reason to depart: when you came into his joint, you had to buy a pie. You could also, if you wished, (and most wished) take your choice of bad beer, bad wine, bad brandy, bad vodka, bad rum — whiskey or gin was not available — the pie was not so bad — not so bad as the other items, anyway. You had your choice of meat or fruit — though not what kind of meat or what kind of fruit. The pies were small and so, for that matter, were the drinks, but as most of Petro's customers were apt to be greeted elsewhere with the words, "Outside, you," few of them ever complained. Petro was believed to have done rather well, and to own the leaseholds on several tenement-courts.

In his usual corner a man in an extraordinarily-ripped frock coat was staring into a wine-cup as though engaged in divination. Bruto's gesture brought wine pouring into the cup, and after the level had gone down again, Bruto spoke.

"Professor. A, like, question."

"Question me," the professor said, after a moment.

"On, like, etiquette." A subject less likely to invite questions in Pie-Petro's, it would have been hard to find. "Supposing there's, like, a queen. And she bobs. Who'd she bob to? Huh?"

Slightly readjusting his torn coat, the professor said it would depend. "Could be to anybody. The Patriarch. The Emperor. Depends. A queen could curtsey even to a muck-raker, if he'd just saved her tiny grandson from tumbling off a dock. . . ." The level of the wine went down again, a bit more was added to raise it, not much. "How deep does this queen bob?"

Bruto looked all around the low dive and there was that in his look which made all shun his glance. He then, and most solemnly, performed a curtsey before the professor's bloodshot eyes.

"That deep, eh?"

"Yeah."

"Only to a fellow-sovereign. Why — ?"

A clumping of boots down the long steps; in came Pishto-the-Avar, drew Bruto slightly aside. "I shadowed'm, Boss. To the Windsor-Lido — *'King'* ? There ain't no kings there. There's a couple counts there, though; they're travellin on Scando-Frorish passports, whatever the Hell *they* are. Huh? Boss?"

But, prior to answering, Boss posed a further question of his own. "Hey, Professor, what's it mean if a king is travelling like a count, like?"

The professor gazed once again into his goblet; divined it was empty; was obliged to look up. His face ceased to be vacant, entirely; a look of faint thought came over it. "It means he is travelling incognito, *incognito,* literally *unknown,* you know. . . ." His title derived from his having been for a while, long ago, a tutor to the junior page-boys at the Palace; he knew, then, presumably, whereof he spoke. "As, for instance, a sovereign wished to visit a foreign country, but not in official state. Could be inconvenient both to him or her and to the host nation; therefore he or she employs what is termed a lesser title, as for example the late King of Illyria visited here as Count Hreb, and . . ." The professor's voice, in its alcoholic monotone, had gotten lower and lower and slower and slower. It next ceased. Then with a look of, almost, terror, on his filthy face, the professor lurched to his trembly feet and took a tottering step towards the door. He was, to employ a polite term, distrained.

Afterwards, the professor having been made comatose with wine, a further conversation:

"Kidnap a king and hold him for ransom. Why, it's never been *done!"*

"Sure it has! Didn't them French capture the old King of Scythia and hold him for ransom, back in them Bonaparte days?"

"Yeah . . . but the French had a army. We ain't got the place, we ain't got the —"

"We ain't got the strennth."

"We ain't got the strennth. Fact. — *Still* . . ."

They gazed at each other, eyes gleaming; mouths open, silent.

"This could mean we swing."

"Yeah . . ." Silence.

"This could mean buckets o' ducats."

"*Yeah. . . .*"

Then —

"Only one man could do it. On-ly *one."*

"Yeah . . . uh, who'd ya mean?"

A hissed-in breath. "Who'd I mean? I mean the Boustremóvitch. Who I mean."

"The Boustremóvitch! Yeah. . . . *Yeah. Yeah!* . . ."

The two young men continued their stroll. Bella was certainly not

Paris, but it was equally certainly larger than St. Brigidsgarth. And far more cosmopolitan. Here one saw men and women whose cut and style reminded one, at least, of Paris — or, at any rate, Brussels. And here were yeoman farmers in the boots and baggy britches of the Gothic Highlands, there a pair of Lowland Hussars in black shakoes, a group of drovers in the characteristic embroidered vests of Poposhki-Georgiou, Mountain Tsigane women in gaudy flounces, River Tartars wearing caftans of many colors, barge-sailors with rings in dirty ears, Avars in low-crowned hats with narrow brims and embroidered bands . . .

"— and," Count Calmar enquired, "besides your duties as equerry, of course, what do you do?"

The young cornet chuckled. " 'Do'? Why should I *'do'* anything? Well, well, you must excuse my levity. My estates are not vast, but at least they are not entailed. I am such a younger son of such a younger son of a cadet branch that what lands came to me were not thought worth tying up; I may sell them if I wish, but there is no hurry. What would I do with the money? Wastrel it away in France? I think not. But . . . why . . . when I am not on duty for the Palace? Well, I hunt a little, I fish a little; very few people of our class do fish here, but I picked it up in England. I have an uncle with an English wife and have spent many summers there; God save us from the winters!"

Magnus said, a touch of reproof, a touch of gloom, in his voice, "The winters of England are tropical in comparison to our Far-Northwestern winters. We have snow instead of rain. And so. And also — ?"

Also Cornet Eszterhazy played cards and billiards. He had a horse — sometimes two. He visited the music halls and, in season, the opera. Now and then he visited the ladies. No, there was no one lady. "I'm afraid it sounds like a rather useless life."

Magnus said it sounded like a rather delightful life. "Everywhere I go at home some minister or chancellor is thrusting papers at me; och! God! Those eternal papers! And not just one set of them. Two! One for each kingdom. Oh why did my thrice-removed grandfather marry my thrice-removed grandmother! 'To unite adjacent kingdoms,' you will say. 'And the House of Olaus-Olaus-Astridson with that of Katzenelenbo̊gen-Ulf-and-Olaus.' Well, the Houses are united. But the kingdoms, not. Always, from the Frores, some new demand. Always. Always. The Scands bother me quite enough, 'Sire, you must not so often get drunk' — why not? If I am sober for the ceremonies, what difference, the rest of the time? 'Sire, you must put on a different uniform,' 'Sire, you must attend for this occasion, for that, you must get up,' 'Sire, you must not do that, Sire, you must do this, Sire, you cannot eat with people of a lower class, Sire' — och! God! So stiff, the Scands! The Scands, so stuffy!" He stopped and shook his head so rapidly that his English-style cap almost fell off; he adjusted it so that it rested more securely on his long, blond hair.

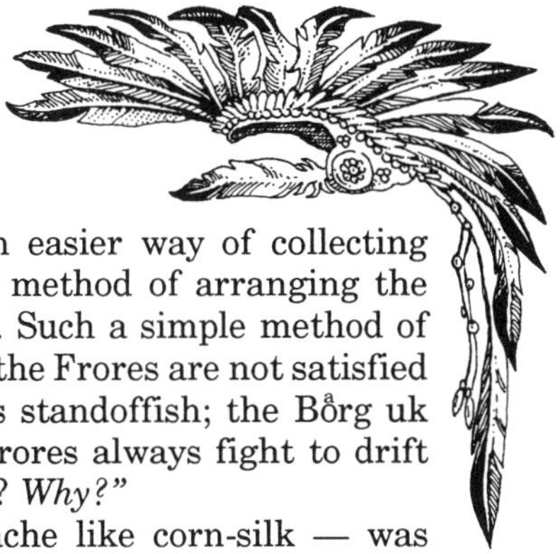

"But the Frores! The Frores! Look: an easier way of collecting taxes: the Frores don't want it. A better method of arranging the Army, the Navy: the Frores don't want it. Such a simple method of satisfying the demands for free education: the Frores are not satisfied at all. Always dour, always scowly, always standoffish; the Bårg uk Bårg said a good word once: said, 'The Frores always fight to drift upstream.' Now, why, my dear new friend? *Why?*"

His dear new friend stroked a moustache like corn-silk — was thoughtful indeed.

"Why?"

"Well . . . Count Calmar . . . it has been my experience that . . . no people, really, wants to be governed by another people, whether it is governed ill or governed well."

Magnus muttered that the Frores really did not want to be governed at all. Then the mutter died away. Then he half-turned. "You spoke of visiting the ladies. Where . . . may one ask . . . as a visitor . . . are the ladies whom one may visit? *Not* one of those 'nice, quiet places, like a boarding-house for parsons' widows. I have in my mind Turkish Gypsy girls with wild, black manes, and for a music there would be drums and concertinas and timbrels, and a wine as red as ox-blood. . . . Eh?"

The Slovatchkoes, third-most numerous (after the Goths and Avars) of the peoples of Scythia-Pannonia-Transbalkania, were divided in their opinion of the Brigand Boustremóvitch. Some still admired their old image of him. Some no longer did so. Some had never admired him at all. Their patriotic painter, Karpustanko, had depicted him with large and lustrous eyes, a heroic stance, and vast curly mustachios worthy of a bashi-bazouk, but time had taken toll. The large eyes were now less lustrous than bloodshot, the stance had declined into bowed legs and a dropped chest, and the mustachios were limp and greyed. Furthermore, he who had once had his nest in a cave whence he preyed upon Turks and Tartars — and, incidentally, upon anyone else who passed by and had not purchased protection — now dwelt in a decayed once-palace in a near-slum section of Bella, and had done so ever since giving his parole and obtaining, with Imperial reluctancy, the Imperial pardon. Did he pass his days reading Boethius' *The Consolations of Philosophy*? No he did not; he had never heard of Boethius, and, save for a faltering and seldom exercised acquaintance with the big red rubrics in the mass-book, the Brigand Boustremóvitch could not read. The Secret Police (uniform: regulation sky-blue trousers, with a crimson tunic) spasmodically reminded the Ministry of Justice that "the reformed Brigand, Boustremóvitch," had a finger (seven or eight fingers) in criminal conspiracies of several sorts, kindly see attached document. The Ministry of Justice eventually invariably instructed the Secret

Police to "continue its most valuable reports, Faithfully theirs, [squiggle]." Translation: "We would rather have him in Bella collecting an illegal tax on radish-wagons (for example), than back in the Glagolitic Alps mounting mounted irregulars. Again." Gradually the Secret Police had grown bored. And so had the Brigand Boustremóvitch. Often he had thought, wistfully, of breaking his parole and absquatulating for, say, Bulgaria, whence he would harry the Greeks. *Or* the Turks.

But the years like great black oxen trod the earth, and he had done nothing.

Ignats Louis —

Ignats Louis, groaning softly from a very recently returned pain to which he had long, at irregular intervals, been a martyr, stood studying an immense sheet of parchment on a table before him. Enter his Prime Minister.

"Your Royal and Imperial Majesty may perhaps wish to ride the Whitey horse this afternoon."

"No he doesn't perhaps either. O God, I am being punished for my sins!"

"But the people will expect it, your —"

"The people must bear the disappointment; O Holy Souls in Purga——"

"But I have taken the liberty of having him saddled, Your —"

"Then take the liberty of riding him yourself. Oh. *Oh.* OH!"

"My constitutional advice —"

"*Stuff* your constitutional advice! I shan't leave the premises — except of course to visit the dear little kiddies in the 'spital-house as usual —"

The First Minister still lingering and seeming about to press further, the Presence, bifurcated beard bristling with rage, addressed to him the following words, of perhaps dubious constitutional aspect: "*Out,* you jumped-up burgomaster! You hangman morphadite and whoreson hostler: OUT!"

The First Minister, thinking enviously of Mr. Gladstone and Mr. Disraeli, bowed deeply and abjectly, and got OUT. Ignats Louis, with a groan and a whimper, returned his attention to the chart on the table. Gradually his moans ceased. Attention to his family tree never failed to soothe him. His finger fondly traced the Lineage in all its ramification, including those marked (MORGANATIC), (ILLEGITIMATE), (NON COMPOS MENTIS), and — none the less Royal, none the less Imperial — (INSANE). So.

Maurits Louis m *Matilda Gertruda*. So. *Ignats Salvador* m *Amelia Carolina*. Quite correct. So he had. *Salvador Ignats. Theresa Matilda*. Hmm. Well, he had not exactly *married* her, Salvador Ignats, but he

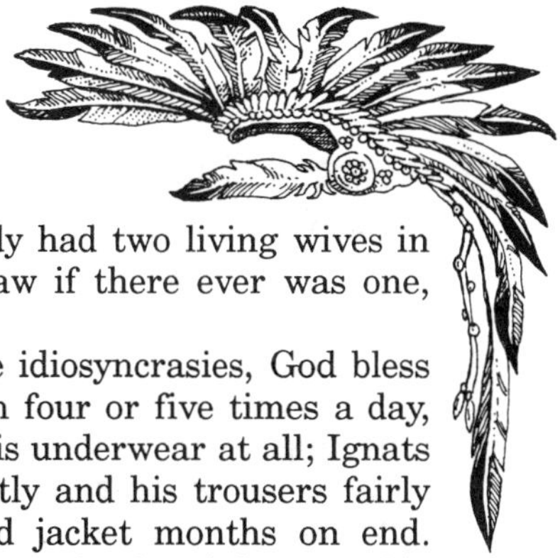

certainly would have if he had not already had two living wives in the dungeons; a stickler for the canon law if there ever was one, Salvador Ignats.

All these monarchs had had their little idiosyncrasies, God bless them. Maurits Louis changed his uniform four or five times a day, but could never be persuaded to change his underwear at all; Ignats Salvador changed his underwear constantly and his trousers fairly often, but wore the same waistcoat and jacket months on end. Maximillian III Ignats considered it *his* constitutional duty to ride around Bella throwing largesse of, so he thought, gold coins to the throngs; actually his purse was kept purposefully filled with newly-minted extra-heavy *kopperkas* constantly coined for the purpose. Salvador Ignats spent most of his time in churches — eikons he could not learn to love — "Mamma, why are there so many ugly saints?" was his, perhaps, most well-known theological comment — but he had an absolute *passion* for the votive paintings which crammed the crumbling, smelly chapels of the Old Town. His favorite was said to be the so-called *Pathetic Exemplum of Makúshushka Daughter of the Master Chimneysweeper Brutsch Being Saved from a Sinking Rowboat by the Personal Intercession of the Archangel Angelo* [the Prince-Archbishop of Bella, for roundly insisting that there was no Archangel Angelo, was forever after referred to by Salvador Ignats as "that freemason"] *Limned in Minimally 37 Colors by the Master Limner-Painter Porushko, Believing without Cavil in the Faith which Was Given to the Saints.* Lucky, lucky Porushko! When votive painting had been scacre, he had done cigar-box covers; now he was enabled by Royal and Imperial patronage to spend six years and six months depicting — of course in advance! — the deathbed of Salvador Ignats: with its many, *many* figures of men and women and of angels. Did it not remind one of the Greco's *Burial of Count Orgaz*?

Not very much.

Presently Ignats Louis rang a bell, the bell was answered by a Gentleman-in-Waiting, a middle-aged nobleman of many quarterings; "Listen, sonny," said the Presence, "tell the Grand Almoner that today for my gifts to the sick kiddies besides the posies let's have some chewy sweetmeats and some of the teeny-tiny toys, hey?"

"Certainly, Sire."

"And, oh, sonny?"

"Yes, Sire?"

The Presence went deep in thought. "Say. Sonny. Where is it, a place called something like . . . ah . . . *Frore*land . . . maybe . . . ?"

The Gentleman-in-Waiting was at no loss for words. "I could go look it up in the Postal Gazette, Sire."

The Presence, regarding this as something akin to brilliance, beamed. Nodded. The Gentleman-in-Waiting began to withdraw. Paused. "Sire. My humble obedience: *Where?*"

As it happened, the Brigand Boustremóvitch had for some while been planning an action involving a recusant boss-fishmonger unwilling to pay his racket-assessments in full and on time. On hearing the proposal of Bruto and of Pishto-the-Avar, the Brigand immediately saw how neatly his planned action would fit, and, placing two fingers into his mouth, gave a brief whistle to summon his henchmen. The negligent fish-dealer could wait . . . or, likelier, be entirely forgotten, in view of what was now to be a great change of scene for Boustremóvitch: with buckets of ducats he would never need to bother with kettles of fish again — he might even skip, or skip through, Bulgaria, and head thence into Turkey-in-Europe (or, for that matter, -in-Asia), turn his coat and swear fealty to the Sultan and purchase the rule of a *sanjak,* or a *pashalik* like Little Byzantia, the southernmost semi-province of the Empire. In his suddenly-quickened mind he saw himself the founder of a dynasty, a new khedive, a new Obrenovitch or Karageorgevitch. . . .

"Yes, Brigand," the henchmen said. "Sure, Brigand! That's the way we'll do it, Brigand!"

"— and you, Vallackavo, go muck out the secret cell in the basement, and toss some clean straw into it —"

"Sorry Brigand, the ceiling's already fall in on the secret cell in the basement."

"Then we'll use the one up in the wall!"

No one had seen the Boustremóvitch so excited since the time he had burned the Tartar's toes; and when he shouted to them to **Get Moving Now!**, they Got.

Count Magnus Calmar and Cornet Engelbert Eszterhazy absently observed a roughly-dressed fellow sitting in a doorway holding an empty bowl in his lap: propped against his body an equally-roughly-lettered sign bearing the initials of the words, MUTE, BLIND. DEAF. MERCY: equally absently dropped coins in it: continued their light-hearted conversation.

"You are sure that you would not rather go to Miss Betty's?"

"I am quite sure."

"Very well, then. I shall speak to my senior colleague, Lieutenant Knoebelhoffer, who is in the Equerries' Room accounted rather knowledgeable on Gypsy dances and dancers; perhaps we may be able to arrange it for, say, later this evening — perhaps only tomorrow."

"The sooner the better."

"Agreed. Ah. By the way. Ahem. As we continue our educational walk," they moved on, "you will observe to the left and across the

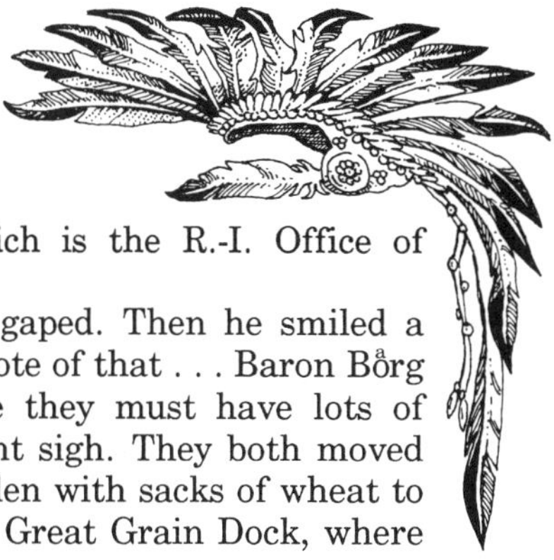

street a rather smart new building which is the R.-I. Office of Commercial Statistics. Ahem."

Magnus made a wry mouth. Then he gaped. Then he smiled a rather rusty smile. "Allow me to make a note of that . . . Baron Bårg uk Bårg will be pleased. Hm. I suppose they must have lots of statistics about stockfish." He gave a faint sigh. They both moved forward to allow a train of six ox-carts laden with sacks of wheat to pass on along to Umlaut's mills from the Great Grain Dock, where they had been unladen off barges.

Eszterhazy said, "You produce a great deal of stockfish, your countries, I mean; do you not?"

Magnus gave a heavy sigh, pressed his hand to his brow. "Och, God! Yes! We catch fish and we dry fish and we catch it and we dry it and . . . You see: Frore stockfish is cheaper, Scand stockfish is better, and so each country feels justified in demanding regulation against the other: quotas, imposts, duties — och, God! And of course neither one wishes to allow the demands of the other. We catch it and we dry it and we boil it and we eat it and we eat it and sometimes we eat it with hot mutton-fat and sometimes without and we have still more of it than we can eat and more of it than we can export. . . . And so, lacking the money to import wheat, often we . . . the people, I mean . . . are sometimes obliged to go without bread —" And he sighed, yet again, heavily.

Eszterhazy gave a sympathetic nod; sympathetic, yet abstracted. The Count Calmar had perhaps told him more about stockfish than he wished to know. The last of the heavy-laden ox-wagons had finally gone by, leaving behind a golden trail of grain spilled from some torn sack, which, as no one bothered to gather it up, the sparrows of the city had now begun to feed upon. Struck by some sudden and inchoate thought, he addressed himself to a woman of the people passing by with her shopping basket — "Excuse me, Mother, but what does stockfish cost these days?"

"Too much!" she snapped. "— when we can git it, that is! Thank God that bread stays cheap."

Magnus's face had assumed once more that familiar vacant, almost rough stare. "My dear Engelbert, I want a drink," he said. "How does one say in your language, 'glåg'? Or, for that matter: 'shnops'?"

Engelbert Eszterhazy noted — and reported — that they were quite near his Club; they at that moment passing in front of the smart new building, he stepped forward and bowed politely to a man who had just descended the steps with a portfolio under his arm. "Pray forgive my impudence, my dear Herra Chiefstatisticscouncillor, but —"

The man, under the double influence of being addressed by a title a full two grades higher than his actual one, and by someone with an immensely upper-class accent, stretched himself to his full height, puffed his chest, and said, "Command me."

"We were wondering . . . at the Palace . . ." The man's eyes began to pop. ". . . if there were any *known* reason why the commerce and trade between Scythia-Pannonia-Transbalkania and Far Northwestern Europe is not greater than it is. Surely my dear Herra *you* will know, eh?"

The chief (merely) clerk was obliged to swallow. Twice. "The reason is, my dear . . . my dear . . ."

"The Cornet Engelbert Eszterhazy for to serve God, the Emperor, and my lord Chiefstatisticscouncillor." He handed his card.

"The reason is one of the economics of geography, a matter to which I, heh-hem, have paid especial attention. To ship, let us say —"

"Let us say . . . oh . . . *grain* . . . wheat . . . just for instance."

To ship grain (for example, wheat) overland through Russia was to observe first-hand that it could be conveyed faster by a Vloxfellow with a wheelbarrow. Via water? Down the Ister to the Danube and thence to the Black Sea, into the Mediterranean, up the Atlantic — one sees the problem? Ideally, such a trade should pass by railroad via a direct northern route into Austria-Hungary, and thence — "Why not?" — Because, why not, there *was* no direct northern route. Such a route would needs pass through the demesnes of the Titular Majesty of Carinthia, and the Titular Majesty of Carinthia refused to allow it on the grounds that all steam engineers were Scotchmen, and all Scotchmen were heretics and had cut off the head of the piously Catholic Virgin Queen Victoria. Furthermore, the smoke of the locomotives would smutch her new-washed laundry. . . .

There being, alas, no glo̊g available at the Club, the two young men had a shnops instead. They had a second shnops. Instead. Eventually and once again they parted in the Grand Lobby of the Windsor-Lido: at any event "Engli" would report back as soon as he could. In an excellent mood, the Count Calmar entered his suite and was about to open the door of the parlor when he noted that, for one thing, it was already open, and, for another, that the room behind it was not unoccupied.

"He is already late," said the dry, grim voice of the Baron Bo̊rg uk Bo̊rg; it was not even an angry or even an annoyed voice. It was only — as always — a disapproving voice. "I have planned to read him this very short minute I have written, it is only ten pages, on the present state of the Triune Monarchy. But he is already late." The scratch of a pen indicated the presence of the industrious Kopperkupp.

Magnus knew he could not, simply could not, enter and sit still for a ten-page minute; he tiptoed out and, observing in the small private lobby a pair of neatly-furled umbrellas, took one and put it under his arm. He could have given no reason why, so perhaps the two glasses of shnops would have to serve as reason.

He had not gone very far, nor did he have any clear idea where he was going, when a rather roughly-dressed man separated himself from a knot of workingmen doing no particular work, and approached. That this fellow bore a very close likeness to the beggarman blind and mute and deaf to whom he had given alms not long ago did not occur to him; he did not remember having given alms. And the man came very close and said, "Hey *meester*, pssst! You like see Turkish Gypsy dancing-girl?"

Later: "Füi! *Ee*yoo! This stuff stinks," said the "beggarman," looking around.

"Otto of roses is one thing," said Pishto-the-Avar. "And chloroform's another."

The Skraeling, when he hunts the walrus on the ice, attempts to convince the walrus that he, the Skraeling, is another walrus, pulling himself along on his elbows as he lies full-length stretched-out. To employ this same tactic in the streets of a large city requires some change of details, but the principle remained sufficiently the same so that Eeiiuullaalaa (a.k.a. "Old Skraelandi," "Ole Frori") was not intercepted. He could not read what was painted on the side of the wagon into which his Sovereign had been swiftly thrust, but his nose told him it was strongly associated with fish . . . and not stockfish, either . . . it went off as rapidly as a fish-wagon could possibly go without arousing suspicion. He walked after it until it turned a corner; then he ran, loped, or trotted; to one who had chased reindeer, a fishwagon was nothing. When he got in sight of it again, he walked again; if it was not in sight he followed its trail of scent until it came in sight. Those who saw and noticed (not the same thing at all) perhaps docketed him as a quarter-cast Tartar in a slightly odd cap; but this was no reason for stopping him. And, in fact, no one did stop him.

He was not even thinking of the possibility that he might eventually become winded when he saw a gate open in a high wall, the wagon roll and rattle inside, the gate close. Nearby to where he stopped was a tree, a mulberry, a rather old and rather tall one. In Skraeland grew no mulberry trees, for in Skraeland grew few trees at all, but the Skrae shamans knew about trees nonetheless, and one of the things they said about them was, "Where there are no crags, eagles dwell in trees." From within the walls wherein his unfortunate Ruler was now captive came, subdued by distance, some shrill whistles; these (the Brigand Boustremóvitch was giving orders to his henchmen) — plus that just-remembered saying, reminded him of what he had to do. The *toom-toom* he had, as always, with him; but the *toom-toom* he had not now *here* with him: it was within its flat case, packed within his box at the hotel. But he had the other thing-of-power with him, and so now he thrust his hand into his bosom and he drew it out. It was wrapped in the skin of an entirely-black ermine tail, worn smooth and darkened by age; the thing-of-power had not been new when the first Court Shaman brought it with him first to Frorigarth and then to S'Brigidsgarth, and no one now remembered the name of the (pre-missionary, entirely pagan) shaman who fashioned it from the wing-bone of the large male eagle he had captured and — after a well-sung apology — killed. Ole chanted the *Beginning Chant* as the *Beginning Chant* was always sung.

Then he placed the whistle in his mouth, there as high in the old tree as it was prudent to climb, and began, in quick, sharp bursts, to blow it.

He did not know to whom he was whistling: to whom, in the realm below, his shrill cry for help was addressed; mainly he had in mind the spirits of the upper and lower air. Partly — though not with much hope — he thought that perhaps there might be shamans here in this distant city or not very far from it . . . if not precisely fellow shamans then at least a one or two with some similar knowledge and who, recognizing the burden of his shrill cry, could come — somehow — to his aid. And besides: what else had he to do? And what else *could* he do?

Having left the Bureau of Parks, Forests, and Lands, Emma Katterina and her suite (popularly denominated as "three witches and a priest") headed outward for the Office of the Privy Purse, there to collect yet another batch of "pensions"; some of them in her own right, and some of them as widow of the very long-late Margrave of the Ister, Ignats Louis's elder half-brother. It had been a tangled Succession-to-the-Throne; and, rather than tangle it further still, the Royal and Imperial Family had preferred to pay. And pay. And pay. It did not, as such things were reckoned, pay much; but — who had known the woman would live so long? — *it was still paying!* The five eventually reached the Five Points, where the major routes through the city disembogued, were obliged to detour along the left side of the road because navvies laying gas-pipes had deeply trenched the east side. Emma Katterina had been waddling wearilessly along; suddenly she stopped, an odd expression on her face. The Baroness Bix and Bix, one of her Ladies in Waiting, asked, a trifle anxiously, "What, The Mamma?"

The Titular Queen of Carinthia was at no loss. "What, you can't hear? What, your ears are stopped with wax and dirt and infidelity? *The Satan is fifing!"* And, in a sudden second of silence, it seemed to them that, lo! the Satan *was* fifing! Had they, the old woman and her chaplain and her three handmatrons, at that moment found themselves in some sort of suddenly constructed sound-trap, a . . . as it

were . . . nexus, where the high thin notes which came from the shaman's eagle's wing whistle were being driven down and along by currents of wind and air and flowed, however briefly, there and thither . . . and thither and there only? However briefly?

Without more to-do, Emma Katterina knelt on the road-bed and, taking out her rosary, began to pray. And so, without more to-do, her Chaplain and her Ladies knelt on the roadbed and, taking out their rosaries, began to pray. Six fish-wives who had been to the Great Market to replenish their wares, on seeing this, set down their baskets and, ceasing to cry, *"Fresh! Fresh! A penny off, a penny off!"* knelt on the roadbed and, taking out their rosaries, began to pray. Seven superannuated housewives who had been on their way to the nearby Church of Saints Cyril and Methodius, knelt on the roadbed, took out their rosaries and began to pray. Eight coal-heavers coming along asked themselves what was going on here, and, reminding one another that it was Lent, knelt (rather rustily) upon the roadbed, and, after patting their pockets ("Got it here *some*where for sure — *ah! Knew* I'd got it!"), took out their rosaries and began to pray. The new-dug ditch was too broad to be leaped, and inside of three minutes the entire Five Points had become impassable. And while the constantly increasing throng knelt reciting endless rosaries (or, in the case of those of Other Denominations, the doxologies in Old High Hyperborean, Ancient Avar, Medieval Slovatchko, Reformed Romanou, and other liturgical languages of the polyglot Empire), the staff of SS. Cyril and Methodius ordered the churchbells to be rung — thus alerted, so did those of the not-quite-so-nearby Churches of St. Gleb, St. Boris, St. Vladimir, Holy Affliction, St. Nicholas of Myra, St. Peter in Chains, St. Catherine the Martyr, SS. Cosmo and Damian Healing the Sick Without Charge . . . the sounds of their bells spread like ripples. While all this was going on, steam-trams, horse-cars, omnibuses, wagons, private carriages, pedestrians, all piled up behind each other, clogging the streets as far as the Swing Bridge, and farther enough to prevent it from swinging, thus tying up the traffic on the Little Ister and even the Ister, and thus — also — preventing the Late Lunchtime Freight from passing across Stanislavs Street, thus tying up rail traffic as far away as Budapest and Belgrade. . . .

Three men in a fruit and vegetable wagon asked each other what was going on? They could fathom out no answer. Said one, "Well, whatever, we can't get through here and we must be at the Palace Children's Infirmary on time; turn at the right —"

"Just as impassable! The devil!"

"Keep on and turn at the next left —"

"No use! What — ?"

"Whip up and head for Garlicstringer's Gulley!" They lashed the horse. They pressed on. And on. But ever they seemed pressed farther and farther from the way they would go, and anxiously they scanned the faces of the church-tower clocks, and, with growing concern, compared their watches.

Three charcoal-burners had come down from the White Mountain to sing for money in the streets according to old-time custom, clad in shaggy goatskins: one with a timbrel, and one with a drum, and one with a rattle and a bell; the intention being to collect enough money to have a good old drunk at the end of Lent before heading back up-hill with what might be left — said, suddenly, one to the other, of a sudden looking up: "Say, brother, ain't that a eagle?"

"A course that be a eagle, brother! That ain't no magpie!"

"Makes a man feel at home . . . almost . . ."

"Say, we ain't comed hear to watch birds, there's a bunch of people up ahead, let's give'm four or five verses of *By the Limpid Forest Pool See the Chaste Gertruda Bathing Bare-ass.*"

By and by the Police traced the bottle to the neck.

No one of course dared order Emma Katterina to arise, but attempts were made to order her Ladies and her Chaplain: "Up with you, Madame. Up, Father, up! Get up, Lady — now!" Lips and fingers continued moving, eyes swung to the Royal Mistress. Her reply was brief. "The Mamma wouldn't let," said she.

The Countess Critz could not restrain a word of triumph to the baffled Police official; "Away, Antichrist!" she cried.

Hers was a very piercing voice.

The word spread to and through the superstitious and ever-turbulent South Ward that "Big Katinka was a-keeping Antichrist at bay," whereat the locksmen in the Grand, the Royal, and the Little Canals downed levers as one, thus blocking canal traffic; with repercussions all the way to 's Gravenhage and Rostov-on-Don; and the stokers in the R. and I. Central Steam Plant raked out the fires under their boilers and sounded the Great Alarm Whistle to blow off all the steam. Then they pissed on the embers to put them all quite out. And then they trooped along to join the throng.

"This bloody Gulley is bloody unpaved!" one of the men in the wagon cried. "Slow down, slow down, slow —"

"We haven't the time," said another, panting, "the clock in the Works is set and no one can break the seal without setting it off — oh God! Oh God!"

Still loyal to his faith in something which could not be proven, namely the nonexistence of Deity, another said, sweaty face gleaming, "There is no God."

"Well, I bloody well believe that! Look, look! The *next* through street is packed and blocked! Oh God!"

"Oh God!"

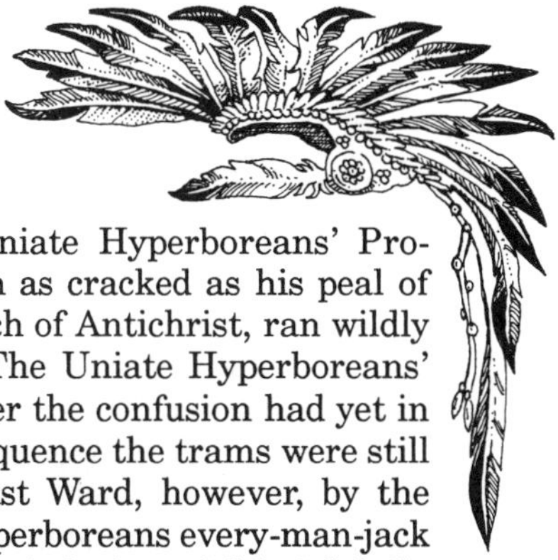

Farther away. The sacristan of the Uniate Hyperboreans' Procathedral, who had in recent years grown as cracked as his peal of bells, on hearing of the attempted approach of Antichrist, ran wildly up into his belfry and pealed them all. The Uniate Hyperboreans' Procathedral lay in the East Ward, whither the confusion had yet in its full form to spread, and where in consequence the trams were still running. The tram-switchmen in the East Ward, however, by the rankest kind of nepotism, were Uniate Hyperboreans every-man-jack of them; no sooner had the tinny tintinnabulation of "their" bells rung out than, taking it for a sign, or at least a signal, they leapt from their hutches and threw their switches. Thirty-three trams were more than sufficient to block Gumbarr Street as it crossed the Avenue Anna Margerita; whereat, puzzled beyond patience as to what was going on, the Royal and Imperial Telegrapher on duty in the Gumbarr St. office tapped along an open wire the query — perhaps unfortunately couched in the form of a proverbial question — THE TURKS HAVE ENTERED VIENNA? It was certainly unfortunate that, having given up spirituous beverage for Lent, his fingers suddenly trembled so that he could not at once add, INTERROGATION POINT . . . for at once all the Receiving Telegraphers still on the wire ran to the doors of their offices and shouted at the tops of their lungs, ***"The Turks have entered Vienna!"***

The duty of the Great Bell Ringer at the Old Tower of the Old Cathedral had traditionally been filled by the largest galley-slave on the Ister, it being assumed that only such labors could develop backs and arms to toll Great Gudzinkas, as the immense Bell (cast in Moscow during the reign of Anna and brought hither at vast expense) was called. Named after Algirdas Gudzinkas, the great Lithuanian metallurgist, engineer, and friend of Dr. Swedenborg, it had last been *officially* rung in celebration of a report that Bonaparte had been killed by an elephant while crossing the Alps (this report turned out to have been false). It had last been *actually* rung when Mazzimilian the Mad had — briefly — regained his sanity: an act so totally impermissible that Authority had ever since steadfastly denied that it had been rung at all.

It was long since there were galley-slaves. The current Great Bell Ringer was a convicted murderer on ticket-of-leave, one Gronka Grimka, called (and for very good reason) the Slovatchko Giant. He was sitting, as usual, scowling in his kennel and smoking the vile black tobacco known as Death-to-the-Vlox, when the Archbishop's cook ran hysterically across the yard, waving her apron and ululating as she ran.

"Why are you *sit*ting there, by-blow of a hobgoblin?" she howled. "*Have*n't you heard? *The Turks have entered Bella!* **Ring the Big Bell!**"

Ordinarily Gronka Grimka would not have cared if the Turks had entered Heaven or Hell, let alone Bella, which he despised; but it was fixed tradition that "whosoever got to ring Great Gudzinkas would receive the Most Gracious Pardon, 17 pieces of gold, a barrel of the best good goose-grease, and a double-pension, too." He rose to his feet rather like the rising of the Nile, and, first crossing himself and then spitting on his immense and horny palms, muttered his national imprecation of "Bugger the Bulgars," and climbed up into the belfry without delay. The immense engine there moved slowly, but by no means silently. The sound of the turning of the huge iron wheels over which the cable-thick bell-ropes passed, presently rumbled through the air, causing all the servants still on their feet within a square mile to fall on their knees, under the impression that they were hearing "Satan's chariots." And soon the dull, clamorous **boom-boom** . . . **boom-boom** . . . of Great Gudzinkas himself sounded throughout almost the whole city.

There was an ancient piece of ordnance, a veteran, in fact, of the French crossing of the Ister, situated on the Old High Rampart; it was of course by now purely ornamental, but Ignats Maurits had ordered it be kept charged. The order had never, somehow, been rescinded: informal motto of the R. & I. Artillery: "Follow an order even if it falls off a cliff." Nevertheless, a certain common sense was employed in regard to the Old French Gun, to wit, "Under no circumstances is the Old French Gun to be fired except at the order of the direct superior officer, or the King-Emperor Himself if there present, or at the sounding of the Great Big Bell." And at the sounding of the Great Big Bell, Cannonry-Corporal Moomkotch performed a neat about-face, bringing his knee up to his belt-level, and down again, **stamp**, produced a large wooden sulfur-match from his pocket, struck it on his boot-sole, and calmly touched it to the touch-hole of the Old French Gun. It went off with an immense **BOOM!** The ball whizzed high, dropped low, struck very near a certain large old mulberry tree, skimmed along the street like a giant bowling-ball, and buried itself in the wall of a mouldering old palace — to the pleasure of a wandering Swiss street photographer who, having set up his equipment, had just then taken a test shot.

"They have us in range!" cried the Brigand Boustremóvitch.

"That's what all the noise is about!" cried a henchman.

"Better beat it, Boss," advised another.

"We will sell our lives dearly!" cried the one-time terror of the Glagolitic Alps.

In the secret cell in the upper wall, Magnus sat up on his straw.

"What was that?" he cried. He had an absolutely terrible taste in his mouth.

Cornet Eszterhazy, having retrieved his horse from the livery stable where he had left it, the better to assist the Count Calmar stretch his train-trip-rusted legs, cantered along towards the Palace, his mind pleasantly at ease as usual. Now and then something beckoned to the corner of his eye . . . a quaint old shop, weather-worn sign, **Bookbinder, Old Books for Sale**, but who would wish to dismount and rummage among old books? Or a mountebank bound in chains from which, when sufficient small coins were produced, he would emerge, straining and groaning, or some drunken wretch lying half in the road, or . . . He turned the horse and cantered back; what else had caught his eye he was not quite aware, but there was some pressing thought to go back and see . . . where had it been? He looked to right and left; presently — sure enough! Halfway up the next, half-empty block, he saw something lying in the road; thither he went to get it.

If it were not the very same English cap which Magnus had been wearing not long before, then it was its twin; and as not that many people in Bella would have had an English cap, very likely it was indeed the same: how came it there?

The drunken wretch in the gutter had pulled himself out of it and was now propped against a lamp-post; he addressed Eszterhazy.

"It fell out of a wagon, like, my lord —"

"When? What wagon? Who — ?"

"A fish-wagon. Come rattling along and knock me right over; help a poor veteran of the Wendish Wars, my lord; no friends at Headquarters and so hence no pension; to buy a nibble of bread, my lord?"

"A noggin of rum would be more like it —"

"Well, there's that, my lord. There's that. 'Man liveth not by bread alone,' as the Scriptures tell us. Thank you, my lord! Thank you!"

The cornet bethought him a moment, trotting back to the broader street. The cap had fallen *out* of a wagon. Why had "Count Calmar," or "Count Calmar's" cap, been *inside* a wagon? A fish-wagon? On the spur of the moment, he turned and headed back to the Grand Hotel Windsor-Lido. And there in the grand lobby he saw the Baron Bőrg uk Bőrg, literally wringing his hands.

"Cornet! Cornet! There's a report that His Maj—— that Count Calmar — he was late, he was late, he did not in fact return — that he was seen being attacked and forced into a fish-wagon! A *fish*-wagon! The King of Scandia and Froreland! Not alone the possible danger to the poor young man, young and impetuous though he sometimes is — and heedless — it is only the Crown which keeps the Two Kingdoms together — it is nothing that I shall surely be forced to resign and that they will send me to be a petty postmaster at some Skrae trading-post on the Arctic Ocean —"

"Is this his cap?"

The courtier seized it, sniffed it, turned it partly inside out. "Essence of Lilac, his very hair-tonic; and look! Look! The label!"

GOUSTAVV GOUSTAVVSON
HABERDASHER, S'BRIG.

"Then immediately we must notify your Minister and the Police."

The Baron moved hand and face in a slight gesture of deep despair. "I have already despatched messengers to both, but — I don't at all understand — they say there is some disturbance in the central section of the city and that the messengers may have some difficulty getting through to —"

The suave and practiced smile on the glossy face of the assistant manager vanished at Eszterhazy's peremptory manner. "Yes, of course, Cornet, the Grand Hotel Windsor-Lido *does* have a private contract telegraph office, just next the cashier's . . . but there seems to be some trouble on the line, and I am afraid that —"

A privy councillor walked by, curling his large moustache and conveying on his arm a handsome younger woman who, whoever she was, was certainly not the frow privy councillor; he raised his eyebrows in acknowledgement of the assistant manager's sycophantic smile; again the smile vanished abruptly.

"This foreign milord, Baron Bo̊rg, is on an important mission; you will go with him and see that constant attempt is made to get his telegrams through and you will remain with him until then or even longer if he asks you. We would hate to commandeer this place." Thus spake Cornet Eszterhazy.

With a word or two and a salute, he left, walking rather rapidly to the alley where the horse waited for him. Yet — upset as he was — he could not but laugh a little as he recalled his own brash words.

We!

He quickly remounted his horse, and, looking up as he did so, he saw, flying rather low overhead, an eagle . . . and another eagle . . . and another . . . and another . . . and another . . . and . . .

The Turkish Legate in Bella at that time was Selim Ghazi Effendi, commonly called "Grizzly Pasha," who had been exiled from Paris for gross peculation and other high misdemeanors; and now spent his days and his nights stupefied with opium, which he smoked (mingled with Latakia and Makedonia and Otto de Rose) in his huge mother-of-pearl-inlaid hookah. Now, as the Great Big Bell boomed on, and he vaguely heard the sole sound which filled the sky, he looked from a dream which he saw very clearly in his charcoal brazier of the Blessed Houri dancing in Paradise . . . a place which he was pleased but not surprised to observe very much resembled his former villa near Neuilly. He said, *"Mmmuhhh?"*

The Legation's *kawas* appeared at his elbow. "Shadow of the Shadow of God," the *kawas* said, "the *giaours* are saying that the

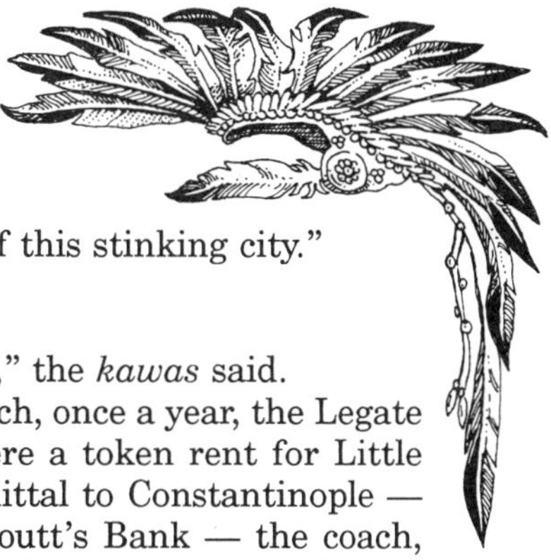

Troops of the Faithful are at the portals of this stinking city."

Grizzly Pasha said. *"Mmmuhhh . . ."*

By and by he gestured.

"At once, Shadow of the Shadow of God," the *kawas* said.

Presently the rather lop-sided coach which, once a year, the Legate was roused to ride to the Exchequer, where a token rent for Little Byzantia was paid over to him for transmittal to Constantinople — the rest being more crisply sent on via Coutt's Bank — the coach, accompanied by five gaunt and elderly Kurd lancers (mounted upon five equally elderly and gaunt horses, and looking like a quincunx of quixotes); the coach rolled out of the grounds of the Legation and into the East Ward . . .

Most of the telegraphers having left their keys to go home and protect their families, the police had resorted to the Army heliograph; this device (aided by telescope) now flashed the news that TURKISH TROOPS HAVE BEEN SEEN IN THE EAST WARD; the sugar, butter, and flour dealers at once doubled their prices and prepared to barricade their premises.

It was in the mind of the Pasha merely to indicate that the building they were approaching was to be appropriated for the benefit of his younger brother; what he said, however was *"Mmm . . ."* and then, his tongue suddenly clearing somewhat, "That one —" The coach turned in the carriage-path, rolled up to the porte-cochère; stopped. The Pasha promptly dozed off. The Bulgarian Minister was playing backgammon with the wife of the Bulgarian First Secretary, when a startled servant informed him that the Turkish Legate had arrived.

"Bozhemoie, what does that impotent old paederast want here?" he asked. But under the porte-cochère he said, *"Altesse, Altesse, mille fois bienvenu!"*

"The keys, *Giaour,"* said Grizzly Pasha. And paused.

"The keys, Your Highness? *At once. Cer*tainly. *Which* keys?"

Another pause. The Pasha had after all been in many cities; if he were not immediately sure which one he was in now, the doubt must be forgiven him.

Yet another pause. "The keys . . . the keys to Belgrade, *Giaour,"* said Grizzly Pasha. *"Mmmuhh. . . ."*

The Bulgarian Minister, who was a Bulgarian, was perplexed; the Bulgarian First Secretary, who was an Armenian, was not. In less than a minute he had returned with the largest keys available (they were those of the potting shed, big and brass and bright), reposing on the red plush cushion which usually served for the repose of his wife's pet poodle. *"Alors, voici, Altesse, les clefs à Belgrade, avec grande submission,"* he said, offering them up. What, after all (his manner enquired) was Belgrade to him, or he to Belgrade?

Grizzly Pasha accepted and dropped them negligently in his lap, whence they slipped unnoticed to the carriage floor. Then he blinked.

Then he said, "Three days looting for the troops." Then he saw a plate, hastily prepared with bread and salt, also being thrust into his hands. "Oh, very well, then," he conceded, in a disappointed tone. "We spare your lives, and your churches need not become mosques, either. But," he licked his dry mouth with a dryer tongue, frowned; "Ah yes! A hundred thousand pieces of gold, a hundred pretty boys — fat, mind you, *very, very* fat! A glass of quince sorbet, and a dancing-girl (also fat). At once, *getir!*"

The sorbet, at least, was quickly brought. And then, to the tune of a music-box, the wife of the First Secretary (she had been born in Cairo, and was of a rather full figure) performed a beautiful belly-dance. Until the *soi-disant* Occupier of Bella fell suddenly asleep. And was wheeled back home in his carriage rather more rapidly than he had come. The Kurdish lancers were getting on in years, and badly wanted their yogurt.

"Bozhemoie!" said the Bulgarian Minister. "The things one has to put up with, here in Scythia-Pannonia-Transbalkania!"

His First Secretary shrugged. "Your Excellency may light a candle to his saint that he has been spared my first post, a place called St. Brigidsgarth, where the sun does not shine from one year to another what with night and fog and mist and where one eats boiled stockfish with mutton-fat."

His Excellency shuddered. "Where was *that?"*

The First Secretary thought for a moment. "It is in Froreland," he said at last. "*Isn't* it?"

"Bozhemoie!" said His Excellency.

Then he said, "*Where?"*

And meanwhile? What of the "three witches"?

Very soon the Countess Bix and Bix began to feel that all prayers might be safely left to The Mamma and her Chaplain. Her own best guns were of another order, and consisted of a deck of worn and greasy old cards concealed inside the lining of her musty old muff of marten-skin. Squatting on the dung-smeared stone paving-blocks, she began to lay them out in the antique — the terribly, terribly antique pattern of the Abracadabra:

ABRACADABRA
ABRACADABR
ABRACADAB
ABRACADA
ABRACAD
ABRACA
ABRAC
ABRA
ABR
AB
A

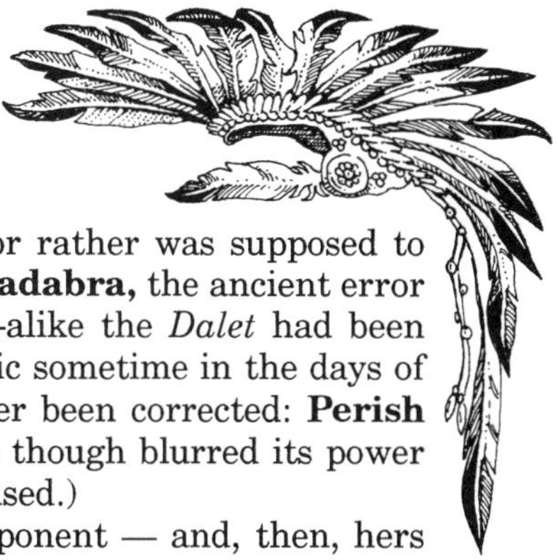

(**Perish like the word** it meant . . . or rather was supposed to mean; actually it should have been **Abdacadabra,** the ancient error of confusing the *Resh* with its near look-alike the *Dalet* had been committed by a scribe unskilled in Aramaic sometime in the days of Darius (or was it Tiberius?) and had never been corrected: **Perish like the word** it should have meant, but though blurred its power was, yet potent, as witness its still being used.)

Hers was no ordinary Adversary or Opponent — and, then, hers were no ordinary cards, for they bore (all of them) the *BAPHOMET* on their backs. What were they *made* of ? Perhaps parchment. What was the *parchment* made of ? Do not ask.

And of the second of the "three witches"? The Countess Critz?

The Countess Critz — as the drone of the growing throng increased — reached through a bottomless pocket in her skirt and rummaged till she found the pouch she wanted: *not* the one with the dried apple for sassy stepdaughters, *no*: the — First she spread out her moth-eaten woolen shawl, then she spread her worn old silk handkerchief. Next from the very small pouch came a smaller ball, the covering of it the scrotum-skin of an all-black bull-calf: the game she played resembled jacks but she used no jacks. Instead of jacks she cast out and gathered in, cast out and gathered in as the small ball bounced, cast out and gathered in the bright-white teeth of a hangman who had been hanged. And all the while she whined and she sing-songed and she chanted in the words of a language so old that (save for this sole incantation) it had quite died before the invention of any signs or letters which could write it.

And the third of the "three witches"? The Highlady Grulzakk had her own rôle to play; taking from a packet concealed in her rusty bosom she shook out into her dirty cracked palm a pair of rude dice carved from the ankle-bones of a wild white jackass, and began to play at dice with the Devil for the fate of Bella; not to give the Prince of Hell too much of a chance, she cast his dice with her left hand — but even so the fate of Bella was far too important to be left to a throw of the dice, and therefore she used loaded dice. "Never give the Devil an even break" was her motto.

Thus, the Highlady Grulzakk.

Down the road from the Bulgarian Ministry and in a somewhat, but only somewhat, larger building: "Gin'ral Abercrombie," asked the wife of the American Minister to the Triune Monarchy, "is they any ice for to make a nice cool glass o' liminade?"

"Not a morsel, my little honey-bee; I have already checked, but for some reason unaccountable the iceman has yet to arrive," said H.A.B. Abercrombie, formerly Sutler-General to the Army of the Missoula.

"Oh, I am jest drinched with presspiration!"

"Endure it, my dear dew-drop, for the sake of Our Great Republic; it is no hotter here than back in La Derriere, Del., and pays much better."

"I b'lieve I'll take off my corset and put on my wrapper and go lie in the hammock you hung between thim funny old iron rengs sut in the walls down in that nice cool deep ol' cellar."

"Do so, my dear, till the cool of the evening. How I wish I might join you and do likewise, but duty calls. 'Toil,' she says. 'Toil on, toil on, toil —' " But Mrs. General had not tarried to hear.

"Safe for hours," muttered the General. He glanced at himself in the tall pier-glass. More than one had commented on his resemblance to the Reverend Henry Ward Beecher, a point which he felt obliged to concede, although his own figure was perhaps a trifle fuller. Next he rang for his butler. General Abercrombie had learned neither Gothic nor Avar, the principal tongues of the Triune Monarchy; and to foreigners wherever he found them, used the language he had learned in a previous diplomatic station (except to servants back home, to whom he might better have spoken in Gullah or Gaelic). "Boy," he said, "washee whiskey glassee in office. Callee my horsee and buggy. And, ah, by the way . . . Boy . . . you know where findee Turkey Gypsy sing-song girly?"

There was at that time in Bella, pitching its canvas tents and touching up the paint on its wagons, in the Old Tartar Paddock, an entertainment entitled the Major James Elphonsus Dandy's Great Texas and Wild West Show; it was really a rather small outfit, a generation or so ahead of its time, but it always managed to pay the bills. Jim Dandy himself, an old goat-looking man and a veteran of the Mexican and Civil Wars, had been giving licks here and there with his paint-brush when along came his partner, Tex Teeter, looking mighty thoughtful.

"Roan Horse has got the spirit up, Jim. Moanin and carryin on. I wanted you should know." He squatted down on his hunkers.

"Drunk again, I spect."

"Nooo. Not drunk a-tall. Keeps moanin that Yellow Hair is in bad trouble. Says he hears the death whistle. And like that."

"Who in the Hell is Yellow Hair?"

"Well now Jim I don't rightly know. But hain't that what the Injuns call George Custer?"

Dandy snorted. "Know whut *I* call George Custer. His outfit was next to mine at Bull Run, he weren't hardly used to war, twas whut you might call his first stand and he hardly stood it a-tall. Well. How come he be sendin smoke signals to Roan Horse — if it *be* him?"

Teeter pushed to one side on his head the high-crowned derby which he like most cattlemen preferred to the broad Stetson with its ridiculous flappy brim, though newspaper and magazine artists

somehow preferred to depict the latter. "Oh it beats *me* Jim. But I say that the Horse has got the spirit up, an — Ho. Hey! Looky thar! In that buggy yander! Hain't that that old jack-ass Hiram Abiff Abercrombie?"

Jim Dandy squinted and peered. "Why I do b'lieve tis. Might's well give'm a hoot and a toot." He moved into the vehicle whose paint he had been touching up. A moment later a blast of steam smote the air, followed at once by a rather rough but immediately recognizable bar of *Rally Round the Flag*. The buggy drew up till it was enveloped in its own dust, the driver stood up and, leaning forward, looked around; then waved his arm, sat down, and drove towards them. "But say, you ott not t'call him a old jack-ass; he is after all a high government official an a veteran of the Great Rebellion."

Teeter snorted. "Great . . . Humbug. Spent the war in them Territories, sellin bad booze to the Injuns an the paroled Rebel prisoners supposed t'ward 'em off, of which I was one — bad *pies*, too! Oh Lordy them was bad pies — crusts soft as mush, and the dried apples hard as leather." And together the two men recited the well-known verse:

I loathe, detest, abhor, despise,
Abominate dried apple pies. . . .

"Major Dandy," said Abercrombie, getting out of his buggy. "Corporal Teeter."

"How do," said the major, offering his grizzled paw.

"Mm," said the corporal. Not doing so.

"Oh come come now. Let us bury the bloody shirt and clasp hands across the something-or-other chasm; boys, my rye's all gone — *got anything to drink?"*

Jim Dandy said he supposed they could broach the barrel of bourbon. "Though mind you, sparingly. The treasury is mighty low, and if no customers show up we'll have to cancel the evenin show."

General Abercrombie said, "Some sort of religious rally has got downtown tied in knots. No idea why; I do not hold with superstitions they being largely spread by Irish Jesuits, no offense to any mackerel-snappers who might be present. As for the other matter, poot! Breach the barrel and pour its contents out with a lavish hand; the Government of the United States shall pay for it; I'll put it down as ENTERTAINMENT OF IRREGULAR CAVALRY." He fluttered his eyebrows and he licked his lips.

After a moment, former-Corporal Teeter asked, only slightly grudgingly, "How's the Mrs.?"

"Sweating. That woman could sweat in the middle of a blizzard." He nodded thanks, raised his glass. "To the glorious American eagle, long may it scream." They drank.

"Well, now, your Mrs. a fine woman. Though the union did seem to me a bit mysterious. You'n her, I mean. *Different.*"

Abercrombie uttered a suspiration of content. "Mystery? Not at all. She was a woman of a certain age who had never been married and I was an office-holder out of office. Her uncle is Senator Adelbert de la Derriere, of Delaware, Chairman of the Senate Foreign Affairs Committee, and a *staunch* Republican with his pockets full of patronage; there is no mystery; say, aren't you going to give all hands a drink?"

Jim Dandy re-entered the cabin of his steam-calliope. Another blast of water music smote the air, followed by the music to the line, "There's Whiskey in the Jar." Figures seemed to arise out of the earth, holding cups, mugs, jam-glasses, and pannikins. "Make you all acquainted," said Tex, as Major Jim poured. "Bloodgood Bixbee; Cockeyed Joe; Deadwood Dick; Vermont Moses; Hebrew Moses; Shadrack Jackson, a former black buffalo soldier; Gettysburg Sims —"

"Gentlemen. Delighted."

"Lance-Thrower, Big Prairie Dog, Minnetonka Three Wolves, Roan Horse, Crow-Killer —"

"Don't stop pouring. My Redskinned friends. Delighted. In war, enemies. In peace, friends. But. Roan Horse. Why the paint?"

In a dolorous chant, Roan Horse announced that Yellow Hair was in trouble, that he (Roan Horse) saw many smokes and heard the deathwhistle and heard the eagle scream . . . and that the sun either wouldn't rise or wouldn't set. He uttered a groan, and began to drink.

"What's all this about, boys?"

Teeter grunted. Smacked his lips. Told him. "Pshaw," said the United States Minister. "More superstition!"

"Well. Gen'ral, you think just as you like, but *last* time Roan Horse had the spirit up, was't the last time — the first time — don't matter; why he set around moaning *Frog, Frog,* complained he had pains in the small of his back something fierce; whut come to pass? Hardly a few days later we heard the French Emperor had a attack a thuh kidney colic something fierce and had surrendered his hull army to the Proosians, now didn't we, Jim?"

"Well, that's for true. We did. Say, who is *this?*"

"This" was a uniformed figure who came galloping up on a light-cavalry-type horse; quickly dismounting, he asked, "Sir. Are you not the American Minister?"

"I am, young sir. And you?"

The young sir said that he was Engelbert Eszterhazy, an Imperial Equerry; he seemed extremely agitated, maintaining his composure with some difficulty. "Ah, thank God, Your Excellency, I thought I recognized your vehicle — Sir! A terrible situation has arisen. The Count Calmar has evidently been kidnapped, and I am unable to get across the city or through the city in order to report it to any of our authorities; I don't know what is happening, and I entreat your help as an emissary."

"Have a drink, Cornet."

"No, no, I —"

"Cornet, as emissary of a friendly nation to the Court of your country, I direct you to have a drink!" A tin cup being put in his hand, young Cornet Eszterhazy drank. To be precise, he gulped. He shuddered. He staggered, put out an arm for balance. The cowboys laughed. Even the Indians smiled.

"*This* is not Tokay!" he gasped.

"Ho, ho. No, it is not Tokay, merely the same color; finish it before you tell me why you want my help. Go on now. Bottoms up!"

The Cornet perforce obeyed, but in some stiff sips rather than one main gulp. Breathing strongly, he wiped his mouth. "I want your help to rescue Count Calmar!"

General Abercrombie gestured that all drinking vessels be refilled. Next, that all drink again. Then he said, "Well, Cornet Um Ahh Um — Well, Cornet. I fear this does not come within the scope of my official duties, sorry as I am for the noble gentleman, Count Who?"

The Cornet removed his pannikin from his mouth. "Your Excellency, but he is only the Count Calmar incognito! In actual fact, he is King Magnus of Scandia and Froreland!"

This was received with no reaction by the assembled rough riders, who continued to stroll to and from the bourbon barrel. But General Abercrombie, whose drinks were being brought to him, allowed a look of deep thought to steal over his face. "Well, this seems to put a different complexion on — A reigning monarch is no mere — 'Scandia and Froreland,' do you say? Yes. Yes? Why, the subjects of the King of Scandia and Froreland have in recent years been migrating very numerously to the United States. They are hard-working, hard-drinking, quick to become naturalized though very much attached to their old homeland; they vote dutifully in all elections and they are almost all of them attached to that same Grand Old Party which has saved the Union. Why —"

Something had occurred to Major James Elphonsus Dandy. "Say. This here king. Hasn't got yellow hair, has he?"

"Why yes. He has. Yes. He has."

The major gave a satisfied jerk of the head. "Well. There *y'are*. And, oh hey! Nother thing! Ain't them two countries whut they call The Land of the Midnight Sun? Why sure! Just like old Roan Horse said, 'The sun either won't rise or won't set,' well! There *y'are*; git your carbines ready, men."

Abercrombie leaned forward. "How do you know all this, my plumed, war-bonneted friend? And what else do you know about it?"

Roan Horse gave an enormous eructation. "Medicine Man send

message. Not know *what* Medicine Man. He blow-em eagle whistle. Roan Horse hear." The Indian's eye-lids drooped. But between them his eyes still gleamed. "Umbrella tree," he intoned. *"Death. Umbrella tree. Yellow Hair. Many smokes. Eagle, eagle. Umbrella tree. . . ."*

Abercrombie asked Now what in the Hell they made of *that.*

Eszterhazy, somewhat more quieted, said that there was something . . . something in a corner of his mind . . . he could not quite . . .

Said Tex Teeter, pouring water (not much water) into his empty glass and swishing it around to collect the residual essence of whiskey: he said, slowly, "Now didn't we see some purely odd-lookin kind a tree down in them Eye Talian provinces, whut was they called but *um ber ella* pines, which shorely they looked like. Now —"

Slowly Eszterhazy put down his own empty glass, not looking as to where it went. And slowly he straightened up again. His air of concentration was almost palpable. It was, certainly, contagious. "The so-called umbrella pine," he said. "I have seen it in Italy, too. Is it here? In the Monarchy? In Bella? Yes. *Yes!* That is . . . a few specimen trees, I have heard, introduced into his palace grounds by . . . by whom? By *whom?"* Again he was silent; scarcely, he seemed to be there. Then his head snapped up. His face was luminous. "Yes, The Duke of Dalmatia! In the palace the old King gave him when the Duke was in exile . . . before there even was an Empire —"

"Well, and who lives there now, my dear young sir?"

Eszterhazy's face went first slack. Then it flooded with color. "It is now the lair of that dirty beast the Brigand Boustremóvitch," he said. His lips writhed up.

"Oh, sugar!" exclaimed the U.S. Minister. He was not noted for having knowledge of the local scene. But he had heard of the Brigand Boustremóvitch. "Well, well. Well, they may fire me for this and I may be lucky to get the post of postmaster in Lump Dicky, Arkansas, but I say Let-tus risk it! A commissioned officer of a great and friendly nation whose capital city lies in temporary disarray asks us to assist in rescuance from durance vile the captured sovereign of another great and friendly, where the Hell *is* the place? — they won't *dare* shoot *me*; I have diplomatic immunity;" (he also had the hiccups) "is there a bugle in the house, I'll sound the charge; I used to, as a boy, play wind instruments in the band of The Great Doctor B.B. Jaspers' Massive Medicine Pill Show; Dr. B.B. Jaspers' Massive Medicine Pills are so skillfully compounded out of benign marsh and meadow grasses and healing woodland herbs as to be good for the de-bilitating diseases of men and beasts alike, one for a man and two for a milch cow, as well as female complaints of a familiar nature, where the *Hell* is this place?"

Eyes swung to the young cornet. He started to gesture.

"The President of the U-nited States to Ignats Louis, Great and Good Friend, we the People of said U-nited States send our Servant

Hiram Abiff Abercrombie in whom there is no guile — Where?"

Cornet Eszterhazy made a gesture of despair. Said, "I have, oh my God, lost my bearings."

"Well. Colonel, cain't you git a native guide?"

Roan Horse rose to his feet and re-adjusted his blanket. White circles were painted around his eyes, his nose was yellow, and red & black stripes ran along his face. "No need-em native guide," he said. "You see-em guide?" He pointed. "Follow," he said, stalking for his mount. Every eye looked up.

Eszterhazy said, "Sweet tears of Christ."

Up, up, and up, yet not so far up that they could not be clearly identified for what they were, from north, from east, from south, from west, four columns of eagles flew in upon the capital in a cruciform pattern: and at some point farther on in the city they converged. And circled.

A shout went up from the men of the show; and, waving their carbines, they ran for their horses. General Abercrombie (in his buggy of course) could not keep up with them, but he made good time, and kept the U.S. and Confederate flags being waved up front well in sight.

"Thish year steam calliope," Major Dandy explained to the watchman, "is made out of prime seasoned English oak and is as hard as iron, if not harder than *some* iron. It was tooken out of the *Lady Washington* steamboat, of which I was once Owner and Master, after she run aground off Garrett's Point; whut toon shall I give'm?" The watchman made no reply; for one thing, the calliope having gotten into motion had started moving forward and lurched out of the Paddock by then. "*Hail C'lumbia,* that's whut I'll give 'em, haw haw haw!" The vehicle did not run smooth. But she ran staunch. And soon the war-whoops and Rebel yells of the horsemen were mingled with the hoarse, steamy notes of the music.

"Chief! Chief! This just come through by heliograph!"

"Give it here. 'MONTEZUMA THE FAMOUS SLAYER OF THE MAXIMILLIAN EMPEROR HAS BEEN SEEN WITH A SQUAD OF IRREGULAR CAVALRY PLEASE FLASH INSTRUCTION.' They've all gone mad, I tell you — *mad!*"

"He must be told, I say!"

"I say, not yet!"

"He must be *told!*"

"Tell him yourself, then —"

"It is not my function!"

"Lower your voice, for God's sake!"

Ignats Louis looked up in some mild annoyance from the interesting marginal gloss about Maurits Louis and the Lovely

Mulatta, from which the (as it was called) Egyptian branch of the Morganatic branch of the Royal Family was descended; why were the officials always bothering him? Why couldn't they make decisions for themselves? What was the use of a Constitution, otherwise? He glanced at the clock, clicked his tongue, and went out through the secret panel and down the secret steps to visit the dear sweet little kiddies in the Infirmary three courtyards away. Sometimes he had half a mind to abdicate and go fish for sardines off Corsica . . . or else Chattanooga in the Americas and hunt wisents with the Red Faced People.

"There, now we have a clear road, make haste! Make haste!"

The driver, sweating, said, "This is not a clear road, it is only a road through a merely crowded street — don't you see the people?"

"Ride them down, then!"

"Ride the *people* down?"

"It would not be our fault but that of the enemy, for it is a definition that the enemy determines the conditions of the war!"

"I tell you, Boss, it's witchcraft — witchcraft — witchcraft!"

"Don't bray in my ear, you jackass!" The Brigand Boustremóvitch spat three times and rapped thrice on the table. The mention of the mere possibility of witchcraft made him uneasy . . . of course he had already had a great deal to be uneasy about. There had been, for example, the thunder-storm. Peals of thunder and bolts of lightning and the day sky as dark as night; bad enough; but it was plain that all that was happening only overhead the old Dalmatian Palace — all roundabout as they looked, lo!, the land was bright and clear! And after that had come the hail-storm, hail-stones big as plums — but only on top of *them*, the henchmen wailed. And after that had come the rain of frogs. And after *that* . . .

"Who'd y' think's doin it all?" demanded the Boustremóvitch.

"Who else?" his henchman asked, jerking his head towards the upper secret cell. "You don't think somebody *that* big is going to travel around without he's got his private wizard, do ya?"

The Brigand struck the table with his huge fist. "I'll cut his throat with my own hands," he cried. "He'll be dead when they get him after the ransom, but we won't be here by then." Yet still he did not move; and now suddenly the walls oozed a liquid red as blood and a most offensive fœtor filled the room; from outside and overhead began a most discordant screaming. The Brigand unsheathed his long curved knife and, with fearful curses, ran out into the courtyard where the by now very old umbrella pines still grew and dripped their needles — and every time he turned towards his destination, the immense convocation of eagles ceased to soar and circle, and, swooping, darted, claws outstretched, screaming, for his eyes. . . .

Up in a tower in another part of the city were four men in uniforms without insignia of any sort. They stood at the windows and gazed out with telescopes. "The set time is very near," said one of them, "and it is possible the clockwork in the infernal machine might go off early."

"Is it possible that we will learn what in Hades is going on down there?"

A third said that he was also very curious, but they would simply have to wait. "Until we either see or hear the explosion. Or both."

"Good God!" exclaimed the fourth. "Is it possible that the Emperor has for some or any reason left the Imperial Palace and that this is the reason for the commotion?"

There were gasps of dismay; then the first speaker said, "It is not possible, he is a creature of indestructible habit. However. I suggest that we coordinate our sightings. Let us each look out on a different direction and say what we see; agreed? Very well. *North,* what do you see?"

"Incredible congestion. A tangle of traffic. Nothing seems to be moving. Nothing at all."

"Just so. *South?*"

"A vast throng of people, choking the streets. They are all on their knees. Can they all be *pray*ing?"

"Who knows? As I am East, I — No. *No.* That cannot *be.* My eyes are suffering from retinal strain. *West,* will you please make your report?"

"Yes. I see lines of halted tram-cars, lines of halted canal- and river-boats, lines of halted railroad trains. Well *East,* will you now report?"

After another silent moment, *East* said, in an oddly-stiff voice, "I see the old Dalmatian Palace, wherein lives the paroled and pardoned Brigand Boustremóvitch. I see . . . I see. . . . Well, I see American Redfaced Indians in full feathers and war-paint and I see American Farvestern *covboyii* in fringed buckskins and they are all on horseback and they are riding round and round the old Dalmatian Palace and firing upon it and now I see a figure strongly resembling the American Minister in the odd horse-drawn vehicle he drives and he is blowing a trumpet and now just now I see an absolutely incredible vehicle which appears to contain a church-organ yet is clearly propelled by steam like a railroad engine and yet as you all know there are no railroad tracks in that part of the city. What can it mean? What does it all *mean?*"

His companions did not tell him what it all meant. Silently, they had one by one joined him and were gazing through their own telescopes out the east window.

Major James Elphonsus Dandy was not riding around the walls of the old Dalmatian Palace, however. Not quite. For one thing, he had slowed down just a bit to get another piece of sheet-music . . . something from *Mazeppa* would, he thought, be suitable.

Up in his secret cell, Magnus III and IV was on his feet. He was quite angry. In the larger sense, he had no idea where he was; in the narrower sense, he knew a cell when he saw one. He shouted and he heard shouts, but he also heard thunder and lightning and what sounded (he decided after a puzzled moment) like hail. And . . . did he hear . . . frogs? He gazed at the door. He tried the door. It was, unsurprisingly, locked. So he threw himself against it. Often. Although Magnus ("Count Calmar") was young and rather strong; and although the door-frame had been already set somewhat askew by the shell of the Old French Gun; and although the door seemed to give a bit; still: it did not open. So he stood back and thought. But he could think of nothing. Nothing, that is, except that his being here was all the fault of the Frores; what did they want of him with their incessant demands? Who *were* they, anyway, that the benign and far more efficient methods of the Scands were not good enough for them? Who were *they,* in their poor and difficult little country with its tiny fields half-way up ragged, rugged mountains and their rocky and inhospitable coast forever split by craggy fiords and their misty forests and unnavigable rivers full of shoals and falls — who were *they* — to make demands? Well, whoever, he would teach them a lesson: *he would sell them to the Swedes!*

Magnus did not know, and neither did Jim Dandy, that when the Patriot-Poet Burli Grumbleson was so suddenly asked to put his great National Poem to music it had equally suddenly occurred to him that a certain piece from *Mazeppa* would suit it perfectly; hence: the immortal anthem, *Froreland Forever,* now, suddenly and amidst a welter of other strange and baffling sounds, soared through the air via the medium of a steam calliope. Magnus may have heard a steam calliope before, he may not; his reaction was not to the medium but to the song. Instantly tears gushed from his eyes. "Froreland!"he cried. "My poor country, my native land, *Froreland! Froreland!"*

That other native, the Skraeling "Ole," had also not been able to make his way back to the Grand Hotel Windsor-Lido by reason not of the congestion alone but because the Swing Bridge was blocked; he had been wandering hither and thither hoping to find a shallow place he might ford, when he heard an allarum of strange cries and the thudding of hooves. Neither he nor Roan Horse had ever seen each other before, needless to say; but there was an instant of recognition, a spark or perhaps even a flame passed between the shaman and the medicine-man. Roan Horse leaned from his saddle and reached out his arm, Eeiiuullaalaa jumped, seized, was lifted up, was sat down, and clutching his horse's mane lightly, charged on with the others and added his Skraeling ululation to their cries.

Round and round the old Dalmatian Palace they rode, and whenever a terrified face appeared over the parapet, they fired on it with whoops and yells. Major Dandy intended to turn his calliope so as to join the encircling pack, but the way thither had been rather rough and the tiller stuck . . . and stuck . . . and so, with full force, the massy engine struck the wall right under King Magnus' cell. The engine was not only massy, it was strong. It drew back, turned slowly and awkwardly, went farther back . . . and then rushed forward at full speed. It struck the gate and knocked it off its rusting hinges at just the moment when the cowboys and Indians came rounding the walls once again. And they poured into the fortress whose defenses had been breached.

Magnus heard and felt the concussion without knowing its cause; at once he attacked the door again: this time it gave way — he was free to go —

— to go — *where?*

There was certain peril down below, he thought (incorrectly . . . but logically). And then he saw the umbrella he had impulsively taken from the lobby of his hotel suite, one of two. He didn't know that he had clutched it tightly under his arm at the moment of his being assaulted; did not know that his captors, with coarse jests about *brolly* and *bumbershoot,* had heaved it into the cell with him; he might use it when the roof leaked, they sneered. "I shall climb to the parapet," Magnus said, "and I shall jump, having first opened the umbrella, which shall slow my descent, as has been done from balloons with something like an umbrella, as I have seen in pictures." He thought this very quickly, made his way to the parapet, and leaped upon it and stood there teetering and afraid to look down and tore off the tape keeping it furled — damned awkward clumsy umbrella, it hadn't even a handle — and, flapping it madly to make it open, looked up and found that he was —

Frightful screams from inside the courtyard, the prisoners half-terrified of being scalped, and half-terrified of something worse: enter the Cornet Eszterhazy, veteran of two previous and rather longer campaigns; he drew his sword and announced that they were his and the Emperor's prisoners: they at once surrendered, all of them. All of them, that is, except the Brigand Boustremóvitch. He lay on his back, right where the keystone of the arch above the gate had in its falling caught him full upon the heart.

One of the prisoners was allowed to show where the barrels of wine were kept; and, as soon as they had finished tying up their captives, the captors began sampling the contents of the barrels. It was not bourbon, it was only the small local wine of the country and it would not travel far. But, then, of course, it was not being asked to.

After a rather wearing and roundabout route of travel, a certain group of foreigners had arrived in Bella earlier that day on one of the last trains to make it in. They had not, however, owing to unexpectedly unsettled conditions, been able to make it to their destination, namely in front of the Grand Hotel Windsor-Lido; they had not intended even to think of staying *at* the fashionable and expensive hotel . . . but they were absolutely determined to stay in front of it. Now, having been dismissed by the omnibus driver with a baffled shake of his hand and head at being unable to go anywhere that anyone wanted to go, they had — for lack of any notion of what to do — unfurled the banners they had brought with them, and simply commenced walking (being prudent, they had carefully noted the location and left one of their number in charge of the baggage). Scarcely had they marched a block or two when the sound of gunfire attracted their attention. And then they heard something which they could not believe they were hearing and next saw something which they could not believe they were seeing. It was at this point that Magnus, the sound of the anthem ringing in his ears, realized (a) that what he was waving was no umbrella but a very familiar flag; and (b) that down below, across the road, was a group of people looking up at him with open mouths and carrying two banners. One of the banners, a new one, read, **Swearing Eternal Fealty to the House of Olaus-Olaus-Astridson-Katzenelenbo̊gen-Ulf-and-Olaus, Froreland Demands a Separate Bureau of Weights and Measures**. And the other, an old one barely legible, read, simply, **A Fourteenth Full-Bishop For Faithful Froreland.**

The Street of Our Noble Ally the Grand Duke of Graustark (usually called Grau Street) was, for a miracle, only half- instead of entirely-filled; taking advantage of this, the driver half-rose from the wagon-seat and began to ply his whip — but the horse, instead of dashing onward at increased speed, came to an abrupt stop. An odd, gaunt, whiskery figure wearing a Norfolk jacket and jodhpur trousers, taking the animal by the head, cried, "Stop, *stop!* How dare you lash this poor old chap? I am Sebastian Allgoode-Freestinghaze, formerly of the Fifth Hyderabad Horse (Piggot's Ponies), and now General Continental Agent for the RSPCA; I am obliged to remove the animal and lead him to our local contract livery stable and veterinary establishment, where he shall be able to receive the rest and medication so obviously requisite." And whilst Col. Allgoode-Freestinghaze was saying all this, and saying it rather rapidly, as though well-accustomed to saying it, he was with even greater rapidity releasing the horse from the wagon. Having done so (and handed over to the dumb-struck trio on the wagon a card printed with his name and local address), he — and the horse — vanished around the corner.

It was too much for the driver. His nerves broke; and, leaping from the seat, he dashed madly away, screaming as he did so, *"The Works! The Works!"* At which almost every living soul on the Street of Our Noble Ally the Grand Duke of Graustark (usually called Grau Street), screaming, ***"The Turks! The Turks!"*** fled precipitately; in a moment no one and no thing remained there except the wagon and the two other men. They had simultaneously decided to follow the example of their fellow conspirator and had, in fact, simultaneously leaped; there was one difficulty — the man on the left had leaped to the right and the man on the right had leaped to the left — the laws of physics being what they are, the two had collided: and it was while they were shouting and screaming and flailing at each other that the clock-works in the infernal machine made it go off.

"Bobbo! Bobbo!" cried the children in the Infirmary, clapping their hands, and using their Sovereign's pet-name.

"Here's the funny old pedlar with his itty-bitty wagon of nick-nacks," said His Royal and Imperial Majesty, wheeling it into the ward. "Who wants a posie? Posies cost one kiss. *Mweh! Mweh!* Who wants a little wooden cavalryman that moves its little wooden legs if you pull the little string? Costs one hand-shake. There you are, sir! Who wants some nice chewy Turkish Delight? Some nice chewy spice-drops, big as Bobbo's thumb? Sweetmeats cost one hug. Oh! What a big squeeze! *Whuh! Whuh!* Who wants . . . ?"

The children were clustering around him when there was a shudder of the whole building, followed by a loud, flat noise. The children immediately looked up at him to see if they should cry. "Practicing the big boom fireworks for Bobbo's birthday, do you like big boom fireworks; do you like big sizzle-sparkle fireworks? Be good kiddies and say your prayers and take your medicine and sit on the potty-chair and make poo when nursey tells you, and you shall be allowed to come and watch the fireworks, see? How's the little footsey? 'Some better?' Not all better? Well, let Bobbo bend over and kiss and it will soon *be* all better because Bobbo is the Lord's Anointed, see, and if Dr. Quaatsch doesn't like it he can go . . . back to Vienna. This little piggy went to market. . . ."

They were all waiting for him when he got outside.

"What dreck-dribbling whoremongering sow-sucking son of a bitch was responsible for that punk-futtering explosion at this hour of the afternoon with no warning given to prepare the kids; I'll geld him like an oxling!"

And then they told him Everything.

The men in the tower were still gazing through their telescopes when the clock in the corner began the brief musical notes which announced that it would next sound the quarter-hour. Only one of them bothered to turn and glance at it, then he turned away. Then — very, very swiftly — he turned back. "Is that the same clock as was always there?" he demanded, his voice gone high and weak. This time they all turned. The clock in the corner began to sound the quarter-hour. They all rushed for the door. They did not quite make it.

The two devices were well-timed, and the explosions had really sounded like one.

Everything, that is, which they knew about to tell him.

"We'll see about this all, later," said the King-Emperor, suddenly not so much angry as weary. "Immediately I must get down there and show myself to calm the people," he said. "Bring the Whitey horse —"

Dr. Quaatsch stepped forward, cleared his throat. "As the Court Physician it is my duty to say that I cannot approve Your Royal and Imperial Highness doing anything of the sort, and Your Royal and Imperial Highness very well knows why."

The Emperor looked at him. "I have my duty, too," he said.

The horse was (of course) white, the Emperor's uniform was white, the ostrich feather in his cap was white, the Emperor had not yet begun to stoop and was still usually tall and straight, and as he now chose for the most part to ride standing in the stirrups he was visible for blocks. "Fun's all over now," he said (and said); "go home now, boys. Go home. Go home. Spread the word."

Or: "Go home, wives. Go home, go home. It's soon time to put the spuds on, if you're not there the man will try to do it himself, scald the baby, and set the house on fire. Go home, ladies, go home —"

At the Five Points: ". . . *Amen*. . . . He doesn't fife no more, upon which I spit," said Emma Katterina, starting to get up, her Chaplain scrambling to help her, the three Ladies-in-Waiting hustling to hide their apparatuses and, this done, to help brush off her skirts. Emma Katterina looked up, looked around. "What, you are still down there?" she asked of those of the multitude yet on their knees. "Up, up, it's over, everything is now all right." She raised her voice as she started walking: "To home or to church! Go! Go!" She shook her skirts as though shooing chickens. *"Go!"*

"Boys [the Emperor], go home. Go —"

Voice from the crowd: "But the Turks, Bobbo! What about the —"

"No more Turks! All gone! All gone!" — which was, historically, quite true, even if they had "all gone" a hundred-odd years earlier. "Go home. . . ."

Voice from crowd: "But what about that there Antichrist, Your Allness?"

Ignats Louis turned upon him in a well-simulated, well, perhaps it was not all simulated, fury. "I'll give you *'Antichrist,'* you dumb son of a bitch; you leave that sort of thing to the Archbishop, the Patriarch, and the Holy Synod! Go home, I say! Go home!"

"Ahh!" they said in the crowd. "That be a real Emperor, hear him cuss!"

If the Frorish delegation was taken aback at seeing their Sovereign atop a palace wall, still, after all, they had come all the way to Bella *to* see him — however, they had not expected to see him waving the Frorish flag just a moment after they had been listening to the Frorish National Anthem. It was at this moment that he cupped his hands and called down to them, "I grant your demands!"

They did not cheer, being after all, Frores. After a moment one of them, The Patriotic Female Helga Helgasdochter, cupped her own hands and called back, "What, both of them?"

"Both of them!"

Silence. *He pressed her so strongly that he might soon have done her a mischief, had she not foiled him by her ready acquiescence. . . .*

Then: "The Scands will never approve!"

Magnus did not hesitate. "Then I shall abdicate . . . as King of Scandia, that is." And, the implications of this slowly dawning on them, they slowly applauded. The Frores, it is well-known, are not a people given to sudden enthusiasms. The Scands, as a matter of fact, *were* indeed loath to approve — until their approval was made contingent to the subsequent Trade Treaty whereby the surplus stockfish of both Scandia and Froreland was sent to Scythia-Pannonia-Transbalkania in return for the Triune Monarchy's surplus wheat; after which the price of breadstuffs went down in both Far-Northwestern Kingdoms and *forefish* (as it came to be known) grew abundant upon even the humblest table in the Triune Monarchy. But this was later. After. After, that is, young Cornet Eszterhazy had persuaded Emma Katterina that all the Scotch steam engineers had gone on somewhere else. Baluchistan, maybe. Or Australia. And that the Royal and Imperial Ironroads could not only be obliged to pay *a thousand ducats a month* towards her charities, but would also build her a glassed-in drying shed for her laundry-drying, thus saying *Make clear the way* to a direct and swifter, cheaper rail route to the North.

Later.

After. After word had meanwhile gotten around of the rôle played by the staff of the Major James Elphonsus Dandy Great Texas and Wild West Show in the capture of the old Dalmatian Palace and the demise of the Brigand Boustremóvitch, the show's business boomed. And it kept on booming. Word, of course, had gotten distorted quite into folklore; but what of that? As for the brute Bruto and

Pishto-the-Avar and the henchmen of the Boustremóvitch, they all became (usually: *again*) "ships' carpenters" in the dockyard/prison; it was hard work, but healthy, seeing that most of it was done in the open air. And perhaps it just might be that they were in some way less degraded as they hauled timber and heated tar and sawed and so on than if they had been confined instead in immense dungeons where they might or might not have tended to *reform* and to become *penitent*.

But this, too, was later.

By the time he had almost circumambulated the center of his city, Ignats Louis's voice was worn to a croak. Observing, then, a sign **Apothecary** over the open door of a shop, and the apothecary in his apron standing in the doorway and thinking perhaps to ask him for a glass of mineral water, the Emperor beckoned. The man came over and the Emperor leaned down; in the man's ear he croaked, "My piles are killing me!"

"So I had assumed from Your Majesty's stance, standing in the stirrups the whole way down the street; so here I take the liberty of offering Your Majesty a pillule of opium and a large glass of mineral water and brandy," and he handed up first the one and then the other.

His Majesty took them, swallowed, swallowed, swallowed; then, with a grateful look, handed back both glass and saucer. In a voice considerably restored, he said, "You may add to your sign, BY APPOINTMENT . . . and all the rest of it." Then he rode on, mostly he gestured; but by now, mostly, they knew the meaning of the gestures.

Go home, boys. Go home . . .

Magnus, "Count Calmar," went home, too. The wandering Swiss photographer had stuck to his place throughout all the excitement and had, thus, been able to take quite a good picture of Magnus as he stood on the wall waving the Frorish flag. It sold forever back home. Only the colors distinguished the two flags, they having the same pattern, and the colors did not show in the photograph: in Scandia they said it was the flag of Scandia and in Froreland they *knew* it was the flag of Froreland. As to details, no one bothered them with details. Their Conjoint King had helped plant a National Flag on the walls of the palace which . . . somehow . . . he had helped be captured from a brigand: they had received a Hero in a time when it was often assumed that Heroism was dead: enough. The few republicans in the Two Kingdoms (mostly bankers, big brewers, and people like that) so to speak slunk back into their lairs, moodily drank their glo̊g and shnops and ate their boiled stockfish with mutton-fat and bitterness. The King's return was a good deal jollier than his departure. As usual not much attention was given in the capital(s) to

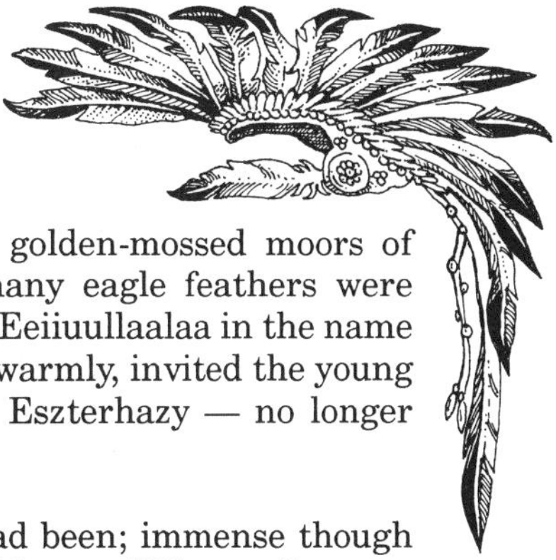

"Old Skraelandi," but — later — on the golden-mossed moors of Skraeland itself the gifts of the many, many eagle feathers were gratefully received from the Court Shaman Eeiiuullaalaa in the name of the King. The King, of course, and most warmly, invited the young Cornet Eszterhazy to come and visit, and Eszterhazy — no longer Cornet — did so. But that was later.

Much later.

Brief though immense the excitement had been; immense though brief. But he had had excitement before. This was different. It was a while, a long while in fitting together all that had happened. (Most people in Bella never *did!*) Even he had "pumped" the shaman and the medicine-man, via interpreters. Even he had gone over the great steam calliope again and again. (Could such vehicles be made to carry people, without rails?) Even he had examined the records of the police, both Public and Secret. Even . . .

It seemed to him that not alone a new world but a new universe had begun to open before his eyes, eyes from which the scales of ignorance had dropped. Gorgeous gates to which he had to find the keys. Knowledge! Knowledge! Science upon science — anthropology, ethnology, criminology, ornithology; history and law; medicine and mechanics; wisdom unsuspected and knowledge unknown. It was no longer possible to pass one's days as a sort of upper servant, a glorified messenger; drinking, dicing, riding, hunting, whoring: these could never again suffice. *Go thou and learn,* somewhere he had heard the words, forgotten where, never mind where, that is what he had to do. First a course, courses, of private studies with tutors, then the university here, then universities elsewhere, then travel. And then again: study . . . study . . . study.

He would of course have to sell his landed estates to pay for it, but no prospect ever gave him more pleasure. These new estates were greater.

Unfortunate Sir Paunceforth! A rumor, writhing slowly and steadily as an eel bound for the Sargasso, made its way eventually down the Baltic and into the North Sea, thence to London, and so, eventually, to Windsor. Sir Paunceforth De Pueue (unfortunate Sir Paunceforth!) thought fit to mention it to the Widow.

"They say, you know, Ma'am, that there was a sort of conspiracy recently in Froreland, don't you know, to depose their king and offer the throne to one of Your Majesty's younger sons; *haw!*"

The Queen looked at him, saying nothing. Perhaps she did not care to hear of Monarchs being deposed; perhaps she was thinking how willingly she would have sent one of her sons to Froreland (had it been possible), though not necessarily a younger son; perhaps she did not like anyone to say *haw!* to her. She said nothing.

Sir Paunceforth tried to save the situation, tried very hard to get across the point that this was a *fun*ny story. "They say, Ma'am, that the main dish there is boiled stockfish with mut-ton fat! . . . in Froreland . . . ***Haw!*** "

She looked at him with puffy, bloodshot, icy-blue little eyes. "We are not amused," she said.

Unfortunate Sir Paunceforth!

Then the Queen said, *"Where?"*

But as to *why* the bears were so bad in Bosnia that year . . .

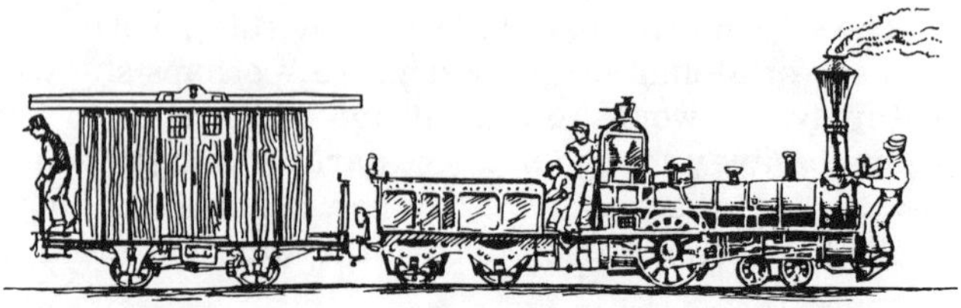

THE AUTOGÓNDOLA INVENTION

The mist was thick and white and wet, and from every side came the sounds of trickling waters. Huge grey rocks loomed, showed their lichenous and glistening contours, fell behind to be succeeded by impossibly steep vistas where tufts of grass and twisted trees lured the stranger on, perhaps only (the stranger thought) to betray him into placing his foot on a narrow and slippery footing whence he would at once plunge into a gorge. From right behind him a voice spoke. "You all right, Lieutenant?" said the voice.

Lieutenant Skimmelffenikk of the Royal and Imperial Scythian-Pannonian-Transbalkanian Excise swore a bit. "How can anybody be all right who tries to climb a saturated mountain in riding-boots?" he asked, next.

He could not see the sergeant, but he was certain that the sergeant shrugged. The sergeant said, "You ought to wear rope-soled sandals, like the rest of us. Ain't that right, Mommed?" The guide was up ahead and equally invisible; he was a Mountain Tartar and a Rural Constable. His reply was a grunt. That is, it sounded like a grunt to the lieutenant, but to the sergeant it had sounded like more. "Hey, that's a good idea," said he. "Stop a bit, sir. Now grab hold of that tree and hold it for balance. Now stick your leg backwards as if you was a mule and I was a-shoeing you. Right leg first." It was a mad-sounding instruction, but no madder than anything else on this tour of duty; and the officer had no one but himself to blame as it was his own misconduct (sleeping off his annual hangover in a public place) which had brought him here as punishment — and lucky he hadn't been cashiered! — here at the wild border of Hyperborea, one of the Confederated Hegemonies of the Empire. Holding onto the moist bole of a tree, he stuck his right leg backwards. The Royal and Imperial Excise was stern. But it was just. He, Lt. Skimmelffenikk, would sweat and suffer and do his damnedest to do his duty, and eventually he would find himself in some civilized jurisdiction again . . . the Scythian Gothic Lowlands, perhaps . . . or near the capital city of Avar-Ister, sometimes called "The Paris of the Balkans" (not often), in the broad plain of Pannonia.

Twisting his head, he looked to see what was being done. It would not have surprised him to see that his sergeant *was* actually preparing to hammer in an iron mule-shoe: not quite: the man produced an immense clasp-knife from which he now unclasped a something for which the tax-officer knew no name: somewhat like an awl and somewhat like a file and, on one edge, somewhat like a saw; and with this the man proceeded to score deep scratches in the soles of his superior's boots. "All right, sir, now the left leg if you please. Aw haw haw! well, better put the right one down first, aw haw haw! Sir."

But his superior was not looking at his feet. His superior was now looking straight in front of him at a slightly upward angle and at undoubtedly the most horrible sight he had ever seen in his life; he was looking at a face in the thicket and this face was diabolical. One side of it was bleach-white, one side of it was jet-black; it had yellow eyes and horns and a wreathed crown and a stinking beard, and it writhed its lips and it sneered as though the next moment it were about to pronounce some dreadful malediction. The exciseman uttered a thin wail and desperately tried to remember a prayer. At once the sergeant appeared alongside and lunged towards the frightful face, hand outstretched. The creature issued a fearful cry. Vanished. A commotion in the thicket. Only the wreathed crown remained. Or . . . was it really a wreath? Or merely a mass of flowering tendrils, adventitiously created as the creature had blundered through the bushes? A sudden small wind blew upon the wreath and it went tumbling out of sight. Meanwhile, in the wake of the commotion, there fell at the exciseman's feet some bits of earth and grass and some other objects, dark and about the size of chick-peas and smoking faintly in the cool misty air. "What *was* it?" he asked.

"Why sir, it was what the usual trouble here is about, a great big billy such as the Hypoes don't want to pay no tax upon it if they can help it . . . there being no tax on a nanny, as you know, sir."

The lieutenant had some faults in character. But he was able to confess them. "I was scared as Hell. I thought it was the Devil's face," he said, now.

And then he said, "Hark. What is that?" The two strained their ears. "Shepherds' pipes?" the officer asked. But his man shook his head, No. It was far too high for shepherds, he said. Nor did they pipe so.

Unlike most excisemen, who seldom read anything except second- or third-hand copies of the so-called "French papers," Skimmelffenikk

was fond of the occasional issue of a monthly which sometimes carried articles about Natural History; he recalled one now about certain "honey-comb" rocks through which the winds sometimes blew with an effect like an aeolian harp, and he now mentioned this to his sergeant.

Who said: "Huh. Well, it might have been." They moved on. Slowly. The rough-cut soles, now both scored, gripped better. "Them Hypoes," the sergeant was a Slovatchko and held the Hyperboreans in great contempt, "Well, it is said they sometimes do worship the Devil, ho, such fools! Don't they, Mommed? — Oh, not *you* o'course for all you're a Tartar and so a kissing-cousin to a Turk; but they others, don't they be sometimes risking their souls by worshiping the Devil?"

The Mountain Tartar's reply may have been of a theological nature and then again it may not. Whatever it was he meant by saying it, he said it over and over again. "Watch step. Watch step. Watch step."

The Monarch was feeling . . . more to the point, was behaving . . . a bit grumpy. The Triune Monarchy had been "protecting" the pashalik of Little Byzantia on behalf of the Turks for a long generation, and now the seemingly interminable negotiations for its annexation to the Empire had taken a great lurch forward. The Sublime Porte had at last agreed to name a sum of money. But in addition to that, the Sultan was also insisting that the Emperor of Scythia-Pannonia-Transbalkania should henceforth be known as Emperor of *only* Scythia-Pannonia-Transbalkania. *"What?"* demanded Ignats Louis. *"What?* You mean that henceforth We've got to give up calling Ourself 'Emperor de jure of New Rome and All Byzantium via Marriage by Proxy'? *What?"* His bulging eyes bulged more and his long nose seemed to grow longer; he gave the ends of his famous bifurcated beard two tremendous tugs. "WHAT?"

"Yes, Sire," said his Prime Minister. He had been saying so for a long time. Or, at any rate, it seemed a long time to him.

"Won't do it," said his Royal and Imperial master. "Won't think of it. Won't yield the point. Never. Never."

They were in the Privy Closet, a vast room jammed with curio cabinets and grand pianos covered with shawls and photographs and daguerrotypes and miniatures, plus the single harpsichord on which *Madame* played for the King-Emperor sixteen minutes twice a day. The Prime Minister was terrified that he might accidentally brush to the floor a sketch on ivory of the infant King of Rome or an early ambrotype of the late Queen of Naples; the Emperor, who could be a sly old fox when he wished, knew this and sometimes chose the Privy Closet whenever he particularly wanted to punish the P.M. by making him be brief. Standing as stiff and motionless as he could, the P.M. said that the point had been repeatedly yielded. "It has been yielded to the Senate of the Republic of Venice, to the Holy Roman Emperor, to the Austro-Hungarian Emperor, to the Vatican, and to the King of Greece. Among others."

Ignats Louis stared stubbornly at an ostrich egg in one of the cabinets. "See? Yield, Yield, Yield," he said. "We shall be little more than a mere petty chieftain if this keeps up. Where has it not yet been yielded?" His first minister informed him that it had not yet been yielded to San Marino, Paraguay, and Mt. Athos. "Besides Turkey, of course." But this merely made the Old Man grumpier. *Mt. Athos!* The very last time the Proxy Claim had been invoked was in a dispute over the placing of a faldstool in the Pannonian Phalanstery at Mt. Athos . . . and had the monks been grateful? Not a bit! "Won't yield. Sorry We yielded to the King of Greece."

The P.M. silently sighed. Then he played his last card. (A threat of resignation was no card at all: each time he tried to play it the Monarch said, Good.) "I am authorized to inform Your Royal and Imperial Majesty that if Your Royal and Imperial Majesty will yield what is after all a mere pretense, and has been since 1381, the Sultan will bestow upon your Royal and Imperial Majesty the style and title of Despot of Ephesus, it being clearly understood that the title is purely of a despotic, I mean, of a titular character, and no longer annually entitles its holder to a caravan of figs, a she-elephant, a eunuch barber-surgeon, or any other of its formal perquisites, including flaying and impalement. Though the Sultan might yield somewhat on the figs. . . ."

Silence. "Despot of Ephesus, hey."

"Yes, Sire."

More silence, Then: "The King of Greece won't like *that,* **will** he?"

This time the Premier did not conceal his sigh. "No, Sire."

"Heh, heh. Take the wax out of *his* moustache! Hey? Where's the ticket?" The P.M. bent down just the slightest bit and indicated the parchment *assumpsit* which, red seals, ribbons, and all, had been in plain sight atop the writing-board on the Monarch's knee all the while; the Monarch dipped the short-trimmed quill into the purple ink, and scribbled **IL RI** (**I**gnats **L**ouis, **R**ex, **I**mperator), called, "Page!" and stood up. The page presented the Premier with a sanding-box, the Premier sanded the signature, the Monarch said There went a thousand years of history down the goo-hole, the Premier said that it was merely 836 years and that the claim had always been dubious and (growing a trifle confused) that Little Byzantia was worth a mass.

"News to *me* the Turks say mass," observed the Monarch, pouncing. The P.M. winced: good. Still **IL RI** felt grumpy over his yielded point and phantom crown, little though he could imagine himself riding his Whitey horse into Yildiz Kiosk and proclaiming, "Stamboul is my wash-pot, over the Sweet Waters of Asia do I cast

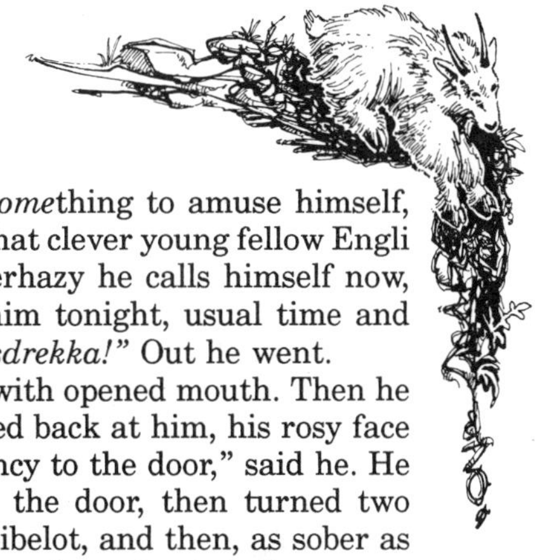

my shoe!" Well, he was entitled to do *some*thing to amuse himself, wasn't he? "Page," said he, "get over to that clever young fellow Engli who used to be Equerry here, Dr. Eszterhazy he calls himself now, and tell him that *Uncle Iggy* will see him tonight, usual time and place; exit the Despot of Ephesus, *shejssdrekka!*" Out he went.

The Prime Minister looked after him with opened mouth. Then he looked down at the page. The page looked back at him, his rosy face perfectly blank. "I will see Your Excellency to the door," said he. He saw His Excellency to the door, closed the door, then turned two cartwheels without disturbing a single bibelot, and then, as sober as before, he went to change from court dress into street clothes.

All was quiet in front of the hotel in the little square at the bottom of the Street of the Defeat of Bonaparte (commonly called Bonaparte Street). It was a rare alley, even, which had no name in Bella, capital of the Triune Monarchy, and this was a rare square, for it had no name at all; the hotel was a private hotel; its owner was one Schweitz, a Swiss, a man for whom the word "discreet" was inadequate. Engelbert Eszterhazy was then engaged in his preliminary studies for the degree of Doctor of Science (a process subsequently completed in Geneva); he had bought the house at Number 33, Turkling Street, and was slowly having it rebuilt according to his plans. For the present, Eszterhazy had rooms in Schweitz's hotel, and on a certain evening at an hour between early and late Eszterhazy had a few guests. By now it had been a while said of him that he was hopelessly eccentric but damnably clever and so best not crossed — on the sideboard tonight, for example, was a collation catered by Colewort — who was *he?* — he specialized in serving up snacks after the funerals of the upper sort of cartmen, that's who he was — on the sideboard tonight was cheese, head-cheese, fruit-cheese, fruit, two sorts of simple cake — if you wanted French kickshaws you could choose to hire a "French" caterer, and Eszterhazy did not choose to — beer, lemonade, and the standard Pannonian wine called bullblood.

A lull in the talk. Another guest entered. "Ah! Uncle Iggy! Welcome, welcome! You are just in time!" Eszterhazy announced, "Tonight we are perhaps going to summon up some familiar spirits. Perhaps some unfamiliar ones. Madame Dombrovski has been so very kind as to agree to see if entities not bound to earthly vessels will tonight be moved to employ her as a medium."

Madame Dombrovski asked that no one be so formal as to call her so. "Pliz, pliz," she begged, extending her ample arms (she had once been prima coloratura at the Zagreb Opera, where, it is well-known, no *thin* coloratura has *ever* appeared); "Pliz. Seemply Katinka Ivanovna. Een You-Rope, eat ease vary furmál, bot I hahv leavèd een América, whar ease vary *enn*-furmál. Not so, Pard?" she asked one of the guests; he nodded and, rising, was perhaps about to speak; but

Katinka Ivanovna went on. "Pair-hops the spear-eats wheel feel movèd, as Dr. Eszterhazy hos sayèd. Pair-hops nought. *Moderne* science hos provide us weeth the planchette, een América we call eat the wee-jee board. Sometimes the spear-eats appear and spik via the planchette. Bot sometimes they peak a human beink. Who con say wheech? Whale, we most see." Beaming, she began to roll a cigarette. Touches of pink petticoat peeped here and there from above and under her frothy blue dress: Katinka Ivanovna was clearly not one of your fanatically neat dressers . . . perhaps that New World informality of which she spoke had accompanied her back to the Old World. Her abundant hair was red, that is, to state it a shade more precisely, henna. Perhaps it was naturally, if unusually, her own hair color; perhaps she had made the Pilgrimage to Mecca. Perhaps *not*.

Who else was present? Well, there was a rather small and pudgy man to whose clothes and shoes the word *glossy* could not have been applied, or, at any rate, not without grave risk of terminological inexactitude; perhaps just as well, for their gloss could not but have suffered under the rain of food fragments produced by his rapid eating — shall we say "guzzling"? yes we shall — at the sideboard: and all the while he rolled his prominent eyes around and around at the company. This was Professor Gronk, in whose scientific mind and work Dr. Eszterhazy was vastly interested. Professor Gronk had been well-known at one time for his having courageously piloted eleven balloons out of, and twelve balloons into, Paris during the Siege. Or, vice versa. The Prussians had referred to him, perhaps a bit sourly, as *der verfluchte Blockaderunner*; "blockade-runner" is a word which does not translate easily into Prussian, but they had done the best they could and dropped the hyphen. Their new Colonial Service in Africa was reputed to be busily working on the many, *many* possibilities of the word *hottentotenpotentaten*. Subsequently Professor Gronk had applied himself to coal-tar derivatives in Montpelier and steam-plows in Silesia, alas *sans* spectacular success, but his past as *balloniste* was always with him and his head remained, so to speak, in the clouds.

Also present was a rather thin woman with rather beautiful eyes who was said to have been once the morganatic wife of a Grand Duke; be that as it may, it seemed to be the case that once a week a courier from the Russian Embassy did call upon her and, being shown that she was still in Bella and not, say, St. Petersburg, proffered a bow and an envelope which might very well contain an order upon a bank in Bella, and not, say, a copy of a poem by Pushkin. The lady was called Countess Zulk and was known to be interested in moral, ethical, and spiritual matters of all sorts.

Hovering over the Countess was a very striking figure indeed. This was the Yankee Far-vestern frontier poet, Washington Parthenopius "Pard" Powell, whose dark-red curls reached halfway down his back

where they left a sort of Plimsoll line of perfumed bear-grease on the blue-flannel shirt which was his trademark. "The children of nature ma'am for so I denominate my beloved Redskin brethren who made me an adopted offspring under the name of Red Wolf Slayer when I lived amongst them as the one and only White Indian Scout and the husband of the great chief Rainmaker's beloved daughter the princess Pretty Deer whose death broke his heart and purt near broke mine too for pretty dear was she to me they have a mighty marvelous appreciation of the great spirit of nature ma'am and whut you might call a extra-ordinary pre-science of things happening afore they really happen oh I recollect many sitch occasions ma'am yessurree." He wore buckskin trousers and moccasins embroidered with porcupine quills in several colors and he sometimes wore over his blue flannel shirt a vest of rawhide with long fringes and he wore a bowie knife and a broad-brimmed hat very much squashed and he smoked a calumet adorned with feathers and he was immensely popular right just then in Bella. Crowds gathered just to watch him stop and scan the city streets with one hand shielding his eyes and then wet one finger and hold it up to see which way the wind was blowing. Even now, Uncle Iggy was regarding him with fascination.

"Oh Mr. Powell —" the Countess began.

"Just 'Pard' ma'am eph yew please fur we ore all pardners in this great trade and commerce which is life ma'am."

The Countess sighed and said How True! Oh How True! and then asked, "In this life with the Redskins, Pard, . . . was this before or after you were in Honduras with William Walker?"

Pard struck a pose. "It was after ma'am it was oh long after though may I not call you Sis instid of Countess fur ore we not all brothers and sisters in this one great human family I may why shore well Sis as I was sayun Sis well now whut *was* I sayun ah yes now it come to me well as I declare in my *Fifth Epic Poem in Honor of William Walker the last Conkwistadoree*:

Whenas a mere lad in Honduras with the great William Walker
Who was a man of action and not much of a talker
It is a vile canard to say he intended to extend slavery
This is said in order to disparage his very manly bravery
He set his calloused hand upon my boyish curly pate
'Pard,' said he, 'love is much richer than hate.'
These words I always recollect when my life is far from ease
He spake them unto me as we galloped through the trees. . . ."

Pard stopped at this point and turned away and brushed his eyes with his forearm; the applause died away in a murmur of sympathy.

The murmur was interrupted by a harsh and argumentative voice, that of Baron Burgenblitz of Blitzenburg, widely known and widely feared and thoroughly disliked as "the worst-tempered backwoods noble in the Empire": even now he was on one of his too-frequent trips to the Capital to complain about some fancied infringement of feudal privilege, threatening as always that if he obtained no satisfaction he would retire to his castle-fortress and haul up its drawbridge and fire his antique but still-functioning cannon upon any interlopers who came within gunshot — and meaning, *anybody*. "Yes yes, Mr. Wash Pard, we have often been informed that you were in Honduras, and we have often read that you were in Honduras, and you have just now told us that you were in Honduras; and so I have only one little small question to speak to you —"

"Speak without fear, my brother."

"Were you ever in Honduras?"

The company froze. Would Pard's hand reach for the scalping knife in its sheath at his belt? Would Pard's hand reach for the tomahawk, set in the other end of the calumet? The company froze. Pard, however, was far from frozen; the look which he looked at Burgenblitz was far from freezing, it was burning hot. "Boss," he demanded, *"say, was Dante ever in Hell?"* Burgenblitz's mouth, already open to sneer, grew round. Then oval. All waited for him to say . . . whatever. He said nothing. Nothing at all. At least for a very long time, and then upon some other subject.

It was, later, felt that Washington Parthenopius "Pard" Powell had had the best of that scene.

But to give a complete roster of those present might be felt tedious; it may however be mentioned that among them was a man in later middle age dressed rather in the manner of a riverboat captain trying to disguise himself as a provincial seed-and-feed dealer.

It was a fact that Ister riverboat captains *did,* often, try to disguise their trade: whatever might have been the case on the Mississippi, it was not looked upon as especially glamorous on the Ister; and those obviously of it were likely to be followed at a safe distance by small boys calling, "Here comes the onion-boat!" and similar indignity. The man was carefully dressed in a suit of best broadcloth obviously tailored by a middling-good provincial tailor of cut at least a generation out of date; his shirt was of staunch linen but it was visibly yellowed from lack of having been sun-bleached.

Nearby rested just such a beaver hat as still found fashion and favor in, say, Poposhki-Georgiou. But the riverboat captain had forgotten to take off his deck-boots, as they were called. And he was still wearing the green-glassed spectacles, even though the yellow-red gaslight of Eszterhazy's room did not glare as did the ripples on the river. So, when Eszterhazy merely waved a hand by way of introduction, saying, "And this is Uncle Iggy from Praz," at the very most the others smiled gently. No one noticed that Uncle Iggy's beard, brushed straight downwards, showed a tendency to part, as if it were

customarily brushed bifurcated; anyway Uncle Iggy fairly often ran his hands down along it, unobtrusively pushing it together again. Nothing could have been done to shorten the nose, but, somehow, the glasses seemed to change it. And the pouched eyes were not obtrusive behind the green glasses. When someone asked, "And what do you do in Praz, ah, Uncle Iggy?" and the answer, "Well, I be in the feed-and-seed trade and also we do a good line in butter and egg," was delivered in a rich Scythian-Slovatchko border accent — well, weren't most riverboat captains from the Scythian-Slovatchko border country? — no one recollected that his R. and I. Majesty was also from exactly there. And who knew how much the Court Gothic accent irked him damnably? For that matter, who called to mind the disguised, nocturnal roamings of Haroun Al-Rashid? Pseudo-bourgeois Uncle Iggy loading up on the black bread and head-cheese with strong mustard was perhaps suspicious, but the suspicion led up the wrong road. As Uncle Iggy meant it to.

At length, during one of those inexplicable pauses which occur in conversations, Katinka Ivanovna made a small sound sufficient to attract attention, tossed the end of her hand-rolled cigarette into the fire-place. Then she gave a frank stretch. Then, glittering with good humor, she said that perhaps it was time to see if the spirits might be ready to come. At her requests the gaslights were turned low and a silence was to be kept until such time as it might appear to the company that she, Katinka Ivanovna, had passed into a trance state: after which, questions might be asked her; she herself requested only that they should not be questions seeking for personal gain. To this rather broad hint that no tips on the bourse would be forthcoming, the company turned up its eyes in horror . . . and perhaps some slight disappointment. . . . She lounged back in her chair and closed her eyes. The inevitable squirming of people who have been told to be quiet died away, there was a very audible stomach-gurgle, a guffaw broken off. Then . . . nothing . . . and again nothing . . . then the breathing of Katinka Ivanovna grew heavier. Her eyes were now partly open. She was not sleeping. She was not awake. Then her host, by gesture, but raising his eyebrows, indicated that it might be question-time.

Countess Zulk sat up straight. "Our dear Katinka Ivanovna has told us many times of a Master Ascended who sometimes comes down from the Ghoolie Hills where his maha-ashram is; that is, in a non-material form he comes down, and if requested will impart messages of the deepest spiritual import. His name . . . his name is Maha Atma Chandra Gupta. I should like to enquire if Maha Atma Chandra Gupta would condescend to say something to us."

There was a long silence. Then, suddenly, the lips of Katinka Ivanovna opened, and a voice spoke through them. It was not her voice. It was the voice of a man and it spoke in English, a clipped British English, but with a trace of something else . . . perhaps a lilt like that of Welsh. *"There is too much coriander in this curry!"* the voice said, sharply. No one else spoke a word. After a while the voice spoke a word, several words, and this time it sounded very annoyed. *"Dal?"* it enquired. *"Do you call this* dal? *An untouchable would not touch it! It causes me the utmost damned astonishment that you should set this before me, purporting it to be* dal!" The voice ceased abruptly. Silence. The gaslight hissed. Again the voice spoke. It said, *"Excellent!"* The tone of sarcasm was unmistakable. *"Excellent! Mango chutney without mango! Excellent!"*

For another long moment the gas-light susurrated without further sound accompanying it. Then, so suddenly that everyone started, Madame Dombrovski was on her feet, her palm pressed to her bosom. *"La!"* she sang. *"Fa so laaa . . ."* In another moment, wide awake now, she burst into hearty laughter, her golden inlays a-gleam. "Pliz," she begged, "pliz tall me, deed a spear-eat spick?"

Sudden embarrassment. . . . Eszterhazy coughed. "The Maha Atma Chandra Gupta —"

"Ah, that great soul! Two hawndred yirs he is stayèd een he's maha ashram een the Ghoolie Heels communing veeth the avatars! *Amrita,* a spear-ritual nectar, they breeng he'm; udder vise only vonse a yir solid food his takèd: *dal* veeth curry, a spoon fool. And mango chawtney, half a spoon fool. — Vhat he sayèd?"

The company looked at each other, looked at Katinka Ivanovna, looked at Eszterhazy. Who again coughed. "Evidently the Great Soul spoke in metaphors which we, with our gross perceptions, were really not quite able to interpret. . . ."

Quite suddenly and with no word of warning — unless, indeed, a somewhat slurping sound caused by licking a blob of mustard off his knife could be so considered — Professor Gronk said, abruptly, "In regard to the Autogóndola-Invention on which I have been working for five years in order to present it to Scythia-Pannonia-Transbalkania, my dearly adopted Parentland —" and there he stopped.

"My dear Professor," said Eszterhazy, smoothly taking the savant gently by an elbow and turning him around, "I perceive that you have not yet tried the very-yellow goat-cheese, although your opinion is one which I particularly value." Professor Gronk calmly reloaded his plate, plopped on some more mustard, and ate with a dreamy air.

" 'Goat-cheese,' hah!" exclaimed Baron Burgenblitz. "The peasants in Hyperborea are cutting up about the goat-tax again, eh, and why? — why, the devil, or some other ancient influence, has gotten into their goat-herds and they don't want to have to pay twice . . . ah I wish those tax-collectors come parading through *my* barony, damn them, I'd get up into my castle-fortress, pull up my drawbridge and bombard the lot with my artillery, damme if I wouldn't!" And he

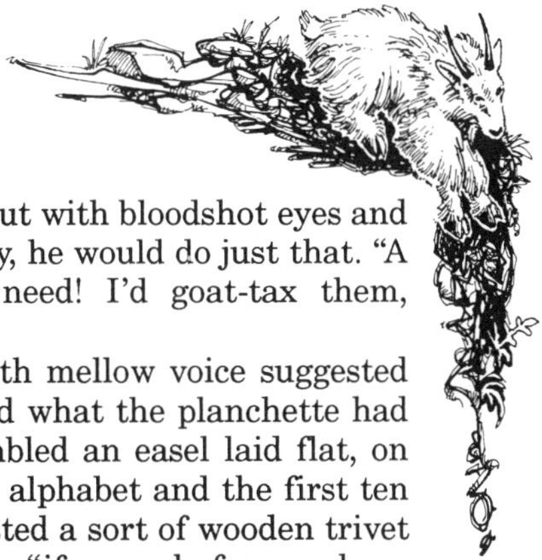

gnashed his teeth and gazed all round about with bloodshot eyes and left little doubt that, given the opportunity, he would do just that. "A whiff of grape-shot, that's what they need! I'd goat-tax them, *rrrrgggghhhh!*"

But at this point Katinka Ivanovna with mellow voice suggested that they sit down at table and try to find what the planchette had to tell. The oui-ja board somewhat resembled an easel laid flat, on which had been painted the letters of the alphabet and the first ten numbers, plus a few other signs. On it rested a sort of wooden trivet with casters. "Now," suggested Eszterhazy, "if several of us, perhaps three, will sit down and place the tips of the fingers lightly on top of the planchette so that no single one person will be able to move it without the two others being aware, it is said that the spirits may guide it to various letters and numbers . . . perhaps by this method spelling out a message. So. If Katinka Ivanovna would be kind enough? If Countess Zulk — ? And . . . Oh? What? I myself ? Oh. Well, very well. Now! Pard, if you will kindly observe the letters which the planchette touches as it moves, and call them out? And if someone else will please use this pencil and paper to write them down? Ah! Uncle Iggy! Thank you very much! Shall we begin?

The three of them sat around the small table with their fingers resting lightly on the light piece of wood. Once more: silence. Nothing moved but the gas-flame and its shadows. Then something else did. The planchette suddenly and very smoothly glided across the board toward the arch of letters. Then it glided back. Then . . .

The lateness of the hour had not prevented Professor Gronk from methodically continuing to graze his way along the sideboard, and the bottle-shaped bulges in his coat-pocket showed where, anyway, some of the otherwise undrunk beer, lemonade, and bullblood wine had gone. At length he paused. Gave a long, slow look up and down. All that remained was a half a pot of mustard. Dreamily, the Professor took up a small spoon and calmly consumed the contents of the pot. He stayed a moment, a long moment, looking into it. Then he gave a huge eructation. Then, the attention of his host and the one other remaining guest having been attracted, he said, "The aerolines."

"The aerolines?"

"The aerolines. For the Autogóndola-Invention. I have just had an idea." And, doubtless thinking deeply of the idea, Professor Gronk glided away, still holding the mustard-spoon in one hand.

Uncle Iggy had looked up, but he did not speak until the inventor was gone. Then he asked, "This . . . invention . . . ?"

Eszterhazy pursed his lips. His moustache was grown thicker; now and then he was obliged to trim it. "It has . . . as an idea . . . some merits. Some . . . possibilities. Perhaps we shall live to see them realized."

Uncle Iggy said that perhaps they might live to see the moon mined for cheese. Then he picked up the paper on which he had written down the letters indicated by the planchette as it moved hither and fro upon the oui-ja board, and lightly smacked it with his free hand. It had been found necessary to eliminate a number of letters; this was perhaps usually the case; out of what was left, one or two statements had been extracted . . . no one had cared to call them *messages.* Eszterhazy issued a slight sigh. "Ah yes, the spirits tonight seemed rather concerned with food. Still . . . I hope you were amused . . . ?"

Guest seemed to wrestle a moment with answer, head crooked earnestly to one side, lips moving before utterance was quite ready. Gas-light reflected on polished wood and brass and glass, made shifting shadows on flowered wall-paper.

"Diverted. Yes. I was amused . . . sometimes. . . . Always, though, I was diverted. And ah my God! how I need diversion. Ah it's not like in the old days, before the Big Union," when, of course, the Two Kingdoms and the Hegemonies had become the Empire; "in those days you could call the Turkish Gypsies or the Mountain Tsiganes into the Old Palace and you could sing and dance and stamp your feet and break wind," (though "break wind" he did not precisely say), "but nowadays, damn it, oh well. — Yes. Now, that American poet from the American Far-vestern Province, his loyalty to that Valker Villiams or whatever name, really a mere adventurer I suspects, but admirable loyalty and his half-wild costume so fascinating, even that beast Burgenblitz was taken with him by and by — hah! the Pard gave Burgen' a very good answer *I* thought! And why of course cut my foot off," (though "my foot" he did not precisely say), "if that Madame Dombrovski ain't a fine full figger of a woman!"

His face, which had lit up, now became somewhat troubled. "But, now, Engli, what d'you make of this here," and he held up the paper.

"HOG-LARD HUNDRED DUCAT A HUNDREDWEIGHT," Eszterhazy read aloud. Such was the first message, if "message" really it was, of the spirits across the board. "Hmm, well, the lard-merchants at any rate should be happy."

"Uncle" raised eyebrows. "Oh *should* they? If the lard alone costs a hundred ducks a hundredw'ight, how much d'you think the rest of the hog's going to cost?"

"Why . . . I had not thought."

Guest made a sound between groan and grunt. "No, I suppose not. Not yours to think about. *Mine* to think about. If hog-lard's so high, it follows that pork be high too; if pork be high, what of mutton, beef, chicking, what of oat, wheat, grain in general, what of spuds? What's the cause of it a-going to be? Drought? Blight? Pest? All? Oh sweet *caro mi Jesu,* not war I do pray?"

Host said that there might well be nothing in the planchette's

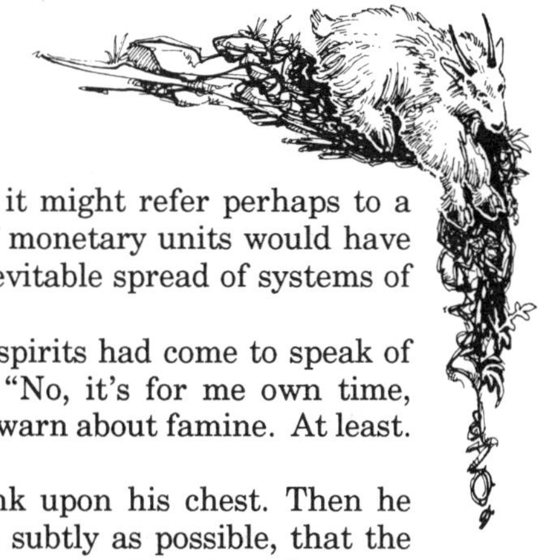

communication at all, or if there were, it might refer perhaps to a century in the future when the value of monetary units would have progressively declined, "owing to the inevitable spread of systems of credit. . . ."

Uncle Iggy did not however feel that spirits had come to speak of the price of hog-lard a century hence. "No, it's for me own time, depend upon it. Some message to *me.* To warn about famine. At least. *What's to be done,* Engelbert?"

Engelbert Eszterhazy let his chin sink upon his chest. Then he brought it up again. "I should see to it, subtly as possible, that the Agricultural Ministry set up or buy up or even long-term lease up very many *dry* places to store Indian corn and then other grain; these gradually to be stocked according to general market price."

His guest stood up. "What do you philosopher fellows call it? Ha, yes, 'a counsel of perfection,' well, it's something to think about and you be sure I am a-going to think about it. Political economy and much such fine phrases I gladly leave to others but when I hear of hog-lard at one hundred ducks a hundredw'ight, why, then I have to think about the Old Man and the Old Woman and the kids at the little old farm in the fields and what might happen to *them* if prices go high as that. — Engli! My thanks! Oh no you don't follow me out, neither. 'Night."

Rather soberly Engelbert Eszterhazy, Doctor of Philosophy, *aspirant* Doctor of Science, considered what had just been spoken. It was said that the great Cuvier could conceive of an entire species on the basis of a single bone; now here was Ignats Louis — always Eszterhazy had thought him a fine man but of never very much mind at all — conceiving of war, famine, pestilence, and death . . . and all on the basis of a single theoretical commodity price. It was remarkable. Whatever it meant. Or whatever it would some day mean.

The Minister of Law was closeted with the Minister of War. The latter, his ministry being the senior, spoke first. "Well, I see we have two reports before us. One is on the possible dangers arising out of a *démarche* on our borders on the part of Graustark and Ruritania, to occur shortly; sons of bitches, why don't they go bother the Bulgars?" The question being rhetorical, he proceeded without waiting for an answer, "And the other is the latest threat of the Baron Burgenblitz of Blitzenburg, etc., an Officer of the Imperial Jaegers, etc., etc.; son of a bitch, why doesn't *he* go bother the Bulgars?" In neither case did he say, precisely, "bother."

The Minister of Law shrugged. "But let us discuss him first, as I am sure that you have already a filed plan in case of invasion by Ruritania and Graustark, whereas we do not have a filed plan in regard to the Baron Burgenblitz. His latest threat is based on his alleged feudal right to refuse to allow one faggot of firewood to be taken from every cart thereof by way of way-tax."

The Minister of War swore frightfully and then very rapidly stuffed snuff up each nostril and sneezed behind his hand and wiped everything with a large and rather unmilitary-looking handkerchief. Then he asked, "And has he said right?"

The Minister of Law looked rather like a Talmudic scholar who, having just presented the most beautifully lucid argument showing how in a certain instance Hillel was right and Shammai was wrong, has at length come to the point where he must needs present the fact that nevertheless in that instance Shammai was right and Hillel was wrong. "Well, in a way. Yes. Technically, if it were presented to the Court of Compurgation and Replevin, there is no doubt that the Court, if pushed into a corner, would sustain him. But, well, for one thing, the Crown has repeatedly offered to present to the Diet a Schedule whereby his and all other such rights would be bought out; and all the Parties have agreed to support it. But the cockchafer won't apply to *be* bought out. And as for forcing him to *sell* out, well, that presents problems, too. The Autarchian Parties would not support it, surrender of feudal privilege must be voluntary and gradual, they say. Just as the Socialists and Liberals will not support his going on and denying himself the duty of paying all the same taxes as others. Son of a *bitch. Son* of a bitch." The Minister of Law pulled at his very full mutton-chop whiskers. But no solution came out of them, pull as he would.

The Minister of War said that Socialist and Liberal leaders might publicly protest Burgenblitz's reactionary actions, but — he thumped the green table between them — perhaps privately they were glad of them. "When he ignored the toll-gates, claiming Special Privilege, who knows how many Conservatives became more liberal or how many Agrarian Smallholders began to think socialist? True, he did pay the tolls eventually, but he might refuse again whenever he feels like it. Same with cattle-tax, same with the church-tax, with his, 'The priest must have a pig?' says he; 'I'll give him the runt of the litter,' now that just promotes freethinking and infidelity — what century does he think he's living in? Keeps roaring and yelling that if he is bothered he'll retreat into his castle-fortress at Blitzenburg and haul up the drawbridge and fire on anyone who comes near him, *ho!* Wish they'd let *me* have a free hand, then! 'My castle is my home?' *what!* Just watch me with one battery of artillery reduce his home to rubble: **boom**-*boom!* **BOOM!** Eh?"

The Minister of Law sighed. "Yes, no doubt. But in this year of his Reign the Emperor does not *wish* to reduce a subject's home to rubble. Why doesn't Burgenblitz of Blitzenburg plant wheat and shoot birds like other country gentlemen?"

The Minister of War had no other reply to this than furiously to

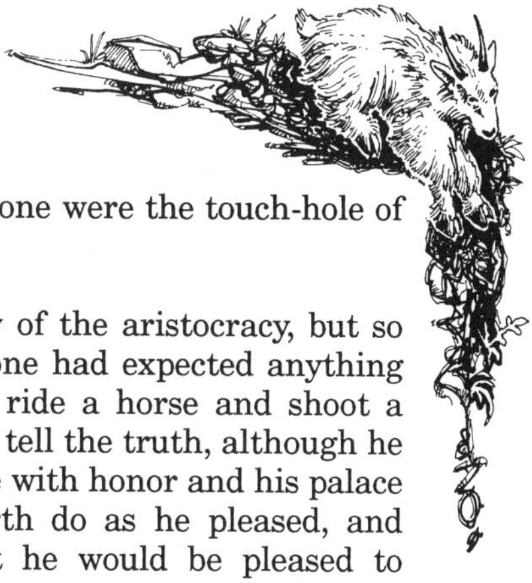

stuff snuff up his nostrils as though each one were the touch-hole of an artillery-piece.

Dr. Engelbert Eszterhazy was certainly of the aristocracy, but so distant from its main branches that no one had expected anything more of him than that, so to speak, he ride a horse and shoot a firearm; he had not even been expected to tell the truth, although he did. He had performed his military service with honor and his palace duty with the same. He might henceforth do as he pleased, and although it had not been foreseen that he would be pleased to undertake a seemingly endless series of studies, nevertheless that is what he had been doing. "He'll get brain fever at this rate," it was said, but he did not get it; neither did he retire to some distant castle to fill its neighborhood with rumor and with terror as did Count Vlad Drakulya; neither did he go to Paris and ride a white mare through the Bois and now and then dismount in order to milk her into a silver tassy from which he then sipped, as did Count Albert de Toulouse-Lautrec. He did not fight duels. He did not join hunting-battues in which thousands of game-birds or -animals were driven before the guns of the shooters . . . but these eccentric non-performances were eventually accepted. Often he had gone abroad, and though he had learned not only to accept the smiles which visited mention of his nation's name but to admit how much the smiles were justified . . . foreign ambassadors invited, for example, to an Imperial Review in honor of the grand opening of a sanitary sewer in Bella: one which turned out to be the first sanitary sewer in the Empire . . . nevertheless it was to his own nation that he always returned.

Incomparably less large and vast than the Russian Empire, incomparably less powerful than the German Empire, incomparably less sophisticated than the Austro-Hungarian Empire — still Scythia-Pannonia-Transbalkania, its mere name a subject for risibility elsewhere, was *his* Empire, his native land. It may not have functioned very well? so much the more he was pleased that it functioned at all. Its Secret Police was a joke? so much the more he too would enjoy the joke; no one laughed at the Secret Polices in the other empires. Its many languages rivalled Babel or Pentecost? let them: at least here no schoolboy was flogged for praying in whatsoever minor mother tongue. One empire had already, fairly recently, gone from the political map of Europe; and although the name of Bonaparte still rang like a tocsin here and there, it was uncertain the Prince Imperial would himself ever ring it successfully.

Day by day others asked, how fared their country's wheat compared with Russian wheat, its butter with Danish butter, its timber with Carpathian timber, its tar with Baltic tar, its cloth with English cloth? Day by day the same spokes of the universal wheel flashed by: love, sorrow, terror, death, success, failure, hunger, joy, growth, decay, weakness, strength: the wheel turned and turned and turned: nothing stayed the same, no one bathed twice in the same flowing water for the water had flowed on and flowed away. *There is no star at the pole of the universe,* young Dr. Eszterhazy recollected the ancient astronomer; and if there was and had long been but blankness in the comparable area in his own country, then might there not be space and place for him? What he hoped for, others did not even think of; what others did not think, might he not think of ?

And, after thinking, do?

As for fuel, if it were burnable, in Bella they burned it. Charcoal, firewood, peat from the bogs of Vloxland (though in Bella only the Vloxfolk burned it, perhaps because only they had the patience to wait for it to boil a pot), coke from the Great Central Gas Plant (It was not *very* great and there was, as a result, not very much coke; but every British firm and office preferred it. Others were suspicious: coke was *new.*), anthracite and bituminous coal . . . Everyone was agreed that anthracite burned better, cleaner, hotter — once it was burning — but there was the trouble of getting it to burn — and if it were necessary to dump it on a fire already burning with some other fuel, why, the feeling was general, why not simply go on using the other fuel . . . instead? There were and had long been not very far from Bella two mines producing a bituminous coal so soft as to be rather friable. One was still in the hands of the descendants of the mine-serfs, who operated as a sort of de facto coöperative; the soft coal hewed out easily enough and the pit was not deep enough to be dangerous, nor was there any new-fangled nonsense about a tipple, grading and sorting the lumps according to size: you either took it as the coalmen brought it, slid and scooped off the coal-carts into ox-hide sacks and thence into the coal-shed in the back by the alley-door . . . or you did without and used something besides soft coal . . . or . . . nowadays . . . perhaps you brought it from Brunk.

Originally the Brunk mine-and-delivery service had operated the same way as the other one did, but bit by bit Brunk Brothers had bought their fellow-miners out. There had been three Brunk Brothers; now there was one. For a quarter century, Brunk Brothers had concentrated on supplying the railroad. And Brunk Brothers still did. But Bruno Brunk had always had in mind that he would someday capture the market for the stoves and fireplaces of Bella, and long he studied it. What was the weakness of the other coaling company in regard to this market? — so he asked. The answer was not hard to find: the local soft coal was so soft that it tended to crumble, and it kept on crumbling; housewife and servant were always busy with broom and shovel sweeping up the little bits and pieces and the coal dust, and dumping it all on the fire. It made things, well, *dirty.* This did not bother the men who brought in the coal from the Old Pit, for

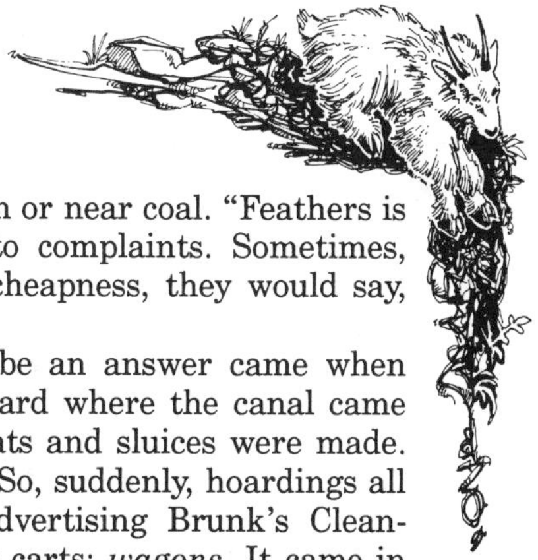

things were dirty anyway if you worked in or near coal. "Feathers is cleaner," was their common comment to complaints. Sometimes, referring to their product's undeniable cheapness, they would say, "Burn gold."

The first hint that something might be an answer came when Bruno Brunk bought a bankrupt wood-yard where the canal came into the Little Ister. Sumps were dug. Vats and sluices were made. Folks hardly knew what was a-going on. So, suddenly, hoardings all around town blossomed with posters advertising Brunk's Clean-Washed Coal. Wagons delivered it — not carts: *wagons.* It came in slabs of several sizes and each slab had, you see, here was the genius of it, had been *washed.* And each slab was wrapped in paper, cheap paper to be sure, but wrapped. And each slab (lumps were also sold but they were in paper *bags*), and each neatly-wrapped slab was tied with twine, cheap twine to be sure, but *tied.* One simply put a small bag of lump-coal on the grate and a slab of wrapped-coal a-top: then one lit the bag (having first, as instructed, nipped a small hole for air). By the time the bag-paper was burned away, the lumps were burning; by the time the slab-paper had burned away, the slab was burning. There was, to be sure, still soot; Brunk had not thought of everything. But still it was cleaner, oh yes it was cleaner, oh God it was cleaner!

. . . well, it did cost a bit more. . . .

The suppliers of the Old Pit coal watched their better-class business vanish, and they watched in dumb surprise. Then they scowled, ground their teeth, kicked their ponies, cursed, got drunk, beat their wives. Their wives, none of whom had ever heard that a voice ever soft and low was an excellent thing in women, beat them back. Presently and with police permission a petitional parade was seen marching through Bella, and it was composed of men whom much boiling and soaping and scrubbing had turned from their usual coal-black to a singular and singularly nasty reddish-grey: these were The Humble and Hardworking Loyal Laborers in the Pit of Coal, as their quasi-partnership was called. In effect, the petition petitioned that Government should Do Something; and what did Government Do? Government's reply boiled down to two words in a language not generally spoken by the local coal-workers, to wit, *Laissez-faire.*

Dr. Eszterhazy, in a general way, had been aware of all this, as Dr. Eszterhazy, in a general way, was aware of everything in Bella. Sometimes, he felt, he was perhaps too much aware; he had just escaped from an original (as it might be kindly to call him) who desired his patronage to perfect a process whereby clarified goose-grease might be used for lamp-oil. Eszterhazy somehow felt that this was a fuel for which the world was not yet prepared . . . generally speaking . . . but this did not mean that the process was yet without value: he had given the original in fact a note to the Semi-permanent

Under-secretary of Natural Resources and Commerce, suggesting that that ministry should have tests conducted. At what temperature would clarified goose-grease freeze? At what, turn rancid? Should the freezing-point prove very low and the rancid-point very high, the product might be promoted to foreign ship-chandlers provisioning long sea-voyages. Not only might it light the lamps but, should supplies run out, it might feed the crews. It would be healthier than lard and tastier than salt-butter; perhaps more economical as well. Bella might even become the anserine equivalent of the city quaintly called "Porkopolis," in the American province of Mid-vest.

. . . and should said ministry, *faute de mieux,* engage Doctor Eszterhazy himself to make those tests . . . well, nothing was wrong with *that,* was there?

This being in his mind, he was perhaps only mildly surprised to see a girl herding geese down Lower Hunyadi Street. She wore the traditional blue gauze fichu of the goose-girls of Pannonia; the goose-girls of Pannonia formed an almost infinite source of folk-lore. Who had not, as a child, and perhaps as an adult, listened to the *Lament of the Poor Little Itty Bitty Goose-girl of Pannonia, Betrayed by A Nobly-born Stinkard,* and failed to shed tears? Who would not recall lying on the floor by the firelight one lowering winter afternoon whilst listening to old Tanta Rúkhellè, spectacles halfway down her nose, reading the story of the poor goose-girl of Pannonia frozen to death whilst faithfully tending her master's goose in a sudden snowstorm? What popular melodrama or even new-fangled operetta could fail to include at least one scene with a poor little goose-girl in it? It was with, therefore, totally benignant reflections that he watched this particular poor little goose-girl from (presumably) Pannonia marching down the street; she was, equally traditionally, bare-footed, and — with her blue gauze fichu and her lament — equally evocative; the effect was only slightly marred by the fact that she weighed about 300 pounds. Eszterhazy, and, doubtless, everyone else watching noted that her bare feet were quite black: and so, from halfway down their traditionally white bodies, were her geese. And after her came about five-and-thirty other such goose-girls, all of approximately the same description and proportions, also driving piebald geese and also lamenting; nor was this all.

Right behind *them* came marching a group of the downstream laundresses, creating rather an effect in their unexpectedly sooty shifts; and, as they marched, they did not merely lament: they banged upon their washboards. And they *yelled.*

*Loud*ly.

He resumed his walk in a rather pensive mood.

What did Brunk say? Brunk preferred to say nothing. What did the Council and Corporation of the City of Bella say? Officially? Nothing. Unofficially? Unofficially they pointed out that it was, after all,

Brunk's coal and Brunk's coalyard and Brunk's riverine rights and there was not a damned thing in the laws preventing Brunk from doing what he wanted to do with any of them. It even suggested (unofficially) that the downstream laundresses might choose to launder upstream; but even unofficially it did not suggest that the entire Kingdom of Pannonia, which also lay downstream, might also choose to move upstream. What did the newspapers say? Very little . . . *as yet* . . . The newspapers did, however, print an occasional "historical essay" indicative of the fact that (a) the Emperor, besides being also King of Scythia, was also King of Pannonia . . . and, incidentally (b) did possess certain feudal powers as Warden of the Waters. Nobody out-and-out pointed out that if the Imperial Crown, as a Royal Crown, were suddenly to exercise its feudal (as distinct from its constitutional) powers, how this might strengthen the position of any feudal-minded nobleman intent upon exercising his own feudal powers.

Things were seldom simple, and this was clearly not one which was.

Meanwhile, *did* the middle-class housewives of Bella, the best customers of Brunk's Clean-Washed Coal, patriotically boycott the product? Well, one . . . it *was,* after all, *clean* . . . it was, after all, not merely convenient, it was fashionable . . . other things were really not the consideration of Women . . . their own laundry was done at home with well-water . . . and what were the waters of Pannonia to them? . . . One fears that, *no,* they did *not* patriotically boycott the product.

The path of progress did not run smooth. Or even smoothly.

"Gracious sir," asked a man who stopped Dr. Eszterhazy on the street; a man in the traditional pink felt boots worn by Hyperborean elders on festal or formal occasions; "Gracious sir, you has the look of a educated and a influential noble: can you tell me where I should git to aks about the spiritual seductions of our he-goats Back Home?"

Used as he was to odd and unusual questions, this one did startle. So much that he instantly wished to learn more. "Uncle Johnus," said he — *Uncle* was merely common good usage in Hyperborea from a younger man to his elder, and half the men Back Home there were named *Johnus* — "Uncle Johnus, if you tell me more maybe I can tell you more, so let us sit down at the tavern table yonder and have fresh rolls and roasted pig-pizzle with a pipkin of raspberry wudky, and do you tell me about that; the cost," he said, smoothly, noting a suddenly-appearing furrow on the other's brow, "will be borne by me out of the revenues of my grandser's estates, which otherwise we gentry might too easily be tempted to spend on champagne wine and gypsy-girl-dancers. Come on over here, Uncle Johnus."

Came Uncle Johnus? Uncle Johnus came. "I can always tell a noble gent when I sees one," he said, contentedly. He skipped upon the rough stone street as though it had been made of velvet. "I take it, my lord YoungLord, that you has travelled amongst us Back Home for you known ezaxtly what we in the High Hyperborea likes for a high snack. . . ."

Eszterhazy, feigning a sudden grimness which he did not entirely feel, said, truthfully enough, "I am the great-great-grandson of Engelbert Slash-Turk, the Hero of Hyperborea, *through two lines of descent.*"

Uncle Johnus attempted simultaneously to kiss the brow, cheeks, hand, knees, and feet of the descendant, etc., but was prevented, the descendant employing the magic formula, *"Don't spill the wudky."*

Having managed to avoid spilling the wudky anywhere but down his bearded throat and having eaten the first dish of rolls with as much delight and relish as if they had been petits-fours, Uncle Johnus began to tell the matter which had, by vote of his home hamlet, sent him to the Imperial Capital; for, said he, "I tried to learn some'at in Apollograd," provincial capital of the Hetmanate of Hyperborea, "but they laugh at me there, me lord YoungLord; they *laugh* at me!" Eszterhazy assured him, with perfect truth, that *he* would not laugh at him; thus assured, the man went on. Goats were very canny creatures, Uncle Johnus said . . . he-goats in particular. They could perfectly well remember that once upon a time in old pagan days they had been worshiped as gods ("They mammals was mommets, in them days," he put it). But since then, generally speaking, being subjected for example along with other animals domestic to an annual aspersion by the priests in blessing, such holy water had driven such unholy ideas clear out of their heads. *Mostly.* However. Lately —

Here the waiter arrived with the bowls of roast pigs' pizzle; Uncle Johnus looked from this to Eszterhazy and from Eszterhazy back to the goodies. Eszterhazy helped himself and gestured that his guest should do so, too; conversation, it being assumed, could wait.

And wait it did. By and by Uncle Johnus licked his fingers and wiped his immense moustaches on some fresh roll pieces and ate them and sipped some more raspberry wudky and swallowed and began to speak again. Them goats, now. Lately, however, through the agency of those whom or that which Johnus was rather he not be asked to name, the he-goats had begun to waver in their allegiance to the new and true religion. "They now runs away from the herds, Slash-Turk. They has crowns and garlands a-put upon their heads as in olden days. And they dances — ah, YoungLord Slash-Turk, yes, to the sound of that evil music they dances! They prances! They like to run wild in that there frenzy! Sometimes they carries on till they be dead, or sometimes they dashes off cliffs. And it's a terror and a worry and a fright to us, Slash-Turk YoungLord, what if they be not a-coming down to serve the she-goats in the breeding-season? We shall have no

goat-kids . . . no kid-skins . . . by and by, so, no more goats . . . no cheese . . . no milk . . . no meat . . . nor no leather. . . .

"And after that, sir: what then?"

The immense wax-lights in the Grand Chamber of the Privy Council were not needed at the moment, but custom required that they be lit, and so lit they were, and their immense wax tears seemed a silent accompaniment to the words being spoken. With an immense sigh, the Prince-President of the Privy Council said that their Intelligence Service was clearly not as keen as it ought to be. The Turks, partly because of British pressure, partly because of Russian pressure, partly because of Prussian pressure, and partly because of no Turkish pressure at all — the Turks had recognized that it was just about moving-day in their two predominantly non-Turkish provinces of Western Wallachia and Neo-Macedonia. The Turks had recognized that they were to leave, and to leave soon. The expectation was that these two provinces would probably become autonomous nations.

"If this is what our non-keen Intelligence Service should have informed us but perhaps failed to," said Privy Councillor, "we may as well cut it out of the Budget and subscribe to the Swedish or the Portuguese newspapers instead. You tell us in effect that applesauce is good with pork. True. We already know it. Applesauce."

The Prince-President raised from his stoop. Again the scarlet ribbon of the Great Order was a taut slash across his bosom. "So. Do you already know *this?* That our neighbors, those two rapacious, tough, absurdly small principalities of Ruritania and Graustark, have between them hatched a scheme to become extremely large at the expense of just about everyone else? Even now . . . now, I mean *now* . . . they are conducting secret manœuvres in the Disputed Areas, where not so much as a sheep-warden or a Rural Constable patrols to prevent them, and if no immediate and tangible gesture intervenes within two days, it has been agreed between them thus: one will annex Western Wallachia and one will annex Neo-Macedonia: thus at one stroke we are to be presented with two newer, bigger, more swollen, more swaggering neighbors upon our eastern borders . . . likely at once to dispute even more than is already disputed . . . and this is a prospect which" — his voice arose over the cries of outrage and the groans of dismay — "a prospect which we never envisaged and for which we are absolutely not prepared . . ."

Someone demanded to know what the Turks were likely to do.

"'Do'? They will protest and demand compensation and they will loot and slay some other Christian folk, one which has the misfortune to live on the Asian and not the European side of the Bosporus —"

"The British?"

"They will make speeches in Parliament and then cry, *'Hear, hear!'* "

The Austrians . . . Russians . . . Prussians . . . French? "A *fait accompli.*"

A silence.

An elderly Councillor asked, "Might not His Majesty, even as a temporary gesture, invoke the powers presumably latent in his Family's ancient title of 'Emperor de jure of New Rome and all Byzantium via Marriage by Proxy?' "

A murmur.

The Prime Minister cast a look of agony upon His Majesty, but His Majesty did not even look up at him, spoke without raising his bowed head. "His Majesty has just immediately recently, at the request of the Turks in connection with the question of Little Byzantia, renounced that title. It has not yet been gazetted, but the *assumpsit* has been signed." And, having signed, Ignats Louis bore the burden, and deftly led the pack on another scent. Another moment they sat and wondered what the Turk would do about Little Byzantia *now* —

A younger Privy Councillor demanded to know, Why were they all just *sit*ting there? Had they not a *Navy?* At this the Minister for Navy awoke with a start which alone reminded them that he had been there all along; the same Privy Councillor at once demanded to know, Had they not an *Army?* Arose the Minister for War. Grimly. Yes [he said], they had an Army. He refrained from telling them why they had not a larger Army [he said], nor would he refer to last year's decision to diminish the Army's share of the Budget [he said]. "The facts are, however, that we have not a very large Army, that our Army is deployed here and there and mostly not near the eastern border, and that the Annual General Militia Call-up had been postponed because the harvest was late and the Militia-men were needed to help bring it in at home. *Which they are now doing.*"

"For if not," interjected the Minister of Agriculture, "perhaps it will spoil, prices will soar, and maybe not enough to eat."

"Hog-lard at a hundred ducats a hundredw'ight," said His Majesty, not bothering with Court Gothic. One great groan rang through the Great Chamber, and the senior socialist Privy Councillor, a notorious Freethinker, was observed to spit three times in the palm of his hand and then surreptitiously to knock on the wooden framework of his upholstered chair. Field Marshals and Ministers, Aristocrats or Political Leaders though they were, still, the facts of farm life lurked never far away from any of them. Asked a labor leader, "O Sire! *That* high?"

Sire said merely, "It ain't mud that puts fat on the hogs, master. It's maize."

The leader of the Opposition asked, " '. . . within two days,' eh? And what is the very soonest that an effective body of our troops could be moved to the eastern borders?"

Said the Minister of War: "Three days."

Meanwhile, Eszterhazy had not only found no answer to the Mystery of the Goats, he had not even found a way perhaps to finding an answer. By the time he returned from his walk he was still perplexed. He made a note of the question; then he turned to his work of the moment, a laboratory experiment he carried on at home as adjunct to the one which formed his current project at the Royal-Imperial Institute of Science. Some time passed: he was thus engaged when a loud knock at the door, a loud voice, and a loud trampling of feet advised him that he had a guest. And which guest he had.

"Why, Doc," asked Pard Powell, "why or yew at home in thuh middle a thee afternoon on sitch a beautiful day? And why not in thuh great outdoor, a-breathin in a thuh sweet soft air? Not ta be found, a course, in thuh middle a town, but shorely we kin rint a couple a ponies and go fur a leetle ride along the river and inter the trees! Why, when I was livin on the boundless prairies as thuh adoptid child a thuh Red Skin People, why my hort beat loud with joy whiniver I buh-held a wild aminal or heard a sweet-singing bird, now —"

Simultaneous with Eszterhazy's suddenly becoming aware that two of the glass pieces of his experimental equipment were unconnected, Pard Powell reached out and imperturbably connected them; almost at once remarking, "I needn't tell you, Doctor, that silver and mercury are incompatible," with no trace of dialect or accent in his voice.

"No," said Eszterhazy. "No, you needn't." Their eyes met. "Nor need you tell me that it was from the Red Skin People that you learned the techniques of analytical chemistry, for I fear I would not believe you if you do." Pard half-turned, made narrow his eyelids. Of a sudden, a certain English word flashed into Eszterhazy's mind as though the very paragraph in the dictionary lay exposed before him. *Glau-cous.* **1.** Of a pale yellow-green color. **2.** Of a light blue-grey or bluish white color. **3.** Having a frosty appearance. **4.** . . . But never mind **4.** It seemed to him that even as he looked, the pupil of the American's eye turned from pale yellow-green to light bluish-grey to bluish white to pale yellow-green again; and . . . always . . . frosty. It was damnably odd. It was uncanny.

Not changing his gaze, Pard said, "Well, no, Doctor, of course not. You see, not only was I once a student, and a good one, too, of the Academy of the State of New Jersey; but I later owned the best pharmacy in Secaucus. If only I could have been content to go on compounding calomel and jalap pills for constipated house-frows and brown mixture for their coughing kids and tincture of cardamom for their flatulent husbands, I might be not merely prosperous now, which I am not: I might be rich. But one day it got to be too much for me, and just then along came a drummer in pharmaceuticals and

I sold out — lock, stock, barrel, mortar, and pestle. And I went out West. And that is how Washington Parthenopius Powell metamorphosed into Pard Powell. Oh, to be sure, I have put a lot of fancy stitches into the splendid cloth on the embroidery hoop of my life. Well, why not? But don't take it for granted that all the gorgeous touches are lies. They're not. — Well . . . Not all."

He gave his head a slight jerk, and all the mass of dark-red waving hair rose and fell. There was a flash from the glaucous eyes. He laid his hand upon his heart. "And as I puts it in my *Fifth Epic Poem in Honor of William Walker the Last Conkwistadoree*:

'Thudding onward o'er the Plains
of wide San Peedro Sula
From whence the dusky Spanish Dons
extracted mucho moola,
We brothe the air that freemen breathe
and all our cry was 'Freedom,'
We relished it like champagne wine,
or Dutchmen relish Edam —'

"Whut say we go fur a ride, Doc?"

Eszterhazy burst into laughter. "By all means, yes let us go for a ride. Let me, first, put some things in order here." Not instantly remembering what the botanical specimens were which he picked up to dispose of, absentmindedly he gave them a sniff and was about to administer an exploratory, if cautious, lick, when Pard Powell cried aloud and dashed forward.

"Don't eat them things, Doc! They'ull drive ya plumb loco! Them's jimson weed!"

Astonished, aghast, Eszterhazy gazed at the plants. "Why . . . these were, allegedly, woven into crowns to garland the heads of he-goats in Hyperborea. What do you —"

The Far-vestern Yankee frontier poet said he hoped to Helen his pal Doc Elmer Estherhazy didn't have him no goats there wherever. "Why looky thar if that ain't the very flower outa the devil's garden, *Datura stromonium,* or I'm a dirtbird!"

Lightning seemed to flash in the makeshift laboratory there in a small scullery-room at Schweitz's hotel. "Surely a relative of the deadly nightshade, a prime ingredient in witches' brew!"

Pard Powell pulled his long red-brown moustache. "Durn tootin! As well as *Hyoscyamus niger,* alias *hen*bane; and — as you so closely perceive the nomenclaytcher — *Atropa belladonna,* or deadly nightshade. Anyone a them will make ya curdle your dander, make ya scamper and cavort and run ginerally *mad.* Or, as we so aptly puts it Out West, *Loco!* As well as which, it might well *kill* ya."

There was a sort of ringing in Eszterhazy's ears. He shook his head

emphatically. "Is there any reason why *she*-goats should be exempt from the effects?"

"None that I kin think of . . . she-*chick*ens ain't. *Hen*-bane. Git it?"

"Could the scent of those plants cause humans to think that they had heard a sound like music? Fifing? Or . . . piping?"

"Not that I — well, durn it, eph yew thenk that, time we got *outa* this stuffy ol' suite! Let's go for a *ride!*"

Somehow or other it happened that they made a few stops in the course of their ride. Professor Gronk was found deep in his plans at his workshop. Without looking up and as though the newcomers had been there all along, he said, "Straw would provide the heat for the ascendant aspects of the Autogóndola-Invention. But straw would not fuel the engine. Wood is insufficiently concentrated, and hence too heavy. Coal, the same. Coke is better, but still too heavy. I have as yet no method of drawing the flammable gases out of the atmosphere."

Scarcely pausing to consider that his question might be considered not serious and therefore resented, Dr. Eszterhazy asked, "What of clarified goose-grease?"

The Professor said that he had not been working with the problem of liquid fuel. "The engine is not set up for it. Then there is the problem of the integument. ["The . . . in*teg*ument?"] Silk is unquestionably still the best. I have no silk. White absorbs too little heat, black absorbs too much heat, red alone will do. Silk. Red." He spoke as though speaking very simply to children. "Of each piece," he made measuring gestures, "such a size. Two hundred and sixty-four such a size pieces. The glue I have only to heat. The wicker I have already framed. The engine is ready. I require only a satisfactory fuel, hot and yet light. Also of red silk, two hundred and sixty-four pieces of such and such a size." He turned upon his two visitors a look of such combined melancholy and appeal that they felt obliged to repeat the measuring gestures until he was convinced they understood.

"Well, Purfessor, that certainly is a wonderful thing," said Pard Powell, slowly edging away. "I'll sure think about that. I'll sure be keepin my eye out for red silk. — Whut the Hell's the little guy talkin about, Elmer?" he asked, once they were outside again.

Outside, in the scarcely paved streets between the old wooden houses, children clapped and sang and danced. A food vendor chanted to them, "Delicate eating? Delicate eating? A nice portion of large beef-gut stuffed with chopped lung and rice, sauced with onion and garlic and red peppers in the Avar style? Two pennikks, only two pennikks, delicate eating?" But they did not pause for it. Eszterhazy assured his friend that it was an acquired taste. They cantered on. At the next corner they stopped in order for Pard to buy a bundle of the small flags of, of course, Scythia-Pannonia-Transbalkania, the sort which are flown, or, rather, waved, at parades. There was no parade due; but the vendor, a wizened cretin from the Friulian Alps, perhaps, did not know this. Nor — seeing that he was, after all *selling* the flags — needed he care. "Be good souvenirs for back home. I'll give 'em to the Injuns. They already got pitchers a them pie-faced Presidents."

Farther along, and in a considerably better-housed neighborhood, if not one where you were likely to meet your maiden aunt or her pastor, a woman waved from a window and called out a greeting which they politely returned. The greeting was followed by an invitation which they politely declined. At the next window, another woman. Another greeting. Another invitation. And at the next window . . . And at the next . . . And . . .

"Dunno why they need any *light,*" said Pard, who had already pushed his sombrero to a rakish angle. "Them red petticuts is bright enough." They rode on a moment or so before the same thought occurred to them. They mentioned the name and the need of Professor Gronk. And . . . it is to be feared . . . they both burst out laughing. "Sure to *be* silk," Pard declared. Still . . . He began to sing:

"I ain't got no use for the women,
the ladies and girls o' the town:
They'll stick to a man when he's winnin,
and step on his face when he's down. . . ."

By and by they found themselves fairly near the mouth of the Little Ister where it disembogued into the Ister proper, and whom should they see sitting on her invariable stool but that well-known character, the Frow Widow Wumple. Wumple ("God rest his soul") had been a master boatwright; his prows were famous: "dumpling-cutters" they were called; and his relict lived by renting out the ways. Right now no vessel was hauled up for repairs, scraping, caulking, painting . . . but who knew what rascal might care to try? . . . and then try getting away without paying! Therefore, as always, the Frow Widow Wumple on her stool. Conversation with her was always interesting, providing only that one had an infinite capacity for hearing the phrase, "Ah, they didn't have none o' them things when *I* was a gal!" — and Dr. Eszterhazy had. Today the list of things which they didn't have none of when the Widow Wumple was a girl included: store-boughten butter, paved roads, a disgusting French disease called *la grippe,* indoor plumbing, and some foreign food named sandwich . . . the Widow Wumple wasn't quite sure what this last was, but was sure it was unwholesome. ". . . bound to be . . ." Another thing, etc., was gentlemen who would light up segars and not offer one to a poor old woman with the affliction in both legs and scarce a pennikk to bless herself with; Eszterhazy was so remorseful and hasty that he forgot to blow out the lucifer match before tossing it away.

". . . and she says to me [puff], 'So you see Mother Wumple [puff], we be getting married in church so I hopes you won't draw the wrong conclusion.' [Puff] *'See?'* says I. 'I ben't *blind,'* says I. 'Wrong conclusion, indeed,' says I. [Puff-puff] 'I've had 11 children of me own and can count up to nine as well as the next one, the wedding feast we needn't ask about but send me some sugared almonds from the chrismation snack,' ah they didn't have such things when *I* was a gal [puff . . . puff]."

Eszterhazy, in mock surprise, said, "Which? Christening or sugared almonds?" The old woman cackled, smacked skinny hand on skinny knee.

The lucifer had begin to burn more and not less brightly, and he felt obliged to dismount and stamp it out. And stayed where he was, looking.

"Ah, that's all that scurf from across the Little River," the old woman said. "First there come all that sawdust. Then come all that coal-dust. The current wash them here, when the seas'nal tides was high. The both of them has sort of conglobulate together and dried out and a body has to be certain careful where she drop or dump a bucket o' hot ashes or that scurf will start blazin; ah they didn't have none 'f them things when *I* was a gal but now I'm just a old woman with the affliction in both legs [puff], and I can't do nothin about anythin [puff]."

Eszterhazy said that he would see to it that the rubbish was cleared away. But he set no date to it. And the two cantered on. And as the two cantered on, the European asked a question and the American delivered an answer. " 'What do I think — ?' Why, I believe old Burgenblitz is not such a bad old son of a bitch for such a bad old son of a bitch as he is, you know, Elmer. Trouble is, he is *bored!* He's *tired!* Bein a European-style, country gentleman *bores* him! Pokin fat pigs, feedin fat cattle, ballroom dancin, opry, why he's done it all, he is *bored* with it. He is *tired* of your make-buhlieve hunts, they air all *fakes,* Elmer — peasants drivin pheasants in front of where he stands a-shootin of them, servants loadin his guns for him, servants countin up his kills for him — why they ain't no good wars he could jine up into right now — folks want to go to Jerusalem they don't go on a Crusade, they go on a Cook's Tour — *he* can't read no books for pleasure. . . . So whut's left for him to do but to dig in his heels and say, 'Nobuddy tells *me* whut t'do!' Jest like some old Florida Cracker."

Much would "Elmer" have wished to ask him more about the Old Florida Crackers . . . from "Old" Florida? and what did they crack, corn? . . . but it was at that moment that everything changed; it was at that moment that he encountered De Bly, the Civil Provost of the Capital and *ex officio* a member of the Privy Council; De Bly was riding his dun gelding and riding him hard, Eszterhazy could not quite make out where, exactly, De Bly was going: and perhaps De Bly at that moment could not have made it out either. And De Bly looked like doom.

He hailed him. The man looked up, mouth open, chops sagging, began a gesture, let his hand fall, made as if to ride on: stopped, suddenly, waved the younger man to come on. Began to talk while they were still not face to face. "They tell me that you are a Doctor-Philosopher now, Eszterhazy, I don't know what that means, but I know you performed well in the Illyrian Campaign, and I know you did something quick and clever in the matter of that Northish King who came here incognito. Oh you better do something quick and clever right now, I don't know what it may be, but damned quick —" And then he told him what he had heard at the session of the Privy Council.

Eszterhazy listened, quite without joy.

Then De Bly went his wild, bewildered way, and left Eszterhazy to go his. Who, as he proceeded back towards the heart of the city, translated for his companion. Who thoughtfully said, "Sort of like . . . oh . . . sort of like, say, Hayti and Santo Domingo tryin to carve up northern Mexico between them. Would *we* like that? No we wouldn't." But Eszterhazy had nothing to say to such a comparison.

And Eszterhazy had nothing to say when he heard Pard say, "How, Burgey. You old galoot." For a moment. He heard a wordless murmur. There, wearing the undress uniform of an officer of Imperial Jaegers, was Burgenblitz. He looked rather tired; and he looked at Eszterhazy, for all that he had recently been his guest, with the same wary indifference with which he looked at most people when he did not look at them with anger. A spark blazed hotly in the younger man's head. He raised his left hand as though, it being his right, he were about to take an oath. "Baron," he said, "I absolutely deny that you have any authority over me whatsoever." He of course gained instantly the Baron's interest . . . if not his understanding. "I also absolutely deny that I have any authority over you whatsoever." The Lord of Blitzenburg was not denying this denial; the Doctor of Philosophy and aspiring doctor of science went on, briskly but not hastily, speaking with clear pronunciation but avoiding any special emphasis of words; "Therefore not as one claiming authority and not as one designating or yielding authority, but simply as one member of the Order of St. Cyril to another, I do ask this of you: that you, acting upon the rank of special constable inherent in your own noble rank, take charge of the field called the Old Fair Grounds. That you take charge of whatever supplies may be sent to it. That you enlist the help of as many soldiers or sailors whom you may need and find at liberty, as you are entitled to do anyway by virtue of your own military rank . . . you are certainly justified in treating them to beer . . . there is a crisis impending and apparently the State cannot act in time." Eszterhazy ceased to speak.

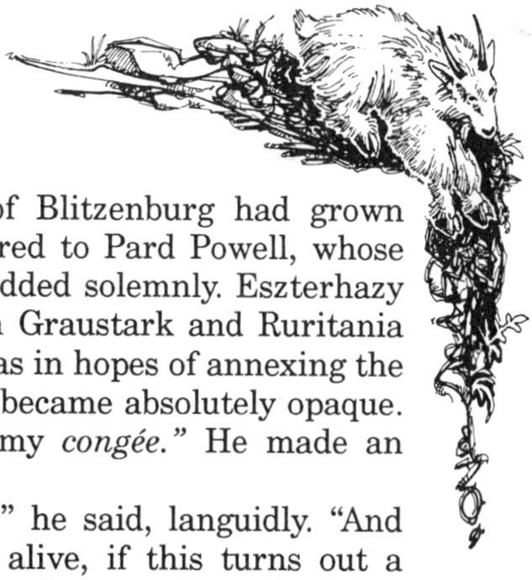

The eyes of the Baron Burgenblitz of Blitzenburg had grown distrustful, then became sly, then wandered to Pard Powell, whose own glaucous glance met his . . . who nodded solemnly. Eszterhazy spoke again. “We have learned that both Graustark and Ruritania may hold a *démarche* in the Disputed Areas in hopes of annexing the Ottoman provinces.” The Baron’s glance became absolutely opaque. “Sir,” said the Doctor, “I now request my *congée.*” He made an informal salute.

Burgenblitz returned it. “You may go,” he said, languidly. “And damned if I don’t flay you, slowly and alive, if this turns out a tarradiddle.” (And doubtless he would, thought Eszterhazy. Claiming a feudal privilege to do so.) The Baron was gone before the thought. Gone slowly. But he had headed his horse towards the Old Fair Grounds.

“Brunk.” Abruptly.

Brunk (aggressively): “Can prove *nothing!* Nothing, *nothing* prove!”

Doctor (calmly): “No? I can prove I know the Emergency Laws of the Year of Bonaparte better than you do.”

Brunk had been prepared to shout about the sludge in the river. Brunk was dressed as usual in a suit appropriate to an upper clerk. Along with this Brunk wore the foxskin hat of a country bailiff, a gorgeous gold watch and chain, and a pair of miner’s boots. Poor Brunk! He did not yet know who he was. Or who or what he might yet be. And, certainly, he was not yet prepared to claim wide knowledge of the Emergency Laws of the Year of Bonaparte — that fierce and frightful Year which first pushed the Confederacy of the Lower Ister on its way towards empery — though certainly he had heard thereof. *“What Law Bonaparte?”* asked Brunk.

“As an emergency measure I can here and now dismount and burn your coalyard to the ground —” See Brunk’s mouth open very, very wide. “— and oh certainly I should be obliged to pay compensation.” See Brunk’s face indicating his calculation how much this could be, plus interest. “Oh of course it would be compensation at the value of the place during the Year of Bonaparte . . . what? A hundred ducats?”

“What a hundred ducks burn my place Bonaparte?!”

“But I won’t.” Eszterhazy. *Very* quietly. Brunk had begun to reel a bit. Things were going too rapidly. He put out both his hands palms down at breast level. He looked rather like a disorganized dancing-bear.

“Now here is what you have to do. . . .” Brunk, mouth a-sag, nodded silently. “You have to take a few good men with wheelbarrows. Cross the Little River. *Now.* Mother Wumple’s Yard. Where all the *stuff* has washed up and dried. You are to break it all up. Into little pieces. About the size of a common hen’s egg. Carefully. *She* won’t prevent you. And then you're to have your chaps wheel it along to the Old Fair Grounds. Pile it on a couple of good large tarpaulins. *Cover* it with a couple of good large tarpaulins. *Got that?"*

Brunk had been nodding, nodding. First he lifted one foot. Then he put it down. Then he lifted the other. Then he put it down. Then he asked *"What I must do next Boss my place Bonaparte don't burn?"*

Eszterhazy thought a moment. Only a moment, though. Then, in the crisp tones of an officer who has allowed the men to take two minutes to piddle into a hedge, and Brunk would certainly still be on the Semi Active Militia Lists, the officer by his tone now indicating that it was back to **Forward! MARCH!**, Eszterhazy said, "Draw four times four rations upper NCO quality plus four times ten rations other ranks quality. And see that it is delivered with the rest, *go!"*

And Brunk, breathing heavily, muttering disconnected words . . . burn, Bonaparte, boss, rations, NCO, break, pieces, eggs . . . Brunk *went.*

Any decade, any year or month or week now, Capital in Scythia-Pannonia-Transbalkania would discover its own power. And leap, roaring, forward. With, right behind it, Labor. And yet and meanwhile? Well. Not today.

Professor Gronk had accepted development as calmly as he had accepted stasis. Washington Parthenopius "Pard" Powell, who had been given his own emergency task to perform, had performed it. And had returned. The inventor's loft was a-blaze with scarlet silk. "What do you mean, 'Did I have any trouble?' Why, harlots is the most patriotic class of people they is, irregardless of nationality or theopompous preference. Course I lied a lot. Told 'em I needed it fer to make belly-bands so the sojers wouldn't ketch the cholera in the humid swamps of them Disputated Territories or whutchewcallem. Even showed whut size to cut they red silk petticuts cuttem up to. Then I give every house one a my little flags. 'N then they all *kiss*ed muh. Well. Here we are. Do we stitch? Or do we glue?"

In the Taxed Domestic Animals Division of the Excise Office.

"What does Skimmelffenikk report from High Hyperborea?"

Chairs were thrust back. Drawers rattled. Files were slapped down. The motto of the Royal and Imperial Scythian-Pannonian-Transbalkanian Excise Office was, "If you have nothing to do, do it very loudly, so nobody will notice."

"Here it is, Chief."

"There it is, Chief."

"Right over there, Chief."

"File Number 345 slash 23 dash 456, the 11th inst. Skimmelffenikk reports from High Hyperborea. . . ."

The Chief 's round whisker-encircled face took on a look of controlled patience. "Yes?" he enquired. "Well? *So?*"

Skimmelffenikk's report from High Hyperborea had been properly received, posted, docketed, filed . . . all the rest of it. However, it was rapidly becoming clear, nobody had read it. Until now. Vows were instantly (and silently) made to The Infant Jesus of Prague, All the Holy Souls, and St. Mammas Riding the Lion, that the Chief not completely blow up, declare Unpaid Overtime, fire them all, cancel the three-o'clock borsht break — None of it. The Chief read to himself without sound, the Chief read vocally in a mutter, then the Chief read altogether aloud. *Skimmelffenikk reports from High Hyperborea that to the sound of like real weird music the untaxed he-goats had been dancing and prancing with like crowns of flowers on their heads. . . .* And this statement had been signed in full by the Officer Reporting (Skimmelffenikk), attested by his Sergeant, one Grotch; and confirmed by the latter's Rural Constable, one Mommed, who makes his Mark, said Mark being herewith identified by the District Imam with Rubric in Turkish according to the Highly Tolerant Imperial *Permittzo. . . .*

There was no use to look in the *Rules and Schedules.* Everyone knew there was nothing on the subject in the *Rules and Schedules.* The Chief, with the near-genius which signifies predestined high rank, simply put his hat on and the file down and went home early.

Brunk — **Bru**nk was by the way the coal-magnate; **Gro**nk was the inventor — Brunk had not got everything quite right. The bit about digging up the entire bed of dried mixed coal-dust and sawdust and carefully breaking it into egg-sized pieces, *this* he had done exactly as directed. It was the rations which had confused him, and this confusion he had passed on to Frow Brunk. Frow Brunk kept a very hearty table, and she did as she thought she was told. She emptied the smoke-house, she emptied the bake-house, she filled a wagon full of bread and cake and sausage and hams and brawns and cheeses and roasted this and pickled that. Who knew what Bonaparte might want? The five soldiers and four sailors whom Burgenblitz had in effect personally conscripted had never had such a feast since . . . since . . . well, likely *never.* And the barrel of home-brewed ale which Frow Brunk had sent along caused the thin and sour beer of the corner tavern to be quite forgotten, something for which the keeper of the corner tavern was thankful, as when he had mentioned the matter of payment the Baron Burgenblitz had given him *such a look* that he had though best to follow the example of that one of whom it was written, "And so he departed, not being greatly desired."

The conscripts had of course wondered what it was all about, but of course they had not asked. True, they were technically on liberty, but they had all spent all their money anyway, and their liberty now amounted to the right to sleep on the Armory floor if they wished. The Baron instead sent them to the Armory with a note for blankets, instead. The Baron set up guard-posts; they stood guard. When the mysterious whatever-it-was arrived, the Baron ordered it put in the middle of his impromptu camp in the middle of the Old Fair Grounds. Food having arrived, he had ordered rations distributed. To be sure, there were no dishes, no utensils, no table nor even table-linen: no matter: his share was neatly served him on a fresh-laundered skivvy shirt from a sailor's ditty-bag. And he ate every bit of it. And when some folk, having noticed the campfire with curiosity, came nosing around, they were promptly told to nose out.

Next morning:

First came the four fellows from the Royal and Imperial Navy, carrying what appeared to be a New England whaleboat, saving only that New England whaleboats are seldom if ever woven out of wicker-work. Almost immediately after that two soldiers came drawing a gun-carriage, and riding on the limber and smoking a pipe and wearing his best ask-me-no-questions look was Baron Burgenblitz. How had he obtained the gun-carriage? If you were an artilleryman alone on duty at the Armory and Baron Burgenblitz appeared at five in the morning saying merely the two words, *"Gun-carriage,"* would *you* not have let him have it, being merely thankful he did not also say, *"Gun-horses,"* as well? Hah. On the carriage was something covered over with oiled cloth. An expert on the subject might have conjectured that under the cover was a steam engine. A very small steam engine. And as to its being on a gun-carriage, this may in fact have been co-source of rumors which long subsequently vexed Graustark and Ruritania, to the effect that "S-P-T has got *steam-cannon!* Oh God!" — a few other vehicles followed.

There was no established drill for what came next. Out of the wicker-work "boat" was produced a pile of bright red silk . . . well, bright red silk *what?* the sailors might have wondered . . . but theirs was not to reason why, theirs was only to fix the *what?* in places ordered by a suddenly in-the-here-and-now Professor Gronk. There were a number of sections of wicker framework. There were cries of, "Belay that rope! Smartly now! Five marlin hitches on the larboard side! A bowline on a bight, I say! Rouse up, rouse up, a bowline on a bight there!" and so on. Before the eyes of those who did not pass the fence around the Old Fair Grounds something rather like the ghost of an immense sausage — also made of wicker — gradually took form. Bright red masses hung in place. A murmur came from beyond the fence, then cries, then shouts. The cover was removed from the gun-carriage, a flat trough of thin wood was hoisted aboard and

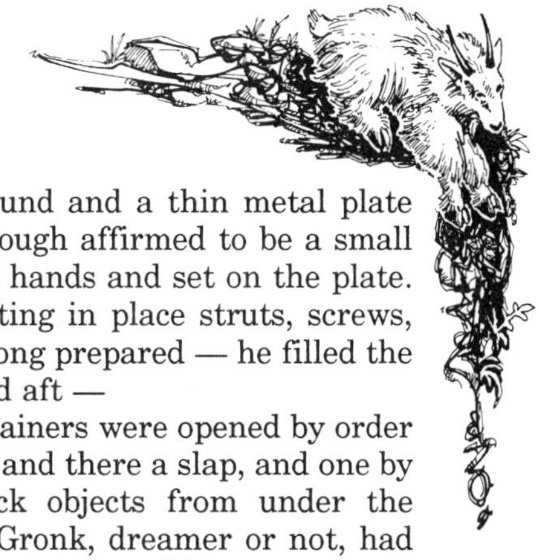

promptly filled with sand from the ground and a thin metal plate placed in it, and what was now sure enough affirmed to be a small steam engine was lifted by many strong hands and set on the plate. And the Professor was everywhere, setting in place struts, screws, braces, all thin, all light, all strong, all long prepared — he filled the boiler and stacked jugs of water fore and aft —

And now a number of pasteboard containers were opened by order of Dr. Eszterhazy and given here a snap and there a slap, and one by one were filled with the curious black objects from under the tarpaulins. What *were* they? Professor Gronk, dreamer or not, had sometimes a way of getting to the heart of things. "What *are* they?" he asked.

Eszterhazy, the wind riffling the short beard which had grown a trifle darker in recent years, said, "This is that new fuel of which I spoke. It is composed of the waste-dust of very soft coal mixed with sawdust of, I should estimate, pine, with of course some residue of resin which acts as both a binding agent and an inflammatory . . . as a sort of phlogiston, to apply a rather *passé* term . . . the whole lavaged with the water of the lower Little Ister, and what semi-solids *that* might contain awaits further analysis. I have had this fuel-substance cut up into small pieces so as to make easier such finer adjustments of the flame as —"

"Get it up," said Gronk, shortly. His pop-eyes darted here and there, rather like those of a chameleon keeping a sharp eye out for the cat. The boxes of fuel were gotten up, the engine was by now fastened in its place, whence, one hoped, any sparks would fall harmlessly into the sand, and a lucifer struck to the first piece of fuel; a briquette it might perhaps be called; perhaps not. It glowed and continued glowing even after the match burned out. It was blown upon. More was added. In a few moments a small fire burned in the grate beneath the engine's boiler. The arrangements above the engine were complex. From the catchment above it led a number of sleeves and each sleeve terminated in one of the drooping masses of red silk. . . .

And now was displayed one of the true beauties of the Autogóndola-Invention, for the fuel was made to do double duty: the same heat which turned the water into steam also filled with heated air the bellies of what were gradually discerned to be five beautiful, big balloons — five they were in number, but the wicker-work frame lashed together according to its inventor's directions held all five cohesively as though they had been *one.* The wicker boat lashed beneath began slightly to tremble.

And then two voices were heard, one of them familiar to the Doctor. *"Bon jour! Bon jour!"* this one cried, in a strong accent not French. "Thee spear-eats sayèd me, *'Ascend!* These morning you shall *Ascend!'* Who knowèd what eat mins, 'Ascend'? So I comb over wheeth Jawnny to find out. These ease Jawnny. *Bon jour! Bon jour!"*

Katinka Ivanovna wore an outfit of brilliant-bright-orange, and a beaming smile, as she climbed into the "boat" and looked eagerly around. Her blue eyes sparkled. Whatever the spirits had meant, it evidently contained none of the gloom of the Road to En-Dor.

Climbing in right after her was a fine large glossy animal of a man, with astrakhan lapels on his surtout, a long thick sleek moustache, and an atmosphere of the very best hair-oil: this, presumably, was Jawnny. "*Buon giorno! Buon giorno!* Gian-Giacomo Pagliacci-Espresso; allow me to present you a cold *fiasco* my very best produced Italian sparkle-wine, *tipo di* champagne, you will prodigiously delight; *marón!* And *achi* also some bearskin lap-robe, plus here an entirety of one case of such my wine, I bottle in Bologna, next my sausage-factory, *brrr!*"

Dr. Eszterhazy looked a bit doubtful as the signor helped place the case in the center of the 'Góndola, but Professor Gronk, with a quick appraising glance, said, very briefly, "Ballast." And returned in controlled frenzy to fastening wires and aerolines, and to spreading out maps and examining various pieces of scientific equipment. "*Laaaa . . .*" sang Mme. Dombrovski, hand on bosom. She waved to what was now a large crowd straining at the fence; the crowd waved back and cheered.

Another figure moved slightly. "Well, Baron Burgenblitz . . . do you come along?" asked Eszterhazy.

"Try to prevent me! — try. In regard to the source material of your pretty red balloons, my patronage has supplied much of it." The Baron settled himself into a pair of the bearskin lap-robes, one of which he slung over his shoulders; applied his pipe to his tobacco-pouch; and growled.

It was at this moment that Sgr. Gian-Giacomo Pagliacci-Espresso, glancing around, said, with a slightly nervous tremor, "Pray inform the sailors be careful with ropes, else this . . . this *cosa* . . . might accidentally go," his eyes rolled, he seemed suddenly to obtain a better grasp of the situation, "**UP!**" He leaped over the side, and from the *terra firma* reached for Mme. Dombrovski; but the abrupt loss of his weight, plus the increased swelling of the red silk balloons, caused the Autogóndola-Invention to strain against the *lines* held by the sailors, who — taking his last exclamation as a signal — stepped back smartly and released them. From inside came cries of annoyance, perhaps alarm, but these ceased abruptly. There was much else to do.

The splendid scarlet Autogóndola-Invention went soaring up into the misty heavens. Gronk, at the scientific instruments, called out courses, Eszterhazy plied the wheel which controlled the tail- and wing-vanes, Pard Powell from time to time stuck his finger in his mouth and held it up to test the breeze, from time to time suggesting slight changes in direction so as to take best advantage of prevailing winds; the engine, as engines will, went **choog-choog, chuff-**

slight changes in direction so as to take best advantage of prevailing winds; the engine, as engines will, went **choog-choog, chuff-chuff;*** and Katinka Ivanovna, waving the tri-national flag, holding now on to one rope and now another, semi-incessantly sang out, "Onward, oh onward, great-glorious-successful Scythia-Pannonia-Transbalkania, hairess to thee future weesdom of the ages!" From time to time she avoided hoarseness by sipping from a *fiasco* of the produce of Sgr. Pagliacci-Espresso's winery; and, now and then, with a merry gesture, she shared it with the others; when it or its successors was empty she tossed it negligently aside . . . on one occasion so much so that it went clear over the side, and hurtling through the clouds, picked up impetus enough to pierce the surface of a certain farm-field known for its dryness, where at once and in the presence of the farmer and his farm-boy a fountain spurted. A hundred years later people were still dipping hankies into it in the belief that it cured warts.

For long periods they flew through clouds and all was grey, then for long periods the skies cleared and down below they saw the land as though cut out of scraps of velvet by some elven artist, fields of vari-colored crops green and greener and yellow and red; here and there a toy-town and its fairy towers. Now and then they were above the clouds and looked down upon fleecy layers towards which, almost, it seemed they might descend and walk upon.

It was at one such moment that Burgenblitz of Blitzenburg said, "We are nearer to Heaven than we were."

Washington Parthenopius Pard Powell silently handed over the peace pipe. The Baron silently took it.

The Conjoint Chiefs of Staff of the Combined Ruritanian-Graustarker Manœuvres Near Or In The Authorized Areas ("Authorized" sounded ever so much nicer — and safer — than "Disputed"), the Margrave Grauheim and the Prince Rupert-Michael, were feeling very pleased with each other. There had been no sign of a sign from Scythia-Pannonia-Transbalkania, no sign was really to be expected from Turkey (the Sick Man of Europe was still very sick; Abdul Hamid's method of preparing himself for the throne was to take courses in mathematics, marksmanship, and magic), and God was in Heaven and the Czar was far away. The Conjoint Chiefs stood at a table looking at a map which a century (and then some) of boundary rectifications has rendered unrecognizable; but as they did not know this, they continued feeling very pleased. The CCs' uniforms had been ordered from the best military (or perhaps theatrical) tailors in Potsdam; with pickelhaube helmets, long overcoats which belted

---

* Also, **wurble-wurble**.

almost under the armpits and reached almost to the insteps, boots with huge spurs, heads shaven, and long goatees and long moustaches upturned, they looked frightful indeed: and when they considered this, they felt even more pleased.

The cookfires had been lit and appeared very welcome, too, what with the evening dews and damps. It was then that the two CCs began to look around; so did the soldiers. "Odd sound," said the Margrave. "Sounds like what they call a locomotive engine; heard one once," said the Prince. Both together they said, "None *here.*" Indeed there was not, and as there were yet none in either Graustark *or* Ruritania either, hardly any of the soldiers had ever seen or heard one.

But the strange noise still persisted, like the transpirations or suspirations of an alien creature; then the mists parted, the troops gave a great shuddering cry, and the great setting sun bathed with its dull rosy rays the . . . the *what?* There it *was!* . . . but what *was* it?

Answer was immediate. A young but zealous and excitable cavalry-corporal cried, "It be the Great Red Dragon and the Woman Clothed with the Sun," possibly a reference to Katinka Ivanovna in her orange outfit of satin and gauze; "Armageddon! The saints be casting down their crowns a-nigh the glassy sea; *re*-PENT!" And, casting down his brimless cap, he commenced beating his brow ritually and rhythmically with his fist as he chanted an immensely long *Recital of Remorse,* ranging from **A**ssembling to Commit Fornication with Two Other Stable-boys and a Tavern Wench; down to **Z**edoary, a Great Quantity of Which I Snitched from an Apothecary to Buy Booze.

Pandemonium in the ranks.

Bearing down at them from an altitude as yet unestimated was *A Thing,* hideous beyond belief, something like (were it possible) an immense aerial insect, although with more body sections than any insect could possibly have, or had it? was that its giant thorax moving in and out? was it merely the wind? were those things jutting out here and there *wings?* Or were — could they be *fins?* Was this all some dreadful dream in the declining day? Was that a Scythian-Pannonian-Transbalkanian flag? Oh Hell and Purgation yes it *was!* — also a perfectly dreadful voice from the heavens barked orders at them and as they milled about in confusion and in terror, *The Thing* swooped and swerved and darted and hissed at them with its scalding breath —

Military marksmanship had nowhere included shooting at a steam-propelled Autogóndola way up in the middle of the sky, nor had anyone been trained to fire at a 35-foot long bird; and though Margrave Grauheim was an excellent stag-hunter, he had never had occasion to hunt a giant stag 100 feet above him: who *had?*

"Halt!" cried that dreadful voice from the heavens. "Halt! Fall in!

Stack arms! Officers, prepare to surrender your swords at an oblique angle! Thrusting the right foot one foot forward and taking hold of the right trouser-leg with the right hand: Ex-*pose* . . . *HOSE!* Sergeants of the 3rd Graustark Chasseurs, take the names of those officers wearing green striped stockings, daresay they patronize the same haberdasher in Port Said, what do you *mean* by wearing green striped stockings at a formal surrender, you dumb sons of bitches!" There was no disobeying that dreadful voice in the sky, and when a battalion of Ruritanian Regulars attempted to sneak away, the Autogóndola sailed along their line of cook-fires (*love*ly up-drafts!) and dropped what were really not howitzer shells but boxes of Brunk-stuff right into the fires; the confected fuel at once pulverized and exploded, sending hot pilaff flying just about everywhere; also the Prince Rupert-Michael was almost struck by an aerial grenade which very oddly left his coat smelling like a rather low-grade champagne; funny.

It was with a complete mixture of humiliation, fear, and relief that they heard themselves being let off with a mere fine for "Having Entered into the Disputed Areas Without the Conjoint Consents of the Emperor, the Sultan, the Woywode of Western Wallachia and the Grand Mameluke of Neo-Macedonia, to the Great Affront of All of Them"; the fine being, well, never mind what the fine being, and officers of flag rank were ordered to take it in large bills from the Pay Chests and drop it into the basket now descending to eye-level; no sooner was the basket filled than it was zipped up out of sight again and a voice with a strong American accent was heard counting its contents.

The implacable Voice from above now announced that torches be lit and that all Ruritanian troops at once march for Graustark and all Graustarker troops march at once for Ruritania: they marched. Long after the huffing-puffing creature had ceased to snuffle and hiss back and forth checking on them, breathing redly in the dark, they kept on marching. They didn't dare *not.*

The Autogóndola descended to take on water and conserve fuel by resting in the deserted camp for the night.

The World Tribunal has long been occupied with the cases of *Graustark* vs. *Ruritania* and *Ruritania* vs. *Graustark.*

Meanwhile, back at the Palace:

Ignats Louis, Emperor of, etc., etc., was gloomily taking his post-breakfast walk in the Gardens when a figure detached itself from a rake, and, bowing, asked permission to speak. Granted. "Guess what I seen this mornin a-comin to work, Your Imperialness?" "Tell me, Genórf. We know you wouldn't lie . . . not to *We,* anyway."

Genórf, I. Pal. Gard. Rakeman, Upper Div., said that in coming to work that morning he passed close by the Old Fair Grounds as usual and was surprised to see there on dry ground a boat like with red sails like. And then come along this red-haired woman Gazinka Somethingovna, what they say she's a witch and in she got to the boat and with no more about it *off* sailed the boat only it like sailed *up* . . . in the very general direction of Wallachia or Macedonia or Graustark maybe or Ruritania rather: and might she lay a curse on all them foreign folk and drive their he-goats mad. Or worse. ". . . Apology to Your Presence, Sire . . . But, now, what might you think? About such witchery . . . ?"

His Royal and Imperial Presence thought about it, stroking his bifurcate beard right-side, left-side. Then he said, "Well, We'll tell you, Genórf. Them country witches such as they had when *We* was a boy, they was good enough to dry up cows or cure the clap, but nowadays things keep getting more modern and we must move with the times." And as a reward for the information, he was Graciously Pleased to direct that Genórf be given a large bowl of suet dumplings plus six and a third skillings plus a big glass of shnops. "And to make certain it be *good* shnops, come, We'll have one with thee; come to think of it, all of ye have one with We," Ignats Louis sometimes had difficulty with his pronouns; "and if the Frow High Housekeep' don't like the smell, tell her to hold her nose as she drinks it: Graustark and Ruritania, oh haw haw! We can't wait to *hear!*"

Avar-Ister, Second Capital of the Triune Monarchy (there really was no "Third Capital," although Apollograd had pretensions), had gone to bed in a rather ugly mood. Not only were traces of some awful bad gunk coming down the Ister from the general direction of the First Capital, but the Post Office had just gotten a new issue three-pennikk stamp (one and one-half pennikks being equal to two-thirds of a kopperka, except . . . but we had perhaps leave that for now) of which the Avar legend lacked a Silent Letter . . . the incomparable richness of the Avar idiom containing *many* silent letters. Avar Nationalists at once revived the traditional cry of, "Are we going to stand for this?" with its terrifying reply of *"Nudgeszemeldinkelfrasz!"* or (in Avar) *No.* Tom-toms did not precisely beat all night, *but* — Shortly after sunrise, well, to be perhaps needlessly blunt, conveniently after breakfast, a concourse of Avar Patriotic Intransigents began to move grimly along the Korszo towards the Viceroy's Castle: when, suddenly from behind a cloud was heard an Angel's Voice singing the Pannonian National Anthem. Not realizing that it was actually the voice of Katinka Ivanovna Dombrovski — she had learned it in Zagreb one bleak winter from an Avar exile who, whenever she slacked learning it, pinched her, severely — the Avars *nat*urally stopped dead. And stood at full attention, only turning their heads to watch the Autogóndola-

Invention fly the full length of the Korszo from east to west, joining in the singing of the first 35 verses; then, the Autogóndola-Invention having unaccountably gone into reverse, turning their heads to watch it fly the full length of the Korszo from west to east backwards, joining in the singing of the second 35 verses: who was not there to hear Madame K. I. Dombrovski render the moving lines:

"Hoy, Pan-n-no-nia, hoy!
Yoy, Pa-n-no-nia, yoy!
O-oy, Pa-n-no-ni-a, oy!"

in full coloratura, has not heard anything.

But must not all things come to an end? Yes.

It was whilst prolonging the final, poignant, patriotic *oy* that the voice of Katerina Ivanovna went briefly hoarse . . . then flat . . . then cracked . . . then gave out entirely. And it was at that moment that the Autogóndola-Invention suddenly went completely out of control and made what may be called, to coin a phrase, a "crash-landing," on the top-deck of the R. and I. Lighthouse Tender *Empress Anna-Gertruda,* fortunately without anyone being injured . . . and with it steamed upriver towards Bella. The cheering Avars then all went back home to put hot compresses on their stiff but patriotic necks.

Who would ever *know?* . . . but somehow Dr. Eszterhazy, having reflected much upon it during free moments of his aerial tour, thought he now understood more of the Mystery of the Goats. There being no tax on the she-goats, there was no need to conceal them. As for the he-goats, they being needed only during the breeding-season, why it was they who were herded up into the far wild pastures in the mountains in hopes of avoiding the tax-collectors — and it was evidently only there that the hallucinatory plants grew — night-shade! traditional in witches' brew! — As for the attested reports of the strange music (surely not upon pan-pipes!?), one must simply, mentally, stamp it: *unsolved.* Eszterhazy might suggest the goat-tax be reduced and its revenues equalized by, say, a fourth-pennikk tax a case on refined sugar, which peasants never used anyway, preferring honey or sorghum or brown sugar-loaf; doubtless then the he-goats would be kept down out of the danger zone. He could suggest. More than that he could not do.

Meanwhile —

Engelbert Eszterhazy, Ph. D., *aspirant* D. Sc., was entertaining guests.

". . . the new fuel caused a build-up which choked all the tubes eventually," Professor Gronk was complaining. Eszterhazy said that the two of them could really call on poor old Brunk shortly and show him how to filter the sludge washed off his soft coal, and re-filter and so on until the wash-water was clear enough to let back in the river. And then they two would work out with Brunk a better formula for mixing the coal dust and sawdust and whatever into a really decent fuel . . . : "For stoves, anyway."

The professor made a gesture. His prominent eyes swiveled all about. "It is not alone the fuel. The design is wrong I see now. The wires snap. The aerolines flap. The framework does not stand the strain. The Autogóndola-Invention does not properly take the helm. The instruments, *yoy mein Dieu* the instruments: I must tell you that not only half the time we really used the wind and not the engine but half of that time the instruments proved there *was no wind* to use! Seemingly, it should never have flown at all! It is as though some witchcraft or magic —"

Eszterhazy stroked his moustache. He looked pensive. "The old magic and witchery is almost everywhere in retreat, Professor. Only here at almost the very edge of the European world does it ever turn and fight. Elsewhere it masks itself and tries to sneak in via the medium and the planchette, but that is not quite the same magic. Nor the same witchery. Well. Eh? 'The Autogóndola-Invention will take years more study and work?' Well, meanwhile let us keep it quiet. It is clearly something for which the world is not yet prepared. Have you tried the sausage? It is . . . *there.*" The Professor's floating eyes ceased to float, concentrated on the sausage. In a moment he had left his host behind.

Instantly the place was taken by Burgenblitz of Blitzenburg; never had the Doctor seen the Baron so voluble. "The castle is doomed, Eszterhazy; the day of the fortress in the forest is over; this little adventure has shown me that anyone may put a motor on a balloon and float over dropping explosives anywhere, so what good's a castle if you can't defy the world from it? Well, I'm selling out. Yes. Giving up. Shall go hunt crocodiles in La Florida by the waters of the Tallahassee and the great Sewanee; my pal Pard has been persuaded to act as guide for the most modest of fees out of which he himself shall pay the native — what? Sioux? — to paddle us in their what? Wigwams? — as I believe the catamaran is called in its native language; we shall go by way of London where the best crocodile-gun and mosquito-netting is made, also to purchase tomahawks, beads, and red cloth to trade with the Crackers as I believe the picturesque aboriginals are also called. . . ."

Eszterhazy's eyes met those of Washington Parthenopius "Pard" Powell, who let his own eyelids slip to half-mast and drew a puff on his calumet. To have the Baron Burgenblitz actually *out* of the country for even whatever length of time was a gift of fortune hardly

to have been looked for. "Ah Burgenblitz how I envy you," he said. "The castle-fortress. Indeed. *Doomed.*" It had, like the walled city, indeed been doomed: since 1453; Burgenblitz was a slow learner. "Hm, crocodiles. Florida, hm. You will not of course wish to hunt the great saurian *all* the time. You would be bored. Fortunately in La Florida there is the legendary life of the *planter* to occupy and amuse you as well. I believe I have read a report that the soil there is excellent for the possible cultivation of the Comparatively Thin-Skinned Yellow-Green Juice Orange, of which cuttings are said to be available at the Botanical Gardens in Kew; pray mention my name to Mr. Motherthwaite, the Curator for Juicy Fruit. Ah. La Florida! You will buy lands there, eh?"

Burgenblitz, who had never once considered doing so, now cried, "But yes of course I shall! That is . . . I hope . . ." he turned to his pal, Pard, ". . . will the picturesque aboriginal Crackers trade land for red cloth?" His pal Pard once more gave Eszterhazy a glance from his glaucous eyes. "Be tickled pink to trade it for most anything," said he. "Money, marbles, or chalk."

Burgenblitz drew out his pocketbook to make a note. "The money is no problem," he said. "As for the marbles, we shall pick up some at Carrara, and I am sure that at Dover we shall be able to procure chalk." As the two of them walked off, deep in talk, Pard Powell was heard to say that when he was in Honduras with William Walker, treacherously executed to death by the people he had come to liberate, William Walker was often heard to say that any man could plant wheat and shoot birds but more than anyone was to be admired a man who could plant orange trees and shoot crocodiles.

The gaslight hissed. There, suddenly, laughing at him, was Madame Dombrovski. A sudden retrospective vision of her clinging now to one rope aloft, now another: *had* he seen her fingers moving deftly, swiftly, through the ropes' ends? . . . and if so *why?* Why . . . *seemingly, it should never have flown at all!* "Ah, Katinka Ivanovna. Tell me. Are you really Russian? Polish? Or —"

" 'Rilly'? Rilly, I am Rahshian Feen. Often comèd famous Lönnrot to my Grandfather house in Karelia, collecting *kalevala*; why ease eat you ask?"

He tweaked his nose. "Oh . . . No particular . . . Tell me. Have you ever heard it said that many 'Russian Finns' are witches and warlocks? That they are said to be able to raise and direct the wind by tying knots in ropes, or even by singing . . . ?" But merely she looked at him, her blue eyes merry and bright. Then she laughed, and, laughing, moved on. *Move on.* As host, he, too, must . . . In the group nearest-by were several of the young liberals, intellectuals and sceptics. *What* were *they* talking about? Not, certainly, about the price of hog-lard, still staying calm and steady at 17 ducats, seven skillings the hundredweight — at *home,* that is; it was reported to have reached such astronomical proportions in Siberia owing to an outbreak of hog-cholera that the peasants were obliged to eat butter.

"No, no," said one, shaking his head. "The hope of education as an adjunct to popularism is a vain one. Why, only now, even now, stories appear that the bulls in Transbalkania are no longer savage and have been seen and heard dancing to strange piping music with wreaths and garlands round their necks! Peasants who believe such stories are not yet ready to vote. No no."

And said another, adjusting his pomaded moustache, "Yes, and the papers encourage that sort of thing. Look, here in today's evening paper, *Report from the Rural Districts,* listen to this, it's being said that a country girl near Poposhki-Georgiou saw a bull with a wreath of flowers round its neck and she climbed up to get it and then the bull ran off with her still clinging to its back. . . ."

"Silly girl!"

"What was her name; it wasn't Europa I suppose?"

"No it wasn't; what kind of name is that; it certainly isn't good Scythian Gothic, what?"

The one with the newspaper gave it a second look. Said, "Olga."

"*Ol*ga?"

"See right here in the paper: Olga. *Here.*"

"Zeus and *Ol*ga? Doesn't have quite the same ring to it as —"

His friend shrugged. "Oh well. Other times, other mirrors."

Eszterhazy felt he liked this, came closer.

"What chap was it who said, nature always holds up the same mirror, but sometimes she changes the reflections?"

The other sipped from his glass of bullblood wine while he considered. "Don't know who said it. You're sure somebody said it? Well, it's either very profound or very silly."

They sipped and talked as they moved on to the quaint buffet; this fellow the Doctor their host, was he carrying his Love of the People too far? . . . head-cheese, sausage, now, really! — And then suddenly a hand was held up for silence. "Oh listen! You can hear the bell of the ten o'clock tram down the road, last one till five tomorrow morning, best hurry! Be hard to find a cab if we miss the tram." Even in Bella, sophistication too had its pains and costs.

Down in the street. "Thank you, Doctor Eszterhazy! Oh it was indeed a pleasure, Doctor Eszterhazy! Good night! Good night! Engelbert! 'Night, Engli . . . !"

For some while he remained there, simply enjoying the mist around the lamplights; suddenly a commotion, there on the next corner was someone shouting and waving his hands and screaming for a fiacre. It was Signor Gian-Giacomo Pagliacci-Espresso. "The Central Station! At once! A fiacre-cab! Pronto!" Would one stop for him, no, one would not, very odd considering the local libel that fiacre drivers "would drive the Devil to mass for a ducat," was this surprising?

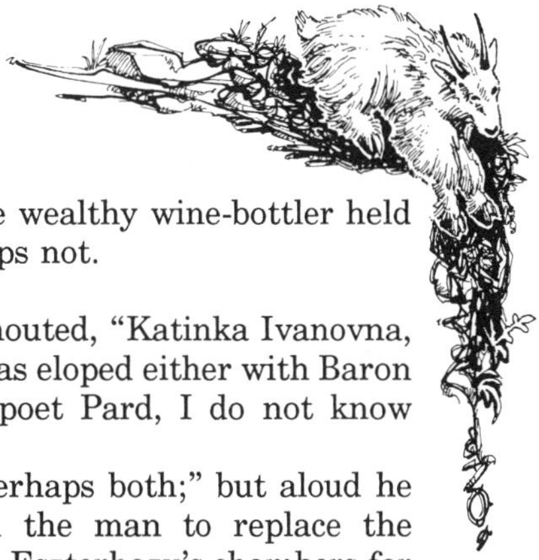

Considering that in one waving hand the wealthy wine-bottler held a stiletto and in the other a pistol, perhaps not.

Then, too, it was *late.*

On recognizing Eszterhazy, the man shouted, "Katinka Ivanovna, that slut, that *buta,* she has left me, she has eloped either with Baron Burgenblitz or the Far-vestern Yankee poet Pard, I do not know which —"

To himself, Eszterhazy murmured, "Perhaps both;" but aloud he spoke so sympathetically he persuaded the man to replace the weaponry of vengeance and to come up to Eszterhazy's chambers for a soothing drink, instead. Sobbing softly into his astrakhan coat-lapels, he agreed.

And so, by and by, once again all was quiet in front of the hotel in the little square at the bottom of the Street of the Defeat of Bonaparte (commonly called Bonaparte Street).

And overhead shone the glittering stars.

DUKE PASQUALE'S RING

The King of the Single Sicily was eating pasta in a sidewalk restaurant; not in Palermo: in Bella. He had not always been known by that title. In Bella, capital of the Triune Monarchy of Scythia-Pannonia-Transbalkania, he had for long decades been known chiefly as an eccentric but quite harmless fellow who possessed many quarterings of nobility and nothing in the shape of money at all. But when the Kingdom of the Two Sicilies (Naples and all of southern Italy being the other one) was rather suddenly included into the new and united Kingdom of Italy, ostensibly by plebiscite and certainly by force of Garibaldean arms, something had happened to the inoffensive old man.

He now put down his fork and belched politely. The waiter-cook-proprietor came forward. "Could the King eat more?" he asked.

"Im[belch]possible. There is no place." He patted the middle-front of his second-best cloak.

"What damage," said the other. His previous career, prior to deserting a French man-of-war, had been that of coal-heaver. But he was a Frenchman born (that is, he was born in Algeria of Corsican parentage), and this was almost universally held to endow him with an ability to cook anything anywhere in Infidel Parts better than the infidel inhabitants could. And certainly he cooked pasta better and cheaper than it was cooked in any other cook-shop in Bella's South Ward. "What damage," he repeated. "There is more in the pot." And he raised his brigand brows.

"Ah well. Put it in my kerchief, and I shall give it to my cat."

"Would the King also like a small bone for his dog?"

"Voluntarily."

He had no cat; he had no dog; he had at home an old, odd wife who had never appeared in public since the demise of her last silk gown. The bone and extra pasta would make a soup, and she would eat.

With the extinction of the Kingdom of the Two Sicilies something had gone flash in the old man's brain-pan: surely Sicily itself now reverted to the status of a kingdom by itself? Surely he was its rightful king? And to anyone who would listen and to anyone who would read, he explained the matter, in full genealogy, with peculiar emphasis on the four marriages of someone called Pasquale III, from one of which marriages he himself descended. Some listened. Some read. Some even replied. But, actually, nothing happened. The new King of Italy did not so much as restore a long-forfeited tomato-patch. The ousted King of Naples did not so much as reply. Neither did Don Amadeo, King of Spain (briefly, very briefly, King of Spain). On the other hand, Don Carlos, King of Spain (pretended or claimed), did. Don Carlos was an exile in Bella at the moment. Don Carlos perhaps heard something. Don Carlos perhaps did not know much about Pasquale III, but Don Carlos knew about being a pretender and an exile. He did not precisely send a written reply; he sent some stockings, some shirts, a pair of trousers, and a cloak. All mended. But all clean. And a small hamper of luncheon.

By the time the King of the Single Sicily had dressed in his best and gone to call on Don Carlos, Don Carlos was gone, and — to Bella, as to Spain — Don Carlos never came back.

That was the nearest which Cosimo Damiano (as he chose to style himself) had ever come to Recognition. Stockings, shirts, and trousers had all worn out; the cloak he was wearing even now. And to pay for the daily plate of pasta he was left to his semi-occasional pupil in the study of Italian, calligraphy, and/or advanced geometry.

"To see again," he said, now rising, and setting upon the tiny table a coin of two kopperkas.

"To see again," said the cook-shop man, his eyes having ascertained the existence of the coin and its value. He bowed. He would when speaking to Cosimo Damiano refer to him in the third person as the king, he would give him extra pasta past its prime, he would even donate to a pretense-dog a bone which still had some boiling left in it. He might from time to time do more. A half-cup of salad neglected by a previous diner. A recommendation to a possible pupil. Even now and then a glass of thin wine not yet "turned." But for all and for any of this, he must have his coin of two kopperkas. Otherwise: nothing. So it was.

D. Cosimo D., as sometimes he signed himself, stooped off homeward in his cloak. Today was a rich day: extra pasta, a soup-bone, and he had a half-a-kopperka to spare. He might get himself a snuff of inferior tobacco wrapped in a screw of newspaper. But he rather thought he might invest the two farthings in the

merchandise of Mother Whiskers, who sold broken nut-meats in the mouth of an alley not far off. His queen was fond of that. The gaunt and scabby walls, street-level walls long since knocked bare of plaster or stucco, narrowed in towards him as he went. The old woman was talking to another customer, not one who wanted a farthingworth of broken nutmeats, by his look. But Mother Whiskers had another profession: she was by way of being a witch, and all sorts of people came to see her, deep in the smelly slums where she had her seat.

She stopped whatever she had been saying, and jerked up her head to D. Cosimo D. "Gitcherself anointed?" was her curious question.

"I fear not. Alas," said D. Cosimo D., with a sigh.

She shook her head so that her whiskers flew about her face, and her earrings, too. "Gitcherself anointed!" she said. "All kinds o' work and jobs I c'n git fer a 'nointed king. Touch fer the king's evil — the scrofuly, that is — everybuddy knows that — and ringworm! Oh my lordy, how much ringworm there be in the South Ward!" Oft-times, when he was not thinking of his own problems alone, Cosimo wondered that there was not much more cholera, pest, and leprosy in the South Ward. "— and the best folks c'n do is git some seventh son of a seventh son; now, not that I mean that ain't *good.* But can't compare to a 'nointed king!"

And the stranger, in a deep, murmurous voice, said *No, indeed.*

Poor Cosimo! Had he had to choose between Anointing without Crowning, and Crowning without Anointing, he would have chosen the Holy Oil over the Sacred Crown. But he was allowed no choice. Hierarch after hierarch had declined to perform such services, or even service, for him. There was one exception. Someone, himself perhaps a pretender and certainly an exile, someone calling himself perhaps Reverend and Venerable Archimandrite of Petra and Simbirsk had offered to perform . . . but for a price . . . a high one . . . it would demean his sacred office to do it on the cheap, said he. And, placing his forefinger alongside his nose, had winked.

Much that had helped.

"Well, if you won't, you won't," grumbled Old Mother Whiskers. "But I do my best for y', anyway. Gotchyou a stoodent, here. See?"

Taking a rather closer look than he had taken before, Cosimo saw someone rather tall and rather richly dressed . . . not alone for the South Ward, richly . . . for anywhere, richly. There was something in this one's appearance for which the word sleek seemed appropriate, from his hat and his moustache down to his highly-polished shoes; the man murmured the words, "Melanchthon Mudge," and held out his hand. He did not take his glove off (it was a sleek glove), and Cosimo, as he shook hands and murmured his own name, felt several rings . . . and felt that they were rings with rather large stones, and . . .

"Mr. Mudge," said Mother Whiskers; "Mr. Mudge is a real classy gent." And D. Cosimo D. felt, also that — though Mr. Mudge may have been a gent — Mr. Mudge was not really a gentleman. But as to that, in this matter: no matter.

"Does Mr. Mudge desire to be instructed," he asked, "in Italian? In calligraphy? Or in advanced geometry? Or in all three?"

Mr. Mudge touched a glossy-leather-encased-finger to a glossy moustache. Said he thought, "For the present, sir. For the present," that they would skip calligraphy. "Madame here has already told me of your terms, I find them reasonable, and I would only wish to ask if you might care to mention . . . by way of, as it were, general reference . . . the names of some of your past pupils. If you would not mind."

Mind? The poor old King of the Single Sicily would not have minded standing on his head if it would have helped bring him a pupil. He mentioned the names of a surveyor now middling-high in the Royal and Imperial Highways and to whom he had taught advanced geometry, of several ladies of quality to whom he had taught Italian, and of a private docent whom he had instructed in calligraphy: still Mr. Mudge waited, as one who would hear more; D. Cosimo D. went on to say, "And, of course, that young Eszterhazy, Doctor as he now is —"

"Ah," said Mr. Melanchthon Mudge, stroking his moustache and his side-whiskers; "that young Eszterhazy, Doctor as he now is." His voice seemed to grow very drawn-out and deep.

Plaster and paint, turpentine and linseed oil had all alike long since dried, inside and outside the house at Number 33 Turkling Street, where lived Dr. Engelbert Eszterhazy; though sometimes he had the notion that he could still smell it. At the moment, though, what he chiefly smelled came from his well-fitted chemical laboratory, as well as from the more distant kitchen where — in some matters Eszterhazy was old-fashioned — Mrash, his man-cook, reigned. Old Mrash would probably and eventually be replaced by a woman. In the meanwhile he had his stable repertory of ten or twelve French dishes as passed down through generations of army officers' cooks since the days of (at least) Bonaparte; and when he had run through it and them and before running through them and it again, Mrash usually gave his master a few days of peasant cooking which boxed the culinary compass of the fourth-largest empire in Europe. Ox-cheek and eggs. Beef palate, pigs' ears, and buckwheat. Potatoes boiled yellow in chicken broth with unborn eggs and dill. Cowfoot stew, with mushrooms and mashed turnips. And after that it was back to *boeuf à la mode Bayonne* [sic], and all the rest of it as taught long ago to his captors by some long ago prisoner-of-war.

Today, along with the harmless game of "consulting the menu-

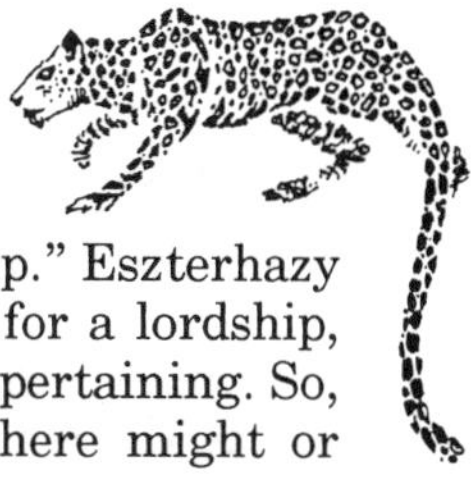

book," Mrash had a question, "if it pleased his lordship." Eszterhazy knew that it pleased Mrash to think that he cooked for a lordship, and had ceased trying to convince him of it not really pertaining. So, "Yes, Mrashko, certainly. What is the question?" There might or might not be a direct answer.

"What do they call that there place, my lordship, a boo?"

Philologists have much informed the world that the human mouth is capable of producing only a certain limited number of sounds, therefore it was perhaps no great feat for Eszterhazy at once to counter-ask, "Do you perhaps mean a *zoo?*"

"Ah," said Mrash the man-cook, noncommittally. He might, his tone indicated, though then again he might not.

Eszterhazy pressed on. "That's the short name for the Royal and Imperial Botanical and Zoölogical Gardens and Park, where the plants and creatures mostly from foreign parts are." Mrashko's mouth moved and seemed to relish the longer form of the name. "It's the second turning of the New Stone-paved Road after Big Ludo's Beer Garden," added 'his lordship'.

Mrash nodded. "I expect that's where it come from, then," he said.

" 'Come from'? Where *what* came from, Cooky?"

Cooky said, simply, "The tiger."

Eszterhazy recalled the comment of Old Captain Slotz, someone who had achieved much success in obtaining both civil and military intelligence. Captain Slotz had stated, "I don't ask them did they done it or I don't ask them did they not done it. Just, I look at them, and I say, ***'Tell me about it.'*** "

"Tell me about it, Mrashko-Cooky."

The man-cook gestured. "See, my lordship, it come up the lane there," gesture indicated the alley. "And it hop onto yon wood-shed, or as it might be, coal-shed. Then it lep up onto the short brick bake-building. Then it give a big jump and gits onto the roof of what was old Baron Johan's town-house what his widow live in now all alone saving old Helen, old Hugo, and old Hercules what they call him, who look after her ladyship what she seldom go out at all anymore," Eszterhazy listened with great patience; "and then it climb up the roof and until it reach the roof-peak. It look all around. It put its front-limbs down," Mrash imitated this, ". . . and it sort of just stretch . . . *streeettch. . . .*"

Silence.

"And then?"

"Then I get back to me work, me lordship."

"Oh."

"Nother thing. I knew that there beast have another name to 't. Leopard. That be its other name. I suppose it come from the boo. I suppose it trained to go back. Three nights I've seen it, nor I haven't heard no alarm." He began making the quasi-military movements which indicated he was about to begin the beginning of his leaving.

"Does it have stripes? Or spots?"

Mrash, jerking his arms, moving stiff-legged, murmured something about there being but the one gas-lamp in the whole alley, there having been not much of a bright moon of recent, hoped the creature wouldn't hurt no one nor even skeer the old Baroness nor old Helen; and — finally — "Beg permission to return to duty, your lordship. ***Hup!***"

"Granted. — And — Mrash! ["Me Lord!"] The next time you see it, let me know, directly."

The parade-ground manner of the man-cook's departure gave more than a hint that the next meal would consist largely of boiled bully-beef in the mode of the Royal and Imperial Infantry, plus the broth thereof, plus fresh-grated horseradish which would remove the roof of your mouth, plus potatoes prepared purple in a manner known chiefly to army cooks present and past all round the world. Eszterhazy looked out the window and across the alley. At ground level, the stones of the house opposite were immense, seemingly set without mortar. *Cyclopean,* the word came to him. Above these massive courses began others, of smaller pieces of masonry. The last storey and a half were of brick, with here and there a tuft of moss instead of mortar. The steep-pitched roof was of dull grey slate. And though he could see this all quite clearly, he could see no explanation for the story which his old cook, never before given to riotous fancy, had just recounted to him. Long he stared. Long he stared. Long he considered. Then he rang the bell and asked for his horse to be saddled.

The old Chair of Natural Philosophy had finally been subdivided, and the new Chair of Natural History been created. Natural Philosophy included Chemistry, Physics, Meteorology, Astronomy. Natural History included Zoölogy, Ichthyology, Botany, Biology. Dr. Eszterhazy, having bethought him of the knot of loafers always waiting on hand near the Zoo to see whose horse shied at the strange odor when the wind blew so, decided to stop off first at the office of the Royal-Imperial Professor of Natural History, who was *ex cathedra* the Director of the Royal and Imperial Botanical and Zoölogical Gardens and Park. Said, "Your tigers and leopards. Tell me about them."

The Professor — it was Cornelius Crumholtss, with whom Dr. E.E. had once taken private lessons — said, crisply, "None."

"What's that?"

"The tiger died last year. The Gaekwar of Oont, or is it his heir, the Oontie Ghook? has agreed to trade us a tiger for three dancing bears and two gluttons — or wolverines as some call them — but he's not done it yet. Leopards? We've never had one. We do have the lion. But he is very old. Shall I have spots painted on him for you? No? Oh."

Eszterhazy had gone to the Benedictine Library. There were things there which were nowhere else . . . and, not seldom, that meant **no**where else . . . once, indeed, he had found the Papal Legate there, waiting for a chance to see something not even in the Vatican Library. It was stark and chill in the whitewashed chamber which served as waiting-room. Who was waiting for what? Eszterhazy was waiting for Brother Claudius, for even Eszterhazy might not go up into the vaulted hall where the oldest books were unless Brother Claudius showed him up; not even the Papal Legate might do so, and it was almost certain that not even the King-Emperor might . . . in the unlikely instance of the King-Emperor's going to the Benedictine Library to look for a book . . . or anywhere else, for that matter. E. assumed that the tall, thin man slumped in the corner was also waiting for Brother Claudius. By and by, in came the lay-brother who acted as porter, and wordlessly set down a brazier of glowing coals before withdrawing.

The man in the corner moved. "Ah, good," he murmured. "One's hands have grown too cold." He got up, and, moving to the fire-chauldron, thrust his hands into it and drew them out filled with hot coals glowing red. His manner seemed abstracted. An odor of singeing hair was very slightly perceptible. Eszterhazy felt his own flesh crawl. Slowly, quite slowly, the man poured the red hot coals back upon the fire. "You are Doctor Eszterhazy," next he said.

The statement required no confirmation. "And you, sir? Who?"

Very slowly the tall body turned. A long finger stroked a long moustache. "I? Oh. I am the brother of the shadow of the slain. The vanguard of the shadows of the living. I —"

Light. "Ah yes. You are the medium, Mr. Mudge."

"I am the medium. Mr. Mudge. As well. Oh yes.

"I am really very pleased to have this occasion to meet the eminent Dr. Eszterhazy," said Mr. Mudge.

"Indeed," murmured the eminent, very faintly questioning. He himself was certainly very interested at meeting the eminent Mr. Mudge. But, somehow, he rather doubted that he was really very pleased.

"Yes, indeed. Ah. You are not here . . . or perhaps you *are* here . . . to consult the Second Recension of the *Malleus Maleficarum*?"

The doctor said that he was not, not adding that both witchcraft and the fury it had once aroused alike tended to be productive of a definite dull pain between and in back of his eyes. "I am here to consult the Baconian Fragment. If it *is* by Friar Roger. Which is doubtless subject to doubt. If it *is* a fragment; the end of the parchment is rather fragmented, but the text itself seems complete."

Mr. Mudge nodded. He seemed, certainly, to follow the comments. But his manner seemed also to be rather faintly abstracted. "Now, I wish to ask you about your former tutor," he said, and touched his full red tongue to his full red lips, and smiled. In fact the smile was not without a certain appeal, an effect, however, spoiled by . . . by what? . . . by the man's having rather yellow teeth?

"Which former tutor? I have had really a great many, as I began my formal education comparatively late, and was obliged to make up for lost time. So . . ."

"He calls himself sometimes Cosimo Damiano, though I understand that this is not precisely his legal name."

Well. Someone learned enough to read old books in Latin, and he wished to ask about poor old — "Yes. And what do you wish to ask?"

Could Dr. Eszterhazy recommend him? Certainly. The old man's Italian knowledge was encyclopedic, his calligraphy was exquisite, and his knowledge of advanced geometry was . . . well . . . advanced. It was at this point that the door opened and Brother Claudius came in, hands tucked inside the sleeves of his habit. "Come with me," he directed in a hollow voice; and, as he did not say to whom he was saying this, and as he immediately turned and left again, they both followed him. Through many an icy corridor. Up many a worn, yet steep, flight of stairs. Into the vast vaulted hall lined to twice a man's height with books whose ancient odors still had, as far as Eszterhazy was concerned, the power to thrill. The monk gestured him to a table on which a book-box reposed. The monk next gestured Mr. Mudge further on and further on, eventually waving him to another table. On which, or so it seemed at a glance, another book-box reposed. Eszterhazy sat at the bench and opened the box.

Immediately he saw that a mistake had been made, but automatically he turned a few pages. Instead of the rather cramped and fuddled Italian hand which he had expected, massive and heavy "black letter" met his eye. One line seemed to unfold itself in particular; had it at one time been underlined and the underlining eradicated? For the parchment was scraped under the line. **The mind of a demon is not the same as the mind of a man.** Indeed, no. And the *Malleus Maleficarum* was not the same as the Baconian Fragment.

"Pray excuse me, most reverend Brother," he heard the voice of Mr. Mudge, "but have you perhaps inadvertently given my item of choice to the learned doctor, and his to me?"

The hollow tone of Brother Claudius said, "Each has that which is proper for him now to read." And he removed a small box from his sleeve, and took snuff. The learned doctor, what was it they called Roger Bacon? Ah yes: **Doctor Mirabilis.** Well — Suddenly he looked up; there was Melanchthon Mudge; had he *float*ed? Usually the old floor sounded. What? The old floor *always* sounded.

Always but now.

"Brother Claudius has gone now. Shall we change books?"

They changed books.

By and by, he having principally noted what he came to note, and the day having grown chiller yet, Eszterhazy rose to leave. Without especial thought, he blew upon his hands. With an almost painful suddenness his hand spun round towards the other man; he had not blown upon *his* hands to warm them! But the other man was gone.

It had been intimated to Eszterhazy that his name had been "temporarily subtracted" from the military Active List for quite some years now, "for the purpose of continuing his education" — that meanwhile he had already obtained the baccalaureate, the licentiate, and two doctorates — and that unless he wished his name moved over to the Inactive List, very well, Engli, better Do Something about this. What he had done was to obtain transfer to the new Militia Reserve (as distinct from the not so new Reserve Militia), and as a result of having done so, found himself the very next weekend serving the twenty-five hours and twenty-five minutes which constituted his monthly service time with the Militia Reserve. (The Reserve Militia, as is well-known, had no monthly service time and instead required an annual service time of three weeks, three days, and three hours.) On reporting to the Armory he learned that although his having obtained a degree in mathematics had automatically shifted him from the Infantry to the Engineers, what was required of him this time had to do with another degree altogether.

"Surgeon-Commander Blauew's got the galloping gout again, Major Eszterhazy, and as you are, it seems, also a Doctor of Medicine, we need you for Medical Officer right now, and you can build us a fortress *next* month; haw haw!" was the adjutant's greeting.

"Very well, Adjutant. Very well. *My* that's a nasty-looking spot on your neck, there, well, well, I'll have a look at it after I've taken care of everything else;" and Temporary-Acting-Medical-Officer Eszterhazy, E., moved on away, leaving the adjutant prey to dismal thoughts; and perhaps it would teach him not to play the oaf with his betters. The T.-A.-M.O. examined a number of candidates for the Militia Reserve, passed some, rejected some; made inspections which resulted in the Sanitary Facilities being very hastily and yet very thoroughly doused down with caustic soda and hot water; and delivered a brief and dispassionate lecture on social diseases to officers and men alike: to the great dis-ease of an elderly paymaster who said he doubted it was right to expose the younger men to such scientific language: perhaps not exactly what he meant. Sounds of drill command rang through the large hall with a surprising minimum of echo, in great measure because Eszterhazy (who had not read Vitruvius's *Ten Books* for nothing) was instrumental in obtaining a theater-architect as consultant during the hall's construction.

Eventually it was time for commissioned officers to withdraw for wine and rusks, a snack traditionally taken standing up even where there might be facilities for sitting down. "Seen you in the Bosnian Campaign," someone said; and, the Temporary-Acting-Medical Officer turning his head, recognized a face once more familiar than lately. The face was not only now older, it was much, much redder. "Just dropped in to pay my respects," said the old soldier. "I am just here on my biennial leave. I am just a retired major in my own country, but I am a full colonel in the service of H.H. the Khedive of Egypt. Can I recruit you? Guarantee you higher rank, higher pay, higher respect, *several* servants, and heaps and heaps of fascinating adventure."

The younger man confessed himself already fascinated. He looked the Khedivial colonel in the man's lightly bulging, slightly blood-shot, entirely blue eyes, and said, "Tell me about it."

He listened without a single interruption until Col. Brennshnekkl got onto the subject of hunting in the Southern Provinces of H.H. — the southernmost boundaries of which evidently did not, as yet, exist. "— at least not on any official map; we intend to push 'em as far south as we can push 'em; now where was I? Ah yes! *Hippo!* Ah, you need a champion heavy ball for hippo! Say, a quarter of a pound. Same as elephant. Same as rhino." Perhaps indecisive which of the three to talk about first, Brennshnekkl paused.

Dr. Eszterhazy heard himself asking, "What about tiger?"

"Tiger, eh. Well, you would naturally want a lighter rifle for soft-skinned game. Say, a .500 . . . or better yet a .577 Express — a Lang or a Lancaster or any of the good ones."

Eszterhazy stroked his beard, trimmed closer than in the mode of fashion. "But *are* there tigers in Africa?"

The colonel appeared to be trying to say *Yes* and *No* simultaneously. To aid him he sipped his wine. Then: "Well, strictly to speak *no:* there are no tigers in Africa. However, lots of chaps call them tigers. Am I making sense? I mean, leopards."

Something somewhere jingled. Or perhaps there was a ringing in the doctor's ears. He repeated, dully, "Leopards?"

Colonel Brennshnekkl explained that in some way leopards were more dangerous than tigers. Tigers, like lions, went along the level ground; leopards sometimes hid up trees. And pounced. Carefully setting down his wine, he bared his teeth, turned his hands into paws and his fingers into claws, and gave something in the way of a lunge which was nevertheless certainly intended to imitate a pounce. It seemed to his younger comrade that people for some reason had lately begun to imitate leopards for him. Was it a *trend?*

"What else do they do up trees? Besides prepare to pounce? Do they have their, no, one would not say 'nests,' do they have lairs — ?"

No. No, leopards did not have lairs in trees. Well. Not precisely. In the manner of colonels the world over since the beginning of time, this one began to tell a story. "— recollect one day my native

gun-bearer, chap named Pumbo — Pumbo? Yes. Pumbo. *Faith*ful chap. Pumbo. Came running over to me and handed me my .577 Express. Said, 'Master, tiger,' which is to say, of course, *leopard,* said, 'tiger up tree, look-see, shoot-quick!' " He raised an imaginary leopard-gun at an angle. "And as I was sighting, sighting, damn me! what did I see? A bloody young zebra or was it an antelope, bloody leopard had killed it by breaking its neck, as they do, and dragged it up into the upper crutch of the tree where I suppose it could *hang,* you know, all that *gal*loping the wild game there does, makes it muscular and tough — 'nother thing," temporarily lowering his nonexistent rifle, the colonel got his wine back, looked at Eszterhazy over the rim of the mug; said, " 'nother thing. Hyaenas can't get to it. Once it's up a *tree.* You know. *Well —*"

But that was the last which Eszterhazy was to hear of the matter, for at that moment a whistle sounded to signal a return to the duties of the twenty-five hours and twenty-five minutes; a whistle? It was the sort of nautical whistle called a boatswain's pipe and it was traditional to sound it at this point. No one at all knew why. That was what made it traditional.

In what had been the oldest and smallest schloss in Bella, long since escheated to The Realm, was the chamber of a gentleman whom rumor connected with the Secret Police. He was called by a number of names. Eszterhazy called him Max.

"Engelbert Kristoffr."

"Max."

Segar and decanters. "How is the great plan for the education going?" "Engelbert Kristoffr" said that it was coming along well enough. He supposed Max knew that he already had the M.D. and Phil.D. Yes? And the D.Sc. and D.Mus. were likely next. Of course degrees were not everything. Right now he was not taking a schedule of courses for any degree, but he considered that his education continued daily nonetheless. Max hummed a bit in his throat. "You shall certainly become the best-educated man in the Empire. I hope you begin to think of some great reforms. Everyone thinks that old Professor Doctor Kugelius is our best-educated man, why? because each year he gives the same lecture on *The Reconciliation of Aristotle and Plato* and it is actually fifty lectures and he delivers it in Latin and what is his conclusion? that, after all, Aristotle and Plato cannot be reconciled; you did not come to hear me talk about Aristotle and Plato." Said Max.

The guest shook his head. "I came to hear you talk about Mr. Melanchthon Mudge," he said.

There was indeed a file on Melanchthon Mudge and Engelbert Kristoffr read it and then they began to talk again. Said Max: "You well recall a Cabinet decision to hold the laws against witchcraft in abeyance. It simply would not do, in this day and age, for our country to start a prosecution for witchcraft. And as we prefer to believe that the matter is confined to harmless old women living in remote villages, there is really no mechanism to handle a latter-day sorcerer."

An ash was flicked off a segar with impatience. "I don't want the man burned or hanged or shackled, for heaven's sake. We have experts in the sophistry of the law. Can't they simply get an excuse to get the man *out* of our country?"

Max very very slightly poured from the decanter to the mug. "Not so easily. Not when he has a lot of powerful friends. One of whom, are you not aware, is the aunt of your cousin Kristoffr Engelbert, of the Eszterhazy-Eszterhazy line; you are *not* aware? Ah, you were not, but are now. Having read the file." The file reminded him of the Sovereign Princess Olga Helena of Damrosch-Pensk; she was of course not sovereign at all, she was the widow of Lavon Demetrius, whose status as one of the once-sovereign princes of the Hegemony had been mediatized while he himself was yet a minor: the family retained titles, lands, money, and had nothing any longer to do with governation at all; was this a good thing? If they were under the spell of Mr. Mudge, probably.

"Nor is she the only one. Not every name is in the file; listen." Max repeated some of the names not in the file. Engelbert Kristoffr winced. "Is it that they are so immensely impressed because he makes the spirits blow trumpets, move tables, ring bells? In my opinion: *no*. They are so immensely impressed because they are weak in character and he is strong in character and he is very, very *bad* in character and his performances are merely as it were items chosen off a menu. Melanchthon Mudge, as he calls himself, has a very long menu, and if he did not impress the credulous by doing such things, well, he would impress them by doing other things. Was it only because Louis Napoleon and Amadeus of Spain and Alexander of Russia believed the spirits of the dead were at this fellow's command, lifting tables and sounding trumpets and ringing bells, that they gave him jewels? *I* don't think so. And I might ask you to look at what happened afterwards: Louis Napoleon deposed, dying in exile; Amadeus deposed and in exile; Alexander of Russia fatally blown up by political disaffecteds." Max banged his mug sharply on the scarred table-top. "And another thing. If he *has* such powers, why does he employ them lifting tables and tinkling bells? Why does he content himself with gifts of jewels from kings and emperors?"

Engelbert Kristoffr Eszterhazy thought of another question: Why is he — via the thought of him? — tormenting me? But he said, suddenly, aloud, "Because the mind of a demon is not the same as the mind of a man."

Said Max, "Well, there you are. There's your answer."

But, wondered Eszterhazy, to which question?

Having left the old, small castle to Max, its present master, Dr. Eszterhazy long wandered and long pondered. Was it indeed his fortune to have become involved with a Count Cagliostro, a century after the original? Was Melanchthon Mudge really "Melanchthon Mudge"? Could anyone be? And if not, who then was he? The learned doctor did not very much amuse himself by conjecturing that perhaps Giuseppe Balsamo had not really died in a Roman dungeon ninety years ago, but —

Of the so-called Pasqualine Dynasty [a learned correspondent wrote Dr. Engelbert] few literary remains exist, and almost without exception they are very dull remains indeed. Only one reference do I find of the least interest, and that is to a so-called Pasqualine Ring. Do your old friends know about it? Legends for a while clustered thick, one of them that "it had been worn upon the very thumb of Albertus Magnus." I cannot even say if thumb-rings were known in the day of the good Bishop and Universal Doctor — you may also have heard it assigned to the thumbs of two anomalous Englishmen named Kelly (or Kelley) and Dee — and in one of the innumerable editions of the *Faustusbuch* — but enough! Do think of me when you see your old and noble tutor, and ask him . . . whatever [and here the learned correspondent passed on to another subject entirely].

Why had not Engelbert Eszterhazy, Ph.D., M.D., long since removed his old and (perhaps, who knows) royal tutor and wife to a comfortable chamber in the house at 33 Turkling Street? He had offered, and the offer had with an exquisite politeness been declined. Why had he not bestowed a pension? To this question: the same reply. Had he, then, to relieve the burden of want, done nothing? No, not nothing. One day he had encountered the owner of the tottering tenement in which lodged the King and Queen of the Single Sicily in Exile, herself (the owner) a widow incessantly bending beneath the burden of many debts, herself; part in sorrow, part in shame, she said that she would shortly have to double their rent: Dr. Eszterhazy easily persuaded her to mention no such thing to them, but to apply instead to him quarterly for the difference: done. So. There he was one day, visiting, and presently he asked, "And the ring of Duke Pasquale?"

"We have it, we have it," said 'the Queen'. In her haggard, ancient way, she was still beautiful. "We have it. So," she said. "It is all that we have. But we have it. So."

Eszterhazy sat silent. "I will have them bring you a cup of chocolate. Clarinda?" she raised her voice. "Leona? Ofelia?" As, not surprisingly, none of these imaginary attendants answered the summons, the Queen, murmuring an apology, rose to "see what they are all doing," and withdrew into a curtained niche behind which (Eszterhazy well knew) reposed the tiny charcoal brazier and the other scant equipment of their scant kitchen. Politely, he looked instead at the King.

The general outlines of the face and form of him who, with infinite sincerity, called himself "King of the Single Sicily," would have been familiar to, at least, readers of the British periodical press; for they were the form and features of Mr. *Punch* (himself originally a native of The Italies, under the name of Signor Punchinello); though the expression of their faces was entirely different. His lady wife did not in any way resemble *Judy*. The King now said, "I shall have the Lord Great Chamberlain bring it." As Cosimo Damiano's former pupil was wondering what piece of gimcrack or brummagem the, alas, cracked imaginations of the pair would work on, the King said, with a gesture, "The view of the hills is remarkably clear today, my son. We are high here. Very high. See for yourself." Eszterhazy politely rose to his feet, went to the window. The window was now graced with a single curtain; there had at one time been two; and some might have seen a resemblance to the other in the garment which the Queen now wore wrapped around her ruined silken dress rather in the manner of a sari.

Clear or not, the view was so restricted by the crumbling walls of the adjacent tenements as to consist of an irregular blur a few feet tall and a few inches wide. Behind him he heard a soft scuffling, shuffling sound. He heard the King say, "Thank you. That is all. You may go." After a moment Eszterhazy felt it safe to say that the view was indeed remarkable. In reply, he was informed that his chocolate was ready. He withdrew slowly from the view, homeopathically of the hills of the Scythian Highlands, and otherwise and very largely of goats, pigs, washing, dogs, children, chickens, rubbish-tips, and other features of the always informal great South Ward; and took his seat. And his chocolate.

It was very good chocolate. It should have been. He had given them a canister of it a while ago and some, with a vanilla-bean in it to keep it fresh. As, each time he visited, there was always a cup given to him, either the canister — like the pitcher of Philemon and Baucis — was inexhaustible, or the royal couple never drank any at all. Well, well. It gave them pleasure to give, and this was in itself a gift.

"And this," said the King, after a moment, "is the ring of Duke Pasquale." And he produced an immensely worn little box not entirely covered anymore with eroding leather and powdering velvet. And, with a dextrous push, sprang up the lid. It made a faint sound.

Eszterhazy with great presence of mind did not spill his hot chocolate into his lap.

Evidently the tarnished band was silver, as — evidently — the untarnished and untarnishable band was gold. They were intertwined and must have been the very devil to keep clean, whenever the task was still being attempted. Though somewhat mis-shapen —

perhaps something heavy had rested on it, long ago? while it was being perhaps hidden, long ago? — the width hinted that it might indeed have been a thumb-ring. Long ago. And set into it was a diamond of antique cut, more antique certainly even than the ring-work.

"There were once many," said the old man.

"Oh yes," said the old woman. "The wonder of it, as it must have been. The Pasqualine Diamonds, as they were called. Who knows where the others are. We know where this one is. He besought us to sell. So, so. Conceive of it. Sell? We did not even show."

Eszterhazy brought himself back to his present physical situation, drank off some of the chocolate. Asked, "And do you wear the ring? Ever? Never? Often?"

The old woman shook her mad old head. "Only on appropriate occasion." She did not say what an appropriate occasion would be; he did not ask. He observed that the ring was on a chain, one of very common metal. His finger touched it. He raised his eyes. "It is the custom to wear it on a chain," she said. "When one wears it, it should be worn on a chain, like a pendant. So, so, so. My late and sainted father-in-law wore it on a silver chain, and his late and sainted father wore it on a golden one. Thus it should be. So. Or," the pause could not be called a hesitation, "almost always so. So, so, so. One does not wear it on a finger, not even on the thumb; certainly not on the finger; on the thumb, least of all. It would be a bad thing to do. So, so, so. Very bad, very bad. It is ours to be keeping and ours to be guarding. As you see. So, so. So, so, so." She coughed.

Her husband the King said, "I shall take it now, my angel." Take it he did; it was done so deftly and swiftly that Eszterhazy was not sure what was done with it. He had some idea. He was not sure.

Need he be?

No.

It was madness to think of these two mad old people living in poverty year after year, decade after decade, when a fortune lay ready to be redeemed. It was mad; it was also noble. Turn the ring into money, turn the money into silk dresses, linen shirts, unbroken shoes, proper and properly furnished apartments; turn it into beef and pork and poultry and salad fresh daily, into good wine and wax candles or modern oil-lamps — turn it as one would: how long would the money last? Did the "King of the Single Sicily" think just then in such terms? Perhaps. He said, as he accompanied his former pupil to the worm-eaten door, this is what he said: "Today's fine food is tomorrow's dung. And today's fine wine is tomorrow's piss. Today's fine clothes are tomorrow's rags. And today's fine carriages are tomorrow's rubble. And after one has spent one's long and painful years in this world, one wishes to have left behind at least one's honor unstained. Which is something better than dung, piss, rags, and rubble. Something more than piss, dung, rubble, and rags. Be such things far from thee, my son. Farewell now. Go with the Good God and Blessed Company of the Saints."

One must hope. Eszterhazy went.

Thus: the Pasqualine Ring.

There had been a meeting of the University's Grand Ancillary Council, to discuss (once again) the private-docent question; and, Eszterhazy being a junior member, he had attended. The conclusion to which the Grand Ancillary Council had come was (once again) that it would at that specific meeting come to no conclusion. And filed out, preceded by dignitaries with muffs and ruffs and chains of office and maces and staves and drummers and trumpeters. About the necessity of all this to the educational process, Dr. Eszterhazy had certainly some certain opinions; and, being still but a junior member, kept them to himself.

The Emperor, who was *ex-officio* Protector, Professor-in-Chief, Grand Warden, and a muckle many other offices, to and of the University, did not attend . . . he never attended . . . but, as always, had sent them a good late luncheon instead of a deputy: this was more appreciated. Eszterhazy found himself in discussion over slices of a prime buttock of beef with a Visiting Professor of one of the newer disciplines, "Ethnology" it was called. Older faculty members regarded an occasional lecture on Ethnology as a permissible amusement; further than that, they would not go. "Where did your last expedition take you?" asked Eszterhazy. Professor De Blaso said, West Africa, and asked Eszterhazy to pass the very good rye bread with caraway seeds. This passed, it occurred to the passer to ask if there were leopards in West Africa. "Although," he added, "that is hardly Ethnology."

De Blaso said something very much like, "Chomp, chomp, gmurgle." Then he swallowed. Then he said, "Ah, but it is, because in West Africa we have what is called the Leopard Society. I believe it to be totemic in origin. *Totem,* do you know the word *totem*? A North-American Red-Indian word meaning an animal which a family or clan in primitive society believes to have been its actual ancestor. Some say this creature changes into human form and back again. — Not bad, this beef. — Is it Müller who sees in this the source of heraldic animals? Can one quite imagine the British Queen turning into a lion at either the full or the dark of the moon? Ho Ho Ho." Each *Ho* of Professor De Blaso was delivered in a flat tone. Perhaps he felt one could not quite imagine it. "Mustard, please."

Eating the roast beef, for a few moments, speaking English between mouthfuls, Eszterhazy could think himself in England. And then the stewards came carrying round the slabs of black bread and the pots of goose grease. And he knew that he was exactly where he now

thought he was: in Bella, the sometimes beautiful and sometimes squalid capital of the Triune Monarchy of Scythia-Pannonia-Transbalkania.

Fourth largest empire in Europe.

The Turks were fifth.

The gas-lights in the great salon in the town-house of old Colonel Count Cruttz were famous gas-lights. Cast in red bronze, they were in the form of mermaids, each the length of a tall man's arm, and each clasping in cupped hands the actual jets for the gas flames as they, the mermaids, faced each other in a great circle: with mouths slightly open, they might be imagined as singing each to each. This was perhaps a high point of a sort in illumination, here in Bella. Well-dried reeds were used to soak up mutton-tallow or other kitchen grease, and these formed the old-fashioned rush-lights which the old-fashioned (or the poor) still used at night. They smelled vile. But they were cheap. Their flickering, spurting light was not good to read by. But they were cheap. They were very, very cheap. Tallow-candles. Whale-oil. Colza-oil, allegedly stolen here and there by Tartars to dress their cole-slaw. Coal-oil, also called paraffin or kerosene. Gas-lamps. From each pair of red-gold hands the red-gold flames leaped high, soughing and soaring. Often attempts had been made to employ the new experimental gas mantles. But Colonel Count Cruttz always shot them away with his revolver-pistol.

Colonel Count Cruttz looked sober enough tonight; of course, that was subject to change, although it was customary for nothing but champagne to be served at such soirées, and it was not in accordance with his reputation to become shooting-drunk (even gas-mantle-shooting-drunk) on such a ladies' drink as champagne. Still. If a bullet from a revolver-pistol, or two or three, could solve a certain problem of which signs were likely to be shown tonight — if so, gladly would Doctor Eszterhazy ply Colonel Count Cruttz with brandy, vodka, rum, gin, shnopps, and whiskey. Or, for that matter, *alcohol absolutus*. As, however, it was not to be more than thought of, he would have to . . . what would he have to do?

. . . something else.

In one half of the great salon, the soirée looked like any and every other soirée in Bella: that is, an imitation of a soirée in Vienna, which in turn would be an imitation of one in Paris. Few things bored Eszterhazy more than a Bellanese soirée, though they were, barring boredom, harmless. The other half of the great salon, under the soaring gas-lights, was not in the least like every other soirée in Bella, for everyone in that half of the room was gathered around one sole person: a breach of good manners indeed. One might give a "reception" for a particular person and that person might be lionized, surrounded; this was to be expected. But a soirée was not a reception, at least it was not intended to be, and it was good manners neither in those gathered round one person nor for that one person to allow it. But — *allow it?*

Mr. Mudge reveled in it.

Those in the other half of the room strolled around for the most part by ones and twos, now and then uttering polite words to those they walked with or to those they encountered. What was going to happen? By now Doctor Eszterhazy knew. Someone would give a polite hand-clap. Others would fall silent. Someone would say what good luck they all had. Someone would speak, obliquely, of the Spirits which — or who — had "crossed over," and how, for reasons not only not made clear but never mentioned, they sometimes were pleased to make use of "the justly-famous Mr. Mudge" as the medium of their attempts to contact the living. Eszterhazy had, he hoped, a most open mind: the received opinion of thousands of years to the contrary, the spirits of the dead were *not* where they could neither reach nor be reached? Very well. Let the evidence be presented, and he would form . . . perhaps . . . an opinion. But he knew no evidence that any of the so-called spirits had passed their time, whilst living, in tipping tables or sounding very tatty-looking trumpets or ringing lots of little bells; and so he did not think they would do so, now that they were dead, as a means of proving that they were not really entirely dead after all. Mr. Mudge did it (assuming it to be Mr. Mudge who did it); Mr. Mudge did it very well.

But did any of it need to be done at all?

Eszterhazy could not think so.

He was not altogether alone.

"Engli, need we got to have all this?" asked a man, no longer at all young, with a weather-beaten and worn . . . worn? eroded! . . . face, stopping as he strolled.

"Not if you do not wish it had, Count."

The Count almost doubled over in an agony of conviction. "I *don't!* I *don't!* Oh, I thought nothing when Olga Pensk asked it of me, that was a month ago, always have had a soft spot in me heart for her, *lovely* young girl her daughter is — But oh I've heard such a lot in that month. And I can't get back to talk to Olga about it. She won't see me. She's become that creature's creature. Look at her, doesn't take her eyes off him, let me tell you what I have heard."

But Eszterhazy, saying that perhaps he had heard it, too, urged that this be put off to another time.

"Do something, do something, do something," begged the Count and Colonel. "I know what I'd love to do, and would *do,* hadn't all of us in the Corps of Officers given our solemn vow and oath to his Royal and Imperial Majesty neither to fight duels nor commit homicides; wish I *had*n't. Engli. Engli. You're a learned chap. You lived how

many a month was it with the Old Men of the Mountains, didn't you learn —"

But Eszterhazy was lightly clapping his hands.

Afterwards, he had brief misgivings. *Had* he been right to have done it at all? To have done it the way he had done? That Melanchthon Mudge thought this-or-that about it: on this he did not need to waste thought. The Sovereign Princess of Damrosch-Pensk, would she *ever* forgive him? Too bad, if she would not. But suppose that collegium of white wizards, the Old Men of the Mountains, to hear of it; what would *they* think? Well, well, he had not depended on what they had taught him for everything he'd done in the great salon of Colonel Count Cruttz's townhouse. Even the common sorcerers of the Hyperborean High Lands dearly loved the rude, the bawdy, the buffoon; they did not rank with the Old Men, but he had taken some pains to learn from them, too.

And though he told himself that he did not need think about Mr. Mudge, think about Mr. Mudge he did. If he had denounced Mr. Mudge as a heretic; a heresiarch, satanist, and diabolist; if he had made him seem black and scarlet with infamously classical sins? Why, certainly the man would have loved it. Swelled with pride. Naturally. But he, Eszterhazy, had not done it. Nothing of the sort. He had parodied the usual ritual of the séance. He had reduced the introductory words to gibberish and, worse by far than merely that, to *funny* gibberish. He had made the table tip, totter, fall back, to the audible imitation of an off-color street-song, as though accompanied on, not one trumpet, but a chorus of trumpets, as played by a chorus of flatulent demons. He had done something similar with his summoning-up, in mockery, of the spirit bells. Was it not enough to show how others could do it? Did he *have* to have them ring in accompaniment to the naughty (recognizable — but who would admit it?) song on the "trumpet"?

Well, "need." *Need makes the old dame trot,* went the proverb.

He had *done* it.

The whole doing was a mere five minutes long; but it had, of course, made it utterly impossible for Mudge, with or without others, to give his own performance. Absolutely impossible, right afterwards. And who knows for how long impossible, subsequently? He had lost the best part of his audience, for certainly the effect was ruined. If he would indeed try a repetition, elsewhere, a week, a fortnight, even a month, months later, he would hardly dare do so in the presence of any who had been there then. A single guffaw would have meant death.

And eloquent of death was the man's face as his eyes met Eszterhazy's. It was but for a moment; then the face changed. No hot emotion showed as he came up to Eszterhazy, the Colonel Count rather hastily stepping up to be ready, in case of need, to step between them. But no. "Very amusing, Doctor," said Mr. Mudge. He bowed and said a few courteous words to the host. Then he left. Leaving with him, her own face as though carved in ice, was the Sovereign Princess Olga Helena. Not icy, but perhaps rather confused, was the face of her daughter, the Highlady Charlotte, own cousin to Eszterhazy's own cousin. Had she, too, believed? Well, it were better she should now doubt. That there were sincere people in the ranks of the spiritualists, the doctor did not doubt. That some were not alone sincere, but, also, even, *good,* he was prepared to admit. But Mr. Mudge was something else, and if indeed he were sincere, it was in the sincerity of evil.

It made of course no difference to the chemistry of Glauber's Salts what name was given them or who had first discovered them. But it was a hobby-horse of Eszterhazy's, one which he so far trusted himself never to ride along the nearer paths which lead to lunacy, that the pursuit of inorganic cathartics marked the real watershed between alchemy and chemistry. The "philosopher" who, turning away from the glorious dreams of transmuting dross to gold, sought instead a means of moving the sluggish bowels of the mass of mankind and womankind, had taken his head out of the clouds and brought it very close to the earth indeed. **Quaere:** How did the dates of Ezekkiel Yahnosh compare with those of Johann Glauber? **Responsum:** Go and look them up. That the figures in the common books were unreliable, E.E. knew very well. He had also known (he now recalled) that there was a memorial to the great seventeenth-century Scythian savant somewhere in the back of the Great Central Reformed Tabernacle, commonly called the Calvinchurch, from the days when it — or its predecessor — was the only one of that faith in Bella.

Q.: Why might he not go right now and copy it? **R.:** Why not? — unless it were closed this hour on Sunday night. But this caveat little recked with the zeal of Predicant Prush, even now ascending into the pulpit, as Eszterhazy tried to collect his information as unobtrusively as possible from the marble plaque set in the wall. "My text, dear and beloved trustworthy brothers and sisters," boomed the Preacher from beneath the sounding-board, "is Jeremiah, V, 6. *Wherefore a lion out of the forest shall slay them, and a wolf of the evening shall spoil them,* ***a leopard shall watch over their cities:*** *everyone that goeth out shall be torn to pieces: because their transgressions are many, and their backslidings are increased.* ***Miserable sinners, there is nevertheless hope in repentance!***" cried out the Predicant in a plenitude of Christian comfort. And went on to demonstrate that the animals mentioned in the text were *types,* which is to say, *foreshadowings,* with the lion signifying the Church of Rome, the wolf

implying Luther; and the leopard, recalcitrant paganism. As for transgressions and backsliding, Dr. Prush gave them quite a number for exempla, ranging from Immodest Attire to Neglect of Paying Tithes. "Woe! Woe!" he cried, smiting the lectern.

But Eszterhazy was not concentrating on the sermon. There rang incessantly in his ear, as though being chanted into it by something sitting upon his shoulder, only the words ***a leopard shall watch over their cities*** . . .

And, when back at home, he examined his scant notes for the dates of Ezekkiel Yahnosh, he found that, really, all that he had written in their place was *Jeremiah, V, 6.*

Many a set of hoopskirts worn in Bella in their time, many a crinoline worn in Bella in its time, many a bustle worn in Bella (around about then or not a long span later being their time) had been fashioned in the ever-fashionable establishment of Mademoiselle Sophie, Couturière Parisienne. Mlle. Sophie was a native of a canton perhaps better known for its cuckoo-clocks than its *haute couture,* but she had nevertheless plied a needle and thread in Paris. She had plied it chiefly in replacing buttons in a basement tailor-shop until her vast commonsense told her to get up and go out of the basement into the light and air. She hadn't stopped going until she reached Bella, and if her trip and her beginnings in business had indeed been "under the protection" of a local textile merchant who sometimes visited Paris on business, why, whose affair was that? That is, who else's affair? Nevertheless, most of the women's garments in Bella owed nothing to the fact that Mlle. Sophie gained her bread by the pricks of her needle; and perhaps a slight majority of the women's garments in Bella owed nothing at all to what was worn in Paris. Even as Eszterhazy paused to throw down and step upon a segar, several women — evidently sisters — passed by dressed in the eminently respectable old high burger style: costly cloth stiff with many a winter day's embroidery, the bodices laced with gold-tipped laces, each stiff petticoat of bright color slightly shorter than the one underneath. No one else even much noticed.

Still, someone laughed, and it was not a nice laugh. Eszterhazy did not move his head, but his eyes slightly moved. Just across the narrow street was Melanchthon Mudge, clad in fur-coat and fur-hat whose gloss must have represented a fortune in sable and other prime pelts: what was he laughing at? Slowly approaching was a woman by herself. She moved with difficulty. She had been limping with a side-to-side motion which caused her short and heavy body to rock in a manner that allowed little dignity. Nothing about her was rich, and certainly not the rusty black cloth coat which covered the upper part of her dingy black dress: truth to tell it was not even over-clean. Her face was not young and it was not comely and it seemed fuddled with effort. Such things as gallantry and pity aside, if one thought the grotesque laughable, then one would understandably laugh at the sight of her. But such laughter, merely the concomitant of a country culture which laughed at cripples and stammerers, was more puzzling when it came from Mudge. The woman clearly heard the laugh, was clearly not indifferent to it. She tried to walk on more swiftly, rocked and swayed more heavily; there was another laugh; abruptly Mudge walked off.

On the poor woman's head was a bonnet of the sort which had been favored, perhaps a generation ago, by fashion in the North-American provinces. So, on the spur of the moment, Eszterhazy, lifting his own hat, addressed her in English.

"You don't have such picturesque native costume," the slightest inclination of his head towards the wearers of the local picturesque costume, "in your own country, I believe, ma'am."

She slowly rocked to a stop and looked at him with, at first, some doubt. "No, sir," said she, "we don't, and that's a fact. We haven't had the time to develop it. Utility has been our motto. Maybe too much so. You don't know who I am, do you? No. But I know you, Mr. Esthermazy, if only by sight, for you've been pointed out to me. Reverend Ella May Butcher, European Mission, First Spiritualist Church, Buffalo, N.Y." She extended her hand, he — automatically — had begun to stoop to kiss it — she gave a firm shake — he did not stoop. "My late husband was very well acquainted with President Fillmore. But you don't know President Fillmore here." She was in this correct. Neither Eszterhazy personally nor the entire Triune Monarchy had known President Fillmore: there . . . or anywhere.

"I've come to show those deep in sorrow that their beloved ones have been saved from the power of the shadow of death. It ain't for me to say why the sperrits of those who've passed over are sometimes pleased to use me as their medium, Mr. Esthermazy. We have settings on Mondays, Wednesdays, Fridays, and Sundays, the Good Lord willing, at eight o'clock P.M. in the room at the head of the stairs in the old Scottish Rite hall. No admission charge is ever made; love offering only." If Reverend Ella May Butcher was offered much such love, there was nothing to show it. The flat level of her voice did not vary as she asked, "Do you know that man who laughed at me just now?"

The shouting of the teamsters and the clash of hooves on the stone blocks obliged him to raise his voice. "We have met," he said.

Widow Butcher looked at him with her muddy eyes. "There are spirits of light, sir; and there are spirits of darkness. That one's gifts never came from the light. I have to go on now. I hope to see you at one of our settings. Thank you for your kindness." He bowed slightly, lifted his hat, she lifted her skirts as high as was proper for a lady to lift them (a bit higher than would have been proper perhaps

in London, but surely not too high for Bella and doubtless not too high for Buffalo, New York, where her late husband had been very well acquainted with President Fillmore), and prepared to cross the broader street. At this signal the filthy scarecrow which was the crossing-sweeper leaned both hands on the stick of his horrid broom and plowed her a way through the horse-dung. Eszterhazy watched as she poked in her purse for a coin; then a knot of vans and wagons went toiling by, laden high with barrels of goose-fat and rye meal and white lard and yellow lard. And when they had gone, so had she.

He had not expected to meet Mr. Mudge within the week, but he had not expected to be in the South Ward within the week, either. Someone had reported to him that a certain item of horse-furniture was in a certain popular pawnshop there, and someone had said that — not having been redeemed when the loan expired — the item (it was a mere ornament, but then, too, perhaps the horse which first had borne it had also borne the last Byzantine Emperor) was now for sale.

"Impossible," said a familiar voice. Outside the pawnshop.

And another voice, less familiar, but . . . familiar . . . said . . . asked, " 'Impossible'? Impossible for you to do it when two Emperors and one King have already done it?"

There was D. Cosimo D., looking as though he would be away, and there was Mr. Mudge, looking as though he would not let him go. "I do not know other than nothing of it," said Cosimo.

Mudge said he would "explain the matter yet again." The briefly reigning King Amadeus of Spain had been pleased to give Mr. Mudge a gift of jewels. Louis Napoleon, Emperor of the French, had given him some other jewels. And a third such royal gift had come from Alexander, late the Czar of all the Russias. "By the merest coincidence," said Mudge, "they contained elements of the so-called Pasqualine Diamonds. That is to say, I now have them all. I can show you the Deeds of Gifts."

"I wish not to see them. *Gifts!*"

"That is to say, all but the thumb-ring of Duke Pasquale. Without it, the set is incomplete. You may name a price. Money, lands; lands and money — whatever. I shall execute a will demising the jewels all to your noble house. I —"

"*I,* sir. Know nothing. Have nothing to sell. Desire nothing to obtain. Ah, my son" — to Eszterhazy — "You have heard? Am I not right?"

And Eszterhazy said, "The King of the Single Sicily is right."

A week later, as Eszterhazy emerged from his club in Upper Hunyadi Street, a tall man seemed to uncoil from a bench, and, in an instant, stood before him. It was Melanchthon Mudge. Melanchthon Mudge was before him, the bench was alongside of him, a stone pillar of the colonnade was behind him. Only one way of passage remained, but he did not seek to take it. The man wished to do it so? Well, let him do it so, then.

"Be quick," he said.

"Dr. Eszterhazy," said the tall, thin man, earnestly; "you have twice affronted me." Eszterhazy looked at him with a face which was absolutely expressionless, and said absolutely nothing. Mudge seemed rather disconcerted at this; and, a moment having passed, he compressed his lips, something like a frown beginning to appear: this vanished almost at once. A smile replaced it; one might easily see how very many had regarded it as a charming smile. Very often. "You have, Doctor, twice affronted me, I say. But I cannot believe that you ever meant to do so. This being the case, you will take no affront when I explain to you what the affronts were" — and still, Eszterhazy did not move. He continued to gaze with motionless eyes.

Mudge cleared his throat. Then he held up one finger of his left hand and he pressed upon it with one finger of his right. "To begin with, although perfectly aware of my perfect reasons for wishing to purchase the Pasqualine Ring, you urged its present owner not to part with it." He paused. No reaction. No reply. A second finger came forward on the extended left hand, was pressed upon with the forefinger of the right. "You also, doubtless purely as a jape, counterfeited — by some species of parlor trick which in another and lesser man I should term 'charlatanry' — counterfeited those great gifts which are mine as donatives of the Spirits. Now, sir, I do urge you, Dr. Eszterhazy, not to presume to affront me a third time. I am in process of taking a most important step in my personal life. It would mean that we would meet so very often that I should desire to be upon no terms with you save the very friendliest. But if you —"

Eszterhazy's eyes shifted suddenly, transfixed the other man with such a sort of look that the man winced. A brief cry, as of pain, was torn from his throat. "Wretch, rogue, and scoundrel," Eszterhazy said; "I well know that you have it in your black mind to propose marriage to my cousin's cousin, the Highlady Charlotte of Damrosch-Pensk. This, it does not lie within my power to prevent; that is, her mother being in something close to vassalage to you, we both know why, you may propose. I shall tell you what does lie within my power. By the terms of her late father's will, the Highlady Charlotte is in effect a ward of the Emperor until her thirtieth year — unless she is lawfully married before that day. I have already seen to it that a full statement of your depraved behavior in other countries, your disgusting statements set by your own hand in writing in regard to another lady, and the abhorrent circumstances under which you became, first famous, and then rich — I have with a great and grim

pleasure seen to it that the Lord President of the Privy Council now knows it all. The present Emperor will never give his assent without consulting the Lord President. And —"

But this next sentence was scarcely begun when something unseen struck Eszterhazy a blow and sent him with great force reeling against the pillar from where he had been standing several feet away. It was of course painful, it left him breathless and without power of speech: all his effort went into remaining upright; he clutched the pillar, backwards, with both his hands.

Even as he felt himself stagger, he saw the medium, face set for one fearful second into a rictus of rage, go striding away and down the steps. His cloak flew almost level with the ground. There was another voice echoing in Eszterhazy's ears, very faint it was, very faintly echoing. *There are spirits of light, sir; and there are spirits of darkness. That one's gifts never came from the light. . . .*

Eszterhazy, coming up the slum stairs to where the old couple lived, was not at first surprised to hear the sounds of altercation. The place was, after all, a *slum,* and slum-dwellers tend when angered not merely to speak out but to shout. What surprised him was to hear the old noblewoman's voice raised, even briefly. What could — Ah. Ahah. The local muckman was trying to collect garbage-fees. So. True, that the work was damnably hard. True that in the South Ward the fees were often damnably hard to collect. True, that it was hard to imagine the old couple's scanty diet producing enough garbage to be worth feeing. And, true, bullying was a time-established way of collecting the fees. Or trying to.

A fat, foul smell, filthy and greasy, announced its owner even before the sight of the fat, foul body on the landing by the door — fat, foul, smelly, greasy — voice coarse, loud, hectoring. "— wants me entitles!" the voice shouted. "Wants me ten kopperkas!" Fat, smeary shoulders thrusting at partially-closed door. " 'r I takes the tea-pot off the cloth and the cloth off the table and —" The third take was never mentioned, the door flew open wider, there stood the dauntless little 'Queen,' something glinted, something flashed. The muckman gave a hoarse howl and fell back, struggling for balance. The door closed. The muckman whirled around, flesh quivering; flesh, where a hand fell for a moment away, flesh bleeding. Scratches on the rank, besmeared arm. Made by — made by what? "That she-cat," grumbled the man, fear giving way to mere astonishment and dull defeated rage — made by small embroidery shears? or —

"That she-cat has claws," said the muckman, and stumped away down. The rank smell of him alone remained.

Inside, a moment later, there was of course no mention of it all. They seemed a bit more haggard, a bit more harried than usual. He asked if there were not, was there not? something wrong. They looked at him with wasted eyes. "The ring. Duke Pasquale's ring. The ring. He shall never have it. Never."

"Cosimo, I saw a very curious thing."

"And what was that, my dear one?"

"I saw a leopard, Cosimo, leaping from roof to roof, till it was out of sight. Was that not curious?"

"Indeed, my dear one, that was very curious indeed. Not many people are vouchsafed to see visions. By and by, perhaps, we will understand. The soup is now very warm. Let me feed you, as I already have our spoon."

If this were a nightmare, thought Eszterhazy, then he would presently shout himself awake, and . . . "*If* this were a nightmare"! And suppose this were *not?* But these thoughts were all peripheral. He felt things he had never felt before, sensed that for which he knew no terms of sensation. Impressions immensely deep, and immensely unfamiliar. And then some sort of barrier was broken, and he felt it break, and things ceased to be immeasurably alien; but he was not comforted by this, not at all, for everything which was now at all familiar was very horribly so: he heard very ugly sounds made by things he could not see and he saw (if only fleetingly or on the periphery of vision) very ugly things doing things he could not hear. In so far as it resembled anything it resembled the grotesque paintings of the Lowlander Jan Bos: but mostly it resembled nothing. Fire bubbled in his brain like lava. To breathe was to be tortured by his own body. Terror was a solid thing sucking marrow from his bones. He caught sight of a certain known face and on the face, its mouth slightly parted and wet yellow teeth exposed, was an expression of lust and glee.

Who was this, suddenly seizing his arm, face now a chalky mask with charcoal smudges under the eyes? "My son, he will not grant it, he will not grant it! I said to his secretary, 'Father, forget that I am the rightful King of the Single Sicily and consider only that I am a child faithful to Mother Church and with a wife who is sick, Father, sick!' But he will not grant it. *Marón!*"

What Cosimo Damiano was doing in the Mutton Market of the Tartar Section, Eszterhazy did not know; but then he did not know at all what he himself was doing there. And if he himself had, in a state of confusion of mind, wandered far — why then, why not his old tutor? "Sir. Who will not grant what?" — though, already, he had begun to guess.

"Why, license for an exorcism! Our parish priest reminds me that he himself, though willing, cannot do so without a faculty from the bishop . . . in this case the archbishop . . . that is, the Prince-

Patriarch of Bella. I begged the secretary, 'Father,' I said — But it doesn't matter what I said. Away he went with his head to one side and back he came with his head to the other side, and he shook his head. His Eminence will not grant it. . . ."

Ancient custom, having the force of canon law, decreed that the Archbishop and Prince-Patriarch of Bella be called "His Eminence" just as though he were a cardinal; and His Eminence's secretary was Monsignor (not merely "Father") Macgillicuddy. Msgr. Macgillicuddy was descended from those Erse warlords whose departure from their afflicted Island has been compared to the flight of the wild geese: unlike the nonmetaphorical ones, those wild geese never flew back, but drifted slowly from one Catholic kingdom to another. Msgr. Macgillicuddy had been 200 years out of Ireland and no one still in Ireland looked as exquisitely Irish as did Msgr. Macgillicuddy. Perhaps it was a shame that there was no Gaelic monarch at whose court he might be serving instead, and perhaps he did not think so. He belonged to no order, he was attached to no ethnic faction of the Empire or the Church, and if he said that the Prince-Patriarch-Archbishop would allow no exorcism, then that — absolutely — as Eszterhazy well knew — was that.

To one side a bow-legged Tartar made a sudden dive at a scaping ram, bucked it shoulder to shoulder, slipped arm and hand between the beast's forelegs, seized a hind leg and pulled forward; the ram went backward, the Tartar swiveled around and, having dropped the leg, from behind seized the animal's shoulders. The ram sat upright, and could not move. Along came the butcher's men with their ropes. Escape had been short-lived. A covey of quaint figures, the old Tartar women of the Section, huddled into shawls and veils and skirts and pantaloons, began to gather, each intent on the fresh mutton for the evening's shashliks. Escape had been very short-lived. For a while the ram had been king of the mountains, defending his meadow of grass and wild thyme and his harem of ewes. But that was over now.

As to *why* Cosimo Damiano wanted a faculty for his parish priest to perform an exorcism, the old man would be anything but specific. His cracked old brain was cracking wider now under the strain of — of what? Of something bad, of bad things, things which were very, very bad: and happening to *him.* And to his sick old wife. Charms were not enough, amulets and talismans not enough, holy water and prayers and Latin Psalms: not enough. Any more. *Cornuto,* usually efficacious against the *strega?* Not enough.

"But . . . Sir . . . do give me an example? — a single sample?"

Almost as though not so much obeying or answering his former pupil as being made a thrall by something else, in a second the body of the old man twisted and the face of the old man twisted and the voice of the old man changed . . . swift, sudden: movement, sound: frightful . . . Eszterhazy tottered back. Another second and the old man was as before, and trembling with terror. With a stifled croaking wail he scuttled off.

The aged females of the Tartar Section were wending their ways to their homes, each with a portion of mutton-meat wrapped in a huge cabbage-leaf. Eszterhazy paid no attention. In the face of the old man a moment ago, in the body of the old man then, in the grum, grim voice, he had for one second, but for a significant one, recognized and been horribly reminded of the same frightful features of his own recent nightmare . . . if such they were . . . the phrase *psychic assault* came to his mind. What was there in his clean, well-furnished laboratory to help them all against this? Eszterhazy muttered, *"Aroint thee, Satan."* And he spat three times.

And all these . . . these assaults . . . against himself, against the old man and the old wife . . . why? Merely affront and pride? Because, come down to common denominators, what were *they?* What was *it? It* was the ring of Duke Pasquale, that antique family heirloom with which the aged couple would not part. Was it indeed because he coveted the jewel as part of a set otherwise incomplete, that the current enemy was setting these waves of almost more than merely metaphysical assault? Could he not obtain, with his own wealth, a replica of real silver, real gold, real diamond? And . . . yet . . . if that was not why he wanted the Pasqualine Ring . . . then why did he want the Pasqualine Ring?

As long as he lived, Eszterhazy was never to be entirely sure. But he was to become sure enough.

And still the assaults continued.

About ten A.M. and there was Colonel Count Cruttz. Unusual. For one thing; for another, what was it the older man was muttering to himself? It sounded like *Saint Vitus.* An invocation? Perhaps. Perhaps not. In Bella —

The Hospice of Saint Vitus in Bella at the time of its founding had been just that — a hospice for pilgrims seeking cure for what might have been (in modern terms) chorea, cerebral palsy, ergot poisoning, certain sorts of lunacy, or . . . many things indeed. By and by most people had learned not to bake bread from mouldy rye, and the rushing torrents of the pilgrimages had slowed to trickles; still, the prolongedly lunatic had to be lodged somewhere, it being no longer fashionable to lose them in the forest or lock them in a closet: and so, by the time of King Ignats Salvador (the Empire did not yet exist), the Hospice had become the Madhouse and St. Vitus's Shrine its chapel. It *was* quite true that besides the common enclosures there was a secluded cloister for insane nuns and, far on the other side, one for mad monks and priests; it was *not* true, common reports not withstanding, that there was also one for barmy bishops.

"Good mid-morning to you, Colonel Count Cruttz; very well, then: *Fritsli.*"

"Mi' morning, Engli. Say, you are a gaffer at St. Vitus, ain't you?"

"I am one of the Board of Governors, yes."

"Well, I want a ticket. Morits. One of my footmen." The colonel-count looked haggard.

Dr. Eszterhazy reached out from a pigeon-hole a dreaded "yellow ticket," a FORM FOR EXAMINATION PRIOR TO COMMITMENT; sighed. "Poor Morits. Well, this should get him seen to, promptly;" he signed it large. And, did he not, "poor Morits" indeed might gibber and howl for hours in the public corridors, waiting his turn on standby. "What has happened to him? Morits, mmm. *Pale* chap, isn't he?"

Master confirmed that man was indeed a pale chap. That was him. What had *hap*pened? Man had gone mad, was what happened. In the night, not long before dawn. Screams had rocked the house — and it was an old house with thick walls, too. Insane with terror, Morits. "Mostly he just screamed and tried to hide himself in his own armpits, but when you could make out what he was saying while screaming, why it was always the same thing. Always the same thing. Always." Cruttz turned his haggard gaze on Eszterhazy.

Who asked, "And what was that? This . . . 'the same thing' . . . ?"

Cruttz wet his lips. Repeated, " 'On the ceiling! On the ceiling! The witch-man! On the ceiling!' "

"The . . . 'witch-man'? Who and what was that?"

Heavily: "That is who and what and which the people call this Hell-hound, Melanchthon Mudge."

Silence. Then, "Very well, then. One understands 'the witch-man.' But. What and what does he mean by 'on the ceiling'?"

A shrug. "I am damned if I know. And I feel that just by knowing the fiend I might be damned. And so poor Morits has been screaming, struggling, be-pissing himself for hours now, and brandy hasn't helped and neither has holy water nor holy oil and so I've come for the yellow ticket. See?"

Eszterhazy saw only scantly. "Had the man . . . Morits . . . ever before showed signs of — ?"

Reluctantly: "Well . . . yes . . . sort of. *Ner*vous type of chap, always was. Which is all that keeps me from shooting down that swine like a mad dog with my revolver-pistol." That, and — the Emperor having indicated a keen dislike for having people shot down like mad dogs with revolver-pistols — that and the likelihood of such an action's being surely followed by a ten-year exile to the remote wilderness of Little Byzantia, where the company of the lynx, the bear, and the wild boar might not suffice for the loss of more cosmopolitan company.

Colonel Count Cruttz took up the "yellow ticket"; and as he was doing so and murmuring some words of thanks and of farewell, his eyes met Eszterhazy's. The latter felt certain that the same thought was in both their minds: was Mudge punishing the house in which he had been humiliated? Was Mudge doing this? Was Mudge not doing this?

And, if so, what might Mudge not do next?

One was soon enough to learn.

Quite late that morning as he was being examined in St. Vitus by the Admitting Physician, pale Morits not only ceased struggling, but — upon being instructed to do so — had stood up. Quietly. Dr. Smitts applied the stethoscope. And Morits, pale Morits, gave a great scream, blood gushed from his nose and mouth, and — "I caught him in my arms. The stethoscope was pulled from my ears as he fell, but I had heard enough," said Dr. Smitts.

"What did you hear?"

"I heard his heart leap. And then I heard it stop. Oh, of course, I did what I could for him. But it never started again. No. Never."

"Never . . ."

Was this what Mudge had done next?

Eszterhazy thought it was.

Later, some years later, Eszterhazy was to acquire as his personal body-servant the famous Herrekk, a Mountain Tsigane, who stayed on with him . . . and on and on. . . . But that was later. This year the office was being filled (if *filled* was not too strong a verb) by one Turt, who had qualified by some years as a barber; and if experience folding towels well enough had not made Turt exquisite in the folding and unfolding of and other cares pertaining to Eszterhazy's clothes . . . well . . . one could not have everything. Could one? Turt awoke him; Turt brought, first, the hot coffee, and next the hot water and the scented shaving-soap. Next Turt would bring the loose-fitting breakfast-gown and on a tray the breakfast, which — perhaps fortunately — Turt did not himself cook. Turt meant to do well, Turt clearly meant to do better than he did, and it was not Turt's fault that he breathed so very heavily. Turt (short for Turtuscou) was a Romanou, and it was a fact of social life in the Triune Monarchy that sooner or later one's Romanou employee would vanish away on what the English called "French leave": and return . . . by and by . . . with some fearsome story of dreadful death and incapacitating illness amongst far-away family; if/when this ever happened, Eszterhazy had determined to terminate Turt's service. But Turt, though not bothersomely bright, was bright enough, and either saw to it that all his near of kin stayed in good health or else he simply allowed them to die without benefit of his attendance in whatever East Latin squalor pertained to them around the mouth of the Ister.

On this morning Eszterhazy, dimly aware of great pain, was more acutely aware of Turt's breathing more heavily than usual. Had Turt gasped? Had Turt cried out? If so, *why?* Eszterhazy sat bolt up in bed. *"Dominů*, Dominů!" exclaimed Turt.

"What? What?" — heavily, anguished.

For reply Turt pointed to the floor. What was on the floor? Turt's *Lord* looked.

Blood on the floor.

Instantly the pain flared up. Instantly, Eszterhazy remembered. He had been sleeping soundly and calmly enough when something obliged him to wake up. Some dim light suffused the room. Some ungainly shape was present, visible, in the room. Something long, attenuated, overhead. Something overhead. Something barely below the ceiling. Something which turned over as a swimmer turns over in water. Something with a human face. The face of Mr. Mudge, the medium. How it glared at him, with what hate it glared down at him. Its lips writhed up, and, ***The ring!*** it said. ***The ring, the ring! I must have the ring!*** It made a swooping, scooping gesture with one long, long, incredibly long lengthened arm. That was the first pain. What was it which the hand now held and showed to him? It was a heart which it held and showed to him; a human heart. And, whilst the words echoed, echoed, ***Ring! Ring!*** the fingers tightened and the fingers squeezed and that was the second pain. The third. The —

It had been a dream, a bad, bad, dream; a nightmare dream. Only that, and nothing more. In that case, why this dreadful pain upon his heart? And why the blood upon the —

"A nosebleed," he heard himself say. And heard Turt say, "No, sir. No. Not."

"Why not?"

Turt began making many gestures, the burden of them being that, for one thing, there was no blood upon his master's nose and none upon his master's sheets. That, furthermore, blood dropping from the side of the bed to the floor would have left a stain of a certain size, only. And that this stain was of a larger and a wider size. Which meant that it had fallen from a greater height. And as Turt's hand went up and pointed to the ceiling, the hand and all the rest of Turt's body trembled; the Romanou are of all the races of the Empire of Scythia-Pannonia-Transbalkania the most superstitious by far, and their legends teem and pullulate with accounts of *uampyri* and werewolves and werebears and werebats and werecats; and of ghoulies and ghosties and things which do far worse in the night than merely go ***boomp.***

— then why this fearsome pain? Eszterhazy started to sit up, cried out, gestured towards the cabinet, gasped, "The small blue bottle —" The elixir of foxglove made him feel better, then (Turt supplying this next bottle unbid) the spirits of wine made him feel better yet. Then he gestured to the still red stain, directed, "Clean it up."

Turt, so often metaphorical and metaphysical, chose now to be literal. And simply sopped a corner of the napkin in the still-steaming coffee, stooped, wipe, wipe: 'twas done. He made the dirtied cloth vanish. Straightened up. Smoothing his sallow face. "My *Dominů*'s coffee," he said. Soon afterward he brought the shaving-water and the scented soap. Eszterhazy had for a while little to do and much to think about (there was not, considering his beard, much to shave, either: the neck and the cheekbones; but Turt trimmed also).

Eszterhazy, while his servant scraped and clipped, considered his own peril. Presumably, Mudge was anyway somewhat in fear of him, whereas he had been in no way afraid of poor Morits. Presumably, he himself was therefore . . . safe? Well . . . safer. . . .

But for how long?

He recalled that face, high up, hateful. To prove the cheat of the servers of the Idol of Bel at Babylon, Daniel had scattered ashes on the floor; would it now be necessary to scatter them on the ceiling?

Eszterhazy was in bed. Bed. Boat. Boat. As he drifted by in the darkness he heard the sound of the district watchman rapping the butt of his staff on the flagstone pave at the corner. Presently he would hear it rapping on the other corner. He did not. He was not there. He was somewhere else. He knew and did not know where. It was in a great yard somewhere, an open waste of rubble and huts. The South Ward, somewhere. Behind a mouldering tenement. Between it and a riven old wall. Up there in that room, that room *there,* with the broken shutter banging aslant, lived an old man and an old woman, there, there in the night. Here, down *here,* concealed in a half-sunken pit, someone was hiding and biding time. Someone tall and sleek and grim. Someone muffled in a cloak. Was waiting. The cracked old bell began to toll in the tower of the Madhouse of Saint Vitus. Someone chuckled. It was not a nice sound. At once Eszterhazy knew who it was. *I am the brother of the shadow of the slain, the vanguard of the shadow of the living. I am the medium, Mr. Mudge. As well.*

Mr. Mudge moved up out of the half-dug pit, and who knew for what gross usage the pit was to have been digged; moved forward, ahead, face intent. Nearer to the tottery old tenement, nearer to the window behind the broken slant shutter, Eszterhazy desperate to stop him, but paralyzed, unable to call out, to move. To *breathe.* Shutter suddenly springing open. Clap. Bang. Cough. Someone springing out and down. Some*one?* Some*thing?* Dark, dark, very dark. Fluid movement, there in the dark. Warn Mr. Mudge? *Why?* No. Mr. Mudge not there. *Where?* His cloak flying, floating, in the blackness night; Mr. Mudge fleeing before it as though, paws on its shoulders, it

coursed him through the night. *No*: Something else coursed him through the blackness night. Scorn and contempt on his face giving way to concentration, concentration to effort, effort to — *Run, Mudge, run!* — to concern, to care, to alarm, faster, *fast*er, *faster,* leap and run and climb and clamber and jump and clamber and climb and run and leap; close behind him something followed faster yet and something else for a second flashed and glinted, something else gleamed at or about the neck of . . . something . . . as sometimes one sees a glint or gleam where the fond master of an animal has fastened a metal sigil advising of its name and owner; or like some ring on a hand moving suddenly in the dim and flaring lamps —

— screamed, Mr. Mudge; **Quaere:** What did Mr. Mudge scream? **Responsum:** Mr. Mudge screamed for help. **Q.:** How did Mr. Mudge scream for help and to what or whom? **R.:** To ***"Belphegor, Belzebub, Baphomet, Sathanas, à mon aide O mes princes, aidez-moi, à moi, à moi, à —"*** The prayer, if prayer it was, decayed into a continuous repetition of the broad **à**-sound as Mr. Mudge fled, leaping; as . . . something . . . leaping, coughing, followed after him; a great, sudden, abrupt coughing sound, a great forelimb chopping down Mr. Mudge: and all his imprecations sank powerlessly beneath even the level of derision. . . .

Eszterhazy, body spent with having followed the hazards of the chase, awoke bathed in sweat and in bed.

One thing alone remained still quick within his ears, and though it seemed not to be from this night before, yet perhaps it somehow was. *That she-cat has claws,* an odd voice said.

That she-cat has claws.

Dawn.

Mrash.

"Your Lordship, that tiger come a-wandering again-time!"

Eszterhazy lifted dulled, fatigued eyes. "The — ? Ah . . . the leopard? You saw it running along and up the roofs?" What was it he felt, now? It was unbalanced that he felt now. He had with infinite difficulties maintained a stance against attack, assault, terror, pain, and worse. He felt this was gone now. But he was infinitely tired now. *Infinitely* tired. He dared be infinitely careful, lest he fall, now. What had and what was happening?

Mrash said, "No, lordship. I seen it running *down* the roofs. And as I looked, so I seen. 'Seen what'? Why, seen summat as was not the tiger nor the leopard. Look out the window there, me lordship. Look out, look up. Look up."

Where was bluff old Colonel Brennshnekkl, who had hunted leopard in Africa, thinking them more dangerous than lion or tiger which course the level ground alone? Back in Africa, out of which, always something new. So Plautus says. Pliny?

Mrash again gestured to the window. "My lordship, look," he said. Added, "There cross the alley, on the roof of old Baron Johan house. On the ridge o' the roof, by the chimbley; look, sir."

Eszterhazy looked; shielding with his hand against the obscuring reflection of the gaslight on the window glass, straining his eyes, wishing — not for the first time — that someone would invent a *light,* a quite bright light, which could (unlike the theatrical limelight) be cast *up* or *across,* across a distance. Well. Meanwhile. Meanwhile, something flapped in the wind, there on the rooftop, on the ridge by the chimney. "What, Mrashko? Some old clothes? Carried by wind — eh?"

"Nay, my lordship," Mrash said. "Clothes, yes. Old or new. But I doubt the wind be that strong tonight to — No matter. That be a cloak and a full suit of clothes, sir, and I be a veteran of more nor one war and I'll tell thee what, Master: inside that suit of clothes does a dead man lie."

Mrash was hired to perform only the duties of a man-cook, but Mrash was no fool, he had indeed been in more than one war, nor had he spent all that time cloistered in the cook-tent; nor had his eyes been worn by much reading. His master said, "Sound the alarm." In a moment the great iron ring rang out its clamor of **ngoyng ngoyng mramha mram, ngoyng ngoyng mramha mram.** In the very faint glim of the single small gaslamp at the alley's far end men could be seen running, casting odd and oddly-moving shadows. But what was on the rooftop cast no shadow. And it never moved at all.

By and by they came with the hooks and ladders and the bull's-eye lanterns and the grapples and the torches. They climbed up from inside the great old house across the alley and then they climbed up the steep-pitched roof. And Eszterhazy climbed with them. (Had he made this climb before? He *had . . . had*n't he?)

"Aye, he be dead. And have *been.* He'm *stiff.*" This from a volunteer fireman, a coal-porter by his sooty look. "See how wry his neck? He did fell and bruck it." And:

"Am these *claw*-marks?" asked another. Answering himself, "Nay, not here in The Town," meaning Bella. "I expects he somehow tore himself when he fall . . . for fall to his dread death 'tis clear he did, may the Resurrected Jesus Christ and all the Saints have mercy on him and us. Aye. Man did fell. . . ."

Dread death. . . . Mercy. . . .

The very-slightly-odd lordship who lived in the smaller and lower house which faced Turkling Street the other side of the alley, he shook his head. "If so, how came he here?" was his question, almost as though asking of himself. "Here — high above the street on the peak of a house with no higher one to fall from? Dead men fall *down.* They don't fall *up.*"

It was so. There being no more to say to that, they brought the dead man down.

Old Helen, Baroness Johan's old housekeeper-cook, served them the traditional hot rum-and-water. While they were sipping it: "Sir Doctor. Pardon, sir. The police want to know who 'tis. The late deceased. Can Sir Doctor — living 'cross the lane — tell them who 'twas and what was doing there?"

Sir Doctor started to nod. Stopped. What indeed? Had it all been a dream which he had earlier seen as he lay upon his bed? Or "a vision of the night"? Or — His mouth moved silently; then, "The deceased called himself 'Melanchthon Mudge,' " he said. He took another swallow of the grog. It was very strong.

Just as well.

Just as well? Aye, well, add it up. That there were rings which were rings of power was a mere commonplace in the lore of legend. And what Dr. Eszterhazy knew about the lore of legend was more, even, than he knew about anything in which he had ever been granted a degree — though who would grant him a degree in it? The thumb-ring of Duke Pasquale (*which* Duke Pasquale? did it even matter?) was a very late entry into the lore of legend, and had come to Eszterhazy's attention only yesterday, as it were. How had Melanchthon Mudge learned of it? — whoever "Melanchthon Mudge" really was? hunted down as though by a leopard and killed as though by a leopard and left high up aloft as though by a leopard. *What* had he done for the third Napoleon of France and the second Alexander of Russia and the first and last Amadeus of Spain, all men of subsequent ill-fate, that they should have given him (doubtless at his request) portions of the time-scattered Pasqualine jewels? Nothing *very* good, one might be sure. (Was it all adding up? Well, one would see. Get on with it. Go on. Go on.)

Was the power of Duke Pasquale's ring that it gave one a capacity to turn for a while into an animal, a beast, a wild beast? Well could one imagine the glee of roaming wild and free of human form — Well. And once again he marveled at what must have been the long, *long,* restraint (if this were all true) of the self-imagined Royal couple in never having made use of the Pasqualine ring. Never? "Never" was a longer word than its own two syllables; *never?* Surely neither of them, old King, old Queen, would ever (never) have used it for mere glee or mere power. Only an inescapable need for defense, for self-defense, the defense of Eszterhazy and the house of Count Cruttz and perhaps of that whole great city of Bella (. . . *a leopard shall watch over thy cities* . . .) against the great evil thing, the vengeful and killing thing which called itself Melanchthon Mudge, could have impelled them to make use of it. If this were all true: *could* this be all true? all of it? any of it? — for, if it was not, what was the other explanation? If there was another explanation.

Try as he might, as he added all this up, Eszterhazy could think of no other explanation.

A dozen frontiers were being "rectified." A dozen boundaries were changing shape, none of them large enough to show upon a single map in an atlas; but, as to matters of straightening here and bending there, here a square mile and there some several kilometres: a dozen frontiers and boundaries were changing shape. And for every *quid* a *quo,* with dust being blown off a thousand parchment charters. In order to assure that a certain area in the Niçois Savoy be restored to its natural outlines, it was necessary to compensate . . . to, well, compensate two municipalities, one diocese, and . . . and what was *this?* to compensate *the heirs of the fourth marriage-bed of the august Duke Pasquale III,* in lieu of dower-rights, rights of conquest, rights of man, rights of women . . . *rights.*

What cared the historians and the cartographers? and for that matter, what cared the minor statesmen around this particular "green table," for the right or plight of *the heirs of the fourth marriage-bed* etc? Nothing. Save that if it were not taken care of, then neither could other boundaries and rights be taken care of, and a certain sand-bar in the Gambia would remain out of bounds and no-man's land, to vex the palm-oil and peanut-oil trade of certain citizens of certain Powers.

"So, you see, Doctor," said Stowtfuss of the Foreign Office of the Triune Monarchy, "you were quite right in your suggestion and *we* passed it on and *they* passed it on; and, now, well, the King of the Single Sicily is still not really King of the Single Sicily and never will be . . . a good thing for Sicily, and a better thing for him. But now at least he can pretend his pretensions at a healthily higher standard of living. A tidy little income, that, from the old estate in the Nice-Savoy."

Eszterhazy nodded. "And his wife needn't scrub the floor on her aged knees," he said. Old woman, old wife, old she-cat with claws. And with that one ring of power which wanton Mr. Mudge had so terribly wanted. That he, too, might have claws? And, turning, changing his spots — and more than alone his spots — use such claws in the night?

"Yes, yes," said Stowtfuss, pityingly. "Yes, poor chaps, the poor old things. He and his old wife are cousins, you know. They are also related to . . . what's the name? her maiden name? . . . a relation to the poet, same as the old man's mother's maiden name, to the poet Count Giacomo — ah yes! Leopardi! Leopardi! Count Giacomo Leopardi was their cousin. I suppose you may guess the animal in that coat of arms."

WRIT IN WATER, or THE GINGERBREAD MAN

The spirit of the wood, the spirit of the water,
and the spirit of the wheat-plant: they three be sib.
— Old Slovatchko saying

The former Chief Eunuch of the Ottoman Empire rode side by side with Madama D'Attila in her trim little chaise through Klejn Tinkeldorff, one of the less-fashionable suburbs of the capital of the Triune Monarchy of Scythia-Pannonia-Transbalkania. Who was the former Chief Eunuch of the Ottoman Empire and who was Madama D'Attila? Madama D'Attila had at various times been the favorite of two European kings, one Turkish sultan, and three Latin American dictators; alas, the Sultan and one of the kings had long ago gone ga-ga, the other king had been ignominiously deposed, and all three of the dictators had met ends too dreadful to be told in detail. Madama D'Attila presently lived very quietly under the aegis of the Triune Monarchy, now and then receiving the calling cards of the oldest (and youngest) members of the nobility. Once a day, bravely wearing a modest assortment of her best paste jewels, she bravely drove her one-horse chaise through the streets of her little suburb. His Royal and Imperial Majesty did not choose that she should come any closer.

"One never knows, you know," said His Royal and Imperial Majesty.

The former Chief Eunuch, a martyr to the gout, had experienced increasing difficulty in the performance of his official duties; and, having taken a (platonic) fondness to Madama, had also (very quietly) taken his departure along with her own — and the privy purse of the *ci-devant* Sultan. "The mad do not need money," he had observed as he bade farewell to his friend the Assistant Chief Eunuch. "By Allah, that is a true word!" replied the new C.E., raking in his own share of the *ci-devant* privy purse. So now the former Chief Eunuch sat upon the front seat (there was no back seat) with Madama D'Attila, and showed to the local burghers his immense pale swollen face with its pink eye-lids and rouged cheeks and rouged mouth and painted eyebrows and painted moustaches. The burghers calmly tipped their hats. "There goes the kings' whore and the funny French gentleman," they said. And tipped their hats again. Respectfully. (The ex-C.E. by the way was wearing a fuzzy brown suit and a fuzzy brown hat and fancied himself in the height of Western fashion; perhaps he *was*.)

A gentleman riding by on his horse just then raised his riding-crop in a polite salute. "Who is *that?*" asked Madama.

"That is the famous Doctoor-Effendim," said the ex-C.E. "His name is Eszter Ghazi."

They stopped at Shueffer's shop and bought marzipan. Then they drove home and really do not appear in this account again. Perhaps this is too bad. One might grow fond of them. But, as King-Emperor Ignats Louis observed, "One never knows."

Dr. Eszterhazy did not stop at Shueffer's shop and he did not buy marzipan.

Engelbert Eszterhazy, having already attained to three of the six learned degrees which he was eventually to have, was then engaged in preparing for the doctorate in music; he had spent a part of that morning in playing a series of Mozarabic masses (of his own arrangement) on the virginals (of his own design), to the great pleasure of the Papal Legate, one of the Examiners for that degree. Now he had come for a lesson with De Metz, in Composition. The great De Metz kept, in addition to his studio in Bella, a cottage in the suburb, regarding said cottage in the suburb as others might regard a chalet in the Alps or a villa on the Riviera. The lesson having been concluded, De Metz was observing as *obiter dictum* something on the nature of music and mathematic: "A single lifetime, sir, is not long enough to devote to the relation between music and mathematic . . . indeed, sir, one may begin by asking: *relation?* Music and mathematic? *Is there a division?* Song is number, sir, and number is song. What else is the Music of the Spheres but that song of all the morning stars singing together for joy?" Eszterhazy, assuming his instructor's question to be rhetorical, forebore to answer it by more than a low, tactful hum, a sort of small, murmuring voice.

And while this **mmmmm** still sounded in the air, De Metz, still regarding his pupil with the same bird-bright gaze, in the same tone of voice asked, "Are you interested, Dr. Engelbert, in investment possibility?"

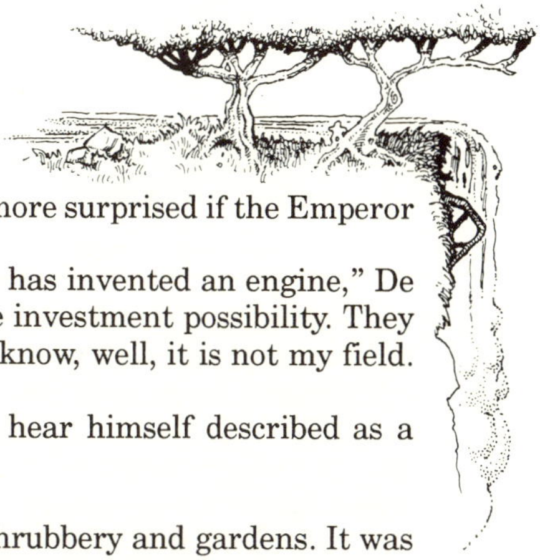

Engelbert could not have been much more surprised if the Emperor had asked him that.

"There is a man down the street who has invented an engine," De Metz said, "and I thought it might have investment possibility. They say that engines do have. I myself, you know, well, it is not my field. But you, Dr. Engelbert —"

"Yes?" asked Engelbert, prepared to hear himself described as a sort of one-man Baring Brothers.

"— you have so many fields. . . ."

The street was lined with trees and shrubbery and gardens. It was not yet what the Indians call the cow-dust hour, but Dr. Eszterhazy knew that when it was, quite a number of many-colored kine would troop back from the common pasturage and, suburb or no suburb, each cow would turn aside and tread the almost invisible path between the street and her owner's cow-house. *The ass knoweth his stall, and the ox his master's crib* . . . But behind one of the houses the cow-house had been converted into a workroom; and though the lineaments of the once-spring-house next to it had been preserved, the cool water flowing from the hill behind no longer served to cool the pans of milk and keep them fresh while the cream rose. "Remind me, Engelbert, to tell you a very amusing story about the Gypsy and the mouse," De Metz was saying; then De Metz said, "Ah, Engineer Brozz! Good later-afternoon. I have the honor to present Dr. Eszterhazy." Engineer Brozz was very tall. And very thin. And Eszterhazy had the fleeting impression that he had seen him before.

His appearance might not have led Eszterhazy to have thought, immediately, in terms of one who had invented an engine with investment possibility. Such a type did not precisely flourish in the Triune Monarchy ("fourth-largest empire in Europe") . . . as distinct from, say, the Nev-England Province of America, where, one understood, every Yankee kept next to his fireplace a device intended to provide either perpetual motion or a supply of wooden nutmegs. . . . Still, some years back, there *had* been Gumm. Gumm lived in the Scythian Highlands and was an engraver of religious woodcuts with brief texts, Gumm had been caught in flagrant delight, stripping the lead from the parson's roof; and Gumm had said that he needed it because he needed a soft metal. For what? For a *notion* of his, that was his own word, the word *invention* seemed not to have been in his vocabulary; for a *notion* which would work a very great change in the production of religious engravings with brief texts: and what might this *notion* be — otherwise — called? Gumm, despite the seriousness of the case, wiggled in something like delight. *"Movable type!"* said Gumm.

Unmoved by the simple splendor of his vision — a mere four hundred years after its time — they had charged him, not with Theft, but with Sacrilege, it having after all been the *parson's* roof; and

Gumm had been sentenced to recite The Ten Long Psalms three times a day for three years. *Without remission.*

Crime almost vanished from the Scythian Highlands.

Brozz began, perhaps inevitably, by saying that *Natura vacuum abhorret* (thus spake Aristotle — or would have, had Aristotle spoken Latin); then he said that Nature didn't either Abhor a Vacuum . . . or, perhaps, it was not quite clear, Nature *used* to abhor a vacuum but had been persuaded by scientific argument not to abhor one all that much. And he spoke about the Column of Mercury and the Column of Water and the Lift-Pump and about Galileo and Viviani and Toricelli and Pascal *father* and Pascal *son* and Air Pressure and Hydrostatics and Hydraulics and Equilibrium and the Experiment in the River and the Sea of Air and von Guericke and the Magdeburg Hemispheres and the Total Force and the Weight of Water and Athanasius Kircher and —

— and he spoke about the three kinds of well-known wheels and the vertical turbine and the hydraulic ram and something called "the Pelton wheel" which was anyway still in the planning stage —

— and Eszterhazy felt himself sitting on a bench in the Great Lecture Hall and listening again to the famous old Professor Kugelius delivering his famous old lecture series *On the Reconciliation of Aristotle and Plato,* concluding that, when all was said and done, Aristotle and Plato could not really be reconciled. . . .

Was Engineer Brozz more or less dotty than Gumm? His voice was monotonous, but his voice was clear. His gestures may have been a bit jerky, but they were moderate gestures, and his words were those of someone speaking sanely on a sane subject — even if not quite persuasively. And the gestures directed attention to this feature and that of a model machine, small but functioning, which . . . when all was said and done and span and spun . . . wound a string which pulled a weight. And let it down. And pulled it up. And — After Brozz had said his say he was a moment silent. A flow of water was heard purling, somewhere very near. "Partly," Brozz began again, "the machinery which you see is on such a small scale because the supply of running water is on such a small scale. Partly, it is because I lack capital to do anything on a larger scale." De Metz again turned his bird-bright gaze upon Eszterhazy. *Investment possibility,* said the bird-bright gaze. "The ancient problem of the Archimedean Screw," said Brozz, "before it was made practicable, I have so to speak turned inside-out. What was its fault, I have made into a strength. The rush of the water works the tuned harmonic turbine which then works the vacuum pump, and thence the compressed-air machine; the compressed-air machine is so clean. . . ." But he began to repeat himself; and besides, his scientific principles seemed . . .

" 'Tuned harmonic turbine!' " exclaimed De Metz. "Music! Mathematic! Marvelous!"

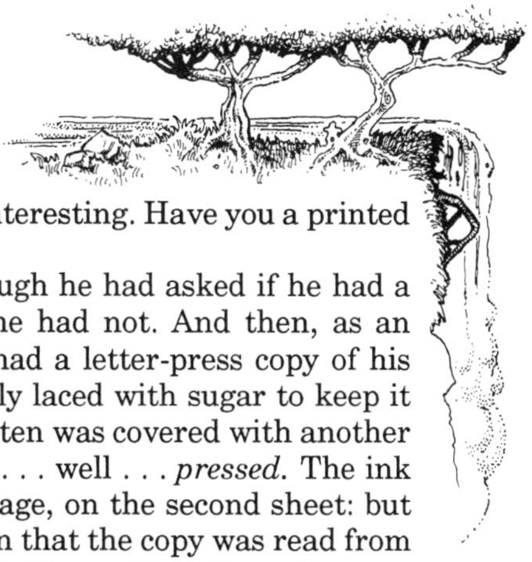

"*Well,* Engineer Brozz! This is most interesting. Have you a printed brochure?" *Had* he not seen the man?

Engineer Brozz looked at him as though he had asked if he had a piece of the moon. Next he said, No he had not. And then, as an obvious afterthought, he said, But he had a letter-press copy of his Statement. Letter-press ink was liberally laced with sugar to keep it from drying rapidly, the paper thus written was covered with another sheet, of different paper, and the press . . . well . . . *pressed.* The ink made, of course, a reverse, a mirror-image, on the second sheet: but the paper of the second sheet was so thin that the copy was read from the obverse, as though it had been right-side up. The alternative was to photograph the original, which was technically possible but so tedious that it was seldom done — or, simply, to *copy* the copy. With pen and ink. Ordinary ink. Brozz did agree to allow Eszterhazy to have the letter-press copy transcribed. But he did not seem at all pleased to have to do so. De Metz might feel bright about the *investment possibility* involved, but, although Brozz had indeed mentioned being hampered by a lack of capital, he did not seem at all concerned with ways of meeting the problem. Eszterhazy was quite sure that the engineer was not engaged in cozenage of any sort, not playing the innocent sitting unsuspecting on a fortune. And Eszterhazy was now quite sure that he *had* seen him before.

"Engineer Brozz has shown me some of the figures involved," De Metz said now. "Some of the physical calculations. I am sure they might form the basis of an extraordinary composition . . . though not one, of course, likely to be familiar to those of purely conventional musical taste. Harmony! Tune! Turbine!"

Somewhere the town-clock sounded. Even in Klejn Tinkeldorff, Time did not stand still. And as Dr. Eszterhazy did not care to dismiss the matter by saying something along the lines of, *You are both too naïf to be left at large for long,* and as he could think of nothing else to say to Brozz which would be neither a lie nor an insincerity, he now said, "You asked me to remind you, *cher maître* De Metz, to tell me a very amusing story about . . . a Gypsy and a — ?"

At once the musician's mask broke into a thousand lines of laughter. "Ah yes!" he cried. "Ah yes! I forget just when it happened. It happened around here, in this picturesque little hamlet. A certain family had a Gypsy working for it and he had his chores and one of them was to skim cream from the milk-pans in the spring-house and ladle it into the crock. You understand. And of course he was most very strictly forbidden to drink any of the cream himself. So. So one day he comes into the spring-house and what does he discover, he discovers that a mouse has gotten into the milk-pan! And drowned! What does he do?" Eszterhazy, smiling, lightly shook his head to indicate his inability to guess what does the Gypsy do; De Metz began to show what, by gesture and by mime. First the Gypsy showed puzzlement. Then surprise. Then — something must after all be done — resolution. De Metz, in the character of *Yanosh,* leaned over, picked up an invisible mouse by its invisible tail, began to throw it away, and then, bringing it level with his face, thrust out his tongue, and — slurp! slurp — and then threw it away.

"Oh ho ho! Ah ha ha! *First* he licked the cream off it! And *then* he threw it away! Oh hoo hoo!"

Eszterhazy chuckled. Engineer Brozz observed, "These Gypsies, they are all such children of nature." A faint, very faint smile, creased his thin and rather weary-looking features. What [it asked], what are Gypsies, mice, and cream to one who lacked capital to prove the larger capacities of the tuned harmonic turbine and compressed-air pump, so potentially efficient in getting energy out of small mountain streams with very high heads of water?

One more call to make. Some of the houses were painted white, some chocolate-brown, some blue, pink, green. And in one of the white ones, with blue trim around the carved window-frames, dwelt the doctor's grandmother's first cousin, Christina Augusta, Tanta Tina. God knows what she might do, were he to ride past her house and *not* go in. Wait till the christening of his first-born child (he was not married) and then appear to utter murrains on everyone's cattle, and blights on all their crops; perhaps. Tanta Tina belonged to an age gone by in more than mere generation; she dressed in the costume of her youth; she had few teeth; she had moles and a slight, white moustache. She and the Emperor Ignats Louis were god-sib. She called him "Loysheck." He called her "Sissy." She did not ever go to Court. And she did not know a word of French.

Well, that is not entirely correct. She knew three.

First she embraced him, then she blessed him, then she fondly stroked his beard. "My dearest little cousin-child," she said, at length, "I shall bring you a cup of *café au lait.* And a piece of gingerbread."

The coffee, in a sense, was already made. But not the *café au lait.* The beans had to come a long way, from Mocha and from Java (described by her as lying "in the lands of the Turks"), in order to be purchased under Tanta Tina's eyes, roasted under Tanta Tina's eyes, ground under Tanta Tina's eyes, and then subjected to an almost alchemical process of . . . almost . . . distillation under Tanta Tina's eyes. Tanta Tina next allowed the coffee to cool and then supervised its being decanted into wide-mouthed glass bottles which, each strictly rotated, remained three days each in the moist cool of the spring-house; the fluid was then poured off the dregs and set to heat in one pan while the milk was heating in another. A dash of cinnamon (fresh-ground), the contents of the two pots commingled at just the right moment: cool slightly, and drink. Who has never drunk *café au lait* made after the manner of Tanta Tina may indeed have drunk

coffee and milk. But he or she has never drunk *café au lait.* And as for a mouse drowning in the cream of the milk in which Tanta Tina made the *café au lait,* no mouse would dare. As for the gingerbread —

"Ha, Tanta Tina, I am reminded of a capital story which I just heard today," and he told it to her, complete with gesture and mime. The old woman laughed heartily; then she said, Ah the poor creature. And when he asked, *Did she mean the Gypsy or the mouse?,* she laughed heartily all over again, then wiped her eyes on her apron, made of hundred-year-old lace the like of which is never made more. And her little cousin-child lifted the gingerbread, sniffed it with zest, smiled . . . what would they say, in fashionable circles, nibbling their petits-fours, if they were to see him about to bite into something as peasant-simple as a gingerbread-man? . . . well, he did not care; he need not care, any more than Tanta Tina; and he knew it and he knew they knew it, too. Then, as his tongue and teeth did their work, he was aware of his experiencing something quite different, quite, well, *better,* than he had expected. He felt his face change.

"It's good, isn't it, Little Engli?"

"But this is extraordinarily good! Is it some new recipe?" Even as he asked, he thought how unlikely it would be if this old woman were to try a new recipe.

She though it unlikely, too. *"Tchah!* A new recipe? From the Old Avar Bakery?" Her tone revealed the all but impossibility of the Old Avar Bakery making anything from a new recipe. Assuming Charles XII, the Swedish "Lion of the North," to have paused long enough in his impetuous ride through the old kingdoms of Scythia and Pannonia to have sampled something from the Avar Bakery; and assuming him to rise from the dead and, returning to sample the same item from the same bakery today, he of "that Name at which the World grew pale" would find the item tasting exactly the same as it had tasted a century and a half before. The Swedish Lion had defeated Danes, Russians, Poles, Turks, sweeping almost insanely across the European continent —

"You can't catch *me,* said the gingerbread-man," Eszterhazy exclaimed, the line coming suddenly into his mind. But a sniper's musket-ball had caught the Lion, at last, in Norway, "on a mean Strand."

"What is that you say, my child?"

He laughed, shortly. "Oh, just something from a children's tale. I learned it long ago, from my English aunt —"

Ah, his English aunt. *Meesis* Emma. And how was *Meesis* Emma? He gave an account of the English Lady Emma Eszterhazy, and then his talk ebbed a moment into silence. He lifted up the remnants of the gingerbread, and, in the silence (. . . had an angel flown overhead? announcing, as the Moslems say, *One God* . . . ?), he heard the old woman murmur, "There is a spirit in this man . . ." And it was his turn to ask, "What was that?"

She blinked, laughed lightly, brushed the matter away with her withered hand. "So my old nurse used to say. I don't know what she meant. You say you like it, but you do not finish? So. A late lunch? An early dinner? Never mind. Let me wrap it up for you to take. The good Lord and Our Lady alone know what they give you to eat in Bella; is it quite wholesome? Yes? Not just foreign kickshaws, I hope?"

Almost back home, the odor of fresh-baked bread brought the matter to his mind again. Where was the — Ah. There. He dismounted, entered the corner bread-shop. Had they gingerbread? They had; he took it. Then he forgot it, until later on, back home at 33 Turkling Street, the slightly unfamiliar weight in each of his pockets reminded him. Really, he mused, looking down, there was not much comparison. The gingerbread man from the antique Avar Bakery, broken though it was, was a sort of modest masterpiece. The outline was as crude as a child's drawing. There was a currant for each eye, two for nostrils to indicate a nose, and a short row of them for teeth. The one from the neighborhood was elaborately confected with brightly-colored sugar icing in several hues. But it was soggy. And its taste was nothing. Let one of the servants remove it and give it to a child. Absent-mindedly he finished nibbling the broken bits from the Avar Bakery. It was good, it was good, it was very, very good. And as the taste filled his mouth, his mind filled with some vague thoughts not unconnected with it.

You can't catch me, *said the gingerbread-man.*

There is a spirit in this man . . .

In came his servant with a small tray; on the tray an apéritif. "Ah, good. Ah. I shan't want this piece of pastry."

Would his Romanou valet lick the cream off a dead mouse before throwing it away? Possibly he might lick the cream off it even if someone else had thrown it away, unlicked.

Or even half-licked.

Ah, well.

Another day. Eszterhazy afoot. A woman called out, not especially to him, automatically, " *'Llyri' an' th' 'Talian 'Lliance . . . 'Llyri' an' th' 'Talian 'Lliance . . . Press, Print, 'Zette. . . .*" Elsewhere in the world, newspapers may have been hawked by newsboys — some of them, Dr. Eszterhazy had observed in his travels, rather well on into rather mature boyhood — in Bella the trade was largely in the hands of soldiers' widows. True, pensions had . . . eventually . . . been instituted; true, pensions had . . . eventually . . . been increased . . . but when it had been hinted that the newswives might now tacitly retire and allow others to take this corner pitch and that: nothing like it! Wrapped in threadbare Army horse-blankets and with their

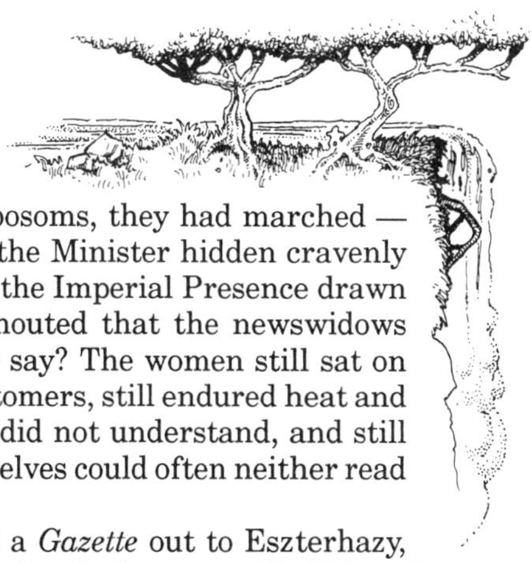

late husbands' medals pinned to their bosoms, they had marched — wailing — to the Ministry of War. *Had* the Minister hidden cravenly beneath his great mahogany desk? *Had* the Imperial Presence drawn his sword and stamped his foot and shouted that the newswidows *must* be allowed, etc.? Who could really say? The women still sat on their stools, still shortchanged their customers, still endured heat and cold, still chanted headlines they often did not understand, and still offered for sale papers which they themselves could often neither read nor wished to learn to read.

Half-automatically this one now held a *Gazette* out to Eszterhazy, half-automatically he gave her a coin and took the paper. He did not greatly desire it. He was not by any means a fanatical nationalist or imperialist, but he certainly preferred to see his own country's flag flying over his own country rather than that of — say — Austria-Hungary, Russia, or Turkey. The news-vendor's late husband may have died in battle or he may have been, whilst drunk, kicked to death by an angry mule. The price of a paper was a very small price.

Illyria and the Italian Alliance. Happy, happy Scythia-Pannonia-Transbalkania, to be fretted by small Illyria! All through the Dog Days and the Silly Season, not over-scrupulous editors would sell off an otherwise perhaps-unsalable edition by smearing a quarter of a page with, in large type, **ILLYRIA AND THE ITALIAN ALLIANCE.** There was somehow a feeling that Illyria ought not to *have* an alliance and that if Illyria nevertheless felt that it must have one, it bloody well ought to have one with Scythia-Pannonia-Transbalkania. And as Scythia-Pannonia-Transbalkania had never had an alliance with Italy, why should Illyria have one? The logic of this seemed irrefutable. At least in Bella. As for the King of Illyria, King Procopio, whose nose (admittedly rather long) had always been good for an affectionate jest in the Bellanese music halls, why, it was to be feared that His Adriatic Majesty's veracity was now come to be questioned on the local musical stage; and that he was even occasionally nowadays being referred to there as King Pinocchio.

Tut-tut.

Eszterhazy gave the front page a glance which was reflexive rather than reflective and had half-folded it again; half he would throw it away, half he would tuck it under his arm for later; he took a half-step forward. He stopped. What. Why. Ah. There *had* been something on that damned page after all. Damn. Much better to have nothing but advertizements on the front page. For Sale, Fine Landau-Barouche. Otto Come Home All Is Forgiven. Philanthropic Gentleman Desires Make Loan to Young Woman in Good Health. — What had it been which had caught his eye . . . aye, and stuck in like a piece of grit . . . ? Of course he could not say. Well . . . a sigh . . . there was nothing for it; he sat down at a bench outside a rough tavern-cum-cookshop which catered to the needs of the coach-for-hire drivers. He was opening the paper when a not very clean apron stopped in front of him. Without looking up, Eszterhazy said, "The usual." When he glanced up, the apron had gone. No waiter would sink pride and admit he did not remember a regular customer . . . which Eszterhazy was certainly not. *Illyria and the* — oh, blast and damn Illyria and the Italian Alliance!

The answer seemed to be, he was obliged finally to admit, that there were *two* somethings. And he would perhaps never be able to learn if he had noticed one before the other, perhaps the two had been read simultaneously; it did not matter. OUTRAGE AT THE SACRED GROVE was one. VERY IMPORTANT NEW INVENTION was the other. Someone, whilst putting an axe to a tree in the so-called Sacred Grove of the Olden-Time Goths at the headwaters of the Little River had had his head cloven by another axe. There was considerable unrest among the peasants. *Huh.* He had notes at home on the subject of the so-called Sacred Grove, et cetera, both from ancient and from modern writers. *Hum.* Well, he could cut this out and compare it and add it to the collection. As for the Very Important New Invention . . . :

> The *Gazette* is able to inform its readers that a very important new invention has been perfected by a subject of the Triune Monarchy which will probably result in our country becoming a most prominent industrial consideration in the economy of Europe. Engineer H. V. Boritz Brozz, a resident of the charming little suburb of Klejn Tinkeldorff, has perfected an engine which operates on water and air. The new engine does not require horse-power or steam. As neither wood nor coal is employed for fuel . . .

Eszterhazy swore very silently. Every practitioner in stock trickery, every promoter of fake companies and worthless schemes, would be sure to get involved in this fine-tuned harmonic hobby-horse, mare's nest, wild-goose chase, what-one-might-call-it. True — and fortunately — there were not many such in Scythia-Pannonia-Transbalkania. But that might leave a clearer field for those there were. At that moment the waiter, saying, "Two kopperkas, sir boss," set something on the unclothed table. And Eszterhazy in a flash realized just how the *Gazette* had got hold of the story: De Metz was a friend of the musical critic of the *Gazette* and told it to him, and he in turn had passed it on to his editor. De Metz knew as much about engineering as Brozz did about music. The bee of *Investment Possibility* had entered his bonnet, and who could say how long it was going to buzz there? Perhaps forever. Certainly — in theory — the harmonic turbine had a potential. Certainly the compressed-air engine had a potential. In theory. So, in the time of Cardinal

Richelieu, had the steam-boiler had a theoretical potential. It had since had two hundred years to develop from a toy suspected of sorcery into the immense engines which sped o'er Land and Ocean without rest. Even electricity had grown from a key on a kite in a rainstorm to something which now began, seemingly, to demonstrate a possible potential capable of perhaps rivaling steam.

What good is your new invention?

What good is a new-born baby?

But surely Engineer Brozz's new model engine, for all its high-toned harmonic title, was now merely at the toy stage, doing nothing more than winding a cord which lifted and then lowered a very small weight. Would it have its century? If the idea got into the hands of scoundrel speculators might not the idea be driven from sight and thought, to lie buried in the Urn for its own several centuries? Well, perhaps that might be what it needed. Meanwhile there were after all and always many other new inventions. *Many* inventions.

What the waiter had set down was borsht. *Cabbage*-borsht.

Wasn't bad. *The usual.* Ha!

But . . . *where* had he seen Brozz before?

The Scotch had not conquered the English nor had the English conquered the Scotch in order for one sovereign to become King of England and King of Scotland and — eventually — King of the United Kingdom of Great Britain. What had brought it about was, firstly, the Scottish marriage of King Henry's sister, and, secondly, the not-marriage of King Henry's daughter: *the Queen of Scots hath a bonny babe and I am but a barren stock.* Neither had any wars at last united Scythia and Pannonia; the Pannonians at a certain point historical had no Crown-Prince? Well, neither had they any Salic Law: the then-Crown-Prince of Scythia was wedded to the then-Crown-Princess of Pannonia; both being tactful enough to die before their conjoint-grandchild, said grandchild became Sovereign of both Scythia *and* Pannonia — and what school-child anywhere did not know that the people of Scythia were (principally) Goths and that the people of Pannonia were (principally) Avars? *What* an occasion for the erasure of frontiers, the unification of armies, the abolition of customs and octrois! There were, however, also all those lesser, minor territories, of which the new Sovereign was Prince of one and Duke of another . . . in the Scythian Line of Descent . . . Grand Hetman here and Chief Boyar there . . . in the Pannonian Line of Descent . . . and so on . . . and so on.

What to do about them, these not-quite-nations already becoming obsolete in an age where every political entity was felt to require a prime minister, a general staff, a set of postage stamps, a — What was done was perhaps cleverer than students of political science realized, for all these "Hegemonies," as they were called, from Ritchli to Little Great Dombróvia to Hyperborea, and including Vlox-Majore and Vlox-Minore, were not absorbed by either Scythia or Pannonia, but were autonomously united to form *Transbalkania.*

The result, rather to the surprise of the gathering which assembled to form the (as it was popularly called forever) "the Big Union," the result was an Empire . . .

And now the cheese of Poposhki, the smoked sturgeon of the Romanou, the brined-pork and the brawn of the Slovatchko Alps, appeared . . . *untaxed!* . . . on the market-stalls of Bella — Avar-Ister — Apollograd — and everywhere else in the fourth-largest empire in Europe. (The Turks were only fifth. Served them right.) Also the wheat of Scythia, and the beef and mutton of the wide Pannonian plains. And, as Dr. Engelbert Eszterhazy composed this paean in his own mind and looked at the ever-thronging streets of what, once a walled town, was now a world capital (yes, it was a small world), he considered the rôle which he himself would play. Which he had intended he should play and had designed (re-designed) his own life the better to play it. You can't catch me, said —

Something light as a feather brushed Eszterhazy's mind. He knew that, usually, he had only to wait a bit, emptying his mind of other things and that fairly soonly whatever the new thought was would silently enter and fill the space. He was mildly surprised that what came, soon enough, to fill the space, was the thought, *newspaper cuttings.* There was a plain, shallow box of some exotic wood on a shelf near his desk, and in it he was accustomed to place any quick-cut items from periodicals which he had not immediately time to dispose of more thoroughly; he rose and looked. Sure enough. From the *Gazette.* VERY IMPORTANT NEW INVENTION was one. That would go under, hm, under, ha ha, *Invention.* In his scrapbooks. With a cross-reference under *Science.* And under *Commerce*? He chuckled. "Investment possibility," ha! And now for the other items so casually cut out a while ago, OUTRAGE AT THE SACRED GROVE. Someone, whilst putting an axe to a tree in the so-called Sacred Grove of the Olden-Time Goths at the headwaters of the Little River had had his head cloven by another axe. There was considerable unrest among the peasants. *This* one —

This one would require cross-references under *History, Ethnology, National, Goths, Religion, Little River,* and — what for its main classification? And did he really want to bother with all of it now? Ought he not now, *now,* in fact, to be in his music-room, doing work on the Mixo-Lydian Mode or the Later Italian Harpsichordists? *Was* music and mathematic really the same thing? How one thought led so easily, swiftly, to another! — and yet and still the feather brushed his mind; what, what? Why? Was there, then, more to it than merely boxing the *newspaper cuttings*? Evidently. So much as a sigh he allowed himself, then he went to looking up things in his books, not

his scrapbooks, though perhaps he might find himself in them before his was finished.

The so-called *Addendum to Procopius* had been printed once, at Leipzig, perhaps fifty years ago; but the text was defective. Eszterhazy had tracked down the original, was able to satisfy himself that it had not been forged by the notorious Simonides — who knew more, probably, about Old Greek Paleography than the old Greek paleographers had known, and did such things as much for pleasure as for profit . . . if not more — and had it painstakingly photographed. It was a very late Byzantine MS, full of abbreviations, ligatures, and flourishes (and lacunae and, more simply, *holes*); and it had taken Eszterhazy a long time to establish exactly what *was* the text: then he had translated it himself. The Faculty of the University of Bella, to whom anything in the way of a Greek text even as late as the New Testament was of but moderate interest, had ignored his work. But he had received letters (one each from Caius College at Cambridge, St. Andrew's in Scotland, and Kansas near Kickapoo in the American Province of Mid-vest) with such praise as more than made up for local neglect. So:

> Another reason which justified Justinian's waging war upon the Goths was their savage rites and customs, totally against religion and morality. For example, in the mountains of Eastern Scythia in a sacred grove by a sacred well or spring, the barbaric Goths are wont to select certain prisoners by lot and to let them loose and to pursue after them. The wretches unfortunate enough to be captured are not alone immolated . . .

. . . *immolated,* an interesting word, although of course all words were interesting; why not more simply say sacrificed? Immolate . . . mol . . . mol . . . surely a cognate with the Magyar *molnar,* miller? and with what else? *Meal*? *Mill*? With a click of his tongue he reached for the dictionary, *immolate*: ah, here: *im-mo-late,* verb transitive, from Latin *immolatus,* past participle of *immolare, in + mola,* spelt grits; from the custom of sprinkling victims with sacrificial meal; akin to Latin *molere* to grind — see MILL. 1. to offer in sacrifice; especially to slay as a sacrificial victim. 2. KILL, DESTROY. . . . Hmm. Hmm. Interesting. Very interesting. Now back to the text . . .

> . . . immolated to the demons who dwelt in the place sacred to them, but portions of their flesh are cooked and eaten. Others say, eaten raw. It is true that some so-called Christians who should know better maintain that though such a cruel rite once pertained there, it had been abolished after the Gothic incursion, and that the Goths themselves merely made effigies of meal and honey and it

is these which they consume. Shame upon the so-called Christians who presume to speak well of the enemies of God and the Empire, they are probably Monophysites or Pelagians, may they be accursed and may they all be burnt alive.

Eszterhazy gave a snort of rueful amusement. The *Addendum* may not have been, probably was not, authentic. This of course did not mean that there had been no Goths, no Justinian, and so on; and certainly it did not mean that there had been "in the mountains of Eastern Scythia" no sacred grove, no sacred spring or well. In fact, it was rather sure that there had been. *Very* likely: more than one. Of each. Of most, reference to the precise site had been lost to both oral and written tradition, and of those sites of which this may not have been so, only one was still known as, and still regarded as, "the Sacred Grove." It was near the headwaters of the Little River. One might have liked it better if the (so-called) *Addendum* — probably never written by Procopius, that spiteful, scandal-loving lawyer — had made a definite reference to a river. One could not have everything. And anyway, the absence of such a reference was a sort of testimony to some sort of authenticity of the text: that the MS was of late Byzantine times did not mean it had been authored in late Byzantine times; had this been so, it likely *would* have mentioned a river, in order to add verisimilitude. No . . . probably it was older than the Middle Ages, if not (perhaps) as old as Justinian and Procopius, and its author, whoever its author had been, merely repeated what others had said. And others had not been interested in providing geographical coördinates.

What then? about the Sacred Grove? Of *the* Sacred Grove?

Eszterhazy had been there, once, briefly. Though the oaks were indeed massy and ancient, of course they could hardly have been *that* ancient. He thought once of the lines of the English poet, Chaucer:

a grove, stonding in a vale

This grove was indeed standing in a vale; it was deeply sunken into the vale. The spring was still there. The river was not the Little River, it was one of its tributaries. A Christian shrine, itself of great antiquity, was there; but the attempt to take the pagan quality away had hardly succeeded. Had not, certainly, entirely succeeded. On every bush and low tree round about, and on whatever low-enough branches of the higher trees, was tied a profusion, a multitude of bright-colored rags, strips of cloth. The people came and the people said their prayers by the proper shrine. And then the people went and made their wishes, and as they did this they tied a strip of bright cloth to a branch. It was a custom so old that it had passed out of anyone's power to rationalize.

So no one tried.

The air was certainly one of more than merely immemorial

antiquity. In the shade of the huge trees one felt intimations of things to which the rosary, the Pater Noster and Ave Maria, hardly seemed to apply. Of course the pilgrims, if so they might be called, hardly could have thought so. From time to time relics of the Bronze Age had been found there. Relics of the *Stone* Age had been found there, and Eszterhazy wondered if these flint knives, mostly now in fragments, had immolated any of the victims in the ancient and horrid rites which had certainly antedated the Goths, to say nothing of the Avars, who had later come to conquer . . . and had stayed . . . and still came and still stayed . . . to pray. One did after all feel something there which one did after all not feel somewhere else. If there were not actually dryads in the oaks, not really naiads in the spring or pool or river, well, then of course, one could not really feel them. But for thousands of years, people had come and had emotional experiences there and had believed that there *were* dryads in the trees and naiads in the spring and pool and stream. And so perhaps it was *that* which one felt.

Because, to be sure, one felt *some*thing.

And as for the incident mentioned in the cutting from the *Gazette* newspaper? Well, there was a superstition that wood fallen from the trees in the Sacred Grove should not be taken from the Sacred Grove. Once a year, at least once a year, certainly on or very near Midsummer's Night, great fires were made of all the wind-fall wood — otherwise the place might have become impenetrable. Heathen would not wish to take wood away, because it was sacred; Christians not, because it was, after all, sacred to heathen gods and spirits. It had been good church doctrine; was it still (he wondered, as the gaslights hissed in the gasolier in his study) good church doctrine that the heathen gods had indeed existed and had been demons? And it was certainly contrary to some deeply-felt regional feeling, call it superstition, that no tree in the Sacred Grove should *ever* be felled —

— furthermore, it was, the entire area and for a league, say rather *leagues,* round about, the property of Prince Preez, who had very stern rules regarding the felling of *any* of his trees — the killing of any of his game — the taking of any of his fish —

But there is perhaps scarcely any rule which someone will not try to break, if it is to someone's interest to break it. Oaken timber had a price, and it was inevitable that from time to time someone would try to earn that price. It was not clear from the paragraph in the *Gazette* which was considered the outrage, the attempted cutting-down of the tree or the successful cutting-down of the attemptor? Or just why there was considerable unrest among the peasants: though presumably in connection with the matter of the tree and the manslaughter.

Well, well, he would try to follow it up; meanwhile he carefully scissored the rough edges of the knife-cut newspaper items, neatly pasted them in their proper places in the scrapbooks, neatly made his cross-references. So much of this was in his head anyway that it wasn't something it would do to depend on a secretary for; and besides: he had no secretary. Though perhaps some day. Meanwhile, and quite apart from the intrinsic value of what he was doing, the storing-up of knowledge as a part of his life-plan, Dr. Eszterhazy found now (as always) that there was a simple and a rather restorative pleasure in doing such simple tasks as using the scissors and applying the paste. If this was — and it was — rather childlike, what of it? There was, after all, a child in everyone; better to minister to it in such harmless and helpful ways.

Just as he was closing the scrapbook there caught his eye the headline, VERY IMPORTANT NEW INVENTION. And, as before, he chuckled.

Fairly soon, however: there it was again.

Arriving for his regular session in Composition, Eszterhazy was met as usual by the housekeeper; and, as usual, she curtsied to him. Then, not as usual, she said, "Master has left word, sir, will you be pleased to go over and meet him at Engineer Brozz's place, behind, in th' old cow-house and spring-house as they've had the builders throw together and they calls it the lavatory."

They were both there in the laboratory. Something had been added, Eszterhazy felt certain, but he was not yet aware what it was. As before, Brozz looked rather weary; as before, De Metz had his head cocked to one side. Greetings exchanged, De Metz, evidently acting as spokesman, said, "It was felt that perhaps the new invention did not sufficiently demonstrate the," and here he paused a second, "*prac-tic-al application* of the invention. Of the tuned harmonic turbine and compressed-air pump. So. Doctor. *There*fore —"

Brozz said, rather as one who speaks as it were weary of having spoken the same thing again and again, almost dreamily said, "It is so clean . . . so clean . . . no fire, no smoke, no ash — Ah. Yes. Instructor De Metz has been kind enough to make some practical suggestions, of the most helpful sort." Sunlight diffused from the whitewashed walls, emphasizing here a ridge and there a whorl in the plaster covering the brick and stone. As though making some sort of effort, Brozz cleared his throat, lifting his head; muscles worked in his lean throat. "Instructor De Metz has assisted me to devise a small device which will —"

"But show him, *show* him, my dear Brozz!"

There was a flurry of apologetic sounds. Brozz moved levers. He turned wheels. The sound of water purling became the sound of water gurgling. Rushing. Brozz made one final movement and pulled a bar. By this time Eszterhazy had noticed the box, of wood and metal,

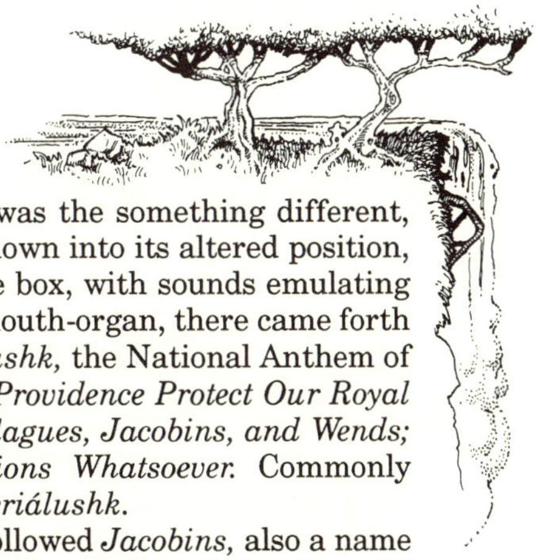

which had not been there before: *this* was the something different, something new. And as the bar settled down into its altered position, there was a distinct *click.* And from the box, with sounds emulating those of the flute, the small drum, the mouth-organ, there came forth the very specific music of the *Imperiálushk,* the National Anthem of Scythia-Pannonia-Transbalkania: *May Providence Protect Our Royal and Imperial Sovereign From Agues, Plagues, Jacobins, and Wends; And, Indeed, From All Other Afflictions Whatsoever.* Commonly called, for purposes of brevity, the *Imperiálushk.*

(Quite another name had originally followed *Jacobins,* also a name of a single syllable, but political considerations indicated that it would be more tactful to substitute the name of a people which did not have a standing army.)

As the last notes — those which would accompany the words, *and even to the humblest grant him and/or her the slice of bread with goosegrease* — died away, Eszterhazy was moved to clap his hands: of course no more appropriate after an anthem than after a hymn. He said, and said quite sincerely, "Charming. Quite charming." The matter of why it was better to have the music performed by water-powered vacuum pump and/or compressed air when music-boxes had done it perfectly well by clockwork . . . and clockwork, after all, operates even during a drought . . . was quite beside the point. Although . . . to be sure . . . a regular music-box might not have done the flute and mouth-organ quite as well.

At once De Metz asked, "And to whom else shall we show this?" He did not add, *investment possibility.* He did not need to.

Eszterhazy rubbed the end of his slightly-pointed nose. "Hm. Let me think. Ah. Have you considered Nuszboum's Arcade?"

They had not considered Nuszboum's Arcade. They considered it now. De Metz gave an entire sequence of his birdy-nods. Brozz said, "I have often enjoyed watching some of the machines and automata in the Arcade. I have no doubt that the principles of the tuned, harmonic, water-powered turbine and compressed-air pump might be successfully applied to them, at any rate to some of them, and of course on a much larger scale." It was clear that they liked the idea.

It was clear, very soon, that Nuszboum liked it, too. Nuszboum made an arrangement with the inventor, Nuszboum provided space for the invention next to his Test-the-Electricity Machine and just after his Slightly Naughty Magic Zoöscope Lantern Peep (fat women in corsets). And in front of the Arcade, Nuszboum posted two masterpieces of posters appearing to be immense enlargements of the small item on the front page of the *Gazette* which had attracted Eszterhazy's attention: IMPORTANT NEW INVENTION: actually, both posters had been painted by the famous Master Sign-Painter Adler. How many people saw them and how many had read them and how many people had been intrigued by them enough to go inside, no one could say. But somebody had gone inside. And someone was not even interested in testing the Electrical Machine or peeping into the Zoöscope Lantern . . . which was just fine with those who were, tinsmiths and plasterers and other such subjects of the Triune Monarchy whose wives were just as fat but never wore corsets . . . and someone asked a question or so of Nuszboum and obtained an answer. And so, *then* —

"And how is our friend Engineer Brozz?" — one day.

"Quite well. He has gone away to set up his full-scale water engine."

Eszterhazy was astonished. "He *has?*"

"Oh yes. Somebody is interested in investment possibility." Eszterhazy asked just enough questions as to reassure himself that Somebody was not a cheapjack or mountebank or floater of bogus shares; Someone was *not.* And further than that, Eszterhazy did not ask and De Metz did not offer and their conversation continued on into a very technical discussion of counterpoint and polyphony. And presently the season of the lessons with De Metz was over and the season for a holiday in the country was at hand, and whilst Eszterhazy was botanizing amidst the crags and high valleys and wildwoods of Little Byzantia, the matter of Engineer Brozz left his mind, and left it as completely (one might think) as though it had never been in it. When next he was in "Big Bella" the mock-newspaper posters were no longer up in front of Nuszboum's Arcade and he had forgotten that they had ever been up. The matter occurred to him, vaguely, when he received the customary letter of felicitation from De Metz upon the award of the Doctorate in Music; but it was very vague indeed. On the vacation following, Eszterhazy went geologizing in the mountains behind Nimtsoran: and nothing there reminded him of Brozz, or of the vacuum-pump and the compressed-air engine. But on the vacation after *that* —

This time Eszterhazy took the Limited Express to Numbitszl, in the Avar Alps, from Numbitszl the mule-drawn diligence went to Gro, and at Gro he was met by a smart mountain wagon; its brightly-painted signs showed a figure with a halo who was mounted on something like a short-legged horse with a ruff of hair around its neck: this was Saint Mammas. *Put a lion on Mammas!* the heathen throng in the amphitheater had shouted, and this was done. Mammas had preached to the lion, Mammas had so to speak converted the lion, and Mammas had calmly ridden out of the arena mounted on the lion. — So at least the legend said, and if orthodox church historiographers and hagiographers said anything different, no one in the Avar Alps knew or cared. And it was at the piously-named (and well-appointed and well-run) Inn of St. Mammas that Eszterhazy was going to stay. For a full fortnight he might not even see a musical score or hear a musical instrument . . . except perhaps a peasant on the zither or the penny-whistle or the woodenhorn.

The road went around and around and up and up and up, the air was clean and clear, not alone different from the thicker air of the city of Bella but certainly far different from the air in the train. In theory the train-carriage's windows were sealed, but the black soot seeped in anyway, and the air grew hot and stale, and if one opened the windows then the smoke from the engine rushed in, and in addition to grime on one's face there was the inevitable cinder in one's eye. Cinders. Eyes. But here all was clean. By the side of the narrow, winding road grew yellow wood-sorrel and the blue blossoms of the cornflower and the blue blue blooms of the chicory.

From the balcony of his two-and-one-half-room suite Eszterhazy could see a broken silver line: the Little River and its several falls, and — past that — the unbroken silver line of the broad ox-bow in its lower course. Eszterhazy's Romanou valet had been given the fortnight off; and he himself was now being tended to by the inn's servants, and tended to well enough; very well, he had to shave himself or submit to the unsophisticated ministrations of the village barber? Tut.

He rode the small rough horses of the mountains, he rode their rough large ponies, once or twice he rode their rusty-colored mules. And he walked. He walked and walked, sometimes botanizing, sometimes bird-watching, sometimes photographing. His face grew red, then brown; his nerves, calmer . . . he had hardly realized that they had been otherwise. And then one night he said, more as a vocal expression of good spirits than an actual question, "Well, landlord, and what shall I do tomorrow?"

Barrel-bodied, immaculately-aproned, vastly-bearded and broadly-moustached, Karrólo the innkeeper answered, "Why, sir doctor sir, a party of the gentry be going cross the frontier a-morrow, and I do wonder if you be not wanting to go with'um."

The frontier ; there had been no "frontier," even officially, since the Great Unification ("The Big Union"), but old manners of speech . . . and of thought, which gives utterance to speech, *That which has no form of its own giving it to that which becomes formed* . . . died hard. When (here is this remote area) they ever died at all. "Going from the Avar Land into Scythia, are they?" he asked, lazily stretching before the fire on which a red-hearted chestnut log burned. "Where there?"

The answer checked his lazy stretch. "Why, sir doctor sir, to the Sacred Grove."

How could this be? The Sacred Grove was far away. It was. Was it not? A moment's reflection showed him that, really, it was not. *He* had gone there before, from Bella: a longish trip. He had come *here,* from Avar-Ister — another longish trip. But from exactly *here,* St. Mammas's Inn, to *there,* the Sacred Grove, was not really that far at all. Eszterhazy had not come to St. Mammas's Inn in Pannonia directly from Bella in Scythia, because there was no direct railroad connection, and even sufficient connection via diligence — "stage coach," they called it in Northamerica — was lacking. But rapidly he conjectured vision of a map, from here to there was but a small way indeed. He might easily go. Why should he not go? He could think of no reason why not. "Yes, Karrólo, I think it an excellent idea. Have them pack me some food . . . and a little brandy."

Idly, he picked up the Avar-Ister newspaper, and turned to the classified notices. He made a mark in a margin.

The picnic went well enough. Karrólo would have felt his house disgraced if there had not been the usual seven sorts of sausages, seven kinds of cheese, and seven of pickled things and seven of pastry. In order to minister to the possibly more finicking tastes of the gentry, Hanni, his wife, who had worked a while in Avar-Ister (sometimes called "the Paris of the Balkans" by people who had spent more time in the Balkans than in Paris . . . a lot more), had prepared *sandwhishkas* — thin slices of this and that between thin slices of bread. She had even made cucumber *sandwhishkas,* though her failure to peel the cucumbers occasioned mild merriment.

"Such a lot of gingerbread," said one of the ladies.

"It is traditional," explained one of the men.

There is a spirit in this man; whatever did that mean?

The air grew rather hot, but there in the shady grove it stayed cool. Now and then a breeze brought wafts of resin from the pines round about. "Look what I've got on my shoe," a young girl whimpered. Her mother made an exclamation of disgust, said that there must be a dog around. One of the guests laughed.

"Not at all," he said. "It is merely some old gingerbread. And the rain and dew have made it soggy. People come here all the time. And every time, they bring gingerbread."

Eszterhazy said, "I don't wonder, it is such good gingerbread. I only wonder that so much of it seems to be lying around, instead of having been all eaten up. Why is that?"

The same man said, "It is traditional." And then, with a gesture, he said, "Look!"

Some distance away the employees of the Inn were also eating. While they watched, the blackbearded coachman took up his piece of gingerbread, broke off a piece, placed it on the ground, straightened up, began to eat the rest. "Why?" asked a lady. And, "Yes, why? Ask him why, do," said the other ladies.

The same man raised his voice, called out, "Hoy, Coachie!" in his citified Avar. "Why do you put a piece of such good ginger bread on the ground to get mucked about? Are you feeding the stoats and the fieldmice?"

It took a while for "Coachie" to understand. Then, with an obvious

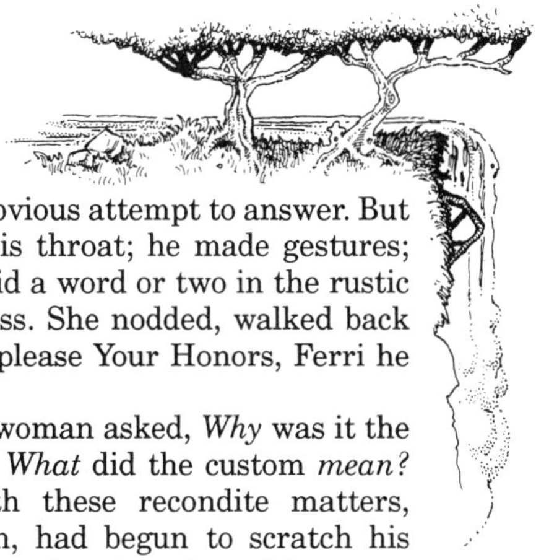

intention to be respectful, he made an obvious attempt to answer. But he felt awkward; the words stuck in his throat; he made gestures; finally, in a voice too low to carry, he said a word or two in the rustic dialect to the woman serving as waitress. She nodded, walked back to the picknickers, curtseyed. "If it do please Your Honors, Ferri he say it be the custom."

This would not do. Not altogether. A woman asked, *Why* was it the custom? Another demanded to be told. *What* did the custom *mean?* "Coachie," not prepared to deal with these recondite matters, scratched his head, scratched his chin, had begun to scratch his armpits: stopped, under some dim apprehension that this was a gesture not socially accepted on all levels of society. All he had wanted to do, really, was drive his coach, tend his horses, eat his victuals, and leave a piece of his gingerbread in the grasses where bloomed the blue cornflower and where the blue chicory blossom blew. And while he thus floundered, the man who had first addressed him, perhaps from pity, perhaps from condescension, said, "Ah, the peasantry, they have their own lot of customs sure enough; for example, when the man comes in from his work, he —" His mouth continued to move but his voice had quite stopped; he grew very red in the face: Eszterhazy, whose own sympathy for the coachman had begun to be aroused, now transferred it to the nearer and more immediate necessitous.

"My legs are stiff from riding and then sitting," said Eszterhazy, getting up awkwardly enough to lend credence to his remark. "A brisk walk is what they need; will you come along for a walk with me, my dear sir? — and point out things to me?"

The man scrambled to his feet, brushed his legs. "Love to," he muttered, avoiding eyes. "Love, love to . . . love to. . . ."

When they were off by themselves, hot sun breathing down, the odor of grass replacing that of leaves and resin sap, Eszterhazy said, "Well, now, you have aroused my curiosity —" He paused.

"Hanszlo Horvath. I know yours. Lord Professor Doctor Eszterhazy."

"I am pleased to meet you, sir. And, oh, simply 'Dr. Eszterhazy' I have never been 'Lord,' my grandfather, yes; not I. And, really, never 'Professor,' either, though I have taught a class or two. Well, now, but what is it that the peasant man does when he comes in from his work?"

Horvath guffawed. "Well, then the woman pulls off his boots. And he breaks wind. And she says, 'Be glad for good health.' Ho ho ho!"

"Ha ha ha!"

"Huh huh huh! Well! So you see, sir. One could hardly tell that story in mixed company among the gentry."

"No, no. Certainly not." Among the gentry, no. And among the aristocracy? Certainly. Well, never mind. "What is that large building there? — down over *there?* I don't remember it from my last visit, a few years ago."

Hanszlo Horvath said, which one? that one? (There *was* only one in sight.) Ah. *That* one. That was the new mill. The new mill? Yes. Some very clever chap from Bella, an engineer chap, had put it up. A faint bell rang in his companion's head. "After all and why not?" declaimed Horvath, his voice ringing and echoing in the gorge down the sides of which they made their way on the old track, half-trail, half-stairs. "Why should all those things be found in Russia and Prussia, why shouldn't we have them here, too?" He gestured. Following the movement, Eszterhazy saw a newly-painted sign. **Great Tuned Harmonic Turbine and Compressed-Air Engine Industrial and Manufacturing Association, Stg.** Sure enough. **Stg.** This was the latest attempt to get Scythia-Pannonia-Transbalkania into the ranks of modern commerce; **Stg.** was the equivalent of **Inc.,** of **Ltd.,** of **Pty.,** and it stood for **Stockholding.**

"Sure enough. Well. Horvath, shall we go and have a look?"

"Might's well," said Horvath. " 'Be glad for good health!' ha ha!"

The tuned harmonic etc. water-power plant was now established, and a factory with ample space had now been established, too. Ample . . . and empty, too. What was to be done with it? What use to be made of it? Brozz was with difficulty brought to bring his mind to bear upon this problem, and, indeed, could not easily recognize it as a problem at all. *He* would have been immensely content simply to watch his engines enginating all the day long, without other consideration. But it had all, after all, been brought into being by a Syndicate largely commercial in nature, and the commercial members of the Syndicate (or Association) had other ideas. They had after all raised what would in other parts of the world have been a lot of money; to the Triune Monarchy — where wealth still tended to be counted in terms of acres and arpents and horses and horned cattle — it was an immense amount of money. The resources of the European industrial world had been summoned to supply the machinery; and if most of it had come from England and Scotland (most of it *had*), some of it had come from Prussia (none of it from Russia), Belgium, Switzerland, and Sweden. So. Set up, was it. Excellent. What next. Brozz had no idea.

Brozz had no idea, but other Stockholders had, and they brought forward one Herra Gumprecht Ruprecht, a foreign thread-spinner. Herra Gumprecht was in search of cheap fibre, cheap labor, cheap space, and — the possibility suddenly occurring — cheap power. The heavy-smelling Upland wool was coarse, coarse, coarse; and . . . perhaps for that reason . . . it was cheap, cheap, cheap. True that for every white strand in a typical clip of fleece of Upland wool there was a grey, a yellow, a brown, and several black strands: but this was all

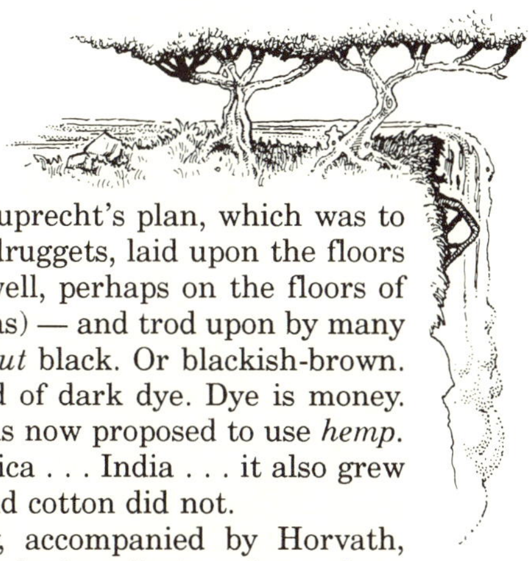

perfectly suited to Herra Gumprecht Ruprecht's plan, which was to supply thread to weave druggets. And druggets, laid upon the floors — not the floors of palaces or villas (well, perhaps on the floors of the servants' quarters of palaces or villas) — and trod upon by many muddy boots, required to be no color *but* black. Or blackish-brown. And the darker the wool, the less need of dark dye. Dye is money. Druggets often had a cotton woof; it was now proposed to use *hemp*. Perhaps hemp grew in Egypt . . . America . . . India . . . it also grew in Scythia-Pannonia-Transbalkania. And cotton did not.

Brozz nodded civilly as Eszterhazy, accompanied by Horvath, appeared. The engineer was supervising the installation of some item and had just called, "A full meter clearance on all sides" to the work-crew. Now he said, as calmly (and as abstractedly) as though they were again (or still) in the suburbs of Bella, "You see how very clean it all is."

"I do see. Yes."

"No fire. No smoke. No cinders. No ash."

"None. True." He didn't add, And no reason why your absurd engine should *work,* either. . . . For if it *did* work, what then? Then it did. And that was that. Brozz was after all the engineer. Eszterhazy had after all not gone over the patents, the blue-prints, plans, specifications, calculations. What he had heard and seen in Bella hadn't persuaded him that it ought all to work — at least not on any large and practical scale. Did it really? Well, well, they would see. Wouldn't they? Now all he said was, "And the water is nice and clean, too."

A very faint cloud came over the face of Engineer Brozz. "Sometimes there is sludge," he said. Eszterhazy was about to ask about this when two gentlemen, investors, board members, appeared, and — seeing new faces — bore them away to the board room, produced cold beer, produced a neatly printed prospectus and an application for the purchase of shares. As he had left the engine-room Eszterhazy had heard Brozz say, yet again, "A full meter clearance on all sides." And then he had heard Brozz catch his breath and he saw Brozz kick something. Heard Brozz say, "I won't have this." The doors closed. Rather odd.

But perhaps not.

There was nothing in the least odd about the way the investment possibility was urged, but something else was odd . . . definitely so. . . . Eszterhazy could not at first have said why. Walls were rising for the new mill-pond, which should produce a very high head of water indeed. Eventually. It was Summer, the water was down, it was more easily diverted to allow the work to go on. What was odd, then? Something certainly was. He sought out Brozz, after they had left the board room. What was the projected height of the new wall? . . . of the new mill-pond? Ah, *that* high. That was more like a lake than a pond! Yes, one had to be assured of a good store and a good fall of water. A good high head of it. It would not of course all be contained by the wall, the dam. The natural features of the landscape would also serve to impound the water? Yes, of course, quite. The vale —

. . . beside a grove, standing in a vale

"Excuse me, Engineer. But, ah . . . ah . . . it seems to me that the new lake or pond or — that it would, if my hasty mental calculations are correct — that it would drown the Sacred Grove. Eh?"

Brozz gave him an abstracted look, turned away, called, "A full meter clearance on all sides," turned back. "Excuse me, one must repeat things very often, else they may not be done. What did you ask? Flood the . . . the what?"

"The Sacred Grove."

The engineer's eyes looked into his own. "What is the Sacred Grove?" Brozz asked.

Perhaps it was not so surprising that the man *had* never heard of the place; were there not many people who *had* and yet had never heard of a vacuum-pump or a compressed-air engine? Brozz had, to be sure, seen the site; he had seen every square meter round about; to him, however, it had been merely a natural declivity in which water might be impounded and made to fall from a considerable height. Its historical associations literally meant nothing to him, and neither did other possible uses for the water. It had seemed to Eszterhazy, and he could not refrain from mentioning the results of his quick calculations, that the water might more profitably be used to turn a dynamo and generate electricity. But this conveyed no more to Brozz than had the phrase *the sacred grove*; his mind for twenty years had been bent in one direction, and it could not now be bent into another. The huge brass and bronze engine parts, the immense segments of iron and steel moved incessantly; the fly-wheel, the walking-beam, the revolving-flying globes, the cogs and all the rest of the equipment. "And all so clean!" over and over again was Brozz's exclamation. "No fire, no smoke, no ash, no cinders: only water and air! So clean! So clean!" (What was a little sludge?) See the great tuned turbine turn!

There was certainly a deal of merit in what he said. Eszterhazy had seen the Black Country of England and its continental equivalents; to compare it to Hell was a simile in a state of fatigue, but what other comparison *was* there? Pillars of cloud, black cloud, by day, and pillars of fire, red fire, by night. Soot falling down like snow, the earth riven open for coal. If indeed it were possible for the inevitable degree of industrialization which the country must experience to be based on water and air, well, so much the better. It would be too bad about the sacred grove or Sacred Grove; one could not have everything, of course. The changes along the Little River and its tributaries would be considerable.

Would, eventually, inevitably, be immense.

Must be immense.

And not there alone.

Eszterhazy realized this, and with something less than an absence of total discontent. But he reassured himself, as most would, that change *was* inevitable — and, in this instance, that change was at least to be minimized. The earth need not be wounded to yield coal, the forests need not be ravished to supply firewood. Only that the water, flowing anyway, would flow through channels. And, if no man ever bathed twice in the same river, the river having meanwhile flowed on; well, the same river would never turn any wheel twice. And, so, what of that?

Nothing.

Back at the Inn of St. Mammas, there on his desk was the Avar-Ister newspaper, folded, as he had left it, to the classified notices.

And there, in the right hand margin, next to the pencil-mark he had made, was *this:*

> Dr. Szilk will receive into his own home a very few gentlemen as residential private patients. Secure care. Full board. Excellent attention. The Rose-colored House, 102 Great St. Gabriel Street near Pannonian Gate.

Why had he marked *this?* There were always such notices in the newspapers; oh very well, there were always such *advertizements*: not always as discreetly worded as Dr. Szilk's was. It was not clear if his "private patients" were shrieking mad or merely moody or nervous. But this was the key to something which had been locked a while in Dr. Eszterhazy's mind. Dr. Szilk's sanatorium in Avar-Ister — had he ever visited there? No. But he had visited others like it, in (for example) Dr. Rothenbueler's, in Bella.

Among the particular ideas of Dr. Rothenbueler's in Bella was that tight clothes were too unhealthy, dark clothes too depressing, bright clothes too exciting. And there, on a visit a few years ago . . . a tall, thin man . . . loose light-grey jacket and loose tan trousers . . . a mere glance. But now proving enough to identify. So. Engineer Brozz had once been treated for a crisis of nerves, eh? This might account for much. And it might account for . . . currently . . . nothing. Nothing at all.

Nothing.

Eszterhazy was now a candidate for the degree of Doctor of

Literature; at times he felt rather as Petrarch must have felt when, having gone all the way to — was it Ghent? — in order to copy a rare text of — was it Cicero? — he discovered that he could get no ink in Ghent. How could they have managed without ink in Ghent? Well, perhaps they had not needed ink just then: one did not copy texts of Cicero every day. Agreed. But — Ghent was a commercial center of no mean size; how had they kept their records? The answer might have been that they used tally-sticks. And not ledgers. It was certainly more easy to make tally-sticks than to make ink; however, one could not copy with a tally-stick.

Still. . . . Was there not somewhere in Scythia-Pannonia-Transbalkania where the tally-stick was still in use? What had this to do with a degree of Doctor of Literature? Eszterhazy decided to adopt for his little motto, *Often pause and turn aside.* And, having paused and turned aside, he recollected that the tally-stick was still in use in the hills behind Gro. *Gro.* What . . . ? He consulted his scrapbooks. This, what: *and in the Late Pre-Christian Era, Gro prospered from the Slovatchko Pilgrimages, as the then-pagan Slovatchkoes passed through on their way to a sacred grove where they worshipped their Twin Gods: Charnibog the Dark and Byellibog the Bright.* Ah, yes, that Sacred Grove again. Peasant unrest again. It was time to look into it again. It was time to consult Grekkor again; Grekkor was an ox-drover who had advanced to being a cattle-buyer, knew the region behind Gro, the Preez country, in and out. Grekkor was often in Bella, was he in Bella just now? He was. And that afternoon he came and brought Eszterhazy up to date on the dam.

The work on the dam was proceeding, but it could not be said that the work on the dam was proceeding in all respects smoothly. An official, or at any rate a semi-official, protest had come from the priest of the chapel in the grove — officially the Chapel of Sts. Ulfilas and Methodius. *Was* this ancient shrine, dedicated to the holy missionaries to the Goths and Slavs, *was* it to be drowned and flooded in order to enable (so the complaint went) the dung-locks of sheep to be spun more expeditiously . . . and more cheaply? But Prince Preez had perhaps been anticipating this, perhaps Prince Preez had already spoken words into ecclesiastical ears: at any rate directions were given that shrine and chapel be removed to higher ground: and, as these directions came from the Bishop, that took care of the objections of the priest. Further remonstrances, that the people were all accustomed from the most ancient times to affix certain bits of cloth to the trees in the grove when they made their petitions and said their prayers, and that they would no longer be able to do so if the trees were flooded and drowned — these remonstrances were met with pontifical censure of a sternness which had not been anticipated. Such customs were superstitious, such customs were heathen and pagan and perhaps even heretical, such customs were best aban-

doned, and the sooner they were abandoned the better. Penitence, prayer, and charity did not, could not, should not depend on such rites and rituals. The Bishop did not indeed say, *Off with their heads!*; bishops could hardly say such things nowadays; but there *were* things which bishops could say nowadays; this Bishop said them: those who persisted in making agitations on the subject (this Bishop said) could hardly expect to apply for dispensations to marry their second cousins. And, as the people in those parts very often *did* apply for dispensations to marry their second cousins, in order to keep old-time properties within the family, resistance ceased.

Or, to employ another terminology, resistance went underground.

Dr. Eszterhazy listened. He asked, "And so the people — ?"

"They won't work on that dam. Goths, Avars, Slovatchkoes, none of them people will work on it. Brought up a team of navvies from The City," *Bella* being understood, "and almost directly, *they* downed tools and made their own way back. I don't know exactly *where* in Hyperborea they found the bunch of backwoodsmen they got working now —"

Eszterhazy's face showed his surprise. "What? Oh, but surely the Hyperboreans are just as prone to superstition as —"

"Oh, *more,* far as that goes, sir. *But they have different superstitions!*"

Oh. Well. Hmm. *Yes*. They *had*. An oak-grove by the river's brim a simple oak-grove was to them. And nothing more. "So. And so the people in the mountains close around? Have they offered any violence? Any —"

" 'Offered,' yes. But, well, the Stockholding folk, they've got the Rural Constabulary on guard. And then Prince Preez, he's got his own men on guard, too. Mind you, no, they won't do a lick of work themselves on this dam. But they keep the others, the locals, from interfering. Prince Preez, he can't call out the *corvée* no more, but . . ."

Prince Preez. As far as living in the country, in his own country, was concerned, Prince Preez could hardly need spend a kopperka from one year to another. Food, wine, wood, even woolen and linen cloth, all were supplied by his own tenantry as part of rent. But Prince Preez did not care to spend all his time on his estates, in his house in Avar-Ister, his house in Bella. More and more often of recent years Prince Preez, glossy-red-faced Prince Preez, liked to travel to Vienna, to Florence, to Paris. To tarry on the Riviera. To turn a hand of cards. Throw a cup of dice. . . .

To *live* . . . as it was called.

All this was increasingly costly (Prince Preez did not always *win!*) and Prince Preez could not pay the costs by giving the railroad a wild boar, however neatly gutted, or even a score of wild boars; his foreign hotels would not take homespun or hogsheads of sour crout or souse;

he could not trade his own vineyards' bullblood wine for champagne. He could not cover the stakes at the casino with cordwood, game, venison, or veal, or ever so many wagonloads of barley. All this required *cash*. Therefore Theobald Dieterich Gabriel Mario Maurits, eleventh Prince Preez, had given a 99-year lease to the new Company, wherefore the new Company had made him a Stockholder in the Stockholding and as soon as the Stockholding produced profits the prince would receive Dividends in the form of cash. *Cash*.

Until then? Until then, nothing.

Hence the huntsmen of Prince Preez and the herdsmen of Prince Preez and the housemen of Prince Preez, lots and lots of them, in their linen and leather livery of red and brown, with their boar-spears and their muskets and their shotguns and their whips and their dirks and their axes and their cudgels: and all on guard. Night and day. Day and night.

But scarcely had Eszterhazy assimilated this, gotten the picture of it formed in his mind, when — "And then there's them gingerbread men, sir."

" 'And then' — *what?* There's **what?**"

So it was that Engelbert Kristoffr Klaudius Eszterhazy, with his baccalaureate, his licentiate, and his (by now) four doctorates, learned of the peculiar — and, rather, pitiful — form of protest to which the people of the mountain had been reduced. Grekkor thought perhaps they had used their children (their very small children) to smuggle these mute protests past the piquets and patrols . . . could there be a milder or a more moderate protest than these edible dolls which it was customary to enjoy in the Sacred Grove? — leaving, of course, a piece behind, uneaten, perhaps by way of quit-rent for the privilege — a more humble reminder? Hardly . . . though . . . even so . . . how even small children managed to get past the lines of guards, with their fires and their torches and their lamps and their lanterns, was a wonder. It was a great wonder.

Later on.

There had been an outbreak of the ailment commonly called "coals of fire," or, in a fancier word, anthrax; and Eszterhazy, both as a qualified physician and as a member of the Higher Consultancy of the Royal and Imperial Hospital (commonly called "The Big Sick-house"), had been discussing the outbreak with Doctor Umglotz, the Assistant Supervisor. Umglotz declared himself to be a "regular old-fashioned physician," given to the traditional and the tried and true. None of your fads for Umglotz.

"Bleeding, blistering, cupping, purging," he said. "If they don't work, well, then nothing works."

Eszterhazy nodded. "I see. Well, which have you tried for anthrax?"

"Tried all of them."

"I see. Well, which one works?"

"None of them works," said Umglotz, with immense calm.

And he was quite right. None of them *did* work. Reading the write-ups on the afflicted, Eszterhazy observed something else. "All of the victims, Doctor, are employed at the Ister Woolen Works, it seems."

"They are? Yes, yes. I see. They are. Well. No surprise. Where folks are working in that line — where you find wool and hair, you know, well, there you find anthrax. Dirty work. The beasts of the field, my good Eszterhazy, they do not employ the *shower-bath,"* he employed the English term: the shower-bath was not greatly used in Scythia-Pannonia-Transbalkania; "but what would you? We cannot always wear cotton and linen. Every trade has its troubles, hatters go mad from the felting-mercury, vintners die from the acid gas in the great vats, trainmen are smashed in wrecks, and . . . and . . . and so it goes. Hazards of the chase, my good Eszterhazy, hazards of the chase. The dirts of the wool and hair get into the lungs. The sick, like the poor, as always with us, you know. Else what should we physician fellows do for our living; eh?" He shrugged and chuckled, then made to ring his bell. "Our good Royal and Imperial master sends us here regularly a pipe of excellent Rainwater madeira, and I am going to make you drink a glass of it before you go."

His good Eszterhazy knew better than to suggest that even a glass of it be sent instead to one of the dying. "Willingly," he said. Then his head jerked. "A sudden thought, Assistant Supervisor. When wool-working was what the English term 'a cottage industry,' when a single family raised sheep, sheared, carded, spun, wove, and all —"

Umglotz rang his bell, begged his good Eszterhazy's pardon. "Yes, yes, quite. Go on, please." Eszterhazy went on to say that in such a situation, if a family had the misfortune to encounter a tainted fleece, the outbreak of anthrax might be at least contained within that cottage and family. Whereas, when a tainted fleece was worked upon by an entire factory-full of people —

"Yes, yes. Quite. I quite see your point. Well, what would you? People don't want to stay in their cottage. They want to come to our beautiful, exciting Big Bella. And who can blame them; not I. Ah, here it is! Let me fill your glass. Sercial is nice, Bual is nice, but as the Emperor is benevolent enough to send us Rainwater, I am loyal enough to maintain that Rainwater is the nicest madeira of all; drink up, my good Eszterhazy. Drink up!"

Having drunk up, and having declined a second glass, and acknowledging that being sent on one's way with a glass of good wine was better than being kicked down a flight of stairs, Eszterhazy nevertheless left The Big Sickhouse with a rather disturbing trend of thought still trending its way through his mind. Not even the beautiful, reflective Ister, of the sight of which anywhere on its course he never tired, was able to distract him. Excellent as Engineer Brozz's intentions were to provide his native nation with a new (and clean) system of power and manufactury, there seemed always some objection, and always some further objection, to arise. And it was of this, in general, and of this latest potential objection in particular, of which he thought and was thinking as he made his way over the beautiful Swedish Bridge, towards his home.

He was *not* thinking of what the Honorable Hiram Abiff Abercrombie, sometime United States Minister to the Triune Monarchy, termed The Remarkable Law of Coincidence as Exemplified by One-Legged Men Wearing Blue Baseball Caps. General Abercrombie (who had been drinking prune brandy purely, as he said, to "maintain the integrity of his intes*tin*eal tract") explained that baseball was a game native to his own Great Republic, that the players wore caps of various colors, that such caps were sometimes worn by men not at the moment playing baseball, that you might go a hundred years without seeing a single one-legged man wearing a *blue* baseball cap, and that — tarnation! — one afternoon you'll see three of them! And Abercrombie was moved to explain to his young friend Elmer Bert the full details of a great game of baseball played on the 4th of July in the year 1800 and 63, at Fort Fillmore, Missoula Territory, between the Soldiers and Indian Friendlies: but his young friend (without much difficulty) persuaded him to have another glass of prune brandy for his stomach's sake. And for his other infirmities.

Yet something of this so-called Law seemed to be at work; for, on Eszterhazy's having barely attained his chamber, there entered Kresht, the day porter, with a card on the flat palm of his hand. (Kresht, later succeeded by Lemkotch, had been provided with a tray for this purpose, but had persisted in using the tray as a way-stop for his glass of coffee, his glass of borsht, and his glass of tea with sliced citron and cherry preserve; until he had finally been excused the use of the tray for holding cards at all.) And the card, engraved in a crisp script, read *Engineer Hildebert V. B. Brozz.*

"Bring the gentleman up, Kresht."

"Yurp, Lord Doctor." And, having brought the gentleman up, Kresht brought himself down again, there to devote himself to his glass of rye-bread-beer, his glass of raspberry juice and hot water, and his glass of whatever else was his by kindness of the upper-kitchen woman with whom he had formed an entangling alliance. Kresht was later (not much later) succeeded by Lemkotch, who never drank anything at all . . . except whatever was in the flat black bottle which reposed in the pocket of his overcoat hanging Winter and Summer in

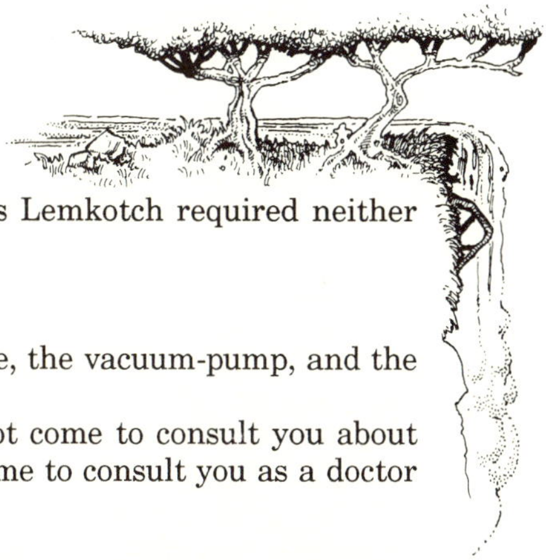

the lower front hall closet: and for this Lemkotch required neither glass nor tray.

But as for Brozz —

Brozz did not look well.

"How are the tuned harmonic turbine, the vacuum-pump, and the compressed-air engine, Engineer?"

Engineer made a gesture. "I have not come to consult you about that. At least . . . not exactly. I have come to consult you as a doctor of medicine."

Again . . . was it that absurd "Law"?

"I am such, it is true, certainly. But it is certainly true that I became such chiefly to mark a milestone on the march to knowledge, not to practice and have patients. Have you consulted, for instance," naming a well-known and "modern" physician, "Dr. Slawk?"

"I have."

"And what did he say?"

"That my liver was out of order. And he offered me a black pill." Brozz gazed at the beautifully-articulated skeleton in its cabinet, but its beautiful articulations did not seem to soothe him.

"Hmm. Well, but — Dr. Hrach?"

"Dr. Hrach, too."

"And he — ?"

"Said that my bowels were sluggish. And offered me a blue pill."

There was one more suggestion to make, and Eszterhazy made it. "The Scottish surgeon is —"

"Dr. MacIllivery. Oh yes. Him, too. He said that the acid in green tea, when over-indulged in, affected the connective fibre of the nervous tissue. Have I over-indulged in the use of green tea? Sir, I have never indulged in green tea at all. And as for the witch —"

It followed. "Yes. 'As for the witch'?"

Engineer Brozz took a slip of paper from a small leather pocket-case. "I wrote it down." He read aloud. " *'Water is thy greater fortune; and water, thy greater infortune as well.'* Now, what does that mean, my good sir?"

Eszterhazy began to say that it meant that she must have been a rather sophisticated witch; desisted. Surrendered. "Any pains in the small of the back? Any swellings of feet or ankles? Any difficulty in making — ? No, eh. We may dismiss a kidney condition or the like. Hmm. Did the witch say anything else?" For sometimes the witch was only a dirty and mean old man or woman, yet sometimes the witch was something else; sometimes a good deal more.

" 'Say anything else'? yes. 'Cross my palm with silver, handsome Christian gentleman.' "

Eszterhazy sighed. "Well, well. Be kind enough to loosen your cuffs and collar, and to open your coat, waistcoat, and shirt. Yes. Just so. Say nothing until I tell you to." The pulse was taken, the stethoscopic horn applied. At length Dr. Eszterhazy said, "There are some occasional, very minor, irregularities, but nothing very divergent from the norm. Pulse, heart, are both strong. Respiration normal. Do you sleep well? Can you eat? Does your vision waver? Any problem in hearing? — you never feel that others are mumbling? Your lungs seem sound." He withdrew the thermometer from the armpit. "Normal. Your eyes are only slightly bloodshot. *Well.* I can tell you nothing more; what is it that you can tell *me?*"

Brozz looked away from the skeleton, looked at the two immense terrestrial and celestial globes. Brozz muttered something very low. He let out his breath in a sudden gust. Jerked his head abruptly from side to side, twice. Then threw out his right hand in a bewildered gesture. "Listen, Doctor, I don't know if you remember, or if you ever saw, perhaps you never saw, years ago there was a mountebank, sometimes he used to stand at the corner of the alley between the Big Wood Market and the Old Stillery, a *very* odd chap —"

Eszterhazy's frown of concentration melted away. "Yes! A *very* odd chap!" His fingers now moved in a rather peculiar manner, wriggling, jerking, bobbing; and he made a crooning sound, a not-quite tune. The effect upon the engineer was not pleasant. His lips and eyelids seemed to snap back. He made a wavering, wordless sound in his throat. Then his widened eyes darted down past the physician's moving fingers, down . . . almost . . . to the carpet-covered floor. And next he uttered a shuddering sigh and for a while remained silent.

The mountebank, yes. He did not, literally, mount a bench. No matter. Who was he? Whence had he come? Whence *had* he come? Whither had he gone? Was he still alive? A slight and sallow man, almost dark his face was, and the skin around his eyes was dark indeed. In all weather he wore a short waistcoat exposing much not-very-clean shirt. His trick? Out of scraps of heavy colored paper a sort of doll or puppet had been made, and from any distance at all it seemed as though the man's mesmeric gestures caused the two-dimensional doll to dance at his command. From right next to him (and only sometimes was he at the corner of the alley between the Big Wood Market and the Old Stillery; sometimes he stood by Sellzer's Spelt Stores or Klungman's Bristles For Brushes, or near the Old Little Uniate Chapel, or the Sailors' Rest) from right next to him it was apparent that a single thread from his right hand kept the marionette up and that threads from each finger of his left hand made head, arms, and legs move and caper. And all the while the odd man keened his odd sub-song. He never indeed seemed to collect much money . . . but then his invested capital was minimal. And his rent was nothing at all. And now Eszterhazy shared the memory of him. And patiently waited.

"You see," Brozz said, by and by, "first I attended the old Bella Pantechnical School in Upper Hunyadi Street. Then I went to

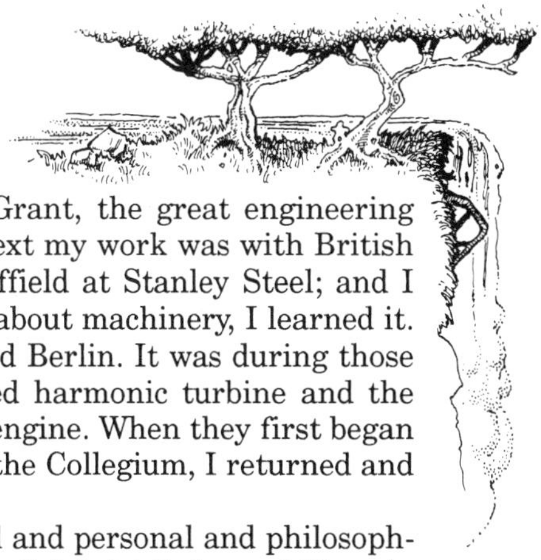

Scotland and worked with Watt and Grant, the great engineering firm in Glasgow and Edinburgh, and next my work was with British Looms Ltd. in Manchester and in Sheffield at Stanley Steel; and I may say: what there was to be learned about machinery, I learned it. I studied in London and in Brussels and Berlin. It was during those years I began to think about the tuned harmonic turbine and the vacuum-pump and the compressed-air engine. When they first began the advanced technical studies here at the Collegium, I returned and obtained the engineer degree. . . .

"My entire adult life, my professional and personal and philosophical *res*; well, though I was raised in the Calvinist Reformed Church, I am not *very* religious, my nature is purely pragmatic and rational, and absolutely I have not a trace of superstition in my nature. So . . . when I say . . . you will not assume that I . . . do I not impress you as sane?"

"As perfectly sane." Brozz may not have been as pragmatic as he thought; but he was certainly sane. Or *seemed* so. So far. Still . . .

"So when I say that I am —" He did not precisely pause or hesitate; only, his voice stopped.

Eszterhazy produced and proffered the (possibly) missing word.

"— haunted —"

Brozz did not react other than to resume speaking. "I am haunted," he said, in a dull, dead voice. His face was thinner than ever.

"You are haunted by paper puppets?"

The man's face showed, fleetingly, first surprise; then, though quickly suppressed, annoyance. "No! What? 'Paper puppets'? No, sir, what makes you think — Oh. I see, I understand. No, *that,*" he moved his own fingers in the manner of the mountebank (if this were not too high a title to have given him, poor starveling wretch); "*that merely* reminded. *That* — reminded me of . . . the other. And . . . the other . . . reminded me of . . . *that.* But no. If I tell you that I am haunted by, oh, ghosts, revenants, vampires, werewolves — whatever — you . . . or anyone . . . might not believe. But even if you were scornful, it would be with a serious scorn. Yet . . ." He looked up, helplessly, as though, almost, his sense of horror was mixed with an equal sense of humiliation.

"At first, merely I saw them by one or two. Just lying around. I thought the workmen had been slipshod, careless. Then these things came more often, and more and more often. Soon one began to realize they were getting into the water supply, dissolving into a sludge, clogging . . . sometimes . . . clogging the machines. And also clogging them with stones, pebbles, fragments of splints. And then next I began to see them out of the corners of my eyes, moving . . . moving . . . walking . . . and when I would, often, at night, lose my self-control and chase after them . . ." His words ended in a soft sound half-sigh, half-groan.

Even softer: "Yes?"

". . . they would run away . . . and never . . . I could never catch them. . . ." His voice had sunk, now it rose. "Who would believe me? Who will ever respect me? They —"

"What are they?"

The engineer's somewhat bloodshot eyes looked at him in a mixture of defiance and shame. "They? What are — ? They are the gingerbread men."

Everyone called it the "Old Avar Bakery." But the place itself did not call itself so, the weathered sign had to be read at a certain time of day with the sun at a certain angle, and the sign read THE FAMOUS OLD GINGERBREAD BAKERY AT WHOLESALE AND RETAIL. It read so in Gothic and it read so in Avar. Everyone knew of it; and everyone knew of the Hospice for the Innocents, the orphanage run by the uncloistered nuns. Eszterhazy had bought a large box of the confections for, as he let it be known, to give to the Hospice, and paid cash: all matters disposing the shopman to answer questions. How did they make their excellent gingerbread men? In old cherry-wood molds. Where did the ingredients come from? "Well, sir, the eyes and mouths we make from them tiny raisins that grows in them Turkish islands where the Greeks do live, currants we call 'em, sir." Yes. The isles of Greece and the cities thereof. Corinth. Currant. Yes. And the other ingredients? "Well, sir, the ginger and the m'lasses they comes from India, from the Indies, sir — Virginia and Jamaica and them-like other Indian places. And — and the what, sir? And the flour? Well — no, not from the Bella Steam Mill, that grinding, well, we doesn't care for it a-tall. 'Twon't taste the same, you see. We use old fashioned style flour. Water-ground meal, we uses. Where it comes from? From the old mills way up the Little River. Sir. And mostly the honey, too."

Rain had washed the soot off the railway-carriage windows, but rain allowed very little to be seen as the train made its way, and that little was so wavering as to convey not much. As Eszterhazy pulled a window up and before he pulled it down again he looked upon a sodden landscape. Not far off another train on the narrow-gauge branch-line seemed to move along like a procession of gondolas crossing the Venetian lagoon. It was after all his own private car and if he cared to keep the window open no one might gainsay him. He did not care: he had a boxful of things to read, and he did not want them rained upon. He would see the scenery later. Another time. When it stopped raining. If it ever did.

Rain in Scythia, rain in Pannonia, rain in Transbalkania — rain in *Cis*balkania, for that matter. The rain was falling on the Acropolis and on the black mountain of Montenegro. All the Italian alliances in the

world could not keep it from raining on Illyria, nor on the Hungarian shepherds in their shaggy capes. In the soggy delta of the Ister the Romanou gathered in their mucky huts, close around their smoky fires, ate smoked eels and thoughtfully wiped their fingers in their arm-pits. Here and there and everywhere the Tsiganes headed for drier ground and kept their keen black eyes open for drowned pigs; they had some very good recipes for drowned pig. In Klejn Tinkeldorff, Eszterhazy's Tanta Tina clicked her tongue, and helped the housekeeper hang the washing in the kitchen. And, a few blocks away, Music Master De Metz sat composing motets. He did not know it was raining.

At the last train stop the diligence-driver helped the porter with Eszterhazy's baggage. "I don't know for sure will we be able to get Your Honor to the last stage, this here rain here be so heavy. They say as God be punishing this here district for that bloody new dam as will drown out the Sacred Grove, what a blasphemous thing to do." He shook his head, scattering more rain, as he tight-hauled the rope on the tarpaulin cover for the baggage.

"Why, man," said Eszterhazy, "this rain is falling not just here and not just on our country but all over Eastern Europe; they say it is the heaviest rain in many years."

The driver looked at him doubtfully. "Not just here? Not just on — How does Your Honor know?"

Eszterhazy was not disposed to stand chatting while his clothes grew soaked. "Telegraphic reports," he said. And got inside.

The driver, who had not a hope of keeping dry, looked at him through the window. "Ah. *Tel*egraph. *Oh.*" He had no more idea of how the telegraph worked than had a child, but he believed in it as surely as he believed in witchcraft. He pulled down the isinglass window, touched his hat, and mounted to the box. If the mica set into the leather flaps failed to keep out the wet, the passengers might lower the canvas curtains on the inside.

The driver proved right, as such drivers generally do: they had *not* been able to get Eszterhazy to the last stage, and so, leaving his baggage in charge of the manager of the post-station at the last stage but one, he had obtained a horse. It was still only afternoon, "though late, late was the hour," yet the rain and mist and clouds so occluded sight that he had ridden through many a night with less trouble. There came a time when he felt he might be better going on foot than on the back of a rain-blinded and nervous horse; and dismounted. He had intended to lead the beast, but the beast had other ideas; with a powerful jerk of neck and head it tore the leathers from his slippery hands and, with one last, loud neigh, made off. For a moment he was in fright for it; then, seeing it heading downhill, the way it had come, he thought the animal was likely to arrive safe enough (if wet enough) at its own stable. In a moment he had forgotten the horse and concentrated on keeping to the road.

He could scarcely see; he could hardly hear. It was no mere rainstorm which made the overwhelming sound now beating incessantly upon his ears, and which bothered him more than the wet. When he reached the new factory he would be out of the wet, into dry clothes; but would he be away from the noise? Soon enough he had an answer of sorts, though not the one he would have hoped for. The road crested at the top of one of the hills, the road was going down, was turning to keep to the river, and —

Lines from an old Scottish poem, again courtesy of his aunt Lady Emma, supplied themselves: *The river was great, and mickle wi' spate. . . .* Had they ever seen anything, though, like *this,* in Scotland? *He* had never before seen anything like it in Scythia-Pannonia-Transbalkania. Incredible sight. The water was a filthy hue of brown; God knows how many farms (in effect) were dissolved in it. To say that the river was swollen was to waste the word. The river had gone mad; the river was insane; the river rioted; and, grown vast and huge, the river seemed to throw challenge at the rainy heavens. There were no banks. There were no bridges. The sound of the waters drowned all other sound, almost it was drowning thought. Limbs of trees hurled and hurtled down that titanic millrace, were thrown high into the air, crashed back down in fume and spray but with no distinct . . . with, even no *in*distinct . . . noise of the fall. Timbers whirled around like straws; several times he saw the forms of cattle appear, whirl, bob, dive, vanish. They must have been long dead by then. And the unstable water made the stable earth tremble and shake.

How could the new dam stand up against all this? Could it? Well, probably. If they, there at the new factory below, so to speak, and alongside the dam, if they opened the sluices and allowed water to escape from the sides as well as over the top. *If* they opened the sluices? By now and in fact long before now, they of course must have.

He had heard much of all the men on guard roundabout this area by night and day, but he saw no one. He saw nothing, neither man nor beast. Animals looking to find refuge on higher ground by now would already have found it . . . found it, or been drowned. The water-birds?, where were they? Somewhere. Somewhere else. Not on the surface of the new-formed lake. He could not soon or easily become used to this new-formed lake. It was too unfamiliar, it was entirely unfamiliar, there was nothing he could recognize —

Stop.

Of course there was.

He recognized the vasty oak trees rising from amidst the waters and knew that he was looking at the Sacred Grove.

How long would and could the Grove's trees survive, half-sunk beneath the waters as they were? He did not know. Bit by bit and very cautiously he advanced, but it was not easy; the road had become in part a stream-bed, and where not that, a mud-slick. And yet (he

saw) he had been rather wrong, for there were living beings moving about; what were they? Children, very small children? No. Marmots, perhaps? Perhaps marmots, moving *en masse* in search of safety? Were there marmots here? Ground-squirrels, perhaps? And yet why did he keep thinking that they might be children, when plainly they could not and —

He saw them coming and increasing. He saw them coming on. He saw them coming, like an army of tiny brown pygmies, waving their stumpy ginger-red-brown arms. Their tiny black-marked mouths opening, wordlessly for all he could hear above the pouring rains and rushing waters. Had they something, each, in their small and fingerless hands? Were those mere meaningless motions, movements, gestures? Were they, seemingly, threatening? Stabbing? Against whom? Against what?

And as he watched, body wet and cold and numb, repeatedly dashing the rain from his forehead, again and again mopping his smarting eyes with his sodden sleeves, he saw the ranks . . . Deucalion's Flood? who had thrown the stones from which this race had sprung? or sown the dragon's teeth? . . . saw the ranks waver, saw them tremble. Saw them melt, melting away. Ebb. Fade. Vanish. Gone.

Had he seen it? How could he have seen it? He could not have seen it, therefore he had not seen it. *Not.*

But how close it had seemed to come to him . . . as close as . . . as that tree. His eyes sank from the rain-soaked bark and bole of the ancient oak (surely of course not one of those there during the ancient days: but how far removed? perhaps grown of an acorn of an oak of an acorn from one of the pagan oaks: only three removes; what said Solomon? *a three-fold cord is not easily broken*), his eyes sank to the ground. He took a step forward, and another, through the quaggy mud and mire. A brown mass overlay the rain-flattened grass. Mud. Merely mud? Ginger-red-brown mud, where all other mud was black? Did it not look rather like melted meal and spice and — ? And another flash, and on the ground something sparkled, sparkling here and sparkling there: mica, it was surely mica, small deposits of it lay all about here and there in this region. Mica. *Was* it? Heedless of the sheets of rain pelting his back, he bent, almost knelt, and picked something up. And another. And another. Incredulous, he felt something a moment later sting his spasmodically closing hand. He forced his fist to open. There among the muck and grass and blood he saw, by lightning flashes, tiny points of sharp flint. *Sharpened* flint. *Flints.* He turned and fled, tottering and slipping; he turned and fled.

Then he turned around again. Turned again, saw again, screamed again, fled again. *Turned* again. There in the gloom, half dark air and half dark water, he saw them again. *Them*: Again they surged forward, again their stone weapons threatened and glistened: again they seemed to melt. He now knew that, whatever they threatened, they did not threaten him. He waited and he waited and the lightnings flashed quite nearby and it was as though — had a signal been given? — had the electric surges animated something inanimate? *that which is formless giving form to that which becomes formed?* To some sort of primal slime, out of some sort of primal sludge? The *them* were larger now, ever so much larger, they were human-sized now, their weapons were larger, still they came on, as rough-shaped, still, as (indeed) the gingerbread-men for ages eaten in this grove, parts of them always left uneaten. An arm. A hand. Head. Leg. He followed, stumbling. Warning himself. Must watch himself. Watch yourself, man. Watch your step. Don't fall or slip. The river. The lake.

(*Where,* now, were the herdsmen, housemen, huntsmen of Prince Preez? And if they had been here, what might they do? Pursue? The words rang in Eszterhazy's ears, *You can't catch* ***me,*** *said the gingerbread man!*)

Once again the crude *them* sank sodden and collapsed. Once more he waited, while the river and (he must suppose) the spillway of the dam roared and thundered. And once more he saw the Figures rise and take form out of the earth, wavering, become firm. Their faces no longer toy-like, doll-like, their faces giant-like. But they were now ruinous and eroded faces; their forms?

Male, female, sexless, androgynous, furious, faceless (now), huge and vast: and the rains came down and the water roared — the Figures leaped forward into the rain and mirk and were lost to sight. And then the almost all-embracing noise for one horrible moment became utterly all-embracing indeed, something like a cataract in reverse heaved up in torrent, the fountains of the deep were truly broken, the saturated earth trembled and quaked; he sank upon his knees.

When he had recovered and was able to stand, though the rains had dwindled to drizzles, though still the waters rushed and foamed, they had ceased to roar and now they only loudly groaned and droned. Thick mud such as might have greeted the eyes of Noah lay all about the Sacred Grove, where . . . long and long ago . . . the ancient Avars and Slovatchkoes and Goths, sometimes together and sometimes apart, had come to perform their heathen rituals, to honor God in the plural before ever they had ever learned to honor God in the singular . . . and, before, even, then, whatever ancient-most kiths and races had dwelt here then: proto-Pelasgians, perhaps, or ur-Hyperboreans and paleo-pagans whose very names were lost . . . but only mud lay round about the giant oak-trees now. The lake was gone. The pond below was gone. The millrace was gone. Save for a shattered stone groin, the dam was gone. The factory was entirely gone. Stripped of limbs and

branches, trunks of trees lay here and there in heaps like giant jackstraws. It was far later and far downstream that, the sun shining as though there had never been rain, Eszterhazy encountered a broken (broken? *shattered!*) piece of machinery which he did not at first recognize. By and by he saw that it had belonged to one of the sluices. *The sluices!* Why had not the sluices been opened to relieve the enormous pressure of the waters inside the dam? He saw the answer to the question which not he alone had raised. The smashed joint or whatever it was had not been opened because it could not have been opened because, doubtless they had tried, but it was jammed shut. And with what, Dr. Eszterhazy now saw.

Aloud he repeated the words, once, long *long* ago (it seemed now) of Engineer Brozz: repeated them aloud: " 'Stones, pebbles, fragments of splints.' " For there they were indeed, there (jammed, crammed) the stones, there the pebbles, and there the — " 'Fragments of *splints'* ?" he cried. What had that meant? Nothing; it was gibberish; his ears had deceived themselves and him. *Fragments of flints,* was what the man had said. Fragments of *flints.* Had, simply, the encroaching waters simply opened up and washed down the remnants of some Stone Age encampment or workshop, or — No. He knew what he had seen.

He looked at the flints. Some of the fracture-lines were new, others as clearly *not.* What trove, troves, of Neolithic, perhaps even Paleolithic weaponry of chipped stone, flaked flint, had lain in the Sacred Grove? as though ancient sacrificers and sacrificial victims had taken once and again, time and again, need never take again, an immense and ultimate revenge against the immolation of that gateway between gods and men, the Sacred Grove.

Was that what had happened? What *had* happened? What had he *seen?* Well, he knew of course what he had seen. But what did it mean? Unbidden, words, entire lines, from the *Addendum to Procopius,* came to his mind as he stood there in the drying mud.

> Another reason which justified Justinian's waging war upon the Goths was their savage rites and customs, totally against religion and morality. For example, in the mountains of Eastern Scythia in a sacred grove by a sacred well or spring, the barbaric Goths are wont to select certain prisoners by lot and to let them loose and to pursue after them. The wretches unfortunate enough to be captured are not alone immolated to the demons who dwelt in the place sacred to them, but portions of their flesh are cooked and eaten. Others say, eaten raw. It is true that some so-called Christians who should know better maintain that though such a cruel rite once pertained there, it had been abolished after the Gothic incursion, and that the Goths themselves merely made effigies of meal and honey and it is these which they consume.

Effigies of meal and honey: mock-men, that is to say; proxies for the actual humans once actually sacrificed and eaten; the pagan Goths were barbarians, they were not savages. And . . . but . . . *effigies of meal and honey* . . . though it was level daylight and no actual lightnings flashed, something like a stroke of lightning now certainly flashed enlightenment upon him: it was not alone in ancient Gothic times that such "effigies of meal and honey" had been made and eaten, but they had been made and eaten ever since; were still being made and eaten right down to the present day, though no doubt the actual recipe had undergone change, changes. The Christian Church had tried to abolish, but had finally accepted this practice, for *You can't stop* **me,** *said the gingerbread man . . . !*

What had lain slumbering in the groves and woods and waters for centuries, perhaps millennia? Had anything? Had not . . . something? Had it or had they been created out of a sort of spiritual effluvium? as the result of immemorial worship, and the rites thereof ? or had worship (and its rites) resulted because Something was already there? Charnibog, for instance, the so-called Dark God of the ancient Slovatchkoes? or Byellibog, their so-called Bright one? But this was infinitely simplistic, and, perhaps, after all, nothing was there. *"Nothing is there!"* he cried aloud. And, *"There is nothing!"* Echo answered, *"Nothing. . . . Nothing. . . ."*

But something else answered, as though out of the mist and rain and sunshine and spray: You can't catch *me,* said the —

"There is a spirit in this man," Tanta Tina's old nurse had said.

It was very suddenly that he saw Engineer Brozz. The man was floating in a new-made backwater, floating on his back, so it seemed; but in fact only partly floating. In part something held him up, held him fast; and this gave a slight illusion to the scene: if one had known nothing else one might have wondered why the man had chosen to float, fully clothed, slightly moving his arms and legs.

Much mud and earth and gravel and sand must indeed have flowed upon and lodged upon him, one saw it lying in deposits all around. But, caught as the back of his belt was by the broken point of a limb of a half-sunken tree, suspended from the muck and mirk at the bottom, all debris and detritus had been washed away by the flowing waters, and only some specks of mica glittered and glistened on him here and there. Eszterhazy remembered and spontaneously cried aloud the man's own words:

"So clean! So clean! And all so clean!"

Though the flood was over, there was still an immense quantity of water which lay impounded by banks and shores and tangled masses of trees and other debris — "jams" or "rafts" this was termed in Northamerica; it had not been common enough in this country to take a name — and not far off this water formed a mere. Birds,

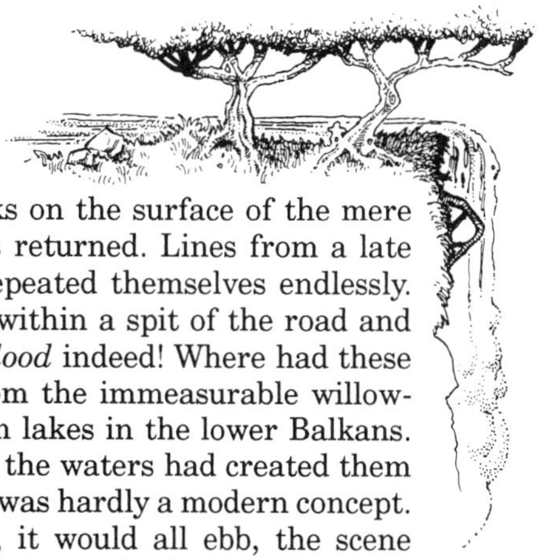

attracted from far away, rested in flocks on the surface of the mere and flew off now and then, but always returned. Lines from a late Roman Latin poet, *the buxom flood,* repeated themselves endlessly. The waters of this mere now came up within a spit of the road and seemed to swell the landscape: *buxom flood* indeed! Where had these birds all come from? Some of them from the immeasurable willow-thickets of the Ister, some perhaps from lakes in the lower Balkans. Others? Perhaps some infecundation of the waters had created them by spontaneous generation, though this was hardly a modern concept. The mere would soon enough subside, it would all ebb, the scene return to normal; meanwhile one might forget death and terror and avalanches and boulders ripped and trundled; here was green grass, green trees, blue skies, birds of many colors, ripple and lap . . .

Buxom flood.

The waters reflected the sky and the sky was an incredible blue, bluer than cornflowers or the blossoms of the chicory (why were all images of it suddenly botanical?), and all nature lay spent, as though after some episode of great passion.

Buxom flood.

"The late deceased learned Engineer was of the Reformed, that is to say, the Calvinist, faith?"

"Yes, Minister."

"Was there not perhaps some line or lines of Holy Scripture to which he was particularly attached? which I might mention in my brief address?"

No one had any reply; then an elderly man in old-fashioned clothing half-livery and half-uniform cleared his throat. "As an Under-sheriff, it's my duty, your reverence, to examine the contents of the clothing of the late deceased. And I find this in his little leather budget as he have in his pocket, wrappit in a piece of oiled cloth. This piece of paper, I mean. Ben't it Scripture?"

The minister — he was young and had yet to learn he might not dawdle whilst the impetuous dead were waiting — took the slip of paper and solemnly read it aloud. " *'Water is thy greater fortune; and water, thy greater infortune.'* Hem. This may be Apocrypha, I cannot say; it is certainly not Scripture as defined by the Reformed, or Calvinist, faith. Hem. I shall briefly speak on the versicle, *Above the voice of many waters, mighty waters, breakers of the sea, mightier by far is the Lord on high.* Briefly."

But when he saw how many graves had been dug, and how many were waiting to get into them, he was very brief indeed.

THE KING ACROSS THE MOUNTAINS

A perilous moment at the puppet-theater. The audience — consisting mainly of the children of the poor, there by themselves, or those of the lower middle-class, accompanied by their country-girl nursemaids; of the meaner class of peasants, up to the city to hawk a wicker-basket-box of dubious eggs; and of super-annuated servants given a penny to spend by Young Master, or of the commonest of common laborers, smelling powerfully of the fish-market or the livery-stable — the audience at the puppet-theater are sitting at the edges of the benches, wondering if Little Handsome Hansli is going to be eaten up by The Ogre. Little Handsome Hansli is wondering, too.

"*Who* will save muh from being eaten by The Ogre?" he cries (or, at any rate, a voice from behind the backdrop understood to be his, cries) allowing his dangling legs to buckle and his dangling hands to be twitched aloft in prayer; *"who* will save muh, will *no*bodduh save muh, will *some*bodduh save muh, will *any*bodduh save muh, and if so, *who?"* A good question. At this, the much bigger puppet, half-man and half-beast, chops its jaws to show its monstrous fangs and tushes, rubs its belly in the nummy-nummy sign, jumps up and down and makes menacing gestures and utters the famous gurgling-growling sound known world-wide* as "the chortle of The Ogre" — "WHO will save muh?" A thirteen-year-old baby-minder at this point beginning to whimper, her four-, five-, and six-year-old charges at once burst into loud wails. *"Help!* ***WHO?"*** cries out the Little Handsome Hansli puppet; whereat observe a not-overbright hostler's helper starting to his feet and being tugged back down by his convives under some dim adumbration that this is really not allowed. And whilst Little

* World-wide throughout Scythia-Pannonia-Transbalkania, that is.

Handsome Hansli's despairing hoot of "***Whoooo?***" rings through every dirty ear and a few clean ones —

— see suddenly appearing from *Stage Right,* a puppet truly marvelously adorned, and crying out, "I will save you, Little Handsome Hansli!" *Much* applause. This figure wears a tall, brimless hat of black samite, with a cross, rather like the archaic headgear of a Hyperborean Uniate mountain archpriest, hat protruding up from a large and battered crown; its garments a mixture of inauthentic military and ecclesiastical rag-tags. "*I* will save you from filling the upper and lower intestines of The Ogre, for I am PURSER-JOHNNY, the Slayer of Frenchmen, Ogres, Monghouls, and Turks! — take *that,* The Ogre, you!, and *this,* and *this,* and —" Much, *much* applause. *Shouts.*

Shortly afterward, having quitted the puppet-theater, "We have really nothing quite like that in The Hague," said Dr. Philosof J.M.R. van der Clooster, Director of the Stateholders' Collegium in the Dutch capital.

"No. Uniquely a part of our own rich cultural heritage, if that is what one would correctly call it," said Dr. Engelbert Eszterhazy, of many degrees and titles, and of the City of Bella, capital of the Triple Monarchy of Scythia-Pannonia-Transbalkania (fourth largest Empire in Europe [Russia, then Austria-Hungary, then Germany; the Turks, their European territories reduced largely to Albania, Thrace, and part of Macedonia, were fifth]). Doctor Philosof van der Clooster, on a trip around anyway the *Old* World, had stopped off briefly in Bella; and Eszterhazy was showing him sights. "I hope you have not picked up anything in that flea-pit. I warned you. But you *would* go."

"I have sprinkled with powder. But tell me, though, Compeer" — Dr. J.M.R. v.d. C. was a fellow-member of the Effectively Noble Order of Saint Bridget of Sweden (Savants' Section) — "who and what is or was *'Purser-johnny'?*"

"Prester John," said his compeer, shortly.

"Ah, ahah!" sang out the Netherlander, in high delight; "Prester *John!"* — as though the emphasis would save from confusion with any possible Prester Jane, Prester William, or (shall we say) Prester Olga. "I did think it would be most unusual for any mere *purser* to achieve apotheosis —"

"Most unusual," agreed Dr. Eszterhazy. Wondered if he should refer to the process for which the British in India had a name, whereby unfamiliar ethnically-exotic words were transformed into ethnically-familiar words — such as assuming that the names of the Prophet's grandsons, *Hassan* and *Hussein,* were actually the home-like *Hobson* and *Jobson.* He decided not to. Van der Clooster was very knowledgeable, but he was (often) very heavy. If, for example, one referred to "the songs of Homer," van der Clooster might ask if one meant

Homer, the Hellenic poet, or Homer Rodeheaver, the American hymn-singing evangelist. Eszterhazy observed, as they proceeded, the perhaps picturesque population of the teeming South Ward; but he for once (*once?*) observed without enthusiasm.

"Tell me, my dear Compeer," avoiding the erratically-located stall of a seller of "green" sausage, "who do you think Prester John really was?" — van der Clooster.

The mid-afternoon chimes of a clock-tower sounded nearby, informing them, musically, of the not-very-latest-news, *viz.,* that Malbrouk had gone to war. A wind, brief but brisk, stirred about the usual South Ward stirabout of old pie-papers, old fruit-peelings, dust, desiccated horse-dung; and blew away the ragged clouds, revealing patches of blue skies, revealing the mountains.

Some might perhaps perform the same tasks day after day, month after month, year after year, without fatigue: His High Highness the Heir, for example, never tired of hunting, or of taking troops on manœuvres; for that matter, Betti and Borri Kratt, who rolled meat-pie-crust in a room in an alley off Lower Hunyadi Street, never tired of mixing flour and water and processing dough. Did Dr. Eszterhazy never tire of reading books, of studying and studying, day in and month-year-out?

Sometimes, yes he did.

"Who do you think wrote the famous so-called Letter from Prester John, claiming to be both priest and king, thus causing medieval Christendom to look upon him as its possible savior from the Mongol Hordes; who?"

A flock of brown-and-white milch-goats followed its piping herdsman, ready to provide strictly-fresh milch as when/where called for, passed by; Eszterhazy, stepping delicately, avoided the evidences of its passage. "*Who?*" echo of Little Handsome Hansli? "One may only guess. *My* guess is that some medieval monk on Mount Athos wrote it, in a fit of boredom and wishful thinking."

Van der Clooster disputed the guess until they reached their next stop, the Archepiscopal Museum; and after that they called at Rudl's Famous Mussels with Fresh Sweet Butter House. And then they went to Dr. v.d. Clooster's hotel rooms for Holland gin. And then it was time to take the visiting savant to catch his train for Zagreb. Ah, Zagreb! Glamorous, sparkling, brilliant Zagreb! Eh? Well, maybe not.

Steam engineering, his current study, had grown lately just a trifle stale, perhaps from overwork; half, Eszterhazy wished to geologize a bit; half, he would study Sympathetic Ethnology, (i.e., Magic) among the Men of the Mountains. And, whilst he hesitated, the voice of a spirit whispered in his ear, "Why not try both?"

Geologists, amateur and professional, had tapped the rocks and stones of the Hyperthracian Hills, and, discovering no mines of gold and silver or precious stones or coal, had departed. Botanists bearing butterfly nets had sallied through them, failed to find exciting new specimens, and also departed. Each mountain (and each valley) was said to have its own peculiar count or prince — and some of them were said to be very peculiar indeed. This profusion of nobility was held, in Bella and in Avar-Ister, to be perhaps not in the best of taste. "If a man there has a cow, he's a count," it was said in those cities. "If he has two, he's a prince." The princes, anyway, were proud, even if poor; Bella and Avar-Ister did not like them? Of no importance, they did not like Bella or Avar-Ister. So there. They stayed in their remote reaches and recesses, reportedly pursuing, barefooted, the chamois from crag to crag, exercising the *jus primae noctis,* and administering the rough and ready justice of the region without much recourse to the larger and more lagging units of government.

Many thought these petty chieftains to be a joke, but Eszterhazy was not among that many. In his first class at the School of Geology, the Lecturer, trying to slide them in easily without the use of too many technical terms right away, had explained that mountains might be divided into two categories: "Young, *rug*ged mountains . . . and old, worn-*down* mountains." And had explained this and explained this forever. Eszterhazy, at least, would never forget it. The Hyperthracian Hills, then, were old, worn-*down* mountains. And their minor nobility were an old, worn-down nobility, dating back to the times of Tsar Samuel and the Bulgarian Wars, and the troubled era which followed. Who had held rule in Little Byzantia and the Hyperthracian Hills, then? who kept the poor man's crops and the widow's goat-kid from the fire? and, who had protected the pedlar's pack and market-stall? when the Palaeologian Dynasty in Constantinople was tottering to its end; and the Ottoman Empire not yet achieved that which was to allow a traveller, even as a conquered subject, to walk one league along a road in safety? Who had exercised *mis*rule was both easier and harder to say: *brigands,* certainly: nature was not alone in abhorring a vacuum, vacuums occurred in power as well as in laboratories; brigandage formed as scum forms on stagnant water. *Who* — in the as yet nameless mountains and wilderness areas later called Greater and Little Byzantia — who had filled that vacuum, who alone had enforced the Natural Law and the Social Contract?

The petty princes, then not so petty; the minor nobility, then not so minor.

That is not to say that they had governed well, for sometimes some of them had governed ill. But, as a certain ancient rabbi (Eszterhazy did not remember his name) was cited as having said, "Pray for the welfare of the government; for, were it not for the fear of it, men would swallow one another up alive."

Of course nowadays, he thought, glancing at this official structure

and that, one placed one's trust in such institutions as the Constitutional Monarchy, the Parliamentary Rule, and the Dedicated Civil Service. And — looking elsewhere around the world — Gad! one had better!

On his way home from the perhaps over-large railroad station, Eszterhazy, glancing helplessly from right to left from the midst of the usual tie-up of jammed wagons and carriages, observed a light landau of the latest design (with royal crest upon the door), the driver of which was rather recklessly plying his whip — and not seeming much to regard upon whose beast or body the lash came down. Seated in the carriage was a young man whose weakly-handsome features were immediately familiar: and not alone because he looked rather like Little Handsome Hansli, and this started another, and yet not dissimilar, trend of thought.

August Salvador Ferdinand Louis Maurits was the son of Ignats Salvador Samuel, Heir to the Triple Crown: in short, he was heir to the Heir. The Crown Princeling was in his early twenties, and some said that his rosy face was adorned with merely whiskers and weak good looks; and some, whatever they may have thought, did *not* say so. True that there were no *lettres de cachet,* no Bastille nor its equivalent: still, why make waves?

Baron Burgenblitz of Blitzenburg knew why — *he **liked*** making waves. "I say that we could learn a thing or two from the Turks in the matter of succession," said he. "Pick the likeliest lad among the next of kin, and as for the rest, strangle the lot!" This prickly Baron was not welcome in many houses in Bella; fat lot *he* cared.

When Bummschkejer's, the great drapers on Austerlitz Crescent, had exhibited its first wax mannequins, there had been enormous excitement. The woman-mannequin had been greatly admired for her Paris fashions, as she stood in the window. But when the throng in Bella had observed the man-mannequin, with his almost-impossibly-regular arched eyebrows, intense blue eyes, Cupid's bow and cherry-red lips, pale strawberry-pink complexion, beautifully fuzzy whiskers, and immaculately-shaven chin — an instant conviction had been formed that the mannequin was actually a statue of the Crown Princeling.

And what else of the Crown Princeling?

Ignats Louis, the King-Emperor, not one of your keen disciples of Pestalozzi or any other professor of theories of education, had said once or twice, "As long as the lad has learned his catechism and can sit a horse, who cares if he knows mathematiccy and the Spanish guitar?" On the few occasions when they — briefly — informally — met, the Crown Princeling addressed the King-Emperor as "Bobbo," and the King-Emperor addressed the Crown Princeling as "Baby."

As for the Heir himself, he was always rather busy slitting up the boars and stags which he hunted to the sound of drums and trumpets according to the custom of the antique *battue;* and when not, he was busy drilling his regiments. To the officers and men of his regiments, he applied more or less the same standard as his sovereign applied to the Crown Princeling, save that he was rather more liberal in regard to the catechism. "Mind you," he said, "I won't have no outright heresy in me ranks; none of them Dacians, Luetics or Pedagogues, or whatever they be called. But I ain't too pertickler if a man's a bit muzzy about the difference between them mortuary and them venereal sins, for I ain't too clear about 'em meself." There were said to be a *few* things which the Heir was none too clear about; never mind.

"But I hate a man who haven't got a good seat. Flog a fellow a few times and he'll sit up straight and do the jumps real good, see if he don't." One saw.

Under the circumstances, it was perhaps not to be expected that strict application to any course of study was required of the Crown Princeling; and this was just as well (Eszterhazy thought), because certainly none was forthcoming. He grew up able to sit a horse well enough on parade, and to hunt the boar and stag; and one saw him often at the lighter theaters and music halls and race-tracks and cabarets; and, beyond that, if there was nothing, well, at least one saw and heard nothing.

In an open and competitive examination for the Throne, Ignats Louis, the King and Emperor (King of Scythia, King of Pannonia, Grand Hetman of Hyperborea, Emperor of Scythia-Pannonia-Transbalkania) would not even have won a scholarship. But what he did not have in wits, he made up for by his immensely paternal personality, as the Heir made up for his own lack with a dogmatic doggedness which at least got things done. But with what did the Heir's heir, August Salvador, the Crown Princeling, compensate? Fortunate that the question was seldom asked, for there seemed seldom any answer.

Well! The King-Emperor was in good health, the Heir was as strong as a bull, one prayed for long life for both of them — and for the rest, one trusted in the principles of Constitutional Monarchy, Parliamentary Rule, and a Dedicated Civil Service —

Gad! One had better!

Eszterhazy had most recently seen the Royal and Imperial Youngling at the latest quarterly levee. Present was the entire Diplomatic Corps, including His Highness Sri Jam Jam Bahadur Bhop, Titular Personal Envoy of the Grand Mogul. The Grand Mogul himself was living, not very grandly, in exile, in Burmah, having (rather rashly) assumed — and not he alone — that the Englishmen visible in India had been all the Englishmen there were . . . and now and then he fretfully complained about the low quality of his opium ration; but these facts had as yet been but dimly perceived in Scythia-Pannonia-

Transbalkania, where the British Ambassador, Sir Augustus Fink-Nottle, saw no reason to press the point. He always bowed very politely whenever he encountered Sri Jam Jam, a nonogenarian who lived chiefly on Turkish Delight. The American Minister, General Hiram A. Abercrombie, not one of your sticklers for protocol, thought that old Sri Jam Jam *was* the Grand Mogul, and always saluted him. The old man, in turn, seeing that Abercrombie (in the democratic-republican manner) wore no uniform, believed him to be one of the butlers, and always gave him a tip. The general always took it. The carpets of the Titular Personal Envoy were regularly cleaned (for free) by the Armenian Lesser Merchants' Guild, which retained fading but still-fond memories of the protection offered by a long-past Grand Mogul to their merchant-shipping in the Indian Ocean at a time when it was being rather vexed by one Wm. Kidd, a Master of Craft, and one with some very *odd* notions of the principles of *meum* and *tuum*.

Also present and accounted for as a fully-accredited member, in fact the Doyen or senior member, of the Corps Diplomatique, was the Nobly Born Legate of the Grand Master of the Sovereign Order of the Knights of Malta; rumor, painted full of tongues, from time to time circulated in Bella to the effect that the Knights were indeed no longer sovereign in Malta; but the Minister of Foreign Affairs had a rather *large* back-log of work, and no time to pay attention to rumors. "Where ***are*** all these places in Southern America?" once he asked Dr. Eszterhazy, distractedly. "What *is* the Argentine Republic? Once there was a Confederation of the La Plata; *why* can I not find it on my map? The Emperors of Hayti and Brazil do *not* answer their *mails*. And — *is* the Confederation of the La Plata the same as the Confederate States, or is it *not?* ***Do*** we recognize these American States, or do we recognize only some of them, and if so, *which?* What and where ***is*** the Republic of Texas? Things were simpler before Bonaparte, don't you agree, Engelbert?" Dr. Engelbert Eszterhazy said that things were seldom simple, and that this was no exception.

"However," said he, "we must take things as we find them. I shall send you a minute on the American question. ["Oh, *thank* you, Engelbert!"] — meanwhile, should we not reply to the request from the Republic of San Marino to lower the excise tax on pasta . . . or is it pizza?"

"I don't know, it is so long since I have studied Dante," said the Foreign Minister, dolefully.

It was on this occasion — i.e., that of the levee — that His Young Highness the Crown Princeling, in reply to the question if *he* thought that Prester John had lived in Abyssinia, revealed that he had never *heard* of Prester John. Or, for that matter, Abyssinia.

"Is that the same as Absentia?"

"Oh, your Young Highness! Surely you will recall [*sotto voce*] that

Prester John was a mysterious and possibly mythical king who, it was hoped, would save the world from the Mongol Hordes? There *is* no such place as Absentia!"

"The which from what? Nonsense. Course there is. Remember What's-his-name, who fiddled the regimental accounts and fled the country? Was tried in Absentia, wasn't he?"

"Oh Your Young Highness! The Mongol *hordes!* Genghis Khan and Tamurlane! Towers of skulls, you know."

"Anything like the Tunnel of Love?"

A nearby and newly-arrived Emissary (from the Ty-coon of Cho-sen, or some such place and title), fortunately at that moment asked if he might hear some example of the native music of Scythia-Pannonia-Transbalkania. Dr. Eszterhazy's tenor immediately began the chorus to a popular tune of which the Noble Infant was sure to have heard; and in a moment the Crown Princeling's baritone enthusiastically joined in with

Port, port, ***port,*** *and*
port, port, ***port,*** *oh*
Heigh*-ho and* ***jolly****-oh,*
Oh, port, port, ***port****!*

If the Congress of Europe could only be run along the lines of a glee club, then Scythia-Pannonia-Transbalkania would be sure to prosper.

Meanwhile, it was certainly time for Eszterhazy to have his holidays — or, as the Americans would call them, vacation.

The Heir considered the boars of Greater Byzantia to be runty, and there were not enough stags; also the topography was not favorable to cavalry charges; and these opinions he carried over to the adjacent regions of the Hyperthracian Mountains. The Heir went there but seldom. And as there was a paucity of light theaters, cabarets, race-tracks, and music halls, the Crown Princeling never went there at all. But every seven and a half years, come drought or flood or whatever, the King and Emperor went there; and on one such visitation, years ago, Eszterhazy had been an equerry, Yohan Popoff a prince-host: and an odd sort of friendship had developed.

And so, soon after van der Clooster had departed for Zagreb, Dr. Eszterhazy put aside steam engineering for a dual-purpose visit to the Hyperthracian Hills.

"And what shall ye do with these wee bits of prettystone ye've gathered?" asked Prince Popoff, at table. *His* table.

"Set some of them, anyway, in brooches, and give them to my

aunties," said Eszterhazy, promptly — not wishing to bother his host with boring descriptions of trituration, spectroscopic analysis, and the like —

— and besides, some of them he ***did*** propose to set in brooches and give them to his aunties.

"Very good," said his host. "Then ye'll not be digging great holes and corrupting my peoples with moneys. Goats *fall* into great holes sometimes, if they be new great holes. And about the only times my peoples see moneys is when some strangers have to pause at the cross-stop and pay the imposts for their goods and gear. Which ain't often, as there are easier ways to get out of Austria than this way. To get *in*to Austria, for that matter."

Eszterhazy was not thinking much about Austria, save that he knew that the forthcoming Congress of Europe was to be held in Vienna. Mostly he was thinking how pleasant it was to be in this mountain fastness so far from Bella (and from Vienna, too, for that matter) and its cares, and how restful and trustworthy not-so-old Popoff was, and how rustic and pleasant he looked. Then at once there entered someone new to him, an old woman who did not think so. At all.

"You have no face, you have no stomach," she squawled at the Prince. "Look, look! Crumbs in your moustache, wudkey on your breath, wine on your waistcoat, your hair looks like badly stooked straw, last week's shirt; what an example for a prince of the mountains and a descendant of His Reverence — *I* don't know — my life has been wasted, poured out like wash-water; you might as well have grown up in the stye, sucking the grey sow's teat; where is the hot bread for the zoop, the hot *bread* for the *zoop?* Holy Souls in Purgatory, is no one at work in the *kitch*en?" Never ceasing to scold and shriek, she hustled out; old and scrannel, not in the least picturesque, boney and rat-toothed, leaving behind her the echo of her voice — like a badly-worn cylinder for one of the new talking-machines — Edisonola, it was called — and an odor of onions and armpits.

Eszterhazy supposed her to have been either mother or mother-in-law, or possibly the invariable "extra-aunt"; had she been mistress or wife, certainly she would long ago have been dropped off the Bear-Tooth Crag, with a couple of pig-irons (to be retrieved later) on each leg. But —

"She was my wet-nurse," said Prince Popoff, whose arcane talents evidently included telepathy; "of course I need a wet-nurse now the way I need another orifice in my fundament, but I can't get rid of her."

"Doubtless she is very faithful," murmured Eszterhazy.

Popoff scratched his thatchy chest, gave a *deep* grunt. "You ***think*** so?" he next asked. "I assure you she would poison my zoop for a penny if she thought she could cheat my sons the way she cheats me. I shall douse you with wine," he said, pouring a nice slop onto the be-sopped table-cloth, and a bit more into his guest's glass. This was old high courtesy, mountain style, and was supposedly to put Eszterhazy at his ease, and make him need not worry if he slopped some himself; how tactful, yes? Not according to the Uniate Exilarch, Venerable Joachim Uzzias, D. Th., III, who declared it to be a pagan libation, and had written a pamphlet denouncing it. The Uniate Exilarch never ventured within a hundred miles of the mountain principalities, for the princes would certainly have burned him alive on general and hereditary principles before the government could have interfered; perhaps to display his scholarship or perhaps from prudence, the Venerable had published the pamphlet in Ancient Armenian, doubtless to the edification and enlightenment of any Ancient Armenians who could read it. The *mod*ern Armenians, most tactful of living men, had bound their presentation copy in tooled morocco, and deposited it in a mesh-fronted bookcase, the key to which was immediately lost, in the Guildhall, in Bella. And had peacefully gone on about their business of roasting and grinding the best-grade coffee, washing carpet-wool, goat-hair, and hog-bristles; cleaning the rugs of all the best houses in Bella (the worst were lucky to have their trod-mud floors covered with fresh rushes twice or thrice a reign), including those of Jam Jam Sahib; and processing a certain quality of millet much favored by the Town Tartars for feeding to their cage-finches — but perhaps no more for now of the Armenians, excellent people; they scarcely enter this account at all. *Some*time maybe. Maybe not.

"Really?" enquired Eszterhazy, the nanny having re-entered with the hot bread and re-exited because there was not enough of it. "One is certainly told that the servants of this ancient house —"

"— been here forever," said Prince Yohan, a trifle mechanically; "or, at any rate, a very long time."

"— are famous for their loyalty and devotion."

"To the ancient *house,*" said the prince, starting to slurp his zoop. "Not to any particular member of it. Wait! Let me crush ye some peppers, else the zoop will be bland as maize-pap," he made a gesture — several gestures, in fact — and a pestle of malachite began to grind in a mortar of chalcedony (both, perhaps, once graced the table of a Grand Comnenus in Trebizond, before the horses and riders of Ottoman the Turk had galloped out of the east . . . and galloped . . . and galloped . . . and galloped . . .) — the mortar and *pestle* ground: no visible and corporal hands ground with them. Certainly not those of the rustic prince, which rested prominently a ways off, on the table. This prince awaited the response of Dr. Eszterhazy his guest.

There was no response.

The reputation of these minor semi-sovereigns for magic was of course well-known. *Well*-known.

"Take," invited Prince Yohan, concealing his disappointment, if any. "Take some on your spoon and stir it about in the zoop." His eyes roved round the setting on Eszterhazy's side of the table. "What!" he exclaimed. "They have given you no spoon? Animals! My father would have had them impaled . . . well, my grandfather . . . certainly my great-grandfather —"

The prince began to whistle, snap his fingers, stamp his foot. "Pray do not bother, Your Vigor," said Dr. Eszterhazy.

"But ye must have a spoon!"

"Certainly. And as you have told me often enough that your guests have the liberty of your kingdom, I shall take the liberty of taking your spoon." Eszterhazy indicated. With his finger. Did he crook his finger? He did something with his finger. And His Vigor, Yohan, Prince Popoff, watched dismally as his spoon slithered across the table, mounted into the mortar, gathered half a load of crushed peppers, and slithered across the rest of the table, coming conveniently to a stop-slither at Eszterhazy's hand. Who calmly stirred it into his zoop, then lifted the stoup to his lips, and drank off its contents.

"Excellent!" he exclaimed. "Delicious! Ah, there is nothing like a good, old-fashioned stoup of zoop!"

Said his host, at last meeting his eyes, "You have learned much."

"And still have much to learn," was the reply.

The prince gave, this time, a merely minor grunt. "Well, as ye have heard, as I have said, ye have, we both have, the liberty of — Well, I shall see what I can do for — You can read the Szekel runes, my guest?"

"Those, and others."

"The language of the Old Men and the Dead?"

"Both."

"Essential. And — Aramaic?"

"Yes. Though it depends a good deal on the characters used. The Hebrew ones I read with fair ease. The Nestorian, rather less so. And as for the Jacobite, I must first transliterate. Then I have comparatively little trouble."

"All right. And as for the medieval Latin and Greek, I am sure I need not ask. So. In the morning —"

"If you don't die in your own dirt by then," interrupted the old wet-nurse, entering with a tray pressed to her bodice. "Some of them pots hasn't been cleaned since Sobieski was King of Poland and Tessie was King of Hungary; much you care. Here. Sweet and sour sow. Certain, I culled the raisins with my own fingers. Who else 'ud do it? Not them high and mighty wenches, who creeps in and out of Someone's bed on their filthy feets. Ah —"

"Put it down, Wetsy," directed the prince. "And you may retire tomorrow and on full pension, as well you know."

She may well have known, but know it or not, she made no reply, but addressed her next remark to her one-time nurseling's guest.

The old woman had set a second dish down, evidently a pasta pudding with fat, spices, and honey; and she put her hands on her hips and looked at him. "So tell me, Sir Philosopher," she said, after a moment, "be's it true that some wiselings such as you, they are a-seeking for to make a machine which it will fly?"

The pudding, the sort which he would have killed for when a boy, looked impossibly heavy, and might have killed him now. There was a bason of small apples; he would numble one of them for his dessert; and in the meanwhile, the longer he could keep the conversation off the pudding, the better. "Yes, Mother," he said — and such a look she flashed at him! He had best remember not to "Mother" her again — "it is true. Some of them are seeking."

She asked, with every sign of sincerity, "Why don't they study trees? Shrubs?"

He asked, a bit puzzled, "Why? Are there trees and shrubs which fly?" She nodded, curtly, as though this itself was a matter well-known, and of not much interest. "*Oh.* How can one tell . . . which, I mean?"

"One goes and learns," she said. Prince Popoff ate silently. "One can tell . . . oh, by the way the knots are formed . . . for instance . . . and by the way the trees reach towards the sky. And the way the shrub-twigs behave."

A piece of the sweetened pasta, browned by the oven, fell from the prince's mouth to his waistcoat. He picked it up and put it in his mouth again.

"No more manners than the piebald dog," the old woman commented.

"Will you teach me, then? I will give —"

"No," she said. "I can't teach you. You are not ready. I can tell that by . . ." she reached out a finger-nail (it had not been cleaned lately) and let it rest a moment between his brows. ". . . the eyes. Maybe some day."

Her look, which had been a trifle abstracted, now came to focus on the present once again. Swiftly she scanned the table, then again she put her gaze on the guest. "And the zoop was no good, I suppose. They makes it better in Bella, I am sure."

Heroic measures were called for, else she might begin asking about the pudding. "First rate it was, Madámka. No, they don't. And here's something to prove it." And something popped up and peeped out of the doctor's pocket and described a parabola as it passed over the table. It was the size, shape, and glitter of a gold *royál,* and so perhaps it ***was*** one — though who can indeed be sure, as it came to rest in

Madámka's left ear, whither one would not have wished to follow and examine. Evidently feeling no such non-wish or scruple, she ***did*** examine it, immediately redeposited it in her bosom, made an antique curtsy (during which at least seventeen bones were heard to snap, crackle, and pop), and left the dining room in such haste as to make one suspect that she may have suspected Eszterhazy of being willing to change his mind.

Eszterhazy had earlier smoked a long pipe of the local, infernally strong *dabág* as it was called; he felt now a desire for the Indian weed, but in a milder and mellower form. Also he desired to remove traces of the meal from face and fingers. So, leaving his host with his own long pipe, his feet into the fireplace, and being smoked by sundry smokes; Eszterhazy ascended with measured tread up to his rooms.

Paradox was plentiful within the halls of Castle Popoff. When Eszterhazy went to wash his hands and face, he saw the basin was marble and the ewer was onyx; but, when having by and by dropped a quantity of segar ashes, he looked for a broom to sweep it up, he found no semblance of the familiar citified item of yellow straw, fitted up and stitched together by Tartar or Gypsy aided by a device like an enormous tuning-fork, no: he saw a bundle of coarse vegetation rudely bound to the butt-end of a stick; in short, a two-penny *bezom* such as one's country-cousin's servants use to expel the dried mud from the porch. Eszterhazy decided to let the ash lie. The Indian segar had been rolled around a reed; withdrawn before smoking, this left quite a nice air-channel, and required no cutting or biting of the end: curiously, as the ash fell upon the dark drugget, it retained the hole where the reed had been, thus clearly identifying itself to be the ash of a Trichinopoly cheroot, as any fool could plainly see, and hardly required reading a monograph on the subject.

Next morning. Going through the Great Hall in hopes of finding some breakfast other than the one deposited in his ante-room — a panikin of coffee astringent enough to tan hides, a pot of quite cold maize-pap, and the pickled head of a large lacustrine fish — passing through the Great Hall, adorned with rude and massive furniture, on or in which giants might have sat cross-legged and smaller men have camped, with rusting and not so rusting stag-spears and boar-spears, spring-guns and man-traps, banners warped and tattered with very great age, a ragged and hairless hide which might just possibly be (he thought, afterwards) the skin of a flayed enemy — walking through the Great Hall, Eszterhazy heard a low, murmuring voice, apparently coming from a room with an open door; automatically, he peeped in and paused.

It was evidently the chapel (or evidently *a* chapel) and within, with a minuscule congregation, someone was celebrating the Divine Liturgy. Or, to use the phrase favored by another facet of the One

Holy Catholic and Apostolic Church, someone was saying mass. Very well, the House of Popoff, though it had not particularly impressed him as being particularly pious, had a chaplain. And the Chaplain was reciting his daily Office. No reason why not. Though it was slightly surprising that the chapel door was almost immediately and silently closed in his, Eszterhazy's, face. Still —

In the immense kitchen where the somewhat surprised staff was giving him such citified foods as a pan of gammon and eggs, browned bread with goose grease (he declined the cracklings, at least for breakfast), and a cup of "weak" coffee — it was quite strong enough to satisfy the Death's Head Hussars, whose coffee was famously strong — in this corner of the huge kitchen, Dr. Eszterhazy let his mind wander back to the scene in the small room. Maybe the chaplain was some hedge-parson with dubious credentials, and that was why they did not want the guest to see him and perhaps inadvertently make a report. Well enough; understandable — but why, in that case, since Eszterhazy knew no such cleric, why was he so sure that he had a least partly recognized the priest, though indeed his face he had not seen?

Then, too, he was — despite the briefness of his glimpse — absolutely sure that the service being celebrated was neither Roman Catholic nor Eastern Orthodox; certainly it was not Uniate (or Eastern Catholic) either; having experienced many an English Sunday, he knew that it was not Anglican: what, then, was it?

Easier to ask, than answer.

Somewhat he had seemed to sense affinities to the Rites of Malabar. But the Malabar Rites had been abolished. *Had*n't they? And, anyway, somewhat he hadn't seemed. So — certainly it was something else. So. In which case, *what* else?

Of a kitchen-hand he asked at a venture, "Is that a *Romi* service they are holding up yonder?"

The kitchen-hand's reply, smacking nothing of the Council of Nicea, was, in toto, "You don't *like* your eggs, my Little Lord?"

It didn't smack of the Council of Trent, either.

"Sure I like them. Let's have another piece of gammon, here —"

"There bain't another piece of gammon, my Little Lord —"

"— and I'll let you have some real good snuff, Swartbloi's, the best in Bella." Eyes gleaming and nostrils twitching, the kitchen-hand departed, walking fast. By and by he returned, depositing on Dr. Eszterhazy's plate something resembling a desiccated bat.

"Cook have locked the larder, my Little Lord, and she keeps the key atween her you-know-whats; but I've brought 'ee a pickled pigeon, my Little Lord, up from the Servants' Cellar; and I've told Cellarman I'll share the nose-baccy with he."

Somehow the "Little Lord," Engelbert Eszterhazy, A.B., Phil. B., M.A., M.S., M.D., D. Mus., D. Phil., Ph.D., D. Sc., and much more,

did not fancy the pickled pigeon; but he gave over the snuff anyway. And, by and by, his host appearing, they went up to the Old Book Room in the South Tower and looked at a lot of old books. And then they went up into the mountains and tried — by word and song and gesture and something more — to move a lot of old boulders.

Some of them they ***did*** move, and some of them they ***did***n't move.

And what with one thing and another, the scene in the semi-secret sanctuary quite went from his mind. And it was a long time before it returned.

The earth of the Red Mountain (not very far off was the Black Mountain, Montenegro, an independent country whose prince-bishops had not very long ago become kings) — the earth of the Red Mountain had been transmuted by spring rain into red mud, and Eszterhazy did not move with perfect ease.

"I don't *mind,* particularly, shooting at a bird with a cross-bow," he said, out in the woods of the mountain with his instructor; "but I think I particularly mind shooting with a cross-bow at a great auk, because I well know it to be extinct; besides it never lived *here.*"

"Less rattlement," warned his instructor, "or I'll make ye shoot at a dodo. Up a little to the right, and forward."

Eszterhazy saw the great auk fall; but when he went to retrieve it (the hound absolutely refused), it had vanished. Some days later, however, he saw it in the muniments room, in a glass case. In the case next to it he saw a clutch of ostrich eggs. And in the glass case next to *it,* he saw the dodo. Both birds were smeared about the feet with what seemed to be dried red mud.

One day, not many days later, as they were standing at an open widow, Prince Yohan suddenly exclaimed, "Hah! This is scrying time. *Fine* time for scrying, this!"

Deeply interested, Eszterhazy asked, "How do you know?"

Prince Popoff showed him a face slightly surprised. "How ***know?*** Why . . . the time of the month — Taurus, upon the cusps of the Ram — the cuspal times are decidedly the best for scrying, one isn't sure why. — And then, too, observe the weather! The air's not flat and dead, such as leaves the living images lying slack all around, no: neither is there a tearing wind or storm, you know, that's no good, that tears the living images all up, and scatters them about, you see.

"But just look now. You see the air is clear and clean; you see how the clouds are scudding along and there's a brisk breeze. That means the living images will move along fairly quickly; it means that you can see them fairly clearly and cleanly in the scrying ink or in the scry-stone or scrying glass. One doesn't always use a pool of ink, you know."

Eszterhazy said he knew. "There are those who use a crystal ball," he said.

Prince Popoff now looked at him in more than mere surprise. "There ***are?***" he cried. He was absolutely astonished.

By and by, having recovered from his astonishment, he took his guest into an inner room where they had not been before. It had been plastered, but it had not been plastered lately, and patches of the primeval plaster had here and there crumbled and fallen, revealing — beneath the place where the plasma and slab of lime, sand, and water had been — areas of the primeval stone walling of the chamber. On the walls hung (often rather askew) badly engraved likenesses of the present emperor, sundry kings and so on; as well as wood-cuts of various voyvodes, counts, boyars, mukhtars and mamelukes and metropolitans and mprets and patriarchs and princes — God help us! — who knew who else? Eszterhazy, widely believed to know everything, knew not all of them — including a likeness of a sombre, brooding, melancholy countenance, a likeness (going by a name scribbled in a corner of the [perhaps] drawing) which he thought was perhaps of that John who was not only the last Catholic King of Sweden (bad timing, John) and enemy of the famous (infamous?) Gustav the Troll, but also the last Swedish King of Poland (bad timing, Poland) — though maybe it wasn't.

There was also a copy of the Martin Behaim map, with gores, presented to the English King Henry VIII, powerful presumptive evidence of the early discovery of Australia; only Henry wasn't interested in having Australia discovered (he was far more interested in discovering what he called the "pretty duckies" of Anne Boleyn), and neither was anyone in Scythia, Pannonia, Transbalkania, or Great or Little Byzantia. How came it here? Who the Hell knows; where it didn't have cobwebs, it had fly-specks. There were old globes almost moist with the foam of perilous seas in Faërie lands forlorn, and here and there were odd skulls of the wisent, the aurochs, the wild mules of the Veneti, and — perhaps, perhaps — the unicorn: and if it wasn't a unicorn, what ***was*** it? the rhinoceros, oryx, or narwhale? Nonsense. What would a skull of a rhinoceros, oryx, or narwhale be doing on the wall of an olden *schloss* in Scythia-Pannonia-Transbalkania? *Ha!* Have you there!

"You can have half my kingdom," said Prince Popoff, seating himself, "but you can't have my chair. Pull up another." And while his guest was pulling, the prince opened a small ebony chest from which he removed a something swathed in somewhat soiled white samite, and from the wrapping extracted a rather glossy black stone. Maybe Doctor *Dee* thought it was coal, and maybe Edward *Kelly* thought that it was coal, and maybe Horace *Wal*pole thought it was coal; but Dr. Engelbert Eszterhazy thought that it was not coal. Prince Popoff took it very carefully in his hands; and, saying, "Hold it like *this,*" held it like *this.*

After some moments, he said, "It is not necessary, but it helps to

repeat what was said by Bishop Albert of Ratisbon — oh, very well, then, *Regensburg* — called 'the Great' — Albertus, I mean, not the city —" and he repeated some phrases, in what some might regard as a rather debased Latin of the Swabian sort; others, on the other hand, might regard it as "Humanistic," and not debased at all.

Eszterhazy watched carefully, sometimes he had rather to squint, he did repeat the phrases as best he remembered them (he remembered them rather well); and then —

"Hm," said Prince Yohan. The surface of the stone, the upper surface, which had evidently once been highly polished, which so far had remained rather glossy or might one say sheeny, suddenly displayed a face. A human face.

At first Eszterhazy could not make it out. It seemed to slide across the face of the stone — or perhaps it was across his own vision — as though imprinted on a piece of silk which moved, passed, at an odd angle and in a way which he could no more identify than he could the likeness itself. Prince Yohan, though, seemed to be having less trouble. But then, he had had more experience. "Who is this mere child, of man size and, I suppose, man's estate?" he asked. Eszterhazy could of course not answer, though he strove to get the image back in focus as his host held it rather slightly obliquely.

"He must be of importance," the Prince went on, staring into the surface, "else why has Psalmanazzar scried him?"

"Psalmanazzar?"

"Yes. Psalmanazzar. Its name. *Ships* have names, do they not? And so do scry-stones. The scry-stone of my uncle-cousin, Baron Big Boris, is named *Agag,* because it walks delicately. A metaphor, of course. Well, as for this youngling, I see passion plain in his face . . . a mere prettyboy? no: more . . . I see lust, and resolution and ***ir***resolution, mixed. . . . Tell me, so, savant, who is he?"

And Eszterhazy again gazed swift into the scry-stone and swift he saw the face one instant fixed before it fled into flux and swift he cried aloud and answered, "O God! O Christ Human and Divine! It is August Salvador, the Crown Princeling! Oh!"

In the brief pause which followed, he noticed that the room smelled of mold. Then he asked, "What is he doing *here?* I mean, *there?* And is he near — or far?"

Said this wise man of the mountains, "Middling near. And getting nearer. What — ?"

Eszterhazy said that they would soon see *"what."* And, "How quickly can I get a message to the nearest telegraph office?" he asked.

Said Prince Popoff, "Write it. And we shall see how soon." He led Eszterhazy to another desk, satisfied himself that it provided paper which would take ink, ink which was not too gummy, a steel pen whose nib he promptly licked to make certain that it would hold the ink, and powdered cuttlefish bone to dry it. Then he began to bellow.

By the time Eszterhazy had finished the message and shaken the powder off the paper —

VON SHTRUMPF, OFFICE OF THE PRIVY PURSE, it ran. KINDLY INFORM WHEREABOUTS HH THE CROWN PRINCELING - E ESZTERHAZY

— someone was waiting to take the message in a large and hairy hand. A mountain pony, saddled and bridled and only a bit hairier, had appeared in the courtyard to carry the messenger.

"Stay for an answer," Popoff instructed. "And — Constable — if anyone tries to wait in the office to observe either the message or the reply, discourage him or them from doing so, d'ye ***hear?*** And all this under the invisible seal of silence; ***go!***"

A clap-clap of hooves and a flurry on the road. Then, "Now we must wait," said the price; "meanwhile let me show you further how holding the scry-stone so as to be best read is like holding the clinical thermometer so as to be best read."

Eszterhazy said, "Axillarily, I see no problem. Orally, I see a small problem. Rectally, I —"

"Haw!" said Prince Yohan. "Now . . . sometimes you have to shake it down first . . ."

IMPERIAL ORDERS, began the reply. DO NOT, REPEAT DO NOT, PERMIT TO PASS THE HIGH PERSON OF WHOM YOU ENQUIRE. SPECIAL DETAILS FOLLOW BY SPECIAL TRAIN. KISSING, VON SHTRUMPF.

" 'Kissing'?" queried the prince. "***Kiss***ing?"

"Undoubtedly the abbreviated idiom of the telegraph, and certainly stands for 'KISSING THE HANDS AND FEET,' and so on."

"Ah, just so, and highly proper," said the prince. "Well, the constable says he has had look-outs posted by the railroad at Zlink, and has given instructions that if a special train approaches *and does not stop,* they are to shoot at the engineer and stoker with powder and ball. Furthermore, we are piling logs upon the tracks a mile farther along, just before what we call Dead Man's Bridge Ravine —"

"I quite see why you do," murmured his guest.

"And whilst we're waiting, let's have some chops off last week's boar, and whilst we're waiting for *that,* let's have a pot of Mokha coffee with some Yah-mah-ee-ka rum. Eh?"

Said Eszterhazy, "Let's."

The "special details by special train" proved to consist, not in any manuscript list, but of elements reposing within the bosoms of two distinguished persons; as their carriage and horses had also arrived by the same special train, those same eventually drew up within the courtyard. And therefrom they debouched. They knew Eszterhazy. Eszterhazy knew them. He proceeded to make introductions.

"Prince," he said, "allow me to present Reserve-Captain Von Shtrumpf, Gentleman-Serjeant of the Black Rod to the House of Peers, and ex-officio Chamberlain of the Office of the Privy Purse;

Captain, my honored host, His Vigor, Prince Yohan Popoff." Both persons announced themselves to be *Enchanted;* and Eszterhazy proceeded to introduce Militia-Major Shtruvvelpeyter, a Principal Secretary to the Foreign Office. By a singular coincidence, once again the persons introduced were *Enchanted.*

It went without saying that the members of the Royal and Imperial Family were above being officially managed by any Government offices. (Brought over the Irish Sea to sign the death-warrant of Charles I after conviction by the so-called High Court of Parliament, Colonel Hercules Hunks — actually — forthrightly told Cromwell, "My Lord General, two things are certain. First, this court can try no man. Second, no court can try the King." Cromwell, not one to stick on ceremony, said, "Thou art a peevish, froward fellow, Col. Hunks. Get thee hence." In private, Cromwell conceded that Hunks may have been technically correct. But he cut off King Charles's head anyway. Oh dear.) Yet the Royal and Imperial money-bags of S.-P.-T. were something else. Hence the politely-named Office of the Privy Purse. Which provided a good deal of management indeed.

One might say, for example, "Surely Your Young Highness's sense of honor and duty will prevent Your Young Highness from taking such a course"; yet His Young Highness's sense of honor and duty might *not* prevent him from taking such a course at all. If, however, one were to say to him (for example), "Alas, there is not currently so much as a single kopperka to Your Young Highness's account in the Treasury. However, should Your Young Highness see fit to preside at the Dedication Ceremonies for the new Mechanical Drawbridge over the Ister and the new Civil Reformatory (dull as such ceremonies doubtless are), no doubt an advance subvention might be applied to the Office of the Privy Purse from the Public Works Accounts"; then one might manage him, if not quite well, then well enough. For a while, anyway.

Hence.

"Where is he, Engelbert, where ***is*** he?"

"Engli! Have you got him?"

" *'He'? 'Him'?* Have I got *whom?*"

Both officials replied in joint voice, *"Baby!"*

"Ah, the Royal Infant. The Crown Princeling," said Eszterhazy. "No, ***I*** haven't got him. I can tell you, on local authority, however, that he is middling near, and getting nearer. But . . . why do you ask?"

They were by now seated on the worn-smooth old front steps of Palace Popoff, or whatever it might be called. Vast vistas stretched in front of them: not merely blue in the distances, but beyond the blue, grey and brown and some nondescript and probably indescribable colors.

"Why do we ***ask*** — ?"

"— it is such a stupid story —"

The stupid story was soon told, unfinished as it was. Not only had the Crown Princeling — who was constitutionally forbidden to marry "a subject," because, as any fool might realize, to do so might and probably would create Faction — not only had he nevertheless made plans to do just that, but the "subject" was already married; a Gypsy dancer, she was already married to a Gypsy dancing-master and fiddler. More, she was estranged from him, and lived under the protection of (translation: was being kept by) a boss-butcher. ("One of the biggest stalls in the Ox Market, he has, Engli.") And what did His Foolship think of these trifling trifles? That they were just that. "Love cares nothing for trifles," he was reputedly reported to have said. Did love care nothing for the Constitution and for Bigamy? Evidently not a bit.

"Anyway, we are going to be married in another country so it will be all right," he had said. It made one want to beat his empty handsome head against a cattle-car.

So much for all hopes that he, only twice removed from The Throne, might get better sense as he grew older — and old enough to assume the three crowns which alone kept three countries together. The royal wittold did, however, take the precaution of travelling under another name; hence the hopeful card-case full of pasteboard imprinted with the name of BILL-SILAS SNEED, DRUMMER IN AMERICAN CLOTH AND CHEESE.

Really!

Of these three countries, one was Scythia, which alone among the Indo-European-speaking nations of the world, spoke a modern dialect of Gothic; one was Pannonia, which spoke Avar, not an Indo-European language at all; and the third, Transbalkania, was not properly speaking, a country or nation at all, but a confederation, the peoples of which spoke a variety of tongues. And none of these nations, countries, or peoples liked each other very much *at all.*

Only the Triple Crown of the Triple Monarchy held them together. And the heir to the Heir was about to contract an illegal, unconstitutional, impermissible, and totally impossible non-marriage, acceptable to ***none*** of his peoples. Oh dear.

More:

Did he not *know* that the city in which he planned his nutty nuptials, *videlicet* Vienna, was about to hospit the Congress of Europe — where Scythia-Pannonia-Transbalkania would attempt finally to rectify its almost-unrectifiable boundaries — and that in consequence S.-P.-T. would become a laughingstock? *No.* (Of course not.) Did he ***care?*** (Don't ask silly questions.) *And,* for a frowzy icing on this very rancid cake, just as Marie Antoinette did not want to flee from France until her diamond-crusted travelling-case was ready (In consequence of which delayed flight . . . well, never mind. Oh dear.), so August Salvador did not want to leave on his not-even-morganatic honey-

moon without his wardrobe. And, lest by an examination at the border of his baggage, with its crest-embroidered underwear, he be discovered, he had hit upon the — for him — brilliant idea of concealing it all beneath a Seal of Diplomatic Immunity. And of which Immune Diplomat was the Seal?

That of the Titular Personal Envoy of the Grand Mogul.

Oh ***dear***.

Popoff hauled out his maps; they were compared to those which Von Shtrumpf and Shtruvvelpeyter had brought with them. On which of the spider's-web of roads (assuming the web to have been spun out the posterior of a very drunken spider) which obtained between Bella and the border might His Young (not to say, infantile) Highness be assumed to be now in progress?

They came to no conclusion.

Popoff was not precisely shy about showing the use of his scry-stones; that is, he turned an enquiring look upon Eszterhazy, who nodded. That was enough for Popoff. Von Shtrumpf wished to be assured that no form of witchcraft was involved; Dr. Eszterhazy showed him in print, fetched down from the prince's shelves, that the last Ecclesiastical Council of Ister, whilst utterly condemning the ceremonial eating of horse-flesh on holy days "after the manner and usage of the pagan and damnable Sarmatians, upon whose so-called sacred places it is permitted, nay meritorious, to micturate"; said absolutely nothing on the subject of scrying: which was good enough for Von Shtrumpf. And Shtruvvelpeyter recollected that "he had read something-or-other about it in a French or German paper once — frightfully scientific these French and Germans were, not so, Engelbert?" — and that was good enough for Shtruvvelpeyter. So Popoff once again uncovered his scry-stones. *Psalmanazzar.* And *Agag.*

Psalmanazzar showed, briefly and rather vaguely, the Crown Princeling's face at the window of a vehicle; *Agag* (on indefinite loan from the prince's cousin, Baron Big Boris) proved to be a bit more precise as to what else the Crown Princeling was doing: he was picking his shapely nose.

"By the color of the mud splashed against the carriage window," suggested Eszterhazy, "I should infer that the carriage is now travelling along the Official Northern Remote Route Road."

"And if so, almost a sufficient punishment for his sins!" cried Shtruvvelpeyter. "The local holders of the electoral franchise so seldom choose to pay the very moderate poll-tax that, as a result, the road there hasn't been paved since . . . since . . . well, since quite a while ago. Or so they tell me. I have never been."

"***I*** have," said Popoff. "I trust that His Young Highness is not obliged to try any of the local hostelries. The fleas there are reported to be large enough to qualify as cavalry remounts."

Von Shtrumpf, however, was not interested in such matters. "If this crack-brained enterprise of August Salvador's is not nipped in the bud," he declared grimly, "our grandchildren may find themselves paying poll-taxes to Austria or Russia or — God help us! who knows what nation or nations which may snap us up as we come apart, like Poland, for lack of a sensible sovereign — Bulgaria, maybe — or Graustark, even — in any of which cases I shall migrate to Egypt, rather than submit. Very well, if 'well' it is, His Nipplehead is on the Official Northern Remote Route Road: what next?" And, before anyone could answer, added that there were worse fates than being bit by fleas, however large.

Eszterhazy rubbed his forehead with his knuckles. "Much as the magnetic telegraph has served to debase human language," he said, "still, it is swifter than any horse, or locomotive engine. The same telegram, in effect, which was sent *me,* should it not be sent to the cross-station at the terminus of the Official Northern Remote Route Road?"

Agreement was that it should; the message was redrafted, and handed over to either the same constable, or another available such; there seeming to be no limit to or shortage of men of that rank in the region of the Red Mountain; who had taken the message of enquiry originally drafted by Dr. Eszterhazy. And so then arose the question, *what* should they do in the meanwhile?

Von Shtrumpf chose to make a speech. "Only the existence of a single sovereign," he said, "keeps the Flemings and the Walloons together in Belgium. The same is true of Scandia and of Froreland. Of Austria-Hungary. And of Scythia-Pannonia-Transbalkania. Let the respected sovereign be removed, and what may the result be? Chaos. That's what."

Eszterhazy, a trifle more testily that was usual with him, said, "And my hair is getting thinner on top. What else is new?"

Popoff, who seldom displayed interest in any events of a political nature more current than the Pragmatic Sanction, which had confirmed Maria Teresa as (among other items) "King" of Hungary — the ancient usages of that nation making no provision for a Queen Regnant — pointed out that Switzerland had remained united as a republic despite its severalty of languages and peoples. It was pointed out to him that Switzerland had had more centuries to grow used to such union than S.-P.-T. had had decades; for a moment he grew silent. Then —

"I know what let's do!" he exclaimed. "Ye all know the trouble with boar-spears is that the momentum of the charging boar sometimes carries him, the charging boar, that is, right up along the shaft of the spear, so that sometimes he can slash his tushes into the huntsman before he dies. Well, I have had cross-guards set onto my new boar-spears, so as to prevent this. In theory. Why shouldn't we, in the

time we're waiting, all go out and see how this works? Eh?"

Shtruvvelpeyter said — let it not be said with haste, but without delay — that, alas, his gout —

And Von Shtrumpf declared that, being a servant of the August House, he had no right to risk his person in anything but service to that House. "Much as I should like to, of course. ***Love*** to."

So it was at length agreed that they should grill some chops off last week's boar (by now growing rather short on chops), and, in the meanwhile, have some good hot Mokha coffee with some good Yah-mah-ee-ka rum. And this was agreed to.

Before and after the grilling of the chops and the eating thereof, a game of whist was played, one of boston, and then another of whist; presently people began to squirm. Von Shtrumpf returned to his theme, but his heart seemed not in it. "And what keeps the Wallachians and the Moldavians united in Romania?" he asked, rhetorically.

"The subventions paid them by the Czar of Russia," was the short reply of Shtruvvelpeyter. As this was not the answer which Von Shtrumpf had expected to get, he followed the way of all flesh, and ignored it.

"What is delaying the fellow?" he asked. "Can he have stopped to drink somewhere?"

Prince Popoff did not appear worried. "Nothing is delaying him, except the fact that his horse has no wings. And when on such a mission, he would certainly not have stopped to drink somewhere. Fierce and faithful are the constables of this mountain region. He will be here in a minute."

With perhaps more precision than appropriate in a guest, Von Shtrumpf took out his heavy gold watch and clicked it open. "He will? Let us see." For a while nothing was heard except the grumbling of a well-masticated chop off of last week's boar as it travelled through someone's stomach and upper or lower intestine. Then the sound of a set of hooves clattering into the courtyard.

"Here he is now," said Popoff. "How long was that?"

"Bind-Satan-and-send-him-down-to-Hell! — ExACTly one minute!" he looked at his host with much respect.

There entered now, still sweating and steaming from his ride, a typical rural constable, which is to say, a typical mountain-man, with a leathern band affixed round his arm; on this was a much-effaced sigil, symbol, or shield, and a much-effaced numeral. The man bore in his hand a folded piece of paper, and this he handed over at once to the outstretched hand of Prince Popoff. Who gave it a quick glance, and swore.

"Bind-Satan-and-send-him-down-to-Hell, indeed! O Thou dear

Cross! But this is the message we gave ye to send. Where is the answer?"

The man brushed moisture from his bristly cheek and chin, and from his great drooping moustache. "There ben't no answer, My Worship," said he. "The clerk, he jiggles and he clickles his little clicket; and, says he, he says the string be broke."

"He says — *what?*"

"The *what* is broke?"

"That there li'-bit wire string as the message they say it pass along, what they *say,*" continued the constable, evidently no great believer in the miracles of magnetic telegraphy. "It has fell."

For an instant this curious image was considered; then, almost simultaneously the four others cried, "The line is down!"

The constable nodded his shag-head. Then he passed the back of his shag-wrist across his lips, a gesture evidently noticed and identified by His Worship. "Down to the kitchen, then," said Prince Yohan, "and tell them to give ye a big drink from the second-best barrel." The man brightened directly, bowed deeply, and was off immediately. Evidently there were barrels below, and perhaps far below, even the second-best. "Well here's a fine how-are-ye," the prince said. "No telegram can get through to the cross-station at the terminus of the Official Remote Northern Route Road."

Outside, a slight and soft Spring rain came mizzling down. Inside, the four men considered this new development. "Outrageous," said Eszterhazy, "that in a country abounding in goodly trees, telegraph wires should continue to be strung in places from shrub to shrub, and from bush to bush! No wonder the line is down . . . again. The wonder is that it is ever up, at all. Well —"

But Von Shtrumpf, still riding the rails of his one-track mind, said, dolefully, "Not alone chaos. Inevitably, civil war. Unless-unless — it may be treason to suggest, but — if not *this* heir to *the* Heir — then *who?*"

Who, indeed.

A moment's silence. Then: "Queen Victoria has many sons," said Shtruvvelpeyter, as though commenting on the weather.

The subject was seldom spoken of, but here perhaps the major, after all a principal secretary to the Foreign Office, had found the kernel in the nut. Not much may have been known about Salvador Samuel, self-styled "Sovereign of the Scythians and Pannonians," but it was known that he *had* married Magdalena Stewart: call her "Mad Maggie" who would, she nevertheless ***had*** been a Stewart (or Stuart) and a Royal Stuart (or Stewart) at that: she had also been an ancestress of the British Queen, however many times removed. And more than once, more than one mind in Scythia-Pannonia-Transbalkania had considered (with more than one emotion) of an almost-endless line of vessels ascending the Ister and bearing as it

might be such names as HMS *Take, Catch, Rake, Snatch, Seize,* and so on and so on; at least one of them conveying, as it might be, Prince Alfred, Prince Arthur, Prince Leopold, or Prince Who, with his umbrella and his cricket-bat and his crown. . . .

"Austria and Russia would never allow it," said Von Shtrumpf. *"Would* they? — we should all have to drink *tea!"* he cried.

But Eszterhazy had something else on his mind than the (possibly) enforced consumption of Orange Pekoe, Lapsang-Souchong, or Oolong. "I suggest that you two gentlemen of the Court consider what you both may think best; meanwhile our host and I will withdraw so as not to disturb you."

Withdrawn into an ante-room the open doors of which debouched upon the vastly wide steps, "Very tactful," said Prince Yohan. *"Very* tactful. And now that ye have got *us* both alone, what is it that ye wish to propose? Eh?"

"Would you very much like to swear allegiance," asked Eszterhazy, "to some, say, King Algernon or King Archibald?"

The prince surveyed the moist landscape. "Not very much, no," said he. "I won't speak of my own ancestral pretentions, every family has those — I suppose that your King Algebra or King Artichoke would be better than some King Vladimir or King Otto — always better King Log than King Stork . . . but . . . what . . . ?"

Eszterhazy shortly gestured to where the light sparse green had begun to grow up along the foothills, ranges, and ridges, of the Red Mountain. *"That* is what I would propose," said he. "Since His Young Highness the Crown Princeling cannot be prevented, via telegraphed orders, from entering Austria along the Northern Remote Route Road, he ***must*** be prevented by some other means; he must, in short, not be allowed to leave the country while this imbecile lust is upon him."

"And therefore?" Yohan looked at Eszterhazy.

Eszterhazy looked at Yohan.

"Need I remind Your Vigor of the ancient parable about Mohammed and the mountain?" he asked.

They were outside. They were by no means out of sight of any part of the castle, but they might by no means be seen from the front parts of it. "Some say that these mountains are worn-down, and not rugged," said Prince Popoff.

"Some do," murmured Eszterhazy.

"But parts of them are rugged enough, that it helps to know the mountain passes if you want to move an army through —"

"Indeed —"

"Not, right here — *here* — through these declivities and between these peaks, ye see —"

"I see."

"This is where he would have to come, Old Ginger I mean, ye see."

"I see," murmured Eszterhazy. *Old Ginger.* What a perfect nickname for the Holy Roman Emperor at the time of the Third Crusade: Old Ginger. That is (or was), Frederick Barbarossa. Of course his real name was no more Barbarossa than it was Old Ginger. Or for that matter, Hobson or Jobson. Still, it was an interesting survival, one which Eszterhazy had not encountered before.

It was an appropriate place for old survivals, here among the men of the mountains; for they were very much old survivors themselves. In fact, recollecting another old legend, that which had them pursuing the chamois, barefoot, from crag to crag, he considered that these men might themselves be compared to chamois, living where others would not live; and then, by adaptation, living where others *could* not live. Those snobby, Frenchified bourgeois nobility of Bella and Avar-Ister, who so looked down upon the men of the mountains — if the men of the mountains, ignorant of cities though they were, if they had to live there, they would survive . . . they would manage . . . if he had to, Prince Popoff could carry carcasses in the Ox Market . . . but let the reverse be true, if Baron This of Bella, or Count That of Avar-Ister, had to live on the Red Mountain, they could not live there at all. Surely they would die.

"Well, enough chatter. To work, to work. . . . I don't suppose that we need go galloping along a cliff-face, *ἄναντα κάταντα πάραντα*, as Homer said about the mules. Here, right here" — the figure of a woman appeared at one of the rear gates, and came towards them almost running — "this here outcrop of rocks right here, they are certainly a genuine part of the mountains —" The woman began waving her apron at them. Eszterhazy peered at her, wondering. "Surely that is your old wet-nurse," he said. "Madámka. I wonder what she wants."

"Wants to poke her hairy nose into what is none of her business, I am sure. Never mind *her.* Here. Get your back up against this big clump of rock just as ye see me doing. Reach behind and grab aholt of it, just dig in your fingers, so —"

Eszterhazy followed the directions. But before the next set might be given, the once-wet-nurse arrived, the very figure of fury.

"No!" exclaimed the old woman, screwing up her features, so that they looked even more unattractive than usual. "No! ***No!*** This is not right! His Reverence may have done it; then again he may not have. *He* would have good reason — *you* have *not!* This is not *right,* this is not *right!*" and she clenched her jaws and face-muscles, and she rolled her eyes, performing in a few seconds a "scene" which might have taken others minutes, quarter-hours, or longer.

His Vigor, the Prince Yohan Popoff, said, with controlled forcefulness, "Wet-woman! Old nurse! Do not interfere! Be quiet —"

"No!" she screamed. "No! I won't be quiet! It is not right! The manners of our mountains do not ***like*** it! The —"

"Smudgy old woman," cried her long-ago nurseling. "Ye know little enough of what is meant by 'the manners of our mountains'! Be gone, I say! Be gone! Or I shall send your sons away to the cities! No law obliges me to retain them here on retainer because long ago I nursed their mammy's pap! Leave off, I say! Be gone!"

She was gone.

She being gone, a gesture from the prince, and again they huddled close to the mass of rock. "Remember," urged Popoff, "what the *Romi*, Lucretius, said about the atoms. You must conceive of these with the most strong conception of which you are capable. Conceive of yourself as amongst the atoms of these rocks. Then conceive of yourself as ***moving*** them, these atoms of these rocks, mounds, and mountains. If you but have faith that you can, you can push and press and shove atoms *A* and *B* — atoms *A* and *B* can then move atoms *C* and *D* and *E* and *F* — and, if you do not yield, atoms *C* and *D* and *E* and *F* can move atoms *G* and *H* and *I* and *J* and *K* —

"Move! Move! *Move!* ***Move!***"

Eszterhazy had thought and conception and belief and faith. He pushed. He *did* push. He shoved. He ***did*** shove. He moved. He ***did*** move. And the rocks, did *they* move? The rocks moved, too.

Did the boulders move? The boulders trembled, shuddered; seemed to ***move.*** Did the **mountains** move?

The mountains moved.

(In the chapel of the Armenian Merchants' Guild in Bella long ago a traveller safely returned from Africa had hung up near the high altar an ostrich-egg in a container of golden filigree on a golden chain, as a thanks offering. Now, suddenly, it began slowly to swing like a pendulum. The phenomenon was duly recorded in the records of the congregation; Eszterhazy, learning of this phenomenon, was moved to make certain researches, and to convey the results to certain of his correspondents; why indeed do we not speak of an eszterhaziograph instead of a seismograph? who indeed can say?)

The Grumpkin Gorge, long unrecognized as a gorge, the roadbed of the Official Northern Remote Route Road, from (and to) Austria, was now blocked. Not entirely blocked, to be sure. Individuals, individual men, *as* individuals, might and could have moved therethrough, carefully picking their way. But no mass or group of men might now move through swiftly. And, certainly, through these mounds of lichen-crusted rocks, schist, granite, what-have-you, no carriages and no baggage-wagons might move at all.

Which left, in that part of the country — unless one wished to carry no baggage other than an alpenstock — only the Official Southern Remote Route Road from Austria.

From (and to) Austria.

Eszterhazy, as he pushed and strained and heaved, and "conceived," had an impression that they appeared like a pair of piano-movers: he knew, though, that it was no mere piano that they were moving. It did not surprise him that there was an intermittent fall of smaller stones and rocks rolling and raining down upon them; but he paid not much attention to it until he heard his co-mover, Popoff, cry out in pain.

"Keep on, keep on, do not stop," said the prince, grimacing.

Dr. E. did not stop; but, looking down, and perceiving some large shadow, he did look *up*. Immediately his impression was that of an enormous bird flying overhead. Almost instantly he realized that it was no bird. Whatever it was, was almost at once out of sight — he could hardly stop what he was doing to run forward and look up to see better. But in a moment the shape came again into sight and view. The old woman did not look down at him. She did not say anything. He had never seen her before — he had *not?* — yes, of course, he had — but never at such a angle. Far high and above, she was, and she was riding on something. She was riding side-saddle, as what woman would not? — for if not, her skirts would bunch up, and Heaven forbid one might observe in daylight with one's eyes that which, properly, one ought to observe only at night-time, with one's hands and fingers. Yes, side-saddle she rode, angry was her face; who was she and on what was she riding?

A few more passing flights she made, she did not swoop, merely she flew riding by, she sat upon a branch of a tree, God have mercy on us, and a bunch or bundle of shrubbery, sticks, twigs, was fastened at the end of it. As he now watched, straining upward as well as straining backward, he saw a rock come falling down. And it did not fall from higher up on the outcrop of rock against which the two men were still straining.

There came to Eszterhazy anyway some of the words of an old text he had seen once — a part of a reply of the then-monarch of part of what subsequently became the Empire, in response to an alleged fall of what would now be called meteorites — it had begun, *We, Isidore Salvador, Vigorously Christian King of all the Scythias,* and had gone on to say that *Reports of stones falling from the skies must suppose that there are stones in the skies, and, as it is well-enough known that there are no stones in the skies, We must reject such reports out of hand . . .*

They were no meteorites which had now fallen; therefor——

"We must stop now," said Popoff. "Here. Help me back. Oh."

Popoff lay reclining with one leg bandaged. Von Shtrumpf and Shtruvvelpeyter were playing another of their endless, two-handed games of cards. Everyone was, in theory, waiting: but everyone had almost forgotten what it was which they were waiting for. . . . Enter another rough-looking fellow with a leather arm-band.

"Ah, it's a constable. What's up, Constable? Found another stray cow?"

"— please Your Princeliness, there are Mongols on the Meadow Road, where the stop-station be. They say they have leave to pass, and us mayn't stop they. So the guards they'm asked we to leave you know, and to instruct them in this matter."

The card-players looked up from their greasy decks. ***Mon***gols in the meadow?" asked Von Shtrumpf.

"What can he ***mean?***" enquired Shtruvvelpeyter.

Popoff moved to rise, sank back with a groan. "No use," said he. "***I*** can't go. So you three had better go."

They went.

The young man there at the border-station *did* look somewhat like Little Handsome Hansli the puppet, and he was shouting. "What do you *mean,* you can't let me cross without orders? How dare you stop me? I have Diplomatic Immunity!" His voice was slightly hoarse, as though he had been shouting for a while; but he might as well have told them that he had Pott's Fracture, for all the good it was doing him. " 'Orders,' what orders?" he cried, literally stamping his foot. "For that matter, *whose* orders?"

Eszterhazy stepped forward; and, as all eyes turned on him, he said, "These orders, sir," and he handed over the document which had been handed him by his host, Prince Yohan — who had copied it, with a sufficiency of moans and groans, as he lay upon his couch of pain — copied it from some older form and model.

The young man took it, not without a look of injury and outrage, and glanced at it.

The document began:

> WE, JOHANNES, to our well-beloved cousins and fellow-Christians of high degree, videlicet the Kings of the Greeks, Franks, Burgundians, and Castillians, as well as to all Hetmans, Woywodes, Chieftains, Dukes, Counts, and Constables . . .

— and went on to describe by title, clothing, and bodily appearance (as revealed by Psalmanazzar *and* Agag) His Young Highness, heir to The Heir, etc., etc., and adjured

> ALL THE AFOREMENTIONED to pay him all worshipful respect — but allow him not to pass without further word and release, and herein fail not, by the Holy Sepulchre and the Anointing Oil, lest they die unshriven and impaled and become meat for pigs and crows . . .

There was a signature, and a very large seal.

His Young Highness, August Salvador, the heir to the Heir, did not bother to carry further the unpersuasive rôle of Mr. Bill-Silas Sneed, Drummer in American Cloth and Cheese. He read the document, and his laugh, as he tossed it down, seemed genuine. His face, which had been petulant and fatigued, once again justified its likeness, appearing (suitably framed) upon the tables of about half-a-million servant-girls and shop-keepers' assistants. The document fell, and one of the wild-looking men picked it up. There were a number of wild-looking men at the scene, many with leather arm-bands and leather badges. They may not ever have done much writing themselves, but they had evidently a respect for that which was written . . . had they lived where more was written, and more often, perhaps they might have had less.

The Crown Princeling said, "You must have ransacked my old Bobbo's trunk to locate this antique mummery, or flummery. Even if those kings were present, do you think that any of them would pay attention?"

"No," said Eszterhazy, "but there are constables present, and *they* will."

So there were. So they did. This ancient office, for long a sort of quiet smile, these ancient officers of the counts' stables, duties now largely confined to the impoundment of cattle, lost, strayed, or stolen; of this ancient office, still they were officers. Hulking, hairy, uncouth, wild-looking, unkempt, a simple badge of office strapped to a sleeve, they passed this odd, *odd* document from hand to hand; and those who could read, read it to those who could not. And always they pointed to the seal. And always they pointed to the signature.

And steadily they continued coming in from the woods. And gradually they blocked the road. And gradually the Crown Princeling wilted. His bravado, his self-assurance, melted away. Mere youth and courage and passion had carried him thus far. If he had simply gone out on this mad-cap scheme in disguise, he might have succeeded. Even if he had added to this mad-cap scheme the hare-brained addition of a false diplomatic immunity, he might have succeeded.

Then again, he might not.

At other border-points, crossings, stop-stations, no one might have ever heard of the Grand Mogul; seeing a diplomatic seal, they might have simply let the baggage and its owner pass on into foreign territory. But here —

Right here — only here — and here alone, they had heard of him quite well. That is, not precisely of *him* — the last him, dying (long after the Sepoy Mutiny) in exile and squalor — but of his ancestors.

Babar? Akbar? Well, anyway — Tamurlane. And Genghis Khan.

And ***Genghis Khan.***

Something about that last name caught in Eszterhazy's mind. It, but not quite exactly it. Had it not other forms? Certainly. *Zinghis* Khan, he had surely seen that one somewhere. But that was not *it.* In a flash and a surge it came to him. *Chinghis* Khan. Well. And what of it?

Old Ginger. That of it. He had been wrong about its having been a nickname for Barbarossa. *This is where he would have come, Old Ginger, I mean . . . it helps to know the mountain passes if you want to move an army through* . . . Well . . . It may have passed out of all common knowledge that, here in Eastern Europe, they had once waited for the Golden Horde to come riding. But it had not passed out of common knowledge here. And here was where August Salvador had come with his preposterous "diplomatic immunity" (probably his valet had bought it from the valet of the tottery Jam Jam Sahib).

The rough, archaic-looking, archaic-thinking rural constables looked grimly at the poor, befuddled, school-and-lessons-shunning Princeling.

"The Mongols shall not pass," they said.

Long after Eszterhazy had uttered the tired, worn-past-satire words — indicating Von Shtrumpf and Shtruvvelpeyter — had said, "Will you go with these gentlemen, please?" for what else could he have said? — still, he looked at the document, smeared as it was by the honest dirt on the rough and calloused hands of the rural constables, the last of whom to read it had passed it on him. He looked at the seal. It had meant something to these wild men. But it meant nothing to him. And the signature? Again — it had meant much to the men of these half-lost, secluded mountains, where the past lived on and the present was not yet born; did it mean anything to *him,* Engelbert Eszterhazy, Doctor of this and Doctor of that?

His own finger traced the large, archaic letters. ***Yohan Popoff.*** Well, and so —

Not quite. He had read — what he had expected to read, not actually what was written. Which was:

Yohan Popa

Yohan Popa, was what the signature actually read. In other words, words which both mystified and made clear, *John the Priest,* in other words. Now he knew who had conducted the clandestine communion service in the chapel; the exotic, divine liturgy, or mass.

"We are waiting for you, Engelbert," someone called from the carriage.

"Been there a long time," that family? Yes, they had. They had indeed been there a long time. A very long time indeed. A "descendant of His Reverence"? To be sure. Celebrated the divine liturgy clandestinely, offered guests the liberty of his kingdom, did he? Of course. To be sure. He was entitled. And *still* he and his men stood guard against the Mongols. John the Priest. Yes.

Or, put in a very slightly different way, Prester John.
Been there a long time, had they?
Yes, a *very* long time.
Indeed.

"I am coming now," called Eszterhazy.

POLLY CHARMS, THE SLEEPING WOMAN

Visitors to the great city of Bella, capital of the Triune Monarchy of Scythia-Pannonia-Transbalkania, have many famous and memorable sights to see, and will find many guides to show them. Assuming such a visitor to be so limited, unfortunately, in his time as to be able to see but three of these sights, and assuming the guide to be of any experience at all, there are three which will under any circumstances however hasty be shown.

One, of course, is the great Private Park, and, of course, the greatest thing about it is that it is no longer private: the first thing which the King-Emperor Ignats Louis having done, upon succeeding the reclusive Mazzimilian the Mad on the throne, being to throw open the Private Park to the public. The park is a marvel of landscape architecture, although this is perhaps caviare to the general. The general prefer to flock there to what is, after all, the largest merry-go-round in the world. And, next to that, the general prefer to stand and watch the vehicles on the New Model Road, which Ignats Louis, with great foresight, established for the exclusive use of what are now coming to be know as "motor-cars," in order (as The Presence sagely said), "In order that they may experiment without frightening the horses or being frightened by them." In a surprisingly brief period of time it became traditional for all owners of "motor-cars," between the hours of three and four in the afternoon, to make at least three complete circuits of the New Model Road. (The order that all such vehicles, whether propelled by steam, electricity, naphtha, or other means, be hauled to and from the Road by horsepower, is no longer enforced.)

The second sight which it would certainly be impossible to leave Bella without having seen is the Italian Bridge. Although this is no longer the only bridge which crosses, at Bella, the blue and beautiful Ister, the gracious parabolas of its eleven arches are always sure to lift the heart; the legend that it was designed by Leonardo da Vinci remains unproven. But of course it is neither the architecture nor the legend which brings most visitors, it is the site, midway across, marked by a marble plaque [*From This Point On The Italian Bridge / The Pre-Triune-Monarchial Poet* / IZKO VARNA / *Having Been Spurned By The Beautiful Dancer, Gretchelle* / LEAPED TO HIS DOOM / *Leaving Behind A Copy Of His Famously Heart-Rending Poem* / FAREWELL, O BELLA / *A Clever Play Upon Words Which Will Not / Escape The Learned*] usually accompanied by some floral tribute or other. The late well-known character, Frow Poppoff, for many years made a modest living by selling small bundles of posies to visitors for this very purpose; often, when trade was slow, the worthy Poppoff would recite Varna's famous poem, with gestures.

The third of the sights not to be missed is at Number 33, Turkling Street; one refers of course, to The Spot Where The Turkling Faltered And Turned Back. (The well-known witticism, that the Turkling faltered and turned back because he could not get his horse past the push-carts, refers to an earlier period, when the street was an adjunct to the salt-fish, comb, and bobbin open-air market. This has long since passed. Nor is to be thought that the fiercest action of the Eleventh Turkish War took place under the bulging windows of Number 33, for the site at that time lay half a furlong beyond the old city wall. The "Turkling" in question was, of course, the infamous Murad the Unspeakable, also called Murad the Midget. It was certainly here that the Turkish tide turned back. According to the Ottoman Chronicle, "Crying, 'Accursed be those who add gods to God!' the valiant Prince Murad spurred on his charger, but, alas, fell therefrom and broke his pellucid neck. . . ." The Glagolitic Annals insist that his actual words were, "Who ordered this stupid charge? He should be impaled!" — at which moment he himself was fatally pierced by the crossbow bolt of one of the valiant Illyrian Mercenaries. But the point is perhaps no longer important.

A uniformed guard with a drawn sword paces up and down by the granite slab set level with the pavement which marks the place where Murad fell, and it is natural that visitors take it for granted that the guard is a municipal functionary. Actually, he is not. A law passed during the Pacification of 1858 has limited private guards with drawn swords under the following terms: The employer of such a guard must have at least sixteen quarterings of nobility, not less than five registered degrees in the learned sciences, and a minimum of one hundred thousand ducats deposited in the Imperial Two Percent Gold Bond Funds.

Throughout the entire Triune Monarchy of Scythia-Pannonia-Transbalkania, only one person has ever qualified under this law: and that one is, of course, the unquestionably great and justly famous Engelbert Eszterhazy, Doctor of Jurisprudence, Doctor of Medicine, Doctor of Philosophy, Doctor of Literature, Doctor of Science, *et sic cetera;* and the guard is his own private guard and patrols in front of his own private home, Number 33, Turkling Street.

One afternoon in the middle late autumn, a heavyset man wearing the heavy gray suit and high-crowned gray derby hat which were almost the uniform of the plain-clothes division of the Municipal Police approached the guard and raised his eyebrows. The guard responded by raising his sword in salute. The caller nodded, and, opening the door, entered Number 33. There was none of this petty-bourgeois business of knocking, or of doorbells. Inside the lower hall, the day porter, Lemkotch, arose from his chair and bowed.

"Sir Inspector."

"Ask Dr. Eszterhazy if he can see me."

"My master is expecting the Sir Inspector. Please to go right up. I will tell the housekeeper that she may bring the coffee."

The caller, who had expelled a slight sough of surprise at hearing the first sentence, displayed a slight smile at hearing the last. "Tell me, Lemkotch, does your master know absolutely everything?"

The stalwart, grizzle-haired servant paused a moment, then said, casually, "Oh yes, Sir Inspector. Everything." He bowed again, and departed on his errand.

The caller trod heavily upon the runner of the staircase, of a dull, ox-blood color which seemed to glow in the gaslight. It had been pieced together from a once-priceless Ispahani carpet which had suffered damages during the Great Fire of '93 and had been presented by an informal syndicate of the poorer Armenian merchants.

"This is for remembrance," the spokesman said.

And Eszterhazy's reply was, "It is better than rue."

He said now, "You are welcome, Commissioner Lobats. You are not, as you know, invariably welcome, because sometimes you bring zigs when I am engaged in zags. But this business of the young Englishwoman, Polly Charms, promises to be of at least mild interest."

Lobats blinked, gave a respectful glance at the signed cabinet photograph of The Presence in a silver frame, considered a few conversational openings, decided, finally, on a third.

"Your porter is well-trained in simple honesty," he said. "He greets me simply as 'Sir Inspector,' with none of this 'High-born Officer,' with the slight sneer and the half-concealed leer which I get from the servants in some houses . . . I needn't say which. Everyone knows that my father is a butcher, and that *his* father carried carcasses in the Ox Market."

Eszterhazy waved a dismissal of the matter. "All servants are snobs," he said. "Never mind. Remember what one of Bonaparte's marshals said to that hangover from the Old Regime who told him, 'You have no ancestors.' 'Look at *me,*' he said; '*I* am an ancestor.' "

Lobats's heavy lips slowly and silently repeated the phrase. He nodded, took a small notebook from his pocket, and wrote it down. Then his head snapped up. "Say . . . Doctor. Explain how you knew that I was coming about this Polly Charms. . . ." His eyes rested upon another framed picture, but this one he recognized as a caricature by the famous newspaper artist, Klunck: a figure preternaturally tall and thin, with a nose like a needle and the brows bulging on either side like a house-frow's market-bag. And he wondered, almost bitterly, how Eszterhazy could refrain from rage at having seen it — much less, framing it and displaying it for all to see.

"Well. Karrol-Francos," Eszterhazy began, almost indulgently, "you see, I get my newspapers almost damp from the press. This means that the early afternoon edition of the *Intelligencer* got here at eleven o'clock. Naturally, one does not look for a learned summary of the significance of the new price of silver in the *Intelligencer,* nor for an editorial about the Bulgarian troop movements. One does not read it to be enlightened, one reads it to be entertained. On hearing about this — this exhibition, shall we call it — upon the arrival of the *Intelligencer* I turned at once to the half-page of 'Tiny Topics' . . . you see . . ."

Lobats nodded. He, too, no matter what he had heard or had not heard, also turned at once to the half-page of "Tiny Topics," as soon as he had the day's copy of the *Intelligencer* to hand. And, even though he had already turned to it once, and already read it twice, he not only turned to see it in the copy which Eszterhazy now spread out over his desk, he took out his magnifying glass. (Lobats was too shy to wear spectacles, coming of a social class which looked upon them as a sign of weakness, or of swank.)

New Interesting Little Scientific Exhibit

We found our curiosity well repaid for having visited a little scientific exhibit at the old Goldbeaters' Arcade where we saw the already famous Mis Polly Charms, the young Englishwoman who fell into a deep sleep over thirty years ago and has not since awakened. In fact, she slept entirely the raging cannot-shot of the Siege of Paris. The beautiful tragic Englishwoman, Mis Polly Charms, has not seemingly aged a day and in her condition of deep mesmerism she is said to be able to understand questions put to her by means of the principle of animal magnetism and to answer the questions put to her without waking up; also for a small sum in addition to the small price of admission she sings a deeply affecting song in French.

Lobats tapped the page with a thick and hairy finger. "I'll tell you what, Doctor," he said, gravely. "I believe that this bit here — where is it? — what rotten ink and type these cheap papers use nowadays . . . move my glass . . . ah, ah, oh here it is, this bit where it says, *'In fact she slept entirely the raging cannot-shot of the Siege of Paris,'* I believe that is what is called a misprint and that it ought to read instead . . . oh . . . something like this: *'In fact, she slept entirely* through *the raging* cannon-*shot of the Siege of Paris,'* or something like that. Eh?"

Eszterhazy looked up. His gray eyes sparkled. "Why, I believe that you are quite right, Karrol-Francos," he said. "I am proud of you."

Commissioner Lobats blushed, and he struggled with an embarrassed smile.

"So. Upon reading this, I looked to see the time, I calculated that the *Intelligencer* would reach you by twenty minutes after eleven, that you would have read the item by eleven-thirty, and that you would be here at ten minutes of twelve. Do you think it is a case of abduction, then?"

Lobats shook his head. "Why should I try to fool *you?* You know as well as I do, better than I do, that I'm a fool for all sorts of circus acts, sideshows, mountebanks, scientific exhibitions, odd bits, funny animals, house-hauntings, and all such —"

Eszterhazy snapped his fingers, twice. In a moment his manservant was at his side with hat, coat, gloves, and walking stick. No one else in the entire Triune Monarchy (or, for that matter, elsewhere) had for manservant one of the wild tribe of Mountain Tsiganes; no one else, in fact, would even have thought of it. How came those flashing eyes, that floating hair, that so-untamed countenance, that air of savage freedom, here and now to be silently holding out coat, hat, gloves, and walking stick? Who knows?

"Thank you, Herrekk," said Eszterhazy. Only he and Herrekk knew.

"I will tell you, Commissioner," Eszterhazy said, *"so am I!"*

"Well, Doctor," the Commissioner said, *"I thought as much."*

Chuckling together, they went down the stairs.

At least one of the goldbeaters was still at work in the old Arcade, as a rhythmical thumping sound testified, but for the most part they had moved on to the New. Some of the former workshops were used as warehouses of sundry sorts; here was a fortune-teller, slightly disguised as a couturière; there was a corn-doctor, with two plaster casts in his window showing BEFORE and AFTER, with BEFORE resembling the hoof of a gouty ogre, while AFTER would have been worthy of a prima ballerina. And finally, under a cheaply painted and already flaking wooden board reading **The Miniature Hall of**

Science, was a sort of imitation theater entrance. Where the posters would have been were bills in Gothic, Avar, Glagolitic (Slovatchko), Romanou, and even — despite the old proverb, "There are a hundred ways of wasting paint, and the first way is to paint a sign in Vlox" — Vlox. The percentage of literacy among the Vloxfolk may not have been high, but someone was taking no chances.

The someone was certainly not the down-at-heels fellow with a homemade crutch who, pointing the crutch at this last bill, enquired, "Do you know what you'd get if you crossed a pig with a Vloxfellow?" And, answering his own question, replied, "A dirty pig." And waited for the laugh.

"Be off with you," said Lobats, curtly. The loafer slunk away.

There was even a bill in French.

POLLY CHARMS	**SLEEPING BEAUTY**
SLEEPING WOMAN	**30 YEARS SLUMBER 30**
ANSWERS QUESTIONS!	**ENGLISHWOMAN ! ! ! !**
MOST REMARKABLE!	**VERY UNUSUAL SIGHT!**

DOES SHE ANSWER FROM THE WORLD OF THE LIVING OR THE DEAD ? ? ? ? ? COME ! AND ! SEE ! ! !

And so on. And so on.

The fat old woman at the ticket window, with dyed hair and wearing the traditional red velveteen dress split under the arms, smiled fawningly at them.

"Permit," said Lobats, putting out his hand.

Nodding rapidly, she reached up to where a multitude of papers hung from a wire on clothespins, took one down, examined it, returned it, took another down, gave it a peep, nodded even more rapidly, and handed it out the window.

"Very well, Frow Grigou," said Lobats, handing it back. "Two tickets, please," putting coins on the counter.

Frow Grigou, instead of nodding her head, now began to shake it rapidly, and pushed the money back, smiling archly. "Guests, the High-born Gentlemen, our guests, oh no no *oh* no —"

Lobats turned as red as Frow Grigou's dress. ***"Tickets!"*** he growled. "Take the money. Take the —"

She took it this time, and hastily, extending the tickets, her head now rocking slowly from side to side, still smiling archly, but now with a puzzled note added, as though the insistence on paying for admission were some bit of odd behavior which required the indulgence of the tolerant. "Always glad to see," she gobbled, her voice dying away behind them as they walked the short, dusty hall, ". . . High-born Gents . . . law-abiding . . . delighted . . ."

Only one of the five or six functioning gas jets inside the Exhibition

Room had a mantle, and at least two of the others suffered a malfunction which caused them to bob up and down whenever a dray went by in the street; the light was therefore both inadequate and uncertain. And a soft voice now came from out of the dimness, saying, *"Billet? Billet?"*

Nature had formed the man who now came forward to look noble, but something else had re-formed him to look furtive. His head was large, his features basically handsome, with long and white side whiskers neatly trimmed so that not a hair straggled, but the head itself was completely hairless, with not even a fringe. The head was canted to one side, and the man looked at them out of the corner of one faded-blue eye as he took the tickets. Eszterhazy, almost as though automatically, and rather slowly, reached over and placed the tips of his fingers upon the man's head and ran them lightly over the surface . . . for just a moment . . .

Then he pulled them away, as though they had been burned.

"A phrenologist," the man murmured in English, indulgently, almost contemptuously.

"Among other things," said Eszterhazy, also in English.

A horrid change came over the man's face; his haggard and quasi-noble features dissolved into a flux of tics and grimaces. Once or twice his mouth opened and closed. Then, *"Come right in, gentlemen, the exhibition will commence almost any moment now,"* he said, unevenly, in a mixture of terrible French and broken German. And, *". . . one of the most remarkable phenomena of the age,"* he whispered, again in English. Then he seemed to fall in upon himself, his head bowed down, his shoulders hunched, and he turned away from them in a curious twisting motion.

Lobats looked with a quizzical face to Eszterhazy and observed with astonishment and concern that his companion was — even in that dim and fitful light — gone pale and drawn, jaw thrust outwards and downward in a grimace which might have been — had it been someone else, anyone else — fright . . .

But, in a moment, face and man were the same as before, save that the man had swiftly taken out a silken pocket handkerchief, wiped his face, and as swiftly returned it. And before Lobats had time to say one word, a thin and almost eerie sound announced a gramophone had added its "note scientific" to the atmosphere. It took a few seconds, during which a group of newcomers, evidently mostly clerks and such who were taking advantage of their luncheontime, entered the room . . . it took a few seconds for one to recognize, over the sudden clatter and chatter, that the gramophone was offering a song in French.

Strange and curious were the words, and curious and strange the voice.

Curieux scrutateur de la nature entière,
J'ay connu du grand tout le principe et la fin.
J'ay vu l'or en puissance au fond de sa minière,
*J'ay saisi sa matière et surpris son levain.**

Few of those present, clearly, understood the words, yet all were somehow moved. Obscure the burden, the message unclear; the voice seemed moreover odd, unearthly, and grotesque through the transposition of the primitive machine: yet the effect was as beautiful as it was uncanny.

J'expliquay par quel art l'âme aux flancs d'une mère,
Fait sa maison, l'emporte, et comment un pépin
Mis contre un grain de blé, sous l'humide poussière,
L'un plante et l'autre cep, sont le pain et le vin.

Lobats dug his companion in the ribs gently and in a hoarse whisper asked, "What is it?"

"It is one of the occult, or alchemical, sonnets of the Count of Saint-Germain . . . if he was . . . who lived at least two hundred years . . . if he did," Eszterhazy said, low-voiced.

Once more the voice — high and clear as that of a child, strong as that of a man — took up the refrain.

Rien n'était, Dieu voulut, rien devint quelque chose,
J'en doutais, je cherchay sur quoi l'universe pose,
Rien gardait l'équilibre et servait de soutien.

The Commissioner uttered an exclamation. "Now I know! I remember hearing — was years ago — an Italian singer —"

"— Yes —"

"He was a . . . a . . . a whatchemaycallit . . . one of *them* —"

"A castrato. Yes . . ."

Once more, and for the last time, the voice, between that of men and women, soared up, magnificent, despite all distortion, from the great, curling cornucopia of the gramophone horn.

Enfin, avec les poids de l'éloge et du blâme,
Je pesay l'éternel, il appela mon âme,
Je mourus, j'adoray, je ne savais plus rien . . .

The moment's silence which followed the end of the song was broken by another and more earthly voice, and one well-enough

---

* From *Poëmes Philosophiques sur l'Homme,* Paris, 1795, quoted in *The Count of Saint Germain,* by Isabel Cooper-Ashley. Steiner, Blauvelt: New York, 1970.

known to both Eszterhazy and Lobats. It was that of one Dougherty, a supposed political exile of many years' residence in Bella. From time to time one came upon him in unfashionable coffeehouses, or establishments where stronger drink was served. Sometimes the man was writing something; sometimes he explained that it was part of a book which he was writing, and sometimes he explained nothing, but scrawled slowly away in a dreamy fashion. At other times he had no paper in front of him, only a glass, into or beyond which he stared slackly. This man Dougherty was tall and he was stooped and he wore thick eyeglasses and now and then he silently moved his lips — lips surprisingly fresh and full in that ruined gray countenance. Officially he described himself as "Translator, Interpreter, and Guide," and he was evidently acting now in the first and second of these capacities.

"Gentlemen," he began (and he used the English word), "Gentlemen . . . Mr. Murgatroyd, the entrepreneur of this scientific exhibition has asked me to thank those of you who have honored him with your patronage, and to express his regret that he does not speak with fluency the languages of the Triune Monarchy, whose warm and frequent hospitality . . ." Here he paused, and seemed to sag a bit, as though bowed beneath the weight of all the nonsense and humbug which convention required him to be saying — and which he had been saying, in one way or another, over and over, for decades. Indeed, he frankly sighed, put his hand to his forehead, then straightened, and took in his hand something which the entrepreneur had given: it seemed to be a pamphlet, or booklet.

"Mmmm . . . yes . . . Some interesting facts, taken from a voluminous work written on the subject of the mysterious sleeping woman, Polly Charms, by a member of the French Academy and the Sorbonne. The subject of this scientific exhibition, the ever-young Englishwoman, Miss Mary Charms, called Polly, was born in —"

His remarks, which had sunk to a monotone, were interrupted by several exclamations of annoyance, amidst which one voice now made itself heard, and distinctly: "Come on, now, Dear Sir ["Lijberherra" — sarcastically], save all this muckdirt ["Schejssdrekka"] for those there *gentlemen* who've got the whole afternoon at their leisure: come on, let's see . . ."

Lobats coughed sufficiently to draw attention. The voice hesitated, then went on, though in tones somewhat less rough and menacing, to say that they were working-people, didn't have much time, had paid to see this here Miss Sharms, and wanted to see her or their money back, so, "Save the French Sorbonne for the dessert course, for them as can wait, and let's get on with it."

Dougherty shrugged, leaned over and spoke to Murgatroyd, who also shrugged, then gestured to Frow Grigou, who did not bother to shrug, but, indicating by a flurry of nods and smirks that she was only too happy to oblige and merely wondered that anyone should think otherwise, trotted swiftly to the side of the room and pulled at a semi-visible cord. The filthy old curtain, bearing the just-visible name of a firm of patent-medicine makers long bankrupt, began — with a series of jerks and starts in keeping with the hiccuppy gaslights — to go up.

And Mr. Murgatroyd, not even waiting for the process to be complete, moved forward and with a smack of his lips began to speak, and then to speak in English, and went on speaking, leaving to Dougherty to catch up, or not, with the translation and interpretation.

"It was just thirty years ago, my lords and ladies and gentlemen, just exactly thirty years ago to this very day —" But his glib patter, obviously long and often repeated, plus the fact of the term **30 Years** appearing in faded letters on several of the bills posted outside, made it at once obvious that the "thirty years" was a phrase by now ritualized and symbolic. Perhaps he, or perhaps another, had endowed Polly Charms with thirty years' slumber at the very beginning of the show's career; or, perhaps, and the thought made one shudder, Murgatroyd had been saying "30 years" for far longer than any period of only thirty years. "That young Miss Mary Charms, called Polly, at the age of fifteen years, accompanied by her mother and several other loved ones . . ."

He trailed off into silence, having been pushed aside by several of those honoring him with their patronage as they shoved up to see; in the silence, Dougherty proceeded with his translations . . . which may or may not have been listened to by any.

Eszterhazy realized that he had been expecting, for some reason, to see either a coffin or something very much like it. What he actually saw was something resembling an infant's crib, though of course much larger, and, at very first glimpse, it seemed to be filled with a mass of —

". . . Professor Leonardo de Entwhistle, the noted mesmerologist," Murgatroyd's voice suddenly was heard again, after the first burst of exclamations had subsided. His eyes shifted and met Eszterhazy's. The Englishman's eyes at once closed, opened, closed, opened, and, as it were desperately, looked away. Where Eszterhazy looked was into the crib, and what he saw it was almost filled with was, or seemed to be, hair . . . long and lustrous golden-brown hair. Coils and braids of it. Immense tresses of it. Masses and masses of it. Here and there ribbons had been affixed to it. And still it went on.

And, almost buried in it, slightly raised by a pillow at the head of the crib was another head, a human head, the head of, and indeed of, a female in early womanhood.

"Can we touch it — uh, *her?*"

Murgatroyd muttered.

"One at a time, and gently," said Dougherty. "Gently . . . *gently!*"

Fingers were applied, some hesitantly. A palm was applied to the side of the face. Another was raised and moving down, though not, by the looks of it, or by the owner's looks, to the face; at this point Lobats grunted and grabbed the man's wrist. Not gently. The man growled that he was just going to — but the disclaimer fell off into a snarl, and the gesture was not repeated. Someone managed to find a hand and lifted it up, with a triumphant air, as though no one had ever seen a hand before.

And Eszterhazy now said, "All right. *Enough . . .*" He moved up; the crowd moved back. He took out the stethoscope. The crowd said *Ahhh.*

"That's the philosopher," someone said to someone else. Who said, "*Oh* yes," although what quality either one attached to the term perhaps neither understood precisely.

God only knew where the girl's garment had been made, or when, or by whom; indeed, it seemed to have been made over many times, and to consist of sundry strata, so to speak. Now and again it had occurred to Whomever that the girl was supposed to be sleeping, and so the semblance of a nightgown had been fashioned. Several times. And on several other occasions the theatrical elements of it all had overcome, and attempts had been made to provide the sort of dress which a chanteuse might have been wearing . . . wearing, that is, in some provincial music hall where the dressmakers had odd and old-fashioned ideas of what a chanteuse might like to wear . . . and the chanteuses, for that matter, even odder ones.

There was silk and there was cotton and there was muslin, lace, artificial flowers, ruches, embroidered gores, gussets, embroidered yokes —

The girl's eyes were almost entirely closed. One lid was just barely raised, and a thin line gleamed, at a certain angle, underneath. Sleepers of that age do not flush, always, as children often do, in sleep. There was color in the face, though not much. The lips were the tint of a pink. A small gold ring showed in one ear; the other ear was concealed by the hair.

"The hair," said Murgatroyd, *"the hair has never stopped growing!"* A kind of delight seemed to seize him as he said it.

Eszterhazy's look brought silence. And another flurry of tics. Several times he moved the stethoscope. Then the silence was broken. "A wax doll, isn't it, Professor? Isn't —"

Eszterhazy shook his head. "The heartbeat is perceptible," he said. "Though very, very faint." The crowd sighed. He removed the ear-pieces and passed the instrument to Commissioner Lobats, who, looking immensely proud and twice as important, attached himself to it — not without difficulty. After some moments, he — very slowly — nodded twice. The crowd sighed again.

"Questions? Has anyone a question to ask of Polly Charms, the

Sleeping Woman? — ah, one moment please. It is time for her daily nourishment." Murgatroyd, with a practiced flourish, produced two bottles, a glass, and a very tarnished, very battered, but unquestionably silver, spoon. "All attempts to make the mysterious and lovely Miss Mary partake of solid sustenance have failed. Nor will her system accept even gruel. Accordingly, and on the advice of her physicians — of the foremost physicians in Christendom —" Here he turned and beckoned to a member of the audience, an elderly dandy, audibly recognized by several as a ribbon clerk in a nearby retail emporium. "I should like to ask of you the favor, sir, to taste and smell of this and to give us your honest and unbought opinion as to its nature."

The man simpered, sniffed, sipped. Smacked his lips. "Ah. Why that's Tokai. Bull's-blood Tokai." And he made as though to take more. Laughs and guffaws and jests. The contents of the other bottle were declared to be water. The girl's manager then ceremonially mixed the glass half-full of wine and half of water. He might have been an alchemist, proving an elixir. "Come on, now, come on. Some of you are in a hurry, you say . . . Questions?"

Snickers, jokes, people being pushed forward, people holding back. Then the ribbon clerk, glancing at his watch, a-dangle and a-bangle with fobs and seals, said, "Very well. One question and then I must go. Gracious Lady: Who is Frantchek? And where?"

Murgatroyd held the spoon to her lips, and, indeed so gently, raised her head a trifle. "Just a spoonful. Polly. A nice spoon of something good. To please Father Murgatroyd." The slick and hairless head bent over, indeed like that of a father cosseting an ill child. Slowly and slightly the lips parted. The spoon clinked against the even rows of teeth. Withdrew.

"Very well, Polly. You're a *good* girl. Father Murgatroyd is very *pleased* with you. And now, if you please, an answer to the question. 'Who is Frantchek? And where?' "

The lips parted once again. A faint, a very faint sigh was heard. And then, in the voice of a girl in her middle teens imitating one much younger, in tones artificial and stilted, Polly Charms spoke.

"Why, Brother, I am in America. With Uncle."

All turned to the old dandy, who had been standing, one hand on hip, with an expression of one who expects to be fooled. But who won't be, even if he is. Because of expecting it. This expression quite fell away. He gaped.

"Well, Maurits. And what about that?" they pressed him.

"Why . . . why . . . Why, Frantchek *is* my brother. He run off, oh, five-and-twenty-year ago. We none of us had a word of him —"

"And the uncle? In America?"

Old Maurits slowly nodded, dumbfounded. "I *did* have an uncle, in America. Maybe still do. *I* don't know —" With a jerk away from the hand on his shoulder, he stumbled out, face in his hands.

Comment was uncertain. One said, "Well, that didn't really prove nothing. . . . Still . . ."

And another one — probably the same who had loudly demanded the biographical details be omitted, now said, loudly, "Well, Miss, *I* think you're a fake, a clever fake. Wha-at? Why, half the people in the Empire have a brother named Frantchek, and an uncle in America! Now, just you answer *this* question. What's this in my own closed hand, here in this coat pocket?"

Another spoonful of wine and water.

Another expectant silence, this time with the questioner openly sneering.

Another answer.

"The pearl-handled knife which you stole at the bath-house . . ."

And now see the fellow, face mottled, furious, starting toward the sleeping woman, hand moving up and out of the pocket. And see Lobats lunge, hear a sudden and sick cry of pain. See a something fall to the ground. And watch the man, now suddenly pale, as Lobats says, "Get out! Or — !" Watch him get . . . holding one hand with the other. And see the others stoop and gape.

"A pearl-handled knife!"

"Jesus, Mary, and —"

"— known him for years, he ain't no good —"

And now someone, first clutching his head in his hands, and then leaning forward, then drawing back and staring, glaring all round, face twisted with half shame and half defiance: "Listen . . . listen. . . . Say — I want to *know.* Is my wife . . . is she all that she should be — to me — *is she* —" He doesn't finish, nobody dares to laugh. They can hear him breathing heavily through heavily distended nostrils.

Another spoonful. Another pause.

"Better than she should be . . . though little you deserve it . . ."

The man will not face anyone. He leans to one side, head bent, breathing *very* heavily.

And soon the last question has been asked, and the wine is all gone. — Or, perhaps, it is the other way around.

And, as Murgatroyd goes to put down the spoon, and the audience is suddenly uncertain, suddenly everyone looks at someone whom nobody has looked at before. Who says, "And so, Professors, what about the French song?" A spruce, elderly gent, shiny red cheeks, garments cut in the fifth year of the Reign, looking for all the world like a minor notary from one of the remoter suburbs ("Ten tramways and a fiacre ride away," as the saying goes) where each family still has its own cow, and probably up to the center of the city for his annual trip to have his licensure renewed; wanting a bit of fun along with it, and, not daring to tell the old lady ("Tanta Minna," probably) that he has had it at any place more risky, has been having it at a "scientific exhibition."

"Wasn't there supposed to be a French song?" he asks calmly.

Murgatroyd, at a murmur from Dougherty, produces a wooden tray lined with worn green velveteen and covertly places in it a single half-ducat, which he watches rather anxiously. "For a very slight additional charge," he says, starting the rounds, "a beautiful song in the French language will be sung by the lovely and mysterious Polly Charms, the —"

Spectators show signs of departing . . . or, at any rate, of drawing away from the collection tray. A single piece of gold spins through the air, all a-glitter, falls right upon the half-ducat with a pure ringing sound. Mr. Murgatroyd looks up, almost wildly, sees Eszterhazy looking at him. Who says, "Get on with it."

Murgatroyd makes the money vanish. He leans over the sleeping woman, takes up her right hand, and slowly caresses it. "Will you sing us a song, Polly dear?" he asks. Almost, one might think, anxiously.

"That sweet French song taught you by Madame, in the old days . . . Eh?" And, no song being forthcoming, he clears his throat and quaveringly begins, " '*Je vous envoye un bouquet . . .*', Eh, Polly?"

Eszterhazy, watching, sees a slight tremor in the pale, pale throat. A slight rise in the slight bosom, covered in its bedizened robe. The mouth opens. An indrawn breath is clearly heard. And then she sings. Polly Charms, the Sleeping Lady, sings.

Je vous envoye un bouquet de ma main
Que j'ai ourdy de ces fleurs epanies:
Qui ne les eust à ce vespre cuillies,
Flaques à terre elles cherroient demain.

No one had asked Dougherty to translate the previous French song, sung by the eunuch singer (surely one of the very last) on the gramophone; nor had he done so; nor did anyone ask him to translate now. Yet, and without his gray face changing at all, his gray lips moved, and he began, " 'I send you now a sheaf of fairest flowers / Which my hand picked; yet are they so full blown, / Had no one plucked them they had died alone, / Fallen to earth before tomorrow's hours.' "*

Still, Murgatroyd caressed the pallid hand. And again, the eerie and infantile voice sang out.

Cela vous soit un exemple certain
Que voz beautés, bien qu'elles soient fleuries,
En peu de tems cherront toutes flétries,
Et periront, comme ces fleurs, soudain.

---

* From Ronsard, *Poems of Love,* selected and edited by Grahame Castor and Terence Cave, Manchester University Press, 1975.

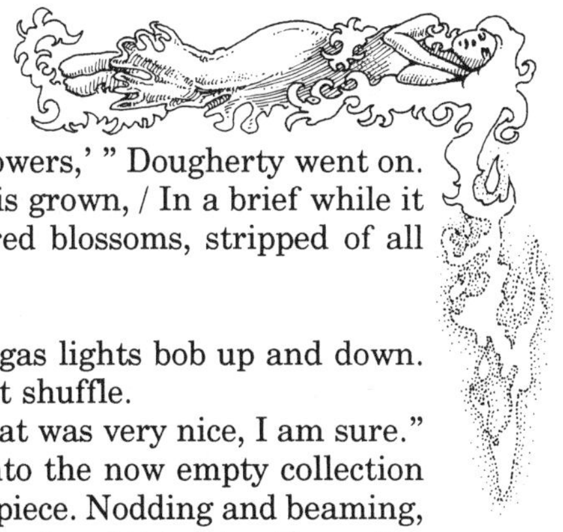

" 'Then let this be a portent in your bowers,' " Dougherty went on. " 'Though all your beauteous loveliness is grown, / In a brief while it falls to earth o'erthrown, / Like withered blossoms, stripped of all their powers . . .' "

Quietness.

A dray rumbles by in the street. The gas lights bob up and down. Breaths are let out, throats cleared. Feet shuffle.

"Well, now," says old Uncle Oskar, "that was very nice, I am sure." Smiling benignly, he walks over, and, into the now empty collection plate he drops a large old five-kopperka piece. Nodding and beaming, he departs. It has been worth every kopperka of it to him, the entire performance. Tonight, over the potato dumplings with sour-crout and garlic wurst, he will tell Tanta Minna all about it. In fact, if he is alive and she is alive, ten years from now, he will still be telling about it; and she, Tanta Minna, will still be as astonished as ever, punctuating each pause with *Jesus, Mary, and Joseph!* or, alternately, *Oh, thou dear Cross!*

Some follow after, some still remain.

"The performance is over," says Eszterhazy.

Lobats: *"Over.* Good afternoon to you."

And Frow Grigou calls after them, anxious as ever, "There is another performance at half-past five, Dear Sirs, and also at eight and at ten!"

Lobats looks at Eszterhazy, as though to say, *What now?* And Eszterhazy looks at Murgatroyd. "I am a Doctor of Medicine and a Titular Court Physician," he says; "and I should like your permission to make an examination of —" he gestures. Dougherty, without looking anywhere in particular, at once begins to translate Eszterhazy's English into Avar, then slowly seems to feel that this is, perhaps, not exactly what is wanted at the moment, and his voice dies away.

Murgatroyd licks his lips, the lower parts of his moustache. Almost, he licks the tip of his nose. "Oh no," he says. "Oh no . . ."

"And this," Eszterhazy says, calmly, "is a Commissioner of Police."

Murgatroyd looks at the Commissioner of Police, who looks back; he looks at Dougherty, who looks away; then he looks for Frow Grigou.

But Frow Grigou has gone, quite gone.

Excerpts from the Day-Book of Dr. Eszterhazy:

> . . . Query Reuters for the precise date of the death by apoplexy of ENTWHISTLE, LEONARD (see Private Encyclopedia), British mesmerist and mountebank, supposedly in the midst of an exhibition or performance . . .
>
> . . . no signs of any callosities whatever on the soles of the

female's feet, or heels . . . degeneration of the muscular tissue, such as is found among the long-senile, was not present, however . . .

Murgatroyd declared, though reluctantly, that passage of waste materials was infrequent, and cleanly . . .

Murgatroyd was almost violent in reply to the tentative suggestion of Lobats that an attempt, by mesmerism, to bring the young woman out of this supposed-mesmeric trance be attempted. MEMO: To re-read story by American writer E. A. Poe, "The Case of Monsieur Waldemar." In this tale, a presumed account of facts, a dying man is placed under mesmeric trance of long duration (exact duration not recalled); removal of trance state or condition discloses that "Waldemar" has actually been dead, body at once lapsing into decay. Cannot state at present if the story is entirely fictitious or not; another story by same writer (Marie Roget?) known to be demi-factual.

Obvious: welfare of young woman, Charms, is first consideration.

Suggestions: Consider question of use of galvanic batteries, but only if —

For some seconds the sound of running feet had echoed in the narrow street below. A voice, hoarse and labored . . . Then the night porter, Emmerman, entered. He was always brief. "Goldbeaters' Arcade on fire, master," he said now. Adding, as Eszterhazy, with an exclamation, ran for his medical bag, "Commissioner Lobats has sent word." The Tsigane had appeared, as though rising from out of the floor (where, indeed, on the threshold of his master's bedroom door he always slept), but Eszterhazy, waving aside the coat and hat, said two words: *"The steam —"* He followed the silently running Herrekk through the apartment and down the back steps to the mews, where the runabout was kept, and they leaped on it. Schwebel, the retired railroad engineer who maintained the machine, had been charged to see that a head of steam was always kept up, and he had never failed. With a sketch of a salute, he threw open the stable door. With a low hiss, the machine, Eszterhazy at the tiller, rolled out into the night. Herrekk had already begun to toll the great bronze handbell to warn all passersby out of the way.

Lobats had said that he was "a fool for all sorts of circus acts, sideshows, mountebanks, scientific exhibitions, odd bits, funny animals, house-hauntings . . ." He might have added: "and fires."

Three fire engines of the newest sort, each drawn troika-fashion by three great horses of matching colors, had come one after another to The Street of the Defeat of Bonaparte (universally called Bonaparte Street), as near as they could maneuver, and made much with hoses into the Arcade. But the watchmen of the neighborhood, many

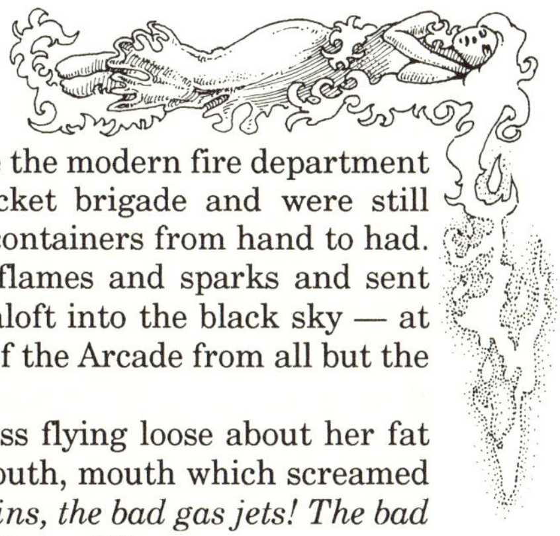

of whom had been employed there before the modern fire department came into being, had set up their bucket brigade and were still passing the old but functioning leather containers from hand to had. A sudden breeze now whipped up the flames and sparks and sent them flying overhead, straight up and aloft into the black sky — at the same time clearing the passageway of the Arcade from all but the smell of smoke.

Off in a corner, her red velveteen dress flying loose about her fat body, Frow Grigou crouched, hand to mouth, mouth which screamed incessantly, *"Ruined! Ruined! The curtains, the bad gas jets! The bad gas jets, the curtains! Ruined! Ruined! Ruined!"*

All at once the firehoses heaved, writhed, gushed forth in a potent flow. The smoke turned back and clouds of steam arose. Eszterhazy felt himself choking, felt himself being carried away in the powerful arms of Herrekk, the Mountain Tsigane. In a moment he cried, "I am all right! Set me down." He saw himself looking into the anxious face of Lobats, who, seeing Eszterhazy on his feet and evidently recovered, gestured silently to two bodies on the pavement in Bonaparte Street.

Murgatroyd. And Polly Charms.

[Later, Lobats was to ask, "What was it that you found out when you put your fingers on the Englishman's head?" And Eszterhazy was to answer, "More than I will ever speak of to anyone."]

Eszterhazy flung himself down beside them. But although he cursed aloud the absence of his galvanic batteries, and although he plied all the means at his behalf — the cordials, the injections, the ammoniated salts — he could bring no breath or motion to either of them.

Slowly, Lobats crossed himself. Ponderously, he said, "Ah, they're both in a better world now. She, poor little thing, her life, if you call that long sleep a life — And he, bad chap though I suppose he must've been in lots of ways, maybe in most — but surely he expiated his sins in dragging her almost to safety, trying to save her life at the risk of his own when her very hair was on fire —"

And indeed, most of the incredible mass of hair had burned away — those massive tresses which Murgatroyd (for who else?) must have daily and nightly spent hours in brushing and combing and plaiting and braiding . . . one must hope, at least lovingly . . . that incredible profusion of light-brown hair, unbound for the night, had indeed burned away but for a light scantling, like that of a crop-headed boy. And this shown in the dim and flaring lights, all a-glitter with moisture, shining with the drops of the water which had extinguished its fire. The girl's face as calm now as ever. The lips of the color of a pink were again so slightly parted. But whatever she might once have had to tell would now forever be unknown.

And as for Murgatroyd, Death had at least and at last released him from all need of concealment and fear. The furtive look was quite gone now. The face seemed now entirely noble.

"I suppose you might say that he'd exploited her, kept her in that state of bondage — but at least he risked his life to save hers —"

One of the watchmen standing by now stepped a pace forward and respectfully gestured a salute. "Beg the Sir High Police Commissioner a pardon," he said now. "However, as it is not so."

"What is not so?" Lobats was annoyed.

The watchman, still respectful, but quite firm: "Why, as the poor gentleman tried, dying, to save the poor missy. But it wasn't so, Sir High Commissioner and Professor Doctor. It was as one might say the opposite way. 'Twas *she* as was trying to get *him* out. *Oh*yes, Sirs. We heard of him screaming, oh Jesus, Mary, and Joseph, how he screamed! We couldn't get in to them. We looks around and we looks back and there she comes, she come out of the flames, sometimes carrying him and sometimes she dragged at him and then her pretty hair went all ablaze and they two fell almost at our feet and we doused them with water. . . . Y'see," he concluded, his eloquence exhausted.

"Ah, stop your damned lies, man!" said Lobats.

Eszterhazy, shaking his head, murmured, "See, then, how swiftly the process of myth-making and legendry begins . . . ***Oh! God!"*** Shocked, speechless, he responded to Lobats only with a gesture. Still on his knees, Eszterhazy pointed wordlessly to the feet of Polly Charms, the Sleeping Woman. The feet were small and slight. They were, as always, naked, bare. And Lobats, following the slight gesture, saw with a shock that even experience had not prepared him for that the bare feet of the dead girl were deeply scratched, and torn and red with blood.

THE CROWN JEWELS OF JERUSALEM, or THE TELL-TALE HEAD

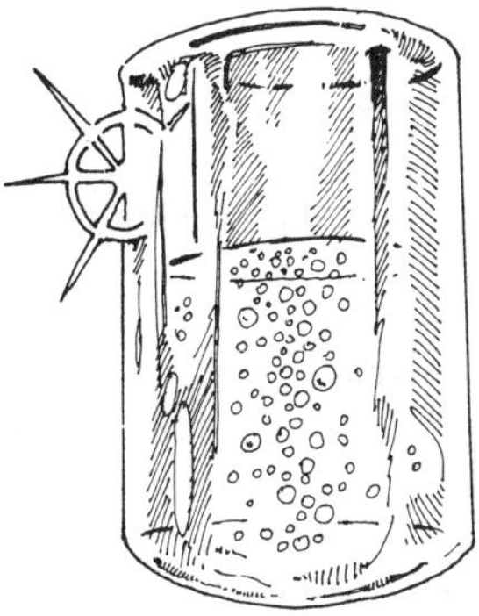

The spa at Gross-Kroplets is not one of the fashionable watering places of the Triune Monarchy, else Eszterhazy would scarcely have been found there. Nor, as he did not practice the curiously fashionable habit of abusing his liver for forty-nine weeks of the year, did he ever feel the need of medicating it with the waters of mineral springs for the remaining three.

It was entirely for the purpose of making a scientific analysis of those waters — or, specifically, those at Gross-Kroplets — which had brought him from his house in Bella, Imperial Capital of Scythia-Pannonia-Transbalkania, to the comparatively small resort high in the Rhiphaean Alps. Two moderately large and three moderately small (four, if one counts the House of the Triple-Eagle) hotels served to provide room and board for visitors to the spa; and although all were privately owned, the Spring itself had been the property of the Royal and Imperial House of Hohenschtupfen since the Capitulations of 1593 and was under the management of the Ministry of the Privy Purse.

Anyone, therefore, not in a condition of gross drunkenness or equally gross nakedness is free to drink the waters (the waters may actually be drunk free in the original, or Old, Pump Room in what is now the First Floor or Basement, but few except the truly indigent care to avail themselves of the privilege; most visitors prefer to employ the drinking facilities in the First, Second, or Third Class Sections of the New or Grand Pump Room reached from the Terrace, where a schedule of fees is in operation); and anyone is, accordingly, free to walk about the pleasantly — if not splendidly — landscaped grounds.

Eszterhazy, therefore, neither said nor did anything when he became aware that someone was not only closely observing him but in effect closely following him. When, of a morning, he walked with his equipment from the small, old-fashioned inn called The House of the Triple-Eagle, someone presently appeared behind his back and plodded after him. When he set up his equipment next to the basin of rough-worked stone whence the Spring welled up and bubbled on its way upstairs and down, someone stood outside the doorless chamber and looked in. When he returned with his samples to the inn, someone followed after him and vanished before he reached the sprawling old building.

In the afternoons, the whole thing was repeated.

In the evenings, when what passed at Gross-Kroplets for A High Fashionable Occasion was at its most, Eszterhazy stayed in his sitting room, making entries in his *Day-Book,* after which he read, first, from some technical work, and, next, from some nontechnical one. He was particularly fond of the light novels of an English writer named G.A. Henty, although he more than once complimented the stories of G. de Maupassant, Dr. A. Tchechoff, and H. George Wells.

It was the morning of the fourth day of his visit, as he was on his knees commencing a check of comparative sedimentation with the aid of a pipette, when someone came to the doorway of the Spring Room and, after coughing, said, "Are you not Engelbert Eszterhazy, Doctor of Medicine?"

Since Eszterhazy felt several simultaneous emotions, none of them amiable, he was for a moment incapable of elegance. Why, for example, was the cough considered a sound worthy of announcing a supposedly polite address? Why not a gasp, an eructation, a hiccough, or a flatulency? But all he first said was, "You have caused me to contaminate the pipette."

The questioner paid as much attention to this as he might have to, say, "Brekekekex koax koax." With his eyebrows raised, he merely made an inquiring sound of "***Mmm?***" which moved his previous question. He was an inordinately ordinary-looking man, in a short jacket, baggy trousers, and string tie, with a moustache which straggled too long on the right side, and pinch-nose spectacles; and had the look of a drummer for a firm of jobbers in odd lots of oilcloth. A writing-master in a fifth-rate provincial *gymnasium.* Or, even, the owner by inheritance of two "courts" in one of the proliferating jerry-built suburbs of Bella, whose rents relieved him of the need to be anything much in particular. And, with only another wiggle of the raised eyebrows, this person again repeated his "***Mmm?***" and this time on a note of higher urgency or pressure.

"Yes, sir, I am Engelbert Eszterhazy, Doctor of Medicine," the scientist said, irritably. "I am also Engelbert Eszterhazy, Doctor of Jurisprudence; Engelbert Eszterhazy, Doctor of Philosophy; Engelbert Eszterhazy, Doctor of Science; and Engelbert Eszterhazy,

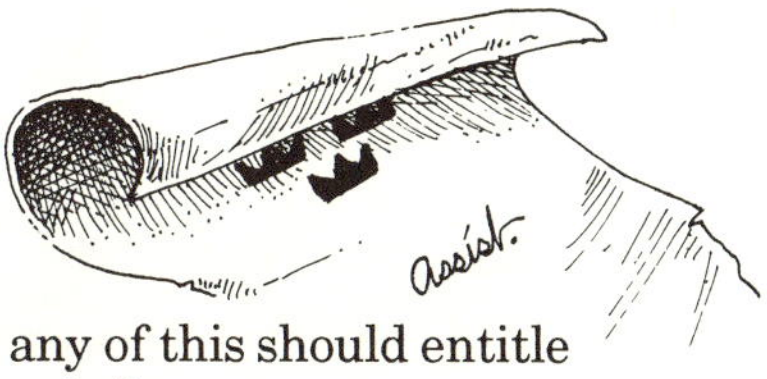

Doctor of Literature. And I do not know why any of this should entitle you to burst in upon my quietness and research."

The other man, as he heard all this, looked all around him, as though inviting spectators (of whom there were none) to witness it; then he said, "I must depart from my invariable incognito to inform *you,* sir, that *I* am King of Jerusalem and that you have unfortunately just prevented yourself from the reception of a *very* important appointment at my court!"

Eszterhazy looked down into the bubbling waters and heaved a silent sigh of self-reproach at himself for allowing himself to be irritated by a noddy. When he looked up, a moment later, prepared to offer a soft and non-committal rejoinder, the man had gone.

During the rest of his stay in Gross-Kroplets, he did not see any more of the man; and his single enquiry met with no information at all.

He recollected the incident next, some months later, at the Linguistic Congress, during the middle of an interesting discussion on the Eastern and the Western Aramaic, with the Most Reverend Salomon Isaac Tsedek, Grand Rabbi of Bella — who, with his perceptive mind and eye, and observing that a different idea had occurred to Eszterhazy, paused inquiringly. "— Your pardon, Worthy Grand Rabbi. Who is King of Jerusalem?"

"Almighty God, King of Heaven and Earth . . . in a theological sense. In a secular sense, I suppose, the Sultan of Turkey." He did not offend against good manners by adding, "Why do you ask," as he — as all sensible men and women should — recognized that if Eszterhazy wished to say why he asked, he would say why he asked. And they returned to their discussion of the construct case, and of the genitive.

Some weeks after the Linguistic Congress, Eszterhazy, passing peacefully through the Pearl Market, where he had been pricing some Russko chalcedonies, observed his friend Karrol-Francos Lobats, Commissioner of the Detective Police, deeply engaged in conversation with De Hooft, the President of the Jewelers' Association. De Hooft, usually reserved to the point of being phlegmatic, was shaking his head excitedly, and even took the Commissioner by the coat lapels. Lobats did notice Eszterhazy, who was going on by, and made as if to disengage himself; after a moment he fell back, as though it had not happened. And Eszterhazy continued on his way.

The visit to the Pearl Market, where gems of all sorts, plus ivory and amber, had been bought, sold, appraised, and bartered for centuries, was a mere brief amusement. Eszterhazy had an overflowing schedule. For one thing, he wished to prepare the final draft of his report on the therapeutic qualities (or otherwise) of medicinal spring water for the *Journal of the Iberian Academy of Medicine.* For another, he had already begun another study, an enquiry into the practice of clay-eating among the so-called Ten Mountain Tribes of Tsiganes (in which Herrekk, his manservant, was of course of invaluable assistance). Eszterhazy liked to have one enquiry overlapping another, in order to avoid the letdown, the lethargy, which otherwise often accompanied the conclusion of an enquiry.

And in addition, the end of the Quarterly Court of Criminal Processes was approaching. Eszterhazy wished few men ill; he was by no means a Mallet of Malefactors; but the chance — which the conclusion of every quarter furnished him — of examining from the viewpoint of phrenology the freshly shaven heads of anywhere from fifty-odd to two-hundred or so newly convicted criminals was one which could not be passed up. Indeed, a few of the regular recidivists looked forward to the examination with an enthusiasm which the fact that Eszterhazy always gave each one a chitty payable in chocolate or tobacco at the canteen in the Western Royal and Imperial Penitentiary Fortress alone could not explain.

"See, this noggin o' mine goes down into history for the third time," one professional thief announced triumphantly to the guard, after Eszterhazy had completed the reading of his remarkably unlovely head.

"The rest of youse has already gone down into history five or six times on the Bertillon System," the guard said.

"Ahah, youse is just jealous, har har! Thanks, Purfessor, for the baccy chit!" And he swaggered off, prepared to spend three to five years under circumstances which no farmer would provide for his dogs or oxen. However, interventions on the part of Eszterhazy had already worked to the abolishment of the so-called Water Cure punishment and of the infamous Pig Pen.

The docket of Doctor Eszterhazy was rather full.

And so he made no much-about the tiny article, almost a filler, in the *Evening Gazette of Bella*:

> The Honorable Police can give no substance to rumors about alleged thefts of certain antique jewelry, it was learned today by Our Correspondents.

And he passed on to the lead *feuilleton* of the issue, entitled, by a most curious coincidence, *The Romance of Old Jewelry.* Liebfrow, the editor of the *Evening Gazette,* was in many ways an old nannykins, but not in so many ways that he was unable to get a point across with a delicacy envied by other editors.

Skimming through the article, noticing references to the Iron Crown of the Lombards, the Cyprus Regalia, and the Crown of St. Stephan (the *feuilleton* seemed somewhat heavy on regalia), Eszterhazy observed some word which triggered a small mechanism deep

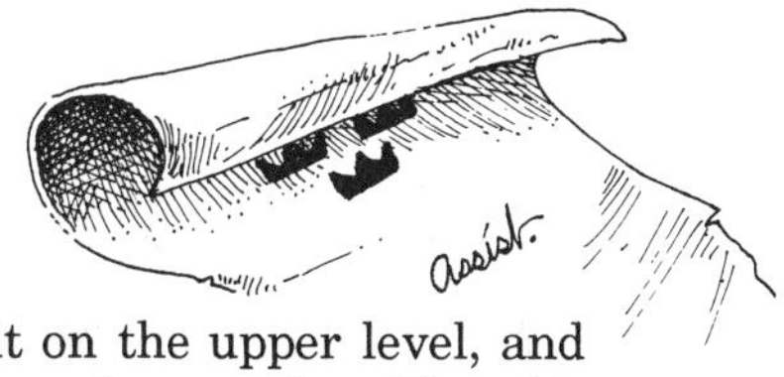

in his mind. He had not quite registered it on the upper level, and was about to go over the article, column by column, when Herrekk silently set upon the table a dish of cheese dumplings. Although the master of the premises at Number 33, Turkling Street, could have endured it very well if cheese dumplings were to be abolished by joint resolution of both Houses of the Imperial Diet, he knew that his housekeeper, Frow Widow Orgats, prided herself on her cheese dumplings — indeed, she regarded it as though an article of faith established by the Council of Trent that her master was deliriously fond of her cheese dumplings — speaking of them in high praise to the Faculties of Law and Medicine — and praising their remarkable lightness and sweetness to the Gentry and Nobility; in fact (Eszterhazy knew damned well from experience) she was certainly even now behind the dining-room door, waiting expectantly.

So he performed.

"Ah, Herrekk, Herrekk!"

"Lord," said Herrekk, a Tsigane of few words.

"Ah, these cheese dumplings of Frow Widow Orgats!"

"Lord."

"How delightfully sweet, how incredibly light!"

"Lord."

"Herrekk, be sure and see she gives you some. Let me know, should she overlook doing so."

"Lord."

Next Eszterhazy made a series of sounds indicating his being reduced to wordless ecstasy by the mere mastication of the cheese dumplings. And then he felt free to continue the rest of his dinner. Should he overlook having done all this, Frow Widow Orgats, an after all truly first-rate cook and housekeeper, otherwise would clump back into her kitchen a prey to injury and grudge, slam about the tinned-copper cookpots, and burn the coffee.

By the time this comedy of manners was completed, Eszterhazy had clean forgotten what it was that he wanted to do about the newspaper piece on the Romance of Jewels. So he set it aside to be boxed for later perusal.

It was over the coffee and the triple-distilled liqueur of plum that the message arrived at the hands of Emmerman the night porter. The message consisted of some words scribbled over, as it happened, a copy of the same *feuilleton*.

"What's this, Emmerman?"

"Someone give it me, Lord Doctor."

"What someone?"

"Dunno, Lord Doctor. He run off." Emmerman, bowing, departed to take up his post of duty from Lemkotch, the day porter.

"Well, Eszterhazy," said himself to himself, "you train your servants to be brief, you must not complain if they are not prolix."

See Sludge, said the message, in its entirety. The handwriting tended toward the script favored in the official Avar-language schools of Pannonia, which brought it down to only seven million or so possible people. Still, that was a start of sorts. As for *Sludge.* The word was an epithet for any of the three and one half to four million Slovatchko-speaking subjects of the Triune Monarchy, and for their language. Its use was rather a delicate matter. "Who you shoving, Sludge?" was, for example, grounds for blows. Yet. Yet the same person who violently objected to the word might easily say, "Speak Sludge" — meaning, talk sense. Or: "What, three beers 'much to drink'? Who you talking to? You talking to a Sludge!" On reflection, and considering that the message had been scribbled on a newspaper . . .

There had always been a kind of genteel pretense in the office of the *Evening Gazette* that the premises constituted a sort of extension of the College of Letters. No such notion had ever obtained in the raucous chambers of the *Morning Report,* where sometimes the spit hit the spittoon, and sometimes it did not, and nobody cared or commented, as long as the details of the interview with the Bereaveds of the latest butcher-shop brawl got set down in full, rich description. Whereas the *Gazette* (if it mentioned the distasteful matters at all) might say, "The deceased was almost decapitated by the fatal blow. One of his employees was taken into custody;" the *Report* would be giving its readers something to the effect that "Blood was all over the bedroom of the Masterbutcher Helmuth Oberschlager whose head was pretty nearly all chopped off by the frenzied blows supposedly delivered in an enraged lovequarrel over the affections of Frow Masterbutcher Helga Oberschlager, third wife of the elderly Masterbutcher Helmuth Oberschlager. The corpse lay almost upside-down propped against the bloodstained bed and the scant undergarment of Journeymanbutcher," etc.

That was the way they did things at the *Report.*

As the editor of the *Report* had been born in the Glagolitic Alps, the very heartland of the Slovatchko, he was not eligible to become President of the United States. So, instead, he had accomplished something almost as difficult, namely, becoming editor of the largest-circulation Gothic-language newspaper in the Imperial (and officially Gothic-speaking) Capital. Where he disarmed all insults in advance by using the nickname of "Sludge" almost to the entire exclusion of his real name.

There would be little point in making references to someone's illegitimacy if he chose to answer his telephone with "Bastard speaking, yeah?"

So.

"Hello, Sludge."

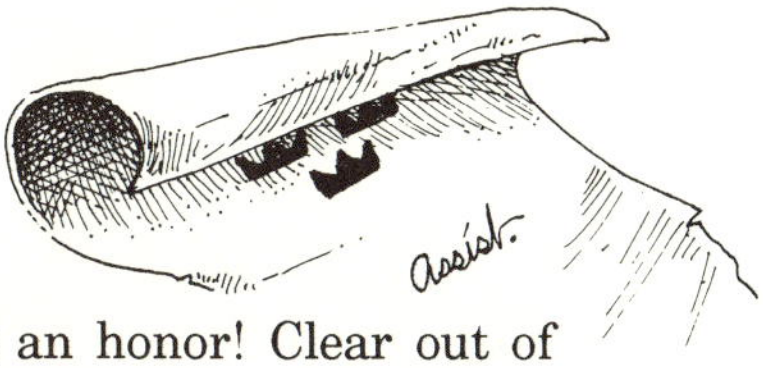

"Hel-lo. Hel-lo! Doctor Eszterhazy! What an honor! Clear out of that chair, you illiterate son of a vixen" — this, to his star reporter, who had in fact already stood up and was offering the chair — "and let the learned doctor sit down."

"Thank you, Swarts."

Sludge, a squat, muscular man with a muddy complexion and prominent green eyes, looked at his visitor with keen appraisal. "I suppose you haven't really come to give us a story to the effect that Spa water is as good for the bowels as an Epsom salts physic, and no Goddam good whatsoever for consumption, rheumatism, liver complaint, kidney trouble, and all the rest of it, eh?"

Eszterhazy did not ask him how he had put two and two together. They looked at each other with understanding. "You may perhaps be interested in a forthcoming article in the *Journal of the Iberian Academy of Medicine.*"

The editor, who had eagerly picked up a pencil, flung his head to one side and put the pencil down again. "Oh, why, certainly, I'll have Our Special Correspondent in Madrid . . ." His voice trailed away; the pencil was taken back, a note made. "I would ask what you would advise about it, eh, Doctor?" What the doctor would advise about it was that the *Report* wait until an abstract had appeared in the French medical journal, which would be excerpted in the British *Lancet.* After that, an article in a Swiss scientific publication of immense standing was inevitable. And the subject would by then be provided with all sorts of guarantees and precedents, and ready to be sprung upon the population of Bella without risk of Sludge spending perhaps thirty days in jail for, say, Libel of the National Patrimony (to wit, its medicinal spas).

"Yeah. Yeah." Sludge scribbled away. "But not me, never, no. Not even thirty days. Not even thirty minutes."

He arose without a word of warning, and, at the top of his lungs, screamed something absolutely incomprehensible, and waited. From somewhere far off, above the clatter of the typewriting machines, the pounding of the steam presses, a voice called up words equally obscure. Sludge smiled and sat down. He looked at his caller again, waiting.

Who was not yet quite ready.

"Why not?" asked Eszterhazy. "You are the Responsible Editor of the *Report.* What?" Sludge rapidly shook his head. The star reporter smiled. "But . . . it says so, on the masthead. 'L. Methodios Hozzenko, Responsible Editor.' "

Sludge smiled. The star reporter laughed out loud.

"That's my Uncle Louie," Sludge said. "The world's worst loafer, bar none. *I* am down on the payroll as L. M. Hozzenko, Nephew, Municipal Editor, see? Trouble comes up, who goes down to the courthouse? Uncle Louie. Who goes to jail? Uncle Louie. We bring him cheap cigars and beer in a bucket and sandwiches and hot-sausage-and-crout, and he plays cards with the cops. . . . *He* don't care! And what really brings *you* here, Doctor E.?"

Eszterhazy said that the Romance of Old Jewelry brought him there. The star reporter choked on a snort. Sludge threw his head back and his arms out.

Eszterhazy said, "Details. Details. Details."

"This won't get out? All right, excuse me, Doctor, of course you won't — Not until our first morning edition gets out. After that — 'Details?' Well, what is it that you don't know? Obviously you do know that the Crown Jewels of Jerusalem have been stolen, and that —"

A multitude of thoughts rushed headlong through Eszterhazy's mind. *"The Cyprus Regalia!"* he exclaimed. Sludge shrugged, indulgently. "That's for you educated folks," he said, without malice. "Us Glagolitski, we never even heard of the Cyprus Regalia. Never even heard of *Cyprus!* But — the Crown Jewels of Jerusalem? Oh, boy, did we ever hear of *them!* Say, one day, down at the little old farmstead, Grandpa rushes up, waving his stick, 'Who let the dogs knock over the barrow of pigshit, was it *you?*' 'Oh, no, Bobbo! It wasn't me! I swear it, I swear it, by the Crown Jewels of Jerusalem, I swear it!' See?"

And the star reporter said it was just the same among the Avars. "Suppose two old peasants have agreed on a deal for the rent of the orchards for the next plum harvest. They join hands and repeat the terms and then each one says in turn, 'I swear to keep this word and I swear it by the Holy Cross and the Avenging Angel and the Crown Jewels of Jerusalem. . . .' You talk to any of them about the Cyprus Regalia and he's likely to think he's being insulted and to hit you with *his* pig-stick."

Eszterhazy slowly, slowly nodded, and looked around the disorderly office, observing with only a sense of the familiar the photograph of The Presence. He observed with mild surprise the photograph of the American President, A. Lincoln. "Yes . . . I could sit here and, without having to send out for research materials, write an entire book to be titled . . . say . . . *The Cyprus Regalia or Crown Jewels of Jerusalem in Law, Legend, and History in the Triune Monarchy. . . .*"

Said Sludge, "And also, *With Added Details As To Their Theft From the Crypt of Saint Sophie* . . . Yeah . . ."

From an article, "The Romance of Old Jewelry," published in the *Evening Gazette* newspaper, Bella, April 7th, 190—

> Among the other items of jewelry pertaining to our beloved Monarchy are those sometimes called The Cyprus Regalia, or the Crown Jewels of Jerusalem. These consist of a crown with pendants, an orb with cross, and a sceptre, which, in turn, bears a

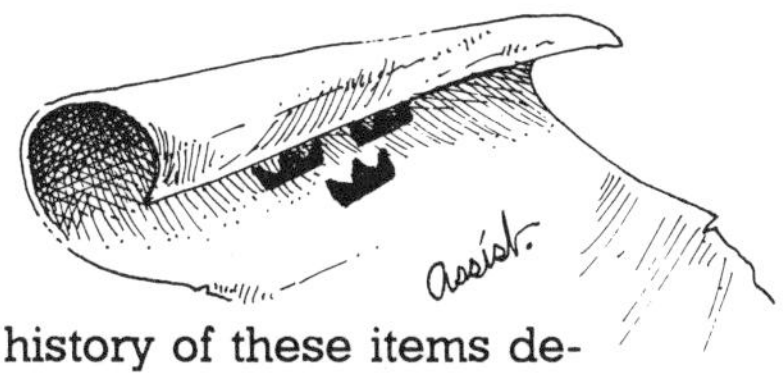

> miniature orb and cross. The popular history of these items derives, ultimately, from the *Glagolitic Chronicle,* composed for the most part by the Monk Mazzimilianos. According to this document of the later Anti-Turkish Resistance Period, these items formed the Crown Jewels of the Christian Kings of Jerusalem during the Crusades. Most modern historians tend not to accept this account. Some, such as Prince Proszt and Proszt, concede that The Regalia did form part of the Crown Jewelry of the Lusignan Kings who reigned over Cyprus prior to the rule of Venice — though only a part — and who were indeed crowned in two ceremonies: one, as Kings of Cyprus, and, two, as Kings of Jerusalem. The learned Prince, however, denies that these same Regalia were ever actually used during the earlier, or Jerusalem period at all. Other modern historical scholars, of whom it may suffice to mention only Dr. Barghardt and Professor Sz. Szneider, do not agree even to this account. The learned Dr. Barghardt goes to so far as to state: "The Turks could not have found them in the vaults of Famagusta when they captured Cyprus, for the very good reason that they (that is, the Jewels) never were in Cyprus at all." And Prof. Sz. Szneider suggests that The Regalia were probably made for the use of one of the many late medieval Christian princes of the Balkania whose brave defiance of the Turks, alas . . .

Eszterhazy sighed, ran his finger farther down the column, grunted, stopped the finger in its tracks.

> But popular opinion prefers to accept the traditional account that these were indeed the very Crown Jewels of Jerusalem, that they were in very truth captured from Prince Murad in single combat by the great and noble Grandduke Gustave Hohenschtupfen, direct ancestor of our beloved Monarch. Popular opinion makes a very definite connection between the possession of these Regalia by the Royal and Imperial House and the August Titles of our beloved Ruling Family: which, as every schoolchild knows, commence with "Holy Roman Emperor of Scythia, Apostolic King of Pannonia, and Truly Christian King of Jerusalem, Joppa, Tripoli, and Edessa," and . . .

Popular opinion, to be sure, was taking the whole thing very, very seriously indeed. Already reports were coming in from the wilder regions of Transbalkania that some of the peasantry were claiming that, with the loss of the Holy Crown Jewels of Holy Jerusalem, the Imperial and Royal power had passed in effect into abeyance, that Satan was now let loose to wage war upon the Saints, and that it was accordingly no longer necessary to pay the salt tax and the excise on distilled spirits.

All things religious were always touchy in the wilder regions of Transbalkania, but even closer to home — in fact, two blocks away — Eszterhazy had heard a drayman shouting to a troika driver, "Did you hear what them Goddamned Turks have done, the dogs?"

"Yes, the dirty dogs," the troikanik had howled, "they stole back the Holy Jewels, we ought to send our gun-boats down the Black Sea and bombard Consta' until they give them back, the dogs!"

The drayman had a caveat.

"We haven't *got* no gunboats on the Black Sea, God-damn it!"

"Well, we better *get* some there, then, blood of a vixen, the dirty dogs, *shove!*" And he cracked his whip over the backs of his horses, as though Ali Pasha, Murad the Midget, and Abdul Hamid themselves were all in the traces.

And now a voice called from the staircase, "Berty, art home?"

Not many people addressed Engelbert Eszterhazy in the *thou*-form. Even fewer called him "Berty."

"To thee, Kristy!" he called back.

Visits from his first cousin once-removed Count Kristian-Kristofr Eszterhazy-Eszterhazy were rare. When he was not acting in his official capacity as Imperial Equerry, the Count preferred, in his purely personal capacities, to visit places much more amusing than the house at 33 Turkling Street. No merely familial duty or memories of boyhood spent much together had brought him here now, his moustache unwaxed, his figure for once unassisted by the usual corset, and smelling rather strongly of Cognac, cologne, and extreme agitation. Without pause or further greetings, he made rapidly for the champagne bucket in the corner and, with a hand which trembled slightly, poured himself a drink from the bottle, tossed half of it off, and —

"No," said Dr. Eszterhazy, "it is not champagne. It is a mixture of geneva with an Italian wine which has been steeped in a profusion of herbs. Courtesy of the American Minister. He calls it 'martini.' I don't know why."

Count Kristy downed the other half and sighed. "Listen, Berty, up, up, and into the saddle. Bobbo has gone round the bend."

It was one of His Royal and Imperial Highness's amiable little habits, which endeared him much to his Slovatchko subjects, that he liked to refer to himself in the third person . . . at *certain times* . . . by the term which meant, varying slightly in the Glagolitic dialects, Grandfather, Godfather, Foreman, Headman, Father-in-law, or — somewhat mysteriously — a boar with either three tusks or three testicles. "What!" he would exclaim, to a delegation from the Hither Provinces. "What! No rain this year? What! Crops bad? What! Want your land rates reduced? Ah, my children, you did right to come to Bobbo! Bobbo will take care of it! Pray for Bobbo! Bobbo is your

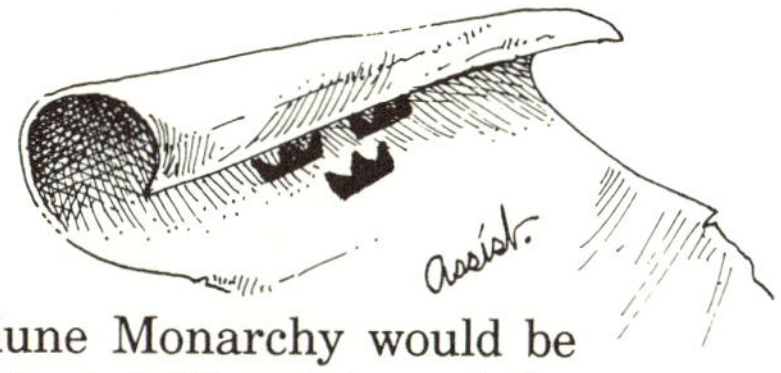

friend!" And so the Dissolution of the Triune Monarchy would be postponed for another five years. At times the intelligentsia and the underground felt certain that Ignats Louis was a stupid old fool. At other times, they were not so sure.

"What? Like poor old Mazzy?"

"Well . . . not quite so bad as that. Doesn't ride his white horse up and down the stairs hunting for Bonaparte. What he *does* do . . . he blubbers, flops on his knees every other minute and prays, shouts, storms, curses, weeps, smacks his riding crop on his desk, and — It's these damned Cyprus Regalia things. (Wouldn't be surprised if they aren't actually *glass,* myself.) Poor old Bobbo, he has the notion that until and unless the Holy Jewels are found, his Crowns, his real crowns, I mean, are in peril."

Eszterhazy, whose devotion to the Person of the Imperial Presence was based on a deep-seated preference for King Log over King (or President, or Comrade) Stork, winced and shook his head.

"This is not quite reasonable," he said.

"When you are seventy-five years old, and an Emperor," Count Kristy pointed out, "you don't have to be quite reasonable. The Old Un is really in a *state,* I tell you! Won't review the Household Troops. Won't read the Budget. Won't sign the Appointments or the Decrees. Won't listen to *Madame* play the harpsichord —"

"Oh! Oh!" If Ignats Louis would not listen to the twice-daily harpsichord performance of Madame de Moulière, whose position as *maîtresse en titre* had, presumably, for many years been so purely titular indeed that it rested chiefly on the remembrance of things past and on the twice-daily performance upon the harpsichord, then, *then,* things were very bad indeed.

"Weeps, prays, storms, stamps," Count Kristy recapitulated. "Reminds everyone that it is still part of the Imperial Prerogative to flay his servants up to and including the rank of Minister — Well. And speaking of which. The Prime —"

"The Prime Minister had ordered extra guards around the Turkish Legation, yes. What else?"

"Aunt Tillie asked me to mention that she is also very disturbed."

The Grandduchess Matilda was the wife of The Heir. And where was The Heir? "Where would he be? If he isn't murdering grouse, stags, and boars, he's on maneuvers. Right now — *fortunately!* — he is on maneuvers just about as far as he can be, in Little Byzantia, with no posts, no telegraphs, and the heliograph limited to matters purely military."

Little Byzantia was, in fact, one of the kernels in the nut. Little Byzantia was, nominally, still a *pashalik,* although the Triune Monarchy had administered it for forty-two years. During all that time, its eventual annexation to the Triple Crowns had been anticipated. And now, though very *sub rosa,* final negotiations with the Sublime Porte were underway. The Sublime Porte did not very much care at all. The Byzantian underground nationalists cared very much. Negotiations were very delicate. Anti-Turkish riots were not desired. Or — and this was another kernel in the nut — they were not desired *now.* The nut, of course, had many kernels. The temper of The Heir, always largely under control when at home and surrounded by ceremony, tended to become less and less under control the farther away from home it got.

There was a very possible and very undesirable order of progression. It went like this: First, Anti-Turkish riots in Bella . . . or, for that matter, in Transbalkania, where a minority of several score thousand Turks still slept away their days over their hookahs and their prayer beads. Following such riots: A Reaction, any kind of a Reaction, on the part of Turkey. Following *that,* and assuming The Heir to find out (and find out he must, sooner or later), precipitate action on the part of The Heir. Following that: Protests by France, Austria-Hungary, Russia, and Roumania. And, following *that*: A stroke, a heart attack, or any of the other disasters lying in wait for an excited old man of seventy-five. And, *following that* —

The Heir had many lovable qualities. One loved The Heir. One wished him many more long years . . . as Heir.

Slowly, Eszterhazy said, "In fact, Kristy, I am working on it now. But I will need time. And I will need help."

Count Eszterhazy-Eszterhazy said, "I can't do a damned thing about time. But as for *help,* well — " He fished something out of his equerry's pouch. "Bobbo ordered me to give you . . . this."

"Jesus ***Christ!***"

"This" was a piece of parchment, deeply imprinted with the Triple Crowns at the top. In the middle, a hand (and Doctor Eszterhazy well knew Whose) had scrawled the one word *ASSIST.* Underneath the *ASSIST,* the same Hand had drawn the initials

I L
I R

And, at the bottom (more or less), in wax, the Seal Imperial. And, in each corner, another initial, forming together the **I N R I**.

"I've never even held one in my *hand* before!"

The Count said, somewhat gloomily, "Neither has anyone else now alive, hardly. — One more glass of that American wine — St. Martin's, you call it? — then I must go."

The old King-Emperor's mind had, under stress and woe, evidently (at least in this one matter) gone back clear sixty-odd years, when the *Provót* (as it was commonly called) had last been used: and that was to harry the horse thieves of the Lower Ister. (Quite successfully, as a matter of fact.) Usually worn out in the course of their

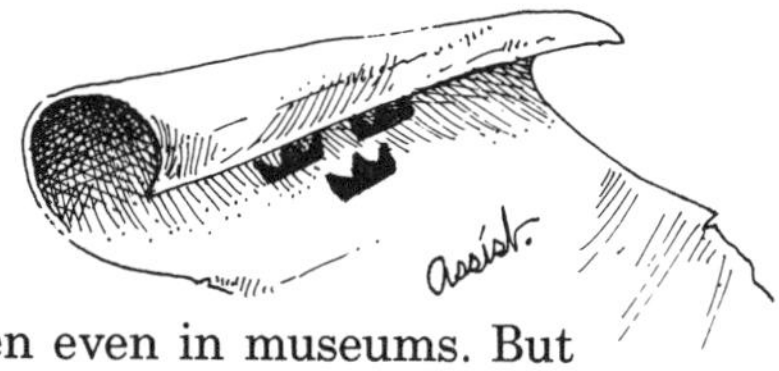

commissions, only a few survived to be seen even in museums. But everyone had seen pictures of them, in newspapers, magazines, even almanacs. Theater bills and posters. They were a staple feature of the popular melodrama.

"Baron Bluegrotz, will nothing stay you from your mad determination to throw me and my aged wife out of our cottage into the snow because we will not allow you to take our promised-in-marriage-daughter into your castle?"

"Nothing [with a sneer]! Nothing, nothing will stay me!"

A commotion, the door is flung open.

"***This*** will stay you!" The ***This*** being, of course, the *Provót* which the hero holds up in his hand. — At which the evil baron and all his henchfellows fall upon their knees and bare their heads and cross themselves and hope they will be merely hanged and not flayed or impaled, and the audience jumps to its feet and shouts and stamps and claps and cheers.

Perhaps the aged mind of Ignats Louis *had* buckled under the strain. Thinking that this relic of the Middle Ages and the Early Turkish Wars was appropriate in the era of the telephone, telegraph, and police force. However. Ignats Louis (**I L**) had, indeed, issued it. He was, indeed, ***I**mperator* and ***R**ex* (**I R**). And it took not much to see clearly the association in his ancient and pious mind between the supposed Crown Jewels of Jerusalem and the letters, traditionally placed around the corners of the parchment, initials of the words ***I**esus **N**azarenus, **R**ex **I**udaeorum. . . .*

"Well," said Doctor Eszterhazy, crisply, "it is not for me to bandy words with my sovereign. He issues, I accept. Make His Imperial Majesty an appropriate reply."

"And what," asked Count Kristy, putting his uniform cap back on, and, with a rather weary shrug, preparing to depart, "what is 'an appropriate reply'?"

A moment's pause. "Tell him," said Doctor Eszterhazy, "tell him I said, '*Adsum . . .*' "

"Lemkotch, I am not at home to anyone."

He had known now for some time that the key word in the *Gazette* article, and the one which had tripped the flare in his mind — he had known now for some time that the word was **Jerusalem.**

"Are you not Engelbert Eszterhazy, Doctor of Medicine?

"I must depart from my invariable incognito to inform you, sir, that I *am King of Jerusalem. . . .*"

Over and over again, head resting in his hands, in the silence and solitude of his study, he went over the odd scene in the old Spring Room at the mountain spa. Was there, now that he deliberately tried to think that there might be, *was* there something else in his memory, besides that single scene, connecting himself with the man behind that totally unmemorable face? Or was this delusion?

After a while he sat up, took a pad and drawing pencil, and, as best he could, made a sketch of the man as he remembered him. The clothing, he somehow felt, the clothing was nothing. *The face* — He discarded the first drawing and sketched, and larger, the face alone. With the pinch-nose eyeglasses. And the absurd moustache, trimmed shorter on one side. And the hair . . . The hair, now . . . Well, the man had worn a hat, a hat like millions. Take off the hat, then, and draw the face without it. Did he part his hair in the middle? Perhaps. Trim it close, like a Prussian officer? Unlikely. Or was he, perhaps, bald? On the whole, and although he could not say why he thought so, Eszterhazy rather thought that the man *was* bald. He finished the sketch. And stared. Still nothing. Or, rather . . . something . . .

Take off the eyeglasses.

Take off the moustache, too.

After another while, he got up and, fixing the latest sketch to a drawing-board, set this one up on an easel. Turned the gaslights down very low. Turned the shade of the electric lamp so that it acted like a spotlight. Sat back in his chair. Allowed all the rest of the world to fall away . . . except for The Face . . .

Had he seen it before?

He *had* seen it before.

Question and answer.

Where had he seen it before?

Question — but no answer.

The stillness grew. There seemed to be no one passing in the street. There seemed to be no carriages in the city. The cathedral bells did not ring. The last voice in the world spoke, many, many blocks away. Then all fell silent.

But if the sense of sound vanished, other senses remained. There was a smell, and a rather bad smell it was. He could not exactly say what the smell was. Familiar, though. Damnably familiar. That face. *Face.* Where had he seen —

Without even being able to recall the steps in between, Eszterhazy was in the kitchen. His housekeeper stared at him, her mouth all agape and askew.

"What did you say?" he was asking her, urgently, urgently.

"Why, High-born —"

"What did you say, what did you *say* —" He forced himself to speak in a softer voice. "Goodwoman, now, do not be afraid. But it is very important. What did you say, a while back, you said something about . . ." He strained memory; memory submitted, yielded up. "Something about needing something. You said," he clenched his fists behind his back in the face of her massive incomprehension, the two moles near her mouth, one with a hair in it, never longer, never

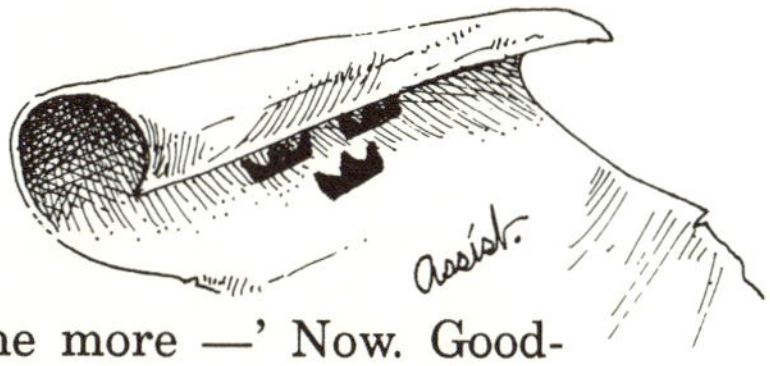

shorter — "You said, 'We need to get some more —' Now. Goodwoman. You need to get some more of what?"

But still she stood frozen. A figure bobbed behind her. A figure in a greasy apron. Probably the scullery maid. "If you please, Frow Widow Orgats," the kitchenwoman murmured, "you had been saying, a minute or so back, how we was needing to get more disinfectant. For the — please to pardon the word — for the servants' privy. In the yard."

Something was out of the ordinary at the Royal and Imperial Penitentiary Fortress, where his card was always sufficient to bring Smits, the Sub-Governor, bowing respectfully, and saluting, as well, when he had done bowing. Smits was a career screw, up through the ranks of the Administration of Guards. It was, of course, the Governor, Baron Von Grubhorn, who interviewed journalists and discussed with them the theories of Lombroso on The Criminal Type. It was the Governor of the prison who made the weekly address to the prisoners as they stood in chains, exhorting them on their duties as Christians and loyal subjects of the Triune Monarchy. But it was the Sub-Governor who checked the bread ration, saw to the cell assignments, and even tasted the prison stew — or, as it was unaffectionately called, "the scum" — and, had the Sub-Governor not done so, the bread ration would have diminished, more murders been committed in the cells, and the stew been even scummier.

Now, however, the Sub-Governor was neither bowing nor saluting. He stood in the mud at the entrance to the Fortress directing the emplacement of what seemed to be a Gatling gun. All about him were guards with rifles at the ready; they poured in and out of the entrance, moiling like ants. Eszterhazy stopped the steam runabout (whose bronze handbell no one here seemed to have heard) about two hundred feet away and proceeded on foot.

"What's wrong, Smits?"

The look Smits flung him was bleak as a rock. "Can't come here now. Away with you!" Peering, he recognized the approaching visitor. "Can't *come* here now, Doctor! Governor's orders! The prisoners are about to riot, sir, they think their bread ration is about to be reduced — a damned lie, but try to tell *them* that — Back, sir! I says, away with you! Don't you *hear* —" He gestured, said some words in a lower voice. Two captains and a number of ordinary guards began to trot forward, holding the rifles at the oblique, to bar his way.

Eszterhazy reached into his pocket, and holding his forearm up at the traditional forty-five-degree angle, thrust out the *Provót.*

Sub-Governor, captains, and guards alike, sweeping off their caps, fell on their knees in the mud, the Sub-Governor, who alone was unencumbered with a rifle, crossing himself repeatedly.

The Governor himself stood on the inner parapet, shouting at the prisoners below. All along the platform were guards, rifles pointing down into the yard. But no one could hear a word the Baron was saying over the noise of the shouting and the ringing chains of the convicts. He turned his head as Eszterhazy approached, and his mouth fell silent. That is, presumably it fell silent. At any rate, his mouth ceased to move. Eszterhazy stepped next to him and held up the *Provót.*

With one great and simultaneous crash of chains, the convicts fell on their knees.

A ringing, echoing silence followed.

"I have received this from the Emperor," Eszterhazy said. "I bring you assurance that the bread ration is not to be reduced."

They did not, after all, give three cheers for the Emperor. Perhaps it was shock. One man, however, in a loud hoarse voice, half-growled, half-shouted: ***"Good old Bobbo!"***

"No punitive measures will be taken . . . this time . . . but you are to return to your cells, *at once."* The words were Eszterhazy's. The Governor, speechless, gestured to the Sub-Governor. The Sub-Governor barked an order. All the rifles went up — straight up. And stayed so. Down in the yard, someone (a trusty, by his red patch) cried, *"**Hump**, tump, thrump, fump!"* The convicts fell into ranks, turned about, and, line by line, in lock-step, began to file out of the yard.

***Clash*-clash-clash-clash.**

***Clash*-clash-clash-clash . . .**

The riot was over.

This time.

The Sub-Governor gave a long look at the sketch which Eszterhazy showed him. (The Governor was drinking brandy, and looking at nothing.)

"Why, yes, Sir Doctor," said Sub-Governor Smits. "Yes, I **do** remember him. You says to me, 'This one's got a bad lung, so keep him out of the damp if you possibly can.' Which I done, Sir Doctor, which I done, inasmuch as we of the Administration of Guards are human beings after all, and not aminals like some would have it said." Even up here, in the middle story of the old tower, far above the cell blocks, the smell of sweat and urine and disinfectant seemed very strong. "Consequently is why he left here alive and in better health than he come in."

Eszterhazy stared. "It has been a fatiguing week, Sub-Governor. A fatiguing week." On the mottled wall, Ignats Louis, bifurcated beard and all, looked down benignly. "Assist my memory, please. When did I say this?"

Smits raised a rough, red hand to his rough, red chin. "Why . . .

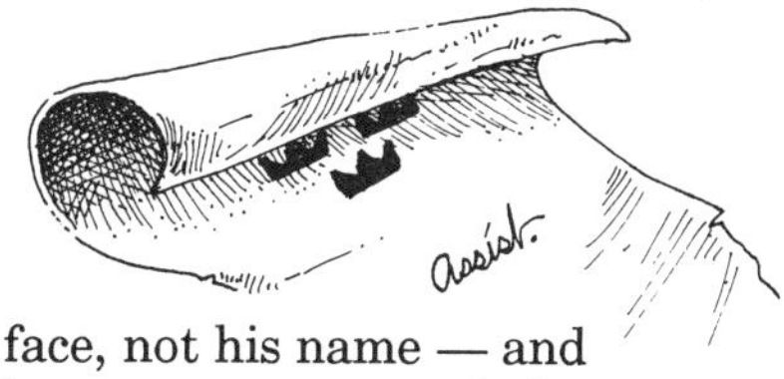

Strange that I should remember, sir — his face, not his name — and you not, with your great mind. But, then, I never was one much for writing and for reading. But I knew by sight, as a boy, every beast in our township. Well. When. Why, when you examine his noggin, sir. Excuse me, Sir Doctor — we are rough men here — when you give the first of them free no-logical examinations. Is when."

And so, after much digging up of old records and after much checking and cross-checking of the prison files, it was found:

NUMBER 8727–6. NAME Gogor, Teodro. AGE 25.
OFFENSE Forgery, 2nd class. STATE Confused.
REMARKS Perhaps Dement. Prae.

And so on.

And so on.

And so on.

"Well, well . . . I am much obliged. And now I must get back to Bella and think about this."

The Sub-Governor rose along with him, saying casually, "And so you think, Sir Doctor, that this old lag, Gogor, he might be the one that's tooken the Holy Jewels?"

Eszterhazy once again looked at his sovereign's face. After a moment, he turned back to Smits. "Why do you think that?"

Smits shrugged and began to hold up Eszterhazy's overcoat for him. "Well, I dunno for sure, of course. But they were cracked from old St. Sophie's Crypt, it's been in all the papers. They say, the papers, that is was an amateurish job. Which it succeeded because the crib they were in, it was so old, the mortar was crumbly and so on. 'Amateurish,' but at the same time they say, 'Professional tools may have been employed,' yes."

Eszterhazy buttoned his coat. "Thank you, Smits. Yes — and so?"

"Well, Sir Doctor. It come into my mind as we were talking, this Gogor, he was in old cell 36-E-2. And who was in there with him? Szemowits, another fancy-writer (forger, that is). Plus a chap I can't recall his name, up for Rape, Second. And Old Bleiweisz. Do you recollect Old Bleiweisz? Well, he was a cracksman. One of the best, they tell me. Anyways, *he* said he was. Always talking about how to do it, and how *he* done it. And so, well, just perhaps, now, the thought come to me, maybe that is how this Gogor — if it *was* him — how he got the idea of how to do it. You see . . ."

Eszterhazy, nodding, buttoned his gloves. "I see. An interesting thought. Would it be possible to speak to this Bleiweisz?"

But the Sub-Governor said it would not be possible. "He's drawn the Big Pardon, as the lags say. He's under the flagstone now. What was it, now, as done for him? *Ah* yes."

He opened the door and gestured the Eszterhazy to pass ahead of him. "It was lungs, that was it. Dunno why. He was healthy when he come in."

Lobats did not seen to have gotten enough sleep lately. He looked at the paper Eszterhazy had given him, blinked, and shook his head. "What is this? Something about somebody sent up for a forgery, Second, seven years ago? — Better take this downstairs to Records, Doctor. I've got something . . . well . . . a lot bigger to worry about."

Eszterhazy said that he was sure of that, that he had suspected as much ever since he had seen Commissioner of the Detective Police Karrol-Francos Lobats so deep in conversation in the Pearl Market. Conversation with Jewelers' Association President De Hooft. So deep that Lobats had not even had time for a word with his old acquaintance and so-often companion, Dr. Engelbert Eszterhazy . . .

Was it unfair for him to be rubbing it in like this? Maybe. Maybe not. Eszterhazy did not want it thought that he, and everything that his immense knowledge and capacity had to offer, could be regarded as the toy of an idle moment, to be picked up, and to be set aside or ignored when someone else might want to . . .

"This Forgery, Second, fellow may be the fellow you are so worried about. We will both need all the information on him you can find . . . in Records . . . or out of Records. Do you take my word for it? Or shall I show, shall we say, authority?" He had begun to have a superstitious notion that he ought to be chary about displaying the *Provót,* lest overexposure might . . . somehow . . . dissipate its power.

Lobats said heavily, "I take your word for just about anything. But I am not so worried about a forger. I'm worried about —"

"A jewel theft. Yes."

For all his heaviness, Lobats got up quickly from his chair. "Well, it has been known for crooks to change styles. I sure hope you are right."

Records, however, had only records. Old records. Seven years old.

If Gogor, Teodro, had committed any more recent offenses against His Royal and Imperial Majesty, His Realm, His Crown and Staff, he had not been apprehended for the crimes.

Those other and perhaps equally important sources of information upon which the police of the world's great cities (and, perhaps, its small ones, too) depend — to wit, informers — had nothing to say upon the subject, either. His former employers, against whom the forgery had been committed (and, interestingly enough, they *did* deal in job lots of oilcloth!), had heard nothing of him since. And wanted to hear nothing of him now. His family, consisting of an exceedingly respectable brother and sister in the provincial city of Praz (and no city is more respectable than Praz), knew nothing of his present or

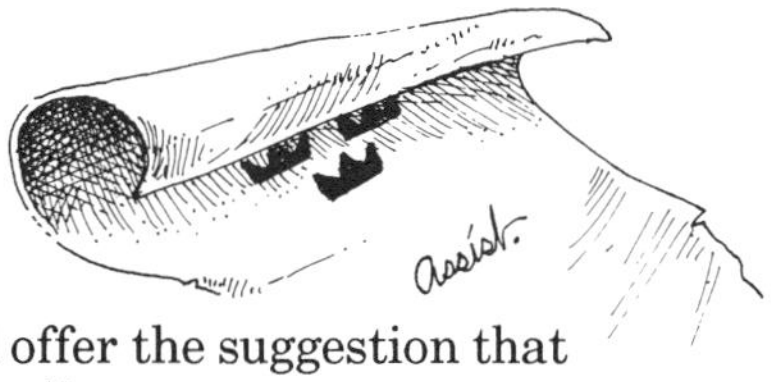

recent or post-prison career, either. They did offer the suggestion that he might have gone to America. Or to Australia.

"He was in Gross-Kroplets this same year," Eszterhazy insisted. "Well. You keep onto that. I have some loose ends of my own which I must try to tie together. I shall see you tomorrow."

On the third floor of the house at 33 Turkling Street, Herra Hugo Van Sltski was (after Dr. Eszterhazy himself) supreme. Here was Dr. Eszterhazy's library. And Herra Van Sltski was Dr. Eszterhazy's librarian. This scholar had a bad complexion, a bad breath, and a worse temper, but he was familiar with all the dialects and languages of the Triune Monarchy — plus French, English, Latin, Greek, and Sanscrit — and he was absolutely indefatigable. His employer had only to send him, via the pneumatic tube, a message to this effect: *Gogor, Teo, in the Criminal Phrenological Examinations, First Series,* for the envelope to reach him, via the same tube, in less than five minutes.

He opened it and drew out the yellow-paper chart. Down the lefthand margin were listed the Proclivities, Propensities, and Faculties. Across the top were the ratings, ranging from Overdeveloped through Underdeveloped to Absent, with graduations between. At the bottom, in a series of small boxes, were the cranial measurements, taken by Eszterhazy himself, with calipers and other instruments (one of them, of his own invention). But he was not greatly interested in the measurements, a glance at them showing that Gogor had an average head as far as size and shape went. It had been his intention, after taking the readings of each quarter, to assess each reading, and to make a summary on the inner leaf of the chart. However, that year — the year he had first taken such readings of a large number of criminals — that year had also been an epidemic year. He had not had time to make the assessments. He had made them each quarter-year afterwards. Somehow, he had never gone back to the First Series.

Ah, well. So, then, now to it.

PHRENOLOGICAL ASSESSMENT OF TEODRO GOGOR, AGED 25, NATIONAL SUBJECT.

The Region of the lower back of the Head:

SOCIAL PROCLIVITIES. Amativeness: Very large. *Conjugality:* Underdeveloped. *Philoprogenitiveness:* Absent. Adhesiveness: Deficient. *Inhabitiveness:* Oddly developed. *Continuity:* Overdeveloped.

The Regions behind and above the Ears:

SELFISH PROPENSITIES. Vitativeness: Average. *Combatativeness*: Uncertain. *Destructiveness*: Weak. *Alimentiveness*: Deficient. *Acquisitiveness*: Strongly but oddly developed. *Cautiousness*: Deficient.

The Regions approaching and reaching the Crown of the Head:
THE ASPIRING FACULTIES, or, *LOWER SENTIMENTS.* *Approbativeness*: Strongly developed. *Self-esteem*: Overdeveloped. *Firmness*: Overdeveloped.

The Coronal Region:
THE MORAL SENTIMENTS. Conscientiousness: Deficient. *Hope*: Excessive development. *Spirituality*: Excessive. *Veneration*: Excessive. *Benevolence*: Deficient.

The Region of the Temples:
THE SEMI-INTELLECTUAL or *PERCEPTIVE FACULTIES. Constructiveness*: Slightly underdeveloped. *Mirthfulness*: Absent. *Ideality*: Strong. *Sublimity*: Overdeveloped. *Imitation*: Overdeveloped.

The Region of the Upper Forehead:
THE REASONING FACULTIES. Causality: Excessive. *Comparison*: Weak. *Human Nature*: Deficient. *Agreeableness*: Average.

The Region of the Center of the Forehead:
THE LITERARY FACULTIES. Eventuality: Well-developed. *Time*: Average. *Tune*: Defective. *Language*: Average.

The Region of the Brows:
THE PERCEPTIVE FACULTIES. Individuality: Slightly underdeveloped. *Form*: Average. *Size*: Average. *Color*: Average. *Order*: Developed. *Calculation*: Odd. *Locality*: Average.

Eszterhazy considered a segar but decided to let the pleasure await him at the end of the task. He did allow himself the pleasure of addressing an observation to himself. "I foresee," he said aloud, "that great possibility, amounting almost to probability, that phrenology must give way to newer and younger sciences, which even now stand waiting at the door to accept, and without acknowledgement, the hard-won discoveries of their elder sister. The intangible aspects, the immaterial ones, will be taken over by psychology. The material and tangible ones, by physical anthropology. Calculations based upon the cephalic index and other cranial measurements have already taught us much about primitive man, and will try to teach us even more about his modern descendants." He bent to his work, then, lifting his head once more, said slowly, "And it may be that these younger sisters of the sciences will find others, younger yet, waiting to supplant them. . . ."

Long he pondered over the yellow-paper chart, and much he pondered. Overhead, in the great gasoliers wrought in red bronze in the shapes of mermaids with naked bosoms, the gas flames (each one

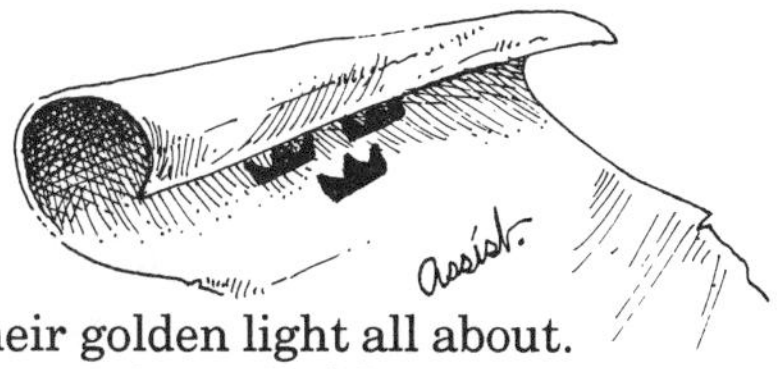

cupped in the hands of one mermaid) cast their golden light all about.

One man may look at a mountain and see only rock. Most men, looking at a mountain, would see only rock. That one man in hundreds of thousands, trained in observation by geology, looking at the selfsame mountain, will see half a hundred different kinds of rock, will see indications of ores buried in mine and matrix deep below the surface (though not so deep as to be beyond delving and discovering), will know what ancient writhings of the Earth — ancientmost of mothers — sent which stratum buckling up or down and which stratum lying level as a rule-yard.

So it was in this case of Teodro Gogor.

And Eszterhazy, having been the first man, now proceeded to be the other.

The faculty of location was merely averagely developed. The fugitive (if such were the proper term) was thus not greatly attached to his native place, which now knew him not. He might indeed have gone to Australia (or to America), but nothing in his innate nature compelled him to be a rolling stone. The Faculties of Form, Size, Weight, and Color were also average. His sense of order was developed, naturally, or he could neither have planned nor carried out the audacious theft, however "amateurishly." His Faculty of Calculation, now. It had been marked "odd." His was no common covetousness, obviously; no desire for mere gold coin had moved him. He had been able to calculate how to commit the crime and how — for the present, anyway — to get away with it. Individuality, slightly underdeveloped. That fitted. He had a conception of himself as an individual — but as the wrong individual. For, whoever might (or might not) be the true King of Jerusalem, it was surely not he.

Dovetailing with this was the fact that both Approbativeness, comprising "the Desire for Fame and Acclaim," and Self-esteem were both overdeveloped — indeed, excessively so. And so was Firmness. No collywobbler could have set out to steal a national treasure . . . and done so. He was deficient in the Quality of Conscientiousness, but in that of Hope, he had far too much. When the Faculty of Spirituality is excessive, as here, there is an inevitable tendency toward the fanatic.

All true, all — now — obvious. And all, so far, just so much locking the stable door after the horse was gone. What did it avail, here and now, to realize that Gogor's Sentiment of Veneration was excessive? He might indeed be venerating the antique treasures. The point was, now, where?

"Deficient in Benevolence," very well, he would not fence the jewels in order to give the money to the poor. Indeed!

"Sublimity excessive, tending toward exaggeration." Obviously. "Imitation, overdeveloped." As true as anything could be true.

Mirthfulness, entirely absent. Hmmmm. No use to look for him enjoying a comedy turn in a music hall, then.

Well. Now for the Reasoning Faculties.

Excessive in Causality: his talents lay more toward the theoretical. He had little analytic ability, for his Faculty of Comparison was weak. Deficient in Human Nature, he would have no discrimination — Eszterhazy sighed and shifted in his seat. So far, all of *this* seemed theoretical. "Merely average in the qualities of Time and Language, deficient in that of Tone." So it was no use expecting to find him at a concert, either. And surely a mere yawn and a nod of the head to see that, owing to a well-developed Faculty of Eventuality, he, Gogor, would probably possess a great interest in history.

"Deficient in Cautiousness." This might be to the good. He might very well tip his hand. "Acquisitiveness strongly but oddly developed." This was but a double confirmation of what had been disclosed in connection with Calculation. "Alimentiveness deficient," eh? Merely eats to live. Not likely to haunt the better restaurants, nor send out for caviar, gooseliver, or champagne. Likely to drink little alcohol or none. "Combatativeness uncertain." Would he fight for his "cause"? — or not? In the propensity toward "Destructiveness, weak." This was somewhat favorable; it seemed to add up to "Not Dangerous."

And in Vitativeness, Gogor was merely average. He had had a bad lung, but he had recovered from it. Mmm, well, so, nothing here, no point in posting watches before the apothecaries'.

And thus, so much for the Selfish Propensities. Now for the Social Ones. And now for a quick prayer that something, at least *some*thing would turn up which would be of help —

"Continuity, overdeveloped." Again, an indication of a possible fanatical devotion to some one thing. Inhabitiveness, or attachment to a place or cause, oddly developed. In other words — now that we have all the *other* evidence — a tendency to form strong attachment to an odd cause. Bully. How often to plow this same furrow?

And now, O God, only four left!

> *Adhesiveness* (that is, friendship or affection): Deficient.
> *Philoprogenitiveness* (love of offspring): Absent.
> *Conjugality*: Undeveloped.
> *Amativeness*: Very large.

And there it was. There it all was. And he might almost as well have skipped all the rest of it.

Eszterhazy clapped his hands in pleasure.

If one rules out Conjugality and Philoprogenitiveness, one rules out desire for home and wife, for children. If even Adhesiveness is ruled out, a mistress is also ruled out. And so, what is left? Amativeness is left. In fact: *"Amativeness is very large . . ."* Here we have a man with

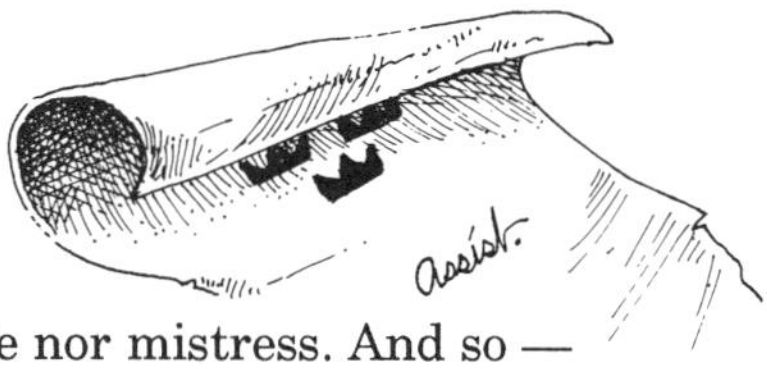

strong sexual passions, who has neither wife nor mistress. And so —

"Lord."

Eszterhazy, slightly startled, looked up. "Ah, Herrekk, what — ? Ah, yes, I clapped, didn't I. Ah . . . no . . . I had not meant — Wait! Herrekk!"

"Lord."

Eszterhazy thought for a moment. Then, "Herrekk. In the attic. The old pigskin traveling bag. The one with the Paris stickers on it. Bring it, please. But, first — take the stickers off . . ."

"Lord."

As the evening express from Praz was drawing into the Great Central Terminal, a man dressed in the height of the fashions of fifteen years earlier, and carrying a pigskin traveling bag of even earlier style, went up the side steps to the central platform. He walked slowly across, mingling with the crowds getting off the express, and went down the main steps and out the main gates —

— and drew back, nervously, from what wits called "the artillery attack."

"Fiacre, sir? Fiacre?"

"High-born Sir! This way! This way!"

"Fiacre, High-born Sir! Anywhere for a half-a-ducat!"

It seemed that half of the hackney coaches in Bella had assembled in the wide street outside the station. And as though, now, half of their drivers had flung down their leathers, and, leaping to the pavement, were intent on rushing the newly arrived passengers into their hacks by main force and what was called "grabbage."

And now see a tall and stalwart figure, an ex-hussar by the height and carriage of him, and resplendent in the uniform of a railroad terminal commissionaire, approach the newly arrived provincial. "All right, sir. Just please to tell me where it is as you'd like to go, and I'll take care of everything."

And he seems to interpose himself between the newcomer and the mob of coachmen, who seeing this, go bawling off and howling for other custom. Of which, after all, there seems no lack.

"Uh, I want, uh, I want to go . . . uh, go to . . . uh," and he gropes in his pockets for an address which is not there. Of course not. It never is when wanted. The commissionaire looks at this familiar scene indulgently. And he glances, with the barest trace of a smile, hid before it begins to show, almost, at the faded dandy.

"Did you want to go to a hotel, sir? I'm afraid one hears that the Grand Beatrix is full-up just now." Oh, what a relief for the visitor! Not to have to explain that he does not really *want* the famous (and justly so) Hotel Grand Beatrix, which would bankrupt him in one day, besides being, really, much, much, much too, well, *grand*. And yet, how flattering to hear that he is obviously thought to be a Grand Beatrix type! "There is the Austerlitz and the Vienna, of course, sir. Nice quiet places." The commissionaire knows full well that the visitor does not want a nice quiet place. "And there's the Hôtel de France, very reasonable rates, the gentry tells me, sir. Of course," her he gives a very slightly roguish look, "of course, some say it's rather a bit too gay and fast there. But I daresay that the gentleman might not find it so."

Hôtel de France! Gay and fast! Almost before he knows it, the commissionaire's whistle has blown, and there the gentleman is, and his luggage, too, luggage with not a single sticker to mar or mark its sturdy old sides, in a fiacre rattling over the stone-paved streets. But not rattling so very loudly. The stone paving-blocks are such smooth stone paving-blocks — quite unlike the streets of Praz, where ghastly primordial cobblestones, shaped like eggs, constitute the paving of the central plaza and adjacent streets, and everywhere else the natural soil and earth allow the streets to be as dusty, or muddy, as it pleases the dear God to ordain.

The sides of the Hôtel de France are painted with enormous letters, three stories in height, which inform the world that **EVERY ROOM IS FURNISHED WITH THE GASLIGHT.**

"A room for *Monsieur*? But certainly! Delighted!" The clerk slaps his hand on the desk bell. "Garçon! Take *Monsieur*'s bags up to Room 30-D!"

Monsieur! And *garçon*!

Sure enough, 30-D, at least, is furnished with gaslight. Sure enough, they rode up in a hydraulic elevator, started and stopped (and, for all the visitor knows to the contrary, Praz not even having a grain elevator, *propelled*) by a cable running through the center from floor to roof.

And, in an alcove in the hallway, only a few doors from 30-D, *there is even running water,* should one's pitcher run dry!

The French know how to live.

Lobats, meanwhile, had started at the bottom. Not, to be sure, at the very bottom. He did not bother with the two-penny drabs, poor wretched things, who plied their trade under the land arches of the Italian Bridge, or in the doorways of the alley round the Rag Market. He had engravings made of a series of sketches by Eszterhazy, and he was now out directing their distribution — not in broadside quantities or by broadside methods, he did not want them on lampposts, it was not intended to take such fairly desperate methods . . . yet. He was having them distributed where he thought they might do the most good.

In a dirty coffeehouse by the Old Fish Wharf, for instance.

"Hallo, Rosa."

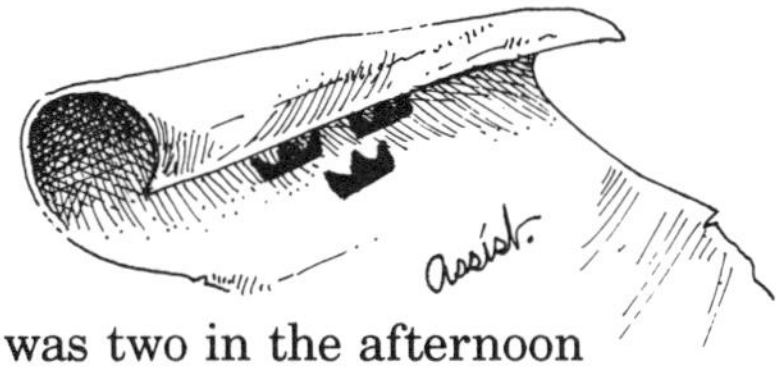

"Oh, God, I'm not even awake yet" — it was two in the afternoon — "and he wants to take me to jail. *I haven't done nothing!*"

"Oh, we know that, Rosa. Look here. Ever see this mug? No? Sure? Well, if you do . . . or think you do . . . well, you know how to pass the word along. Somebody might do herself a very good turn. Particularly if she needed one done. 'Bye, Rosa."

In a disreputable tavern behind the Freight Yards, for instance.

"Hallo, Genau."

A greasy, shriveled little man in a torn jacket of the same description seems about to dive beneath the counter. But he only dives deep enough to come up with a piece of paper. Also greasy and shriveled.

"Oh, I don't want to see your tax receipt, Genau. Look here. Ever see this mug? No? Sure? Well, if you do . . . Somebody might be able to make a very good deal for himself, if you know what I mean."

Genau seems to know what he means.

In front of a cheap bakery in the South Ward.

"Hey, you, Tobacco. Come here."

Tobacco comes here, eyes bulging with honesty. "I'm clean, Your Worship. Search me, 'few like. Haven't picked a tip since —"

"— since last night. Never mind. Take a look here. Eh?"

Tobacco takes a look. Shakes his head. "Not a regular."

"We'd like to see him, just the same. Twig? Secret fund. Twig?"

Tobacco twigs. "I'll be sure and letcha know. We don't like irregulars, anyway. Mucking things up and making things difficult for the trained hands. *Sure. I'll* letcha know."

"Hallo, Lou . . ."

"Hallo, Frou . . ."

"Hallo, Gretchen . . ."

"Hallo, Marishka . . ."

Marishka blinks her painted eyes. Gives a nod. A *very* tired nod. Genteelly smothers a yawn. "Sure. He's a bit dotty, ain't he? But not *dangerous.*"

Lobats: "You *have* seen him, then? When?"

Marishka sips, licks whipped cream off her painted lip. "Last night," she says, indifferently. "All night. Nothing special." She means, first, that her last night's guest had no very *odd* habits, and second, that he had paid only a standard fee.

"Where? Know where he might be?"

Marishka no longer even bothers to shrug. "He came in from the street," she says. "And he went back out into the street." She returns to her cup of coffee. It is all so very dull, life and its demands. They come in from the street. And they go back out into the street.

Over and over. However. Others can do that work. There is one thing more, which Doctor Eszterhazy had advised not be neglected.

And Lobats, who has a little list (written, this time — he has many little lists, and quite a few long ones, in his head). One by one he checks them off, shop after shop, and fitting-room after fitting-room. Then, scratching his head, he goes farther afield.

Frow Widow Higgins, Theatrical Costumière, was not from England, as the rich accents of her native South Ward testified. But the late Higgins had been born there. The late Higgins, however, was very late indeed, and his widow made little mention of him. She looked up from her sewing machine, through which she was running a tunic of 16th-century design . . . one which much needed the restorative attentions of the machine, and which, in fact, might indeed have been in semi-continual use since that century. She looked up from her sewing machine, and for a moment rested her foot at the treadle.

"Yeah," she said.

"When?"

"Oh . . . Maybe last month . . ."

Lobats wants her to tell him all about it. And, politely, for Frow Widow Higgins is of an entirely respectable and, God knows, hard-working character, he asks that she understand that he means *all* about it. Frow Widow Higgins runs her fingers over her tired eyes. Then she sums it up.

"He paid in cash," she says.

Many are the brightly dressed ladies who pass in and out of the saloon bar of the Hôtel de France, rich in lace, with very rich color in their cheeks, and with very large hats that many egrets have died to adorn. They are agreeable to letting the gentleman from Praz buy them a richly colored drink. They listen with arch interest to his story. After all, every gentleman has a story. They make remarks indicating interest. "And you can't settle the estate without him?" they repeat. "*Oh*-what-a-*shame!*" Well, any excuse will serve when a dandyish gent from the provinces wants to come up and have his bit of fun. There are few nicer pigeons to pluck than these dandyish gents from the provinces, after all. But the gentleman from Praz can't seem to take a hint. And so, one after another, hints as to dinner . . . the theater . . . supper . . . champagne . . . the opera . . . not only not being forthcoming, all such hints even on the ladies' parts meeting with no more response than, "Yes, but surely *some*one must know my brother; *he has lived in Bella for years!*" . . . well, sooner or later, the richly dressed ladies sigh and excuse themselves and move on.

Even if only to another table.

It is late.

Mlle. Toscanelli.

Mlle. Toscanelli is from Corsica. And if that is not French enough to suit any of the customers of the saloon bar of the Hôtel de France,

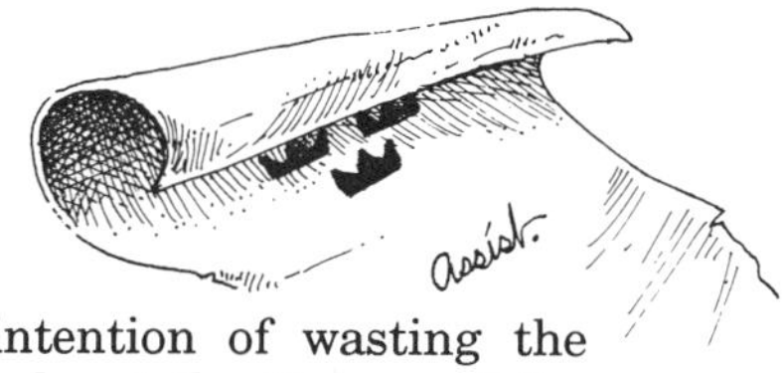

well, *oh-la-la!* Mlle. Toscanelli has no intention of wasting the evening over a peppermint shnops. She looks at the tintype of the brother of the gentleman from Praz. "This has been retouched," says Mlle. Toscanelli.

"It is my brother Georg. We cannot settle the estate, you see, without him."

Mlle. Toscanelli has a question, one which seems to indicate that emotions other than the purely sentimental sometimes animate the bosom of the daughters of the warm south.

"How much is it worth to you to find him?"

A faint change seems to come over the gentleman from Praz, in his obsolete finery, and with his funny-fancy manners. He meets the hard, bright, black little eyes of Mlle. Toscanelli.

"Fifty ducats," he says. ***"But no tricks!"***

Mlle. Toscanelli says, *"In advance."*

She counts the five notes of ten ducats each, snaps the tiny beaded and be-bijou'd reticule, starts to rise. "One moment, I wish to send a note," says the gentleman from Praz. "He is — where?"

He is in Hunyadi Street, Lower Hunyadi Street; Mlle. Toscanelli does not recollect the number, but there was an apothecary on the corner and a bicycle shop next door to it.

It was as she said. However, the entire block had been erected by a builder who had used one set of house plans. All the houses look alike, and Mlle. Toscanelli could not remember which one it was. Not even the sight of the police, while she was still gazing up and down the block, aided her memory. And, when even the offer of another fifty ducats failed, it had to be assumed that she was telling the truth.

Ah, how may police, and so suddenly, in Lower Hunyadi Street! And in the streets behind. And all around —

The apothecary's lips trembled. "But there was nothing illegal about it," he protested. "I have a *license* to sell opium. Fifty pillules of the anhydrous, here, all properly noted in my Record Book. See? See? Well, if I am shouted at, I cannot *think* what house!"

By the time he had gotten his nerves and his memory together, the police were being reinforced by soldiery. The residents of Lower Hunyadi Street seemed divided between a desire to utilize the best seats, those by their windows, and view the show — whatever its purpose might be — and a desire to barricade their windows with bedding, china closets, and clothes cabinets.

"Open up, Number Forty-four! Open up! Concierge! Porter!"

Fifty years of almost unbroken peace under the Triune Monarchy had not fully persuaded the inhabitants out of the habits formed during fifty previous decades of almost unbroken war. The gates of the houses in Bella tend to be thick.

"Well, may as well send for the firemen," said Lobats.

Axes, ladders, a full siege. Eszterhazy was sure that the porter — or someone — was watching. Someone who could open the doors without a violent assault — if he — or she — wished to.

"Hold up," he said. The police drew back. Then the soldiers. Eszterhazy walked across the street toward Number 44. Halfway across he stopped, drew his hand from his pocket, and, arm at the traditional forty-five-degree angle, held up the *Provót.* A great sigh seemed to go up all around him. A moment later the gates swung open. He gestured to Lobats. They walked in.

A woman, not so old as concierges are generally assumed to be, stood to one side, sobbing. "The poor man!" she cried. "The poor man! So suppose he *is* cracked. What if he does think he is King? Does that hurt the real King?" The two men went on through the empty courtyard and started up the stairs. "Don't be hurting him!" the woman screamed. "Don't you be hurting him . . . the poor man . . ."

He sat facing them, as they went in — and it had not taken them long to get in — but in a moment they realized that he was not really facing *them* at all. He was facing a full-length mirror. Somehow he had made shift to fix up a dais, and he had draped the chair all in crimson. It made do for a throne. He sat in his sleazy "robes" of state, cape and gown and collar of cotton-wool spotted with black tufts to resemble ermine. It was all false; even across footlights it would have looked almost false. His head was slumped to one side.

But the crown was on his head, his telltale head; the crown with its glittering jeweled pendants was on his head, so tightly that it had not fallen off, and the orb and sceptre, though his hands had slid into his lap, still his hands clenched them tightly.

For most of his life he had been no one and nobody. For now, however, he was as much King of Jerusalem as the Crown Jewels could make him — or anyone — King of Jerusalem.

The crown and orb and sceptre of the ancient and mysterious Regalia. They, and the fully fatal dose of the fifty pillules of anhydrous opium.

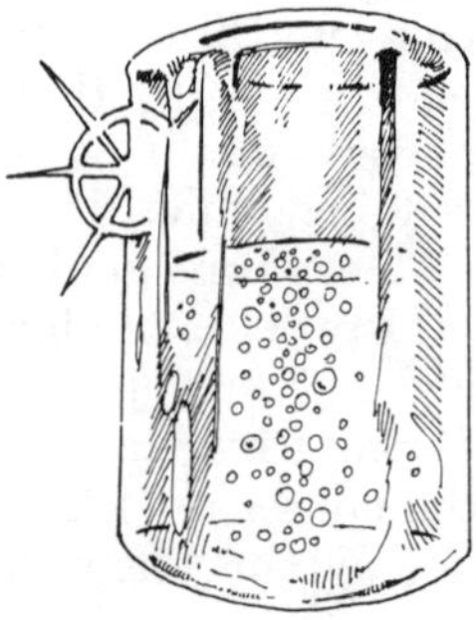

THE OLD WOMAN WHO LIVED WITH A BEAR

The traditional descent of the Mountain Goths (or, for that matter, the Lowland) of the Triune Monarchy may be open to question. What is not open to question is that the Mountain (if not the Lowland) Goths believe this tradition implicitly. This makes them very, very indulgent to the handful of Italians — makers and vendors of ice cream, chiefly, in the market towns — who have trickled into and taken up residence in the Gothic Alps. However, this indulgence is always hedged about with qualifications.

"Mind you give us full measure of that there sweet snow," they sometimes warn Luigi, or Giovann', "else we'll go and capture that there Rome of yours again."

Their Lowland kinfolk have long ago become accustomed to the probability that their forefathers migrated in the early Middle Ages from the Gautlands of South Scandia, and hence — their forefathers — never even smelled Rome, burning or otherwise. As long as the price of butter, eggs, and milk, the three pillars of the Gothic Lowland economy, hold up, the Lowland Goths will listen calmly to any historical account, even if it has them descended from giraffes. The rich bosom of the Gothic Lowlands, upon which the Imperial City of Bella floats, or perhaps it doesn't float, rests, then, like a jewel: this is the central fact of the Triune Monarchy.

The mountains of the Gothic hegemony are something else, of course.

Eszterhazy had dedicated the first week in May to botanizing in the hills behind Graach. Not that he could not have botanized elsewhere just as well, but his Aunt Emma wished it. Even the Dr.

Eszterhazys of this world have Aunt Emmas, and when Aunt Emma takes a notion to be insistent, even unreasonably so, the nephew is likely to do nothing more than sigh and say, "Very well, Aunt Emma," . . . even as you and I.

"Engelbert, you always go in May, I know, to recruit your health by picking flowers and such-like, near Graach —"

"By no means always near Graach, Aunt Emma. I did go to the Graachs once, to be sure, but I like to spend that week in a different place each year, if possible, in order to obtain wider samples of flora, so —"

He might just as well have said, *Mumblety-peg, Minnie-and-Meg,* for the good it did.

Lady Emma Eszterhazy said to her English maid, "More tea for Dr. Engelbert, Churchwarden, please." And she said, "As you know, your dear Uncle Ferdinando left all *sorts* of bits and pieces of estate here and there and everywhere; and, thank you, Churchwarden, I shall ring when we need you. Has she quite gone, Engelbert? Engelbert, take a cheroot from the box there, one for yourself if you like, and of course, one for *me.* You know that I dearly love a cheroot, but Churchwarden, though she has been with me ever since before I met your Uncle Ferdinando and was swept off my feet and into Scythia-Pannonia-Transbalkania, has never learned to accept these Continental customs. So she must never know. Now, S'Graachs."

S'Graachs was certainly one of the late Ferdinando Eszterhazy's bits and pieces of estates. He was the cadet of a cadet branch of a line of the family with a proclivity for difficult inheritances. Consequently it was not perhaps to be expected that the best part of the settlement should have gone to him. He left his English-born widow bits and pieces of estates because bits and pieces were what he had inherited, and, as he was in no sense a canny hand at management, what he had to leave, viz., the same bits and pieces he had inherited. Including S'Graachs.

"S'Graachs," said Lady Emma, cheerfully puffing her cheroot, "S'Graachs is the bane of my existence. The steward cheats me, I am sure he does. I want you to *check up* on him, Engelbert. I of course do not wish to interfere with your rambles and such, but it will be quite easy, I shall give you a note, and you will be put up at S'Graachs, and you can ramble around *there.* And see how the steward cheats me."

Dr. Eszterhazy sighed, but it was an inward sigh. Outwardly, he said, "Very well, Aunt Emma."

And, after some more discussion of details, Lady Emma rang and Churchwarden came and removed the tea tray and the ashtray. Her coeval and mistress gave him a triumphal stare and hissed, "See? She never knew a thing! Never suspects!" Churchwarden, one supposed,

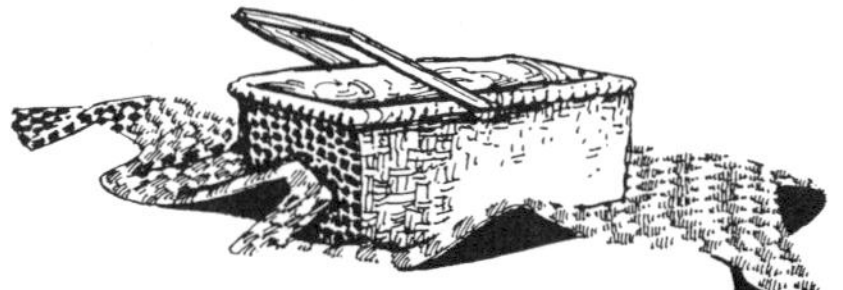

simply supposed that Eszterhazy chose to smoke two cheroots. Simultaneously.

The steward of S'Graachs clearly did not believe for one moment that Eszterhazy had come looking for stamens and rhizomes.

After having seen the best room shaken down and Eszterhazy installed in it, he stood with both gaitered legs apart and hands behind his back, for all the world like a soldier who had received the command *At ease!* and said stiffly, "I suppose Your Excellency will want to see the Account-Books."

"Nonsense, Chilperits, why should I want to see the Account-Books? And I repeat, I am not Your Excellency. I am Doctor Eszterhazy." He gazed around the room. Despite the walls bearing far too many evidences of former lords of the manor and their fondnesses for slaying the wild fauna of the area, it was rather a nice room. Frow Chilperits had provided a choice sampling of the flora of the area, but she had put them all into vases of water.

"And me who has known you since you were Master Engelbert," the steward said, dolefully.

Eszterhazy sighed. "Oh, very well, then, Chilperits, let me *see* the damned Account-Books!"

"There, and I knew that Your — that the Sir Doctor would be wanting to see them, so here they are." And he set them down on the table.

They were bound in leather, as they had been bound since Time Immemorial by the one bookbinding establishment in Graach, and no doubt would be of some interest to students of Mountain Gothic bookbinding. Eszterhazy gave them a stare apiece. "There, now I've seen the damned things, so take them away," he said.

But they were not taken away.

Eszterhazy, his kit full of specimens, had passed through the picturesque small town of Graach — that is, he had halfway passed through it, when he saw a lime tree spreading out its branches and giving such a tempting shade that he simply had to sit at the table beneath it. And since the table and its chairs were part of the teeny-tiny tavern set back a bit behind the tree, it seemed only courteous that he order something. He could not, however, make up his mind what to order, so the pleasant young woman ventured to make it up for him.

"I will bring My Sir a glass of sorrel soup," she said.

The notion that he might like a glass of soup, any kind of soup, was remote from finding acceptance. But it would have been impolite to refuse. It did not look very nice, it looked rather nasty, being of a greenery-yallery color, and full of flocculencies. It had a strange, astringent taste . . . it was not entirely unpleasant . . . it was perhaps an acquired taste . . . and before it was gone for more than a second or so, he discovered that he had in fact just now acquired a taste for it.

He took his time over the second glass of the sorrel-grass soup. The afternoon had some time left to it. He would let the cool of the day catch up with him before getting up to finish his walk back to S'Graachs. There was no hurry. And there, back at S'Graachs, he would have a bath and then a leisurely supper. And then, well . . . then he would arrange the results of the day's botanizing. And then he would retire early, adjust his traveling lamp (the lamps at S'Graachs had been formed to burn whale, or perhaps it was rape-seed, oil, and tended to resist kerosene), and read another soothing chapter of *With Clive in India,* by that excellent English author, Mr. G.A. Henty. Then, then, amidst the sweet scents and soft noises of the mountain country, then he would turn out the lamp, turn over on his left side, and . . .

He must have fallen asleep right there. But *there.* And at first he thought that perhaps twenty years had passed, as in the quaint American tale of Rip Von Winkle, for he saw, standing solemnly before him, the same — surely the same — set of faces he had seen when, his Uncle Ferdinando being still alive, they had received the Village Council on some occasion or other. A Loyal Address to the Throne was perhaps the subject. Or perhaps a request for a rebate on the season's rents.

But the dregs of the sorrel soup still stood in front of him. So twenty years had not passed, after all.

"Yes," he said, feeling slightly embarrassed. "Yes . . . ah . . . Mayor Odopfacker. I greet you in the name of God."

"And the Holy Company of the Angels," replied old Odopfacker. "Tell us, High-born and August Excellency, you being, as we hear, a Master Jurisconsult, is it lawful for an old woman to live with a bear?"

Eszterhazy did not feel it appropriate at the moment to tell them that the title of Master Jurisconsult had been obsolete since the Confederacy of the Middle Ister had gone down to defeat before the forces of Napoleon. Nor did he allow his face to show either astonishment or mirth.

He considered the question with furrowed brow for a moment. "Well, Master Mayor . . . This is no simple question which you raise. However, it is held, *ipso facto* and *ipse res* in the Code of Justinian, that a bear is a wild creature, just as a stag or an eagle is a wild creature. And that no one may hold a right of property vested in a wild creature, for the sufficient reason that a wild creature, being wild, is not subject to control. And what we cannot control we cannot own. However, as the Pandects of Charlemagne tell us, *Abeunt studia in mores,* which is to say: 'Practices zealously pursued become habits,'

and also, *Medio tutissimus ibis*: 'With a middle course one goes most safely.' "

The venerable heads before him nodded their assent.

"Since, therefore, the bear in question cannot belong to anyone, it cannot belong to anyone else, either. And if the old woman in question is otherwise a civil and a law-abiding subject of His Imperial Majesty —"

"Whom God spare for many years," chorused the elders.

"— one does not see that it can be unlawful for her to live with the bear in question. — Eh?"

There fell a silence. And then one of them, by his looks even more ancient than the mayor, declared, "Well, that be true, a bear do *be* a wild animal, and no denying of the factual."

They bowed and expressed thanks, bowed again, and filed away, but it cannot be said that they looked in all manner satisfied, and Eszterhazy's conscience prickled him a little bit. But at the moment he could think of nothing to do about it, and perhaps after all, he had done all that he or anyone else could do. So he paid his bill and went home by way of the Chapel of Saint Ulfilas, a move he soon had a mind to regret, for whom should he see in the outer garden, with his cassock tucked into his cincture, but Father Alarits, parish priest and one who dearly delighted in a good religious wrangle out of the pure and disinterested principle of Christian love. Thinking to avoid a frontal attack, Eszterhazy attempted a feint.

"Good evening, Father, and what can you tell me about the old woman who lives in a — I mean, who lives with a bear?"

But the wily cleric popped up out of an earthwork, so to speak, and fired a bombard.

"Better ask what I can tell you about your own sins! When was the last time you made your Easter duty? Down there in Bella and up to your neck, I have no doubt, with opera singers and Freemasons," the fiery little priest began, with relish.

"My dear Father, up here and out of touch with things, are you not aware that nowadays most opera singers *are* Freemasons?"

Exit Eszterhazy, under cover of a sapping operation.

That night at dinner, all was very traditional. The steward standing At Ease and supervising the gardener's boy, who acted as waiter (it was not *that* traditional that they washed the guest's feet, but both wore towels in their belts to show that they remembered); and, on a stool in the corner, the manorial zither-player playing songs from the Gothic Wars. And the steward, of course, tasting each dish first, and then they all waited a full minute to see if he had been poisoned by (as it might have been) a Turkish spy.

Frow Chilperits [at the door and in a whisper]: Sweet and sour hare.

Waiter-boy [in a pubescent rottle]: Sweet sow rare, Boss.

Chilperits: Most Excellent Guest! A humble hare, sauced both sweet and sour! [Takes a gobbet on a spoon, puts the spoon back in the tureen, chomps the gobbet].

Old Emyil [in the corner]:

Oh, four and twenty redhaired maidens
In the high tower, In the high tower
[**pringle prangle**]
Oh, Cunigunda, Cunigunda, Oh!
[**pringle prangle**]

Eszterhazy: Tell me, Chilperits, as soon as you've got a mouth free, what is all this about an old woman who lives with a bear?

Waiter-boy: [Drops the tureen]

Chilperits: The dish was not worthy of the Most Excellent, and, as he has tasted it by proxy, no one else may taste of it.

Eszterhazy: Quick thinking, Chilperits. . . . But if you drop dead in the course of the meal, I shall take a hasty emetic.

Frow Chilperits: Roast capon with gooseberries.

Waiter-boy: [On his knees, cleaning up the mess, and dodging Chilperits's boot]

Chilperits: Most Excellent Guest! A roast capon, sauced with gooseberries!

Eszterhazy [Waits till the fowl is safely on the table]: About the old woman, now —

Chilperits: I have left the Account-Books on the bedside table for the Most Excellent Guest, if he pleases.

Old Emyil:

Oh, four and twenty Gothic knights
To the high tower, to the high tower
[**pringle prangle**]
Oh, Cunigunda, Cunigunda, Oh!
[**pringle prangle**]

Finally it was time for his bedtime read; he picked up *With Clive in India* and opened it to the bookmark with a subliminal feeling that the bookmark was the wrong color and in the wrong place.

> . . . although the wools have not the fine texture of merino, the market at Kicxpolakx each year . . .

Damn, what the Hell was this! The wool market at Kicxpolakx had no business being in India, not even with the wildest notions of boundary revisions. He looked at the spine; the spine was faded. He tried for the title page, which resisted him, coyly interposing the piece of bound-in tissue paper which was supposed to protect the half-color plate. Hah! Of course *With Clive in India* had no such frontispiece —

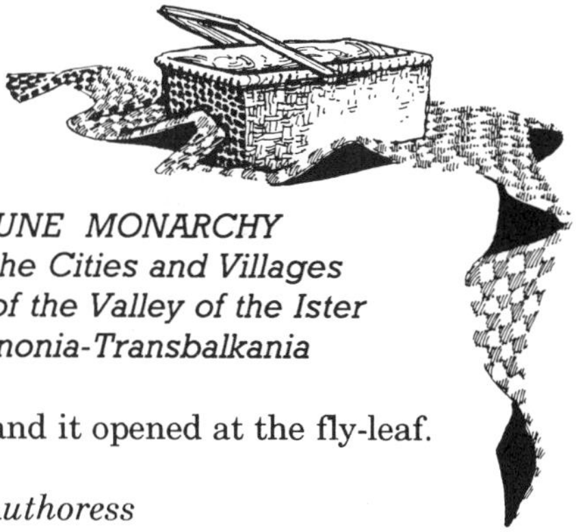

TWELVE YEARS IN THE TRIUNE MONARCHY
Experiences of a Consul's Wife in the Cities and Villages and Among the Picturesque People of the Valley of the Ister and the Mountains of Scythia-Pannonia-Transbalkania

Here the book slipped, he clutched it, and it opened at the fly-leaf.

To my dearest Emma Eszterhazy
Compliments of the Authoress
Sissy Potlatch-Snurph.

He grunted and flipped to the title page once again. "Potlatch-Snurph" was too good. Ah, yes. Cecily Piggot-Smith. Husband used to be H.B.M. Consul at Avar-Ister. And what was the book doing here? Well, for one thing, it was about the same size and color of binding as *Clive.* And, for another, Eszterhazy's manservant, Herrekk the Mountain Tsigane, who had packed the kit for the journey, could read and write no language but the Szekel Runes. That he had happened to pack the wrong book, but one in the same language, was mildly curious, no more.

Well. Mrs. Piggot-Smith's comments on the wool market in and around Kicxpolakx were not really what he wanted right now. What else might there be? There might be, and in fact was, a small volume entitled *A Nosegay of Nocturnal Devotions For the True Humble Soul, Plus Ten Curses Against the Turks.* And, hmm, what were *these,* looking faintly familiar?

To one gallon turps @ ducat 1/2 per gal
To 1 pr best bristle brushes @ 1 a a

What the Devil?

Cottage and byre Ye Wolfenspring
Rent @ ducats 100 per an
Tribute @ eggs 6 score lambskins 1 cockerel 2

Ah, it was those damnable Account-Books! Had Aunt Emma really missed an egg? Still, how was it that Chilperits, over a hundred miles away in the Highlands, seemed to know very well that he was suspected of malfeasance at Lady Emma's, down in Bella? Well, no great mystery. Doubtless some letters had been written. Pish tush.

Not yet *time* for sleep! Well, then back to Mrs. Cissy and her twelve picturesque years. *Sigh . . .*

The best place to begin in such a case was at the index. The index here was copious, beginning with *Abernathy, Duke of, shoots grouse in Rhiphaean Alps,* and concluding with *Zimlac, Pyotro, Patriot Poet of Hyperborea, a sonnet by.* Idly running his eyes back up the columns, Eszterhazy blinked and stared.

Bears, allegedly eaten, Little Byzantia.
Bears, skins of, use of for shakoes.
Bears, dancing, Gypsies, trained.
Bears, hunted, Pannonia.
Bears, Hyperborea.
Bears hunted, Scythia.
Bear grease, exported.
Bear, old woman who lived with.
Bears, myths and legends.
Bear, cub, pet.
Bear . . . Bear . . . Bear . . .

Slowly the book slipped down. His head snapped back. Slowly, Herrekk rose from his usual sleeping place by the door and on silent feet came and blew out the lamp.

And this was rather odd, because Herrekk had stayed behind, on orders, in Bella.

Eszterhazy slept.

When he looked, only half-remembering, for the book next morning, it was gone. The Account-Books, though, were not. Odd.

He had told Frow Chilperits, after dinner, that he would be going up the mountain the following day, and she had packed him a lunch. "Only a small one, now," he had warned. And she, oh, to be sure, she had understood perfectly. She said. And, of course, she had not. Not only did the basket contain more than he wished to eat, it contained more than he wished to carry. Frow Chilperits had not understood the first, but she had anticipated the second. And so Eszterhazy, who had wanted to be by himself, learned that he was to be by himself, along with the company of the garden-boy-*cum*-waiter, who carried the basket.

Feudal traditions worked more than one way. But of course he had known that for a long time.

"How call they thee?" he asked the boy, as they walked along an overgrown but fully serviceable path, the tinkle of goat-bells in their ears.

"Cosmo, to serve God, the Emperor, and Your Highness." It interested Eszterhazy to be reminded that the old ways were best discerned among the very young as well as the very old. The gardener, in whose company Cosmo passed most of his time, must have been close to eighty, and no doubt it was the gardener who had taught the boy these antique expressions.

Graach, looking more than ever as though it had been made out of marzipan by some guild of fairy craftsmen, appeared, briefly, far

below, then vanished as the path turned. "Listen, Cosmo. I am not called His Highness. My *grand*father was called His Highness. I am called Sir Doctor."

"*Oh*-hh," said the boy, in naïve surprise. He was perhaps thirteen, perhaps fourteen, and had evidently recovered in full from the mishap of the previous night, for he smiled contentedly as he met Eszterhazy's eyes. He was what some boobling professor would doubtless describe as "a pure Gothic type" — that is, his hair had once been blond and would probably become brown and was now brownish-blond, and his eyes were blue, or anyway bluish, or one might say, hazel . . . somewhat. His nose was freckled and tended toward the snub, as — in both cases — traditional in boys; but long before he was the age of the gardener, who was probably his great-uncle, it would be almost as hooked as the old man's was. And as for his complexion, why, one might call it fair, or suntanned, or olive. His cheekbones? He had cheekbones.

The Scythian Goths, like any other wandering people (i.e., at one time or other, every people) of the days of yore, had certainly not taken genealogical tables along with them; and, equally certainly, they certainly had taken along with them as many nubile women as they could possibly pick up along the way.

"Does the plant called blue-friar grow in these parts?" In between great rocks, detritus of ancient avalanches, the path wound.

"My granny would know."

"Ah, pity, then, she's not here," Eszterhazy said, indulgently.

"Ah, but she is, she is! For there's Wolfensprings now!"

The mountains had sagged here, long, long ago, had subsided as though intended to make land level enough — if not very, very level — and land wide enough — for a small peasant farmstead. One cottage. One byre and byre-yard. A garden. Small orchard. Some pasture. And the spring itself, purling prettily out of its conduit in the wall of the low byre. And one woman. One old woman, starting to throw out her arms at sight of the boy, stopping at sight of Eszterhazy. Being very, very still for a moment, long enough for Cosmo to cry, "Granny, I've brought thee a doctor!" Then again moving, doing traditional oh-a-stranger-is-coming things.

A handsome old woman. "Well, Granny of Wolfensprings," Eszterhazy said, "I haven't brought my medical bag . . . but if I can hear, I may be able to advise." His medical bag was in Bella, and as to his advice, well —

There was no false shyness. "Ah, sir, when people grow to an age, their joints ache. As Doctor Engelbert must know." He had no idea who she was, but word would have gotten around of his being here. "Sometimes my wrists and hands. Sometimes my knees, my ankles. And feet."

He examined wrists and ankles. She was, of course, barefoot;

probably carried her shoes as far as the church lane before putting them on, Sundays. The knees he took on faith.

"An infusion of willow bark may be of help," he suggested. "I'll give the apothecary a prescription, and Cosmo can bring up the medicine. Warm poultices, with very warm water, as often as you have time." Probably she did not have much time. The farm was small, but there was no sign of a farmer — no boots, no musket, no shirt being mended, no hunt-cap. "Recollect to keep the joints warm, come winter — come fall, even. Is the house dry?" She said the house was dry. She thanked him, with dignity, and offered him simple hospitality. Coffee. Curds. A dish of preserves. He did not stay long.

Something came to him as they were about to leave. "Is the rent too much? Or the tribute?"

A curious look she gave him. Then shook her head. "It is not too much. Pray, my duty and respects to Lady Emma."

It was not till later that the lad said, softly, regretfully, "Ah, we did forget to ask about the blue-friars plant."

A feeling, as of the rightness of the moment, stole over Eszterhazy. "Tell me now, Cosmo," he said, "about the old woman who lived with a bear."

It had been a good lunch for Cosmo. He had eaten the black bread and cheese and sausage-end which Frow Chilperits had included for him. He had also eaten half of the sandwiches and almost all of the pastry which she had packed for the guest, and the better part of the fruit. "Well, sir . . . Sir Doctor . . . It is a very curious thing." A sidelong glance. "A *very* curious sort of thing. There was a man, Sir Doctor, who was an infidel. And there was a woman, Sir Doctor, as was a witch. Being an infidel, he didn't believe as she was a witch, you see. So what does she do, she charms him and turns him into a bear. And she makes him live with her. Because that is his punishment for being such an infidel." He reëxamined the ruinations of the lunch, and turned a piece or two over again with a finger. But that was all he did. It had been a *very* good lunch for Cosmo.

"I see, I see. And the priest? Can he do nothing?"

Very firmly, Cosmo shook his head. "Not without the Bishop gives him leave. And the Bishop, *he* lives in Dominets. *Ever* such a long ways off."

And that, as far as Cosmo was concerned, was clearly that. As for Dominets, it was a full twenty-five miles away. And even before the New Road had been put through, a decade past, it would have been considered a scandal had not the Bishop made the trip at least once a year, to confirm the children. A piece of the story appeared to be missing. Well, well, perhaps it would fall into place . . . sometime. And if not, not.

The apothecary did not so much attempt social equality — a matter to which Eszterhazy was indifferent — as scholastic co-eminence. "Do

you know whom they mean here, when they say 'the doctor'? Me? You? Never!" He brought his round, red face close. "The barber, that's who. *The* ***bar-****ber!* And, in a way, why not? Eh. Doctor. Why not? Doesn't he draw blood every time he shaves? Eh? Ah ho ho haw? Nay, but really, because he cups, he sets leeches, he lances boils, he makes liniments. Well, if that is progress, if that is science, then we may as well retire, you and I. *I* think it is retrograde, I think it should be illegal, and to that effect I have written our delegate, Dr. Juris. Alarits, the priest's cousin. And do you know the nature of his reply?" Again he leaned across the counter. "His reply was to this effect, and concluding in these words: *My colleagues and I intend to give your views the most intense reflection. . . .*" He gave an emphatic nod, and slapped his hand on the counter. And, picking up the prescription once again, he once again read it aloud, in round rolling tones, giving each common abbreviation its full form, and lending to the recitation an air of one pronouncing a valedictory address (of course, also in Latin) at a *gymnasium* graduation.

"You will know, then," Eszterhazy said, in a tone which took it for granted that the learned apothecary really would know, of course — and the learned apothecary, nodding rapidly at each word — "this old woman who lives with a bear?"

And, of course, he did know. "Knew him, too," he said. "He was in the Fifth Regiment, the 'Famous Fifth,' you know. It was a piece of shellfire that he took in the head, during the Serbian War. *Af*-fec-ted-the-*brain! Nat*u-ral-ly! Ran off from the hospital. Fetched him back. Ran off again. Fetched him *back.* Were going to court-martial him. Was found Unfit-to-Plead! By reason of Insanity! So they let him go. But they wouldn't give him any pension, of course. Can't reward desertion. Can we?"

Skyrockets went off in Eszterhazy's head. The "Famous Fifth" Regiment of Hussars! Of course. Eszterhazy had always considered that he had as good a command of the colloquial as anyone of his level, and far better than most. But that the word was, in this local, immediate sense, slang — no, this had never occurred to him. Many examples occurred to him now:

"Tilda, thinks she's much, keeping company with a Bear."

"Tried to get into the Bears, my sister's son, they turn him down for a lousy half-inch below the minimal height, so now he's mucking in the mucking muck with the mucking Sappers, instead."

Very faintly he smiled, remembering the boy Cosmo's account. Folktale had turned a common case of concubinage into something — almost — out of the *Odyssey.* Well. It wouldn't be the first time.

"Ah, by the way, Doctor," the apothecary said, suddenly confidential. "I see that there Fillyi's in town. Always looking for trouble. Don't know why the High-born Lady hasn't turned him out long ago, of course it *is* none of my — Many times I have thought that he and Steward

Chilperits, they would come to blows. Hm, well." The apothecary seemed suddenly to think that he had said enough, if not too much, so he looked at the antique clock standing between two equally antique shelves of medicine jars, *Tinc. Bel., Elix. Opi., Ther. Ven.,* and even *Pulv. Corn. Uni.*! "Time I was getting started on this prescription, Doctor. You may have confidence. Thank you! Thank you!"

Only about a third of Graach village formed part of the S'Graachs estate, and if one took care and remembered correctly, one might avoid the third which did. And if one didn't, well, how many suggestions about the rents could one listen to, how many fireplaces-in-need-of-repair-never-mind-what-Steward-says could one inspect; how many parlors stifling with camphor and polish and never-opened windows could one sit in and drink coffee . . . and how much coffee could one *drink?*

Eszterhazy had been all through this before, on his last visit to Graach. Which was one reason why he had not wanted to make this visit, either.

Nor had he calculated that he could not in any case keep away from the estate if the estate, or part of it, came looking for him. Which it now did.

He had met Fillyi two or three times, that last time. He had no desire to take up an acquaintance which had never really existed. But he did recognize the man, who had not much changed. He was grayer of head, redder of face, and even more of a bullock, as to body, than before. More of a bullock as to mind, one would not have thought it possible to be. He was also the largest tenant of the estate. And so, of course, paid the largest rent. Was the rent too large? Fillyi thought so. Who was there who paid rent who did not think so? The old woman at the Wolfenspring must have been one of the two.

But times were not bad, times were not so hard, certainly not for a prosperous peasant. Farm produce held its own level; wheat did well. There was no sign that Fillyi was suffering hunger or thirst. How account for his rage?

For the rage was there, it was plain from the first sight of the man. He was polite, but words seemed to choke him. It may not have been personal, but Eszterhazy felt the man's emotions like a blast of heat. The few phrases of civility aside, the man, in his good clothes and boots facing Eszterhazy there on the shady street and grinding his teeth, said: "It must come off. It can't go on. I can't pay it. Can't go on. Won't. Must tell Her Ladyship. Have written. No good." Then, as Eszterhazy said nothing (understanding almost nothing), the heavy face grew purple, the heavy mouth drew up under the heavier moustache, the bristly cheeks swelled.

If he had raised one fist, Eszterhazy might have struck him, or, likelier, drawn back and warned him. But he raised both fists. His eyes rolled up. Growls rattled in his thick throat.

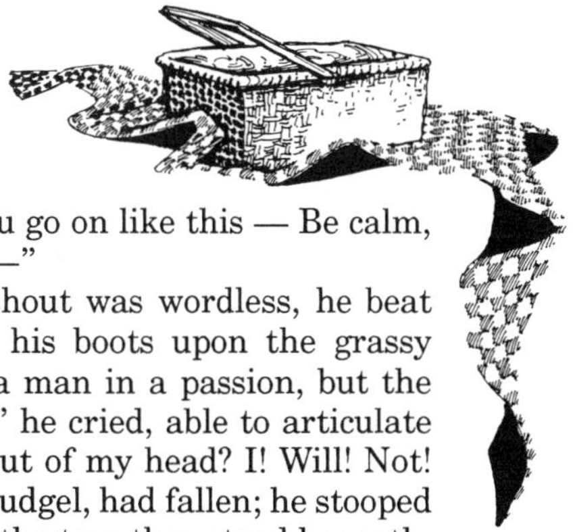

"Fillyi, you will have an apoplexy if you go on like this — Be calm, open your collar, cool off for a moment —"

But Fillyi was past hearkening. His shout was wordless, he beat his fists against his head, he stamped his boots upon the grassy roadside. It was almost a caricature of a man in a passion, but the man *was* in a passion. "God in Heaven!" he cried, able to articulate again. "Do they want to burn the eyes out of my head? I! Will! Not! Pay! It! More!" His stick, half-staff, half-cudgel, had fallen; he stooped and snatched it up and struck it against the tree they stood beneath. Again. Again. Again. The tree trembled; showers of twigs and leaves fell; surely the stick must break?

But the sticks in the Gothic Highlands are made of hard and tough wood. The stick did not break. Sweat poured down the man's face. He groaned aloud.

Eszterhazy stretched out his right arm, stretched out his right hand, stretched out the index finger and pointed it. It did catch Fillyi's eyes. The eyes followed the finger. The finger swung round. The insane attack upon the tree paused, the stick upraised to renew it. The index finger of the right hand swung round to the left pocket of Eszterhazy's coat. The hand delved in the pocket and came out with something between the index and middle fingers. A small notebook. Red. Bright red. The eyes of the rich tenant farmer followed it as the eyes of a bull are said to follow a red cape or other garment.

Next a pencil appeared. Softly: "You wish me to tell my Lady aunt? That you will no longer pay it? Very well. I promise nothing. But I shall write it down before your eyes: *Fillyi says he will no longer pay the required rent —*"

The man swung his head up, away from the notebook. His eyes were full of blood. "It is not the rent! Not the rent, man — it is the encumbrance!"

Ah . . . Eszterhazy had not known that Fillyi's farm was encumbered, but there was no reason why he should have. However, he nodded, and he wrote it down. And Fillyi burst into tears. They were not tears of gratitude, nor were they tears of rage. The Scythian peasant does not shame to cry, even publicly. Such tears as these, though, one might see shed at the gravesite of a wife or child. He had crossed his hands and bowed his head upon them, and he sobbed aloud, and he wept.

"Remember! Nothing is promised. But I will look into it."

He heard the man behind sobbing for a long while.

In the Account-Books, the rent on Fillyi's farm stood at a thousand ducats, and the tribute . . . ah, well, Eszterhazy could not attempt to calculate what the monetary value of the tribute might be, and in any case it would vary, not only from year to year but from season to season. Items on it must have come down, unchanged, since God knows when. *Item One halberd-leather,* for instance! It was doubtful that either Fillyi or Chilperits could have defined a halberd to save their own hides. As for so much hemp, so much flax, pounded, so much flax, unpounded, so many jars of goose grease — did they know of all this, back down at the Royal and Imperial Institute of Agriculture and Commerce, in Bella?

Never mind, it was not the goose grease nor the down and feathers, nor any of that, which was behind Fillyi's rage and torment. "The encumbrance," he had said. And, so, here it was.

Alperits-stead [that was the farm's name] *is encumbered with a pension in amount of an hundred and fifty ducats payable,* the handwriting of the Steward was very pleasant to observe but not always the easiest to read, *payable to Elisapheta Hencko, at Wolfenspring: on Old Christmas and on Ascension Day.*

In effect, then, Fillyi was paying an extra rent — though, of course, the second one, the pension, bore no comparison to the first one, the rent proper. The situation was not unusual. Landowners had clear notions of *noblesse oblige,* and if someone on an estate required support, why, landlords would see that the support was forthcoming. However, as was only human nature, they did not care to have their own direct incomes diminished by such support. Chilperits, for example, if Chilperits were obliged to retire, suddenly, by reason of, say, illness or accident not directly connected with his work as steward, why, Chilperits would still certainly be pensioned. But Lady Emma's attorney would certainly not advise her to pay the pension herself. The amount of the pension would be levied, in the form of an "encumbrance" upon . . . well, upon some other farm which formed part of the estate in the Graachs area. This was the way it was done.

"Cosmo," he asked, "what does it mean, to 'burn the eyes out of someone's head'?"

A sort of sadly knowing smile came over the boy's pleasant face. "Well . . . Sir Doctor . . . suppose, now, two fellows are wanting to walk out with the same girl. And one of them gets to walk out with the girl. And he swanks it over the other, 'Yah yah, it's me as is walking out with Cunigunda!' And then by and by the other fellow, he takes her away from him. See? And so what do he do, every time they walk out together, why, he makes sure they walk right where the first fellow can see them doing it, and . . . well, they burn the eyes out of his head . . ."

So, Eszterhazy, not much the wiser, went back to the Account-Books, which were increasingly taking on aspects of the higher mysteries. And, by and by, from page to page, and from one week's entry to another week's entry, he observed one iterated and reiterated note. *To charity, three eggs. To charity, one pullet. To charity, loaf of*

bread and jar of honey. All very traditional. Some of these items no doubt came from the home farm, S'Graachs itself. Others must have come from the tributes. Lady Emma could eat only so many eggs, put but so much honey on her bread; and the bread, if baked hereabouts, would be stale by the time it got to Bella. Charity was its logical destination.

Loud groans came from the gardener and audible mumbles about his age and his work-burdens and the ingratitude of boys who went traipsing out on excursions and never made up their proper work afterwards. After a repeated statement by Eszterhazy that he desired a light, light, very light and very much lighter lunch, finally he was allowed to go out botanizing by himself, all day long. Though Frow Chilperits clearly was not sure that sheer inanition might not lay him low, a mere two sandwiches and a piece of fruit . . .

The red, red of the rowan seemed to lead him on a certain way the next day; that rowan-tree whose wood was half-haunted and half-a-charm all by itself. But one tree turned out not to be a rowan at all, another one was indeed a rowan but so unhealthy by reason of sour soil or what have you that he scorned to stop by it, and at length when he saw what seemed just what he wanted he was obliged to go down a steeper slope than he had bargained for. But it was a rowan, all right, and it was a good one.

"Ah, Young Lord, thee knows the right tree!" a high, clear voice said, near behind him. He turned to see what boy this was who addressed him in the *thou*-form, and saw no boy at all but an old woman, a veritable old woman, archetypal hag and crone by her looks, stooped, bent, ragged, filthy, but sound enough in health for all of that.

"And thee knows it, too, Granny," he said, making her a bow.

"Ah, Unda knows 'em all, all. Unda knows 'em all. An thee be's pleased to come along down to my cot, I'll show thee some nice ones."

An old herb-woman, then; good! He came along willingly. "Cot," she called it, it was not much of a cottage, it was a hovel of the classical sort, straight out of the grimmer fairy tales. She had a stool in front and gestured him to sit down. Inside the cottage where she could be seen flitting back and forth, she was speaking . . . saying what? . . . talking to herself, no doubt . . . or to someone inside . . . someone? . . . speaking to a cat or a dog, perhaps . . .

"Now, here is a stoop of metheglin, Young Lord, as I made myself out of the best honey and such. And whiles ye drink, Unda will show off her yarbs, for word's come her way as the Young Lord be's interested in the like."

She had of course no notion of "preserving" her plants; her interest in them was not his. They were all shrunken-dried, or in process of drying, but by no means without interest even so. He sipped the metheglin. He took samples. He made notes. There was a mighty bad smell coming from somewhere nearby, though. And, by and by, it grew upon him that there were some mighty odd sounds, too. Old Unda saw that.

"Thee'll be wanting a look, Young Lord," she said simply, laying down a twist of herbery. Getting up, she beckoned him after her to the cottage door.

Inside, half the hovel was barricaded from earthen floor to thatched roof — to the beams of the roof, anyway. Something passed back and forth in there, glimpses showing between the palings, stout and thick poles. And, oh, the stink — ! He stepped forward. But not very much so.

Back and forth, back and forth, a man was walking, walking on all fours. Not on hands and knees, not with legs bent. A man was walking, back and forth, on the flats of his hands and feet, his rump elevated, but, somehow, it was odd, not so much as one would think it would be. A man with clotted hair and filthy rags. A man staring either down or straight ahead, but never up. He stared out, unseeing, as he turned to begin his pacing once again. And Eszterhazy shuddered.

The face oh so briefly turned his way was as blank as any beast's face in a cage, but it was a man's face, though not much save the physical semblance of a man's face was left to it. The face wrinkled and made a snuffling sound. The face only partly wrinkled, a face horribly scarred, the scar reaching from the tangled scalp down into the tangled beard, obliterating one eye.

Softly, softly, old Unda said, not as though speaking to anyone, "Ah, my God, my God, ah my darling and my beau . . ."

The wretched remnant of a man halted, uncertainly, and growled. Unda, as deftly as one who does an act done often and over and over, took up a pole and poked it between the palings of the cage. Something came up out of the heap of stinking straw, something all stuck-about with straw, something dark — "There it be, my darling," she said. "There! There! It's all right."

The man-thing nuzzled it, toyed about with it, seemed briefly comforted by it, then, once more, the ceaseless pace began again.

It might indeed — that which she had fetched up from where he had last forgotten it — it might indeed have been, once, and long ago, a shako. One of those hats, uselessly ornamental, and made of bearskin, which sat so smartly upon the heads of the Hussar troops.

And little enough protection had it served him when the Serb shell sprang open into horrid glory, so close to his once-brave head.

"Ah, my God, my God," old Unda breathed. "My darling, my darling, and my beau . . ."

So that night he called Chilperits up into his room and he said, "All right, Chilperits, now let's hear the whole story, if you please."

The steward's face was wearing his formal and stiff expression, but beneath it he seemed a bit relaxed, even if not happy. "Your Ex— the Doctor has read the Account-Books, then," he said.

The Doctor had. "These charities, then. They're all for old Unda, aren't they?"

Again, the impression of relief. "Yes, sir. Oh, well, not all of them, no. Now and then Father Alarits, he suggests we do this or that, and of course, Doctor, we do. But, as a regular thing, yes sir, all most these charities are for she, for old Unda; yes, sir." At once, the formal air fell away. "She'd starve, sir, weren't it for the charities of S'Graachs; those bits of pennies the women give her for herbs and charms, how much do they buy?"

Eszterhazy said nothing, he only looked on.

"And she shouldn't starve, no not she. Not whilst a loaf of bread is baked at S'Graachs, or elsewhere in the Graachs, for that."

"Chilperits, there is no desire on my part, and none, I am sure, on Lady Emma's, that old Unda or anyone else should starve. But *why,* Chilperits, why all the mystery?"

The steward stared. "Can it be, Doctor, that you don't *know?"*

"No more than I know why Fillyi should be encumbered with a pension for the boy's grandmother, up at Wolfenspring — *Ah! There is a connection!"*

Still Chilperits shook his head, amazed. Then he said, "Oh, yes, sir, a connection indeed. And I see you really do not know. Why, sir, it was his late Lordship, don't you see, sir."

Eszterhazy still did not see. That is, he would then and there have said that he did not see. And yet, when next he heard the steward's voice, he realized that the possibility of it had lain in his mind for some time now, unrecognized but seen.

"What? Uncle Ferdinando?"

"Yes, sir. Ah, speak no word of evil of the dead, and all, but — Well, Doctor, in a word or so, his late lordship was a very devil with the women, sir. But those two, the most."

That Captain Eszterhazy had his favorites among the girls of the district surprised no one. They would have been surprised if it had not been so. And that there were involved aspects of these expected passions was not in itself unexpected. However, no one can predict the end of an affair in all its details. And the affair or affairs were not done with, even yet. Not even yet.

The late Captain's nephew listened long and with chin in hand, and now and then he asked a question, as the twigs snapped in the stove, filling the room with their scent; and now and then he made a statement; and now and then he merely nodded. For the most, he was silent.

Elisapheta's parents were subtenants, of which the Graachs had not many, few of the farms being large enough to allow of it. Somehow, though, the parents, three children (she the oldest), and one cow were fitted into the economy of Fillyi's holding. And for the small plot of rye and the small plot of wheat, the truck garden, and the grazing right, the firewood — for all these Elisapheta's family paid. Paid in cash, paid in tribute, paid in labor. And then, Elisapheta growing tall and comely, Fillyi began to make it plain that he expected another kind of payment, too. His suggestions did not include marriage. Her parents, already old in their middle age, suffered the hail and the drought when they came. They could not, after all, resist them. Nor could they resist Fillyi. Still, Elisapheta did not yield. The suggestions became threats, and the threats became menaces.

And then Captain Eszterhazy (who became Uncle Ferdinando) appeared, back from military service, on leave. He saw Elisapheta. Elisapheta saw him. The old couple who rented Wolfenspring suddenly found themselves en route to join their son on his homestead in the distant America — all expenses paid by Captain Eszterhazy. And, equally suddenly, Fillyi had no subtenant family to menace. Small as Wolfenspring was, it was spacious in comparison. And Elisapheta no longer vanished when the caller came . . . or, if she did, it was only to vanish with him.

However. No one expected the lord of the manor to content himself with one woman, nor did he. Cunigunda's father, by old right, cut wood in the hills. His daughter grew up wild, and wild she stayed. Rumor attributed her black hair and black eyes and her wild ways to some long-dead Mountain Tsigane. Rumor told of the young captain's suit. Rumor called the suit successful, but even rumor conceded that the success was not lasting. Cunigunda was wild, and her affections wandered. That is, they wandered until the day she met the young Hussar — in his own turn, back on leave. The captain stormed. Cunigunda simply tossed back her wild black hair, laughed, and laughing, ran off. Did Captain Eszterhazy pull strings? Exert influence? His nephew, now, so long later, preferred to hope not. Perhaps it was only the quickening pace of the Serbian War which caused the Hussar's leave to be cancelled. Cunigunda wept. But still she ran off when her former lover appeared.

"When Gabro came back, that first time, having run off from the hospital, you see," Chilperits explained, "she saw at once that he could never be the same — mad, and so awfully wounded as he was. Ah, sir, Sir Doctor! A woman't love is a wondrous thing! She took it on herself to care for him. And finally, as you know, sir, the authorities, they stopped trying to take him back. Of course they paid him no pension for all his wound, since he was termed a deserter for having run off from the hospital. Unda, she never made no never mind of that. When there was no food, she worked for it. When there

was no work, she stole it. And she never would take Captain's orders to send Gabro-Hussar away. So, by and by, he stopped trying."

By and by, also, retired from military service, and, first, spending most of his time in Bella, and, then, travelling abroad . . . married, finally . . . he had agreed that the affair with Elisapheta was lawfully finished. She married, had a daughter, was widowed when still young, and her days passed in the cycle of work and of Sunday church and the festivals, and work, again. And so passed the years.

Ferdinando Eszterhazy's will was may pages long. One of the clauses included the prescription that "all benefices and encumbrances shall continue as recorded" — and the Notary in Graach, removing the records from the files, discovered that Elisapheta's years of age were to be assisted by a pension. It not being in the will proper, Lady Emma never learned of it. Nor did it come in any way out of her own income. It was to be paid by Fillyi.

"You see, then, Doctor, this was his late Lordship's way of getting back at Fillyi for having tried to bother Elisapheta. And, then, too, Fillyi is rich, and can afford it."

Rich in money, yes. But the paying of the pension cost him more than money. Twice a year, year after year, decade after decade, to have his old passions dug from their grave — though, perhaps they had never died! — in which case, how much worse! Never to be able to forget, loss kept forever fresh. No wonder he had stormed, wept. Indeed, in his own brute, peasant way, he must have loved Elisapheta, too.

"Though I do know," the steward said, "the he writes to her Ladyship in Bella, and he complains."

Ah, indeed. Never would Fillyi have brought himself to lay his whole case bare and open. Rage would have found vent in mere complaints, perhaps barely coherent, in insinuations and innuendoes. And to no aid to his cause. And to what aid, then? Simply to plant in the mind of his landlady a single thought. *I am sure the steward cheats me . . .*

"To old Unda," Eszterhazy mused, "my uncle left nothing. That was his punishment for *her*. Tsk. He ought to have done better. I believe, though" — He forced back memory, and back she went, unwillingly — "that he may have had this on his mind, in his last days. I . . . think . . . so. . . ."

Chilperits thought so, too. "But he did not get around to do it in writing. So I has taken it upon myself to do it for him. I believe it is for the good of his soul, and that he rests easier for our doing of it." By *it,* meaning the doles and the boons, the trickle of charities which helped keep alive old Unda and her old and so terribly afflicted Hussar lover. "Though I do not care to explain it to her Ladyship, and I am sure than she thinks the worse of me for all."

Doctor Eszterhazy nodded. A sudden swift yawn, not of boredom, but of fatigue, rose from within him. He checked it and started to rise. A sudden thought — "Now, an idea has just come to me, Chilperits. Do you suppose Fillyi would exchange? What is the name of the next-largest farm here? — Gothenford, isn't it? Yes. Surely whoever has the Gothenford would accept Alarits-stead. And then Fillyi, well, his income would be less, but he need pay no encumbrance. It would not be forever reminding him —"

The steward, with a sigh which was only half-reproach, said that he had thought of that long ago — and long ago, and more than once since then suggested it to Fillyi. "Sir, I have, you might say, *pressed* it on him. But he won't do it. He says it would be a come-down for him. And that people would talk. That's what he says, Fillyi. That people would talk . . .

People came and talked to Eszterhazy as he lay in his bed in the best guest room at S'Graach. There was his Uncle Ferdinando, again young and dashing. There was Elisapheta, grown young, for another miracle. Old Unda was Young Cunigunda and beside her was the equally young Gabro, in his Hussar's shako with its death's-head emblem. They talked and they talked. But not a word of what they said reached his ears. Not even a sound of it.

The sound which did reach his ears, rousing him up from slumber and from bed, contained none of these voices. There were screams and shouts and snarls and growls — all from below and to the rear of the house.

Eszterhazy leaped from his bed, into his trousers, took up a lantern, and made his way through the dark old house.

The lantern beam fell first upon Frow Chilperits, her hair down around her shoulders, upon the back steps of the house, and wringing her hands in that age-old symbol of feminine distress.

"What is this, my frow — ?"

"Ah, sir, 'tis a bear, raiding the smokehouse for the meat — Ah, sir, do take care — ***Otho!***" she screamed into the darkness, as Eszterhazy darted off into it. "***Otho!*** *Take care! Take care! The Young Lord is out here — !*"

Her husband called back something which Eszterhazy did not understand, and then Eszterhazy stumbled and fell, the lantern fell also, and, in its beam, wasting itself on the upper boles of a tree before it sank into extinction, Eszterhazy saw the bear. He saw it but for a moment as it shuffled past him at half a run. It was upright. It was upright, holding something in its forepaws — a side of smoked pig, probably — and it tore at it, growling, as it fled. This was seemingly not its first incursion at some farmstead, for it had been wounded once, long before — there was a huge scar on its head, long healed, and reaching from scalp to cheek. Whatever had torn into the bear's head, perhaps some farmer's ax, had in so doing torn the very eye from the beast's head.

Eszterhazy cried out and simultaneously a gun went off. A woman screamed. *"Oh, God, Otho, if you've shot the Young Lord!"*

He called out to them, assured them he had not been shot at all, but demanded that the guns be put up. "Or someone may *be* shot, you all stumbling about in the blackness like this," he added, feeling decidedly grumpy about the whole thing. His grumpiness seemed to reassure them all. A grumpy gentleman was a figure familiar in type and fact, something with which one could deal.

" 'Tis past time we did fix that smokehouse door," they agreed, apologetically.

And in the morning they showed him the bear's prints in the soft earth between the smokehouse and the spring.

Old Unda, late that morning, rose and curtsied to him. She blessed him and his gift of money, but did not offer to show him more herbs, nor did she offer another stoop of metheglin. In fact, she said nothing more at all. And when Eszterhazy went into the cabin, she accompanied him and sighed a sigh which may have meant anything at all.

Nothing was moving behind the palings. Something was lying on the sad, stale straw. Eszterhazy felt himself chilled, felt an oppression in his chest. Gabro-Hussar sat crouched in a corner. It would have been the last touch if he had been bleeding from a bullet wound. But there was no sign of blood or wound. The wretched man merely crouched, staring blankly, and fondled the filthy remnant of his once-proud Hussar's hat.

"Is he . . . all right?" Eszterhazy finally asked.

She did speak, now. "As always," she said.

With that, the man crouching in the corner eased out on all fours and began the same mindless pacing back and forth, back and forth. "When it is very hot," she said, in a tired, subdued voice, "and he is very tired, he will often let me bathe him." And that was all she said.

All the way back to S'Graachs, Eszterhazy turned the matter over in his mind.

Very well: lycanthropy was a mere legend born of ignorance, descended out of dimly remembered totemism on the one hand and buttressed by outbursts of simple, animal-imitative insanity on the other. Men did not turn into bears, any more than into wolves, this last being merely the commonest form of the legend, and giving it its name.

This being the case, one had only to acknowledge the existence of two living and entirely different creatures, though both living in this same area of the province, one a man and one a bear, each of which bore identical scars and each scar in the same place on their heads and each of which had lost an eye and in each case the same eye.

That was all one had to accept.

It might almost be easier to accept lycanthropy.

Of course, one was not absolutely obliged to accept either.

One simply acknowledged the phenomena, and one simply said: "No explanation."

It was certainly a mistake to think that one had to supply an explanation for everything. It was perhaps a mistake to think that there had to *be* an explanation for everything.

The railroad had not yet reached Graach and perhaps never would. The New Road was well-built, and smooth enough; the ride in the diligence required no effort. No effort, that is, besides holding on to the leather straps provided at each seat, each time the coach turned a bend. The New Road, however, was full of bends. To read a book or paper would not have been impossible, but it would have been inconvenient. The ride to the railhead at Dominets gave Eszterhazy time to pass in thought as he wished. He did not particularly wish to think about the scene he had left behind him. But think about it he did.

What, after all, had he done?

He had, after all, done nothing. He had left things just as he found them, just as they had been, before he arrived. As they had been, all along. And for some reason, a few lines came to his mind from a *Life* of Luther which he had once read. "One day Doctor Luther said to Doctor Melanchthon, *'Philip, this day thou and I will go fishing, and leave the governance of the universe to God.'* "

Sometimes the right thing to do was to do nothing.

And, back in Bella, when Lady Emma asked, "And so now, tell me, doesn't the steward cheat me?" he answered, "Well, just a little bit," and she said, contentedly, "I thought so," and at once forgot.

THE CHURCH OF SAINT SATAN AND PANDAEMONS

"Have you seen this, Engelbert?" asked Judge Baltazaro Gumperts, tapping the newspaper — one of a dozen or two provided daily by the thoughtful proprietors of the Crow's-head Coffeehouse.

"What is that — the *Report* ? — haven't seen it today."

"Did you know there is a woman newspaper editor in the American province of Far-vest?"

"I did not know, and am not surprised."

"Incredible province."

The judge sucked in coffee and shook his head.

Judge Gumperts smacked the newspaper, perhaps as much to reprove it as to straighten it out for easier reading. "She says that the farmers there should raise less corn and more Hell; fact, just what it says: 'Raise less corn and more Hell' — what do you think it *means?"*

Doctor Engelbert Eszterhazy watched the waiter pour boiling milk into his cup from one vessel and hot coffee into it from another, with simultaneous dexterity: half and half. "Why . . . I suspect that it is an invitation to the always embattled farmers of America to devote fewer energies to the cultivation of maize in order that more energies may be devoted to politico-economic agitations." He observed the milk forming a skin and nodded his satisfaction. The waiter withdrew. Eszterhazy raised the glass and held it a moment as he followed a thought. "Something to do with railroad rates, I seem to recall. Our railroads are owned by the Crown, but as there is no Crown in America, the railroads there are owned by what are called *investors."* He bent his head and sipped.

Judge Gumperts said, "Ahaah!"

"What 'ahaah!'?"

And the member of the Court of the Second Jurisdiction said that this was perhaps why American railroads sometimes imported quantities of peasants from the Triune Monarchy. "Of the odder sort, too. Give them free land, and all. Which ones was it? Those odd chaps who wouldn't vote or do military service — oh yes, Mennonites. *They* won't make politico-economic agitations, I am sure. All *kinds* of different religions they have there in America, Engelbert. Fact. Read it in the *Gazette*. All privately owned too! Like their railroads. All equal, you know. Fact. No State Church and no Concordats, you know. And women can be editors, too, it seems. Well, women can *vote* there, you know, in the Province of Far-vest." Once more he sipped and licked his moustache. "In-CRED-ible," he said.

On that same morning in the late Spring, Count Vladeck, the Minister of Cults to the Triune Monarchy of Scythia-Pannonia-Transbalkania, was laying out a game of patience on his inlaid ebony desk when a soft double knock followed by an equally soft cough announced the presence of Brno, the Ministry's Principal Secretary.

"Come, most worthy servant," the Minister said, his eyebrows rising slightly in surprise. Brno, a stickler for protocol in all its most antique forms, did not usually call upon his superior without having previously sent a note beginning *Exceedingly August and High-born,* and concluding, *Kissing thus the Feet,* and so on. Count Vladeck, accordingly, did not merely look up from the cards, he laid them down entirely.

Entered Brno, tall, thin, clad in black, pale as wax: the perfect civil servant, treading almost upon his toes. With lips compressed, he laid upon the Minister's desk a document headed, in very large letters, and in the Gothic, Glagolitic, and Latin alphabets, **PERMISSION FOR THE LAWFUL RECOGNITION OF THE CONVENTICLE HEREUNDER DESCRIBED.**

Count Vladeck did not exactly wince, he did not exactly make a move, certainly he did not grind his teeth: but his teeth did indeed meet, with a perceptible click. And Brno, with a certain air which combined satisfaction and gloom, said, "Exactly so, Exceedingly August and High-born Lord Minister and Count."

If the conventicle (thereunder described) had been a congregation of the Holy Orthodox Church, no such permission need have been sought of the Ministry of Cults, such matters being purely the concern of the Metropolitans of Pannonia and Scythia, and/or the Holy Synod of Transbalkania. If it had been a Roman Catholic or Greek Catholic matter, the preliminary documentation would have been handled by the Papal Delegate, with the advice and consent of the Primus of Pannonia or the Ethnarch of Scythia or the Byzantine Exilarch of Balkania. And, inasmuch as Count Vladeck had received preliminary

visits from neither the Grand Rabbi nor the Grand Hodja, clearly no newly planned synagogue or mosque was involved.

More — and on arriving at this point in his cogitations, the Minister of Cults sighed and reached for his snuff-box — more: If it were merely a matter of a new Lutheran or Reformed church congregation, not only would Brno not have come to consult with Count Vladeck, the Regional Secretaries of the Ministry would not have bothered bringing the matter to the attention of Brno.

All of which added up to the prospect of another Evangelical Dissenting Group. And from that point on, there was really no knowing.

The last time this had occurred there were riots in Cisbalkania, the Byzantian delegates in the Diet had voted against the Budget, the Hyperboreans had refused to pay their head-tax, and the Papal Delegate, Monsignor Pinocchio, pleading severe indisposition, cancelled the twice-monthly sessions at which he and Count Vladeck (plus Field Marshal Dracúlya-Hunyadi and Professor Plotz of the Medical Faculty) played "poker" — a game which Monsignor Pinocchio had learned as a parish priest in Bruklín, a provincial city on Great Island in the American province of Nev-jork.

All most disturbing, of course.

Count Vladeck took snuff rather gloomily.

"Which is it this time, Brno?" he asked, with a sign and a snuffle. "The Two-Seed-in-the-Spirit Predestinarian Baptists? Or the Seventh Day Antinomians?"

Brno pointed without words to the line reading, NAME OF THE CONVENTICLE FOR WHICH LAWFUL RECOGNITION IS SOUGHT, and upon which, in a neat and clear hand indicating nothing of any of the emotions which the copying clerk might be supposed to have felt, was written, *The Church of Saint Satan and Pandaemons.*

It was Brno who broke the silence, although it was the Count who twitched convulsively. "The petition," he said, as softly as usual, "is signed by the requisite nineteen respectable and loyal subjects, all of whom were registered in the last Census, all of whom have paid head-tax for the previous five years, all of whom have performed military service, and none of whom have ever been placed under arrest. The requisite engrossing fee has been paid, and in gold, and so has the stamp tax on the receipt for one year's rent of the premises designated for worship."

All, in short, was in order, perfectly in order. There was no lawful ground for the Minister of Cults to refuse his seal and signature. And, of course, if he were to apply them, the results . . . the results —

"I shall resign," he said, in a broken voice. "Resign — and take up my duties as Master of the Boarhounds in the remote border province of Ptush, as one is automatically obligated to do after resigning without having been requested to do so by the Throne. Resign . . .

and give up my cosy little ten-room flat on the Corso, my so-amiable plump mistress who sings coloratura soprano in the Opera, my electrical landau, my membership in the Jockey-Sport Club, and my English manservant. . . ." He thrust his knuckles into his mouth to prevent a sob escaping. It was impossible even to think of adequately heating a single room in Schloss Ptush, and the Minister was a martyr to chilblains.

Brno, to his superior's infinite surprise, said, softly but firmly, "The Exceedingly August and High-born Lord Minister Count must do no such thing."

Hope was not yet to be thought of. But surprise alone checked the tear which brimmed in one of Count Vladeck's eyes. "Then what must I do?" he whispered.

Said Brno: "You must consult Dr. Eszterhazy."

Engelbert Eszterhazy, Dr. Juris., Dr. Philosoph., Dr. Med., D. Litt., etc., contemplated the cedar box before him. At length he opened it, extracted a panatela Caoba Granda, sniffed it, put it to his ear, did things to it and listened. Next he cut an end off it with a small ivory-handled knife (a gift of the late Hajji Tippoo Tibb, of Zanzibar and Pemba). Next he put that end in his mouth and the other end in a small gas flame. He took in a puff of smoke, a puff of smoke, did things with his mouth to it, at length allowed it to dribble out, took another, longer puff and kept this one in for a longer time. Then he pursed his lips and, as though scarcely aware of what he was doing, blew a smoke ring. The ring floated through the air, and settled down over the single gloved finger which protruded from the hands clasped upon the gold-topped cane of his caller.

"This is a very good Habana," he said. "This is a very difficult thing which you ask of me. You are in effect asking me to place an official *imprimatur* upon the rumors which even now already and for some years past have circulated among the more ignorant, *videlicet*: 'Eszterhazy trafficks with the Devil.' Why should I do it?"

Count Vladeck blinked and removed his gaze from a richly colored porcelain phrenological head which gave the impression of floating in mid-air about five feet equidistant from floor and ceiling. "Patriotism," he said, after a moment, and cleared his throat.

A faint movement which might have been a preliminary blink or an unfinished tic disturbed for a moment the corner of Dr. Eszterhazy's left eye, and another thin film of segar smoke ebbed from the left corner of his mouth.

"*Not* patriotism?" asked Count Vladeck.

"The most patriotic man I ever met," Dr. Eszterhazy observed, "was Sergeant-Major Moomkotch, the mass murderer. Remarkable head that man had. Re*mark*able. You remember Moomkotch's head, of course."

Perhaps a trifle nervously, perhaps a trifle crossly, Count Vladeck said, "No, I do *not* remember the head of Sergeant-Major Moomkotch!"

"Really," his host said, with faint surprise. "Well, it is almost directly behind you, in a large vessel of formaldehyde." Count Vladeck, issuing a sound rather reminiscent of a large bat during the rutting season, leaped from his chair and gave the impression of trying to move two ways at the same time. Then he sat down heavily and cast a look of cold displeasure at the man who still calmly and with placid pleasure smoked the segar given him.

"Eszterhazy —"

"Yes, Vladeck?" Their eyes met, locked.

After a moment: "Really, Eszterhazy, you must not allow yourself to forget that you are addressing a Royal and Imperial Minister —"

"I do not for a moment forget it, nor do I expect that a Royal and Imperial Minister will find it unreasonable that when a man has been awarded seven doctorates he be addressed by at least one of them —"

But Count Vladeck could contain himself no further. With a sound no louder than an involuntary puff, he spun about in his chair and exclaimed, "Jesus, Mary, and Joseph!"

"No, no, no. Monosh Moomkotch, Sergeant-Major, First Pannonian Hussars (Star of Valor, 5th Class, Carpathian Campaign, with Bar). Convicted on seventeen counts of Infamous Murder. Went to the block singing the National Anthem. The Protuberance of Patriotism is *very* strong . . . as Your Excellency can see —" He gestured with his segar.

"Looks like a wart, to me."

Dr. Eszterhazy looked at his own hands, then at the back of the barbered and crisply collared neck of his guest, moved all of his fingers once or twice, giving the impression of a spider about to spring, then sighed, very, very faintly.

"That *is* a wart, Your Excellency," he said. "The Protuberance of Patriotism is approximately four and one half centimeters to the left oblique." He placed both his hands in his pockets, and, leaning back in his chair once more, cocked up the segar and watched the smoke.

"*Very* good Habana . . ."

At length Count Vladeck turned. "Depressing sight," he murmured. "Yes, yet, I am sure it is also educational. Well. Enough of all this . . . this . . ." He avoided his host's gaze, then he met it.

"Well, well, Doctor Eszterhazy. Well enough. You know the nature of the problem. Will you take the case?"

Another ring of segar smoke. Another. And another.

"Will you name your . . . your *honorarium* . . . Doctor Eszterhazy? Doctor Doctor Eszterhazy? Doctor Doctor Doctor Eszterhazy? Doctor Doctor Doctor Doctor Eszterhazy? Doc——"

But the host waved away any further repetition. "Those will do. The other three are honorary. 'Honorarium'? Yes. Well —" He sat up.

All boredom, all mockery, all indifference, was now gone. He leaned forward.

The marketplace in Poposhki-Georgiou smelled like a barn — that is, assuming a barn to have borne, in addition to the usual odors of hay and dung and animals, a strong scent of ripe fruit, cheap perfume, kerosene, hot grease, fried meat, and fresh-baked pastry.

A rather unlikely combination for a barn, it must be admitted. But there you are. And here *we* are. In the marketplace of Poposhki-Georgiou. Tuesday, since time immemorial (that is, for the past seventeen or eighteen years), has been Little Market Day. Great Market Day is Friday. Little Market Day is largely reserved for trading in mules, oxen, and he-goats; only the men come to Little Market Day. Little Market Day really smells like a barn — that is, a barn in which someone has been spilling a great deal of beer and a great deal of the cheapest variety of distilled spirit (known in the local dialect as Maiden's Breath). Few cooked or baked goods are offered on Tuesday, the men bringing their own lunch, and "lunch" to the peasantry of Poposhki-Georgiou traditionally consists of a hunk of goat sausage, a hunk of goat cheese, a hunk of bread (not exactly black, more like gray), and a bunch of dried sour cherries. Sour cherries are believed to be good for the lower intestine. In Poposhki-Georgiou the lower intestine is regarded as the seat of the deeper emotions. "When my best mule broke his left foreleg," one might hear it said, "it felt like a Turkish knife in my lower intestine."

Also, they tell this story:

First Peasant: Yesterday I came home and found my wife in bed with the goatherd-boy.

Second Peasant: What did you do?

First Peasant: I ate some sour cherries.

On hearing this story, particularly after the first half of the second bottle of Maiden's Breath, your Poposhki-Georgiou peasant will clutch at his embroidered vest with both hands, wet his knee-breeches, fall into spasms, and roll into dungheaps.

But on Friday there come to town not only the peasant, but the peasant's wife, the peasant's daughters, the peasant's mother, and the peasant's mother-in-law. So things are somewhat different. In addition to the goodies aforementioned, there is a considerable trade in ribbons, whistles, preserved gingerbread, milch-goats, religious artifacts in gold — in pure gold, and in real gold — as well as a brisk traffic in herbs, some for love potions, some for laxatives.

Up to the herbalist's stall falters an aged *bobba-bobba* in sixteen petticoats and twenty-seven shawls, all rusty black.

The Herbalist: What way may I serve the High-born Lady?

The *Bobba-bobba*: [Groans, putting both withered fists into the small of her back] Something for the lower intestine?

The Herbalist: I have just the thing.

After that, up comes the *bobba-bobba*'s great-grand-daughter.

The Herbalist: What way may I serve the High-born and Beautiful Lady? Parlé-voo Italyano, Maddom?

The Girl [blushing]: [In a whisper] Something for the lower intestine?

The Herbalist: I have just the thing for you.

And then, by and by, up comes the girl's father.

Peasant: Say, ain't you new here? What become of Old Yockum, used to keep this pitch, hanh? [Hawks a phlegm and spits]

The Herbalist: Yockum was gored by a boar in Hyperborea.

The Peasant: May the Resurrected Jesus Christ and All the Saints have mercy on his soul, goring was too good for him, the son of a bitch. Got something for the lower intestine?

Ah, the pawky peasantry of Poposhki-Georgiou!

Meanwhile, and just to show that the Machine — symbolized by (a) the narrow-gauge railroad from (and, for that matter, to) the District Capital, (b) the one-boiler engine in the local mill, which grinds grits and goat fodder, and (c) — but there is no (c) — just to show that here the Machine has not destroyed the spirit of the countryside, traditional music is being supplied by an old man on a one-drone bagpipe, a crippled boy who clashes cymbals which are not mates, and a drunken fat woman with a tambourine. The peasants show their keen appreciation for this old tradition by dancing traditional jigs, breaking wind when the music pauses, and — when the crippled boy holds out his hand — giving him their bad coins or else spitting in his dirty paw.

And whenever this last piece of prime wit is performed, oh see the peasants — that is, see the other peasants — clutch at their embroidered vests with both hands, wet their knee-breeches, fall into spasms, and roll into dungheaps.

Also traditional, although missing from the local scene for many years: a mountebank in a cherry-colored coat, blue trousers which fasten under his shoes, and an enormous and ancient gray top hat — The old folks, when they catch sight of him, poke each other and say, "Ahaha, a Russian jester! Now we'll hear something good!" and they quicken their pace and crowd up close; the mountebank juggles three pomegranates, which he subsequently auctions off, keeps up a prolonged patter full of coarse jokes . . . and somehow the fruit turns into bundles of booklets, almanacs, which he proceeds to hawk for a few groushek each . . . "All the Days of the Saints, in Gothic, Glagolitic, and Latin, with the right signs of the moon and the time to plant turnips, plus many excerpts from the Sacred Psalms." Here he says something, with a pious look and a learned air, something which the peasants assume to be Old Slovatchko, High Romanou, or Church Gothic; next he summons up a small boy and pulls pigeon's egg out of his ear; anon there are suddenly two balls which he juggles, anon suddenly there is only one —

The "Russian Jester": Funny, I had two when I started! [Slaps at himself]

And the peasants clutch their embroidered vests and —

Afterwards, the mountebank, off in a corner by himself, the unsold almanacs in his huge hat, a red kerchief spread out in his lap, is counting his pile of coppers. Most of the crowd is watching an unscheduled bit of entertainment, to wit, a dog fight. This is as much fun as anything else and has the added advantage that no one will try to take up a collection afterwards.

"Greetings, purest one," someone says to the juggler. The juggler looks up slowly, one hand upon the coppers, and says not a word.

The newcomer is a yellow-faced man, a man with a hairless face, deeply grooved; he wears the costume of a *tchilditz,* an itinerant sow-spayer. "Greetings, purest one," he repeats.

The mountebank smiles the faintest of smiles. "Say," he says, "you look a sight purer than I am."

The *tchilditz* nods. "I am a white dove," he says. "Received the removal of fleshly cares when I was a boy. Wasn't any law against it, then. But you, no, you are a purest one. You know the Old Tongue. I heard you say it, back then, when you's talking about their false Psalms, yes I did. Didn't I?" The two give swift glances around; their hands meet and are covered by the red kerchief. Does the kerchief move in the wind? Do their fingers move beneath the kerchief ? — fingers touching fingers in some ritual play? It is all over in a moment.

"There are more of us around now than there used to be, aren't there?" the "Russian jester" says.

The white dove nods head, strokes long chin. "Yes, more. More. Not many. Never many. Nowhere many. Not since olden times. But all this is going to change. Soon. Changes be starting. You know?"

The jester shrugs, waggles his hands, cups an ear. "I hear. I just . . . *hear.* But I don't really *know.*"

The *tchilditz* (his name, he says, is Jaaneck) comes closer and brings his mouth close to the mountebank's ear. Then he seems to think better of it. "Look here, what I be going to show you . . . *thee* . . . So look here. Look down here. Look —" With his long stave he begins to draw something. Something like a map. "And I'll see thee, then, there," he concludes. And starts away.

"Come, brother, only two groushek, only two for this here

almanac," the mountebank calls after him, holding one up, as if still trying to make a sale. There are faint smiles on both faces.

It is a feature of the Triune Monarchy, indeed, it is of its essence, that His Most Serene and Apostolic Majesty, Ignats Louis, is simultaneously Emperor of Scythia, King of Pannonia, and Basha of Transbalkania. However, as Engelbert Eszterhazy himself so often said, "Things are not simple." Nor are they. Transbalkania is itself a *Confœderats,* consisting of Vlox-Minore, Vlox-Majore, Popushki, and Hyperborea. H.M.S.A.M., Ignats Louis, as every schoolchild knows, is thus High Duke of the Two Vlox, Prince of Popushki, and Grand Hetman of Hyperborea: *Pop. (1901): 132,756. Principal exports: Sheepskins, boars' bristles, dried artichokes, eisenglass, and musk. Capital: Apollograd (formerly Apolloöpolis).*

Apollograd is thus the smallest National Capital of the Triune Monarchy. Dr. Einhardt, the statistician, has calculated, in one of his droll moments, that it takes anything new an average of 17.5 years to move the 300-odd miles between Bella, the Imperial Capital, and Apollograd. ("That is," he adds, with the familiar twinkle in his kindly, myopic eyes, "when it moves at all!") Even now, one may see a group of boar-herds crossing themselves in awe at sight of "the samovar on wheels," as they call the Apollograd steam tram; as it happens, the last steam tram in Bella was discontinued over seventeen years ago. Provincial nobility still find it necessary to warn their servants on no account to blow out the gas-lights in the Grand Hotel Apollo and Ignats Louis. Even in the Saxon and the Armenian quarters the majority of homes are illumined by kerosene lamps, while most of the Tartars use rush-lights. The rubble-strewn streets of this last sector, formerly a by-word, are now, under the benevolently stern and progressive administration of the Governor of the City, Count Blops, entirely a thing of the past.

The gas mains have as yet to reach most of the streets in the older parts of town. Street lamps burning colza oil were tried by Count Blops, on an experimental basis, early in his term of office; but it was found that the Tartars used to drain the oil and use it for cooking purposes. Visitors may, on payment of a small fee, obtain the service of a municipally licensed porter with a lamp.

"I ain't seen *you* here before, Brother," the porter Karposh commented one night, in the dipping and bobbing lamplight.

"Things in the bristle business are not what they were," his hire said, gloomily. "One must get closer to sources of supply." He might have been considered tall, had he not stooped so much. Perhaps conditions in the bristle trade were weighing him down.

"That's what they tell me, Brother. Say, Brother, how about a drop of brandy before we get into Tartar Town? No brandy *there,* you know, being all Musselmens," and he spat, *pro forma,* in the rutted, pitted road.

The traveler muttered something about the brandy not evaporating before they got back, and with this hint of future kindness Karposh had to pretend contentment. The houses huddled far back from the way, thatched-roofed and low-set. Now and again a dog, chained by a melon patch, lifted its snouzle and bayed at the lemon-rind moon. And at length they came to their destination.

"See this here warehouse, Brother?" the guide asked, lifting the lamp as though to show to better advantage the peeling plaster and the rubble-and-stone walls beneath. "Used to be a what they call a caravanserai in the old days of the Turks. Camels they had here in them days. Fact! My old granddad he told —"

But perhaps what was told by Karposh *grandpère* may never be known to any other living soul, for at that moment the small door set into the big door opened, the traveler spoke a few words into the opening, the door opened a bit more, the traveler entered, and the door creaked shut. Karposh grunted, set the lamp into a niche, lowered the wick, then lowered himself onto the turf and, thinking of brandy, prepared to wait.

Many, many camels indeed could have been accommodated during the great days of the caravanserai; one thinks of them, Bactrians for the most part, wool peeling off in great patches, necklaces of big blue beads round their thick, crooked necks, padding and bobbing and pressing on, league after hundred leagues, all the way from the Court of the Great Khan at Karakorum — perhaps — and even, perhaps, farther. There were courtyards within courtyards, and warehouses which might have lodged the bristles of all the boars of Hyperborea and bales more precious than that, by far: galingale and benjoin, reels of silk, Indoo veilery thin as mist — but now nought but a few bare halls containing hair from the stinking swine of the Hyperborean ranges, destined to make paintbrushes for to whiten the walls of Christendom.

The doorkeeper had a torch.

At each corner of each rectangle within the great serai, another stood with a torch.

Within a chamber so large its hither parts were only a lostness of shadows, two lines of men stood an arm's span apart, and each of them with a torch.

A Voice: *This will be the last. None more may enter now.*

The last passed down between the rows of torchbearers and the torchbearers fell into step behind him.

The gathering was not very large, and neither was the inner room. At one end was a table with the embroidered tablecloth one saw on

high occasions in the kitchens of prosperous farmhouses, and a modern oil lamp sat on it, frosted chimney semi-covered with a bright pink globe. Three respectable men with side whiskers sat at the table, and one was rendered twice-respectable by reason of his wearing eyeglasses with rather small, oval lenses. A stout woman, all in black, sat at a small harmonium; if she herself was not the widow of a prosperous butcher, surely she had a sister who was. Eszterhazy sat as near the back of the fairly small congregation as was possible for him to do; the diaconal-looking man in spectacles nodded to the woman, she threw back her ample shoulders and began to play, with fairly few false notes, what one would automatically assume to be a hymn, but which Eszterhazy after a moment recognized as the Grand March from *Aïda.*

She did not play much of it.

The harmonium subsided on a sort of sigh, the deacon arose, took a handkerchief from his sleeve, and in a voice heavy with emotion said, "Beloved brethren, dear saints who have kept the Faith, I have come to deliver unto you the joyful and so-long-awaited tidings: Saint Satan has at last been released from Hell, and, with all his Holy Demons, even now begins to prepare for his rule over all the Heavens and over all the Earth . . ."

The congregation burst into sobs, shouts, cries of ecstasy, throwing out their arms, clasping their hands, beating their bosoms, doubling forward in their seats, and, in a moment, first one by one, then by twos, then three and four at a time, leaping to their feet. A white-haired man in worn broadcloth, with the look and smell of a backwoods apothecary, turned to Eszterhazy and, with tears running down his furrowed face, embraced him and cried out, *"Satan is risen! Satan is risen!"*

And Eszterhazy, somewhat returning the embrace, said in the tones nearest to enthusiasm which at the moment he felt capable of, "Is he indeed?"

Not the least of the interesting features of the Pannonian Presbyterian Church is that it sustains seventeen bishops, of whom fifteen are in Pannonia proper, and two — *in partibus infidelium,* as it were — preside over the Synods of Scythia and Transbalkania. Skeptical Calvinists have been known to come all the way from Scotland (*especial*ly from Scotland) to check upon this, and to them the learned divines of the Reformed Faith explain that, firstly, the institution was in a sense forced upon them by the Capitulations of 1593, that, secondly, the bishops are chosen by lot and after fasting, meditation, and prayer, and without any hint of an Apostolic Succession, the bishop being in his synod merely first among equals to the other Calvinist clergy, and that, thirdly —

But these visitors rarely desire to hear of thirdly. They say, "Hoot!" and "Wheesht!" they exclaim. And, "*Beesh*ops, did ye say!" they murmur, casting up their eyes and hands.

Bishop Andreas Hogyvod walked up and down in his garden in the precincts of the Great Old Reformed Church in Apollograd. He was a man of enormous girth and stature, in a Geneva gown, a huge starched ruff, and a tricorn hat; he gave the impression of being a sort of catafalque stood on one end and moving under its own locomotion. In one hand he held — almost, indeed, engulfing — volume XXII of the octavo edition of Calvin's *Institutes,* with a tiny agate snuffbox pressed against the morocco binding; the other hand, or, at any rate, two fingers of it, he pressed to his nose. There was, let us say, a certain nobility to the bishop's nose. A certain grandness, an amplitude of architecture, rococo . . . or, perhaps, baroque. A painter, engaged by the Committee of the Presbytery to fix the bishop's likeness in oils, had once, and only once, and most unwisely, declared the nose to be "Roman." So unchristian an emotion as wrath would certainly not have disfigured the episcopal countenance; however, he let it be known that he did not agree, and let us, therefore, leave it so: the nose of the Calvinist Bishop of Apollograd and All Transbalkania was not Roman. And, certainly, it was not Roman Catholic.

Walking to and fro in his garden, meditating doubtless upon the doctrines of Election, Predestination, and Total Depravity, he gazed with an unwinking solemnity at the approaching visitor. The visitor was tall and walked in a somewhat stately manner, one hand clasped behind him in the small of his back. His frock coat was spotless, in itself somewhat unusual in Apollograd, which the bishop himself had more than once humorously referred to as "Apollograd the Dusty." And when he removed his equally spotless silk hat and bowed, he revealed an imposing head whose silvery hair had receded just sufficiently to remind one of Gogol's comment, in another context, "Forasmuch as he is wise, God hath added unto his brow." This visitor's head bulged appreciably on both sides, indicating that his hatter, at least, must certainly and most certainly have been aware of the unusual quality and quantity of brain matter between the frontal and occipital bones.

The bishop, experienced in judging physiognomy and other matters indicative of profession, allowed the hand at his nose to fall away and the snuff to dissipate in the wind (and, if not, to be joined to other dust motes of the National Capital, where, as has been hinted, they would scarcely be noticed), transferred book and box to that hand, and held the newly unencumbered one out to the visitor, remarking as he did so, "Sir Advocate."

"Engelbert Eszterhazy, of the Faculty of Law, and for to serve Your Reverence. But how did Your Reverence *know?*"

His Reverence waved the matter aside. "One knows," he rumbled. "One knows." He gave the visitor's hand another squeeze. "Well. Doctor Eszterhazy. So. Well. From Bella? Of course. From Bella. You see. One *knows.*" He gave a slight shrug.

Merely a provincial bishop he might be, the shrug said, but he was well aware of a thing or two, *videlicet* that, firstly, the visitor was an Advocate at Law, secondly, that as such he bore the title of Dr. Juris., and that, thirdly, such a smart get-up was just the sort of smart get-up worn by and only by members of the Society of Advocates in the Imperial Capital, but that, and after all, fourthly, it was thus no use trying to humbug the bishop and maybe try to cozen him out of any of his first fruits, tithes, annates, and/or other presbyterial perquisites — *no* use to try.

"Well, well, Your Reverence is of course quite correct. I have *not* come here to buy bristles!"

"Ho ho!" the bishop rumbled. "Ahahah. Bristles! Ha! That's good. That's a rich one. Bristles, no. But as for . . . ah, hum, *musk?*" He raised his eyebrows and twisted his mouth. "Concerning this the humble shepherd had better not ask; therefore he won't. *Ho!*"

Eszterhazy's manner, as he gave his head a slight shake, indicated that he was all too well aware of the reputation, in matters of amour, of the Faculty of Law. He said nothing of the fact that it had been decades since musk had been regarded as a proper gift by the higher-priced courtesans of the Imperial Capital.

"What shall I say to my excellent and revered acquaintance, Pastor Eckelhofft, on your behalf, Bishop, when I return?"

"Eckelhofft, ah, Eckelhofft!" The bishop had deftly hiked up his gown and stuck the snuffbox in one pocket and the little book in another. He now raised both hands, palms out, and his eyes as well . . . so to speak. "There is a soul for you! There is a mind! *Smart?* Smarter than six Jesuits! Christian souls in doubt and danger," he apostrophized them from his garden, with the rosebushes and the linden trees as witnesses, "such as are subject to hazards innumerable, temptations and licentious doctrines being ever found in the great cities above all places under the sun, have no fear! Sebastian Eckelhofft stands like a beacon light! Hearken unto *him,* dwellers in the great imperial high city! Sit at *his* feet on the Lord's day! Eschew Lutheranism in all its forms, not to speak of even worse errors —"

The jurisconsult rubbed his long nose as though appreciative of these admonitions. "Quite a scholar, Pastor Eckelhofft," he said.

"None better. Cicero at his fingertips, Erasmus in the hollow of his hand. I was once a bit of a scholar myself," the bishop said, a trifle wistfully. "Though little enough use one finds for learning here, amidst the heathen hordes of Hyperborea."

" 'Heathen,' ah yes. Your Reverence refers to the Tartars?"

His Reverence was not so sure. Tartars, he said, Tartars were but simple souls, honest and hard-working, deceived by a false and so-called prophet, true. But there was worse than Tartarism by far to be found in Hyperborea. A Tartar after all was a mere shadow of a Turk, and the Turks, bestial devotees of Lust in all its forms, still, even the Turks had recognized in the Reformed Faith a faith free from idolatry in all *its* forms. . . .

"There are those here worse than Tartars by far," he repeated, darkly.

The visitor seemed both troubled and fascinated. "I would not dream of contradicting the immense wealth of knowledge and experience," he said, "on which Your Reverence must base his statements. No doubt it was to these historical events which Pastor Eckelhofft referred once or twice when we were discussing — he and I — the surprising hold which the Manichaean heresies used to hold, so long ago, upon so many of the inhabitants of this once-flourishing (I refer to pre-Turkish times) district . . . eh?"

But the Bishop of Apollograd did not seem inclined to assent to the *eh?* "Historical events? Used to hold? *Used* to hold? Pre-Turkish times? Ha. *Ha!*"

Why . . . surely Bishop Hogyvod did not mean to imply that — ?

But Bishop Hogyvod *did* mean to imply. That.

Had Doctor Eszterhazy ever been in Poposhki-Georgiou?

Doctor Eszterhazy touched his own long nose thoughtfully. Yes, he had.

Did Dr. Eszterhazy know the famous cheeses of Poposhki-Georgiou? Doctor Eszterhazy did; so. And so then he must know the method in which these cheeses were ripened. By being carefully wrapped in a clean pig's bladder, and then wrapped inside of seven sacks, and then buried beneath a dungheap for two months. "Is it two months?" he pondered. "Well, no matter. Two months or — or whatever. The dungheap, foul as it is, produces an even and continuous heat; a fact pointed out and utilized by the old alchemists. Though maybe not to make cheese. Never mind. Nevertheless. You put the green cheese under the dungheap, and, if you wait long enough, what do you get? *Ripe* cheese. *Over*-ripe, to my own way of thinking; blood of a she-wolf, how they stink! So now you understand." He gave his head a portentous nod and stamped one of his huge feet on the herb-bordered flagstones of the garden path.

Evidently it took a moment for the visitor to clear his throat and pluck up courage to admit that he did *not* —

"What! Not understand? What, *not?*" The back door of the Bishop's Seat opened and an elderly but spry woman came out, smoothing her apron. "What is there not to understand? You take the green cheese, that is to say, the Manichaean or Dualist heresy, the damnable doctrines of the so-called Cathari, or Pure Ones, the abominable teachings of the Bulgarian Daemonolaters — you take this and you

bury it beneath the dungheap: that is, obviously, the long, long rule of the Orthodox, the Romanist Catholic, and the Turk: centuries of hiding beneath the surface of the world, like the worms they are, like the serpents which they be. And what do you get? Why, what *would* you get, man? You would get stinking cheese, wouldn't you? Or, in other words, Christian Diabolism. What else?"

The old woman came up and curtsied in the high, antique style. "Good early evening, Sir Bishop. Cook says dinner is ready, and will the gentleman be staying — ?"

The bishop's scowl, on the mention of the word DINNER, vanished like ice in a hot samovar. "Of course the gentleman will be staying, Mrs. Umlaut, do you take him for a fool, why should he eat those greasy kickshaws at the Grand Hotel when he can eat here?"

The gentleman murmured something about regretting, and indeed tugged at a watch; but the bishop waved the watch back into its pocket. "What? *Not* eat here? *Not* have dinner at Apollograd Bishop's Seat? *Not* have . . . not have . . ." Here his erudite nose went up a few inches, the nostrils dilated and gave an educated sniff . . . or two. . . . "*Not* have cock-and-pullet soup with sour cream, fresh dill, Bosnian prunes? Not have grilled squabs farced with pounded chicken livers and shallots? Not have sweet and sour red cabbage and caraway seeds? Roast breast of heifer with crisp cracklings, potato dumplings and sour crout, fresh homemade noodles and pot cheese, plum brandy, fresh-roasted coffee with fresh-ground cinnamon, apple-strudel-walnuts-raisins? *What?* **NOT?**"

Doctor Eszterhazy sighed. "Ah. Your Reverence has a certain way of putting things."

His Reverence said, "Ho ***Ho!***" and, putting his hands between his guest's shoulderblades, gave him a friendly shove which might have staggered someone less sure on his feet. "Yes," said the bishop, "Christ-ian Di-***ab***-o-lism . . . And would you believe — no: the fleshpots of Egypt (that is to say: Bella) you know, but of this particular canker sore you know nothing and would not believe. But *we* know and *we* believe! Yes! These scoundrels are stirring after their insufficiently long slumber and sleep. Yes, these rogues are actually whispering about coming out into the open! Well, let them try! Tolerant we may be, but even tolerance has its limits, and, after all, we are not the descendants of mice or of sheep. Let me tell you a tale or two of that godly man, Duke Vladimir the Impaler, **rrrrr!**"

But, by this time, they had washed their hands and it was time for the bishop to say grace.

The Bureau of the Royal and Imperial Posts and Mails (Division of Semaphores and Telegraphs) had closed for the night, but it opened as a courtesy to the Faculties of Law, Letters, and Medicine . . . plus a small gratuity.

"You have no objection to the use of American standard commercial code?" asked Eszterhazy.

"Doctor," the Royal and Imperial Telegrapher said, as he sat down at the instrument, "for another such amount, you may, if you please, send the entire corpus of the *Legends of the Saints* — in Glagolitic."

But Eszterhazy said he thought that the rather briefer message which he had prepared would do. At that moment the incoming set burst into a clatter.

" 'MOST IMPORTANT,' " the clerk translated, and, brightening, suggested that it was the results of the soccer tournament held that afternoon in Bella, but no.

" 'BULGARIA MAY INVADE TURKEY,' " Eszterhazy interpreted.

" 'MOST IMPORTANT'!" The telegrapher shrugged sarcastically, and clearing his throat, began to tap the outgoing message.

That night the congregation of the illicit conventicle in Tartar Town was larger by several dozen. "Beloved brethren," the deacon began, "the glad tidings have begun to spread. It is our duty to help them spread, indeed. It is also, as always, our duty to accept martyrdom, and I am sure that oppression is as inevitable as — this time — it is bound to be transitory. For is not our local saying that 'We are in debt to the landlords' kerchiefs for the very sweat of our brows' as true as ever? Which of us indeed owns the fields he tills, the shops wherein he toils? Scarcely a one. Scarcely a one. If the monks, bishops, and archimandrites do not own the fabric of our livelihood, then some nobleman does. It is in their evil interests to defy holy Saint Satan and to wage war upon his saints, but . . ."

His voice stopped upon the interval for breath and in the shaveling of a second his voice, like that of everyone present, rose and fell upon a deep sound of **ô**, which prolonged itself.

To his left, and in what had been until that second the darkness and dimness of the corner of the room-top, there appeared a head and face. In appearance it reminded one of the portrait in the Royal and Imperial Art Museum in Bella, entitled *The Boyar Bogdanovich, after a Long Resistance to the Vlox, Being Led away to Impalement on His Castle Walls* — the same air of ruined grandeur and defiant nobility — but it was more than twice the size of any merely human head or face, and tears of blood coursed from the glowing yellow eyes and fell silently into the darkness. The congregation fell with one accord upon their knees, and the lips opened and began to speak.

"Children of Light, falsely called 'of Darkness'," the head spoke, in tones sonorous and echoing, *"the way which you intend is not the way. Not* . . . not . . . *the* . . . *way* . . . the . . . *way* . . . *way* . . ."

The deacon broke the numinous silence. "O blessed Saint Satan," he asked, imploringly, "what *is* the way?"

The lips writhed as though in anguish; the golden and glowing eyes

rolled; at length the voice said, *"I shall send you a messenger and the token shall be the verse of the former scriptures about the land spread forth as though on wings . . ."*

And, as the last words still throbbed in the ears, the vision and the visage began to fade, and again the congregational voice rose and fell and prolonged itself upon a deep sound of **ô**.

The great central platform of the railroad terminal in Avar-Ister, capital of Pannonia, is seldom uncrowded. Here arrive and here depart the great expresses to and from Bella, almost their last stop this side of Constantinople, many of the fashionable travelers getting down to stretch their legs during the half-hour pause, to walk up and down, and buy the famous roses and the famous sweetmeats of the Co-Capital (as it is called, often, in Avar-Ister and, seldom, in Bella). Here one changes for all the branch lines which connect the second city of the Triune Monarchy with all places east and south (including Apollograd). Here one sees Yanosh, the once famous Gypsy dancer — that is, still famous, but no longer a dancer, not since losing two of his toes as the result of a bite inflicted during a lovers' quarrel by a jealous mistress — and his by now almost equally famous dancing she-bear, Yanoshka. There is a well-known saying to the effect that "Whoever sits upon the middle bench of the great central platform of the railroad terminal in Avar-Ister, if he sits long enough, will see pass in front of him everyone whom he or she knows"; at least, there is a saying to that effect in Avar-Ister . . . called "the Paris of the Balkans."

Sometimes.

At the moment (the moment being midnight) it was difficult to see just who *was* sitting on the middle bench, for a crowd of travelers was milling around watching Yanosh beat his Gypsy tambourine, shouting hoarsely as Yanoshka, head up, shuffled up and down upon the soles of her huge feet. A thin gentleman in a high starched collar with rounded ends looked around uncertainly. At that moment someone rose from the middle bench and approached him.

"Mr. Abernathy?"

The thin gentleman removed a finger from its place between his collar and his neck, adjusted his eyeglasses, and said, "Sir, I *am* Silas Abernathy, sole representative in ***Sky***thia-Pannonia-Transbalkania of the Atlantic, Pacific, and Southwestern Nebraska Railroad; might you be Doctor Eszterhazy? You *are!* Well, say, I want to thank you for your wire, and — say, are you a doctor of philosophy, or a doctor of jurisprudence?"

"Yes," said Eszterhazy.

Mr. Abernathy blinked, gave an uncertain chuckle, then plunged ahead. "Say, I don't know how you learned that those ten townships alongside our right-of-way have finally come out of litigation, but you are one hunderd percent right that the A, P, and SN Line desires to settle them with You-roe-pene settlers of an industrious nature. The soil is deep, sir, the soil is fer-tyle, it can grow corn (maize, as you call it), it can grow pertaters, it can grow winter wheat, and the A, P, and SN Line is not only willing to sell it to the right parties for nothing down and three dollars a acre over twenty-five years, but we are also willing and eager to pay all of their moving and traveling expenses for their persons and baggage. Say, they can be their own landlords in no time flat, with a good crop er two, and they can also enjoy freedom of the press if they are of a literary pursuit in their spar time, as well as freedom of speech and assembly, needless to add mention of freedom of rulligion —"

"Needless," said Eszterhazy. "And, pray, do not forget to mention, when you speak to their leader, Deacon Philostr Grotz, that according to many exegetes and scholars, North and South America in the singular shape of the conjoined continents, may have been mentioned in the Old Testament as 'the land spread forth as though on wings' —"

"Say," said Mr. Abernathy, "that's *right.* No, I sure *won't* forget. They'll be good customers for our line, Doctor, we prefer above all other types of settlers your You-roe-pene settler of a deeply rulligious nature. Say, we certainly must have you over for Sunday morning breakfast sometime in Bella, Mrs. Abernathy she makes *waf*fles, sir, she makes *pan*cakes —"

Eszterhazy with a look of apology, having received consent, raised his right index finger and touched a part of Abernathy's skull. "You are of a philoprogenitive nature, I see."

"Well sir (say, it is almost time for my train), well sir, the Mrs. and I are both children of the great and fer-tyle prairies (the steppies, as you call um), and I don't hesitate to say that we have five little ones of whom I am, yes, *very* fond, with promise of a sixth one in nothing flat, that is, in about five weeks three days, give er take a day er two. Say, are those *gongs* them guards are beating? Say, I really must go now. Say, I'll be sure to give your regards to Apollograd. Say, I sure do thank —"

In the brief lull following the departure of the Hyperborean Hawk, Yanosh could be heard laboriously counting his take and then commenting on it, as follows: "They call this alms? Blood of a vixen! May they catch the cholera! Alms, they call this? May an aurochs gore them!" The curses of Yanosh are famous, and known to be as vivid as they are archaic.

At first sight of him, the bull lunged into a wooded declivity and was lost to sight for the rest of the morning. "Lunged" is perhaps too swift a word. It lumbered. About mid-afternoon he was able to obtain

brief and broken glimpses with his binoculars. About mid-morning of the second day, it came slowly up and out of the declivity, and began to graze. And by the third morning it came up to him, very, very shyly, and accepted a lump of salt.

It was a bull, and an old, a very old bull indeed; and it was huge, even though its head with the huge and vast-spread horns seldom raised up even to shoulder level. And it smelled, Lord God how it smelled!

When the old Warden shambled over, a little before noon, it merely acknowledged him with a glance and a flick of the tail. "I take the liberty, High-born Sir and Noble Doctor, of bringing you some lunch, same as yesterday," said the old Warden. "Since you was so good as to accept of it yesterday and the day before. Today being your last day," he said, with respectful and sympathetic firmness. "Three days being the term stated in your honorable pass."

"Yes, yes," said Eszterhazy. "Thank you very much indeed. No need to worry. I'll leave at sundown. I fully appreciate the privilege." The great and ancient beast nuzzled his hand and was rewarded with some thinly-shaved slices of apple.

"That's a old beast, sir," said the Warden. "It's most twenty year old. There was a half-a-dozen when first I come here, but, somehow, they others all died off. Don't know if there is another anywhere, I don't."

"There isn't," said Eszterhazy. He never took his eyes off it.

The old man breathed noisily for a few minutes. Then he nodded. "The only other visitor ever allowed," he said, "was the King of Illyria. Didn't stay long, on finding our Sovereign Lord the King-Emperor wasn't going to let him shoot at it; fancy! Ah — now it's come to me, what it's called. 'Old Methusaleh,' of course, that's only our name for it. The *kind* of aminal it is," he said, "is a naurochs."

Eszterhazy never took his eyes from it. "Yes," he said, after a moment. "I know."

MILORD SIR SMIHT, THE ENGLISH WIZARD

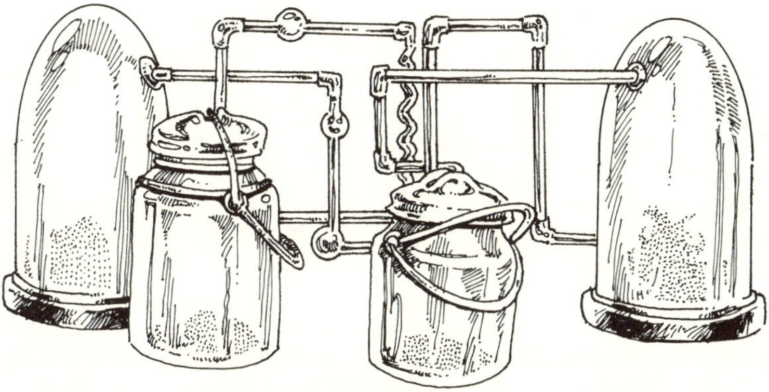

The establishment of Brothers Swartbloi stands, or squats, as it has done for over a century and a half, in the Court of the Golden Hart. The inn, once famous, which gave its name to the court, has long since passed off the scene, but parts of it survive, here a wall, there an arch, and, by sole way of access, a flight of steps (so old had been the inn, that Bella, Imperial Capital of the Triune Monarchy, had slowly lifted the level of its streets around about it). The shops in the Court of the Golden Hart are an odd mixture. First, to the right of the worn three steps, is Florian, who purveys horse-crowns, though the sign does not say so. (All, in fact, that it says is **Florian.**) There is nothing on display in the window, the window being composed of small pieces of bull's-eye glass set in lead, a very old window, with the very old-fashioned idea that the sole duty of a window is to let light in through a wall. What are horse-crowns? Has the reader never seen a funeral? Has he not noticed the crowns of ostrich plumes — black, for an ordinary adult, white for a child or maiden-woman, violet for a nobleman or prelate of the rank of monsignor or above — bobbing sedately on the horses' heads? Those are horse-crowns, and nobody makes them like Florian's.

To the left of the steps is Weitmondl, who makes and sells mother-of-pearl buttons in all sizes. However great must be the natural disappointment of the fisher in the far-off Gulfs of Persia when he opens his oyster and finds no pearl within, he can still take comfort in the thought that the shells, with their nacreous and opalescent interiors, must find their way to the great city of Bella, where Weitmondl will turn them into buttons: all the way from the great buttons which adorn the shirts of coachmen down to the tiny buttons which fasten children's gloves.

Facing the steps in the Court of the Golden Hart is the shop of Brothers Swartbloi, who are purveyors of snuff-tobacco.

There are other shops, to be sure, in the Golden Hart, but they are of a transitory nature, some of them lasting a mere decade. Florian, Weitmondl, and Brothers Swartbloi are the patriarchs of the place; and of them all, Brothers Swartbloi is the oldest.

The shop contains one chair, in which scarcely anyone dares to sit, a wooden counter, and, behind the counter, a wooden shelf. On the shelf are five stout jars, each the size of a small child. One is labeled RAPPEE, one is labeled MINORKA, one is labeled IMPERIAL, one is labeled HABANA, and one is labeled TURKEY.

Should anyone desire a snuff of a different sort, some upstart sort of snuff, a johnny-come-lately in the field of snuff — say, for example, *Peppermint! Wintergreen!* or *Cocoa-Dutch!* — ah, woe upon him, he had better never have been born. Words cannot describe the glacial degree of cold with which he will be informed, "The sweet-shop is across the Court. *Here we sell only snuff-tobacco.*"

One day comes Doctor Eszterhazy to the shop in the Court of the Golden Hart. He is not walking very fast, in fact, as he has been following someone, and as that someone was taking his own good time, it may be said that Engelbert Eszterhazy, Doctor of Medicine, Doctor of Jurisprudence, Doctor of Science, Doctor of Literature, etc., etc., was walking decidedly slowly. The man he was following was tall and heavy and stooped and wore a long black cloak lined with a dull brown silk. Now, long black cloaks were not then the fashion, and Lord knows when they had been. It would be supposed that anyone who wore one did so in order to create a certain impression, to draw upon himself a certain amount of attention. In all of Bella, so far as Eszterhazy knew, there were only two other men who went about in long black cloaks. One was Spectorini, the Director of the Grand Imperial Opera. The other was Von Von Greitschmansthal, the Court Painter. And both had their long black cloaks lined with red.

To wear a long black cloak and then to line it with brown . . . with *brown* . . . this indicated an individualism of the very highest order. And, as he could scarcely in good manners stop this strange man on the street and confront him with his curiosity, therefore he followed him. Down the Street of the Apple-pressers (no apples had been pressed there in decades), left into the Street of the Beautiful Vista (the only vista there nowadays was that of a series of dressmakers' shops), down the Place Maurits Louis (containing six greengrocers, two florists, a French laundry, a café, and a really awful statue of that depressed and, indeed, rather depressing monarch), and thence into the Court of the Golden Hart.

And thence into the establishment of the **Brothers Swartbloi, SNUFF-TOBACCO.**

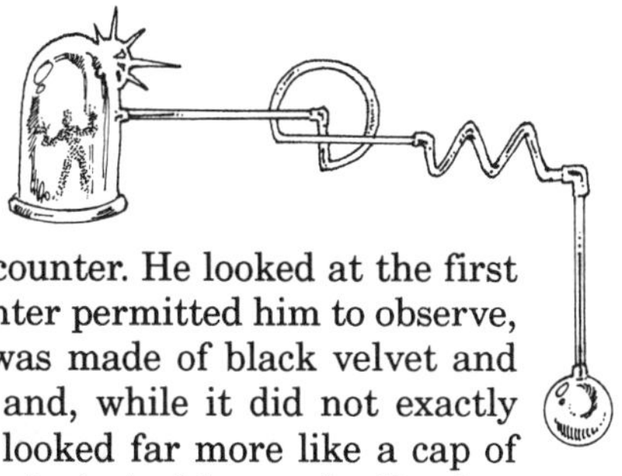

One of the brothers was behind the counter. He looked at the first newcomer, from as far down as the counter permitted him to observe, all the way up to the curious hat (it was made of black velvet and bore a silver medallion of some sort; and, while it did not exactly appear to be a cap of maintenance, it looked far more like a cap of maintenance than it did like anything else). And he — the Brother Swartbloi — permitted himself a bow. The first newcomer drew from his pocket an enormous snuffbox, set it down, and uttered one word.

"Rappee."

The brother took up a brass scoop, reached it into the appropriate jar, removed it, set it on the scales, removed it, and emptied it into the snuffbox.

The quantity was just enough. One hundred years and more in the business of estimating the capacities of snuffboxes gives one a certain degree of skill in the matter.

The tall man placed on the counter a coin of five kopperkas (the snuff of the Brothers Swartbloi does not come cheap) and a card, allowed himself a nod of thanks, and turned and left.

His face was craggy and smooth-shaven and indicative of many things.

When the door had closed behind him the Brother again bowed — this time more warmly. "And in what way may I help the August Sir Doctor?" asked he.

"By supplying him with four ounces of Imperial."

Small purchases at Swartbloi's are wrapped in newspaper, when not decanted into snuffboxes. Larger purchases are wrapped in special pleated-paper parcels, each supplied with a colored label. The label shows a gentleman, in the costume of the reign of Ignats Ferdinando, applying two fingers to his nose; his expression is one of extreme satisfaction. These labels are colored by hand by old Frow Imglotch, whose eyesight is not what it was, and the results are more than merely curious: they are proof of the authenticity of the label and of the product.

"I had the honor of seeing the August Sir Doctor some months since," said the Brother, "when I was at Hieronymos's" — he named Eszterhazy's tobacconist, the source of the famous segars — "obtaining of our usual supply of Habana clippings for our famous Habana snuff-tobacco. I am wondering if the August Sir Doctor is giving up segars in favor of snuff . . . ?"

He was a dry, thin sort of man, with a few dark curls scattered across a bony skull. Automatically, Eszterhazy took a sight reading of the skull, but it did not seem very interesting. "Ah, no," he said. "It is for one of my servants — a saint's-day present. However, were I to take to taking snuff, be assured that it would be the I-have-no-doubt-justly-famous snuff of the Brothers Swartbloi. Who was that gentleman who was just in here?"

The brother, with a bow at the compliment, passed the card over.

MILORD SIR SMIHT
Wizard anglais
Specializing in late hours & By appointment

In a very elegant copperplate hand had been added:

Hotel Grand Dominik.

"One does hear," the brother said, "that the British nobility are of a high and eccentric nature."

"So one does. Often," Eszterhazy agreed. It might not have been high, but it would certainly have been eccentric for a member of the British aristocracy to put up at the Hotel Grand Dominik. He reflected, not for the first time, he knew, and not for the last, he expected, on the persistence of the Continental usage of *Milord,* a rank not known either to Burke or Debrett. As for the name Smith, no one to the south or east of the English Channel has ever been able to spell it right, nor ever will.

He put down his money and prepared to depart; now that he knew where the stranger was to be found, it was no longer necessary to dog him about the streets.

He looked up to find a familiar, if not a welcome, expression on the face of the brother, who proceeded as expected: Might he take the very great liberty of asking the August Sir Doctor a question? He might. Ah, the August Sir Doctor was very kind. But still the question was not forthcoming. Eszterhazy decided to help him along; most such silences, following such questions, followed a certain pattern.

"If the question involves past indiscretions," he said, gently, "I should represent that Doctor LeDuc, who has a daily advertisement in the popular newspapers — It is not that? Well. If the question involves a failure of regularity, I should recommend syrup of figs. What? Not that, either? Then you must come right out with it."

But the man did not come right out with it. Instead, he began a sort of history of his firm and family. The first Brothers Swartbloi were Kummelman and Hugo. They were succeeded by Augsto and Frans. And Frans begat Kummelman II and Ignats.

"I am the present Kummelman Swartbloi," he said, with an air of dignity at which it was impossible to laugh. "My brother Ignats — he is at present in the mill, salting the Turkey — has never married, and it does not seem that he ever will. My wife and I — she is the daughter and only child of my late Uncle Augsto — we have been wed for fifteen years now. But there have been no children. After all, no one lives forever. And how would it be possible, Sir Doctor, for there to be no Brothers Swartbloi in Bella? How could we leave the business over to

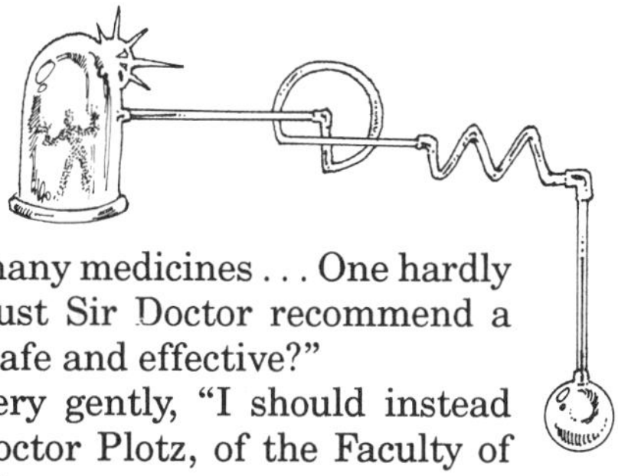

strangers? And . . . and . . . there are so many medicines . . . One hardly knows where to begin. Could the August Sir Doctor recommend a particular medicine, known to be both safe and effective?"

The August Sir Doctor said very, very gently, "I should instead recommend my colleague, Professor Doctor Plotz, of the Faculty of Medicine. You may mention my name."

The Hotel Grand Dominik has come down in the world since the days when it formed a stop on the Grand Tour. Long after having ceased to be fashionable among the gentry, it retained an affection on the part of the more prosperous of the commercial travelers. But it was at that time near the East Railroad Terminal. It is still, in fact, near the East Railroad Terminal, but since the completion of the Great Central Terminal, the shabby old East only serves suburban and industrial rail lines. Consequently, the commercial travelers who stop at the Grand Dominik either are very uninnovative or very old and in any event very unprosperous, or else they are merely unprosperous by reason of such factors as not selling anything worth buying. In fact, for some several years the Grand Dominik has stayed open solely because its famous half-ducat dinner, served between eleven and three, is deservedly popular among the junior partners and upper clerks of the many timber firms who still hold out in the adjacent neighborhood. The rooms are thus ancillary to the hotel's main business. So the rooms are, in a word, cheap.

They are also — no management having been vigorous enough to undertake architectural changes — rather large. Milord Sir Smiht sat in a chair and at a table in the middle of his room, lit by the late afternoon sun. The rear of the room was dim. One caught glimpses of an enormous bed, hugely canopied and reached by a small step-ladder, of an antique clothes press, a washbasin of marble and mahogany, a sofa whose worn upholstery still breathed out a very faint air of bygone fashion — and a very strong odor of present-day Rappee snuff — although it was actually rather unlikely that this last came from the sofa, and vastly likely that it came from the *wizard anglais* himself.

Who said, "I've seen you before."

Eszterhazy said, "You left a card in the Court of the Golden Hart, and so —"

"— and so that was why you followed me halfway across Bella, because you knew I was going to leave my card in a snuff shop. Eh?"

The conversation was in French.

Eszterhazy smiled. "The *milord* is observant. Well. It is certainly true. My interest was aroused by the distinctive, I may say, distinguished appearance —"

The *milord* grunted, took out an enormous watch, glanced at it, shoved it across to where his visitor could see it. "My terms," he said, "are two ducats for an half-hour. It has just now begun. You may ask as many questions as you please. You may do card tricks. You may spend the entire time looking at me. However, if you wish the employment of the odyllic force, then we should commence at once. Unless, of course, you are willing to pay another two ducats for any fraction of one-half hour after the first."

Eszterhazy wondered, of course, that anyone so seemingly businesslike should find himself a wanderer in a country so distant from his own — let along a lodger at the Hotel Grand Dominik. He had learned, however, that the rôle which people see themselves as playing is not always the same rôle in which the world at large perceives them.

"To begin with," he said, taking one of his own specially printed forms from his pocket, "I will ask Sir Smiht to be kind enough to remove his hat for the length of time which it will take me to complete my examination —"

The Englishman gazed at the forms with the greatest astonishment. "Good God!" he exclaimed. "I did once, long ago, at Brighton, to be sure, pay a phrenologist to fumble and peer about my pate — but I never thought that a phrenologist would pay *me* for the privilege!"

"Ah, Brighton," Eszterhazy said. "The Royal Pavilions — what an excursion into the *phantastique!* Do you suppose that the First Gentleman of Europe might have been the first gentleman in Europe to have smoked hasheesh?"

Smiht snorted. Then his face, as he began to take his hat off, underwent a certain change. He completed the gesture, and then he said, "Brighton, eh. I suppose you must speak English, although I don't suppose you *are* English?"

"As a boy I often spent my holidays with the family of my aunt, who lived in England."

"Then let us cease to speak in French. Much better for you to struggle than for me. *Furthermore* — If you have been in England you ought to know damned well that the title *Sir* never precedes the family name without the interposition of the Christian name, although in such instances as that of Sir Moses Montefiore one would employ another terminology — A point which I can*not* get across to the Continental mind, confound it! I consent to *Milord,* because it is, I suppose, traditional, as one might say; and I submit to S-M-I-H-T because I realize how difficult the T-H is to speakers of any other language except Greek and I suppose Icelandic . . . speakers? spellers . . . ?"

Here he paused to draw breath and consider his next phrase, and Eszterhazy took the opportunity to approach him from behind and gently place his fingers on the man's head. He was slightly surprised

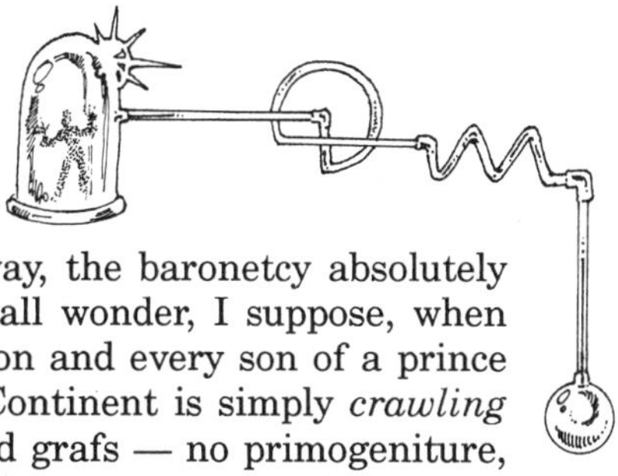

when the other went on to say, "Anyway, the baronetcy absolutely baffles the Continent of Europe — small wonder, I suppose, when every son of a baron here is also a baron and every son of a prince here is also a prince. No wonder the Continent is simply *crawling* with princes and barons and counts and grafs — no primogeniture, *ah* well . . . Now suppose you just call 'em out to me and I'll write 'em down, can't read this Gothic or whatever it is, so you needn't fear I'll get me back up if you decide I'm deficient in honesty, or whatever. Just say, oh, second down, third over — eh?"

"First down, first over," said Eszterhazy.

Without moving his head, the Englishman reached out his long arm and made a mark in the first column of the first row. "I was christened George William Marmaduke Pemberton," he said. "Called me *George,* was what me people called me. Marmaduke Pemberton was a great-uncle by marriage, long since predeceased by the great-aunt of the blood. Made *dog*-biscuit, or some such thing, grew *rich* at it, or perhaps they were digestive biscuits, doesn't matter. As he'd never gotten any children on Aunt Maude and never remarried after *she* died, couldn't get it *up,* I suppose; rest of me people they thought, well, let's name this 'un after him and he'll leave him all his *pelf,* you see, under the condition of his assuming the name of Smith-*Pem*berton. Baronetcy was to go to me oldest brother. *Well,* old Marmaduke left me *beans,* is what he left me, rest of it went to some fund to restore *churches,* sniveling *par*sons had been at him, don't you see.

"Second down, fourth over, *very* well. Tenny rate, say what you will, always tipped me a guinea on me birthday, so out of gratitude and because I couldn't *stand* the name George, have always used the style Pemberton Smith. Can I get *any* Continental printer to spell Pemberton correctly? Ha! Gave up trying. *Now,* as to the odyllic force or forces, in a way it began with Bulwer-Lytton as he called himself before he got *his* title — ever read any of his stuff ? *Aw*ful stuff, don't know how they can read it, but he had more than a mere inkling of the odyllic, you know. What's that? Fourth down, first over, dot and carry one. And *in* a way, of course, one can say, 't all goes back to Mesmer. Well, tut-tut, hmm, of course, Mesmer *had* it. Although poor chap didn't know what he *had.* And then Oscar took a Maori bullet at a place called Pa Rewi Nang Nang, or *some* such thing, *damn*able is what I call it to die at a place called Pa Rewi Nang Nang, or *some* such thing — sixth down and four, no five over, *aiwah, tuan besar.* Next thing one knew, Reginald had dived into the Hooghli, *likely story,* that, and never came up — 'spect a croc got him, poor chap, better mouthful than a hundred scrawny *Hin*doos, ah well."

George William Marmaduke Pemberton Smith fell silent a moment and helped himself to two nostrils of Rappee snuff.

"And what's the consequence? Here is my sole remaining brother, Augustus, heir to the baronetcy. And here's *me,* poor fellow, name splashed all over the penny press, because *why?* Because of a mere accident, a Thing of Nature, here am *I,* as I might be *here,* demonstrating the odyllic forces before a subcommittee of the Royal Society, one of whom, Pigafetti Jones, *awful* ass, having kindly volunteered to act as subject, dis-a-*pears!* — leaving nothing but his *clothes,* down to the last brace-button, belly-band, and ball-and-socket truss — Well! *After all. Is* this a scientific experiment or is this *not?* Are there such things as the hazards of the chase or are there *not* such things as the hazards of the chase? *First* off, laugh, then they say, very well, bring him *back,* then they dare to call me a *char*-la-tan: ME! And then —"

Dimly, very dimly, Eszterhazy remembered having read, long ago (and it had not been fresh news, even then), of the singular disappearance of Mr. Pigafetti Jones, Astronomer-Royal for Wales. But what he was hearing now provided more details than he had ever even guessed at. It also provided, if not a complete explanation, for at least an assumption as to why "Milord Sir Smiht" was and had long been wandering the continent of Europe (and perhaps farther) a remittance man, as the British called it. That is, in return for his keeping far away and thus bringing at least no fresh local scandals to his family's embarrassment, the family would continue to remit him a certain sum of money at fixed intervals.

It was still not clear, though, if he were already a baronet or was merely assumed to be because his father was one. Or had been.

And as for the odyllic force . . .

"Forces," said the tall old Englishman, calmly. "I am quite confident that there is more than one."

And for the moment he said no more. Had he read Eszterhazy's mind, then? Or was it merely a fortuitous comment of his own, in his own disjointed manner?

"Or, for that matter," the latter went on, in a generous tone of voice, "take Zosimus the Alchymist, if you like. *Come in!"* The hall-porter came in, bowed with ancient respectfulness (the hall-porter was rather ancient, himself), laid down a salver with a card on it, and withdrew. "Ah-hah. Business is picking up. Fifteen down, three over . . ."

Eszterhazy had not stayed beyond the half-hour, but made a semi-appointment for a later date. The card of the further business awaiting Milord Sir Smiht was facing directly toward both of them, and he could hardly have avoided reading it.

And it read:

BROTHERS SWARTBLOI
NUMBER 3, COURT OF THE GOLDEN HART
SNUFF-TOBACCO

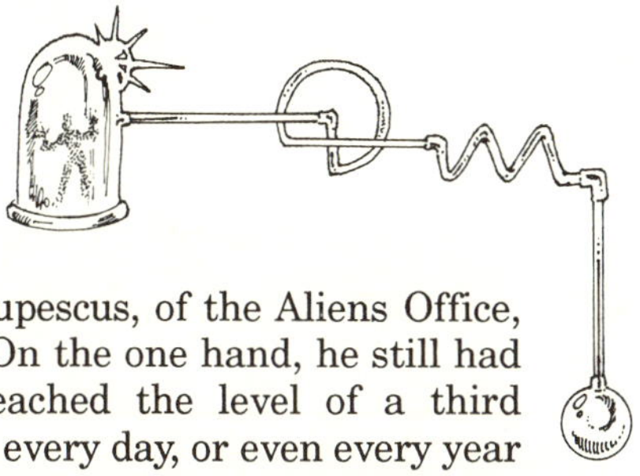

Third Assistant Supervisory Officer Lupescus, of the Aliens Office, was feeling rather mixed, emotionally. On the one hand, he still had the happiness of having (recently) reached the level of a third assistant supervisory official; it was not every day, or even every year that a member of the Romanou-speaking minority attained such high rank in the Imperial Capital. On the other hand, a certain amount of field work was now required of him, and he had never done field work before. This present task, for instance, this call upon the Second Councillor at the British Legation, was merely routine. "Merely routine, my dear Lupescus," his superior in the office, Second ASO Von Glouki had said. Easily enough *said,* but, routine or not routine, one had to have something to *show* for this visit. And it did not look as though one were going to get it.

"Smith, Smith," the Second Councillor was saying, testily. "I tell you that I must have more information. *What* Smith?"

All that Lupescus could do was to repeat, "Milord Sir Smiht."

" *'Milord, Milord,'* there *is* no such rank or title. Sir, why, that is merely as one would say *Herra,* or *Monsieur.* And as for Smith — by the way, you've got it spelled wrongly there, you know, it is S-M-I-T-H — well, you can't expect me to know anything about anyone just named *Smith,* why, that's like asking me about someone named Jones, in Cardiff, or Macdonald, in Glasgow. . . . Mmm, no, you wouldn't know about those. . . . Ah, well, it's, oh, it's like asking me about someone named Novotny in Prague! D'you see?"

Lupescus brightened just a trifle. This was something. Very dutifully and carefully, he wrote in his notebook, *Subject Milord Smiht said to be associated with Novotny in Prague . . .*

With his best official bow, he withdrew. Withdrawn, he allowed himself a sigh. Now he would have to go and check out Novotny with the people at the Austro-Hungarian Legation. He hoped that this would be more productive than this other enquiry had been. One would have thought that people named Smiht grew on trees in England.

Eszterhazy's growing association with the white-haired Englishman took, if not a leap, than a sort of lurch, forward one evening about a month after his first visit. He had sent up his card with the hall-porter, who had returned with word that he was to go up directly. He found Smith with a woman in black, a nondescript woman of the type who hold up churches all around the world.

"Ah, come in, my dear sir. Look here. This good woman doesn't speak either French or German, and my command of Gothic is not . . . well, ask her what she wants, do, please."

Frow Widow Apterhots wished to be placed in communication with her late husband. "That is to say," she said, anxious that there be no confusion nor mistake, "that is to say, he is dead, you know. His name is Emyil."

Smiht shook his head tolerantly at this. "Death does not exist," he said, "nor does life exist, save as states of flux to one side or other of the sidereal line, or astral plane, as some call it. From this point of view it may seem that anyone who is not alive must be dead, but that is not so. The absent one, the one absent from here, may now be fluctuating in the area called 'death,' or he or she may be proceeding in a calm vibration along the level of the sidereal line or so-called astral plane. We mourn because the 'dead' are not 'alive.' But in the world which we call 'death' the so-called 'dead' may be mourning a departure into what we call 'life.' "

Frow Widow Apterhots sighed. "Emyil was always so healthy, so *strong,*" she said. "I still can't understand it. He always did say that there wasn't no Hell, just Heaven and Purgatory, and I used to say, 'Oh, Emyil, people will think that you're a Freemason or something.' Well, our priest, Father Ugerow, he just won't listen when I talk like this, he says, 'If you won't say your prayers, at least perform some work of corporal mercy, and take your mind off such things.' But what I say —" She leaned forward, her simple sallow face very serious and confiding, "I say that all I want to know is: Is he happy there? That's all."

Pemberton Smith said that he could guarantee nothing, but in any event he would have to have at least one object permeated with the odyllic force of the so-called deceased. The Frow Widow nodded and delved into her reticule. "That's what I was told, so I come prepared. I always made him wear this, let them say what they like, he always did. But I wouldn't let them bury him with it because I wanted it for a keepsake. Here you are, Professor." She held out a small silver crucifix.

Smith took the article with the utmost calm and walked over and set it down upon a heavy piece of furniture in the dimness of the back of the room. There were quite a number of things already on the table. Smith beckoned, and the others came toward him, Frow Widow Apterhots because she was sure that she was meant to, and Eszterhazy because he was sure he wanted to. "These," said Smith, "are the equipment for the odyllic forces. Pray take a seat, my good woman." He struck a match and lit a small gas jet; it was not provided with a mantle, and it either lacked a regulatory tap or something was wrong with the one it did have — or perhaps Smith merely liked to see the gas flame shooting up to its fullest extent; at least two feet long, the flame was, wavering wildly and a reddish gold in color.

Certainly, he was not trying to conceal anything.

But *these* were interesting, certainly, whatever else they were, and Eszterhazy took advantage of the English wizard's at the moment administering to himself two strong doses of Rappee — one in each

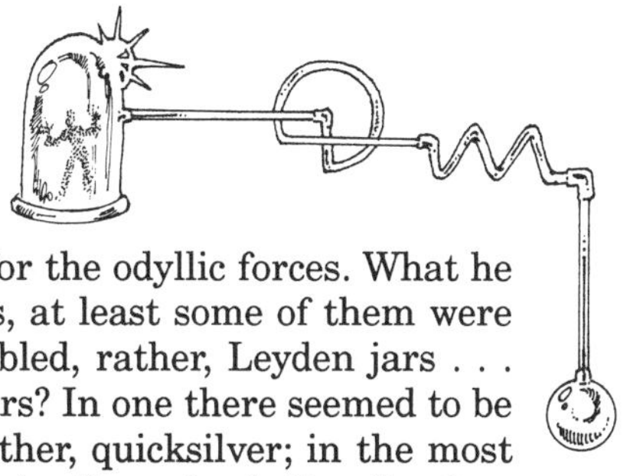

nostril — to scrutinize the equipment for the odyllic forces. What he saw was a series of bell jars . . . that is, at least some of them were bell jars . . . some of the others resembled, rather, Leyden jars . . . and what *was* all that, under the bell jars? In one there seemed to be a vast quantity of metal filings; in another, quicksilver; in the most of them, organic matter, vegetive in origin. Every jar, bell or Leyden, appeared to be connected to every other jar by a system of glass tubing: and all the tubes seemed fitted up to a sort of master-tube, which coiled around and down and finally upward, culminating in what appeared to be an enormous gramophone horn.

"Pray, touch *nothing,*" warned Milord Sir Smiht. "The equipment is *exceedingly* fragile." He took up a small, light table, the surface of which consisted of some open latticework material — Eszterhazy was not sure what — and, moving it easily, set it up over the horn. On it he placed the crucifix. "Now, my dear sir, if you will be kind enough to ask this good lady, first, to take *these* in her hands . . . ? And, to concentrate, if she will, entirely upon the memory of her husband, now on another plane of existence." The Widow Apterhots, sitting down, took hold of the *these* — in this case, a pair of metal grips of the sort which are connected, often, to magnetic batteries, but in this case were not — they seemed connected in some intricate way with the glass tubings. She closed her eyes. *"And,"* the wizard continued, "please to cooperate in sending on my request. Which, after all, is *her* request, translated into my own methodology."

He began an intricate series of turnings of taps, of twistings of connections at joints and at junctions, of connectings; at length he was finished. "Emyil Apterhots. Emyil Apterhots. Emyil Apterhots. If you are happy, wherever you are, kindly signify by moving the crucifix which you wore when on this plane of existence. *Now!*"

The entire massive piece of furniture upon which the equipment for the odyllic force (or forces) was placed began to more forward.

"No, *no,* you Gothic oaf!" shouted the *milord,* his face crimson with fury and concern. *"Not* the sideboard! *The crucifix!* Just the *cru-ci-fix* —" He set himself against the sideboard and pressed it back. In vain. In vain. In vain. In a moment, Eszterhazy, concerned lest the glass tubings should snap, reached forward to adjust them, so that the intricate workings should not be shattered and sundered — the wizard, panting and straining against the laboratory furniture as the heavy mass continued to slide forward . . . forward . . . forward . . .

— and suddenly slid rapidly backward, Milord Sir Smiht stumbling and clutching at empty air, Eszterhazy darting forward, and the two of them executing a sort of slow, insane *schottische,* arm in arm, before coming to a slow halt —

And then, oh so grumpy, wiping his brow with a red bandana handkerchief, of the sort in which navvies wrap their pork pies, hear Milord Sir Smiht say, "I must regard this session as questionable in its results. And I *must* say that I am not *used* to such contumacy from the habitants of the sidereal line!"

Frow Widow Apterhots, however, clearly did not regard the results as in any way questionable. Her sallow, silly face now quite blissful, she stepped forward and retrieved the crucifix. "Emyil," she said, "was always so *strong . . . !*"

And on that note she departed.

Herr Manfred Mauswarmer at the Austro-Hungarian Legation was quite interested. " 'Novotny in Prague,' eh? Hmmm, *that* seems to ring a bell." Third ASO Lupescus sat up straighter. A faint tingle of excitement went through his scalp. "Yes, yes," said Herr Mauswarmer, "we have of a certainty heard the name. One of those Czech names," he said, almost indulgently. "One never knows what *they* may be up to." Very carefully he made a neat little note and looked up brightly. "We shall of course first have to communicate with Vienna —"

"Oh, of course!"

"And they will, of course, communicate with Prague."

Herr Manfred Mauswarmer's large, pale, bloodshot blue eyes blinked once or twice. "A Czech name," he noted. "An English name. Uses the code cypher *Wizard.* Communicates *in French."* He briefly applied one thick forefinger to the side of his nose. He winked. Lupescus winked back. They understood each other. The hare had had a headstart. But the hounds had caught the scent.

One of the bell jars was empty — had, in fact, always been empty, although Eszterhazy had merely noted this without considering as to why it might be so. He did not ask about it as he listened, now, to the Englishman's talk. Milord Sir Smiht, his cap on his head, his cloak sometimes giving a dramatic **flap** as he turned in his pacings of the large old room, said, "The contents of the vessels in the large part represent the vegetable and mineral kingdoms — I don't know if you have noticed that."

"I have."

"The *an*imal kingdom, now . . . well, each man and woman is a microcosm, representing the macrocosm, the *un*iverse, in miniature. That is to say, we contain in our own bodies enough of the animal and mineral to emanate at all times, though we are not aware of it, a certain amount of odyllic force —"

"Or forces."

"Or forces. Point well *made*. However. Now, although the average human body does include, usually, some amounts of the vegetable kingdom — so much potato, cabbage, sprouts, let us say — undergoing the process of digestive action," **flap** went his cloak, "as *well* as

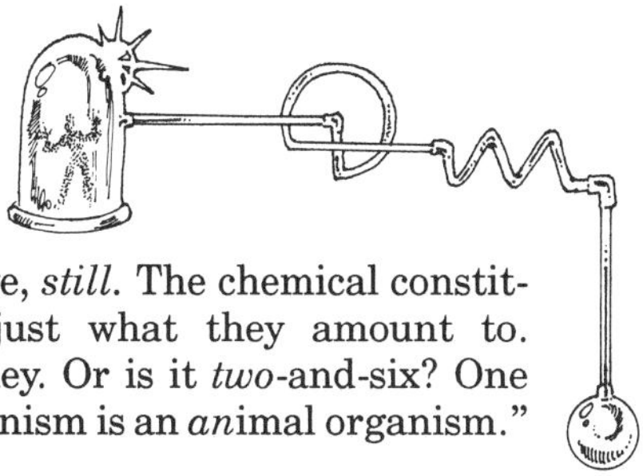

the ever-present bacteria, also vegetative, *still.* The chemical constituencies in our body, now, I forget just what they amount to. Four-and-six, more or less, in real money. Or is it *two*-and-six? One forgets. *Still.* Primarily, the human organism is an *an*imal organism."
Flap.

Eszterhazy, nodding, made a steeple of his hands. "And therefore (Pemberton Smith will correct me if I am wrong), when the human subject takes hold of that pair of metallic grips, the three kingdoms, animal, vegetable, and mineral, come together in a sort of unity —"

"A sort of Triune Monarchy *in parvo,* as it were, yes, co-*rect!* I see that I was not wrong in assuming that yours was a mind capable of grasping these matters, [**flap**] and then it is all a matter of adjustment: One turns *up* the vegetative emanations, one turns *in* the mineral emanations. . . . And then, then, my dear sir, one hopes for the best. For one has not as yet been able to adjust the individual human beings. They are what they are. One can turn a *tap,* one can open a valve or close a valve, plug in a connecting tube or *un*plug a connecting tube. But one has to take a human body *just as one finds it.* . . . Pity, in a way . . . Hollo, hollo!"

Something was happening in the empty bell jar: mists and fumes, pale blue lights, red sparks and white sparks.

Milord Sir Smiht, dashing hither and thither and regulating his devices, stopped, suddenly, looked imploringly at Eszterhazy, gestured, and said, "*Would* you, my dear fellow? *Awf* 'ly grateful —"

Eszterhazy sat in the chair, took the metal grips in his hands, and tried to emulate those curious animals, the mules, which, for all that they are void of hope of posterity, can still manage to look in two directions at once.

Direction Number One: Pemberton Smith, as he coupled and uncoupled, attached and dis-attached, turned, tightened, loosened, adjusting the ebb and flow of the odyllic forces. Animal, vegetable, *and* mineral.

Direction Number Two: The once-empty bell jar, wherein now swarmed . . . wherein now swarmed *what?* A hive of microscopic bees, perhaps.

A faint tingle passed through the palms of Eszterhazy's hands and up his hands and arms. The tingle grew stronger. It was not really at all like feeling an electrical current, though. A perspiration broke forth upon his forehead. He felt very slightly giddy, and the *wizard anglais* almost at once perceived this. "Too strong for you, is it? *Sorry* about *that!*" He made adjustments. The giddiness was at once reduced, almost at once passed away.

And the something in the bell jar slowly took form and shape.

It was a simulacrum, perhaps. Or perhaps the word was homunculus. The bell jar was the size of a child. And the man within it was the size of a rather small child. Otherwise it was entirely mature.

And "it" was really not the correct pronoun, for the homunculus (or whatever it was) was certainly a man, however small: a man wearing a frock coat and everything which went with frock coats, and a full beard. He even had an order of some sort, a ribbon which crossed his bosom, and a medal or medallion. Eszterhazy *thought,* but could not be sure, that it rather resembled the silver medallion which Milord Sir Smiht wore in his hat.

"Pemberton Smith, who *is* that?"

"Who, that? Or. Oh, that's *Gomes* —" He pronounced it to rhyme with *roams.* "He's the Wizard of Brazil. You've heard of *Gomes,* to be sure." And he then proceeded to move his arms, hands, and fingers with extreme rapidity, pausing only to say, "We communicate through the international sign language, you see. He has no English and I have no Portagee. Poor old Gomes, things have been ever so slack for him since poor old Dom Peedro got the sack. Ah well. Inevitable, I suppose. Emperors and the Americas just don't seem to go together. Purely an Old World phenomenon, don't you know." And once again his fingers and hands and arms began their curious, rapid, and impressive movement. "Yes, yes," he muttered to himself. "I see, I see. No. Really. You don't say. Ah, too bad, too bad!"

He turned to Eszterhazy. Within the jar, the tiny digits and limbs of the Wizard of Brazil had fallen, as it were, silent. The homunculus shrugged, sadly. "What do you make of all *that?*" asked the Wizard of England (across the waters).

"What? Is it not clear? The ants are eating his coffee trees, and he wishes you to send him some paris green, as the local supply has been exhausted."

"My dear chap, *I* can't send him any paris green!"

"Assure him that I shall take care of it myself. Tomorrow."

"I say, that *is* ever so good of you! Yes, yes, ah, pray excuse me now whilst I relay the good news."

In far-off Petropolis, the summer capital of Brazil, the Wizard of that mighty nation, much reduced in size (wizard, not nation) by transatlantic transmission, crossed his arms upon his bosom and bowed his gratitude in the general direction of the distant though friendly nation of Scythia-Pannonia-Transbalkania. All men of science, after all, constitute one great international confraternity.

The saint's-day gift of snuff was so well received by Frow Widow Orgats, Eszterhazy's cook (who had taken his advice to stock up on coffee), that he thought he would lay in a further supply as a sweetener against the possibility of one of those occasions — infrequent, but none the less to be feared — when the Frow Cook suffered severe attacks of the vapors and either burned the soup or declared (with shrieks and shouts audible on the second floor) her intense inability to face anything in the shape of a stove at all. So,

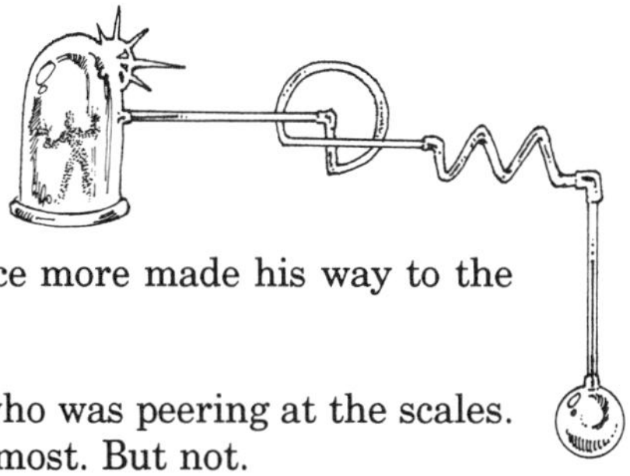

on the next convenient occasion, he once more made his way to the Court of the Golden Hart.

"Four ounces of the Imperial."

He peered at the Swartbloi brother, who was peering at the scales. "You are not Kummelman," he said. Almost. But not.

"No sir, I am Ignats," said the brother. "Kummelman is at the moment —"

"In the mill, salting the Turkey. I know."

Ignats Swartbloi looked at him with some surprise and some reproof. "Oh, no, sir. Kummelman always grinds the Rappee, and I always salt the Turkey. On the other tasks we either work together or take turns. But *never* in regard to the grinding of the Rappee or the salting of the Turkey. I had been about to say, sir, that Kummelman is at his home, by reason of his wife's indisposition, she being presently in a very delicate condition."

And he handed over the neatly wrapped packet of pleated paper bearing the well-known illustrated label — this one, old Frow Imglotch had tinted so as to give the snuff-taker a gray nose and a green periwig, neither of which in any way diminished the man's joy at having his left nostril packed solid with Brothers Swartbloi Snuff-Tobacco (though whether Rappee, Imperial, Minorka, Habana, or Turkey, has never been made plain, and perhaps never will be).

"Indeed, indeed. Pray accept my heartiest felicitations."

The brother gazed at him and gave a slight, polite bow, no more. "That is very kind of you, sir. Felicitations are perhaps premature. Suppose the child will be a girl?"

"Hm," said Eszterhazy. "Hm, hm. Well, there is that possibility, isn't there? Thank you, and good afternoon."

He could not but suppose that this same possibility must have also occurred to Brother Kummelman. And, in that case, he wondered, would a second visit have been paid to the large, antiquated room in the Grand Dominik where the *Milord anglais* still prolonged his stay?

Herr von Paarfus pursed his lips. He shook his head. Gave a very faint sigh. Then he got up and went into the office of his superior, the Graf zu Kluk. "Yes, what?" said the Graf zu Kluk, whose delightful manners always made it such a pleasure to work with him. More than once had Herr von Paarfus thought of throwing it all up and migrating to America, where his cousin owned a shoe store in Omaha. None of this, of course, passed his lips. He handed the paper to his superior.

"From Mauswarmer, in Bella, Excellency," he said.

The Graf fitted his monocle more closely into his eye and grunted. "Mauswarmer, in Bella," he said, looking up, "has uncovered an

Anglo-Franco-Czech conspiracy, aimed against the integrity of the Austro-Hungarian Empire."

"Indeed, Your Excellency!" said von Paarfus, trying to sound shocked.

"Oh yes! There is no doubt of it," declared Graf zu Kluk, tapping the report with a highly polished fingernail. "The liaison agent — of course, in Prague, where else? — is a man named Novotny. The password is 'wizard.' What do you think of *that?*"

"I think, Your Excellency, that Novotny is a very common name in Prague."

Graf zu Kluk gave no evidence of having heard. "I shall take this up with His Highness, at once," he said. Even Graf zu Kluk had a superior officer. But then, long years of training in the Civil Service of Austria-Hungary cautioned him. "That is," he said, "as soon as we have had word on this from our people in London, Paris, and Prague. Until then, mind, not a word to anyone!"

"Your Excellency is of course correct."

"Of *course.* Of *course.* See to this. *At once!*"

Von Paarfus went out, thinking of Omaha. Not until the door had closed behind him did he sigh once again.

Oberzeeleutnant-commander Adler had had a long and distinguished career in the naval service of a neighboring power. "But then," he said, stiffly, "I — how do you put it, in English? That I copied my blotting-book? I of course do not desire to go into details. At any rate, I thought to myself, even if I shall not be actually at sea, at any rate, at least I shall be able to put my finishing touches on the revision of my monograph on the deep-sea fishes. But the High Command was even more loath with me than I had thought; ah, how they did punished me, did I deserved such punishedments? And so, here I am, Naval Attaché in Bella! In *Bel-la!* A river port! Capital of a nation, exceeding honorable, to be sure." He bobbed a hasty bow to Eszterhazy, who languidly returned it. "But one which has no deep-sea coast at all! Woe!" For a moment he said nothing, only breathed deeply. Then, "What interest could anyone possibly find in a freshwater fish, I do enquire you?" he entreated. But no one had an answer.

"Mmm," said Milord Sir Smiht. "Yes. Yes. Know what it is to be an exile, myself. Still. I stay strictly away from politics, you know. Not my pidjin. Whigs, Tories, nothing to me. Plague on both their houses. Sea-fish, rich in phosphorus. Brain food."

But the commander had not made himself clear. What he would wish to propose of the Milord Sir Smiht was not political. It was scientific. Could not Sir Smiht, by means of the idyllic — what? ah! thousand pardons — the odyllic force, of which one had heard much — could not Sir Smiht produce an ensampling of, say, the waters of

the Mindanao Trench, or of some other deep-sea area — here — here in Bella — so that the commander might continue his studies?

The *milord* threw up his hands. "Impossible!" he cried. "Im-*pos*-sib-le! Think of the pressures! One would need a vessel of immensely strong steel. With windows of immensely thick glass. *Just to begin with!* Cost: much. Possibilities of success: dubious."

But the Naval Attaché begged that these trifles might not stand in the way. The cost, the cost was to be regarded as merely a first step, and one already taken; he hinted at private means.

"As for the rest." Eszterhazy stepped forward, a degree of interest showing in his large eyes. "At least, as for the steel, there are the plates for the *Ignats Louis* . . ."

The *Ignats Louis*! With what enthusiasm the nation (particularly the patriotic press) had encouraged plans for the construction of the Triune Monarchy's very first dreadnought, a vessel which (it was implied) would strike justly deserved terror into the hearts of the enemies — actual or potential — of Scythia-Pannonia-Transbalkania! A New Day, it was declared, was about to dawn for the Royal and Imperial Navy of the fourth-largest empire in Europe; a Navy which had until then consisted of three revenue cutters, two gunboats, one lighthouse tender, and the monitor *Furioso* (formerly the *Monadnock,* purchased *very* cheaply from the United States after the conclusion of the American Civil War). Particular attention had been drawn to the exquisitely forged and incredibly strong steel-plate, made in Sweden at great expense.

Alas, the day of the Triune Monarchy as one of the naval powers of the world had been exceedingly short-lived and more or less terminated upon the discovery that the *Ignats Louis* would draw four feet more than the deepest reaches of the River Ister at high water in the floods. The cheers of the patriotic press were overnight reduced to silence, subsidies for the dreadnought vanished from the next budget, the skeleton of the vessel slowly rusted on the ways, the exquisitely forged and incredibly strong steel-plating remained in the storage sheds of the contractor; and the two gunboats and the monitor alone remained to strike terror into the hearts of, if not Russia and Austria-Hungary, then at any rate Graustark and Ruritania.

The downcast face of the foreign naval commander slowly began to brighten. The countenance of the English wizard likewise relaxed. And, as though by one common if semi-silent consent, they drew up to the table and began to make their plans.

"Qu'est-ce qu'il y a, cette affaire d'un vizard anglais à Scythie-Pannonie-Transbalkanie?" they asked in Paris.

"C'est, naturellement, une espèce de blague," they answered, in Paris.

"Envoyez-le à Londres," they concluded, in Paris.

"What can the chaps *mean?*" they asked each other, in London. "'*English vizar Milor Sri Smhti'?* Makes no sense, you know."

"Mmm, well, *does,* in a way, y'know," they said in London. "Of course, that should be *vizier.* And *sri,* of course, is an Injian religious title. Dunno what to make of Smhti, though. Hindi? Gujerathi? Look here. Sir Augustus is our Injian expert. Send it up to him," they said, in London.

"Very well, then . . . but, look here. What can this be about *Tcheque novothni?* They simply can't *spell* in Paris, you know. Check up on the Novothni, what are the Novothni?"

"Blessed if I know. Some hill tribe or other. Not our pidjin. Best send it all up to Sir Augustus," they said, in London.

But in Prague they sat down to their files, which, commencing with *Novotny, Abelard,* ran for pages and pages and pages down to *Novotny, Zygmund.* They had lots and lots of time in Prague, and, anyway, it was soothing work, and much more to their tastes than the absolutely baffling case of a young man who thought that he had turned into a giant cockroach.

They had directed the old hall-porter at the Grand Dominik to inform all would-be visitors that Milord Sir Smiht was not receiving people at present. But Frow Puprikosch was not one to be deterred by hall-porters; indeed, it is doubtful if she understood what he was saying, and, before he had finished saying it, she had swept on . . . and on, and into the large old-fashioned chamber where the three were at work.

"Not now," said Smiht, scarcely looking up from his adjustments of the tubing system to the steel-plated diving bell. "I can't see you now."

"But you must see me now," declared Frow Puprikosch, in a rich contralto voice. "My case admits of no delays, for how can one live without love?" Frow Puprikosch was a large, black-haired woman in whom the bloom of youth had mellowed. "That was the tragedy of my life, that my marriage to Puprikosch lacked love — but what did I know then? — mere child that I was." She pressed one hand to her bosom, as to push back the tremendous sigh which arose therefrom, and with the other she employed — as an aid to emphasis and gesticulation — an umbrella of more use to the ancient lace industry of the Triune Monarchy than of any possible guard against rain.

"And what would Herra Puprikosch say, if he knew what you were up to, eh? Much better go home, my dear lady," she was advised.

"He is dead, I have divorced him, the marriage was annulled, he is much better off in Argentina," she declared, looking all around with great interest.

"Argentina?"

"*Some*where in Africa!" she said, and, with a wave of her umbrella,

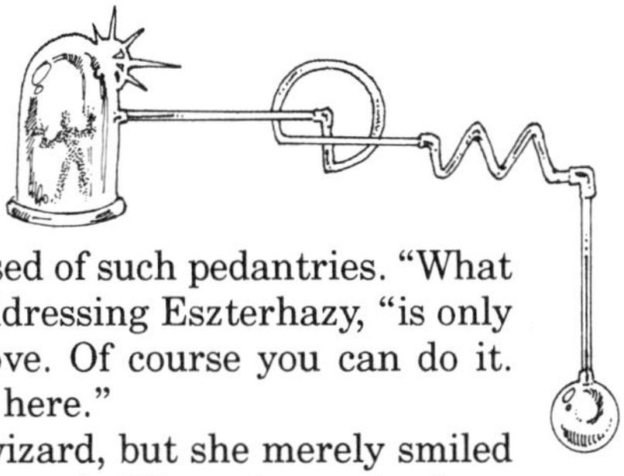

or perhaps it was really a parasol, disposed of such pedantries. "What I wish of you, dear wizard," she said, addressing Eszterhazy, "is only this: to make known to me my true love. Of course you can do it. Where shall I sit down here? I shall sit here."

He assured her that he was not the wizard, but she merely smiled an arch and anxious smile, and began to peel off her gloves. As these were very long and old-fashioned with very many buttons (of the best-quality mother-of-pearl, and probably from the establishment of Weitmondl in the Court of the Golden Hart), the act took her no little time. And it was during this time that it was agreed by the men present, between them, with shrugs and sighs and nods, that they had better accomplish at least the attempt to do what the lady desired, if they expected to be able to get on with their work at all that day.

"If the dear lady will be kind enough to grasp these grips," said Sir Smiht, in a resigned manner, "and concentrate upon the matter which is engaging her mind, ah, yes, that's a very good grasp." He began to make the necessary adjustments.

"Love, love, my true love, my true affinity, where is he?" demanded Frow Puprikosch of the Universal Aether. "Yoi!" she exclaimed, a moment later, in her native Avar, her eyebrows going up until they met the fringe, so pleasantly arranged, of glossy black hair. "Already I feel it begins. *Yoi!*"

" 'Yoiks' would be more like it," Smiht muttered. He glanced at a dial to the end of the sideboard. "Good heavens!" he exclaimed. "What an extraordinary amount of the odyllic forces that woman conjugates! Never *seen* anything like it!"

"Love," declared Frow Puprikosch, "love is all that matters; money is of no matter, I have money; position is of no matter, I expectorate upon the false sham of position. I am a woman of such a nature as to crave, demand, and require only *love!* And I know, I know, I *know,* that *some*where is the true true affinity of my soul — where *are* you?" she caroled, casting her large and lovely eyes all around. *"Oo*-hoo?"

The hand of the dial, which had been performing truly amazing swings and movements, now leaped all the way full circle, and, with a most melodious twang, fell off the face of the dial and onto the ancient rug.

At that moment sounds, much less melodious, but far more emphatic, began to emanate from the interior of the diving bell. And before Eszterhazy, who had started to stoop toward the fallen dial hand, could reach the hatch-cover, the hatch-cover sprang open and out flew — there is really not a better verb — out flew the figure of a man of vigorous early middle age and without a stitch or thread to serve, as the French so delicately put it, *pour cacher sa nudité . . .*

"Yoiii!!!" shrieked Frow Puprikosch, releasing her grip upon the metal holders and covering her face with her bumbershoot.

"Good heavens, a woman!" exclaimed the gentleman who had just emerged from the diving bell. "Here, dash it, Pemberton Smith, *give* me that!" So saying, he whipped off the cloak which formed the habitual outer garment of the *wizard anglais,* and wrapped it around himself, somewhat in the manner of a Roman senator who has just risen to denounce a conspiracy. The proprieties thus taken care of, the newcomer, in some perplexity, it would seem, next asked, "Where on earth have you gotten us to, Pemberton Smith? — and why on Earth are you rigged up like such a guy? Hair whitened, and I don't know what else. Eh?"

Pemberton Smith, somewhat annoyed, said, "I have undergone no process of rigging, it is merely the natural attrition of the passage of thirty years, and tell me, then, how did you pass your time on the sidereal level — or, if you prefer, astral plane?"

"But I don't prefer," the man said briskly. "I know nothing about it. I'd come up from the Observatory — *damn*ed silly notion putting an observatory in Wales, skies obscured three hundred nights a year with soppy Celtic mists, all the pubs closed on Sundays — and, happening to drop in on the Royal Society, I allowed myself to act as subject for your experiment. One moment I was *there,* the next moment I was *there* —" He gestured toward the diving bell. Then something evidently struck his mind. "'Thirty years,' you say? Good heavens!" An expression of the utmost glee came across his face. "Then Flora must be dead by now, skinny old bitch, and, if she isn't, so much the worse for her, who is this lovely lady *here?*"

The lady herself, displacing her parasol and coming toward him in full-blown majesty, said, in heavily accented but still melodious English, "Is here the Madame Puprikosch, but you may to calling me Yózhinka. My affinity! My own true love! Produced for me by the genius of the *wizard anglais!* ***Yoi!***" And she embraced him with both arms, a process which seemed by no means distasteful to the gentleman himself.

"If you don't mind, Pigafetti Jones," the wizard said, somewhat stiffly, "I will thank you for the return of my cloak. We will next discuss the utmost inconveniency which your disappearance from the chambers of the Royal Society has caused me throughout three decades."

"All in good time, Pemberton Smith," said the former Astronomer-Royal of Wales, running his hands up and down the ample back of Frow Puprikosch — or, as she preferred to be called by him, Yózhinka. "All in good time . . . I say, Yózhinka, don't you find that corset *most* constrictive? *I* should. In fact, I *do.* Do let us go somewhere where we can take it off, and afterwards I shall explain to you the supernal glories of the evening skies — beginning, of course, with Venus."

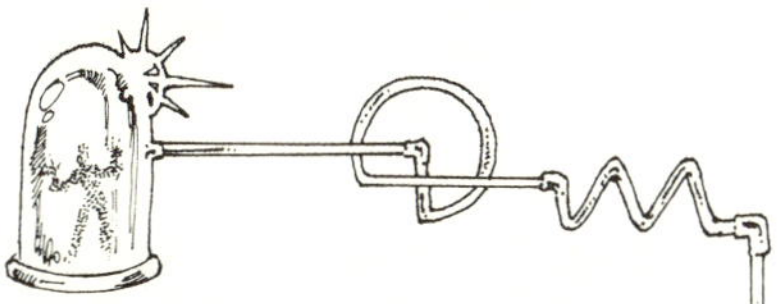

To which the lady, as they made their way toward the door together, replied merely (but expressively), *"Yoi . . . !"*

Standing in the doorway was a very tall, very thin, very, very dignified elderly gentleman in cutaway, striped trousers, silk hat — a silk hat which he raised, although somewhat stiffly, as the semi-former Frow Puprikosch went past him. He then turned, and regarding the *wizard anglais* with a marked measure of reproof, said, *"Well,* George."

"Good Heavens. *Augustus.* Is it really you?"

"It is really me, George. *Well,* George. I suppose that you have received my letter."

"I have received no letter."

"I sent it you, care of Cook's, Poona."

"Haven't been in Poona for years. Good gad. That must be why my damned remittances kept arriving so late. I must have forgotten to give them a change of address."

Sir Augustus Smith frowned slightly and regarded his brother with some perplexity. "You haven't been in Poona for years? Then what was all this nonsense of your calling yourself Vizier Sri Smith and trying to rouse the hill tribes with the rallying cry of 'No votny'? Votnies were abolished, along with the tax on grout, the year after the Mutiny, surely you must know that."

"I haven't been in Injia for eleven years, I tell you. Not since the Residency cut up so sticky that time over the affair of the rope trick (all done by the odyllic forces, I tell you). As for all the rest of it, haven't the faintest idea. Call myself Vizier Sri Smith indeed, *what do you take me for?"*

Sir Augustus bowed his head and gently bit his lips. Then he looked up. "Well, well," he said, at last. "This is probably another hugger-mugger on the part of the Junior Clarks, not the first time, you know, won't be the last," he sighed. "I tell you what it is, you know, George. *They let* **anyone** *into Eton these days."*

"Good heavens!"

"Fact. Well, Hm. Mph." He looked around the room with an abstracted air. "Ah, here it is, you see, now that I have seen with my own eyes that Pigafetti Jones is alive and playing all sorts of fun and games as I daresay he has *been* doing all these years, ahum, see no reason why you shouldn't come home, you know, if you like."

"Augustus! Do you mean it?"

"Certainly."

The younger Smith reached into the clothes press and removed therefrom a tightly packed traveling bag of ancient vintage. "I am quite ready, then, Augustus," he said.

There was a clatter of feet on the stairs in the corridors beyond, the feeble voice of the hall-porter raised in vain, and into the room there burst Kummelman Swartbloi, who proceeded first to fall at the younger Smith's feet and next to kiss them. "My wife!" he cried. "My wife has just had twin boys! Bella is guaranteed another generation of Brothers Swartbloi (Snuff-tobacco)! Thank you, thank you, thank you!" And he turned and galloped away, murmuring that he would have stayed longer but that it was essential for him to be at the mill in a quarter of an hour in order to grind the Rappee.

"Do twins come up often in the chap's family?" asked Sir Augustus.

"I'm afraid that nothing much comes up often in his family at all, any more. I merely advised him to change his butcher and I may have happened to suggest the well-known firm of Schlockhocker, in the Ox Market. Old Schlockhocker has six sons, all twins, of whom the youngest, Pishto and Knishto, act as delivery boys on alternate days. Wonderful thing, change of diet . . . that, and, of course, the odyllic forces."

Sir Augustus paused in the act of raising his hat to his head. "I should hope, George," he said, "that you may not have been the means of introducing any spurious offspring into this other tradesman's family."

His brother said that he didn't know about that. Fellow and his wife were first cousins, after all. Sir Augustus nodded, again lifted his hat, and this time gestured to the multitudinous items upon the heavy old sideboard. "Do you not desire to remove your philosophical equipment?" he asked.

Smith the younger considered. He looked at his own hat, the velvet cap of curious cut with the curious silvern medallion on it. He took it in both hands and approached Doctor Eszterhazy. Doctor Eszterhazy bowed. George William Marmaduke Pemberton Smith placed the cap upon the head of Engelbert Eszterhazy (Doctor of Medicine, Doctor of Jurisprudence, Doctor of Science, Doctor of Literature, etc., etc.). "You are now and henceforth," the Englishman said, "the Wizard of the Triune Monarchy, and may regard yourself as seized of the entire equipage of the odyllic force, or, rather, forces. Sorry I can't stay, but there you are."

The brothers left the room arm in arm, Sir Augustus inquiring, "Who was that odd-looking chap, George?" and his junior replying, "Phrenologist fellow. Can't recollect his name. Does one still get good mutton at Simpson's?"

"One gets *very* good mutton, still, at Simpson's."

"Haven't had good mutton since . . ." Voices and footsteps alike died away.

Doctor Eszterhazy looked at the equipage of the odyllic forces, and he slowly rubbed his hands together and smiled.

THE CASE OF THE MOTHER-IN-LAW OF PEARL

It was a bright afternoon after much rain and Doctor Eszterhazy decided to take the steam runabout on the fashionable three turns along the New Model Road in the great Private Park. He had put on his duster and was reaching for his cap when the day porter came in.

"Yes, Lemkotch."

"Sir Doctor, Housekeeper asks if you would be so graciously kind as to leave this here off at Weitmondl, in the Golden Hart, to be repaired," and he set down a box upon the desk, bowed, and withdrew.

If the housekeeper's master had been a boss butcher or an advocate of the Court of First Jurisdiction, he probably would have said, "What, damn it, does the woman think I am, a messenger boy?" but as he was Engelbert Eszterhazy, Doctor of Medicine, Doctor of Jurisprudence, Doctor of Science, Doctor of Philosophy, and Doctor of Literature, he merely said, "Yes, of course." He took up the box — it was a small one, inlaid, with part of the inlay missing and part about to be, evidently a sewing-box — and he put it in his pocket.

His manservant, Herrekk, sat beside him, ringing the large bronze bell; Schwebel, the retired railroadman, sat behind, carefully stoking the fire. They were trying out a new fuel which Eszterhazy had been working on for some time now — the late Count Tunk and Tunk, for many years Consul for the Triune Monarchy at Boston in the American province of Nev-England, had been enamoured of a tree called "hickory" and had planted thousands on his estates in Transbalkania and the Gothic Midlands, but the present Count found that he could make no commercial use of the wood, which was not known in East Central Europe. Eszterhazy, an old school-mate of

Count Béo Tunk and Tunk, desired to see if bricquets made of the hickory sawdust might not be an utile fuel.

"Nothing to lose," Count Béo had said, with a shrug. "All that my stewards hear, they say, when they offer the wood for sale, is a variation on the phrase, 'Ai' — or, 'Yoi' — 'us never hear of no *khickory* tree,' and that, of course, is that. But if we call it, say —" Here he paused, at a loss as to what to call it, say.

"Tunkfuel," said Eszterhazy. *"Tunkfuel, Patént Amerikánsko."*

The Count had thought that *Tunkfuel, American Invention,* was an excellent idea, and so did his friend, but the former had nothing in mind but an economic use for a crop planted out of sentiment, and the latter hoped to advise something which might tend to retrench the reprehensible increase — slight but evident — in the use of hydrocarbon vehicles. He was aware that even many steam-propelled road vehicles now used either kerosene or naphtha, or both, to say nothing of the cars now powered entirely by petroleum derivatives, but he steadily preferred fuels less offensive to eye and nostril. They might be preferable to coal; other than that, he had nothing to say for them.

As though to prove his point for him, he observed, some streets ahead, the enormous vehicle of Glutlovicx the sweets magnate. The magnate himself had no social ambitions, but as his wife could not be persuaded to be happy in a brand-new castle set in the semi-exact center of forty thousand acres of sugar beets (the *exact* exact center was occupied by the refinery), Glutlovicx, with a shrug, had agreed to move to Bella. There he had, among other things apparently needful for the happiness of Frow G., a motor vehicle. Neither one had any other standard of judging the value of new things save by cost and size: their vehicle was an hydrocarbon talley-ho, and, as they rode along, enabled them to look into the windows on the second floors of buildings. Glutlovicx always looked to see if his candies, his sugars, or his preserves were on the tables; she only looked at her reflection in the mirrors or the windows.

And always, driving along, Eszterhazy at the tiller, Herrekk tirelessly tolled the bell. This not only alerted nervous pedestrians to get out of the way, it enabled drivers of nervous horses to make necessary adjustments of the reins, even — if deemed needful — to jump down and take the horse by the head. Sometimes bystanders had thought it funny to see a horse rear upon hind legs and whinny, but the horse had not thought it funny; sometimes horses had gone mad with fear and dashed up on the sidewalks and spilled drivers or passengers and trampled people, and sometimes they had galloped through the new-fashioned plates of window-glass, slashing themselves so that they had to be destroyed.

But such incidents were now becoming less frequent.

After the traditional three turns around the "Motor Road,"

Eszterhazy drew off to the side. "How is the new fuel behaving, Stoker?" he asked. (It would perhaps have been fashionable to address him in the French equivalent, but Schwebel, for one thing, would not have known what *chauffeur* meant; and, for another, he was very proud of having been what he had been on the Royal and Imperial Ironroads S.-P.-T.)

"Sir, a hot fire, a clean smoke, a clean ash," he answered.

"Good, good. Very well, let us change places. The Court of the Golden Hart."

The boiler required no fresh fuel for a while now, and, even if it had, Eszterhazy might have stoked it without soiling white gloves, the new fuel was so clean.

The interior of Weitmondl's consisted chiefly of drawers, shelf after shelf of them, up to the ceiling; moving ladders ran on wheels along rails, and someone seemed always restocking the drawers or else taking stock out; each drawer had in its front a little window, as it were, containing samples of the size and style of button contained within.

One of the clerks from aloft called something into the back, and the proprietor himself appeared. Seligman Weitmondl was himself a little blanched almond of a man who managed to be serious and cheerful at the same time. He took the sewing box from Eszterhazy with small crows and clucks of pleasurable recognition. "Oh yes, oh yes! Done in my father's day, my father's day," he affirmed. "That was the style then, lozenge-work, lozenge-work," he said, tapping the inlay with his finger. "*Cheap* stuff," he said, a moment later.

Eszterhazy looked at it more closely. The nacre seemed indeed faint, the opalescence rather dim. "It does not appear to be the highest quality of mother-of-pearl," he conceded. "Although I might have supposed it merely faded —"

Weitmondl chuckled. "Faded here, faded there," he said; "it wasn't bright and it didn't fade. It isn't even mother-of-pearl, be blessed, my dear sir: it's what we in the trade call mother-in-law of pearl. It doesn't come from the South Sea or the North Sea or the Gulfs of Persia or the Gulfs of Anywhere-else. It comes from a mere river mussel, somewhere in the Vlox-Minor. And if you had come to us last week, I'd have had to say, 'No, sir, we can no longer repair the article in the same material for the reason that we haven't got it in stock and haven't had it in stock for long years, long years.' " And he nodded seriously. Then, seemingly out of nowhere, perhaps from each nostril, he produced two shells. "*This* one, you see at once, dear sir, is mother-of-pearl, the real and genuine article. Look at it — beautiful. Though not from Persia, to be sure, from Australia, which is a large island, my dear sir, to the south of Persia — *this* one, you see at once the difference, my dear sir, day and night, day and night, is the river mussel, such as we used to get in as a staple, ever so much cheaper, of course."

And, sometimes stimulated by questions and sometimes volunteering the data, Seligman Weitmondl went on to explain that, for one thing, the price of standard-quality mother-of-pearl had come down — owing to the opening of new grounds in such places as Australia and the South Seas — and the purchasing power of the public had gone up, owing to manufacturing, railroads, abolition of the octroi, the defeat of the Serbians and the Graustarkers, benevolent laws, and the immense benign influences of the Throne — consequently the demand for the cheaper article had dropped. "Nobody would buy it any more; it took a long time for us to sell out what we had on hand; soldiers wouldn't even buy it in snuffboxes for their sweethearts, you see. And *then,* then when, what with one thing and another, we could have sold some items in the cheaper material, why, we couldn't get it any more."

Eszterhazy, his mild curiosity desiring to have the matter wrapped up, asked *why* they couldn't get it any more. And the button-maker, with a shrug and a smile, said *They* hadn't brought it in. *They?* The dealers. That is, the dealers in such odds and ends — he implied that the odds were very odd, coming as they did from the ends of the Empire. Until the previous week. When one of the *They* had brought a lot of it in.

"So we should have this repaired and ready for the dear sir in very short order. Say, two weeks?"

Eszterhazy said two weeks. Weitmondl smiled, bowed, and withdrew. Eszterhazy was withdrawing when a voice from above said, "You see, sir, the lurlies stopped bringing the shells."

Down from one of the movable ladders, where, presumably, he had heard the whole conversation, climbed one of the stock clerks — a man somewhat on in years, with a sallow little face framed in a curl of sallow little whiskers.

"The lurlies stopped — ?"

The elder clerk now reached the floor and gave a short stiff bow. "As in that song, sir, about She combs her golden hair with a golden comb, sitting on the rocks by the river, and he feels so sad."

"The lorelei, ah yes, go on." Eszterhazy marveled how the man managed to get every element of the beginning of Heine's beautiful poem into one sentence and into impeccably incorrect order. "But the poem — song — says nothing, surely, of shell — ?"

"*It* says nothing. *I* says something. What the song calls, as the sir says, a lorelei, we-folks back home calls it a lurley, which is its correct name. And the old people always say, in the old days, how a lurley will bring ye gold or gems or such things, if you make right with her. But, by and by, don't know what happen, the old people they say 'the lurley stop bringing it,' sir, you see."

"And now has started again?"

But the old clerk's only response was to call, as he moved the ladder

farther along the wall of drawers, "Number Twenty-two twenty, Coachman Gloves, two dozen short!"

More than once Eszterhazy had noticed that, once an idea or a notion had entered his mind, not long afterwards something bearing upon it would enter his ken in some material way. Whether, by only thinking about it, he had released it — so to speak — into the Universal Aether, where it would grow and send forth intangible but none-the-less effective "tentacles," or whether, contrariwise, someone else had implanted it in the Aether by thinking about it, and so forth . . . but he had never completed the concept. Nor could he tell why, now, he felt his eyes more than once straying to the telephone instrument in one corner of the room, or why he seemed to feel a sort of straining in his ears. Again and again he bent to his work, again and again he looked up from it: looked through the Swedish crystal-glass at the huge dry-cell batteries within the mahogany telephone case. And it was with a sense of great relief that he did hear, at last, the clear, brisk tinkling of the instrument's bell.

"Eszterhazy is here," he announced into the mouth-piece.

A voice asked him if he would graciously attend another moment "to facilitate a far-distant call." In another moment, more or less, a second voice, somewhat weaker in volume, identified itself as the Avar-Ister exchange, and made the same request. After a somewhat longer wait, a somewhat even more distant voice proclaimed itself as "Second Princely Fortress of the Pious and Loyal Velotchshtchi" — in other words, Vlox-Minore. It had not quite finished when another voice, entirely different in tone and quality, broke in to say, "Engli, this is Roldri Mud," and all — or, at any rate, much — became clearer.

Official maps of the Triune Monarchy bore none of those curious sad cross-hatchings, likelier to be found on maps of South America, and which mean — the key at the bottom informs us — *Disputed Territory*. Nevertheless. While some matters were certainly undisputed — the Romanou had never penetrated to the Gothic Highlands, for instance; the Slovatchko made no claims to Central Pannonia — *nevertheless,* there was not a single nation-state component of the Empire around whose borders things did not tend to become somewhere liqueous and in some measure subject to confusion, ethnicism, infra-nationalism, linguistic conflicts, and appeals to the tribunal of history; woe betide whoever must bring his case to *that* much-crowded court!

Long ago the Goths and the Avars had fought over the Sable River — but the famous *Kompromis* of the Year '60 had declared the area to be a part of Vlox-Minore, and so it still stood. To this district the Avars had in their customary fashion affixed one of their ponderous and polysyllabic names, meaning (in this case) "Estuary of the dark river where grow many reeds of the quality used for weirs and baskets"; the Goths, in their own fashion, had termed it "Mud." To be sure, the Vloxfolk doubtless had another name for it, but enough.

And all this area was the property of the Princes Von Vlox, who, with their sixty-four *proven* quarterings of nobility, their boresome plethora of available names and titles (*fitz-Guelf zu Borbon-Stuart,* as exemplum), disdained not to describe themselves, in the person of Prince Roldrando, descendant of Charlemagne and the Lusignan kings of Cyprus, as Lords of Mud. The fens had in part been reticulated and drained a century back and constituted some of the richest farmland in the Monarchy. Probably sixty-four banks bulged with the quit-rents of the Lords of Mud, but one seldom saw these Lords in Bella, even, let alone Paris or Monte Carlo: and legend pictured them as having returned altogether to the primitive, lolling about on rush-strewn floors, guzzling bread-beer, clad in wolf-skins.

"Ah, Roldri," Eszterhazy said, aloud, "the lurlies have begun to bring up pearl-shell again after all this time — eh?"

And prince Roldrando, his voice like an organ note, said, "Ah, . . . *then you already know. . . .*"

Prince Roldrando was not wearing wolfskins — that had been a misunderstanding — he was wearing shaggy Scottish tweeds of such antique design that they must have been cut for a father or an uncle, and they had not been recently cleaned or pressed. "Damnedest story you ever heard, Engli," he said, as easily as, a moment later, he pointed out the stationmaster's office, "if you want to wash up." The door of the place of public convenience, brightly painted with the internationally recognized double-zero and W.C., he ignored as though it were not four feet away, or perhaps inscribed in Hittite. "Or, we can stop by the roadside," he offered as an alternative suggestion.

"I won't ask if you've had a good journey," he went on, "one never has a good journey by the cars. If the window is not open, one swelters; if the window is open, one gets cinders in one's eyes." Baggage had been picked up by two attendants, one of whom wore a footman's coat and the other a footman's hat; the trousers of both, as well as those of Prince Roldrando, gave evidence that a deer or boar had recently been killed, drawn, and flayed.

Very recently.

"Lunch in the hamper, whenever you like," said the host, with a gesture. And, with another gesture, "Care to take the coachman's seat?"

"Where is the coachman?" asked the guest.

"Coachman? There's no coachman," the Prince said, mildly surprised. "Do you think you're in Bella?"

Sure enough. One of the attendants vaulted onto the near horse —

it *had* been saddled! — gave a guttural growl — both horses sprang forward — the servant playing the rôle of tiger uttered a bloodcurdling squawl (no bronze bells hereabouts!) — the Town of the Princely Fortress (etc.) flashed by. Eszterhazy murmured to himself a few words from his favorite guide-and-phrase-book, " *'Help! My postillion has been struck by lightning!'* "

Prince Roldrando turned a face twisted with astonishment and concern, his golden-brown eyes wide. "Too bad!" he exclaimed. "Oh, why *didn't* he wear a *charm?*" Then, in an instant, the eyes vanished, the face split into a half-hundred wrinkles, the mouth exploded into laughter. "Ha — ha! Oh, you had me there! 'Postillion struck by lightning,' he says! Oh, oh, sweet little Saint Peter in Chains!" And he rolled about in such a manner as to give Eszterhazy the most extreme concern for his safety. Prince Roldrando, however, did not fall off the coach, and neither did he forget the phrase: from time to time during his friend's visit — and, indeed, often at the oddest times — he would repeat it, the words usually varying in their order, until, at last, it passed into the common speech of the district as a sort of by-word, as it might be, "May the black pox pass us over and may our postillions ne'er be struck by lightnings. . . ."

The farmhouses of the Vlox countryside were painted in an absolutely Mediterranean profusion of colors — pink, yellow, brown with white trimmings, green with white trimmings, blue, lavender with brown trimmings, and many, many other shades, tints, permutations, combinations — as though to make up in splendor what they lacked in straightness of line. Presently the houses began to thin out, and the real and still-untamed Mud spread out on both sides and all about.

The road itself was lined with trees, but through the trees one could see nothing but an endless profusion of marsh: water, reeds, hummocks, water, blue sky, white clouds, canals, here and there a man in a flat-bottomed boat . . . and, everywhere, everywhere, sometimes floating on the surface of a pool, sometimes diving and bobbing for food, sometimes wheeling and screaming, sometimes conducting a parliamentary inquiry in a clump of trees, the birds . . . more birds than Eszterhazy had ever seen in one place before, certainly more birds than he could identify . . . although, like a familiar motif recurrently introduced into some half-wild sort of symphony, there were often swans. Sometimes they sailed majestically upon the waters, and sometimes they squatted like pigs in the mudbanks.

Prince Von Vlox, who had fallen silent, suddenly sat up. Eszterhazy followed his host's gaze.

Through a fortuitous gap in the trees, Castle Vlox could be seen, perhaps less than a kilometer away, and it seemed to float upon the surface of the waters as though designed for a pageant out of some insubstantial substance. It had, seemingly, everything a castle traditionally should have: walls, a gate, a drawbridge, a moat, towers.

"How often one thinks," Eszterhazy said, musingly, "that a castle must be upon a high hill, a peak. That they often were had nothing to do with any desire for scenery or prospects, vistas. It is clear that the marshes afford every bit as much protection to this place as any mountain top. It has a moat, to be sure, but the Mud itself is one vast moat. . . ."

Prince Roldrando gave a rich, deep chuckle. "Ferdy tried to besiege it once," he said — probably the only living person who would even *think* of referring to that long-dead Holy Roman Emperor by a nickname — "a nice ball-up he made of it, too, trying to get his engines and his artillery through the Mud! So, after sitting and a-thinking about it a while, he sends word he'll settle for a titular submission — say, the gaffer's staff, and a silver bowl. Ha ha! Ah, the gaffer" — here he referred to none other than Sigismundo, Prince Von Vlox, 1520–1583 — "the gaffer sends him a copper pisspot and a gumph-stick, ho *ho* . . ." In the sixteenth century and at this remove from the centers of soft living, a copper urinal was after all indeed a luxury of sorts, but a gumph-stick was a mere common appurtenance in every privy which hung out from a castle wall. What "Ferdy" had thought about it all need not trouble conjecture, but he had certainly never come back.

Eszterhazy gazed at the castle, slowly growing larger, appearing and vanishing as they came nearer and nearer. "It gives one a definite feeling of reassurance," he said, "to know that tales like that are told of this old place. It is certainly neither Castle Dracula nor Castle Frankenstein —"

Roldrando nodded. "As for Vlad Drakulya, he was a Rumanian, need more be said? And the Franckensteins," he said, indulgently, "one hears well of them, they are, after all, *barons,* is what *they* are. After all, *any*body can be made a baron, but nobody can be made a prince; one is either born a prince or one is not, and the personal caprice of a monarch or a minister has nothing to do with it." Eszterhazy was reminded of the great Duke of Wellington and his comment that what he liked about the Order of the Bath was that "there was no damned nonsense about 'merit' to it!" Such attitudes transcended snobbery. If one were, on one side, descended from the Lusignan kings (one of whom quite casually married a mermaid), and on the other side descended — somewhat further back — from Charlemagne, the great-grandson of Big-footed Bertha, *la reine pédauque* — then one either automatically appropriated the stationmaster's private *pissoir* or one merely "stopped by the side of the road" — either one indifferently acceptable.

Prince Roldri took up a battered post-horn and blew a blast or two on it. Almost, one expected the drawbridge to fall, and men-at-arms

to appear on the battlements. Actually, it was a signal to light the samovar. The coach rattled over the bridge, and, making one half-turn around the courtyard, came to a stop. Several men half-rose, half-bowed, and returned to their duties. Duties which, Eszterhazy noticed, consisted respectively, of cleaning the latest-model shotgun, and of sharpening the head of a boar spear.

He really did not know whether it was the latest model boar spear.

They had the boar that night, with wild apple sauce, and with it a wine of the district, one which did not keep and so was never sent for sale; now between sweet and sour, and slightly effervescent, it might have tempted angels.

Prince Roldri, gazing at the church-ransom of beeswax candles all a-glimmer, improved the vision by regarding it through his glass of wine. "Try it, Engli," he urged. "Do the same. See if you can see the monkey in the glass."

Eszterhazy complied. The flames winked, winked, wept, wept. Odd bits of things seemed to come into vision, then fall out of focus again. "The monkey?" he inquired, pleased, pleasantly tired, enjoying his dinner.

" 'Es. We had an old family doctor once. Said he could make monkeys. Long ago. The gaffer didn't want him to make monkeys. Wanted him to make *gold,* I daresay. *Aw*ful quarrel. Don't know why the gaffer didn't drop him in the sink. Eh? The sink? Don't you know what the — Ah, the . . . what do they call it . . . dunjeon. *We* call it the sink. He didn't, though. Chap rode away, swearing the sky sulfur-colored. Ever since then we always say, 'Look through the wine into the flame and you'll see the monkey old Theo made. . . .' "

It was news indeed to Eszterhazy that Doctor Philippus Aureolus Theophrastus Bombastus von Hohenheim, called Paracelsus, had ever come this way. Sooner or later, he thought, must have a look in the library and the archives. Had "old Theo" actually made himself a homunculus here? One hardly knew. Still, the legend — however transmuted — the legend had persisted.

"You have more trouble brewing now, you say, Roldri, than many monkeys might cause . . . ?" It seemed the right moment to broach the cask.

It was.

"Yes . . . damn it. . . ." The prince sat up, set down his glass, and shook his head. "If 'tisn't settled, there'll be no buckwheat. If there's no buckwheat, then they'll start eating the wheat and the potatoes. If they eat the wheat and the potatoes, then they'll not be having enough to make wudkey. And if they'll not be having enough to made wudkey, they'll have to be *buy*ing wudkey. — And the Vloxi, may the Almighty God of Heaven and Earth defend us from evil, when the Vloxi start *buy*ing wudkey. . . ."

Eszterhazy had made only the first, faintest of beginnings at an understanding. It would not do to push, it never *did* do to push. *Any*where. So he said one sole word. *"Lurley?"*

"So they *say* —" His friend pushed his hands through his hair and sighed. "So *they* say. . . ."

After a moment. "And you say . . . ?"

The prince shrugged. "Perhaps it's not a lurley. Perhaps it's — perhaps she is . . . an undine. . . ."

Candles weeping golden-brown tears. Guest saying nothing. Waiting, waiting. Sipping the rich red wine. Thinking of old thoughts. Of old beliefs . . . could one indeed call them "old" when they were so evidently still being believed? After a long, long wait, and a long, long sigh, Prince Roldrando said, "Maybe she is an undine. Maybe one that old Theo made. Let go loose, out of anger, you know, with our gaffer. And so, maybe . . . maybe she's been waiting . . . waiting . . . ever since . . ."

Sweet scent of beeswax, mingled with sweet scent of wild apples.

What century were they living in now, here, on the wild border marches of the Vlox, where the Avars and the Goths alike had left their bones to moulder and their angry spearheads to rust and their ghosts, their still-vexed and angry ghosts, to wander, muttering and unshriven . . . ?

"Because, you know, Engli, the old story of old King Baldwin's bride? You know what the common folk say about old King Baldwin's bride?" Eszterhazy was fairly sure the story had not been originally told about old King Baldwin, but it was of the same blood; he summed the long and uncanny story up in a few words: How the noble lord had wedded a beautiful and a strange woman, how her only condition was that she must never be seen bathing. How for some several years the marriage had been happy enough, until . . . one ill-fated day . . . the husband coming home unexpectedly (ah, those eternal stories of husbands and their fatally unexpected returns!) and hearing sounds of song and of the splashing of water, had dared to break his own word . . . had espied his wife in her bath . . . espied, over the side of the tub, her glistening, glittering mermaid's tail. . . .

"Yes. . . . Yes. . . . Such is the common story. But it's not the true story, you see. We know it. We of the family. She wasn't a mere mermaid, you see. She was an undine. He espied her, she sprang out and into the moat, and thence to the open flood. But they often used to hear her, wailing for her children. 'Es. An undine. She wedded him — for what? Gold? Hadn't she, hadn't they all of them gold enough, and silver and jewels as well, there at the bottom, where the rich ships sank? Ah, no; you know what it is that undines want: a soul, a soul is what undines want! She wedded him to gain a soul by reason of the Christian wedding, you know that, for the undine has no soul to start with. . . .

"And so maybe this is what she's come for. Come back for. Is waiting

for . . ." The prince's voice droned on in the growing darkness, the last lights of the sunken day sinking into the horizon behind it, the candles sinking wetly into their sockets.

Eszterhazy felt his head snap up. Therefore, it must have dropped upon his bosom. A day's travel by train and by coach. The full belly, stuffed with roast boar. The monotone narration. Narration stopped. Had Roldri noticed this breach of manners? What was the last thing he'd said? Ah . . .

"Waiting for her soul, eh?" the guest said.

"No. No." The host nodded emphatically. "Not her soul. She hasn't *got* a soul. Don't you see?

"She's waiting for a soul, all right. *But it's* ***my*** *soul she is waiting for . . . !*"

Ephraim the trader was clad in velveteens, worn, clean velveteens. Tied at the knee in clumps of cords. High cross-gaiters. In Bella, such costume had not been seen offstage in half a century. Here it was a suit of working clothes. And the man and his trade were as archaic in terms of imperial commerce, as his costume. But he was a man for all of that, and a civil man, too. It did not occur to him, as it often seemed to occur to others in this country scene — and in others, for that matter — that the stranger from the big city was asking him about his own affairs for an ill purpose certain to involve the country fellow's loss — or, what was just as bad, the stranger's gain!

"Well, sir," the trader said, "I have four sisters. And 'tis our custom to dower them, not with much money, for our trade here doesn't bring in much money, we don't hunger or go in rags, but we don't find ourselves with much in the way of cash. My old dad, he give the girls furniture and featherbedding and of course they already has their own linens in their chests. And my old dad, he gives the bridegroom a gold watch and a chain, as is the custom with us. Well, sir, as I say, I've got four sisters, long may they live, and after the third, Estella is her name, after she was wedded off, 'twas like the house had suffered a fire. Oh, how she wept, 'Father, Father, don't forget me!' and afterwards my old dad he says, in his wry way, 'Forget her, how can I forget her, she's tooken the last stick of furniture and the last feathertick off the pads!' And yet there was the fourth sister, Marrianna, well *she* gets betrothed, and there *was* a problem, how our old dad he did weep. 'A shame to my name,' he says. 'I've got not a groushek nor a bed-stool to dower her with, not to mention the gold watch and chain for the bridegroom.' Had I mentioned the gold watch and chain for the bridegroom, sir?"

Eszterhazy listened patiently. A prosecutor or an examining magistrate might — at least in fiction — allow himself the luxury of asking crisp, incisive questions — short, to the point. But an enquirer such as himself, a stranger, among a strange-enough people, and involved in as strange a matter as this one — the best thing by far was simply to start with a general subject and then to listen. And listen and listen.

And listen . . .

"Well, sir, we are not like how we hear the children in the cities are, we respect our old elders, our gaffers, as we say, and it pains us to see them weep. So I says, 'Dad, never fear, I'll help thee.' And I gets in the wagon and off I goes, not half-knowing as to where, to tell the truth; and then it bethinks me, 'No one has gone down along the little river of late years, so off with thee, Ephraim, and see what God may send thee.' And among other things He sends me, sir, is a whacking great pile of mussel shell, and so that's the story, sir."

Someone, somehow, must have brought word to old Hakim the River Tartar that a High-born Guest was coming, for not only was rude hospitality already prepared on the table — a much scratched old pewter plate piled with nuts and mulberries, a gourd of milk, a pile of flatbread on a clean cloth — but the old man had put on his embroidered caftan: for usually the River Tartars — those few who remained — usually they wore the cast-downs of the local Rag Market. The River Tartars had forgotten most of their own tongue without ever having gathered much mastery of the common speech. The old man muttered a long greeting which had once, perhaps, been current in the courts of Karakorum. Then he pulled a boy from behind him and shoved the lad forward. There was no robe for the lad, perhaps had been none such for a century. But the boy's rags were at any rate clean.

"Where me get the shell? Me get she from the lurley-girley." Broken, the boy's speech, but straightforward enough. "Me see a great pile of 't by Lurley Bend, and me leave a bowl of milk one time and me take some shell, wrap up in me sark." He gestured and he grinned; stripping off his shirt had evidently posed no problem, likely he went most ways and most days in his breech-clout, no more. "And a nex' day me go, take some more shell, leave some more milk, and a nex' day me go," and so on and so on. " 'Es, me pay milk, take shell. 'Nen come pedlar-khan and give me crockery and we trade crockery for we don't be needin' it, us eats outen table-holes. 'Es, us trades it for salt and matches and lamp oil, an' —"

Eszterhazy barely followed. To Joachim-the-Groom (thus, to distinguish him from Joachim-the-Smith, Joachim-the-Shrewd, Joachim-Cuckold, and a few score more) he said, "Ask how he knows it was a lurley."

The old man answered, in some surprise at the question, "Why it be find to Lurley Bend, who else, me khan, would leave it shell there?"

But the boy had a word of his own. "Me do see she, all a-bare!"

The gaffer clouted his shaven pate, "For shame! Giaour!"

Perhaps the clout, perhaps the guffaw which Groom-Joachim had not felt able to constrain — well, for whatever reason, the boy had no more to say. They sipped the sour milk, pecked at the mulberries, put some bread and some nuts into their pockets, and left something beneath the cloth — at least Eszterhazy did — something which was not salt or matches or lamp oil. And, with bows here and there, they departed.

Riding away, on the heavy horses whose feet were so accustomed to the mud, Eszterhazy asked, "Have these mussels any other use, Joachim?"

The groom scratched his beard. "Aye, Sir Doctor. Can be eaten."

"Ah. And how do you eat them?"

A shocked look was his first answer. *"I?* Ah, Sir Doctor, *I* don't eat them!"

"Oh. So. Who does, then?"

Again, a sidelong look. Another scratch at the beard. "The lurley, then," said Joachim-the-Groom.

The map of the area, as it hung in the office of the bailiff (half tack-room, half gun-room, another half of it somehow made shift to serve for business: if there are not three halves in one whole in most places, be sure that the Mud is not one of them) of the estate, might not have passed inspection at the Royal and Imperial Institute of Cartography. But it sufficed to locate the cove of the little river —

"Does it have a name, bailiff ?"

"Does, Sir Doctor."

A silence.

A sigh.

"And what, then, is its name, bailiff ?"

"Its name? Its name is Little River, sir, Sir Doctor."

The cove called Lurley Bend had, so far as could be recalled, always been called that. There seemed no local legends of any golden-haired sirens sitting on rocks and luring men to their certain deaths there. There seemed, in fact, no local legends about it at all — save the one local legend, so strange and totally unfamiliar to Eszterhazy, that the appearance of the lurley meant certain death to the buckwheat crop.

"It's certain death to the buckwheat crop," Prince Roldrando burst out, "if you will all neglect to tend it!"

The bailiff said nothing, but one of the older men, wagging his head, said, respectfully but nonetheless doggedly, "Ah, me Lord Prince, this easy for you to say, but 'tis a known fact that whenever there be a lurley-girley in the river, us buckwheat crop do blight and die, and then us have no kasha for the winter, lulladay!"

His lord prince pointed out, again, that the only certain fact was that the buckwheat had to be tended; but this brought nothing but a certain clarification, to wit, that if anyone were to dare to tend the buckwheat while the lurley-girley was in the river, he or she or they would by so doing incur certain death.

It was certain, to be sure, that buckwheat was the staple foodstuff for the winter thereabouts. Some wheat was saved to make bread, some potatoes were saved for the borsht, much wheat and potatoes went to pay rent or be sold for cash (or, likelier, to pay against credit). The main use for wheat and potato, however, as far as the fact of good crops of either one gladdening the hearts of the farmer-folk, was that much of both went into the making of the local wudkey. To have used wheat alone would have seemed a wanton extravagance; to have used potatoes only would have seemed a degree of coarseness to which they were unwilling to descend. They sought a balance, and — usually — they found it.

And if, instead of bowl after bowl of familiar buckwheat grits winterday after winterday, if, instead of this, they had need to fill their bellies with bread, with potato — why, a twofold sadness would surely come upon them: One — no kasha. Two — no home-made wudkey. None of this meant, of course, that they would do without wudkey! The very thought was alien, would have brought unbelieving grunts. But sometimes the buckwheat failed for natural reasons. The results were familiar to all. One sold what one could, sometimes the wife's gold trinkets — and the wife never cared for that — or the silver frames of the ikons, when one went to town to buy town-made wudkey. And, once in town, once at the tavern, did one — could one — have a quiet and thoughtful sip, as one always did at home? Never a bit of it. There was always the urging to pass the pint around . . . to stand someone else a round . . . before one knew it, the pint was gone . . . so quickly!

And then, one by one: The wagon. The harness. Even the horse.

And then the first fight. And then the second fight. And —

"Ah, sirs, she lurley ha' been seen up and down the river, yes. 'Tis bad, oh, bad." It was clear that more than one, as Eszterhazy and his princely friend made their rounds, had anticipated whatever might come by dipping in the wudkey already. Not only the buckwheat was suffering, the district itself had begun to suffer. The fishermen no longer set their nets; the fowlers feared to go abroad in the fens.

"Now, sir," said the fellow whom the bailiff had sent as guide, "it's just as you follow that bit of path, there, and you come, you are bound to come, as easy as easy, to within sight . . . within sight of . . ."

"Of Lurley Bend?"

The man threw him a reproachful look. *Speak not the word, lest it come to pass. . . .* "Within sight of it," he said, after a nervous swallow, visible and audible. He asked, stiffly, "Will Your Honor be wanting to come back before noontide? — or after? What I means is —" What he meant, clearly, was that he had no intention of accompanying

Eszterhazy but was, however, willing to return for him — here. Thus far would he go, and no farther. Eszterhazy shrugged. "Tether the horse, then," he said. "I daresay I can find my own way back." And, as the man hesitated, painfully, he added, "And if I can't, no doubt the horse knows the way."

How eagerly the man was about to grasp at this easy way out of it! But then, something which may have been duty, or may have been a fear of something other than the lurley — the prince, perhaps — or may have been honest concern, came over the man's face. It was, God knows (Eszterhazy thought), an honest face. The man shook his head. "I shall meet Your Honor here," he said. "At when the shadows are like so." He drew in the soft dirt with his stick. About three hours after noon hour, Eszterhazy calculated. "Surely Your Honor will be here then?" It was less a question than a plea. And then he stayed and watched as his master's guest walked down the path.

The day was warm, and growing warmer, but here all was cool. Ahead, the trees thinned out. The path was already thinning out, itself. And then the path came to a hollow, and that was the end of the path. It was less a pool than an eddy, less an eddy than a backwater. Flocculent bits of decayed leaves and such floated, dotting the surface and the subsurface of the dark water. Ahead, some good way ahead, there was the shine of the unobstructed sun upon the water. The river, then.

Lurley's Bend, then.

He sat down and took out his binoculars. And he waited.

The quality of the light, the quantity of the light, was never the same two seconds in a row. The trees and the bushes wavered in the slow, soft wind; and the light, filtering between and amongst them, wavered with them. Sometimes the air was bright, then it went into flux and turned green. Now one corner was yellow from the sun, and now another. In a way, it was like being under water. And he fell into a sort of revery in which he was, in deed and fact, underneath the waters. He rose and fell with the waves. And then, from somewhere in the dim and aqueous distances, came the daughter of the wave, the child of the *unda,* of the undulating wave, there came the undine herself. And she —

He had the glasses to his eyes before he realized what he was doing.

The movement was too abrupt. Far away as the woman was, still, she had noticed. Something, at least, she must have noticed. As swiftly as she had come out of the waters, even more swiftly did she return to them.

But the glimpse, brief as it had been, had been enough.

There were two or three with their heads together at the curve of the road. That is, one man, one woman, and one child straining on her toes. They drew apart as the horse ambled up. One of them was his guide. His face went almost weak and loose with relief on seeing Eszterhazy. "Ah, thank God, Your Honor, well, the horse, and now, although 'tis nowhere near time," he babbled.

"Well enough, Augsto," said Eszterhazy. "Look here." They looked. "The fact is," he began. "A touch of the sun, you see. Only a touch. No more, but my skin, well, I am a city fellow. I am afraid I don't tan, I may burn. I was wondering. A salve? An ointment? Is a shop around where such things are sold? An apothecary?" They shook their heads. Nooo. . . . Nothing like *that*. . . . Not around *here*. . . . And it was the woman's face which first lighted with a sudden thought. As he had known it would.

"Ah, sir! Ah — the midwife!"

"To be sure, Mamma, the midwife!" the girl echoed. And even Augsto had understood, and, happy that all was well and that the new matter was merely something which could be settled by the ministrations of one well-known and familiar, added his own exclamations of, "The midwife, to be sure, Your Honor, the midwife! She does make all salves and such, as well as her tending to the women in their time! And if Your Honor will be so kind as to allow it, I'll —"

But His Honor declined to be so kind as to allow it. He insisted on being given directions. And, indeed, it was not very far. The woman was tending to her sunflowers, already beginning to droop their heads, so heavy with seed; she was barefoot and had her outer skirt tucked up, showing a perfectly respectable profusion of petticoats. She looked up, bobbed him a curtsey, and waited for him to dismount and enter the yard. A woman with a seamed face, and pale blue eyes. She waited for him to speak.

"I am His Highness's guest," he said. She gave a nod of knowing much — and, indeed, he wondered how much she might really know. He repeated his story and she looked at him, somewhat doubtfully. Then, "If you will step inside, sir," she said.

The house was as neat as anyone had any right to expect and smelled of herbs and of flowers and of something cooking on the stove . . . a chicken in paprika sauce, probably. "Well, sir," she said, still looking at him with the same doubtful expression, "the best thing for sunburn, you know, is simply oil and vinegar, mixed."

"I don't wish to smell like a salad," he said, entirely honestly.

She gave a sudden snort of laughter. Obviously she was in no great awe of him. This might be all to the good. On the other hand —

"Perhaps you have a salve," he suggested.

She nodded, slowly. "I have a number. I suppose the best thing might be the zinc oxide, although —"

Despite himself, he was startled; he had expected, perhaps,

something along the lines of, say, swallow's fat, mixed with the juice of cornflowers plucked in the light (or the dark) of the moon.

"Zinc oxide! What do you know about zinc oxide?"

The look she gave him was heavy with reproof. "I have the diploma of the Provincial School for Midwifery and Nursing, sir. The late Prince Von Vlox sent me there, he paid my expenses, so that his people should have good care. I know a good deal about zinc oxide, sir, and a great deal more, besides. . . ."

At once he said, "Then you know who or what was born in these parts about fifteen or sixteen years ago and is now frightening the present Prince Von Vlox's people into imbecility — don't you think it is time for you to come out into the open with it?"

She threw back her head. If he had expected her — and, to a degree, he had — to break into tears, to sigh or sob or cross herself, well, he was mistaken, to that extent. The pale blue eyes were quite steady. "So it *is* her, then," she said, calmly. "I half-thought it might be. I have been thinking. Thinking. Even just now, as you came up, I was thinking. But no clear answer came to me. But, sir, have some mercy on her! It is no matter of 'what,' it is a matter of a human child, begotten in secret, to be sure, and born in even more secrecy . . . a child sadly afflicted . . . but a child, a human child all the same. . . ."

"Forgive me that lapse," he said, "Of course you are entirely right. Go on, then. Go on."

Less may be hidden from the midwife than from most, but it can happen, and not seldom does it happen, that even from the midwife a thing may be hidden until the last moment. "I did not want you to see me," the woman said, tight-lipped, sweat already beginning to break out upon her face. And then the first cry broke. And then the waters broke. And then all such thoughts as secrecy fell into the shadows where all but the essentials fall. And the woman herself began to writhe, as though she herself were a broken thing.

"But for all of that, it was a normal labor," the midwife said. "The *labor* was normal. . . ."

And Eszterhazy said, "The child, though . . ."

"The flesh of the lower limbs was fused. In appearance, there was but one lower limb. Ah, God, how she did indeed break down at that. I told her, 'Helena, this may very probably be cured through surgery,' but she knew nothing of such things. And she was in agony for her child and said it was a punishment for sin, for her sin in getting the child —"

He said, "Ah . . ."

The woman shrugged. "I do not sit in judgment. I do not make reports. I did not even tell the priest, he is a monk; if he had been a married priest, well . . . In fact, I told no one. Until now."

He tried to imagine what it must have been like, trying to keep such a secret for such a length of time. . . . Not the midwife — the mother. "Surely the child's mother must have guessed, though," he said. "How could she have escaped hearing? How far into the woods do they live, that the mother hasn't heard these stories, these few past months?"

Said the midwife, "That is it, you see. She died, the mother — I mean, Helena, I mean. She died only a few past months ago."

It took a few seconds for the meaning of it all to be clear to Eszterhazy. Then he said, softly, "Oh, my God. . . ."

To have lived a life, even a life of only fifteen or sixteen years, a life of concealment, even if not complete concealment, to have spent those years pretending to be a cripple in a chair . . . a chair from which one never moved during the daylight hours . . . clad in a dress so long that no one would see . . . or guess . . . or even suspect. . . . A life largely confined to one's self and one's mother, and then, of a sudden stroke — half the world gone out. After a life of being warned, and warned, and warned, *"No one must know. . . . No one must ever know —"*

"Well, the rest can wait," he said. "We must find that child. And find her soon. What is her name?"

The midwife said, "The same as mine. Maria Attanasia. I baptized her. Yes. Find her." She thought a moment, then nodded. "A boat, to begin with."

It was not so hard as one might have thought, nor did it take very long, either. He had one more question, and asked it as they went toward the boat mooring. "As to the child's father . . ." He paused. Maria the midwife stopped and swung about. Again the pale blue eyes gazed at him.

"You do not know, then," she said. "I never knew if Helena ever told him. Evidently she did not. This, too, must wait."

She would not let him in the boat. The child, she said, must not be frightened further. She had food with her, and drink, and she had clothing, too. But most of all, he thought, as he saw her get calmly into the flat-bottomed boat and take the oars in her own deft hands, most of all she had her own calm heart and her own unfearing soul.

"At first, she said," Maria the midwife told him later, "she had intended to drown herself. She took off her dress, there, where she had crawled down to the bank, and she threw herself in. But by the sure mercy of God, she did not sink, she must have floated, I think, for at least as long as it took her to discover that she could swim. I have known that to happen with children; sometimes the older boys will throw a young one in, and they scream and kick and before they quite know it, there they are, swimming." This newfound way of motion, perhaps even more than the shock of the water, brought her to another way of thinking. And the young woman did not think again of dying. What had hindered her upon the land was no hindrance in

the water. She was formed after the manner of a seal, and in that manner she found her way with ever-increasing confidence upon the river. She ate the mussels and left the shells; it had been only coincidence that the secluded cove was named Lurley's Bend, she had not known it. And there were berries, windfallen fruit; and then, for a while, at least, the milk which the River Tartar lad had so innocently and so honestly left "for pay for shell."

But someone had to be told, of course. And Eszterhazy told the natural person to tell.

"Helena?" said Prince Roldrando Von Vlox. "Helena — Oh, God. I do remember now. I wondered what had happened. For a while. And then I forgot. Helena . . ."

He took the rest of it very well indeed. "After all," he said, "it is in the blood. She is descended from King Baldwin and his undine wife on the one line, and on the other we are out of the body of Charlemagne himself, the great-grandson of the Webfooted Queen. Yes, yes," he said — almost to himself, almost, one might have thought, almost proudly — "the blood will tell. . . ." After a while he agreed that the younger Maria should go up to Bella and be examined by the Medical Faculty. "If she wishes to try what they can do, she is free to do so. And if not, not. She will lack for nothing which I can provide, of course."

The story which soon spread all around the fens and farmlands was that the Lord Prince's friend had caught the lurley-girl and had taken her up to Bella to show her to the Emperor, whom God preserve for many years. . . . For a moment, as the news spread, each one who heard it reflected what a fine thing it was to be the tenant of a prince whose friend could capture a lurley and take her up to the capital city and show her to the Emperor.

And then, without exception, after a moment of such reflection, the same thought would occur to each and every of them. "Oh, *Jesus, Mary, and Joseph!*" they cried. "The ***buckwheat!***"

Fortunately, the days were long, the weather stayed clear, they toiled like serfs . . . and they saved the crop.

THE CEASELESS STONE

The Clock — *the* Clock, in the old Clock Tower, the clock which was meant when anyone said, without other word of qualification, "So let us meet by the Clock" — this was the one. Annually the gold leaf of its numerals was renewed and refreshed, and the numerals were Roman, not as any deliberate archaicism, but because no other numerals were known thereabouts when it was made; the "Arabic" numbers, in their slow progression out of India through Persia into Turkey, had nowhere reached that part of Europe when the Clock was made; and furthermore, as a sign to us how our fathers' fathers lived without a need for graduations of haste, the great dial had but one hand to turn the hours.

The pulsebeat of the heart of Imperial Bella, capital of the Triune Monarchy of Scythia-Pannonia-Transbalkania, is no longer as perceptible round about the Old Town Hall as it once was: to be sure, on Saints Cosmo's and Damian's Day, the City Council still in full regalia comes for the formal ceremony of electing the Chief Burgomaster, but the rest of the year not much happens. Tourists come to see the tower as part of the regular tour offered by Messrs. T. Cook, beggars and pedlars follow the tour as birds follow a boat, and country-folk — to whom the new Municipal Building, with its mansard roof, marble lobby, and typewriting machines, means nearer to nothing than nothing at all — country-folk make the Clock Tower the center of their perambulations, as they have done for centuries. It is too old a joke to raise even a smile any more that some of them expect to see the Emperor emerge when the automata come out to strike the hours. It makes no difference if they have come up in those huge and huge-wheeled wagons stuffed with feathers, down, hams, cabbages, sour-crout, hides, nuts, eggs, fruit, and all whatever, from barrel-staves to beeswax; or if they have come on foot behind a drove of beeves for the Ox Market; or if they have come up on the railroad. As soon as they can manage, they go to the old Clock Tower, as though to reassure themselves that it is still there, for all their directions start from there: *Take the first lane facing the old Clock Tower and count two turnings but take the third,* and so on. Unless they have paced the way thence to the spectacle-makers or the watchmakers or the thread-and-button shop or the gunsmith's or wherever it may be, nothing can persuade them that they may confidently trade with a spectacle-maker, a watchmaker, a thread-and-button shop, or a gunsmith. Who knows who *they* are? May not their merchandise turn to dust like so much fairy gold? Who could trust even to find them again? Whereas, should one have either dissatisfaction or satisfaction with the tradesmen whose way is known via the old Clock Tower, well, what could be easier — or, rather, as easy — but once again to make one's way to the old Clock Tower, and thence, as safe as by Great God His Compass, return to the same tradesman once again?

It is on a clear, dry day in later February, as near as any subsequent report affirmed, that a young man from the country — let us call him Hansli — finds his way to the very foot of the Old Clock and commences to look about him a bit nervously. A man sitting on a piece of faded rug on the step calls Hansli over, and, very kindly and soberly, inquires if he can assist him. Hansli is relieved.

"Honored Sir," he says, "it's the lane that leads to the lane as is where the goldsmiths are. What it is I'm looking for."

The man nods. "Was it for a wedding ring, perhaps?" he asks.

Hansli is astonished to the point where he does not even at first turn red. Then he reflects how clever the city people are. As for the man himself, the city man, he looks both clever and respectable. "Like a philosopher," he explains, afterwards. This description is clear to Hansli, and to Hansli's father and mother and his promised bride and *her* father and mother. Otherwise, it lacks precision, might mean anyone from the lay instructor of algebra at a seminary school to a civil engineer getting ready to plot out a canal. Equally, it might mean a perfect rogue selling a mixture of salt water and methylene blue as a cure for infertility in cattle or dropped stomach in children.

"Because," the man explains, "if it was for a wedding ring, I have a few for sale."

The man looks at him without a trace of a smile, and this is very reassuring, for Hansli had feared — who knows what — they might laugh at him, at the goldsmiths, make rude jokes. This quiet gentleman is certainly doing nothing of the sort. "It's for Belinda," Hansli explains. The gentleman nods, takes out from a pocket a piece of cloth and unwraps it. Sure enough, a ring. Sure enough, it is gold. But wait. It *looks* like gold . . . sure enough. But —

He buys time. "What might the price be?" The price is half-a-ducat. This is also a relief, a great relief. Hansli can bargain an ox, a horse,

a harness, with the best of them. As for rings, he has no idea. Still, still, "That seems very cheap," he declares. *Is it gold, real gold, pure gold?* is what the wee voice is asking in his ear.

The gentleman nods, soberly. "It is cheap," he concedes. "A goldsmith must charge more, because he has to pay rent. And a very high rent, indeed. But I, here, I need pay no rent, for my place of business" — he gestures — "has for the landlord the Emperor himself, whom God bless and preserve for many years —"

"Amen, amen." Hansli takes off his hat and crosses himself.

"— charges me no rent. Do you see," he says. And he takes out of another pocket what some would call a jeweler's loupe, but which Hansli calls "a look-see," a term covering everything from a magnifying glass to a telescope, and he tenders it. Hansli peers through the glass at the ring, all round the ring. How bright it looks! How it shines in the clear winter air! And then Hansli sees something. A triple-headed eagle, and the numerals LXI. This is good enough for Hansli. He takes out his purse and selects a half-a-ducat. The philosophical gentleman blesses him and he blesses the philosophical gentleman.

Back home, Hansli's father peers inside the ring. "Never seed no gold like this," he says. Then his clear eyes, which (they say locally) can spot a goat-kid three miles off in the dark woods, observe something. "Ah, th' Imper'al Eagle! So. 'Tis good gold, then, and, lets me see." He calculates slowly. "Ah, the sixty-first year o' the Reign, hm, twas made a year ago . . . or so . . ." He lifts the ring. It has passed the test. Hansli kneels. His father raises the ring and blesses him with it. Now all plans for the wedding may proceed. As soon as the sunny days are sure, Belinda will begin to bleach the linen.

Who knows how often this was all repeated? Not Lobats, the Commissioner of the Detective Police. Not De Hooft, the President of the Jewelers' Association.

"It is always the same story," says De Hooft, a dapper Fleming with dyed hair and a waxed moustache. "Very soon the ring begins to bend, or sometimes it breaks even if it is not too big or too small. They come to town, they look for this chap, this, ah, 'phil-os-o-pher,' " he parts the word sarcastically (and incorrectly); "they don't find him, they go to a respectable jeweler or goldsmith. The gold is tested, it proves pure, it is explained to them that it is in fact *too* pure, that it is too soft to take pressure. The idea that the goodwife will have to be bought another ring in order to testify that she is in fact married, this does not please them. Not at all. But what can one do, eh?" He shrugs.

Lobats is there, listening. He has heard it all before. Also there, and not having heard it all — or any of it — before, is Engelbert Eszterhazy, Doctor of Medicine, Doctor of Philosophy, Doctor of

Jurisprudence, Doctor of Science, and Doctor of Literature. Who now asks, "And reports of stolen gold?"

"None that fit. Spahn, the tooth-surgeon, had a robbery. But this is not dental gold. And Perrero's had reported a robbery, but this is not coin gold. We have never settled that matter of the theft from the Assay Office in Ritchli-Georgiou, but that was the regular Ritchli gold, very pale yellow. Not *this* —" Lobats gestures. Several rings lie on a soft piece of paper before them, rings which the Jewelers' Association has succeeded in buying back, so to speak. Usually they could not be bought back.

Eszterhazy takes up the loupe and has a look. He puts it down and De Hooft says, "I've seen all sorts of gold, you know. This is new to me. I've seen yellow gold, I've seen white gold, red gold, even green gold, yes! But this, *this,* shining with the sheen of a . . . of a Chinese orange! This I have never seen before."

Lobats paused in the act of brushing his high-crowned gray bowler hat with the sleeve of his gray overcoat. "Naturally, our very first thought was that the rings themselves must have been stolen," he explained. "But that didn't stand up for long."

Eszterhazy nodded. "Exactly what laws are being broken here?" he asked.

Lobats raised his eyebrows thoughtfully. "Well . . . hmm . . . well, of course, the man is in violation of the municipal street-trading ordinances. But that is a small matter. And his method of marking the rings is technically illegal, for they haven't been proofed either at the Goldsmiths Guild, the Jewelers' Association Testing Room, or any Imperial Assay Office. However, as we all know, they are of a purer gold than any rings which are."

De Hooft frowned. "Obviously the man is dishonest," he said. "Probably the gold was stolen abroad and he is trying to dispose of it bit by bit, without attracting attention."

Lobats put his head at an angle and shook it. "But we've had no reports from abroad of any thefts which would fit. We've even checked back to reports a few years ago, for example, from California, and from Australia. But this just isn't their kind of gold."

Doctor Eszterhazy once again examined the rings. "And yet," he said, "if he came honestly by it, why is he selling them so far below normal price? Evidently, by the way he impresses the people he sells to, he speaks as a man of anyway moderate education. And as such, he ought to know that even if the gold was dug up in a hoard, somewhere, by the law of treasure trove, the Throne will concede him a half-portion . . . provided, that is, that he made an immediate and honest disclosure. . . ."

Lobats lifted his brows and pursed his lips. "Well, Doctor, it may be that you have hit upon it. Maybe it *is* a buried treasure that he found, maybe his greed got the better of him and he started to dispose

of it in what he thought was a clever way. And, now he knows that we are on to him, well, maybe he thinks it's too late for him to come forward. Just think, gentlemen!" — he poked the rings with a thick and hairy forefinger — "this might be pirate gold . . . or maybe even dragon gold . . . !" He laughed hastily and twisted his face.

Eszterhazy caught at something before the telltale slip; it was perfectly all right with him if a plainclothes police commissioner believed in the hoards which folk-belief still held that dragons from the ancient days of the Goths and Scythians had planted here and there in many a hidden valley and many a haunted hill; no one was ever the worse off for such a belief, and the thought of them added a touch of color which the modern age could well use.

"What do you mean, Karrol-Francos, that now he knows you are onto him? How does he know?"

Commissioner Lobats told him that a plainclothesman had been assigned to the area around the old Clock Tower, but that no further signs of the stranger had been seen since.

Doctor Eszterhazy, having left the other two to further talk and consideration, engaged in a bit of reflection as he walked away. Selling cheap rings to the visiting peasantry was almost a natural notion — that is, if one had cheap rings to dispose of. And suppose that one still had? Where else, and to whom else, might it be equally natural to attempt a sale?

The puffing railroad trains had stolen away much of the old river trade, but much still remained; it was not as quick, but it was cheaper. Coal and timber and pitch, salt and gravel and grain and sand were still moved in great quantities by sailing-barge up and down the Ister, even if the boats no longer caught the winds in scarlet sails and even if the bargees no longer wore their hair in pigtails. A good place to find the bargees, when their minds and eyes were not preoccupied with snubbing lines or disputing precedence at the wharfs, was the Birch Walk.

Conjecture vision of a stone embankment crowned with a paved walk planted on both sides with birch trees, a walk which winds perhaps a third of a kilometer along the River Ister. It had at one time been contemplated to continue the Walk, and to plant an equivalent number of birches more, for a much greater distance; this had not been done. But the experiment could not be said to have failed. People of the class who can afford simply to amuse themselves at hours when the sun still shines, and on a weekday, too, found that the prospect was pleasant from the Birch Walk; some, indeed, compared it to portions of the Seine, although not always to the same portions. Those establishments which offered refreshment, and which were willing to make more than merely minimal gestures in the way of cleanliness and good order, found that ladies and gentlemen (and those who wished to be taken for ladies and gentlemen) were now willing to patronize them. These new customers found an interest in watching the barge-people at their food and drink, and the barge-people, it is possible, perhaps found an almost equal interest in watching these same people at theirs. Though perhaps not.

Those captains, mates, and deckhands (most sailing-barges carried a deckhand, in addition to a captain and a mate) who wished, their duties done for the day, to get drunk as quickly as possible, as cheaply as possible, or to enjoy the company of some barefoot trull, also cheaply and quickly, did not come up to the Birch Walk to do so. One found there, instead, barge-folk well-bathed and well-combed and cleanly clad, either strolling decorously, or, with equal decorum, sitting at an outside table, enjoying a dark beer or a plate of zackuskoes. Often they merely hung over the railings, enjoying a sight of the river from a different angle than the deck of a barge affords.

Eszterhazy paced slowly along, waiting for a familiar face . . . not any one particular familiar face, nor even just any familiar face; he waited for one of a general category. And, as so often happens, as long as one is not in great need of borrowing money, he found one.

Or one found him.

As it turned out, there were three of them, and at least two of them hailed him to "Sit down and take!" The verb *to take* has perhaps fewer meanings than many another which one might name, but among those who traffic in and labor around the wide waters called the Pool of Ister, the definitive definition is liqueous . . . and hospitable.

The older two were the brothers Francos and Konkos Spits, the captain and mate, respectively, of the sailing-barge *Queen of Pannonia,* and the other was their deck-hand — presumably he had a Christian and a family name, but Eszterhazy had never heard him referred to as anything but "the Boy." The brothers were dark, the boy was fair, and Eszterhazy had met all three in connection with a singularly mysterious affair involving an enormous rodent of Indonesian origin.

Conversation was at first general. The current state of the river trade was discussed, which of course entailed discussion of the river trade for many years past. Some attention was given to the perennial rumor that the Ruritanians, or perhaps the Rumanians, were going to place a boom across the Danube, or perhaps, as some said, a bomb. The merits and demerits of the current methods of marking channels, shoals, and wrecks came in for much commentary, little of it favorable. By the next drink, conversation became more personal. Eszterhazy asked if many young men showed a disposition to take up the bargee trade. The brothers Spits simultaneously insisted that recruitment was flourishing and that none of the recruits were worth

recruiting: they twirled their huge mustachios and banged their vast fists upon the table to emphasize this point. The Boy blushed. Eszterhazy glanced at him, in a friendly fashion, and the Boy blushed even more.

"Nowadays," Eszterhazy said, "the younger bargees do not pierce their ears any more, do they?"

At this, rather to his surprise, the captain and the mate burst into rough, loud laughter, and the Boy turned absolutely crimson, with a tinge toward purple.

"Why, what is this joke?" the guest inquired. "Can I not see for myself that his ears are not pierced?"

"Har har har!" guffawed Captain Francos Spits.

"Hor hor hor!" chuckled Mate Konkos Spits.

Between them they secured the Boy's head — for some reason he had turned shy and declined cooperation — and twisted it about, giving Eszterhazy some fear that he was about to witness a non-judicial garroting. But evidently the Boy had a sufficiently limber neck. It was certainly true that the Boy's left ear had not been pierced. It now proved to be equally true that his right ear had. This was red and swollen about the lobe, and a thread, of an off-white tint, hung through and from it.

"I was like drunk when I done it," the Boy muttered.

Both of the brothers Spits sporting a golden ring in their right ears, they did not receive this in good spirit; Captain Francos, in fact, aimed a cuff. "What do you mean? You mean you got like sense and you done it! Ain't it good for the eyesight, ain't it, Doctor, ain't it?"

"So it is often said," Eszterhazy answered, adding, "The custom is exceedingly ancient, and I for one am glad to see it kept up."

The Boy seemed more disposed to take this for good than the growls of his superiors. Eszterhazy seized the moment to ask, "And what about the ring?"

The Boy fumbled in his pocket. Would it be some wretched brass trinket? — or even one which, though it might be fully lawful, would still be of infinitely less interest than — Out came a screw of filthy paper which showed signs of much wrapping and unwrapping. And inside that was the ring. It did, indeed, shine somewhat with the luster of a very fine mandarin orange. Eszterhazy took out the small leather case in which he carried an excellent magnifying glass.

"See th' eagle?" the Boy inquired. "Don't that mean it's good? Cost me half-a-duke."

"It is certainly as good as gold — that is," he hastened to explain, "it is certainly of very good gold."

"But it didn't have no pissin' gold wire loop, like. I hadda go to a reg-lar jooler for that. Wasn't he pissed off, 'cause I didn't git the whole pissin' works from him! 'Don't get your piss hot, lardy,' I say t' him."

The Boy's address was vigorous though, in the matter of adjectives, somewhat limited.

"Did you buy it from that philosopher chap?" asked Eszterhazy. The Boy nodded and commenced to rewrap it. "What did he say?" The Boy thought for a moment as he engaged in this difficult task.

"Said, 'The free lynx of the south . . .' Is what he said . . ." The Boy finished his task, put the wad back in his pocket, and, taking up from the table a toothpick which already showed signs of wear, proceeded to attend to his teeth. Clearly, the matter of the philosopher's discourse was over, as far as the Boy was concerned.

Captain Francos Spits wrinkled up one side of his face in a half-scowl of concentration. " 'The *south,'* " he repeated. "There ain't no lynxes in the *south,* brother —"

"Nor I never said there was! In the *north,* now —" He turned to Doctor Eszterhazy. "Our old gaffer, he killed a lynx up north, for it was catching all his turkey-birds, and —"

"Waiter!" Eszterhazy caught all eyes. "Cognac all around," he ordered. Every lynx in the Monarchy was at once forgotten. It took a second order of the same before he was allowed to depart.

Back at Number 33 Turkling Street, he asked his librarian, Herra Hugo Von Sltski, "Do we have — we do have a copy of Basil Valentine's *Twelve Keys,* do we not?"

"We do. And we don't." Having uttered this statement, almost delphic in its tone, Von Sltski proceeded to explain. "Our copy has gone to the binders. As I had indicated it must, on last quarter's list. It is now in the press. I daresay we might get it out of the press. But I would instead propose that you consult the copy in . . . the copy in . . ." He rolled his eyes and thought a moment. "Not the Imperial Library, they haven't got one. And the one in the University is defective." The eyes rolled down again. "There is a good copy in the collection at the Library of the Grand Lodge. I will give you a note to the Keeper of the Rare Volumes." He took out his card, neatly wrote a few words and a symbol upon it, and handed it over.

Eszterhazy thanked him and departed, thinking — with some irony, with some amusement — that there was at least one place in this great city, of which he had thought himself free, where he . . . even he . . . with his seven degrees and his sixteen quarterings, might not go with firm hopes of success without an introduction from one of his own employees.

The card sufficed to get him into the silent chambers high up in the blank-faced building marked only with the same symbol. No one prevented him from access to the catalogue, which consisted of shelf after shelf of huge bound volumes chained in their places. He found his entry, carefully copied down what he saw into one of the forms provided, took it to the desk and there handed it over, along with the puissant pasteboard. The man at the desk held the form in one hand

and his spectacles with the other and read aloud, as though he were a rector conferring a degree.

" *'Volume V, of the Last Will and Testament of Basil Valentine, VIDELICET, a Practical Treatise together with the XII Keys and Appendix of the Great Stone of the Antient Philosophers.'* "

There was the sound of a chair being scraped, a throat was cleared, and a voice asked, "Is that Master Mumau?" and a very tall, very thin, very pleasant-looking man came strolling forward from an adjacent office.

"No, it is not," the man at the desk said.

"Have I the opportunity of addressing the Honorable Keeper of the Rare Volumes?" asked Eszterhazy, handing over his own card — the assistant having already handed over the other.

"*Ye*-es," the Keeper said, as though struck by the remarkable coincidence of someone recognizing him whilst in his official capacity. "How do you do. I did think that you might be someone else. We do not often have many calls for such books. Ah-hah. Oh-ho. Yes. Yes. I know *him* very well. He was the Tiler at the Lodge of the Three Crowns. *My* lodge, you know." These last remarks referred, however, to Eszterhazy's librarian, not to Master Mumau, about whom Eszterhazy would have wished to inquire, would have wished to very much indeed, had he but been given opportunity. The Keeper was very kind, very thoughtful; he provided Eszterhazy with a desk by himself, brought him a better chair (he said) than the one already there, ordered a floor lamp, provided notepaper and sharpened pencils, regretted that ink could not be allowed, regretted that smoking could not be allowed, offered a snuffbox, had brought a printed list of the recent acquisitions, and somehow, before Eszterhazy quite knew it, the Keeper, the desk assistant, and the floor assistant had all withdrawn. Leaving him, if not entirely alone, at least alone with *Volume V of The Last Will and Testament of Basil Valentine,* etc., an absolutely vast volume, perforated here and there on its still-clear pages with neat little wormholes. It opened with the cheerful and reassuring notice that anything against the Holy Christian Faith which the work might ever have contained, if it contained any, had been purged and removed, according to the Rule laid down by the Council of Trent; the date of publication was 1647. It was not the first edition.

Nothing would have pleased Eszterhazy more than to have reread the entire volume through then and there. However. He was in search of a particular reference, and, as it happened, he found it in the Preamble.

> The Phoenix of the South hath snatched away the heart out of the breast of the huge beast of the East, for the beast of the East must be bereaved of his Dragon's skin, and his wings must vanish, and

then they must both enter the Salt Ocean, and return again with beauty . . .

Well, obscure, and typically obscure, as all this was, there was anyway no obscurity in the guess which he had formed about *the free lynx of the South.* Considering that the Boy had certainly never in his life heard of Basil Valentine. Or of any of his works.

Or of his Work.

On a sudden impulse, Eszterhazy carefully took the volume and shook it, gently, gently, for it was, though sturdy in appearance, still, quite old. A slip of paper dropped out of the back pages, and, although hastily he set down the volume, almost it escaped him. Almost. It was half of a form of application for books, neatly torn in two; and on the back of it, which side was facing him as he took it up, Eszterhazy saw, in a neat school-masterish hand, the words *Ora Lege Lege Lege Relege Labora et Invienes.*

Pray, Read, Read, Read, Read Again; Toil and Thou Shalt Find.

Thoughtfully, he turned the slip over. What was left of the original application were the words:

——au, K.-Heyndrik

The Annual Directory of Loyal Subjects Resident in the Imperial Capital and Registered According to Law, etc., had certainly been up-to-date . . . once. However, Master Karrol-Heyndrik Mumau had not moved since its last publication. That is, his name was known to the porteress in the shabby-genteel block of flats.

"Yes, the Master do live here, but he have a work-shop at th' old Spanish Bakery, where he be now, I expect. Thank 'ee, sir."

Once there had been an Emperor who had wedded an Infanta of Castille. That was long, long ago. And it had been long, long, since any farduelos or other Hispanic pastries had been produced from the oven at the Spanish Bakery. Had he not known what the letters were supposed to intend, it is doubtful that Eszterhazy could have made them out. The windows were curtained and dusty, and dust lay so heavily in the corners of the front door that it was doubtful anyone had used it for decades, perhaps. However, there is always a "round the back." Thither he went, and there, upon the door in the faded russet brick wall, he knocked.

The door opened fairly soon.

"My dear Master Mumau," Eszterhazy said, gently, "you mustn't make gold any more, you know. You really, really mustn't. It is forbidden according to law."

"Will they put me in the galleys?" the man whispered.

"I'll see to it that they won't," Eszterhazy said. He had never made a promise he felt safer of keeping.

"I was about to stop, anyway," the man said. His manner was that of a schoolboy who has been caught roasting apples at the bunsen burner. For a moment he stood there, irresolute. Then he said, "Would you like to come in . . . ? You *would? Really?* Please *do!*"

Everything that one might have expected to find there was there: the furnace, the crucible, the athanor, alembic, pelican. It was all there. One thing more was there, which Eszterhazy did not recognize. He turned away, urging himself to forget its very outlines. "That . . . piece of equipment," he said, gesturing. "*That* one. *Break it at once.*"

The man made a huffling sound, clicked his tongue, sighed. At length there was a smash. "Oh well. I *said* I wouldn't make any more, didn't I? Well, I meant it. So I don't need it."

"And you are not to make another one like it."

He turned back and looked around once again. Yes, a bakery was a very good place to have chosen. God only knew what they would do, there at the Mint, and at the Treasury, if they knew what had been baked here recently.

"I used to be chemistry master at the Old Senior School, you know," Mumau said. "And I was a very good one, too. Till I got sick. Father Rector was very kind to me, 'Master Henk,' he said, 'we've agreed to give you a nice pension, so just take it easy, and don't you read any more of them big thick books, do you hear?' And I said, 'I won't, Father Rector.' But of course I *did.* And so of course I have to confess it. 'Father, I've been reading those big thick books again, that I'm not supposed to,' I tell the priest. It's not Father Rector, just the parish priest, and he says, he always says, 'Say three Our Fathers and a Hail Mary and don't play with yourself.' "

Eszterhazy had taken off his hat and was fanning his face with it. "But why did you sell the rings?"he asked. "*Why?*"

Master Mumau looked at him. "Because I needed the money for my *real* project," he said.

"I don't care about the gold, puff-puff with the bellows, *oh* what a nuisance! I just needed more money because the pension couldn't stretch that far, and I needed fifty ducats and so I had to make enough to sell a hundred rings. Well, now I've *got* the fifty ducats." His face lit up with an expression of glee such as Eszterhazy had almost never seen in his life before.

"— and now I can work on my *real* project!"

Eszterhazy nodded. "The elixir of life," he said, wearily.

"Of *course,* the elixir of life!"

For once, Doctor Eszterhazy could think of nothing to say. He racked his brains. Finally he murmured, "Keep me posted."

Later, he said to Lobats, "You may consider the case as closed."

"You mean that? You do. Well. Very well. But . . . at least tell me. *Where did he get it?*"

And Eszterhazy said, in a way perfectly truthfully, "It was dragon gold."

He was never sure, afterwards, that Lobats ever forgave him for that.

THE KING'S SHADOW HAS NO LIMITS

The Late Renascence historian known as Pannonicus had written that "The names of nations are often changed; the names of rivers, never." Had he contented himself with observing that the names of nations changed more often than those of rivers, his comment would have been more correct. The name of Triune Monarchy of Scythia-Pannonia-Transbalkania had been officially adopted only in the fifth year of the Reign of the present Monarch; the name of the Ister is found upon the earliest maps; the so-called *Addendum to Procopius* quotes a fragment of Tacitus, now lost, to the effect that "The river of the Galans flows into the Ister," and so forth. Gaul, Gael, Galicia, Gallego, Galatia, all mark the marches of that once widespread people, whose languages are now spoken only upon the headlands, highlands, and islands of the misty Atlantic. The lesser of the two streams on whose banks came into being the great City of Bella still bears, officially, the name of Galants . . . but to every non-scholar in the Capital of the Triune Monarchy it is only the Little Ister.

For a long time the lower part of this stream, particularly where it flowed through the South Ward, had been little better than an open sewer; now, however, it was announced, "the Council and Corporation of the City of Bella" — a phrase which lacked, somehow, quite the majesty of, say, *Senatus Populusque Romanus* — was going to embark upon a twofold program of flood control and beautification in regard to the lesser river, and this project was to be dedicated as a birthday present to His Royal and Imperial Majesty, Ignats Louis. With a certain degree of caution, it had not been made entirely clear *which* birthday it was going to commemorate. The King-Emperor, in no great period of time, would be eighty-two.

Some alterations to adjoining property were, of course, inevitable;

and one property-owner, a parvenu brewer, had been gauche enough to protest. The lawbooks had been opened wide enough to acquaint him with the law of eminent domain and then slapped shut in his face, so to speak; whilst the slap was still echoing, the Court of First Jurisdiction had seen fit to add, perhaps as *obiter dictum,* the old saying, "The King's shadow has no limits . . ."

Doctor Eszterhazy, one fairly fine day, thought that he would go and have a look at the work in progress. He did not take any of his carriages, and neither did he take the steam runabout — the last time he had taken his steam runabout into the South Ward an aggressive drunkard had staggered up and insisted on being supplied with two pennyworth of roasted chestnuts. Eszterhazy took the tram.

The rains that spring had been less than usual, and this portended trouble for the farmers' crops, and, eventually, for the poor, for whom a rise of . . . say, two pennies . . . in the price of a commodity meant tragedy. But even this much drought made work on the Little Ister easier; a series of dams had, first, reduced the flow to a trickle, and then the last one had cut it off entirely. Where the old stream had in freshet inundated slums and junkyards, an enormous excavation was now preparing the way for a tree-lined pool. Exactly how much the poor would appreciate this park was not yet certain, but certainly they must have appreciated the great increase in employment which the project afforded. It would have been most ungrateful if they had not, for this did more than merely supply them with wages, it helped "dissipate unrest," as the *Gazette* newspaper reminded its readers . . . few of whom were likely to be seeking employment on the project, however.

Eszterhazy progressed through the crowd over the Swedish Bridge (it had once been crossed by Charles XII, fleeing the Turks, among whom he had brief refuge after fleeing the Russians), and eventually found a place on the railing. He seemed to be looking down upon an anthill which had been roughly broken open.

"Unrest" there certainly was in more than usual quantity. The Royal Pannonian Government had again refused Slovatchko-language rights to the Slovatchko minority in the schools of Avar-Ister, capital of Pannonia, whilst vigorously insisting upon an extension of Avar-language rights for the Avar-speaking minority in the schools of Bella: the Serbians, as usual, had been far from slow in pointing out that such a situation would never arise in a (projected) Kingdom of the Serbians, Slovatchkos, and Dalmatians. The Romanou had revived their old practice of driving swine to market through the Turkish and Tartar sections of the towns; the regular routes would have been shorter, but it would not have been as much fun. The Concordat with the Vatican was shortly due for its quinquennial confirmation, and the Byzantian delegates in the Diet were again announcing that, if it were confirmed, they would vote

against the Budget. The grain merchants, in anticipation of a shortage, had already begun to hoard supplies. And the Hyperboreans were again refusing to pay their head-tax.

Long lines of men reached from the bottom of the excavation to its top and passed up leathern buckets of dirt from hand to hand. Steam shovels would have been quicker, but there were only a dozen or so of these smoking monsters in all of Bella, whereas the number of the underemployed was beyond count. Some of the workers, had they belonged to a class higher in the social scale, would have been still in school. Others must certainly have had wives and children to support. A surprising number were quite on in years, and one of these for some reason kept repeatedly attracting Eszterhazy's attention: an old, old man, white-haired and -bearded, clad in tatters, who moved slowly to receive his bucket of dirt, strained to maintain it, slowly turned to pass it on. Again and again the eyes of the watcher returned to this single figure, though he could not have said why.

It took less time to withdraw from the railings of the bridge than it had to get to them. Eszterhazy crossed over to the south side, wandered a while through the mazy little streets where the fishwives were forever slapping herring on the chopping blocks and hoarsely shouting, "A penny off! A penny off!" and came back again within sight of the work. Slowly, slowly, the sides of the great pit were being peeled back at an angle, the dirt tossed down into a huge heap. The heap itself was in constant flux, shovels moving it continually to several points, whence by buckets it slowly moved to the top and into the wagons which carried it off, he did not know where. The men in the bucket brigade swayed to and fro, from side to side. The leathern containers moved up, up, up. When they had been emptied, they were tossed down into the pit again.

Eszterhazy's eyes were seeking something . . . someone . . . he had not realized whom until he found him once again. He was nearer, this time, and in a moment or two, he realized what it was about the ragged old man which had been attracting his gaze.

For some reason, the old toiler reminded him of the old Emperor. And this brought him a recollection of some words of Augustine about astrology: of two men known to him whose births, having occurred upon an estate "where even the births of puppies were recorded," were known to have been under the same sign at the same hour and minute — yet one grew up to inherit the estate, and the other toiled on "without the yoke of bondage being lifted for a moment . . ." The reflection disturbed him. Had the old man been near, he would have given him alms; as it was . . .

He boarded the tram which had taken him to the South Ward, but — on impulse — got off quite a ways before his home stop. He had seen a crowd where crowds were not usually to be seen, and he walked across the street and into the square where it was. He saw an old, neglected-looking church and the high iron palings and tottering tombstones of a neglected churchyard. People were swarming in and out. An old woman, her bosom covered with a tattered sack, hurried past him, one hand clutched tightly upwards as though to contain and protect; behind her another old woman, and an old man, and a youngish woman, and a child — all in sackcloth and all with expressions of great wonder and all with a clutched fist.

"What is it that you have there, Mother?" he asked one.

She shot him a look of resentful astonishment, and said, as she hurried by, "Dust of Saint Dominik . . ."

"Ahhh . . ." he murmured. All was now clear. He made his way through the church and into the churchyard. The throng was clustering round a tomb of incredibly antique design; it had been whitewashed, and a number of priests were standing next to it. One was scraping the side of the tomb with a short knife of exactly the sort which painters use to remove old paint before putting on a fresh coat. A second priest gathered the powder into a paper, and, when the first paused, transferred it into a bowl, whence a third spooned it up, tiny spoon by tiny spoon. The fourth and last priest stood a slight bit apart, reading aloud from the psalter.

Two men, evidently the verger and the sexton, allowed the pilgrims to approach the tomb one by one; each knelt, and (presumably) prayed a moment, arose, held out a hand, received a tiny spoonful of dust, withdrew. This, then, was the somewhat famous tomb of Saint Dominicus Paleologus, a younger son of a cadet branch of the Imperial House of Byzantium. His missionary labors had included the free treatment of the sick; so great his reputation that his very tomb had repeatedly been, and literally, torn to pieces in order that the hallowed fragments might prove medically utile. At length the ecclesiastical authorities had fenced and walled the Saint's last resting place; the present ceremony was already hundreds of years old — once a year the dust was scraped from the tomb and distributed. Doubtless the ceremony had been fashionable, but not for long years now; those clustering here and straining for the puissant dust were all from the poor.

The pious rich had other places.

The bell began to ring in the church tower, a flock of doves wheeled up and around, the crowd set up a melancholy howl and pressed closer round the priests at the tomb, who began to move faster and faster. The ceremony was coming to its conclusion. In front of Eszterhazy was an old man dressed in blue canvas, worn soft, worn full of holes, scarcely in any better condition than the remnant of a sack which he had about his back and shoulders. The aged supplicant knelt, received his bit of dust, hastily spooned out, and had begun to hobble away when a heavy old woman, perhaps a fishwife by the sound and smell of her, hurrying so as not to miss out, fell full

against him. The hand he had clenched fell out, fell open, and in a second was empty.

The old man gazed at his empty hand, still lightly covered by the dust of lime, with stupefaction. He hooted once, twice, in grief and senile disbelief, turned as though to return for another portion, was pushed aside, pushed back. Tears ran from his rufous eyes into his snowy beard. Then, with a sudden and unexpected movement, he plunged his head forward, tongue out, and licked the dust adhering to his hand. Then he tottered away, and Eszterhazy tried to follow after him. But the press was too great.

The last toll of the bell echoed in the air, the last spoon of dust was distributed from the bowl, the priest with full deliberateness lifted the bowl and smashed it, and the unsatisfied remnant of the crowd gave voice to one more howl of sorrow. . . .

The ceremony was over.

As fast as he could, as soon as he could, Eszterhazy scuttled from the churchyard, his eyes darting everywhere around the square. He darted, first up one street, then back to the square and then up another — all, all in vain. The old man was not to be seen, was nowhere to be seen.

Old man whose face was the face of the old man who was Emperor.

Eszterhazy at last sat down in a low dram-shop and ordered Cognac. The rough, pale spirit in the dirty glass had never been to France, had been nowhere near France. No matter. He sipped, then he gulped. Then he coughed, choked. Then he made himself be calm and still, and he made himself reflect, there in the stifling room with the rough concrete walls and the flies and the stench from the privy in the nearby yard.

First he forced himself to consider what might have been the state of his own mind to have created this sudden obsession that every white-bearded old man he saw had the Emperor's face. . . . Then he reproached himself for the exaggeration; still, there had been two, in little over an hour's time. Briefly, he considered protesting this last ceremony to the Cardinal-Archbishop, to the Minister of Cults, but decided not to; in the six centuries which had passed since the death of St. Dominicus Paleologus (himself close kin to an Emperor) the ceremony had been repeatedly — and uselessly — forbidden. Now, at least, it was reduced to one hour, once a year; no one nowadays was injured . . . and, perhaps, he thought, wryly, the lime content of the dust might be of some use to the body!

But, back to his own state of mind . . . Certainly he had been increasingly, if somewhat unconsciously, uneasy about the state of the nation. And to him, as to almost everyone else, the Emperor *was* the nation. Had he not been uneasy, too, about the state of the aged Emperor's health? Did not every report of even a cold send ripples of uneasiness throughout the land, cause prayers, most of them genuine, to be offered for old Bobbo's health? So it was perhaps not a completely unreasonable thing if he had seen his sovereign's face in the face of other old men who suffered. . . . He suddenly sat up. Suppose (his heart thumped) suppose it was *not* an illusion! Suppose — could it be possible! — that it *was* Ignats Louis himself whom he had seen? The first old man, laboring in the pit, no, that was impossible, he could not have had the strength, that one had been too far off for him to have been sure. But this other, this second one? The pouched, protruding, and reddened eyes, the bifurcated beard, the long nose, the very stoop and gait . . . Could the Emperor have suddenly taken a notion to play Haroun al-Rashid and go about incognito to take the pulse of the city, so to speak? This pilgrimage just now over, for instance —

For although the King-Emperor reigned and lived in an age of telephones and gramophones and motorcars, he had been born in an age when the steamboat was only a toy on a pond. Born to an obscure princeling in a house — not even a castle — on the Gothic-Slovatchko border-marches, deep in the forests, raised in infancy and early childhood not by nannies, mademoiselles, frauleins, but according to antique custom by his wet nurse in her own cottage, what tales of ages even earlier yet had he heard day after day and night after night? He had already had his first beard when destiny, in the form of a court circle alarmed at the growing insanity of the then-emperor, had plucked him from the hunting lodge and the wilderness and the village priest-teacher and sent him to military school — their idea and their only idea of how to fit the Heir for the heavy task ahead.

Small wonder that religious eccentrics of all sorts, not to say outright charlatans, were able to find access, increasingly as his hearing diminished, to his ancient ear; yes, it just might be possible that he had of his own mere whim and fancy decided to participate in the now-brief pilgrimage for the Dust of Saint Dominik. One might find out.

One would *have* to . . .

He had by this time left the dram-shop, and, wandering about in a deep study, marked not his steps, and, looking up, found himself, as the bells tolled to mark noon, at another of the scenes continued from ancient ages: the distribution of the Beggars' Dole. Only a single arch of heavy masonry remained to mark the location of the City Gates. Down to the early years of the present Reign the Imperial Capital had remained a walled city, its gates literally locked at sunset, the keys ceremonially handed over to the Emperor to keep till shortly before dawn. The city had since spread far and wide, the walls for the most part demolished. But the City Gates remained, or, at any rate, one of the arches of the Main Gate still remained. And at this spot, where once assembled the lame, the halt, the blind, the pauper and the leper, to beg for alms, at this same place forever commemo-

rated in living legend and in folklore, each noon the ancient beneficence of bread and milk was still distributed.

Slowly the line of recipients moved forward. Doubtless there were no longer any lepers among them. Even the standards of raggedness had improved. There were a few more old women than old men, shuffling forward to accept the mug of milk and the chunk of bread from the "one friar, one sister, and one knight" traditionally charged with the duty. The "knight" was usually a very junior member of the Household; Eszterhazy did not know the one on duty today. Eszterhazy drew near. The two policemen stationed there looked at him, indifferently, and yawned. Eszterhazy examined the recipients one by one. Why? Absurd! What did it matter? Ah-hah, a Tartar, few to be seen nowadays . . . This next one still in fragments of the old-style costume of the sailing-bargees . . . This one a Goth . . . The next —

So. Yes. In shapeless coat, rags wrapped about shuffling feet, cap torn in two places, bread in one hand and milk in the other, with dim purpose heading for the worn old steps at the side to sit and eat and drink — if this was not Himself the King-Emperor, it was no one else. Only a sudden flash of memory of the fatal identification of Louis and Marie Antoinette by the innocent priest at Varennes, some dim caution flaring up, prevented Eszterhazy from bowing, from kneeling. But he was sufficiently taller than the sunken, shrunken figure to justify bending, and he made of this merely physical motion an act of homage; he inclined his head as he said softly, "Sire."

The old eyes, rheumy and filmed, looked at him. The old head nodded once, twice. The old hands started to dip the bread in the milk and paused. The old man slowly crossed himself. Once again the bread went toward the mug, and once again it stopped.

"Long, long ago," he said, in his high, now somewhat tremulous voice, "a delegation of the Jewish notables came to see me, to thank me for something or other. And I, may God forgive me, I was young then, there was a rabbi among them, and I said to him, jovial, I said, 'And is your Messiah here?' God forgive me, God forgive me . . . And he looked at me, this old man who had looked as it were on Pharaoh, and this is what he said, he said, 'Do not seek him here. Seek him among the sickly beggars at the City Gates.' " Again the bread went toward the milk, and this time it went in, came up dripping, and with dexterous haste he caught the sop and took it in his mouth before, sodden, it could fall.

Eszterhazy said nothing. The old man munched and sucked and swallowed. It did not take him long to be done with the refreshment. Then he said, "God has given this weary old body such length of days so that this Empire and its many nations might have some few more years of peace, you see. What did the old France say? He said, after him the deluge . . . and the Deluge swept away his house. But, now, after me, after me . . . what? Tell me, learned fellow, what was the name of that old empire which in olden days sank beneath the sea?"

"Sire, Atlantis."

"Yes, so. After me, this Empire will sink like Atlantis, and the children of these children," he gestured to a few boys and girls playing near, "will look for it upon the maps in vain." He was long silent. Then, in a whisper, *"Sed Deus spes mea."*

When Eszterhazy raised his head, the place beside him was empty.

Up and down and back and forth through the ancient-most quarters of the city, Eszterhazy sought his Sovereign; what his Sovereign was seeking, he did not know.

A voice close by said, "Watch!" He looked up, started, stopped. There had been no great danger; indeed, the caution may have been less to prevent his walking into the horse and hearse than to adjure him to take off his hat, which he now did. There was but one horse; there were no carriages of mourners to mark the sad bobbing of the jet-black ostrich plumes. Alongside and behind this modern version of the death-cart walked a half-dozen figures in the robes and the hoods of the Penitential Brotherhood who had once been charged with burying the victims of the Plague and were still charged with conducting the funerals of paupers. If equality existed anywhere in the many nations of the Triune Monarchy it existed in the ranks of the Penitential Brotherhood. The knight of many quarterings might be found therein, and therein, too, the convict on ticket-of-leave. He did not know the one who called out, as the hearse rattled and creaked over the stone blocks and the tram tracks, *"Thou too, thou too!"* nor did he know the one who echoed this call with another, *"Pray for him and pray for us . . ."* He recognized none of the faces beneath the hoods of those who bore lighted candles till one of them casually half-glanced in his direction, and so again he saw the bloodless, weary countenance of his Emperor.

When the day wore to a close, he found his way to his home. A while he spent in thought, then he thought to send a message, then he got up and went to his telephone. The number he announced was one of two digits and below fifty; the call went through immediately.

"The Equerries' Room," a voice said. What emotions could he imagine in the voice? Best to imagine none.

"Pray ask Count Kristofr Eszterhazy if he will speak with his cousin, Doctor Engelbert."

Almost at once the familiar voice. "Yes, Engli, what — ?"

"Kristy, forgive the presumption, but . . . how is it with The Presence?"

A short silence, heavy breathing, then, "Engli, you frighten me, how *could* you have known?"

He felt his heart swell. "What? What?" he mumbled.

"We thought he had fainted, he was unconscious for most of the day, he seemed to be saying something from time to time, it made no

sense, ever; things like . . . oh . . . 'How heavy is the dirt,' maybe, or 'Quick, quick, the dust,' or, 'The dole,' and 'Is he here?' But he was mostly silent — all day long! We feared the worst; no one but the doctor was allowed in, and no one of course was allowed out. But about an hour ago he suddenly regained consciousness. The doctors say that he is as well now as he was yesterday. So we must say, 'Thank God'!"

The call was soon ended.

What had happened? Was it possible? Had he, Engelbert Eszterhazy, suffered and shared in suffering an hallucination of the most fantastic kind conceivable? Dreamed, constructed an entire phantasm out of the depths of his own mind — a phantasm which . . . somehow, somehow . . . in some way seemed to fit in with the phantasm of this other and so much older man, lying motionless on his hard bed halfway across the City? Incredible as this was, still, it was the likeliest explanation. The likeliest, which may not have been the best and truest . . .

Or had some . . . some *aspect* of the aged Monarch left its fleshly mansion, and, as the kaffirs of Africa said, gone wandering about whilst the body slept . . . or . . . or what?

Long, long he pondered the matter, pacing back and forth in his study, back and forth.

At length, and longing for fresher air, he went up to the roof of his house. It stood on no great hill, but stand upon a hill it did: all, all about him, on every side, the Imperial Capital lay spread out to his view, gas and electric lamps in streets and houses; and with naphtha and acetylene flares as well, where the markets were — necklaces and pendants and clusters, a coffer full of jewels spread out before him. And above, every tower and crenelation and door and gate of the Castle on the bluffs above the glittering, reflective Ister was illuminated.

He heard, over and over again, in his mind, as though even now spoken next to his ear, the words which either the aged Sovereign or else his very simulacrum or doppelganger had said. *After me, this Empire will sink like Atlantis, and the children of these children will look for it upon the maps in vain. . . .*

And he asked himself, again and again: Could these words be true? Dare he even think they might be true?

Below, all about, the lights dwindled. Above, the stars wheeled. And then came the mists from the river. And then the cold wind.

THE INCHOATION OF ESZTERHAZY
An Afterword by Avram Davidson

The time was the late middle '70s; the place was the picturesque little city of Mill Valley, California. (California, like Washington State, *has* no other form of municipal incorporation — no towns, boroughs, villages, townships — they are all cities.*) I had, I think, been living in the not-quite-so-picturesque little city of Novato, California, a mile from the nearest bus stop. Nobody walked in Novato — except me — there weren't even any sidewalks: everybody drove. This was par for California, but Mill Valley was somewhat of an exception: a few people did walk in Mill Valley.

Partly because it was near to San Francisco, partly because its topography included lots of hills and bluffs and a wandering stream or two or three, Mill Valley, not lending itself to large-scale tract housing, had become so very popular that housing was hard to find. One resident dingbat (quite a number of the inhabitants were — ah — picturesque, too) greeted me and my ten-year-old and then-long-haired son with a cheerful "And how are you and your little granddaughter today?" We left him wallowing in his gore — but not before we had extracted the news of a possible rental.

This was the old, wooden, and run-down building which I have called The Flea Circus; it was actually the second-oldest house in town, but unsympathetic Authority had declared it "without architectural merit" (true), and it was eventually to be destroyed and replaced by a bland office building. But that was later.

The set-up was not exactly that of a commune, but neither was it an ordinary lodging house. Mike and Sue paid the rent to the landlord and then collected it share by share from the tenants — no, it was

* Except for the City-*and*-County of San Francisco, which is, of course, unique.

the other way around. Sometimes the rent was not always entirely collectable (I may have been the only tenant who always paid promptly), at which time see the large, indignant landlord appear with a List. "Where is Tom Piano?" he would demand. "Don Smike, where is he? I want to know where Floradora Hopkins is. Where *are* these people? Jesus!"

Nobody ever informed Mr. Sevagram that Tom was probably playing piano in a loose bar, which probably paid in left-over drinks; that Don was in his pick-up truck testing burgundy with his Mexican hairless dog, Señor; or that Floradora was probably upstairs copulating with Benny, whose name wasn't even on the rent-roll, although he lived there in whatever unrented corner of the upper floor he could find. And, on occasion, when he couldn't find one, he and Floradora would copulate on my threshold — why *mine*, I couldn't tell you — maybe they liked to listen to classical music. They were usually kind enough to stop whenever I had to step over them. Mr. Sevagram had a neat, orderly mind and had accumulated a neat, orderly fortune; and it was impossible for him to realize that the tenants didn't even *care* that when the rent was late he was put into the position of *Losing The Interest On His Money.*

Never mind that Floradora was never so kind to *me,* or that the rent on her front room, *right,* was being paid by Snark (perhaps a certain nicety prevented her from using it to entertain Benny). Snark, in the course of a quarrel, busted the window out and was promptly visited by two policemen; this being Marin County (hey, I guess I forgot to mention that), they were perhaps not *a priori* interested in the fact that Snark was filled up to his dandruff with (un)Controlled Substances; but on finding out that he had $35 in unpaid traffic offenses, they promptly put the cuffs on him and hauled him away.

Floradora drifted off into the sunset, and Benny was as unconsolable as he could be considering his discovery that he had somehow contracted a Social Disease, which he maybe got off a door-knob.

The front room, *left,* was occupied by Nikk, who was a feather artist. He would buy the hides and plumage of wild ducks and pheasants from Mike and other hunters, and convert them into garments of various kinds. Sue painted very nice flowers, but no one ever paid 40 million zopnicks for them, maybe because she didn't paint irises or sunflowers; with taste and scent, no argument.

This did not by any means cover the roster, the muster cut or uncut, of those who lived at The Flea Circus. People came and people went. "Another chick, good!" someone said about a new denizen. "Good. They mellow out the vibes." Which is as it may be; what they also did was — constantly — sample one another's shampoo in the (one, count them, one) bathroom. Loud shrieks of "But I just *bought* it last *week!*" always filled the air.

My small son, still learning, said, "Why do ladies hafta take so long in the bathroom?" I informed him that, to a man, a bathroom was just a place where one went to do something, did it, and left; whereas to a woman, a bathroom was a sort of living room with running water, and that he (my son) had in such cases better use the bushes. He ran off, happy to be told to do what he preferred to do anyway.

There was the time that I was visited by the Rev. Mr. Niwa, and there was the sound of a stampede and of much plumbing being worked. Bip appeared in my door later, asking, "Who was *that?*" I told him *that* was a minister of the Tenrikyo faith. "A MINister!" cried Bip, rolling his eyes and smacking his brow; "When I seen that dark suit and white shirt, I said to myself *'A Narc!'* and I run and flushed my joints down the john." What he also done, alas, was to attempt later to enter the heavier drug scene; and, on his first try, he sold something illict to an Agent. Thus putting himself in the position of a would-be deer hunter who shot cows, or a naturalist who, saying "Nice doggie," tried to pet a wolf.

Was I not afraid that these characters might corrupt my son? No. Did they even try? Not a bit of it. In fact, one Sunday afternoon when he announced that he was hungry — and there was Nothing To Eat — one of them walked blocks through the rain and brought him back a spaghetti dinner, thoughtfully covered with another plate so that the sauce should not get diluted.

Meanwhile, what of my professional life? Well, what *about* it? It was during these months that ⇒Harlan Ellison⇐ sent me a 30-page Xerox® copy of a manuscript (not one of mine), I forget just why. And, after I had read it, a very strong, wet wind blew a hunk of something out of one wall in my room, letting in the elements. The MS fitted it just fine.

All this, however, did not serve entirely as a substitute for Cash. The Mill Valley merchants were pleasant, but their motto was "Take the cash and let the credit go." It by and by became apparent that I would have to write something to sell. During this decade I had long been engaged on research for the background to my *Vergil Magus* books*; and, much though I loved the work, it brought in no monies; so I resolved to write something which I could do without getting up from my desk (unless perhaps to use the facilities, if they weren't already being used by a chick mellowing out the vibes, reading magazines, eating healthful granola, and testing some other chick's new hair tonic/shampoo, or by some dude engaged in joint-flushing).

I thought that I'd do a sequel to *The Cabinet of Dr. Caligari,* but no less a Someone than the Custodian of Enemy Property informed me that, all the records having been destroyed during the war, they could not grant me a clear title. But those arcane syllables, *The*

* *Vergil in Averno* and *The Phoenix and the Mirror.*

Cabinet of Dr. Caligari, remained and rustled in my mind. They weren't quite the right syllables, but what were?

Gradually it came to me that there had been an empire in Eastern Europe which had been so completely destroyed that we no longer even remembered it, rather like the Kingdom of the Serbs, Croats, and Slovenes, or the Dual Monarchy of Austria-Hungary; that being an empire, it had an emperor; that the emperor had a wizard; the wizard drove about the streets of Bella (**Bel**grade/Vienn**a**) in a steam runabout (remember Tom Swift and his electric runabout?) (then you're much older than I); that the emperor's name was **Ignats Louis**; and that the wizard's name was . . . was . . . was **Engelbert Eszterhazy**: and suddenly, in exactly the same space and with exactly the rhythm as *The Cabinet of Dr. Caligari,* there appeared before my eyes as if illuminated by gaslight, *The Enquiries of Dr. Eszterhazy.* The presence of the ***z*** showed that this was not the same family as that of the noble and august House of E***s***terhazy, the patrons of Haydn, and certainly not of the probably illegitimate and unsavory "Count Wallis-Esterhazy" claimant of Dreyfus case fame.

I sat down at the typewriter, and in six weeks wrote all eight stories of the first series. No rewrites were ever even suggested. The only interruption was occasioned by my descending the unbanistered stairs to investigate a grisly shriek — which had been made by an unwary **rat** rash enough to have intruded on the territory of *Etta,* the Kitchen Kat, a gaunt, working-class mother cat with one dirty little kitten. Rough on rats? Boy, you wanna believe it! It was as big as she was, but little did reason of size avail him. (Soon afterwards my two-year-old godson Seth Davis proudly and happily pointed out the kitten and cried, *"Cow!"*)

Everything came so clear to me, the bulging eyes and bifurcated beard of Ignats Louis the fatherly King-Emperor, the teeming streets of the South Ward of Bella, where foodsellers hawked stuffed intestine, the fusty blackish-green dress of Emma Katterina, Titular Queen of Carinthia, the urban telegraphic system and the trams and the canal and the Little Ister River and the French Gun and the Great Big Bell and the sub-Rabelaisian peasants of Poposhki-Georgiou with their embroidered waistcoats and dung-smeared boots, the Avars of Avar-Ister (Pannonia) and their ever-prickly nationalism, the endless and legend-haunted fens of the Vloxlands, the snuff shop and the pearl buttons shop, the ever-bubbling mixture of races and ethnoi and dialects and religions, the very mature goose-girls — and all the rest of it — came so clear to me . . . that now I recognize that I did not at all "make them up," that Scythia-Pannonia-Transbalkania *did* exist!, as surely as Courland, a Baltic duchy which once had colonies in America and Africa; and Lemkovarna, land of the Lemkos, those Slavs forgotten by everyone save themselves; and the Kingdom of the Two Sicilies and the Free City of Fiume did exist: could *you,* for example, point out *Livland!*, to name but several *No Longer on the Map*, in the felicitous phrase and title of Ray Ramsay's fascinating book. I had an immensely clear picture even of the maps of Scythia-Pannonia-Transbalkania, as they would have appeared in a Baedecker Guide-Book of the turn of the century; and these very maps are certainly as "real" as any which we are likely to see of the Kingdom of Montenegro, the Union of Kalmar, and the Republic of Nueva Cartagena.

More than once, real persons have emerged to provide something like models for the fictional (*fictional?*) characters in the Eszterhazy stories. Scarcely was the ink dry on the magazine which told the story of the exiled King of the Single Sicily ("Duke Pasquale's Ring"), than there emerged from the shadows the exiled "Man Who Would Be King" of Serbia — if Serbia still had a king — if that king were still of the House of Obrenovitch instead of the House of Karageorgevitch, which had twice deposed them. "King" Obrenovitch was living on next to nothing in a tiny apartment in Rome, and would give you a title in the peerage of his "kingdom"; a donation was of course expected: I had never before heard of him. Some have seen in the Kingdom of Scandia and Froreland a reference to the now-dissolved union of the Kingdoms of Sweden and Norway; and if "Melanchthon Mudge" may seem in any way similar to "Mr. Sludge the Medium" in Robert Browning's poem of that name, why not connect Mr. Sludge with Daniel Dunglass Home, unofficial medium to Napoleon III and Alexander II? — but I disdain to suggest others; go do your homework: spend 58 years reading omnivorously as I have done; do you think that even a little line like, "The Byzantian deputies voted against the Budget," and all it implies, fell into my lap like a flake of dandruff?

Well, well, no hubris. Doctor Eszterhazy has his admirers (and fie and a pox upon the reviewer who described him as a "pastiche of Sherlock Holmes," scurvy fellow, may his teeth fall out), but he has failed to set even the Ister on fire. Just this week I have read that a writer ("a certain writer") of many, many best-sellers reports that when he first began to send out his stories the only thing other than a routine rejection slip which he received was "a crusty but supportive note from Avram Davidson, then editor of *F&SF*." And has he bought me a pipe-organ, an old Ford, or a hovel in the country? Probably he thinks I'm dead. ("Avram Davidson? I thought you were younger and taller!" a fan once said. I told her, "I used to be." And I *was*.) Among the admirers of Engelbert Eszterhazy, Ph. D., D. Phil., Dr. of Science, Dr. of Music, Dr. of Literature, of Laws, of Engineering, etc., is George Scithers, then editor of *Amazing Stories,* who first encouraged me to write a story of Eszterhazy as a young man. Which I did (It appeared as "Young Doctor Eszterhazy" . . . *my* title for that adventure was "Cornet Eszterhazy."); and from which came the other four stories of the second series. (An Eszterhazy novel is now in progress.)

This account must soon cease. The Triune Monarchy of Scythia-Pannonia-Transbalkania was not a cold despotism, Ignats Louis was not a cold despot, Eszterhazy was not a cold wizard, neither were any of them angels frolicking in Eden (as exiles sometimes tend to remember things); S-P-T was not Eden. Often there was mud in the streets, and dung in the mud, and often came a cold wind off the river, and often one felt that cold sharply. Ignats Louis dimly, and Dr. Eszterhazy keenly, felt the wind, and tried in their different and often odd ways to make things a bit warmer. Alas, it is now clear that they did not succeed . . . enough.

But let us, if you will, as we may, let us watch them try.

Herrekk! The steam runabout! If you please . . .